# Short Fiction
## by Black Women,
### 1900–1920

THE SCHOMBURG LIBRARY OF
NINETEENTH-CENTURY BLACK WOMEN WRITERS

# Henry Louis Gates, Jr.
## General Editor

Titles are listed chronologically; collections that
include works published over a span of years are listed according to
the publication date of their initial work.

# Short Fiction
*by*
# Black Women,
# 1900–1920

*Collected with an Introduction by*
ELIZABETH AMMONS

*New York   Oxford*
OXFORD UNIVERSITY PRESS
1991

Oxford University Press

Oxford   New York   Toronto
Delhi   Bombay   Calcutta   Madras   Karachi
Petaling Jaya   Singapore   Hong Kong   Tokyo
Nairobi   Dar es Salaam   Cape Town
Melbourne   Auckland

and associated companies in
Berlin   Ibadan

Copyright © 1991 by Oxford University Press, Inc.

Published by Oxford University Press, Inc.,
200 Madison Avenue, New York, New York 10016

Oxford is a registered trademark of Oxford University Press

Library of Congress Cataloging-in-Publication Data
Short fiction by black women, 1900–1920 /
collected with an introduction by Elizabeth Ammons.
p.   cm.   Includes bibliographical references.
ISBN 0-19-506195-0
1. Short stories, American—Afro-American authors.   2. Short stories,
American—Women authors.   3. American fiction—20th century.
4. Afro-Americans—Fiction.   5. Women—Fiction.
I. Ammons, Elizabeth.
PS647.A35S56   1991
813'.01089287'09041—dc20   90-35233

2  4  6  8  10  9  7  5  3  1

Printed in the United States of America
on acid-free paper

The
Schomburg Library
of
Nineteenth-Century
Black Women Writers
Is
Dedicated
in Memory
of
PAULINE AUGUSTA COLEMAN GATES

*1916–1987*

# PUBLISHER'S NOTE

# FOREWORD TO THE SCHOMBURG SUPPLEMENT

*Henry Louis Gates, Jr.*

The enthusiastic reception by students, scholars, and the general public to the 1988 publication of the Schomburg Library of Nineteenth-Century Black Women Writers more than justified the efforts of twenty-five scholars and the staff of the Black Periodical Literature Project to piece together the fragments of knowledge about the writings of African-American women between 1773 and 1910. The Library's republication of those writings in thirty volumes—ranging from the poetry of Phillis Wheatley to the enormous body of work that emerged out of the "Black Woman's Era" at the turn of this century—was a *beginning* for the restoration of the written sensibilities of a group of writers who confronted the twin barriers of racism and sexism in America. Through their poetry, diaries, speeches, biographies, essays, fictional narratives, and autobiographies, these writers transcended the boundaries of racial prejudice and sexual discrimination by recording the thoughts and feelings of Americans who were, at once, black *and* female. Taken together, these works configure into a literary tradition because their authors read, critiqued, and revised each other's words, in textual groundings with their sisters.

Indeed, by publishing these texts together as a "library," and by presenting them as part of a larger discourse on race and gender, we hoped to enable readers to chart the formal specificities of this tradition and to trace its origins. As a whole, the works in the Schomburg Library demonstrate that the contemporary literary movement of African-American women writers is heir to a legacy that was born in 1773, when Phillis Wheatley's *Poems on Various Subjects, Religious and Moral* first unveiled the mind of a black woman to the world. The fact that the Wheatley volume has proven to be the most popular in the Schomburg set is a testament to her role as the "founder" of both the black American's and the black woman's literary tradition.

Even before the Library was published, however, I began to receive queries about producing a supplement that would incorporate works that had not been included initially. Often these exchanges were quite dramatic. For instance, shortly before a lecture I was about to deliver at the University of Cincinnati, Professor Sharon Dean asked me if the Library would be reprinting the 1859 autobiography of Eliza Potter, a black hairdresser who had lived and worked in Cincinnati. I had never heard of Potter, I replied. Did Dean have a copy of her book? No, but there *was* a copy at the Cincinnati Historical Society. As I delivered my lecture, I could not help thinking about this "lost" text and its great significance. In fact, after the lecture, Dean and I rushed from the building and drove to the Historical Society, arriving just a few moments before closing time. A patient librarian brought us the book, and as I leafed through it, I was once again confronted with the realization that so often accompanied the research behind the Library's first thirty volumes—the exciting, yet poignant awareness that there probably exist *dozens* of works like Potter's, buried in research libraries, waiting only to be uncovered through an accident of contiguity like that which placed Sharon Dean in Cincinnati, roaming the shelves of its Historical Society. Another scholar wrote to me about work being done on the poet Effie Waller Smith. Several other scholars also wrote to share their research on other authors and their works. A supplement to the Library clearly was necessary.

Thus we have now added ten volumes, among them Potter's autobiography and Smith's collected poetry, as well as a narrative by Sojourner Truth, several pamphlets by Ida B. Wells-Barnett, and two biographies by Josephine Brown and Frances Rollin. Also included are books consisting of various essays, stories, poems, and plays whose authors did not, or could not, collect their writings into a full-length volume. The works of Olivia Ward Bush-Banks, Angelina Weld Grimké, and Katherine Davis Chapman Tillman are in this category. A related volume is an anthology of short fiction published by black women in the *Colored American Magazine* and *Crisis* magazine—a collection that reveals the shaping influence which certain periodicals had upon the generation of specific genres within the black women's literary tradition. Both types of collected books are intended to kindle an interest in still another series of works that bring together for the first time either the complete *oeuvre* of one writer or that of one genre within the periodical press. Indeed, there are several authors whose collected works will establish them as major forces in the nineteenth- and early twentieth-century black women's intellectual community. Compiling, editing, and publishing these volumes will be as important a factor in constructing the black women's literary tradition as has been the republication of books long out of print.

Finally, the Library now includes a detailed bibliography of the writings of black women in the nineteenth and early twentieth centuries. Prepared by Jean Fagan Yellin and Cynthia Bond, this bibliography is the result of years of research and will serve as an indispensable resource in future investigations of black women writers, particularly those whose works appeared frequently throughout the nineteenth century in the principal conduit of writing for black women *or* men, the African-American periodical press.

The publication of this ten-volume supplement, we hope, will make a sound contribution toward reestablishing the importance of the creative works of African-American women and reevaluating the relation of these works not only to each other but also to African-American *and* American literature and history as a whole. These works are invaluable sources for readers intent upon understanding the complex interplay of ethnicity and gender, of racism and sexism—of how "race" becomes gendered and how gender becomes racialized—in American society.

# FOREWORD
## *In Her Own Write*

### *Henry Louis Gates, Jr.*

One muffled strain in the Silent South, a jarring chord and a vague and uncomprehended cadenza has been and still is the Negro. And of that muffled chord, the one mute and voiceless note has been the sadly expectant Black Women, . . . .

The "other side" has not been represented by one who "lives there." And not many can more sensibly realize and more accurately tell the weight and the fret of the "long dull pain" than the open-eyed but hitherto voiceless Black Woman of America.

. . . as our Caucasian barristers are not to blame if they cannot *quite* put themselves in the dark man's place, neither should the dark man be wholly expected fully and adequately to reproduce the exact Voice of the Black Woman.

—Anna Julia Cooper
*A Voice From the South* (1892)

The birth of the African-American literary tradition occurred in 1773, when Phillis Wheatley published a book of poetry. Despite the fact that her book garnered for her a remarkable amount of attention, Wheatley's journey to the printer had been a most arduous one. Sometime in 1772, a young African girl walked demurely into a room in Boston to undergo an oral examination, the results of which would determine the direction of her life and work. Perhaps she was shocked upon entering the appointed room. For there, perhaps gathered in a semicircle, sat eighteen of Boston's most notable citizens. Among them were John Erving, a prominent Boston merchant, the Reverend Charles Chauncy, pastor of the Tenth Congregational Church; and John Hancock, who would later gain fame for his signature on the Declaration of Independence. At the center of this group was His Excellency, Thomas Hutchinson, governor of Massachusetts, with Andrew Oliver, his lieutenant governor, close by his side.

Why had this august group been assembled? Why had it seen fit to summon this young African girl, scarcely eighteen years old, before it? This group of "the most respectable Characters in *Boston*," as it would define itself, had assembled to question closely the African adolescent on the slender sheaf of poems that she claimed to have "written by herself." We can only speculate on the nature of the questions posed to the fledgling poet. Perhaps they asked her to identify and explain—for all to hear—exactly who were the Greek and Latin gods and poets alluded to so frequently in her work. Perhaps they asked her to conjugate a verb in Latin or even to translate randomly selected passages from the Latin, which she and her master, John Wheatley, claimed that she "had made some Progress in." Or perhaps they asked her to recite from memory key passages from the texts of John Milton and Alexander Pope, the two poets by whom the African claimed to be most directly influenced. We do not know.

We do know, however, that the African poet's responses were more than sufficient to prompt the eighteen august gentlemen to compose, sign, and publish a two-paragraph "Attestation," an open letter "To the Publick" that prefaces Phillis Wheatley's book and that reads in part:

> We whose Names are under-written, do assure the World, that the Poems specified in the following Page, were (as we

verily believe) written by Phillis, a young Negro Girl, who was but a few Years since, brought an uncultivated Barbarian from *Africa,* and has ever since been, and now is, under the Disadvantage of serving as a Slave in a Family in this Town. She has been examined by some of the best Judges, and is thought qualified to write them.

So important was this document in securing a publisher for Wheatley's poems that it forms the signal element in the prefatory matter preceding her *Poems on Various Subjects, Religious and Moral,* published in London in 1773.

Without the published "Attestation," Wheatley's publisher claimed, few would believe that an African could possibly have written poetry all by herself. As the eighteen put the matter clearly in their letter, "Numbers would be ready to suspect they were not really the Writings of Phillis." Wheatley and her master, John Wheatley, had attempted to publish a similar volume in 1772 in Boston, but Boston publishers had been incredulous. One year later, "Attestation" in hand, Phillis Wheatley and her master's son, Nathaniel Wheatley, sailed for England, where they completed arrangements for the publication of a volume of her poems with the aid of the Countess of Huntington and the Earl of Dartmouth.

This curious anecdote, surely one of the oddest oral examinations on record, is only a tiny part of a larger, and even more curious, episode in the Enlightenment. Since the beginning of the sixteenth century, Europeans had wondered aloud whether or not the African "species of men," as they were most commonly called, *could* ever create formal literature, could ever master "the arts and sciences." If they could, the argument ran, then the African variety of humanity was fundamentally related to the European variety. If not, then it seemed clear that the African was destined by nature to be a slave. This was the burden shouldered by Phillis Wheatley when she successfully defended herself and the authorship of her book against counterclaims and doubts.

Indeed, with her successful defense, Wheatley launched two traditions at once—the black American literary tradition *and* the black woman's literary tradition. If it is extraordinary that not just one but both of these traditions were founded simultaneously by a black woman—certainly an event unique in the history of literature—it is also ironic that this important fact of common, coterminous literary origins seems to have escaped most scholars.

That the progenitor of the black literary tradition was a woman means, in the most strictly literal sense, that all subsequent black writers have evolved in a matrilinear line of descent, and that each, consciously or unconsciously, has extended and revised a canon whose foundation was the poetry of a black woman. Early black writers seem to have been keenly aware of Wheatley's founding role, even if most of her white reviewers were more concerned with the implications of her race than her gender. Jupiter Hammon, for example, whose 1760 broadside "An Evening Thought. Salvation by Christ, With Penitential Cries" was the first individual poem published by a black American, acknowledged Wheatley's influence by selecting her as the subject of his second broadside, "An Address to Miss Phillis Wheatly [*sic*], Ethiopian Poetess, in Boston," which was published in Hartford in 1778. And George Moses Horton, the second African American to publish a book of poetry in English (1829), brought out in 1838 an edition of his *Poems By A Slave* bound together with Wheatley's work. Indeed, for fifty-six years, between 1773 and 1829, when Horton published *The Hope of Liberty*, Wheatley was the *only* black person to have published a book of imaginative literature in English. So central was this black woman's role in the shaping of the

African-American literary tradition that, as one historian has maintained, the history of the reception of Phillis Wheatley's poetry *is* the history of African-American literary criticism. Well into the nineteenth century, Wheatley and the black literary tradition were the same entity.

But Wheatley is not the only black woman writer who stands as a pioneering figure in African-American literature. Just as Wheatley gave birth to the genre of black poetry, Ann Plato was the first African American to publish a book of essays (1841) and Harriet E. Wilson was the first black person to publish a novel in the United States (1859).

Despite this pioneering role of black women in the tradition, however, many of their contributions before this century have been all but lost or unrecognized. As Hortense Spillers observed as recently as 1983,

> With the exception of a handful of autobiographical narratives from the nineteenth century, the black woman's realities are virtually suppressed until the period of the Harlem Renaissance and later. Essentially the black woman as artist, as intellectual spokesperson for her own cultural apprenticeship, has not existed before, for anyone. At the source of [their] own symbol-making task, [the community of black women writers] confronts, therefore, a tradition of work that is quite recent, its continuities, broken and sporadic.

Until now, it has been extraordinarily difficult to establish the formal connections between early black women's writing and that of the present, precisely because our knowledge of their work has been broken and sporadic. Phillis Wheatley, for example, while certainly the most reprinted and discussed poet in the tradition, is also one of the least understood. Ann Plato's seminal work, *Essays* (which includes biographies and poems), has not been reprinted since it was published a century and a half ago. And Harriet Wilson's *Our Nig*, her compelling novel of a black woman's expanding consciousness in a racist Northern antebellum environment, never received even *one* review or comment at a time when virtually *all* works written by black people were heralded by abolitionists as salient arguments against the existence of human slavery. Many of the books reprinted in this set experienced a similar fate, the most dreadful fate for an author: that of being ignored then relegated to the obscurity of the rare book section of a university library. We can only wonder how many other texts in the black woman's tradition have been lost to this generation of readers or remain unclassified or uncatalogued and, hence, unread.

This was not always so, however. Black women writers dominated the final decade of the nineteenth century, perhaps spurred to publish by an 1886 essay entitled "The Coming American Novelist," which was published in *Lippincott's Monthly Magazine* and written by "A Lady From Philadelphia." This pseudonymous essay argued that the "Great American Novel" would be written by a black person. Her argument is so curious that it deserves to be repeated:

> When we come to formulate our demands of the Coming American Novelist, we will agree that he must be native-born. His ancestors may come from where they will, but we must give him a birthplace and have the raising of him. Still, the longer his family has been here the better he will represent us. Suppose he should have no country but ours, no traditions but those he has learned here, no longings apart from us, no future except in our future—the orphan of the world, he finds with us his home. And with all this, suppose he refuses to be fused into that grand conglomerate we call the "American type." With us, he is not of us. He is original, he has humor, he is tender, he is passive and fiery, he has been taught what we call justice, and he has his own opinion about it. He has suffered everything a poet, a dra-

matist, a novelist need suffer before he comes to have his lips anointed. And with it all he is in one sense a spectator, a little out of the race. How would these conditions go towards forming an original development? In a word, suppose the coming novelist is of African origin? When one comes to consider the subject, there is no improbability in it. One thing is certain,—our great novel will not be written by the typical American.

An atypical American, indeed. Not only would the great American novel be written by an African American, it would be written by an African-American *woman:*

Yet farther: I have used the generic masculine pronoun because it is convenient; but Fate keeps revenge in store. It was a woman who, taking the wrongs of the African as her theme, wrote the novel that awakened the world to their reality, and why should not the coming novelist be a woman as well as an African? She—the woman of that race—has some claims on Fate which are not yet paid up.

It is these claims on fate that we seek to pay by publishing The Schomburg Library of Nineteenth-Century Black Women Writers.

This theme would be repeated by several black women authors, most notably by Anna Julia Cooper, a prototypical black feminist whose 1892 *A Voice From the South* can be considered to be one of the original texts of the black feminist movement. It was Cooper who first analyzed the fallacy of referring to "the Black man" when speaking of black people and who argued that just as white men cannot speak through the consciousness of black men, neither can black *men* "fully and adequately . . . reproduce the exact Voice of the Black Woman." Gender and race, she argues, cannot be conflated, except in the instance of a black woman's voice, and it is this voice which must be uttered and to which we must listen. As Cooper puts the matter so compellingly:

It is not the intelligent woman vs. the ignorant woman; nor the white woman vs. the black, the brown, and the red,—it is not even the cause of woman vs. man. Nay, 'tis woman's strongest vindication for speaking that *the world needs to hear her voice*. It would be subversive of every human interest that the cry of one-half the human family be stifled. Woman in stepping from the pedestal of statue-like inactivity in the domestic shrine, and daring to think and move and speak,—to undertake to help shape, mold, and direct the thought of her age, is merely completing the circle of the world's vision. Hers is every interest that has lacked an interpreter and a defender. Her cause is linked with that of every agony that has been dumb—every wrong that needs a voice.

It is no fault of man's that he has not been able to see truth from her standpoint. It does credit both to his head and heart that no greater mistakes have been committed or even wrongs perpetrated while she sat making tatting and snipping paper flowers. Man's own innate chivalry and the mutual interdependence of their interests have insured his treating her cause, in the main at least, as his own. And he is pardonably surprised and even a little chagrined, perhaps, to find his legislation not considered "perfectly lovely" in every respect. But in any case his work is only impoverished by her remaining dumb. The world has had to limp along with the wobbling gait and one-sided hesitancy of a man with one eye. Suddenly the bandage is removed from the other eye and the whole body is filled with light. It sees a circle where before it saw a segment. The darkened eye restored, every member rejoices with it.

The myopic sight of the darkened eye can only be restored when the full range of the black woman's voice, with its own special timbres and shadings, remains mute no longer.

Similarly, Victoria Earle Matthews, an author of short stories and essays, and a cofounder in 1896 of the National Association of Colored Women, wrote in her stunning essay,

"The Value of Race Literature" (1895), that "when the literature of our race is developed, it will of necessity be different in all essential points of greatness, true heroism and
real Christianity from what we may at the present time, for
convenience, call American literature." Matthews argued that
this great tradition of African-American literature would be
the textual outlet "for the unnaturally suppressed inner lives
which our people have been compelled to lead." Once these
"unnaturally suppressed inner lives" of black people are unveiled, no "grander diffusion of mental light" will shine more
brightly, she concludes, than that of the articulate African-
American woman:

> And now comes the question, What part shall we women
> play in the Race Literature of the future? . . . within the
> compass of one small journal ["Woman's Era"] we have struck
> out a new line of departure—a journal, a record of Race
> interests gathered from all parts of the United States, care-
> fully selected, moistened, winnowed and garnered by the ablest
> intellects of educated colored women, shrinking at no lofty
> theme, shirking no serious duty, aiming at every possible
> excellence, and determined to do their part in the future
> uplifting of the race.
>
>     If twenty women, by their concentrated efforts in one lit-
> erary movement, can meet with such success as has engen-
> dered, planned out, and so successfully consummated this
> convention, what much more glorious results, what wider
> spread success, what grander diffusion of mental light will
> not come forth at the bidding of the enlarged hosts of women
> writers, already called into being by the stimulus of your
> efforts?
>
>     And here let me speak one word for my journalistic sisters
> who have already entered the broad arena of journalism. Be-
> fore the "Woman's Era" had come into existence, no one
> except themselves can appreciate the bitter experience and sore

disappointments under which they have at all times been
compelled to pursue their chosen vocations.

If their brothers of the press have had their difficulties to
contend with, I am here as a sister journalist to state, from
the fullness of knowledge, that their task has been an easy
one compared with that of the colored woman in journalism.

Woman's part in Race Literature, as in Race building, is
the most important part and has been so in all ages. . . . All
through the most remote epochs she has done her share in
literature. . . .

One of the most important aspects of this set is the republication of the salient texts from 1890 to 1910, which literary
historians could well call the "Black Woman's Era." In addition to Mary Helen Washington's definitive edition of
Cooper's *A Voice From the South*, we have reprinted two novels by Amelia Johnson, Frances Harper's *Iola Leroy*, two
novels by Emma Dunham Kelley, Alice Dunbar-Nelson's two
impressive collections of short stories, and Pauline Hopkins's
three serialized novels as well as her monumental novel,
*Contending Forces*—all published between 1890 and 1910.
Indeed, black women published more works of fiction in these
two decades than black men had published in the previous
half century. Nevertheless, this great achievement has been
ignored.

Moreover, the writings of nineteenth-century African-
American women in general have remained buried in obscurity, accessible only in research libraries or in overpriced and
poorly edited reprints. Many of these books have never been
reprinted at all; in some instances only one or two copies are
extant. In these works of fiction, poetry, autobiography, bi-
ography, essays, and journalism resides the mind of the
nineteenth-century African-American woman. Until these
works are made readily available to teachers and their students,
a significant segment of the black tradition will remain silent.

Oxford University Press, in collaboration with the Schomburg Center for Research in Black Culture, is publishing thirty volumes of these compelling works, each of which contains an introduction by an expert in the field. The set includes such rare texts as Johnson's *The Hazeley Family* and *Clarence and Corinne*, Plato's *Essays,* the most complete edition of Phillis Wheatley's poems and letters, Emma Dunham Kelley's pioneering novel *Megda*, several previously unpublished stories and a novel by Alice Dunbar-Nelson, and the first collected volumes of Pauline Hopkins's three serialized novels and Frances Harper's poetry. We also present four volumes of poetry by such women as Henrietta Cordelia Ray, Adah Menken, Josephine Heard, and Maggie Johnson. Numerous slave and spiritual narratives, a newly discovered novel—*Four Girls at Cottage City*—by Emma Dunham Kelley (-Hawkins), and the first American edition of *Wonderful Adventures of Mrs. Seacole in Many Lands* are also among the texts included.

In addition to resurrecting the works of black women authors, it is our hope that this set will facilitate the resurrection of the African-American woman's literary tradition itself by unearthing its nineteenth-century roots. In the works of Nella Larsen and Jessie Fauset, Zora Neale Hurston and Ann Petry, Lorraine Hansberry and Gwendolyn Brooks, Paule Marshall and Toni Cade Bambara, Audre Lorde and Rita Dove, Toni Morrison and Alice Walker, Gloria Naylor and Jamaica Kincaid, these roots have branched luxuriantly. The eighteenth- and nineteenth-century authors whose works are presented in this set founded and nurtured the black women's literary tradition, which must be revived, explicated, analyzed, and debated before we can understand more completely the formal shaping of this tradition within a tradition, a coded literary universe through which, regrettably, we are only just beginning to navigate our way. As Anna Cooper said nearly one hundred years ago, we have been blinded by the loss of sight in one eye and have therefore been unable to detect the full *shape* of the African-American literary tradition.

Literary works configure into a tradition not because of some mystical collective unconscious determined by the biology of race or gender, but because writers read other writers and *ground* their representations of experience in models of language provided largely by other writers to whom they feel akin. It is through this mode of literary revision, amply evident in the *texts* themselves—in formal echoes, recast metaphors, even in parody—that a "tradition" emerges and defines itself.

This is formal bonding, and it is only through formal bonding that we can know a literary tradition. The collective publication of these works by black women now, for the first time, makes it possible for scholars and critics, male and female, black and white, to *demonstrate* that black women writers read, and revised, other black women writers. To demonstrate this set of formal literary relations is to demonstrate that sexuality, race, and gender are both the condition and the basis of *tradition*—but tradition as found in discrete acts of language use.

A word is in order about the history of this set. For the past decade, I have taught a course, first at Yale and then at Cornell, entitled "Black Woman and Their Fictions," a course that I inherited from Toni Morrison, who developed it in the mid-1970s for Yale's Program in Afro-American Studies. Although the course was inspired by the remarkable accomplishments of black women novelists since 1970, I gradually extended its beginning date to the late nineteenth century, studying Frances Harper's *Iola Leroy* and Anna Julia Cooper's *A Voice From the South*, both published in 1892. With the discovery of Harriet E. Wilson's seminal novel, *Our Nig* (1859), and Jean Yellin's authentication of Harriet Jacobs's brilliant slave narrative, *Incidents in the Life of a Slave Girl* (1861), a survey course spanning over a century and a quarter emerged.

But the discovery of *Our Nig,* as well as the interest in nineteenth-century black women's writing that this discovery generated, convinced me that even the most curious and diligent scholars knew very little of the extensive history of the creative writings of African-American women before 1900. Indeed, most scholars of African-American literature had never even read most of the books published by black women, simply because these books—of poetry, novels, short stories, essays, and autobiography—were mostly accessible only in rare book sections of university libraries. For reasons unclear to me even today, few of these marvelous renderings of the African-American woman's consciousness were reprinted in the late 1960s and early 1970s, when so many other texts of the African-American literary tradition were resurrected from the dark and silent graveyard of the out-of-print and were reissued in facsimile editions aimed at the hungry readership for canonical texts in the nascent field of black studies.

So, with the help of several superb research assistants—including David Curtis, Nicola Shilliam, Wendy Jones, Sam Otter, Janadas Devan, Suvir Kaul, Cynthia Bond, Elizabeth Alexander, and Adele Alexander—and with the expert advice of scholars such as William Robinson, William Andrews, Mary Helen Washington, Maryemma Graham, Jean Yellin, Houston A. Baker, Jr., Richard Yarborough, Hazel Carby, Joan R. Sherman, Frances Foster, and William French, dozens of bibliographies were used to compile a list of books written or narrated by black women mostly before 1910. Without the assistance provided through this shared experience of scholarship, the scholar's true legacy, this project would not have been conceived. As the list grew, I was struck by how very many of these titles that I, for example, had never even heard of, let alone read, such as Ann Plato's *Essays,* Louisa Picquet's slave narrative, or Amelia Johnson's two novels, *Clarence and Corinne* and *The Hazeley Family.* Through our research with the Black Periodical Fiction and Poetry Project (funded by NEH and the Ford Foundation), I also realized that several novels by black women, including three works of fiction by Pauline Hopkins, had been serialized in black periodicals, but had never been collected and published as books. Nor had the several books of poetry published by black women, such as the prolific Frances E. W. Harper, been collected and edited. When I discovered still another "lost" novel by an African-American woman (*Four Girls at Cottage City,* published in 1898 by Emma Dunham Kelley-Hawkins), I decided to attempt to edit a collection of reprints of these works and to publish them as a "library" of black women's writings, in part so that I could read them myself.

Convincing university and trade publishers to undertake this project proved to be a difficult task. Despite the commercial success of *Our Nig* and of the several reprint series of women's works (such as Virago, the Beacon Black Women Writers Series, and Rutgers' American Women Writers Series), several presses rejected the project as "too large," "too limited," or as "commercially unviable." Only two publishers recognized the viability and the import of the project and, of these, Oxford's commitment to publish the titles simultaneously as a set made the press's offer irresistible.

While attempting to locate original copies of these exceedingly rare books, I discovered that most of the texts were housed at the Schomburg Center for Research in Black Culture, a branch of The New York Public Library, under the direction of Howard Dodson. Dodson's infectious enthusiasm for the project and his generous collaboration, as well as that of his stellar staff (especially Diana Lachatanere, Sharon Howard, Ellis Haizip, Richard Newman, and Betty Gubert), led to a joint publishing initiative that produced this set as part of the Schomburg's major fund-raising campaign. Without Dodson's foresight and generosity of spirit, the set would not have materialized. Without William P. Sisler's masterful editorship at Oxford and his staff's careful attention to detail, the set would have remained just another grand idea that tends to languish in a scholar's file cabinet.

I would also like to thank Dr. Michael Winston and Dr. Thomas C. Battle, Vice-President of Academic Affairs and the Director of the Moorland-Spingarn Research Center (respectively) at Howard University, for their unending encouragement, support, and collaboration in this project, and Esme E. Bhan at Howard for her meticulous research and bibliographical skills. In addition, I would like to acknowledge the aid of the staff at the libraries of Duke University, Cornell University (especially Tom Weissinger and Donald Eddy), the Boston Public Library, the Western Reserve Historical Society, the Library of Congress, and Yale University. Linda Robbins, Marion Osmun, Sarah Flanagan, and Gerard Case, all members of the staff at Oxford, were extraordinarily effective at coordinating, editing, and producing the various segments of each text in the set. Candy Ruck, Nina de Tar, and Phillis Molock expertly typed reams of correspondence and manuscripts connected to the project.

I would also like to express my gratitude to my colleagues who edited and introduced the individual titles in the set. Without their attention to detail, their willingness to meet strict deadlines, and their sheer enthusiasm for this project, the set could not have been published. But finally and ultimately, I would hope that the publication of the set would help to generate even more scholarly interest in the black women authors whose work is presented here. Struggling against the seemingly insurmountable barriers of racism *and* sexism, while often raising families and fulfilling full-time professional obligations, these women managed nevertheless to record their thoughts and feelings and to *testify* to all who dare read them that the will to harness the power of collective endurance and survival is the will to write.

The Schomburg Library of Nineteenth-Century Black Women Writers is dedicated in memory of Pauline Augusta Coleman Gates, who died in the spring of 1987. It was she who inspired in me the love of learning and the love of literature. I have encountered in the books of this set no will more determined, no courage more noble, no mind more sublime, no self more celebratory of the achievements of all African-American women, and indeed of life itself, than her own.

# A NOTE FROM
# THE SCHOMBURG CENTER

*Howard Dodson*

The Schomburg Center for Research in Black Culture, The New York Public Library, is pleased to join with Dr. Henry Louis Gates and Oxford University Press in presenting The Schomburg Library of Nineteenth-Century Black Women Writers. This thirty-volume set includes the work of a generation of black women whose writing has only been available previously in rare book collections. The materials reprinted in twenty-four of the thirty volumes are drawn from the unique holdings of the Schomburg Center.

A research unit of The New York Public Library, the Schomburg Center has been in the forefront of those institutions dedicated to collecting, preserving, and providing access to the records of the black past. In the course of its two generations of acquisition and conservation activity, the Center has amassed collections totaling more than 5 million items. They include over 100,000 bound volumes, 85,000 reels and sets of microforms, 300 manuscript collections containing some 3.5 million items, 300,000 photographs and extensive holdings of prints, sound recordings, film and videotape, newspapers, artworks, artifacts, and other book and nonbook materials. Together they vividly document the history and cultural heritages of people of African descent worldwide.

Though established some sixty-two years ago, the Center's book collections date from the sixteenth century. Its oldest item, an Ethiopian Coptic Tunic, dates from the eighth or ninth century. Rare materials, however, are most available for the nineteenth-century African-American experience. It

*A Note*

is from these holdings that the majority of the titles selected for inclusion in this set are drawn.

The nineteenth century was a formative period in African-American literary and cultural history. Prior to the Civil War, the majority of black Americans living in the United States were held in bondage. Law and practice forbade teaching them to read or write. Even after the war, many of the impediments to learning and literary productivity remained. Nevertheless, black men and women of the nineteenth century persevered in both areas. Moreover, more African Americans than we yet realize turned their observations, feelings, social viewpoints, and creative impulses into published works. In time, this nineteenth-century printed record included poetry, short stories, histories, novels, autobiographies, social criticism, and theology, as well as economic and philosophical treatises. Unfortunately, much of this body of literature remained, until very recently, relatively inaccessible to twentieth-century scholars, teachers, creative artists, and others interested in black life. Prior to the late 1960s, most Americans (black as well as white) had never heard of these nineteenth-century authors, much less read their works.

The civil rights and black power movements created unprecedented interest in the thought, behavior, and achievements of black people. Publishers responded by revising traditional texts, introducing the American public to a new generation of African-American writers, publishing a variety of thematic anthologies, and reprinting a plethora of "classic texts" in African-American history, literature, and art. The reprints usually appeared as individual titles or in a series of bound volumes or microform formats.

The Schomburg Center, which has a long history of supporting publishing that deals with the history and culture of Africans in diaspora, became an active participant in many

# INTRODUCTION

*Elizabeth Ammons*

The fiction in this volume comes from two monthlies, the *Colored American Magazine* (1900–1909) and the *Crisis* during its first decade (1910–1920). The *Colored American* originated in Boston, where its literary management fell under the control of Pauline Hopkins. The *Crisis*, founded as the official publication of the National Association for the Advancement of Colored People and edited by W. E. B. Du Bois, was highly influenced in its literary offerings throughout the teens by Jessie Fauset, who formally became the journal's literary editor in 1919 and then served in that capacity for the following seven years. The presence of these two women in powerful editorial positions no doubt contributed significantly to the publication of work by women (particularly by Hopkins and Fauset themselves) in both journals. Although other periodicals existed in which stories by African American women appeared, the *Colored American* and the *Crisis* provided the two largest secular, national outlets for short fiction by black women at the turn of the century.[1]

The *Colored American Magazine* clearly articulated its literary mission during the years that it was managed and published in Boston. Announcements in early issues stated that the magazine would run short stories of special worth, giving the most careful attention to all submissions, and the magazine frequently emphasized its commitment to publishing work by black authors. The editors declared in October 1900: "We want a magazine *Of the Race, By the Race, For the Race*." In December of the same year, a publisher's

announcement reiterated: "We urge OUR PEOPLE to send
to the Magazine their ideas, stories, poems, etc." Reviewing
the progress made by May 1902, the journal announced:
"Our short stories, by our Race Writers, are becoming more
and more literary in style, and we shall soon see an era of
strong competition in the field of letters."[2] The magazine
was not solely literary. It ran news items, often clipped from
other publications and commented upon by the *Colored American*'s editors; special feature essays about events or individuals
of particular interest such as Hopkins's multipart series,
"Famous Men of the Negro Race" and "Famous Women of
the Negro Race"; and analyses and arguments by various
writers on aspects of the race issue in the United States.
Nevertheless, in its early years, showing the strong influence
of Hopkins, the magazine was predominantly literary. It
aimed to be "distinctly devoted" to the concerns of African
Americans and to "the development of Afro-American art
and literature" (1 [May 1900]). An announcement for 1903
declared that "our readers expect and must have the very best
that the literature of the race can produce, in the form of
Serial Stories, Short Stories and Poems" (5 [Dec. 1902]:
n.p.).

In the early spring of 1904, Hopkins restated the editors'
initial vision of the *Colored American*'s purpose. The March
1904 issue, which named Hopkins as editor on the masthead,
announced that the magazine was "intended to show that the
colored people can advance on all the lines of progress known
to other races, that they can be more than tillers of the soil,
hewers of wood and drawers of water—that they can attain to
eminence (both the men and women among them) as thinkers,
as writers, as doctors, as lawyers, as clergymen, as singers,
musicians, artists, actors, and also as successful business men,
in the conduct of enterprises of importance" (7 [March

1904]: 152). Later in the issue an advertisement proclaimed that the *Colored American Magazine,* among other things, led in the work of "making our white brothers and sisters realize the work we are doing, and that, in a single generation after the abolition of slavery, we have produced not only farmers and mechanics, but singers, artists, writers, poets, lawyers, doctors, successful business men, and even some statesmen" (7 [March 1904]: n.p.).

Hopkins's effort to preserve both the predominantly literary character of the magazine and her power as an editor failed. Struggling financially, the magazine was secretly bought by Booker T. Washington, of whom Hopkins was not a champion, and relocated to New York in 1904, where it remained until it ceased publication in 1909. The move signaled a major change. The lead essay in the June 1904 issue, "What A Magazine Should Be," announced: "The materialism of the age upon which we have come compels us to revise the view-point we maintained in the past. . . . The world now cares very little for what is said but a great deal for what is being done in any given direction, by individuals as well as races. It wants the results of effort and a clear statement of how they were got" (7 [June 1904]: 394). The November issue stated outright: "We are proud and feel honored in having the friendship of Dr. Booker T. Washington and we shall always take pleasure in publishing in the Magazine any matter in which he is interested, or which he desires us to publish" (7 [Nov. 1904]: 693). After 1904 the *Colored American Magazine* occasionally published fiction, some of which appears in this volume, but mainly it reflected Washington's views and concentrated on articles about African American economic and industrial progress. Essays about the National Negro Business League, Masonic Lodge activities, events at the Tuskegee Institute, and accomplishments of

black entrepreneurs and businessmen dominated the revamped
*Colored American.*[3]

This change in the management and philosophy of the
magazine represented a fundamental change for black women
writers. In contrast to the original publication, which was
committed to black authors, the new *Colored American,* shortly
after its move to New York, featured a long serial by the
white author Harriet Martineau. Also, the magazine, along
with being avowedly more material and less literary, became
markedly more male. The cover illustrations, the writers,
and the subject matter after the journal's removal from
Boston, and with it the removal of Hopkins from power,
became strikingly more male-focused and male-dominated,
especially immediately following the relocation and reorgan-
ization.

The literary character of the *Crisis* in the years represented
in this volume was more constant. Operating under the
editorship of W. E. B. Du Bois, himself a writer of fiction,
the magazine did not specifically announce the inclusion of
fiction as a principal objective. Rather, the first issue named
four goals, all focused on illuminating and addressing racial
prejudice "particularly as manifested to-day toward colored
people": to print news, to review new publications, to feature
short articles, and to issue editorials (1 [Nov. 1910]: 10).
However, the magazine quickly evolved a steady literary
component. Although not dominated by creative writing,
from the beginning most issues contained some poetry or
fiction or both, in addition to the literary reviews that Jessie
Fauset wrote; and she officially took over the management of
the literary part of the journal in 1919. Although conflicts
surely existed,[4] Fauset and Du Bois were friends who shared
a strong belief in the importance of literature, and a solid

literary dimension to the *Crisis* developed early on. Because it was the official journal of the NAACP, which welcomed all people as members, the *Crisis*, unlike the early *Colored American*, regularly included some work by white people.

The appearance of short fiction by African American women in these two journals at the turn of the century was not unprecedented. As Penelope L. Bullock explains in *The Afro-American Periodical Press, 1838–1909*, the black periodical press in the United States from the beginning included work by women. It is thought that the first short story by an African American writer published in the United States was "The Two Offers" by Frances Ellen Watkins (later Harper) in the *Anglo-African Magazine* in 1859. Moreover, before the first issue of the *Colored American Magazine* even appeared, Alice Moore Dunbar (later Dunbar-Nelson) had published two volumes of short fiction, *Violets and Other Tales* (1895) and *The Goodness of St. Rocque and Other Stories* (1899). What the *Colored American* and then the *Crisis* offered black women writers were two highly supportive, national, secular outlets for short fiction at a particularly critical juncture in American history: the first two decades of the twentieth century. Those decades witnessed, on the one hand, the virulent intensification of institutionalized racism in the form of lynching, Jim Crow legislation, the convict lease system, and the campaign for disenfranchisement; and, on the other hand, the blossoming of what historians and literary critics now call the Woman's Era, a time of burgeoning social and political self-empowerment and activism among middle-class black women.[5] The short fiction in this volume contributes to our growing understanding of the turn of the century as a crucial period in the development of African American women's literary traditions. Certainly more short fiction by more black women reached more people in the United States during the first two decades of the twentieth century than ever before in the nation's history.

Simply because a person's work appeared in either the *Colored American Magazine* or the *Crisis* does not automatically mean that she was African American. As Bullock points out, "Contributions by white persons became a significant part of the *Colored American Magazine* in the latter period of [its] publication,"[6] and the *Crisis* regularly, even if not often, published white writers—Mary White Ovington, Jane Addams, Jacob Riis, Dorothy Canfield. These white writers, however, were usually well known; the likelihood of lesser-known authors in this volume not being African American is very small. Still, it is important to recognize that there may be one or more errors of inclusion in this book.[7] One of its obvious functions, in fact, is to encourage scholarship on the writers so that more about them becomes known. Our ignorance today results from the fact that for most of the twentieth century the people officially designated to preserve and hence create the national literary record—scholars trained and hired by colleges and universities, a group that until very recently has been almost exclusively white and male (and is still predominantly so)—have almost totally ignored the writing of African American women. Learning more about a number of the women whose work appeared in the *Colored American Magazine* and in the *Crisis* in its first decade is one of the many important, long-range scholarly projects suggested by The Schomburg Library of Nineteenth-Century Black Women Writers.

Some of the writers, of course, are not at all obscure. Pauline Hopkins, Angelina W. Grimké, Jessie Fauset, and Alice Dunbar-Nelson are well-known authors. Pauline Hopkins (1859–1930) published the long novel *Contending Forces* in 1900 and then published in the *Colored American* three serialized novels, the stories reprinted here, and numerous uncollected essays. Angelina Weld Grimké (1880–1956), author of the play *Rachel* (1916), is probably best known as a Harlem Renaissance poet. Jessie Redmon Fauset (1882–1961), in addition to the short stories and novellas reprinted here from the *Crisis*, published poetry and many essays as well as four novels, *There Is Confusion* (1924), *Plum Bun* (1929), *The Chinaberry Tree* (1931), and *Comedy: American Style* (1933). Alice Dunbar-Nelson (1875–1935) wrote the volumes of short fiction already mentioned, several plays, a diary that is now in print, and poetry; she also edited an anthology of African American writing.[8]

Generally not thought of as fiction writers, Gertrude Mossell (1855–1948) and Fannie Barrier Williams (1855–1944) were well-known race leaders at the turn of the century. Using her married name, Mrs. N. F. Mossell, Gertrude Mossell published in 1894 a collection of original essays and verse titled *The Work of the Afro-American Woman*. Fannie Barrier Williams wrote and lectured extensively on the race issue at the turn of the century, often explicitly addressing the racism of white women.[9]

Some information about other writers can be found in the magazines or other sources. Marie Louise Burgess-Ware, the author of a story in the *Colored American*, is specifically identified in a preceding issue of the magazine as "a well known race educator who has lived and labored in the South for some years" (6 [July 1903]: advertisements, n.p.). Appearing in the United States Census for 1900 with her birthdate listed as August 1876, Gertrude Dorsey Browne, who published as Gertrude H. Dorsey before her marriage and changed or corrected the spelling of her last name from

Brown to Browne in later issues of the *Colored American,*
evidently was a sales and distribution agent for the magazine
in Newark, Ohio; and a picture of her appears in the
publication a couple of times (10 [Jan. 1906]: publisher's
announcements, n.p.; 11 [Dec. 1906]: 418). Also named in
the 1900 Census, Ruth D. Todd is identified as a black
servant working in the home of George M. Cooper in
Philadelphia. She was born in Virginia, and her birthdate is
given as September 1878. Leila Amos Pendleton, who continued to publish in the *Crisis* in the 1920s, opens her
impassioned "An Apostrophe to the Lynched" in the June
1916 *Crisis* with this clear affirmation of her African ancestry:
"Hang there, O my murdered brothers, sons of Ethiopia,
our common Mother!" (12: 86). Finally, a biographical note
at the opening of Minnibelle Jones's story in the *Crisis* in
1914 states that she wrote the piece when she was ten years
old (the story appeared in the October issue, which was
regularly devoted to a focus on African American children).

Written by more than two dozen different people over a
period of twenty years, the stories that follow provoke no easy
generalizations. Rather, they illustrate—if they can be said to
illustrate any one thing—the widespread insistence on self-
definition of their authors.

In 1903 Pauline Hopkins replied furiously to a white
reader who said that fiction in the *Colored American* should
quit focusing on interracial relationships: "It is the same old
story. One religion for the whites and another for the blacks.
The story of Jesus for us, that carries with it submission to
the abuses of our people and blindness to the degrading of
our youth" and—presumably—all sorts of stories for white
people. The right to tell whatever story she wished was what
Hopkins angrily laid claim to. She told her self-appointed

white critic who fantasized about an American Dickens rising up and writing about the "neglected colored people of America":

> If he had been an American, and with his trenchant pen had exposed the abuses practiced by the Southern whites upon the blacks—had told the true story of how wealth, intelligence and femininity has stooped to choose for a partner in sin, the degraded (?) Negro whom they affect to despise, Dickens would have been advised to shut up or get out. I believe Jesus Christ when on earth rebuked the Pharisees in this wise: "Ye hypocrites, ye expect to be heard for your much speaking"; "O wicked and adulterous (?) nation, how can ye escape the damnation of hell?" He didn't go about patting those old sinners on the back and saying, "All right, boys, fix me up and the Jews will get there all right. Money talks. Divy on the money you take in the exchange business of the synagogue, and it'll be all right with God." Jesus told the thing as it was and the Jews crucified him!

Hopkins complains: "You are between Scylla and Charybdis: If you please the author of this letter and your white clientele, you will lose your Negro patronage. If you cater to the *demands* of the Negro trade, away goes Mrs. ————." But she concludes: "Let the good work go on. Opposition is the life of an enterprise; criticism tells you that you are doing something" (6 [March 1903]: 399–400).

Hopkins was not alone in her determination to define her own art. The diversity of the stories in this volume emphasizes the same determination of many black women writers at the turn of the century. Common themes and shared stylistic and formal preferences do exist, but at the same time, the stories do not resolve into any tidy set of types, much less one type. Differences in subject matter, tone, style, form, political perspective, class alliance, and regional bias permeate the volume. The stories talk about the church, schoolteaching, love, poverty, lynching, passing, sisterhood, uplift, slavery, marriage, mothering, dreaming, lying, laughing, dying. They dramatize relationships between blacks and whites. They ignore whites and examine life in the black community. They voice opinions on political issues—American imperialism, white racism, industrial education for African Americans, black men's sexism, color prejudice within the black community, votes for women, the sexual exploitation of black women by white men. They celebrate community—the strength of black men and particularly of black women and of the black family—and they criticize the black community. Above all they refuse to give in to despair. They register pain and anger and frustration, but they seldom elect pessimism.

In provocative ways, the opening story by Hopkins, "The Mystery Within Us," comments on this refusal to despair by tying it to the issue of writing, a crucial subject for all of the authors in this volume. Although gender is displaced and race is never mentioned, the autobiographical importance of "The Mystery Within Us" is clear. Hopkins's story records the temptation to commit suicide of a young doctor who finally realizes that he cannot kill himself because his life is not his own. Through him a brilliant dead physician writes. If the young man kills himself, he kills two people.

"The Mystery Within Us" says that writing is corporate—not a singular but a collaborative act, one in which the otherwise lost voices of the past find expression. Writing constitutes communion across generations, a link between the living and the dead. To despair of life, to give up and give in to silence—the young physician's temptation to kill himself—is to render voiceless not only the present but also the past, the literally life-saving words of those who have gone before. It is no accident that the two writers in the story are doctors. (The need to make them such, I think, explains Hopkins's use of men in this story.) Writing heals. The written word can relieve pain, restore wholeness, give hope, and provide comfort in the face of death. The written word can enable the past and the present to join in life.

Ruth D. Todd's light-hearted love story, "The Taming of a Modern Shrew," offers a quite different perspective on being a black woman writer. Beginning with its title, the story plays with men writers. Todd's heroine announces that she will marry the hero on one condition: if he writes a novel or poems worthy of publication. Able only to write doggerel, the young man desperately pens outrageous nonsense verse and a story in modern slang, and his horrified sweetheart declares that she will marry him immediately if he will only promise not to publish these terrible creations in the local paper.

Todd's comedy celebrates the nonsense of young love—in itself a political act given the pressures on serious African American authors, as Jessie Fauset would complain in print some years later, to produce nothing but protest.[10] The story ignores pain and evil and injustice and thinks instead about love between a black man and a black woman untouched by racial issues. It enjoys the lovers' stubbornness and rivalry in a modern revision of Shakespeare that, true to the original, relishes the battle of the sexes and leaves us wondering who "won." Simultaneously, however, "The Taming of a Modern Shrew" is a black woman writer's sly but serious story about writing, gender, jokes, and literary masters and models. The tale declares Todd's right to write herself into any tradition—the highest (Shakespeare) or the silliest (the nonsense verse)—and in so doing, it flaunts her freedom to own form. Playfully expressed, the story broadcasts its author's license. It dramatizes a young black woman's demand for literature, a young black man's simultaneous success and failure in meeting that demand, and behind the scenes, another black woman's (Todd's) perfect mastery of all of the forms involved: the Shakespearean comedy of the sexes, the trendy nonsense verse and slang fiction, and—what the woman in the story really craves—a genuine love story.

Referring explicitly to Thomas Dixon's 1905 racist best-seller, *The Clansman,* which in 1915 would be turned into the critically acclaimed racist film *Birth of a Nation,* Gertrude Dorsey Browne in "A Case of Measure for Measure" also plays with form and invokes Shakespeare. However, Browne's rewrite of Shakespeare—and rebuttal to Dixon—is anything but light-hearted. She appropriates the favorite fictive form of nineteenth-century white racism, the black-face minstrel show, and uses it to write her own dark comedy about the racism of white people. In her story of white people blacking up (an inversion of the more usual passing plot which shows black people whiting up), the whites cannot shed the insulting form they have created: They try to "unmask" but the paint will not come off. The "make-up" sticks. Form holds. It traps and turns against the formers—the form-makers—and won't let them out. As a metaphor for how racist form, visual or narrative, deforms its makers—and even more important, as a demonstration of the black woman writer's adept reversal of racist form onto itself—"A Case of Measure for Measure" (itself measured out originally over six issues of the *Colored American,* making it the longest serialization of any in this book) hints at both the powerful anger and the creative release that Gertrude Dorsey Browne could tap as a black woman writing.

Jessie Fauset comments most directly on being a woman and a writer in "My House and a Glimpse of My Life Therein." It is a complex and unusually surreal fiction for

Fauset. Obviously allegorical, what is the "house" in this story? Where are we? The place to which Fauset takes us is solitary, gorgeous, scary, highly intellectual, and specifically literary. The speaker acknowledges an insidious destructiveness about the place: The house can unfit one for the duties and real struggles of life, as well as for ordinary enjoyments. Fauset was well educated and brilliant, a Phi Beta Kappa graduate from Cornell: Is this story her nightmare vision of her own life? Who is "Kathleen" and what is the quarrel to which the speaker alludes? What do we make of the image of the speaker as "queen" in a tiny secret attic space? The house Fauset describes is beautiful, sensuous, and luxuriant, but it is also haunted by isolation, irrelevance, and incapacitation. Is this lifeless, silent house a metaphor for the creative life of a modern middle-class black woman as the contemporary West has constructed it?

Considerable formal variety appears throughout the volume. Some stories are cast as dream-visions, such as Fauset's "My House and a Glimpse of My Life Therein" or Angelina Grimké's "Black Is, As Black Does." Others, though posing as realism, are really parables—for example, a number of the Christmas tales or a story such as Hopkins's "As the Lord Lives, He Is One of Our Mother's Children," which, hard to accept as realism, gives new form to old New Testament truths (the story revolves around a minister for good reason). A number of stories such as "Aunt 'Ria's Ten Dollars," "Bro'r Abr'm Jimson's Wedding," "Mizeriah Johnson: Her Arisings and Shinings," and "Aunt Calline's Sheaves" draw heavily and deliberately on oral tradition, attempting to re-create in print, often but not always through dialect, a sense of direct, spoken delivery. The popularity of first-person narration—"The Mystery Within Us," "Black Is, As Black Does," "Talma Gordon," or "Mary Elizabeth"—likewise shows certain authors' interest in manipulating form to create immediacy, intimacy, complexity, or suspense. The nine-teenth-century sketch tradition can be felt in various pieces— "The Wooing of Pastor Cummings," "Mizeriah Johnson: Her Arisings and Shinings," and "Aunt Calline's Sheaves"— all of which attempt to capture character and environment as much as or more than they try to work out plot. "A Dash for Liberty" draws directly on the male slave narrative, with its emphasis on singular heroic action and combat, while parts of other stories—stories within stories—reproduce fictively the more familial dynamic of many women's slave narratives, as in "The Octoroon's Revenge," "After Many Days," "Scrambled Eggs," or "Mary Elizabeth." [11] True to Hop-kins's particular fascination with form, a story such as "Talma Gordon" almost visibly stirs together disparate genres: the after-dinner male smoker, the Gothic thriller, the revenge plot of slave narrative, the contemporary murder mystery, and the tragic mulatto or passing plot.

This last, the passing plot, may present the most challenge to a modern audience. Switched babies, dead mothers, duped fathers, and deceived children are used repeatedly to produce fictions in which racial identity is confused or hidden until at some crucial point in a young person's life, such as engage-ment or marriage, she (sometimes he) must confront directly the full force of American racism. "Talma Gordon," "The Octoroon's Revenge," "The Test of Manhood," "After Many Days," "Bernice, The Octoroon," "Scrambled Eggs," "Emmy," and "The Sleeper Wakes" all work variations on this plot.

The problems posed by the passing plot are considerable. Viewed realistically, how common a figure in the United States at the turn of the century was the African American woman who passed knowingly or unknowingly for white?

Certainly most African American women at the beginning of the twentieth century were not leading privileged middle- or upper-middle-class lives in either the white or the black world. Why the literary obsession with a figure so far removed from the ordinary problems and issues of African American life, except that she is all that her class-bound creators know, or want to know? Viewed from this perspective, the black character so fair that she can pass for white is highly problematic. She is an elite heroine who allows her middle-class creators to parade their class biases without compunction. Not only does her whiteness play into the hands of white racism— she is refined, virtuous, and ladylike, the racist argument runs, precisely because she is white—but she also reinforces discriminatory attitudes about color within the black community.

While these problems are real and must not be dismissed or denied, it is also important to look at the passing plot as a literary strategy that serves quite different purposes. The plot exposes the insanity of white racism—the mania of the dominant culture with cups and teaspoons and thimblefuls of "blood"—and affirms African American community, sanity, and struggle. When the blonde heroine of Marie Louise Burgess-Ware's "Bernice, The Octoroon" first identifies herself as an African American, she does so because she has no choice. Thrown out of the white world in which she was raised, she is labeled "black" by white America, a negative identity—a terrible fate—from the dominant point of view. However, when she stays with that identification at the end of the story, she does so because she *chooses* to. Black has become a positive identity, a proud, difficult, and worthy fate. From this perspective, the passing plot does not reinforce elitist, racist attitudes. Rather it gives Burgess-Ware a way to take her character fully into both white and black America and to force upon her the critical moral question: Which does she choose? With which America will she stand?

In *The Work of the Afro-American Woman* (1894), Gertrude Mossell observed: "Every one engaged in literary work, even if but to a limited extent, feels greatly the need of a quiet nook to write in." [12] For many of the authors collected in this volume we remain a long way from being able to picture the "quiet nook," literal or symbolic, in which their fiction took form. For some we may never be able to reconstruct that biographical space. However, the stories that follow immediately open the door into an equally important world, a broad and rich imaginative space. In them, like the healer in Hopkins's opening story, we can meet directly a past once thought dead—gone, even nonexistent—and catch living voices.

## NOTES

1. For excellent, detailed discussion of the black periodical press in the United States up to the founding of the *Crisis* in 1910, see Penelope L. Bullock, *The Afro-American Periodical Press, 1838–1909* (Baton Rouge: Louisiana State University Press, 1981).

2. *Colored American Magazine* 1 (Oct. 1900): prospectus for 1901, n.p.; 2 (Dec. 1900): 157; 4 (May 1902): 76. All subsequent references to the *Colored American Magazine* and the *Crisis* will be indicated parenthetically in the text.

3. For description and analysis of this change in ownership and management of the *Colored American Magazine*, see Bullock, pp. 108–18, and Abby Arthur Johnson and Ronald M. Johnson, "Away from Accommodation: Radical Editors and Protest Journalism, 1900–1910," *Journal of Negro History* 62 (Oct. 1977): 325–29.

4. Du Bois, for example, received credit for a number of editorial decisions actually made by Fauset. See Carolyn Wedin

Sylvander, *Jessie Redmon Fauset, Black American Writer* (Troy, NY: Whitson Publishing Co., 1981), pp. 114 ff.

5. Excellent discussion of this period can be found in Paula Giddings, *When and Where I Enter: The Impact of Black Women on Race and Sex in America* (New York: Bantam, 1984), and Hazel V. Carby, *Reconstructing Womanhood: The Emergence of the Afro-American Woman Novelist* (New York: Oxford University Press, 1987).

6. Bullock, p. 115.

7. I welcome information about authors in the volume, most of whom do not show up in the usual sources: the National Union Catalog, the Schomburg Catalog, the Schlesinger Women's History Archives, *The Encyclopedia of Afro-American Writers, Who's Who of the Colored Race, 1915, Who's Who in Colored America, 1927, The Club Movement among Negro Women* by Fannie Barrier Williams (1912), *History of the National Association of Colored Women's Clubs* (1984), accessible genealogical reference books such as *American Negro Women during Fifty Years,* or the Accelerated Indexing System (AIS) of the United States Census 1850–1906 available in the Church of the Latter Day Saints Family History Center in Weston, Massachusetts.

For generous help and advice already received, I wish to thank Wilson Fleminster at Atlanta University, Dr. Debora Newman at the Library of Congress, Professor Penelope Bullock in Atlanta, Georgia, Dr. Dorothy Porter Wesley at the W. E. B. Du Bois Institute, Professor Gerald Gill of the History Department at Tufts University, and especially Ann Allen Shockley at Fisk University. Above all, I am grateful to Dr. Katherine Kleitz, who provided me with outstanding research assistance on very short notice. In particular, I am indebted to Katherine for the hunch—held onto despite my skepticism—that Gertrude Dorsey Brown, Gertrude D. Browne, Gertrude H. Dorsey, and Gertrude Hayes Brown were all the same person—which turned out to be true.

8. Hopkins's novels and Dunbar-Nelson's collected works are available in The Schomburg Library of Nineteenth-Century Black Women Writers (New York: Oxford University Press, 1988). Those volumes, edited by Richard Yarborough, Hazel V. Carby,

and Gloria T. Hull, contain excellent introductions to the two authors. For further discussion and information, see Carby on Hopkins in *Reconstructing Womanhood;* Hull on Dunbar-Nelson in *Give Us Each Day: The Diary of Alice Dunbar-Nelson* (New York: W. W. Norton, 1984) and on both Angelina Grimké and Dunbar-Nelson in *Color, Sex, and Poetry: Three Women Writers of the Harlem Renaissance* (Bloomington: Indiana University Press, 1987); and Sylvander on Fauset. Also I discuss Hopkins, Dunbar-Nelson, and Fauset in my book *Conflicting Stories: American Women Writers at the Turn into the Twentieth Century* (New York: Oxford University Press, 1991).

9. Mossell's *The Work of the Afro-American Woman* (New York: Oxford University Press, 1988) has also been reprinted in The Schomburg Library of Nineteenth-Century Black Women Writers, with an excellent introduction by Joanne Braxton that contains biographical information and analysis. For discussion of Williams and excerpts from her speeches, see Giddings, *When and Where I Enter,* as well as Gerda Lerner, ed., *Black Women in White America: A Documentary History* (New York: Pantheon, 1972).

10. In a 1920 review in the *Crisis* Fauset praised "the launching of an essay by Negro writers into the realm of pure romantic fiction" and goes on immediately to say: "This is a relief when one considers that nearly all writing on the part of colored Americans seeks to set forth propaganda" (20 [June 1920]: 80).

11. Discussion of differences between men's and women's slave narratives can be found in Valerie Smith's introduction to Harriet Jacobs, *Incidents in the Life of a Slave Girl,* in The Schomburg Library of Nineteenth-Century Black Women Writers (New York: Oxford University Press, 1988).

12. Mossell, p. 126.

# THE MYSTERY WITHIN US

*Pauline E. Hopkins*

"Speaking of spiritualistic phenomena, and the existence of guardian angels, and that there are means of actual communication between the denizens of earth and those bright spirits—why, my dear Jack, I *do* believe in these things."

"Then you agree with the immortal bard that 'there are more things in heaven and earth than are dreamt of in *our* philosophy.' "

When I left home five years before, I had fretted a good deal about my friend Tom Underwood. I knew that he was in financial difficulties, but his indomitable pride was such that I dared not offer him the pecuniary help which I longed to give and which I felt was sorely needed. I had learned nothing from his occasional letters except that he was well. Upon my return from a long exile we met and resumed our friendly relations, to an extent, although there was, I felt, a something which he held back from me, and which would, if told, explain the state of great success and eminence which he had attained in his profession as a physician, and as an author, too, of eagerly sought scientific works on subjects pertaining to the science of the preservation of life. I found, indeed, a great fascination in reading the most wonderful work of its kind that I had ever chanced upon, entitled "The Ethics of Life," and I did not wonder at his success.

To-night he had invited me to a *tete-a-tete* dinner at his bachelor quarters; this was the first time we had so dined

*Colored American Magazine* 1 (May 1900): 14–18.

since my return. After finishing our repast, I settled myself
in the most comfortable position I could assume, and while I
silently waited for my friend to give me the confidence which
I felt would be natural to the time and place, I enjoyed
his fine Havanas and admired the elegance of his surroundings.

Tom's rooms formed the top floor of one of those wonderful
apartment houses with which large cities now endeavor to
cater to the refined tastes of those men who have, apparently,
foresworn matrimony, to the despair of the fair sex and the
delight and profit of the speculator to whom the bachelor
apartment house is a veritable mine. I glanced curiously about
me at the rich furnishings which betokened the man of wealth
and culture. An attentive man servant glided in and out and
ministered to our comfort. It was like a story from the
"Arabian Nights"—the luxury, the ease, the elegance. Outside the twilight shades gathered over the roofs of the busy
city and mingled and melted into each other; the clouds,
tinged with the gold of an exquisite sunset were, for a
moment, radiant angel forms, clad in celestial garments of
light, covering the city with their heavenly mantles before
they were lost in the rapid descent of the night shadows. Tom
threw his cigar stump away, and turning to me, said:

"The thoughts expressed by the bard so many years ago
prove the inspiration of his genius, and could the many
strange things which happen in our individual lives be recorded we would be justified in calling ourselves a world
mentally unbalanced.

"When you left home, Jack, I was, as you doubtless
surmised, a bankrupt. My patients were as poor as myself
and I treated the most of them for nothing. I had drawn a
blank at every turn of Fortune's wheel. Love, at one time,
had seemed to present a happy augury for a happy future.

Poor fool that I was! *She* turned from me with scorn for my poverty.

"One evening I sat in my cheerless room and weighed carefully each event in my life—struggles and disappointments, against the few successes which had come to me. The result was too much for me. I went to my mineral cabinet and deliberately selected a bottle of prussic acid with the intention of ending it all right there. I seated myself on the edge of my couch and watched the dying candle as it prepared for its final disappearance, just as the clock in a neighboring room struck twelve. So shall I be in a short time, I thought, as I watched the dying candle. What is life anyhow, I argued, but a flame easily extinguished by the rude hand of destiny or misfortune. And is it not manlier to take arms against a sea of trouble and end all, than to tamely bear the buffets of misfortune and the cold scorn of the world? I raised the bottle to my lips with the intention of draining it. Halfway there my arm lost its carrying power, and I sat upon the edge of my couch startled into momentary forgetfulness of my project as I mentally analyzed the condition of the arm. Again I essayed to raise the member, but although my mind was more active than it had been for some time, I found that my *entire body had lost the power of volition!* Imagine my sensations! In no way could I account to myself for this condition. My bodily health was perfect.

"To say I was astonished is putting it mildly. I was dumbfounded! I was wont to boast, if you remember, Jack, that my nerves were impervious to fear, but now I felt absolute terror. I arose from my couch, and then, overcome by an irresistible impulse of weakness, sank back again and closed my eyes. The next instant a voice sounded in my ears:

" 'Be not afraid; it is I.'

"My mind worked with lightning-like rapidity; I con-

cluded that I was having a psychological experience, so trying
to overcome my fear, I endeavored to put in practice certain
rules governing such phenomena. *I thought a question and the
answer came:—'Look and see.'*

"At these words I felt compelled to unclose my eyes and
sit upright. A faint light had settled about the only armchair
the room contained and my mind seemed forced to centre
itself upon this halo. Gradually the shadowy outlines assumed
the form of a man, and I could even trace the features, but
no one feature attracted me so much as the eyes; they dazzled
me, they were so bright—like piercing wells of light.
All sensations of fear ceased as I gazed into their limpid
depths. Sorrow left me and peace took the place of black
despair.

"At last the Presence spoke. I say *spoke*, but, indeed, no
sound broke the silence of the room. The Presence *seemed* to
speak, although I was well aware that *it did not*. I had heard
and read much of the power which lies in the action of one
magnetic mind upon another, but never before had I experienced a vivid electrical impression.

" 'What would you do, rash man? Overcome by the petty
obstacles that have filled a pathway intended to end in benefit
to yourself and others, after the needed lessons necessary to
develop the latent faculties with which you have been most
generously endowed, would you destroy the life that is not
yours? By the divine will of God you were designed as an
instrument for the accomplishment of certain plans formed
before your birth. Would you in the rash despair of human
short-sightedness destroy the tenement and reduce the spirit
of life within you to the impenetrable darkness and wild
tempests of the ocean of regret to which the self-destroyed
are forever doomed?'

"I sat in silence, receiving the impressions that emanated

from the shape before me. Over the shadowy features various emotions passed: stern denunciation, pity, and finally, grief, as it continued:—'Once, like you, I lived in the flesh, although I know now that I never lived until I died to earth and left my body to assume the form of my Creator; for only in our spiritual essence do we assume the image of God. This clay house is but the casket within which God created man in His own image—that is the ethereal, fleeting animation which we call life, and which comes we know not how, and goes we know not where.'

"The Presence paused again in the midst of impressions made upon me like waves of electrical shocks most delicately given. I seemed to recognize the ideas expressed, and even the language was familiar. Gradually my mind was led to thoughts of a physician who had instituted a new epoch in medicine in the cure of certain chronic diseases called incurable by the medical profession. This man died just at the time when his fame was nearing its zenith, and physicians were seriously contemplating the adoption of methods quite foreign to accepted ideas. Dr. Thorn's books (he was the author of three wonderful treatises on 'The Philosophy of the Three Ethers') were my daily companions, and I had often wished it had been my privilege to know the man and to have seen something of his mysterious cures. As I reached the name of Dr. Thorn, in my mind, I glanced at the Presence. The outlines wore a shadowy smile, and I received the impression that I was right in thinking that I beheld the spiritual essence of the great physician.

" 'Yes, I was Dr. Thorn, and I would have given the whole of my hard-earned fortune to have remained in the body a few years longer. The transgression of certain laws in the matter of my physical being caused the failure in my own case of the formula which I used for the cure of blood poisoning, and so the vitiated corpuscles dominated my whole system and I made the great change before I realized that it had come. In the midst of my grief for those I had left and my lost art, I received the promise from the Divinity that my discoveries should not be lost, and that one should be given me who should revive and restore the whole of my system. You are he. Be pure in thought and aspiration; diligent and contented; seek and find.'

"When I came to myself in the early morning hours, I awoke as one from a long sleep. I still sat upon the side of my couch, but the bottle of poison I have never seen since. The room was cold and cheerless and upon the table which stood at my elbow was the full manuscript of the book that has made me famous and has brought me a fortune. *I invariably find prescriptions and treatises upon chronic cases on that table by my bedside in the morning when I awake.*

"I cannot account for all of this except by quoting the words which you have used: 'There are more things in heaven and earth than are dreamt of in our philosophy.' "

# BLACK IS, AS BLACK DOES
## *(A Dream)*

*Angelina W. Grimké*

It came to me one dark, rainy morning as I was half awake
and half asleep. The wind was blowing drearily, and I listened
to the swish of the rain upon the glass and the dripping from
the eaves. As I lay listening I thought many things, and my
thoughts grew hazier and hazier, and I fell into deep slumber.

Then methought a great feeling of peace came upon me
and that all my cares were falling from me, and rolling
away—away into infinity. As I lay with my eyes closed this
great feeling of peace increased, and my heart was glad within
me. Then some one touched me lightly upon the shoulder
and eyes, causing my heart to give a great bound, for I was
not prepared for the loveliness of the scene which now burst
upon my sight. Stretched all around was a wide, green, grassy
plain. Each little blade of grass sang in the gentle wind, and
here and there massive trees spread their branches. The leaves
and the birds made music, while the river passing through
the meadow sparkled and sang as it sped on its way. Listening,
I heard no discord, for all the voices blended with each other,
mingling, and swelling, and making one grand sweet song.
I longed to sing too, and I lifted up my voice, but no song
came, so that I wondered. Then a voice at my side answered:
"Thou art not one of us yet." The voice was sweeter than the
babbling brook, more tender than the voice of a mother to
her erring child, lower than the beating of the restless surf

*Colored American Magazine* 1 (Aug. 1900): 160–63.

on the shore. Then I turned to see whence this voice came. As I looked I fell upon my face weeping.

For there stood before me a figure clad in white. As she moved she seemed like a snowy-white cloud, which sails o'er the sky in summertime. A soft light shone above, around, behind, illuminating her. It was not for this I fell to weeping. I had looked upon the face, and the truth which shone forth from the mild eyes, the sweetness which smiled around the mouth, and all the pity, the mercy, the kindness, expressed in that divine countenance, revealed to me how wicked I was, and had been. But she took me by the hand, bidding me arise, and kissed me on the brow. Between my sobs I asked: "Where am I?" The low voice answered: "This is heaven." I said: "Who art thou?" She answered: "One of the lovers of God." And as she spoke that name the heavens brightened, the grass sang sweeter, as did the leaves and the birds, also the silvery river. Looking up I saw that she was no longer by my side, but was moving o'er the plain, and turning she beckoned to me. I followed without knowing why.

Thus we passed silently over the velvety grass, o'er hill and dale, by laughing brooks and swift-flowing rivers. Often turning she smiled upon me, but on and on we went; now and then other bright spirits passed us, all smiling kindly upon me as they went their way. Some came and kissed my forehead and said they were glad to see me, and I was happy, *so* happy. Then methought we came to a city, but ah! so unlike our cities: no hurrying this and that way, no deafening roar of passing wagons, no shrieking hucksters, no loud talking, no anxious, worried faces. All was peace. And as we passed up the noiseless streets many spirits clad in spotless white, and gleaming with that ineffable light, passed, and all smiled and greeted me tenderly as they went their shining way.

Then we came to a great hall. The doors thereby were three and opened wide, and I saw many people going in through the first door, but they were not clad in snowy white, and I could see no light illuminating their bodies. I asked: "Pray tell me who are these?" And the spirit said: "These are those, like you, who have just come from earth." And as she spoke I saw some passing forth from the second door, clad in white, but I saw no light, and I said perplexed: "Pray who are these, and why does no light illuminate them?" She answered: "These are they whom our *Father* has blessed of those who have just come from earth, and they will have the light when they have been with us a long time, when they have done some service which has particularly gratified *'our Father.'*" She had scarcely ceased speaking when I saw several ragged ones, with looks downcast, coming through the third door; and I asked: "Pray who are these?" As she answered her voice trembled, and gazing upon her I saw a tear glide down her cheek, as she answered, simply: "The lost." And, groaning within me I said: "Pray what is this place?" And solemnly she answered: "This is where God weeds out the wicked from the good." And as she ceased speaking she glided to the first door and beckoned me.

We came within a hall, large and gloomy, and we passed down one end, and looking up I saw a great, dazzling light, that was all; for I fell upon the floor, overcome. I had looked upon *God!* As I lay I heard his voice now low and tender beyond expression, now stern and mighty, like the roll of thunder. When I took courage I gazed around, but I dared not look upon *His* face again.

I saw a vast multitude of those lately come from earth, waiting to stand before the bar of judgment; also those who had been tried, passing out through the doors. Looking at my companion I saw that she was gazing upon *God*, and his brightness shone upon her face, and I was dazzled and looked down. When I glanced upon the throng of the lately dead, I saw one pass to the bar, and fall with a loud cry for mercy. I heard him weeping and confessing all his sins, excusing himself in nothing, and I saw that his skin was black; looking closer I saw that he was lame, torn, and bleeding, and quite unrecognizable, for most of his features were gone. I saw him waving his poor stumps of arms, begging for mercy. By these tokens I knew that he came from my country, and that he was one of an oppressed race; for in America, alas! it makes a difference whether a man's *skin* be black or white. Nothing was said, but I perceived that he had been foully murdered.

I heard *God's* voice speaking to him and I was lost in its sweetness. It seemed to me I was floating down a stream of loveliness, and I was so happy. When He ceased I thought I had gently come to some bank, and all was peace and rest. And I saw the man pass from the bar, and that he was clad in pure white. Beautiful spirits came and tended his wounds, and lo! he stood forth glorified, a dim light shining round him. I looked at my companion and she smiled, and then I understood. And behold another stood before the *Judgment-seat*. I did not hear *him* beg for mercy, but I heard him telling all the good he had done, and I heard a sound as of distant mutterings of thunder, and I felt the angry flashings above the *Judgment-seat*. And I saw the man waiting calmly in his own conceit. And I heard the muffled thunder of God's voice asking: "And didst thou treat all my children justly?" And I heard the man say: "Yea, yea, O Lord!" And I heard God again: "Whether their skin was black or white?" And the man answered: "Yea, yea, Lord," and laughed.

Then I heard the thunder of God's voice saying: "I know thee, who thou art; it wast thou who didst murder yon man,

and upon that day occurred the monthly rhetoricals, he had made the school the favorite rendezvous of his evenings. It was only the night before that he had attended the Alumni Banquet, and made himself the cynosure of all eyes, and subject of many comments, by his bold but *very* courteous manner, handsome person and fashionable apparel. I noticed, as did everyone else, that he paid marked attention to Louise. She told me that during the progress of the fete he came to where she and Tom were having a fond tete-a-tete within the bay window of the library. But no; I will let Louise tell you her own story.

"Mr. Warwick came to us with his usual suave smile and punctilious manner, Beth. I introduced him to Tom, which was no sooner done than he asked that dear boy if he would excuse me for a short interval. He had dogged my steps all the evening, and just when I thought I had escaped him, he surprised me with such audacity as this! Tom looked quickly, entreatingly at me, and said blandly—too blandly in truth: 'Just as Miss Trent wishes it.' My lips had framed a haughty refusal. But before I spoke I looked (truly the woman who deliberates is lost) at that evil genius, and when his piercing black eyes met mine, I said *yes* as mechanically as someone in a dream, and took his arm. He turned our steps toward the library porch, where hung Japanese lanterns and floral decorations of all kinds. A premonitive shudder shook my form—I truly dreaded the interview—and this dread was accentuated by the knowledge that I was powerless to avert it. He is a wicked, unscrupulous man, Beth, and he did not use any preliminary at all, but taking my hand, and compelling my eyes to meet his by the power of an implacable will, he said as truthfully as a better man might have done: 'I asked you here, Louise, because I love you and I wish to take you away as my wife. I have never loved any woman before you, and that is saying a good deal, taking into consideration the fact that I am not a young man. You have been evading me, and I am not one to brook evasion or thwarted purpose. I have the license in my pocket; the minister I have caused to be an invited guest. All is ready. Marry me tonight and I will remain in the city as before, keeping the marriage a profound secret until after Commencement night; then we leave for my home in the western part of the state. A refusal will do no good; if you do not marry me now, you will never know what peace is until you do.'

"Oh, Beth, and all that time his great, dreadful eyes were telling me to acquiesce. I do believe that there is some snake nature in that man, and it is all concentered in his eyes.

"As I realized my danger, all my past life spread out before me with its kaleidoscopic features, mostly bright and beautiful; all my future misery with him aroused in me a revulsion of feeling greater than any magnetic power of his could master. I sprang deftly aside, evaded his grasping hand, and ran to my room.

"What must I do, Beth? Tom is surprised and angry; this man is my shadow. If I report to the President it will necessitate a faculty meeting, and you know that will incur scandal; true, I could tell Tom, but his temper and headstrong, thoughtless action will do more harm than good. A week from tonight is Commencement night; I am valedictorian, and don't want to leave for home till school closes."

I was surprised, indignant, but could only sigh, and say uningenuously, that it is too bad to be only a woman. "Ah!" she said, with more than her usual spirited impatience: "I expected you to help me, tell me something of which I am ignorant. I would not have told you had I known that you, like myself, could only sigh, sigh! I looked for more than that from you, the *brilliant, gifted, scholastic Beth.*"

There was a note of bitterest irony in her voice as she spoke, and I looked at her in blank amazement; feeling toward her at that moment, as I never had before, and hope to never feel again. Women do not bear with one another's caprices as readily as they should. Louise had not the temper or fortitude allotted to angels, yet she had never spoken crossly to me before. And now, I did not even think she cared for the wound she had inflicted, because she left me and walked hurriedly up the path; the stile was reached, she hesitated a moment, and returning wound her arms around me, saying in a scarcely articulate whisper: "Can you ever forgive me, darling little sister?"

I returned her pressure with vengeance, and told her that I understood. Probably my voice sounded a trifle lachrymonious, for she looked hastily down, and asked quizzically, "Are *you* crying, Beth?" I had never been known to cry during my six years' stay at school (something unheard of in a girl!). So to her question I answered with a merry laugh, in which she joined, and the threatening gulf between us was abridged.

Naturally, I was not as much worried over the confidential disclosure as Louise. I regarded it as a contingency to be looked for in any love affair where there are too many lords to a lady. Every such condition of affairs invariably ends the same—disastrously. In some cases of course the ruin is greater than in others; but that also is a law from nature's code, and he who offends must of necessity accept fate's allotment (whether it be great or small). Truly said the sage: "Experience is that dear school in which fools deign to take their only lessons." And that very truth has made every man a fool.

Luncheon bell rang—at school it is the salve that heals temporarily, even grief's wound, and we went slowly back to the dining-hall.

The girls had an unpleasant habit of privately calling our dear (?) matron "Eyes"; whose real name by the way was Smith, but she affected a more pretentious way of spelling it by inserting "y" and ending it in "e,"—it looked well in print too;—dear soul, I wish I could say the same of her picture I saw in a paper once. Well, as the Romans do, so do I,—this same "Eyes" came bouncing toward us (she could bounce, for she had an excellent figure, but what she paid for it I am at present unable to say) saying in her usual hurried, flurried, scared sort of way: "Girls, where in the world have *you two* been?" Her emphasis was called for,— *we two* were likely to be found just anywhere impromptu curiosity or premeditated plans took us. Fan—I mean Louise had cried, and it is simply wonderful how these aquatic emissions relieve persons addicted to them—and was now looking and acting like her old self again; so to "Eyes' " query she replied with a knowing nonchalant shake of the head, and her gay little laugh: "Ah, mater" ("Eyes" liked that word, it sounded young and caressing), "were we wanted?"

"Yes, dear; you had a visitor—Mr. Warwick."

"Well," Louise said brusquely, "I'm glad I wasn't here," and we passed into the dining-hall.

I scarcely saw Louise after luncheon, for she would never, not even for her dearest friend, or for ignorance of a certain lesson on the morrow, miss her afternoon nap; sometimes it was ten minutes, again two hours that she slept,—but whether long or short, it came. So I went to play tennis and left her to entertain Morpheus.

At supper she reappeared looking as immaculate as ever, that immaculateness which gives the other girl a loose feeling, forces her hand involuntarily to her head to smooth the wind-tossed hair,—and also opportunity to make a covenant saying that tomorrow evening I'll wear my new pink shirtwaist.

*My* room-mate as it happened was a Prep.; moreover, she had a hearty disliking for *her* room-mate, and would "bunk" out, making frequent and sometimes long nocturnal absences. After taps had sounded she would mightily please me by evading the vigilance of "Eyes," and visit the girls who knew how to appreciate her garrulous proclivities better than I did. Tonight a bargain had been struck, and contract signed, that she would remain from home one week, relinquishing her place to Louise. Hence eight o'clock finds two members of the "T. S. T." (a club to which we belonged) domiciled and chatting gaily. "Eyes" ruled the back corridor, or Prepdom, at night, and another good little teacher, whose memory among others I really hold dear, was too far away on our hall to know that *we two* were cooking chocolate or talking above a whisper.

Ten o'clock found us in bed. Between then and the time I awoke to find myself sweltering in perspiration, and scared out of my wits, seemed an age. I had dreamed, and such a dream! Was it the outcome of our talk of the morning? Did it bring the traditional warning? Or had it no significance other than that the effect had been caused by the piece of refractory meat that I had eaten the night preceding? I am not superstitious, nor easily frightened, but don't think it pleasant to be awakened after a mysterious dream in the wintery gloom of the early morning, when every black-robed piece of furniture seems to say: "I am here to prove that your dream was not at all a dream, but reality." You can't explain anything to your companion, because she is a sleepy-head, and worst of all, should you arouse her, what have you to tell? In my case I should have said: 'Oh, Louise, I have had such a terrible dream,'—and she—well, would have given an indescribable grunt, and again yielded herself to the caresses of sleep. Next morning I was mum on the subject, but when on the two following nights my presence in Slumbertown was greeted by the same denouement, I resolved not to remain silent. Night, because of these suggestive visitations, had grown terrible to me. I dare not sleep for fear I would dream. Not that I was afraid of a mere dream, but I was afraid of its persistence, its apparent truthfulness to life, and if true, its malignant effect upon the lives and destinies of my loved ones. I must tell some one, and yet—who? Louise? No; she had enough to keep her morbid and thoughtful.

But, ah! why had I not thought of him before? There is De. I was sure that he would listen, and not say that it was only a romantic, womanish fancy of mine, even if he thought so. No one loved De more than we, his classmates did—and no one deserved that affection more than he. If we remained in our rooms with real or pretended headaches, he was solicitous; the other young men might laughingly insinuate that our Psychology, or a certain unwritten paper, had more to do with our absence than the headache; but it was De who sent the consoling box of bon-bons, and the little: "I hope you will be down in the morning." If things went wrong, it was De who offered to right them, and who never forgot that a Senior girl was not the only one to whom he owed a tip of the hat and the social courtesies. He was a brother, especially to the T. S. T. We called him De, and it was a contraction of his real name; while it had no special significance, it had an endearing sound. I could easily see him, since we were allowed this week as a merited respite from months of most careful work. I believe there was only one who would not acknowledge that she was satisfied with our progress; for after we had long since crossed the line where we might have been termed novices, "Eyes" remarked that she would like to see the "prospective Seniors" after school hours. We were more conscious of the height we had attained, and careful lest our dignity be not recognized at that time than we were upon graduation, so none of us fell in love with the woman or her appellation, and I am afraid we showed that we did not.

# PART II

The opportunity to tell De my troubled state came almost unsought. He was a resident of the city, and on Thursday our club (which was analogous to one composed of young men) with these young men, were invited to dinner at De's mother's. After the coupling off incident to such occasions had taken place, I found myself with De in a cozy retreat formed by climbing roses and honeysuckle, where the very pestering bees and silver-throated birds seemed to prate of the many secrets that had been told in this ideal home of theirs. The proximity of another night and this scene made me doubly determined to unburden my mind, so after a few casual observances upon the banquet, weather and the coming Commencement night, I led uncertainly to a subject that was nearer home.

"De," I said with a familiarity warranted by years of Platonic friendship: "Do you know this Mr. Warwick,—the latest lion in town?"

"Yes; I—at least I have seen him. Why?"

"Well, I came here to tell you, and I intend to do so, but first you must promise not to repeat what I tell you to anyone unless I give you permission; looking and acting according to the ethics of the case, I have no right to tell you; I was not told not to repeat it, and yet I think I understand that secrecy was meant." He faithfully promised to do as I

requested. Then occurred to me the words so aptly written
by the French novelist,—and I laughingly expressed them:
"Is it difficult for a woman to keep a secret? Then I know
more than one man who is a woman." De refuted the quotation
as unjust to the memory of the many times he had prudently
acted in capacity of confidant and adviser. I acknowledged
the injustice, and grew serious. I told him almost verbatim
the story that Louise had intrusted to me only three mornings
before; at which he looked so fierce and angry that I declared
positively I would not finish the narrative unless he took it
all more passively than that. He told me to proceed, and
became tacitly thoughtful.

"Now, De, I have yet to tell you something which you
will probably call superstition. It is about a dream that I
speak, and I don't want you to class it as 'bosh' or anything
else, until you have heard me. The night succeeding the
morning on which Louise made me her confidante, I had a
dream of possible fearful significance, I believe. We cannot
always attribute dreams to either physical or natural causes.
When there is a special cause, and an undeniable one, we
may judge it to be the source from which sprung a certain
effect; but acknowledge that there is a limit to any one natural
source. And when mystical affairs stupefy us by their varied
and intricate innuendoes and the revelation of our own ignorance of the supernatural and spiritual existence, it is the
acme of egotism to assume that all unsolved problems which
taint of the weird are the outcome of superstitious illiteracy.
The day of Jacobs, Josephs and seers, whose dreaming has
foretold great good or evil, has passed, 'tis true, but since all
admit that history repeats itself,—why allow it to be robbed
of its repetitous power in this instance alone? I do not attempt
to attach any importance to my dream in your mind by any
especial effort or convincing argument, but as for myself I

shall continue to believe that its persistence meant more than doctrinaire scoffers of mental and spiritual communication would have us believe.

"I only wish that I could impress the central points as indelibly upon your imagination as they seem on my brain; the sensible connections, and location of place, people, and the peculiar but clear unraveling of a drama in that dream-world of mine, which would have made gold for its author and fame for its histrionic abettors.

"A high, level, fertile country, noisy cattle, and everywhere a mark of rural plenty. An old roomy red-brick farm-house, and straggling, tumble-down Negro quarters of ante bellum days. Taken in all, the place reminded me of the description Professor Gregory had given me of the springs where our club intends spending July. He said that if we did not care to stay at the hotel, that there was a large brick house near, kept by two elderly persons, who would be very likely to accommodate our party; there were no children only a son,— a traveling hypnotist of considerable renown. To this point my dream had accurately coincided with all given statistics, but here, too, occurred a diversion.

"Our club of three girls, with Mrs. Wyatt as chaperon, completed the party. I do not know how long we had been there, or when we came—we were there; and enjoying the novelty of our freedom as only girls can, when restrictions incident to plaits and aprons are removed. I can't explain, but we seemed to have lived weeks in the placid calm of those surroundings, before any sense of danger came to me. We had finished our luncheon, and were standing on the veranda waiting for our hats which Louise had gone to get, when a thought as lazy as I am, came to me. 'Girls,' I said, 'it's too warm now to walk over to the springs. I tell you what—let's explore the upper regions of this ante-bellum-looking house.

Mrs. Warwick says the top story isn't used, except for the stowing away of odds and ends, but I am sure that making legends for its musty curio will furnish a more pleasant respite than a walk in the sun.'

" 'Twas peculiar, but even here Louise's opinion carried more weight than mine. She had heard my remark, and called out from the hall: 'No, we won't; Mrs. Wyatt, you and Lucy let Miss Beth go spook-hunting alone if she wants too,—we are going to the springs.' And to the springs they went.

"I remained from sheer pique, and five minutes later walked stealthily down the gloom-curtained hall of the top story. I was afraid of my own foot-fall, the silence was so oppressive. The last door on the hall was open,—I wondered why,—and crept softly forward. The inner door to that room was also open, and displayed a picture intense in its suggestive pathos. The room was cozily furnished, but arranged in untidy confusion of sofa-pillows and chairs. In its center stood a quaintly dressed little lady, with white hair, save for a few shining threads of black in the careless knot. She was holding a baby in her arms and speaking to her companion, a man who stood with face turned from me. He was after the Yankee fashion: tall, large, and might have been called angular, had he not lounged against the mantel with such easy grace. My interest in the group was heightened as I listened to her words. She was saying in a frightened, petulant voice:

" 'But Jerome, the doctor says that my malady is not dangerous, nor ever likely to prove so; then why is it you want to take baby away? I have *never* complained till now; you and Doctor Bell say that I am a victim of a mild form of insanity, and I have believed you; yet there are times when you are away for a long while and a weight seems lifted from my brain,—I feel free, oh, so free, and perfectly rational, doubting those who say I am crazy. Oh, my husband, give

me some hope! See, I can even reason with you; I consider
your welfare; I read, and do not see that I understood better
in the old days than I do now; look at our baby, darling,—
there has never been one moment since he came to us that I
have had a desire to do other to him than kiss his round, fair
limbs, and pray God to at least let me keep my beautiful boy
till the shell that holds my poor doubting, loving, aching
heart, is hidden beneath his verdant grasses and glistening
snows. Jerome, Jerome, I kneel to you—do not take my
baby. I am not mad; it is only weakness I feel. I *know* that I
am not mad; I am not even weak now. I wish that dear Jesus
would let my little child speak, and plead his own cause.
Dearest husband, don't you love me? Then look at our boy—
he cannot speak, but let his silent helplessness and his mad
mother's sorrow plead for him. Listen; I read it this morning:
"Yet a little slumber, a little folding of the hands to sleep;"
let me keep baby till then, Jerome; you won't wait long—I
tell you I know it, I feel it.' The highly tensioned nerves
relaxed,—her husband caught her fainting form, took the
baby from her convulsed clasp, and with it still in his arms,
turned to the door from which I had silently witnessed his
pathetic domestic scene.

"When Mr. Warwick—for it was he—saw me standing
in the hall, I felt that I was more frightened than he was. As
far as I know he did not even start, or show the least surprise.
I realized in a moment that I was the dove and he the snake.
He came to me just as suave as he is now.

" 'Ah, you must pity me after this scene; my crazy widowed
sister; poor girl, she thinks me her dead husband. I must
take the baby away; she might injure it. The doctor says she
may become raving mad at any time now. Heavens! Watch
out! Run for your life, she will kill you; she is clutching for
your throat! See how mad and wild she looks. The long-

dreaded has come,—my poor, poor sister. Help me to hold—'

"I waited to hear and see no more; when I came to my senses I was back on the last hall, standing panting in the door. Where had I been? What had I seen? I declare to you, De, that I did not remember at that time one thing that had happened. I knew that some terrible experience had shattered my nerves, but all power of associating ideas had left me. I could not have told any one what had transpired—I did not know.

"This was my dream for three consecutive nights. I do not know that it varied one iota. Why could not there be some truth in it, De? This Mr. Warwick need not be a lawyer because he says so. And, too, compare Louise's incapability to act or think clearly in the library the night of the banquet, with the swift oblivion that envelopes my mind; the illusion produced by his words,—of the fainting woman becoming suddenly mad. She did not come to herself or clutch at my throat—it was in the dream as true as reality, and showed the marvelous control that strong wills exert over weaker systems. The points clustering around the dream were true—and I believe that it was true, also. I believe deep in my soul that Mr. Warwick is no lawyer; that he has a wife and child, and lives much nearer to us than he acknowledges. If we can prove him the fraud that my hypothesis tells me he is, he will not only cease to destroy Louise's happiness, but will leave town."

"And so, Beth, you want the much-abused me to trot off to Farmville vicinity and follow up a nightmare that involves a crazy woman in the top story of a brick house?"

"Please don't jest, De. This chase is not so wild as you think. You have two play-days in which to ease my heart, if it does no greater good. The distance is not great—please go."

I expect that the so-called incorrigible Beth is crying again, for De adds hastily:

"Of course I will go; it's a little favor, and I don't mind in the least, Beth. What say you to tomorrow evening at 3:45?"

"De," I replied, "I could not love my brother more. You are the very dearest boy in the world."

"Pshaw! it's nothing; don't thank me, you make me think that I was a wretch to hesitate."

After that evening I did not see De until Sunday at church, and then his face wore a troubled expression—something rare for him.

"So glad you are alone; may I accompany you?"

"Beth, you are a brick, after all. I never was so surprised in my life. I stayed with Mrs. Warwick all night, in the very house you described. There is one difference: her son's wife is not so very closely confined, and Mrs. Warwick does not seem to think secrecy is necessary. The girl—she is a girl, though her hair is nearly white—thinks herself crazy, and so do other people. I do not; she is no more crazy than I am at present, but will be, if there is not a change in her surroundings. How she worships that baby! It is a pitiful sight to see her crying and moaning over it; calling herself its poor crazy mother, who is going away soon. Once I caught her saying to her mother-in-law: 'Please don't let Jerome take baby; I am not mad.' Just as you told me before I left, and you have no idea how strangely it moved me, Beth. Yet I am glad, for now you, Louise and Tom will be happy. You must not worry one bit over the matter. Tom and I will see that this hypnotist incognito finds suddenly that L ———— is not a very good climate for his health, or some excuse equally transparent. Leave it to me, and your ears will not be surprised by tidings of any rash act, either."

"I am perfectly willing to trust you, De." And I was.

Tuesday morning Louise ran to me her face all radiant with happiness: "Oh Beth, little sister, De tells me, positively, too, that horrid old Mr. Warwick got in some kind of trouble, and had to leave town! Aren't you so glad? Say that you are, quick!" I answered, and got a kiss for my pay.

Few who saw and heard the happy, queenly girl on Commencement night, whose pathetic eloquence melted tears from the frozen eyes of the usually impregnable faculty, would have thought that only a week before she had almost unconsciously escaped being heroine in a tragic episode. She did not know; and her ignorance made De and I happy. Her sun had passed so close to the storm-cloud and had not touched it.

# TALMA GORDON

*Pauline E. Hopkins*

The Canterbury Club of Boston was holding its regular
monthly meeting at the palatial Beacon-street residence of Dr.
William Thornton, expert medical practitioner and specialist.
All the members were present, because some rare opinions
were to be aired by men of profound thought on a question
of vital importance to the life of the Republic, and because
the club celebrated its anniversary in a home usually closed
to society. The Doctor's winters, since his marriage, were
passed at his summer home near his celebrated sanatorium.
This winter found him in town with his wife and two boys.
We had heard much of the beauty of the former, who was
entirely unknown to social life, and about whose life and
marriage we felt sure a romantic interest attached. The Doctor
himself was too bright a luminary of the professional world
to remain long hidden without creating comment. We had
accepted the invitation to dine with alacrity, knowing that we
should be welcomed to a banquet that would feast both eye
and palate; but we had not been favored by even a glimpse
of the hostess. The subject for discussion was: "Expansion;
Its Effect upon the Future Development of the Anglo-Saxon
throughout the World."

Dinner was over, but we still sat about the social board
discussing the question of the hour. The Hon. Herbert
Clapp, eminent jurist and politician, had painted in glowing
colors the advantages to be gained by the increase of wealth

*Colored American Magazine* 1 (Oct. 1900): 271–90.

and the exalted position which expansion would give the United States in the councils of the great governments of the world. In smoothly flowing sentences marshalled in rhetorical order, with compact ideas, and incisive argument, he drew an effective picture with all the persuasive eloquence of the trained orator.

Joseph Whitman, the theologian of world-wide fame, accepted the arguments of Mr. Clapp, but subordinated all to the great opportunity which expansion would give to the religious enthusiast. None could doubt the sincerity of this man, who looked once into the idealized face on which heaven had set the seal of consecration.

Various opinions were advanced by the twenty-five men present, but the host said nothing; he glanced from one to another with a look of amusement in his shrewd gray-blue eyes. "Wonderful eyes," said his patients who came under their magic spell. "A wonderful man and a wonderful mind," agreed his contemporaries, as they heard in amazement of some great cure of chronic or malignant disease which approached the supernatural.

"What do you think of this question, Doctor?" finally asked the president, turning to the silent host.

"Your arguments are good; they would convince almost anyone."

"But not Doctor Thornton," laughed the theologian.

"I acquiesce which ever way the result turns. Still, I like to view both sides of a question. We have considered but one tonight. Did you ever think that in spite of our prejudices against amalgamation, some of our descendants, indeed many of them, will inevitably intermarry among those far-off tribes of dark-skinned peoples, if they become a part of this great Union?"

"Among the lower classes that may occur, but not to any great extent," remarked a college president.

"My experience teaches me that it will occur among all classes, and to an appalling extent," replied the Doctor.

"You don't believe in intermarriage with other races?"

"Yes, most emphatically, when they possess decent moral development and physical perfection, for then we develop a superior being in the progeny born of the intermarriage. But if we are not ready to receive and assimilate the new material which will be brought to mingle with our pure Anglo-Saxon stream, we should call a halt in our expansion policy."

"I must confess, Doctor, that in the idea of amalgamation you present a new thought to my mind. Will you not favor us with a few of your main points?" asked the president of the club, breaking the silence which followed the Doctor's remarks.

"Yes, Doctor, give us your theories on the subject. We may not agree with you, but we are all open to conviction."

The Doctor removed the half-consumed cigar from his lips, drank what remained in his glass of the choice Burgundy, and leaning back in his chair contemplated the earnest faces before him.

We may make laws, but laws are but straws in the hands of Omnipotence.

> "There's a divinity that shapes our ends,
> Rough-hew them how we will."

And no man may combat fate. Given a man, propinquity, opportunity, fascinating femininity, and there you are. Black, white, green, yellow—nothing will prevent intermarriage. Position, wealth, family, friends—all sink into insignificance before the God-implanted instinct that made Adam, awakening from a deep sleep and finding the woman beside him, accept Eve as bone of his bone; he cared not nor questioned whence she came. So it is with the sons of Adam ever since, through the law of heredity which makes us all one common family. And so it will be with us in our re-formation of this old Republic. Perhaps I can make my meaning clearer by illustration, and with your permission I will tell you a story which came under my observation as a practitioner.

Doubtless all of you heard of the terrible tragedy which occurred at Gordonville, Mass., some years ago, when Capt. Jonathan Gordon, his wife and little son were murdered. I suppose that I am the only man on this side the Atlantic, outside of the police, who can tell you the true story of that crime.

I knew Captain Gordon well; it was through his persuasions that I bought a place in Gordonville and settled down to spending my summers in that charming rural neighborhood. I had rendered the Captain what he was pleased to call valuable medical help, and I became his family physician. Captain Gordon was a retired sea captain, formerly engaged in the East India trade. All his ancestors had been such; but when the bottom fell out of that business he established the Gordonville Mills with his first wife's money, and settled down as a money-making manufacturer of cotton cloth. The Gordons were old New England Puritans who had come over in the "Mayflower"; they had owned Gordon Hall for more than a hundred years. It was a baronial-like pile of granite with towers, standing on a hill which commanded a superb view of Massachusetts Bay and the surrounding country. I imagine the Gordon star was under a cloud about the time Captain Jonathan married his first wife, Miss Isabel Franklin of Boston, who brought to him the money which mended the broken fortunes of the Gordon house, and restored this old

Puritan stock to its rightful position. In the person of Captain Gordon the austerity of manner and indomitable will-power that he had inherited were combined with a temper that brooked no contradiction.

The first wife died at the birth of her third child, leaving him two daughters, Jeannette and Talma. Very soon after her death the Captain married again. I have heard it rumored that the Gordon girls did not get on very well with their stepmother. She was a woman with no fortune of her own, and envied the large portion left by the first Mrs. Gordon to her daughters.

Jeannette was tall, dark, and stern like her father; Talma was like her dead mother, and possessed of great talent, so great that her father sent her to the American Academy at Rome, to develop the gift. It was the hottest of July days when her friends were bidden to an afternoon party on the lawn and a dance in the evening, to welcome Talma Gordon among them again. I watched her as she moved about among her guests, a fairylike blonde in floating white draperies, her face a study in delicate changing tints, like the heart of a flower, sparkling in smiles about the mouth to end in merry laughter in the clear blue eyes. There were all the subtle allurements of birth, wealth and culture about the exquisite creature:

> "Smiling, frowning evermore,
> Thou art perfect in love-lore,
> Ever varying Madeline,"

quoted a celebrated writer as he stood apart with me, gazing upon the scene before us. He sighed as he looked at the girl.

"Doctor, there is genius and passion in her face. Sometime our little friend will do wonderful things. But is it desirable to be singled out for special blessings by the gods? Genius always carries with it intense capacity for suffering: 'Whom the gods love die young.' "

"Ah," I replied, "do not name death and Talma Gordon together. Cease your dismal croakings; such talk is rank heresy."

The dazzling daylight dropped slowly into summer twilight. The merriment continued; more guests arrived; the great dancing pagoda built for the occasion was lighted by myriads of Japanese lanterns. The strains from the band grew sweeter and sweeter, and "all went merry as a marriage bell." It was a rare treat to have this party at Gordon Hall, for Captain Jonathan was not given to hospitality. We broke up shortly before midnight, with expressions of delight from all the guests.

I was a bachelor then, without ties. Captain Gordon insisted upon my having a bed at the Hall. I did not fall asleep readily; there seemed to be something in the air that forbade it. I was still awake when a distant clock struck the second hour of the morning. Suddenly the heavens were lighted by a sheet of ghastly light; a terrific midsummer thunderstorm was breaking over the sleeping town. A lurid flash lit up all the landscape, painting the trees in grotesque shapes against the murky sky, and defining clearly the sullen blackness of the waters of the bay breaking in grandeur against the rocky coast. I had arisen and put back the draperies from the windows, to have an unobstructed view of the grand scene. A low muttering coming nearer and nearer, a terrific roar, and then a tremendous downpour. The storm had burst.

Now the uncanny howling of a dog mingled with the rattling volleys of thunder. I heard the opening and closing of doors; the servants were about looking after things. It was impossible to sleep. The lightning was more vivid. There was a blinding flash of a greenish-white tinge mingled with the crash of falling timbers. Then before my startled gaze arose columns of red flames reflected against the sky. "Heaven help us!" I cried; "it is the left tower; it has been struck and is on fire!"

I hurried on my clothes and stepped into the corridor; the girls were there before me. Jeannette came up to me instantly with anxious face. "Oh, Doctor Thornton, what shall we do? papa and mamma and little Johnny are in the old left tower. It is on fire. I have knocked and knocked, but get no answer."

"Don't be alarmed," said I soothingly. "Jenkins, ring the alarm bell," I continued, turning to the butler who was standing near; "the rest follow me. We will force the entrance to the Captain's room."

Instantly, it seemed to me, the bell boomed out upon the now silent air, for the storm had died down as quickly as it arose; and as our little procession paused before the entrance to the old left tower, we could distinguish the sound of the fire engines already on their way from the village.

The door resisted all our efforts; there seemed to be a barrier against it which nothing could move. The flames were gaining headway. Still the same deathly silence within the rooms.

"Oh, will they never get here?" cried Talma, ringing her hands in terror. Jeannette said nothing, but her face was ashen. The servants were huddled together in a panic-stricken group. I can never tell you what a relief it was when we heard the first sound of the firemen's voices, saw their quick movements, and heard the ringing of the axes with which they cut away every obstacle to our entrance to the rooms. The neighbors who had just enjoyed the hospitality of the house were now gathered around offering all the assistance in their power. In less than fifteen minutes the fire was out, and the men began to bear the unconscious inmates from the ruins. They carried them to the pagoda so lately the scene of mirth and pleasure, and I took up my station there, ready to assume my professional duties. The Captain was nearest me; and as I stooped to make the necessary examination I reeled away from the ghastly sight which confronted me—*gentlemen, across the Captain's throat was a deep gash that severed the jugular vein!*

The Doctor paused, and the hand with which he refilled his glass trembled violently.

"What is it, Doctor?" cried the men, gathering about me.

"Take the women away; this is murder!"

"Murder!" cried Jeannette, as she fell against the side of the pagoda.

"Murder!" screamed Talma, staring at me as if unable to grasp my meaning.

I continued my examination of the bodies, and found that the same thing had happened to Mrs. Gordon and to little Johnny.

The police were notified; and when the sun rose over the dripping town he found them in charge of Gordon Hall, the servants standing in excited knots talking over the crime, the friends of the family confounded, and the two girls trying to comfort each other and realize the terrible misfortune that had overtaken them.

Nothing in the rooms of the left tower seemed to have been disturbed. The door of communication between the rooms of the husband and wife was open, as they had arranged it for the night. Little Johnny's crib was placed beside his mother's bed. In it he was found as though never awakened by the storm. It was quite evident that the assassin was no common ruffian. The chief gave strict orders for a watch to be kept on all strangers or suspicious characters who were seen in the neighborhood. He made inquiries among the servants, seeing each one separately, but there was nothing gained from them. No one had heard anything suspicious; all had been awakened by the storm. The chief was puzzled. Here was a triple crime for which no motive could be assigned.

"What do you think of it?" I asked him, as we stood together on the lawn.

"It is my opinion that the deed was committed by one of the higher classes, which makes the mystery more difficult to solve. I tell you, Doctor, there are mysteries that never come to light, and this, I think, is one of them."

While we were talking Jenkins, the butler, an old and trusted servant, came up to the chief and saluted respectfully. "Want to speak with me, Jenkins?" he asked. The man nodded, and they walked away together.

The story of the inquest was short, but appalling. It was shown that Talma had been allowed to go abroad to study because she and Mrs. Gordon did not get on well together. From the testimony of Jenkins it seemed that Talma and her father had quarrelled bitterly about her lover, a young artist whom she had met at Rome, who was unknown to fame, and very poor. There had been terrible things said by each, and threats even had passed, all of which now rose up in judgment against the unhappy girl. The examination of the family solicitor revealed the fact that Captain Gordon intended to leave his daughters only a small annuity, the bulk of the fortune going to his son Jonathan, junior. This was a monstrous injustice, as everyone felt. In vain Talma protested her innocence. Someone must have done it. No one would be benefited so much by these deaths as she and her sister. Moreover, the will, together with other papers, was nowhere to be found. Not the slightest clue bearing upon the disturbing elements in this family, if any there were, was to be found.

As the only surviving relatives, Jeannette and Talma became joint heirs to an immense fortune, which only for the bloody tragedy just enacted would, in all probability, have passed them by. Here was the motive. The case was very black against Talma. The foreman stood up. The silence was intense: We "find that Capt. Jonathan Gordon, Mary E. Gordon and Jonathan Gordon, junior, all deceased, came to their deaths by means of a knife or other sharp instrument in the hands of Talma Gordon." The girl was like one stricken with death. The flower-like mouth was drawn and pinched; the great sapphire-blue eyes were black with passionate anguish, terror and despair. She was placed in jail to await her trial at the fall session of the criminal court. The excitement in the hitherto quiet town rose to fever heat. Many points in the evidence seemed incomplete to thinking men. The weapon could not be found, nor could it be divined what had become of it. No reason could be given for the murder except the quarrel between Talma and her father and the ill will which existed between the girl and her stepmother.

When the trial was called Jeannette sat beside Talma in the prisoner's dock; both were arrayed in deepest mourning. Talma was pale and careworn, but seemed uplifted, spiritualized, as it were. Upon Jeannette the full realization of her sister's peril seemed to weigh heavily. She had changed much too: hollow cheeks, tottering steps, eyes blazing with fever, all suggestive of rapid and premature decay. From far-off Italy Edward Turner, growing famous in the art world, came to stand beside his girl-love in this hour of anguish.

The trial was a memorable one. No additional evidence had been collected to strengthen the prosecution; when the attorney-general rose to open the case against Talma he knew, as everyone else did, that he could not convict solely on the evidence adduced. What was given did not always bear upon the case, and brought out strange stories of Captain Jonathan's methods. Tales were told of sailors who had sworn to take his life, in revenge for injuries inflicted upon them by his hand. One or two clues were followed, but without avail. The judge summed up the evidence impartially, giving the prisoner the benefit of the doubt. The points in hand furnished valuable collateral evidence, but were not direct proof. Although the moral presumption was against the prisoner, legal evidence was lacking to actually convict. The jury found the prisoner "Not Guilty," owing to the fact that the evidence was entirely circumstantial. The verdict was received in painful silence; then a murmur of discontent ran through the great crowd.

"She must have done it," said one; "who else has been benefited by the horrible deed?"

"A poor woman would not have fared so well at the hands of the jury, nor a homely one either, for that matter," said another.

The great Gordon trial was ended; innocent or guilty, Talma Gordon could not be tried again. She was free; but her liberty, with blasted prospects and fair fame gone forever, was valueless to her. She seemed to have but one object in her mind: to find the murderer or murderers of her parents and half-brother. By her direction the shrewdest of detectives were employed and money flowed like water, but to no purpose; the Gordon tragedy remained a mystery. I had consented to act as one of the trustees of the immense Gordon estates and business interests, and by my advice the Misses Gordon went abroad. A year later I received a letter from Edward Turner, saying that Jeannette Gordon had died suddenly at Rome, and that Talma, after refusing all his entreaties for an early marriage, had disappeared, leaving no clue as to her whereabouts. I could give the poor fellow no comfort, although I had been duly notified of the death of Jeannette by Talma, in a letter telling me where to forward her remittances, and at the same time requesting me to keep her present residence secret, especially from Edward.

I had established a sanitarium for the cure of chronic diseases at Gordonville, and absorbed in the cares of my profession I gave little thought to the Gordons. I seemed fated to be involved in mysteries.

A man claiming to be an Englishman, and fresh from the California gold fields, engaged board and professional service at my retreat. I found him suffering in the grasp of the tubercle-fiend—the last stages. He called himself Simon Cameron. Seldom have I seen so fascinating and wicked a face. The lines of the mouth were cruel, the eyes cold and sharp, the smile mocking and evil. He had money in plenty but seemed to have no friends, for he had received no letters and had had no visitors in the time he had been with us. He was an enigma to me; and his nationality puzzled me, for of course I did not believe his story of being English. The peaceful influence of the house seemed to soothe him in a measure, and make his last steps to the mysterious valley as easy as possible. For a time he improved, and would sit or walk about the grounds and sing sweet songs for the pleasure of the other inmates. Strange to say, his malady only affected his voice at times. He sang quaint songs in a silvery tenor of great purity and sweetness that was delicious to the listening ear:

> "A wet sheet and a flowing sea,
> A wind that follows fast,
> And fills the white and rustling sail
> And bends the gallant mast;
> And bends the gallant mast, my boys;

>       While like the eagle free,
>       Away the good ship flies, and leaves
>       Old England on the lea."

There are few singers on the lyric stage who could surpass
Simon Cameron.

One night, a few weeks after Cameron's arrival, I sat in
my office making up my accounts when the door opened and
closed; I glanced up, expecting to see a servant. A lady
advanced toward me. She threw back her veil, and then I
saw that Talma Gordon, or her ghost, stood before me. After
the first excitement of our meeting was over, she told me she
had come direct from Paris, to place herself in my care. I
had studied her attentively during the first moments of our
meeting, and I felt that she was right; unless something
unforeseen happened to arouse her from the stupor into which
she seemed to have fallen, the last Gordon was doomed to an
early death. The next day I told her I had cabled Edward
Turner to come to her.

"It will do no good; I cannot marry him," was her only
comment.

"Have you no feeling of pity for that faithful fellow?" I
asked her sternly, provoked by her seeming indifference. I
shall never forget the varied emotions depicted on her speaking face. Fully revealed to my gaze was the sight of a human
soul tortured beyond the point of endurance; suffering all
things, enduring all things, in the silent agony of despair.

In a few days Edward arrived, and Talma consented to see
him and explain her refusal to keep her promise to him.
"You must be present, Doctor; it is due your long, tried
friendship to know that I have not been fickle, but have acted
from the best and strongest motives."

I shall never forget that day. It was directly after lunch
that we met in the library. I was greatly excited, expecting I

62 *Pauline E. Hopkins*

knew not what. Edward was agitated, too. Talma was the only calm one. She handed me what seemed to be a letter, with the request that I would read it. Even now I think I can repeat every word of the document, so indelibly are the words engraved upon my mind:

MY DARLING SISTER TALMA: When you read these lines I shall be no more, for I shall not live to see your life blasted by the same knowledge that has blighted mine.

One evening, about a year before your expected return from Rome, I climbed into a hammock in one corner of the veranda outside the breakfast-room windows, intending to spend the twilight hours in lazy comfort, for it was very hot, enervating August weather. I fell asleep. I was awakened by voices. Because of the heat the rooms had been left in semi-darkness. As I lay there, lazily enjoying the beauty of the perfect summer night, my wandering thoughts were arrested by words spoken by our father to Mrs. Gordon, for they were the occupants of the breakfast-room.

"Never fear, Mary; Johnny shall have it all—money, houses, land and business."

"But if you do go first, Jonathan, what will happen if the girls contest the will? People will think that they ought to have the money as it appears to be theirs by law. I never could survive the terrible disgrace of the story."

"Don't borrow trouble; all you would need to do would be to show them papers I have drawn up, and they would be glad to take their annuity and say nothing. After all, I do not think it is so bad. Jeannette can teach; Talma can paint; six hundred dollars a year is quite enough for them."

I had been somewhat mystified by the conversation until now. This last remark solved the riddle. What could he mean? teach, paint, six hundred a year! With my usual impetuosity I sprang from my resting-place, and in a moment stood in the room confronting my father, and asking what he meant. I could see plainly that both were disconcerted by my unexpected appearance.

"Ah, wretched girl! you have been listening. But what could I expect of your mother's daughter?"

At these words I felt the indignant blood rush to my head in a torrent. So it had been all my life. Before you could remember, Talma, I had felt my little heart swell with anger at the disparaging hints and slurs concerning our mother. Now was my time. I determined that tonight I would know why she was looked upon as an outcast, and her children subjected to every humiliation. So I replied to my father in bitter anger:

"I was not listening; I fell asleep in the hammock. What do you mean by a paltry six hundred a year each to Talma and to me? 'My mother's daughter' demands an explanation from you, sir, of the meaning of the monstrous injustice that you have always practised toward my sister and me."

"Speak more respectfully to your father, Jeannette," broke in Mrs. Gordon.

"How is it, madam, that you look for respect from one whom you have delighted to torment ever since you came into this most unhappy family?"

"Hush, both of you," said Captain Gordon, who seemed to have recovered from the dismay into which my sudden appearance and passionate words had plunged him. "I think I may as well tell you as to wait. Since you know so much, you may as well know the whole miserable story." He motioned me to a seat. I could see that he was deeply agitated. I seated myself in a chair he pointed out, in wonder and expectation,—expectation of I knew not what. I trembled. This was a supreme moment in my life; I felt it. The air was heavy with the intense stillness that had settled over us as the common sounds of day gave place to the early quiet of the rural evening. I could see Mrs. Gordon's face as she sat within the radius of the lighted hallway. There was a smile of triumph upon it. I clinched my hands and bit my lips until the blood came, in the effort to keep from screaming. What was I about to hear? At last he spoke:

"I was disappointed at your birth, and also at the birth of Talma. I wanted a male heir. When I knew that I should again be a father I was torn by hope and fear, but I comforted myself with the thought that luck would be with me in the birth of the third child. When the doctor brought me word that a son was born to the house of Gordon, I was wild with delight, and did not notice his disturbed countenance. In the midst of my joy he said to me:

"Captain Gordon, there is something strange about this birth. I want you to see this child."

Quelling my exultation I followed him to the nursery, and there, lying in the cradle, I saw a child dark as a mulatto, with the characteristic features of the Negro! I was stunned. Gradually it dawned upon me that there was something radically wrong. I turned to the doctor for an explanation.

"There is but one explanation, Captain Gordon; there is Negro blood in this child."

"There is no Negro blood in my veins," I said proudly. Then I paused—*the mother!*—I glanced at the doctor. He was watching me intently. The same thought was in his mind. I must have lived a thousand years in that cursed five seconds that I stood there confronting the physician and trying to think. "Come," said I to him, "let us end this suspense." Without thinking of consequences, I hurried away to your mother and accused her of infidelity to her marriage vows. I raved like a madman. Your mother fell into convulsions; her life was despaired of. I sent for Mr. and Mrs. Franklin, and then I learned the truth. They were childless. One year while on a Southern tour, they befriended an octoroon girl who had been abandoned by her white lover. Her child was a beautiful girl baby. They, being Northern born, thought little of caste distinction because the child showed no trace of Negro blood. They determined to adopt it. They went abroad, secretly sending back word to their friends at a proper time, of the birth of a little daughter. No one doubted the truth of the statement. They made Isabel their heiress, and all went well until the birth of your brother. Your mother and the unfortunate babe died. This is the story which, if known, would bring dire disgrace upon the Gordon family.

To appease my righteous wrath, Mr. Franklin left a codicil to his will by which all the property is left at my disposal save a small annuity to you and your sister."

I sat there after he had finished his story, stunned by what I had heard. I understood, now, Mrs. Gordon's half contemptuous toleration and lack of consideration for us both. As I rose from my seat to leave the room I said to Captain Gordon:

"Still, in spite of all, sir, I am a Gordon, legally born. I will not tamely give up my birthright."

I left that room a broken-hearted girl, filled with a desire for revenge upon this man, my father, who by his manner disowned us without a regret. Not once in that remarkable interview did he speak of our mother as his wife; he quietly repudiated her and us with all the cold cruelty of relentless caste prejudice. I heard the treatment of your lover's proposal: I knew why Captain Gordon's consent to your marriage was withheld.

The night of the reception and dance was the chance for which I had waited, planned and watched. I crept from my

window into the ivy-vines, and so down, down, until I stood
upon the window-sill of Captain Gordon's room in the old
left tower. How did I do it, you ask? I do not know. The
house was silent after the revel; the darkness of the gathering
storm favored me, too. The lawyer was there that day. The
will was signed and put safely away among my father's papers.
I was determined to have the will and the other documents
bearing upon the case, and I would have revenge, too, for
the cruelties we had suffered. With the old East Indian
dagger firmly grasped I entered the room and found—that
my revenge had been forestalled! The horror of the discovery
I made that night restored me to reason and a realization of
the crime I meditated. Scarce knowing what I did, I sought
and found the papers, and crept back to my room as I had
come. Do you wonder that my disease is past medical aid?

I looked at Edward as I finished. He sat, his face covered
with his hands. Finally he looked up with a glance of haggard
despair: "God! Doctor, but this is too much. I could stand
the stigma of murder, but add to that the pollution of Negro
blood! No man is brave enough to face such a situation."

"It is as I thought it would be," said Talma sadly, while
the tears poured over her white face. "I do not blame you,
Edward."

He rose from his chair, wrung my hand in a convulsive
clasp, turned to Talma and bowed profoundly, with his eyes
fixed upon the floor, hesitated, turned, paused, bowed again
and abruptly left the room. So those two who had been lovers,
parted. I turned to Talma, expecting her to give way. She
smiled a pitiful smile, and said: "You see, Doctor, I knew
best."

From that on she failed rapidly. I was restless. If only I
could rouse her to an interest in life, she might live to old

age. So rich, so young, so beautiful, so talented, so pure; I grew savage thinking of the injustice of the world. I had not reckoned on the power that never sleeps. Something was about to happen.

On visiting Cameron next morning I found him approaching the end. He had been sinking for a week very rapidly. As I sat by the bedside holding his emaciated hand, he fixed his bright, wicked eyes on me, and asked: "How long have I got to live?"

"Candidly, but a few hours."

"Thank you; well, I want death; I am not afraid to die. Doctor, Cameron is not my name."

"I never supposed it was."

"No? You are sharper than I thought. I heard all your talk yesterday with Talma Gordon. Curse the whole race!"

He clasped his bony fingers around my arm and gasped: *"I murdered the Gordons!"*

Had I the pen of a Dumas I could not paint Cameron as he told his story. It is a question with me whether this wheeling planet, home of the suffering, doubting, dying, may not hold worse agonies on its smiling surface than those of the conventional hell. I sent for Talma and a lawyer. We gave him stimulants, and then with broken intervals of coughing and prostration we got the story of the Gordon murder. I give it to you in a few words:

"I am an East Indian, but my name does not matter, Cameron is as good as any. There is many a soul crying in heaven and hell for vengeance on Jonathan Gordon. Gold was his idol; and many a good man walked the plank, and many a gallant ship was stripped of her treasure, to satisfy his lust for gold. His blackest crime was the murder of my father, who was his friend, and had sailed with him for many a year as mate. One night these two went ashore together to bury their treasure. My father never returned from that expedition. His body was afterward found with a bullet through the heart on the shore where the vessel stopped that night. It was the custom then among pirates for the captain to kill the men who helped bury their treasure. Captain Gordon was no better than a pirate. An East Indian never forgets, and I swore by my mother's deathbed to hunt Captain Gordon down until I had avenged my father's murder. I had the plans of the Gordon estate, and fixed on the night of the reception in honor of Talma as the time for my vengeance. There is a secret entrance from the shore to the chambers where Captain Gordon slept; no one knew of it save the Captain and trusted members of his crew. My mother gave me the plans, and entrance and escape were easy."

"So the great mystery was solved. In a few hours Cameron was no more. We placed the confession in the hands of the police, and there the matter ended."

"But what became of Talma Gordon?" questioned the president. "Did she die?"

"Gentlemen," said the Doctor, rising to his feet and sweeping the faces of the company with his eagle gaze, "gentlemen, if you will follow me to the drawing-room, I shall have much pleasure in introducing you to my wife—*nee* Talma Gordon."

# GENERAL WASHINGTON
## *A Christmas Story*

*Pauline E. Hopkins*

### I

General Washington did any odd jobs he could find around the Washington market, but his specialty was selling chitlins.

General Washington lived in the very shady atmosphere of Murderer's Bay in the capital city. All that he could remember of father or mother in his ten years of miserable babyhood was that they were frequently absent from the little shanty where they were supposed to live, generally after a protracted spell of drunkenness and bloody quarels when the police were forced to interfere for the peace of the community. During these absences, the child would drift from one squalid home to another wherever a woman—God save the mark!—would take pity upon the poor waif and throw him a few scraps of food for his starved stomach, or a rag of a shawl, apron or skirt, in winter, to wrap about his attenuated little body.

One night the General's daddy being on a short vacation in the city, came home to supper; and because there was no supper to eat, he occupied himself in beating his wife. After that time, when the officers took him, the General's daddy never returned to his home. The General's mammy? Oh, she died!

General Washington's resources developed rapidly after this. Said resources consisted of a pair of nimble feet for

*Colored American Magazine* 2 (Dec. 1900): 95–104.

dancing the hoe-down, shuffles intricate and dazzling, and the Juba; a strong pair of lungs, a wardrobe limited to a pair of pants originally made for a man, and tied about the ankles with strings, a shirt with one gallows, a vast amount of "brass," and a very, very small amount of nickel. His education was practical: "Ef a corn-dodger costs two cents, an' a fellar hain't got de two cents, how's he gwine ter git de corn-dodger?"

General Washington ranked first among the knights of the pavement. He could shout louder and hit harder than any among them; that was the reason they called him "Buster" and "the General." The General could swear, too; I am sorry to admit it, but the truth must be told.

He uttered an oath when he caught a crowd of small white aristocrats tormenting a kitten. The General landed among them in quick time and commenced knocking heads at a lively rate. Presently he was master of the situation, and marched away triumphantly with the kitten in his arms, followed by stones and other missiles which whirled about him through space from behind the safe shelter of back yards and street corners.

The General took the kitten home. Home was a dry-goods box turned on end and filled with straw for winter. The General was as happy as a lord in summer, but the winter was a trial. The last winter had been a hard one, and Buster called a meeting of the leading members of the gang to consider the advisability of moving farther south for the hard weather.

" 'Pears lak to me, fellers, Wash'nton's heap colder'n it uster be, an' I'se mighty onscruplus 'bout stoppin' hyar."

"Bisness am mighty peart," said Teenie, the smallest member of the gang, "s'pose we put off menderin' tell after Chris'mas; Jeemes Henry, fellers, it hain't no Chris'mas fer me outside ob Wash'nton."

"Dat's so, Teenie," came from various members as they sat on the curbing playing an interesting game of craps.

"Den hyar we is tell after Chris'mas, fellers; then dis sonny's gwine ter move, sho, hyar me?"

"De gang's wid yer, Buster; move it is."

It was about a week before Chris'mas, and the weather had been unusually severe.

Probably because misery loves company—nothing could be more miserable than his cat—Buster grew very fond of Tommy. He would cuddle him in his arms every night and listen to his soft purring while he confided all his own hopes and fears to the willing ears of his four-footed companion, occasionally poking his ribs if he showed any signs of sleepiness.

But one night poor Tommy froze to death. Buster didn't—more's the wonder—only his ears and his two big toes. Poor Tommy was thrown off the dock into the Potomac the next morning, while a stream of salt water trickled down his master's dirty face, making visible, for the first time in a year, the yellow hue of his complexion. After that the General hated all flesh and grew morose and cynical.

Just about a week before Tommy's death, Buster met the fairy. Once, before his mammy died, in a spasm of reform she had forced him to go to school, against his better judgment, promising the teacher to go up and "wallop" the General every day if he thought Buster needed it. This gracious offer was declined with thanks. At the end of the week the General left school for his own good and the good of the school. But in that week he learned something about fairies; and so, after she threw him the pinks that she carried in her hand, he called her to himself "the fairy."

Being Christmas week, the General was pretty busy. It was a great sight to see the crowds of people coming and going all day long about the busy market; wagon loads of men, women and children, some carts drawn by horses, but more by mules. Some of the people well-dressed, some scantily clad, but all intent on getting enjoyment out of this their leisure season. This was the season for selling crops and settling the year's account. The store-keepers, too, had prepared their most tempting wares, and the thoroughfares were crowded.

"I 'clare to de Lord, I'se done busted my ol' man, shure," said one woman to another as they paused to exchange greetings outside a store door.

"N'em min'," returned the other, "he'll wurk fer mo.' Dis is Chris'mas, honey."

"To be sure," answered the first speaker, with a flounce of her ample skirts.

Meanwhile her husband pondered the advisability of purchasing a mule, feeling in his pockets for the price demanded, but finding them nearly empty. The money had been spent on the annual festival.

"Ole mule, I want yer mighty bad, but you'll have to slide dis time; it's Chris'mas, mule."

The wise old mule actually semed to laugh as he whisked his tail against his bony sides and steadied himself on his three sound legs.

The venders were very busy, and their cries were wonderful for ingenuity of invention to attract trade:

"Hellow, dar, in de cellar, I'se got fresh aggs fer de 'casion; now's yer time fer agg-nogg wid new aggs in it."

There were the stalls, too, kept by venerable aunties and filled with specimens of old-time southern cheer: Coon, cornpone, possum fat and hominy; there was piles of gingerbread and boiled chestnuts, heaps of walnuts and roasting apples. There were great barrels of cider, not to speak of something stronger. There were terrapin and the persimmon and the

chinquapin in close proximity to the succulent viands—chine
and spare-rib, sausage and crackling, savory souvenirs of the
fine art of hog-killing. And everywhere were faces of dusky
hue; Washington's great negro population bubbled over in
every direction.

The General was peddling chitlins. He had a tub upon his
head and was singing in his strong childish tones:

> "Here's yer chitlins, fresh an' sweet,
> Young hog's chitlins hard to beat,
> Methodis chitlins, jes' been biled,
> Right fresh chitlins, dey ain't spiled,
> Baptis' chitlins by de pound,
> As nice chitlins as ever was foun."

"Hyar, boy, duz yer mean ter say dey is real Baptis'
chitlins, sho nuff?"

"Yas, mum."

"How duz you make dat out?"

"De hog raised by Mr. Robberson, a hard-shell Baptis',
mum."

"Well, lem-me have two poun's."

"Now," said a solid-looking man as General finished waiting on a crowd of women and men, "I want some o' de
Methodess chitlins you's bin hollerin' 'bout."

"Hyar dey is, ser."

"Take 'em all out o' same tub?"

"Yas, ser. Only dair leetle mo' water on de Baptis' chitlins,
an' dey's whiter."

"How you tell 'em?"

"Well, ser, two hog's chitlins in dis tub an one ob de hogs
raised by Unc. Bemis, an' he's a Methodes,' ef dat don't
make him a Methodes hog nuthin' will."

"Weigh me out four pounds, ser."

In an hour's time the General had sold out. Suddenly at his elbow he heard a voice:

"Boy, I want to talk to you."

The fairy stood beside him. She was a little girl about his own age, well wrapped in costly velvet and furs; her long, fair hair fell about her like an aureole of glory; a pair of gentle blue eyes set in a sweet, serious face glanced at him from beneath a jaunty hat with a long curling white feather that rested light as thistle-down upon the beautiful curly locks. The General could not move for gazing, and as his wonderment grew his mouth was extended in a grin that revealed the pearly whiteness of two rows of ivory.

"Boy, shake hands."

The General did not move; how could he?

"Don't you hear me?" asked the fairy, imperiously.

"Yas'm," replied the General meekly. " 'Deed, missy, I'se 'tirely too dirty to tech dem clos o' yourn."

Nevertheless he put forth timidly and slowly a small paw begrimed with the dirt of the street. He looked at the hand and then at her; she looked at the hand and then at him. Then their eyes meeting, they laughed the sweet laugh of the free-masonry of childhood.

"I'll excuse you this time, boy," said the fairy, graciously, "but you must remember that I wish you to wash your face and hands when you are to talk with me; and," she added, as though inspired by an afterthought, "it would be well for you to keep them clean at other times, too."

"Yas'm," replied the General.

"What's your name, boy?"

"Gen'r'l Wash'nton," answered Buster, standing at attention as he had seen the police do in the courtroom.

"Well, General, don't you know you've told a story about the chitlins you've just sold?"

"Tol' er story?" queried the General with a knowing look. "Course I got to sell my chitlins ahead ob de oder fellars, or lose my trade."

"Don't you know it's wicked to tell stories?"

"How come so?" asked the General, twisting his bare toes about in his rubbers, and feeling very uncomfortable.

"Because, God says we musn't."

"Who's he?"

The fairy gasped in astonishment. "Don't you know who God is?"

"No'pe; never seed him. Do he live in Wash'nton?"

"Why, God is your Heavenly Father, and Christ was His son. He was born on Christmas Day a long time ago. When He grew a man, wicked men nailed Him to the cross and killed Him. Then He went to heaven, and we'll all live with Him some day if we are good before we die. O I love Him; and you must love Him, too, General."

"Now look hyar, missy, you kayn't make this chile b'lieve nufin lak dat."

The fairy went a step nearer the boy in her eagerness:

"It's true; just as true as you live."

"Whar'd you say He lived?"

"In heaven," replied the child, softly.

"What kin' o' place is heaven?"

"Oh, beautiful!"

The General stared at the fairy. He worked his toes faster and faster.

"Say, kin yer hab plenty to eat up dar?"

"O, yes; you'll never be hungry there."

"An' a fire, an' clos?" he queried in suppressed, excited tones.

"Yes; it's all love and plenty when we get to heaven, if we are good here."

"Well, missy, dat's a pow'ful good story, but I'm blamed ef I b'lieve it." The General forgot his politeness in his excitement.

"An' ef it's true, tain't only fer white fo'ks; you won't fin' nary nigger dar."

"But you will; and all I've told you is true. Promise me to come to my house on Christmas morning and see my mother. She'll help you, and she will teach you more about God. Will you come?" she asked eagerly, naming a street and number in the most aristocratic quarter of Washington. "Ask for Fairy, that's me. Say quick; here is my nurse."

The General promised.

"Law, Miss Fairy, honey; come right hyar. I'll tell yer mawmaw how you's done run 'way from me to talk to dis dirty little monkey. Pickin' up sech trash fer ter talk to."

The General stood in a trance of happiness. He did not mind the slurring remarks of the nurse, and refrained from throwing a brick at the buxom lady, which was a sacrifice on his part. All he saw was the glint of golden curls in the winter sunshine, and the tiny hand waving him good-bye.

"An' her name is Fairy! Jes' ter think how I hit it all by my lonesome."

Many times that week the General thought and puzzled over Fairy's words. Then he would sigh:

"Heaven's where God lives. Plenty to eat, warm fire all de time in winter; plenty o' clos', too, but I'se got to be good. 'Spose dat means keepin' my face an' han's clean an' stop swearin' an' lyin'. It kayn't be did."

The gang wondered what had come over Buster.

## II

The day before Christmas dawned clear and cold. There was snow on the ground. Trade was good, and the General, mindful of the visit next day, had bought a pair of second-hand shoes and a new calico shirt.

"Git onter de dude!" sang one of the gang as he emerged from the privacy of the dry-goods box early Christmas Eve.

The General was a dancer and no mistake. Down at Dutch Dan's place they kept the old-time Southern Christmas moving along in hot time until the dawn of Christmas Day stole softly through the murky atmosphere. Dutch Dan's was the meeting place of the worst characters, white and black, in the capital city. From that vile den issued the twin spirits murder and rapine as the early winter shadows fell; there the criminal entered in the early dawn and was lost to the accusing eye of justice. There was a dance at Dutch Dan's Christmas Eve, and the General was sent for to help amuse the company.

The shed-like room was lighted by oil lamps and flaring pine torches. The center of the apartment was reserved for dancing. At one end the inevitable bar stretched its yawning mouth like a monster awaiting his victims. A long wooden table was built against one side of the room, where the game could be played to suit the taste of the most expert devotee of the fickle goddess.

The room was well filled, early as it was, and the General's entrance was the signal for a shout of welcome. Old Unc' Jasper was tuning his fiddle and blind Remus was drawing sweet chords from an old banjo. They glided softly into the music of the Mobile shuffle. The General began to dance. He was master of the accomplishment. The pigeon-wing, the old buck, the hoe-down and the Juba followed each other in

rapid succession. The crowd shouted and cheered and joined
in the sport. There was hand-clapping and a rhythmic accompaniment of patting the knees and stamping the feet. The
General danced faster and faster:

> "Juba up and juba down,
> Juba all aroun' de town;
> Can't you hyar de juba pat?
>     Juba!"

sang the crowd. The General gave fresh graces and new
embellishments. Occasionally he added to the interest by
yelling, "Ain't dis fin'e!" "Oh, my!" "Now I'm gittin' loose!"
"Hol' me, hol' me!"

The crowd went wild with delight.

The child danced until he fell exhausted to the floor.
Someone in the crowd "passed the hat." When all had been
waited upon the bar-keeper counted up the receipts and
divided fair—half to the house and half to the dancer. The
fun went on, and the room grew more crowded. General
Wash'nton crept under the table and curled himself up like
a ball. He was lucky, he told himself sleepily, to have so
warm a berth that cold night; and then his heart glowed as
he thought of the morrow and Fairy, and wondered if what
she had said were true. Heaven must be a fine place if it
could beat the floor under the table for comfort and warmth.
He slept. The fiddle creaked, the dancers shuffled. Rum went
down their throats and wits were befogged. Suddenly the
General was wide awake with a start. What was that?

"The family are all away to-night at a dance, and the
servants gone home. There's no one there but an old man
and a kid. We can be well out of the way before the alarm
is given. 'Leven sharp, Doc. And, look here, what's the
number agin?"

Buster knew in a moment that mischief was brewing, and he turned over softly on his side, listening mechanically to catch the reply. It came. Buster sat up. He was wide awake then. They had given the street and number where Fairy's home was situated.

# III

Senator Tallman was from Maryland. He had owned slaves, fought in the Civil War on the Confederate side, and at its end had been returned to a seat in Congress after reconstruction, with feelings of deeply rooted hatred for the Negro. He openly declared his purpose to oppose their progress in every possible way. His favorite argument was disbelief in God's handiwork as shown in the Negro.

"You argue, suh, that God made 'em. I have my doubts, suh. God made man in His own image, suh, and that being the case, suh, it is clear that he had no hand in creating niggers. A nigger, suh, is the image of nothing but the devil." He also declared in his imperious, haughty, Southern way: "The South is in the saddle, suh, and she will never submit to the degradation of Negro domination; never, suh."

The Senator was a picture of honored age and solid comfort seated in his velvet armchair before the fire of blazing logs in his warm, well-lighted study. His lounging coat was thrown open, revealing its soft silken lining, his feet were thrust into gayly embroidered fur-lined slippers. Upon the baize covered table beside him a silver salver sat holding a decanter, glasses and fragrant mint, for the Senator loved the beguiling sweetness of a mint julep at bedtime. He was writing a speech which in his opinion would bury the blacks too deep for resurrection and settle the Negro question for-

ever. Just now he was idle; the evening paper was folded
across his knees; a smile was on his face. He was alone in the
grand mansion, for the festivities of the season had begun
and the family were gone to enjoy a merry-making at the
house of a friend. There was a picture in his mind of
Christmas in his old Maryland home in the good old days
"befo' de wah," the great ball-room where giggling girls and
matrons fair glided in the stately minuet. It was in such a
gathering he had met his wife, the beautiful Kate Channing.
Ah, the happy time of youth and love! The house was very
still; how loud the ticking of the clock sounded. Just then a
voice spoke beside his chair:

"Please, sah, I'se Gen'r'l Wash'nton."

The Senator bounded to his feet with an exclamation:

"Eh! Bless my soul, suh; where did you come from?"

"Ef yer please, boss, froo de winder."

The Senator rubbed his eyes and stared hard at the extraordinary figure before him. The Gen'r'l closed the window and
then walked up to the fire, warmed himself in front, then
turned around and stood with his legs wide apart and his
shrewd little gray eyes fixed upon the man before him.

The Senator was speechless for a moment; then he advanced
upon the intruder with a roar warranted to make a six-foot
man quake in his boots:

"Through the window, you black rascal! Well, I reckon
you'll go out through the door, and that in quick time, you
little thief."

"Please, boss, it hain't me; it's Jim the crook and de gang
from Dutch Dan's."

"Eh!" said the Senator again.

"What's yer cronumter say now, boss? 'Leven is de time
fer de perfahmance ter begin. I reckon'd I'd git hyar time
nuff fer yer ter call de perlice."

"Boy, do you mean for me to understand that burglars are

about to raid my house?" demanded the Senator, a light
beginning to dawn upon him.

The General nodded his head: "Dat's it, boss, ef by
'buglers' you means Jim de crook and Dutch Dan."

It was ten minutes of the hour by the Senator's watch. He
went to the telephone, rang up the captain of the nearest
station, and told him the situation. He took a revolver from
a drawer of his desk and advanced toward the waiting figure
before the fire.

"Come with me. Keep right straight ahead through that
door; if you attempt to run I'll shoot you."

They walked through the silent house to the great entrance
doors and there awaited the coming of the police. Silently the
officers surrounded the house. Silently they crept up the stairs
into the now darkened study. "Eleven" chimed the little silver
clock on the mantel. There was the stealthy tread of feet a
moment after, whispers, the flash of a dark lantern,—a rush
by the officers and a stream of electricity flooded the room.

"It's the nigger did it!" shouted Jim the crook, followed
instantly by the sharp crack of a revolver. General Washington felt a burning pain shoot through his breast as he fell
unconscious to the floor. It was all over in a moment. The
officers congratulated themselves on the capture they had
made—a brace of daring criminals badly wanted by the
courts.

When the General regained consciousness, he lay upon a
soft, white bed in Senator Tallman's house. Christmas morning had dawned, clear, cold and sparkling; upon the air the
joy-bells sounded sweet and strong: "Rejoice, your Lord is
born." Faintly from the streets came the sound of merry
voices: "Chris'mas gift, Chris'mas gift."

The child's eyes wandered aimlessly about the unfamiliar
room as if seeking and questioning. They passed the Senator
and Fairy, who sat beside him and rested on a copy of Titian's

matchless Christ which hung over the mantel. A glorious
stream of yellow sunshine fell upon the thorn-crowned Christ.

> "God of Nazareth, see!
> Before a trembling soul
> Unfoldeth like a scroll
> Thy wondrous destiny!"

The General struggled to a sitting position with arms
outstretched, then fell back with a joyous, awesome cry:

"It's Him! It's Him!"

"O General," sobbed Fairy, "don't you die, you're going
to be happy all the rest of your life. Grandpa says so."

"I was in time, little Missy; I tried mighty hard after I
knowed whar' dem debbils was a-comin' to."

Fairy sobbed; the Senator wiped his eyeglasses and coughed.
The General lay quite still a moment, then turned himself
again on his pillow to gaze at the pictured Christ.

"I'm a-gittin' sleepy, missy, it's so warm an' comfurtable
here. 'Pears lak I feel right happy sence I'se seed Him." The
morning light grew brighter. The face of the Messiah looked
down as it must have looked when He was transfigured on
Tabor's heights. The ugly face of the child wore a strange,
sweet beauty. The Senator bent over the quiet figure with a
gesture of surprise.

The General had obeyed the call of One whom the winds
and waves of stormy human life obey. Buster's Christmas
Day was spent in heaven.

.    .    .    .    .

For some reason, Senator Tallman never made his great
speech against the Negro.

# AUNT 'RIA'S TEN DOLLARS

*Georgia F. Stewart*

"Ria, I hate ter ax you, but can't you gin me dem ten dollars w'at you's ben savin' all dis long time?"

"Who dat? You, 'Lije? You git back mighty soon. I hope an' trus' yo' quick settlement wus a good un. W'at yer say 'bout ten dollars? Dat all yer got in de settlin' wid dem six five hunderds?"

Elijah Davis had gone from home that morning with six bales of cotton, weighing five hundred pounds each, and his wife had been looking forward to his return, though not so early, with a great deal of anxiety. All this year she had guarded ten dollars which represented their income from eight bales the previous year, hoping to increase the sum with this year's receipts.

Elijah seated himself on the block of oak at the door, on which was a tin basin, recently polished with sand and soft soap. This he and Maria used for bathing their faces, and there was another of smaller size near by for the use of the little ones, of whom there were six, ranging from four months to nine years.

"I be dah pres'n'y. Dese greens'll sho' be good an' greazy." After pressing down the greens, which seemed to prefer any place to the kettle in which they were boiling, she put more fresh coals on the cover of the oven, which contained the bread. Before joining her husband she turned to the other side of the chimney which was five feet wide, and from a

*Colored American Magazine* 3 (June 1901): 105–8.

large oven about the size of a half bushel measure she took perhaps two dozen sweet potatoes, put them on a large tin and left them on the hearth to cool.

"W'at yer want? Bread? Eat dem taters while I's talkin' ter yer daddy." This remark was addressed to the children, who realized the hour.

"Come out in de shade, Ria. Too hot to talk business in deah."

"De wedder 'pears cool to me. I bin feelin' lak a chill all dis mawnin'. Yer know my min', and yourn, too, is turned agin so much 'spishuns, but somehow I cud'n he'p sayin', "dis cool air mak' me feel onezy 'bout 'Lije'. Ain't dat foolish fer me, who 'tends so many good meetin's at de church an' up to de school whar all de good books an' papers is read to us, an', Oh! de fine talks o' de folks fum de Norf."

"Go long wid it, 'Lije. I'se ready now." With this she smoothed her clean check apron, which she had drawn from its accustomed hook as she passed from the house, and her soiled one left in its place, and folded her hands in her lap.

"You's er 'oman w'at laks things dun right. I allus wus proud on yer. Ef you 'member—an' you is too business-fied to furgit—year fo' dis las', seben bales fotch us out twenty-five dollars behin', but dere wus plenty co'n to las' fur stock an' all. See?"

"Yes, but—"

"Now to git de understandin', lemme finish. Las' year de crop remounted to eight bales. All de back debts wus paid an' Mister Bradley said: ' 'Lijah Davis, you's de first man dis year to come out an' hav' cash in year hands. A red cross goes down by yo' name.' "

"Yes, an' since den, Ria Davis bin holdin' dem ten dollars, an' keepin' count on all dat comes fum Mister Bradley's sto', too. Listen to me, now. 'Two piece o' check fur me an' de chillun, five dollars; one piece o' sheet'n, two dollars; fo' pair shoes, five dollars; dat's twelve dollars an' er—"

"Wal, I promus to be back soon wid de ten dollars, 'kase I knowed yer didn want no 'counts caid over ter nex' year, an' so I 'spect yer feelin's an' come ter splain matters ter you."

"Wa'r de ten dollars yer talkin' 'bout?"

"Yo' ten dollars, Ria. It's de bes' step ter take, ef yer want ter hav' clean 'count Krismus day."

" 'Lije Davis, dem ten dollars is now part er me, an' I specks fur it ter stay so. You an' Mister Bradley bin doin' yo' kind er settlin' ev'y year, an' yer kin do it de same dis year."

"Folks allus called yo' a sensible 'oman, now den don' lose yer rep. Tain't no use puttin' yer hands akimbo an' marchin' up an' down lak yer min' is made up ter argify wid de Madestry. Be kam. All I can do is to stick ter de plow 'n make the chil'n stick ter de books; so der'll be somebody else to figger 'long wid Mister Bradley. W'at yer doin', Ria? Is you gwine down wid me?"

"I's gwine war I orter been gone years ago."

About four o'clock in the afternoon Mr. William Lyons, a young lawyer of the town of Milton, was seated in his office, reviewing the day and congratulating himself on his success, when some one rapped at the door. The face which responded to his "Come!" was indeed a familiar one, much to his surprise.

"Well! Well! How have you been, Aunt Maria, and what brings you here?" She curtsied, and began by laying the ten dollars on his desk, and giving its history along with her trials for the past years, since she and "Lije" had been working for themselves.

"Yer know 'bout de morgig' sistum. Ev'y time yer feel

yer gittin' free somp'n come over yer an' press yer down
ag'in. When I felt today lak my heart gwine break to part
wid dis money, Miss Ad'line's, yer dear mudder's words, I
'membered, an' so I's come ter you. She told me nebber ter
suffer, but ter go ter her William, an' he wud he'p me.
Now, Mister William, all I wants is a patch o' my own, an'
dis ten dollars 'll pay yer fur lettin' me hav' it; an' w'en I
raise my crop I'll pay yer fur de land."

"Sit down and rest yourself, Aunt Maria. In a few moments
I shall be back."

Aunt Maria was very tired, as she had walked seven miles.
While she rested on one of the comfortable chairs everything
in the office seemed to breathe comforting messages to her.
She determined then and there that her ambition would assert
itself; that she would not wait for the children, but would do
her part towards educating them—she would make a home
for them. On Mr. Lyon's return he read to Aunt Maria as
follows:

"For and in consideration of ten dollars paid to me this
twenty-ninth day of November, 1899, by Maria Davis, I,
William Lyons, do hereby sell, grant and convey to said
Maria Davis, her heirs and assigns, two acres of farming
land," etc.

On her way home she stopped to speak to Mr. Bradley,
telling him what she had done, and that the ten dollars had
gone to pay for her land, but that she would pay him if he
would trust her. He willingly accepted her word as guarantee
of the payment. When she reached home she unwrapped the
paper, and said to Elijah, "Here's my ten dollars, 't hav' an'
to' hol' two acres o' farmin' lan'. Yer must set ter work ter
git out de timbers termorer mornin'."

The distance to Simon Reese's, the nearest neighbor's, was

not less than two miles, but the joy of her new possessions had made the distance much less for Aunt Maria this evening. The news, which was too good to keep, was hailed with delight by the Reese family.

"Woen er good 'oman lak you set her heart 'pon doin' somp'n de Lord 'll he'p her. Ain't nuttin' lef' here er li'l scrap cotton, an' I kin pick dat ober myse'f; den I'll start Simon an' de boys ober deah by daylight. Good night, Sis' Ria. God he'p you."

Meanwhile Elijah had not been idle. His plans had been made while he watched "de house an' de chil'n."

Squire Evans had used Elijah and his team at odd times during the year, in consideration of which he had promised to run the plow for him in the spring. At early dawn next morning Elijah "steps over" to Squire Evans', a distance of three miles, and "arranges" for help in getting out timber instead of plowing.

"I 'spec' yer hav' to bake right sharp er bread, Ria, 'kase Squire Ivins lemme hav' fo' han's today."

"W'at yer say? Lawd bless me! Ain't it s'prisin' w'at ten dollars kin do w'en it starts to workin'? All de year it jes' was er lone ten dollars, an' now in two days it done git to be two acres o' farmin' land', Bre'r Simon Reese an' his two boys fur de whole day, an' fo' good han's fum Squire Ivins."

"Sis' Ria! Oh, Sis' Ria!"

"Git me some mo' trash chil'n; dis dinner orter been gone, for now de sun at twe'v' o'clock, already."

"Oh, Sis' Ri-a-h-!"

"Hush! 'Pears ter me I hear 'em callin' me."

"Sis' Ria!"

" 'Pon my soul, ef dat ain't Sis' Reese! Step over an' come along, chile."

"Jes' run 'ere to de fence, Sis' Ria."

Aunt Maria had just patted in the last "pone" of bread, and heaped her "lid" with coals.

"All right, Sis' Reese, but I pow'ful rushed."

She immersed her hands in a basin of cold water, which caused the cornmeal dough to fall from them, for she used her hands from beginning to finish in preparing the lovely oval-shaped "pones." On reaching the fence she had finished wiping her hands on the bottom of her apron.

"I jes' run 'cross de fiel' to fetch yer some bile dinner, ter help you out. I dunno ef you know'd it, but Simon stepped over ter see Bre'r Collins an' Bre'r Ha'is, dis mornin', an' 'bout dem t'aint no need ter 'splain, 'kase dey split 'nough boa'ds in er day ter kiver Miss Ad'line's big house, an' dey can eat 'cord'n'ly."

With this she handed over a pail and a bag.

"Dem mighty fine, juicy, yaller yams, an' you'll see, for short, de bread, I jes' drapped in de pot an' biled it all to-gedder."

"De good angel sont you heah ter day. Uphm! Doan' de smell good!"

"Here's yer dinner, 'Liji. Dis is er lubly place ter res, 'g'in' de fence, under dese shade trees."

Aunt Maria, with the assistance of two of the children, had brought down the dinner. Both quantity and quality delighted the men, as they beheld the feast.

Parson Davis, as his neighbors commonly called him, had never failed to ask a blessing upon the scantiest meal. Now, standing in the shade of the sweet-gum trees, he took Aunt "Ria's" hand in his, and raising his eyes to Heaven, gave God thanks for what was truly a Feast of Thanksgiving.

# A DASH FOR LIBERTY

Founded on an article written by
Col. T. W. Higginson,
for the Atlantic Monthly, June 1861

*Pauline E. Hopkins*

"So, Madison, you are bound to try it?"

"Yes, sir," was the respectful reply.

There was silence between the two men for a space, and Mr. Dickson drove his horse to the end of the furrow he was making and returned slowly to the starting point, and the sombre figure awaiting him.

"Do I not pay you enough, and treat you well?" asked the farmer as he halted.

"Yes, sir."

"Then why not stay here and let well enough alone?"

"Liberty is worth nothing to me while my wife is a slave."

"We will manage to get her to you in a year or two."

The man smiled and sadly shook his head. "A year or two would mean forever, situated as we are, Mr. Dickson. It is hard for you to understand; you white men are all alike where you are called upon to judge a Negro's heart," he continued bitterly. "Imagine yourself in my place; how would you feel? The relentless heel of oppression in the States will have ground my rights as a husband into the dust, and have driven Susan to despair in that time. A white man may take up arms to defend a bit of property; but a black man has no right to his wife, his liberty or his life against his master! This makes me low-spirited, Mr. Dickson, and I have determined to return to Virginia for my wife. My feelings are centred in the idea of liberty," and as he spoke he stretched his arms

*Colored American Magazine* 3 (Aug. 1901): 243–47.

toward the deep blue of the Canadian sky in a magnificent gesture. Then with a deep-drawn breath that inflated his mighty chest, he repeated the word: "Liberty! I think of it by day and dream of it by night; and I shall only taste it in all its sweetness when Susan shares it with me."

Madison was an unmixed African, of grand physique, and one of the handsomest of his race. His dignified, calm and unaffected bearing marked him as a leader among his fellows. His features bore the stamp of genius. His firm step and piercing eye attracted the attention of all who met him. He had arrived in Canada along with many other fugitives during the year 1840, and being a strong, able-bodied man, and a willing worker, had sought and obtained employment on Mr. Dickson's farm.

After Madison's words, Mr. Dickson stood for some time in meditative silence.

"Madison," he said at length, "there's desperate blood in your veins, and if you get back there and are captured, you'll do desperate deeds."

"Well, put yourself in my place: I shall be there single-handed. I have a wife whom I love, and whom I will protect. I hate slavery, I hate the laws that make my country a nursery for it. Must I be denied the right of aggressive defense against those who would overpower and crush me by superior force?"

"I understand you fully, Madison; it is not your defense but your rashness that I fear. Promise me that you will be discreet, and not begin an attack." Madison hesitated. Such a promise seemed to him like surrendering a part of those individual rights for which he panted. Mr. Dickson waited. Presently the Negro said significantly: "I promise not to be indiscreet."

There were tears in the eyes of the kind-hearted farmer as he pressed Madison's hand.

"God speed and keep you and the wife you love; may she prove worthy."

In a few days Madison received the wages due him, and armed with tiny saws and files to cut a way to liberty, if captured, turned his face toward the South.

\*     \*     \*     \*     \*

It was late in the fall of 1840 when Madison found himself again at home in the fair Virginia State. The land was blossoming into ripe maturity, and the smiling fields lay waiting for the harvester.

The fugitive, unable to travel in the open day, had hidden himself for three weeks in the shadow of the friendly forest near his old home, filled with hope and fear, unable to obtain any information about the wife he hoped to rescue from slavery. After weary days and nights, he had reached the most perilous part of his mission. Tonight there would be no moon and the clouds threatened a storm; to his listening ears the rising wind bore the sound of laughter and singing. He drew back into the deepest shadow. The words came distinctly to his ears as the singers neared his hiding place.

> "All dem purty gals will be dar,
>     Shuck dat corn before you eat.
> Dey will fix it fer us rare,
>     Shuck dat corn before you eat.
> I know dat supper will be big,
>     Shuck dat corn before you eat.
> I think I smell a fine roast pig,
>     Shuck dat corn before you eat.
> Stuff dat coon an' bake him down,

> I spec some niggers dar from town.
>   Shuck dat corn before you eat.
> Please cook dat turkey nice an' brown.
> By de side of dat turkey I'll be foun',
>   Shuck dat corn before you eat."

"Don't talk about dat turkey; he'll be gone before we git dar."

"He's talkin', ain't he?"

"Las' time I shucked corn, turkey was de toughes' meat I eat fer many a day; you's got to have teef sharp lak a saw to eat it."

"S'pose you ain't got no teef, den what you gwine ter do?"

"Why ef you ain't got no teef you muss gum it!"

"Ha, ha, ha!"

Madison glided in and out among the trees, listening until he was sure that it was a gang going to a corn-shucking, and he resolved to join it, and get, if possible some news of Susan. He came out upon the highway, and as the company reached his hiding place, he fell into the ranks and joined in the singing. The darkness hid his identity from the company while he learned from their conversation the important events of the day.

On they marched by the light of weird, flaring pine knots, singing their merry cadences, in which the noble minor strains habitual to Negro music, sounded the depths of sadness, glancing off in majestic harmony, that touched the very gates of paradise in suppliant prayer.

It was close to midnight; the stars had disappeared and a steady rain was falling when, by a circuitous route, Madison reached the mansion where he had learned that his wife was still living. There were lights in the windows. Mirth at the great house kept company with mirth at the quarters.

The fugitive stole noiselessly under the fragrant magnolia

trees and paused, asking himself what he should do next. As he stood there he heard the hoof-beats of the mounted patrol, far in the distance, die into silence. Cautiously he drew near the house and crept around to the rear of the building directly beneath the window of his wife's sleeping closet. He swung himself up and tried it; it yielded to his touch. Softly he raised the sash, and softly he crept into the room. His foot struck against an object and swept it to the floor. It fell with a loud crash. In an instant the door opened. There was a rush of feet, and Madison stood at bay. The house was aroused; lights were brought.

"I knowed 'twas him!" cried the overseer in triumph. "I heern him a-gettin' in the window, but I kept dark till he knocked my gun down; then I grabbed him! I knowed this room'd trap him ef we was patient about it."

Madison shook his captor off and backed against the wall. His grasp tightened on the club in his hand; his nerves were like steel, his eyes flashed fire.

"Don't kill him," shouted Judge Johnson, as the overseer's pistol gleamed in the light. "Five hundred dollars for him alive!"

With a crash, Madison's club descended on the head of the nearest man; again, and yet again, he whirled it around, doing frightful execution each time it fell. Three of the men who had responded to the overseer's cry for help were on the ground, and he himself was sore from many wounds before, weakened by loss of blood, Madison finally succumbed.

\* \* \* \* \*

The brig "Creole" lay at the Richmond dock taking on her cargo of tobacco, hemp, flax and slaves. The sky was cloudless, and the blue waters rippled but slightly under the faint breeze. There was on board the confusion incident to departure. In the hold and on deck men were hurrying to and fro, busy and excited, making the final preparations for the voyage. The slaves came aboard in two gangs: first the men, chained like cattle, were marched to their quarters in the hold; then came the women to whom more freedom was allowed.

In spite of the blue sky and the bright sunlight that silvered the water the scene was indescribably depressing and sad. The procession of gloomy-faced men and weeping women seemed to be descending into a living grave.

The captain and the first mate were standing together at the head of the gangway as the women stepped aboard. Most were very plain and bore the marks of servitude, a few were neat and attractive in appearances; but one was a woman whose great beauty immediately attracted attention; she was an octoroon. It was a tradition that her grandfather had served in the Revolutionary War, as well as in both Houses of Congress. That was nothing, however, at a time when the blood of the proudest F. F. V.'s was freely mingled with that of the African slaves on their plantations. Who wonders that Virginia has produced great men of color from among the exbondmen, or, that illustrious black men proudly point to Virginia as a birthplace? Posterity rises to the plane that their ancestors bequeath, and the most refined, the wealthiest and the most intellectual whites of that proud State have not hesitated to amalgamate with the Negro.

"What a beauty!" exclaimed the captain as the line of women paused a moment opposite him.

"Yes," said the overseer in charge of the gang. "She's as fine a piece of flesh as I have had in trade for many a day."

"What's the price?" demanded the captain.

"Oh, way up. Two or three thousand. She's a lady's maid, well-educated, and can sing and dance. We'll get it in New Orleans. Like to buy?"

"You don't suit my pile," was the reply, as his eyes followed the retreating form of the handsome octoroon. "Give her a cabin to herself; she ought not to herd with the rest," he continued, turning to the mate.

He turned with a meaning laugh to execute the order.

The "Creole" proceeded slowly on her way towards New Orleans. In the men's cabin, Madison Monroe lay chained to the floor and heavily ironed. But from the first moment on board ship he had been busily engaged in selecting men who could be trusted in the dash for liberty that he was determined to make. The miniature files and saws which he still wore concealed in his clothing were faithfully used in the darkness of night. The man was at peace, although he had caught no glimpse of the dearly loved Susan. When the body suffers greatly, the strain upon the heart becomes less tense, and a welcome calmness had stolen over the prisoner's soul.

On the ninth day out the brig encountered a rough sea, and most of the slaves were sick, and therefore not watched with very great vigilance. This was the time for action, and it was planned that they should rise that night. Night came on; the first watch was summoned; the wind was blowing high. Along the narrow passageway that separated the men's quarters from the women's, a man was creeping.

The octoroon lay upon the floor of her cabin, apparently sleeping, when a shadow darkened the door, and the captain stepped into the room, casting bold glances at the reclining figure. Profound silence reigned. One might have fancied one's self on a deserted vessel, but for the sound of an occasional footstep on the deck above, and the murmur of voices in the opposite hold.

She lay stretched at full length with her head resting upon her arm, a position that displayed to the best advantage the perfect symmetry of her superb figure; the dim light of a lantern played upon the long black ringlets, finely-chiselled mouth and well-rounded chin, upon the marbled skin veined by her master's blood,—representative of two races, to which did she belong?

For a moment the man gazed at her in silence; then casting a glance around him, he dropped upon one knee and kissed the sleeping woman full upon the mouth.

With a shriek the startled sleeper sprang to her feet. The woman's heart stood still with horror; she recognized the intruder as she dashed his face aside with both hands.

"None of that, my beauty," growled the man, as he reeled back with an oath, and then flung himself forward and threw his arm about her slender waist. "Why did you think you had a private cabin, and all the delicacies of the season? Not to behave like a young catamount, I warrant you."

The passion of terror and desperation lent the girl such strength that the man was forced to relax his hold slightly. Quick as a flash, she struck him a stinging blow across the eyes, and as he staggered back, she sprang out of the doorway, making for the deck with the evident intention of going overboard.

"God have mercy!" broke from her lips as she passed the men's cabin, closely followed by the captain.

"Hold on, girl; we'll protect you!" shouted Madison, and he stooped, seized the heavy padlock which fastened the iron ring that encircled his ankle to the iron bar, and stiffening the muscles, wrenched the fastening apart, and hurled it with all his force straight at the captain's head.

His aim was correct. The padlock hit the captain not far from the left temple. The blow stunned him. In a moment Madison was upon him and had seized his weapons, another moment served to handcuff the unconscious man.

"If the fire of Heaven were in my hands, I would throw

it at these cowardly whites. Follow me: it is liberty or death!"
he shouted as he rushed for the quarter-deck. Eighteen others
followed him, all of whom seized whatever they could wield
as weapons.

The crew were all on deck; the three passengers were seated
on the companion smoking. The appearance of the slaves all
at once completely surprised the whites.

So swift were Madison's movements that at first the officers
made no attempt to use their weapons; but this was only for
an instant. One of the passengers drew his pistol, fired, and
killed one of the blacks. The next moment he lay dead upon
the deck from a blow with a piece of a capstan bar in
Madison's hand. The fight then became general, passengers
and crew taking part.

The first and second mates were stretched out upon the
deck with a single blow each. The sailors ran up the rigging
for safety, and in short time Madison was master of the
"Creole."

After his accomplices had covered the slaver's deck, the
intrepid leader forbade the shedding of more blood. The
sailors came down to the deck, and their wounds were dressed.
All the prisoners were heavily ironed and well guarded except
the mate, who was to navigate the vessel; with a musket
doubly charged pointed at his breast, he was made to swear
to take the brig into a British port.

By one splendid and heroic stroke, the daring Madison
had not only gained his own liberty, but that of one hundred
and thirty-four others.

The next morning all the slaves who were still fettered,
were released, and the cook was ordered to prepare the best
breakfast that the stores would permit; this was to be a fête
in honor of the success of the revolt and as a surprise to the
females, whom the men had not yet seen.

As the women filed into the captain's cabin, where the meal was served, weeping, singing and shouting over their deliverance, the beautiful octoroon with one wild, half-frantic cry of joy sprang towards the gallant leader.

"Madison!"

"My God! Susan! My wife!"

She was locked to his breast; she clung to him convulsively. Unnerved at last by the revulsion to more than relief and ecstacy, she broke into wild sobs, while the astonished company closed around them with loud hurrahs.

Madison's cup of joy was filled to the brim. He clasped her to him in silence, and humbly thanked Heaven for its blessing and mercy.

* * * * *

The next morning the "Creole" landed at Nassau, New Providence, where the slaves were offered protection and hospitality.

Every act of oppression is a weapon for the oppressed. Right is a dangerous instrument; woe to us if our enemy wields it.

# THE WOOING OF
# PASTOR CUMMINGS

*Georgia F. Stewart*

"Whoa! How do you feel this morning, Brother Olmstead?"

"Wal, jest toler'ble. You looks well an' happy, but sich a good man allus gits along."

"Step in Brother Olmstead, I suppose you are on your way to church. How I wish they all were as true to their church as you are."

"Yas, dey kin all say w'at dey please, but I said it fus an' I says it las'—you's de man fur to lead dis congashun—a man w'at eddication doan mak too high strung to retch down an' he'p a po man to a seat in his ca'age. I dunno a nuther one ez'd tek notice o' me hobblin' long heah. Dey tek it a mohenjus crime to speak to a po' man lak me; an' ez fur set'in 'long side 'm' lak I's by you, well I nebber gwine smell dat."

Reverend E. Z. Cummings, as he always signed his name, had created between his congregation, which was composed of good, honest people, and what he termed "eddicated niggers," an impassable chasm. Shortly after his settlement in this parish, he said to some of the officers of his church: "I should not be with you long, were I to listen to people who appear to be friendly to this church." He often intimated to them that they were considered an ignorant body, and were not worthy of an educated minister, but he would pledge himself never to leave them if they would support him in the many battles that must inevitably be fought. Being naturally

*Colored American Magazine* 3 (Aug. 1901): 273–76.

pessimistic, they needed little argument to confirm his statement.

Now, the true state of affairs was this: Rev. E. Z. Cummings lacked strength of character. Soon after his invasion into a community this quality asserted itself, and he was invariably requested to resign his pastorate. Yet, in the face of this, his next victims would receive glowing reports of his last "charge."

"We missed you at prayer-meeting Friday evening, Brother Olmstead."

"Yer mout 'a' Knowed it wuz jes my plan to go 'mongst dese folks w'at raise dis 'sturbment an' see how de lan lays. I bleves you's a hon'able man, I does, an' ef Miss Mandy Lucas w'ats a spread'n all de talk 'bout you an' sartin parties wuz a christon w'ats not jelous, de poperlation 'd soon stop pint'n at you."

For sometime the critics had not dealt gently with Rev. E. Z. Cummings, and the sentiment he feared was not favorable to him. He had always been able to lead his flock to the water and generally force the majority to take a drink regardless of their will. With that thought in mind he determined to fortify himself as strongly as possible. He consciously misled every woman who would accept his attentions and give ear to his flattery, assuring each that she was his choice and the one whom he most desired for a companion.

"Here we are at the church," he said.

"Jes a minit, Revend. I wuz say'n dat my gal Luc' Ann w'at is so sorter ezy in her way 'bout tend'n Meet'n an' all, mout some day suit de fancy of some eddicated sheperd. She's a lakly gal, she is."

He had no idea that this introduction came entirely too late, and that the pastor had already shown his daughter much attention; which accounted for her constant attendance upon the services.

"I must confess that her admirable qualities have attracted me since first I met her," said the pastor.

This Sunday was one which called into use all of the summer apparel. As a special meeting always meant a new gown for the sisters, a gorgeous array of cheap muslins, flowers, and ribbons met the pastor's eye, as he strode forth with lordly air, that they might be inspired by his presence, while he stood with compressed lips and bowed head, as if communing with the saints. Finally he said:

"If it were not for faith, how could we stand the persecutions of our fellowmen! Day after day I have walked meekly on and said nothing. Now, today, I offer myself to this body of brothers and sisters who have ever supported me, and for which I am thankful. Though I have been persecuted by man, right will prevail. I love every member of this church. I love to eat with them; sleep with them; and pray with them every day of my life."

"Amen! I knowed he wuz a' innercent man fum de fus."
"Love to be wid us po' creeters. Ain't he good."

"You been sont to lead us." "I means to stand by you." "Lemme shake your han."

Such expressions came from all parts of the church. "Now my dears," said the pastor, "before we go farther let us give thanks for this privilege of assembling, believing that the Lord will make it alright." At the end of three minutes of silence the pastor began singing softly:

"A little mo-re talk with Jesus makes it right, alright;
A little mo-re talk with Jesus makes it right, alright.
In trouble of every kind, thank God I always find,
That a little talk with Jesus makes it right, alright."

Shouting and weeping were indulged in very freely, while the pastor with folded arms, walked slowly back and forth across the rostrum. One sister, as she looked up at him said, "Too good! Too good! for dis earth."

Elder Jackson came forward at this juncture, and placing a small table just at the end of the centre aisle, told them in a few words that he knew they were anxious to give the pastor substantial signs of their high esteem of him.

"We are much in need of finance, and if you will march right up to the table, and put down your dues, it will relieve our dear pastor, who feels the responsibility of all debts connected with the church. Will the choir please give us some music? Then you shall have a chance to come up while some of the sisters sing. Come right along now, and as soon as this is done, Reverend Eli McLemore will give us a stirring talk on the 'Agonies of Christ,' since our beloved pastor is not well."

"Still we lack four dollars. We must give him fifty dollars tonight! That's right, brother Williams. Now we need three more. Ah! here come two sisters and two brothers. Thank you, thank you, thank you. Just twenty-five cents and all will be over. Won't some dear sister give five cents of that? There, three, four, five, six sisters! That's good, a little more doesn't matter."

The minister drew from his pocket a small bag which showed signs of dust as well as wear, and handed it to the deacon. Into this bag the money was put and it was left on the floor by the pulpit where the Reverend could get it on going out.

Brother McLemore's talk, picturing the sufferings of Christ, served only to increase the excitement which began earlier in the service. The effect of his appeals to them to adhere to one who had suffered for them were tragic beyond description.

Some ran to and fro, shaking hands; some wept and walked, while those who were less demonstrative sat swaying their bodies from side to side to the accompaniment of piteous moans, which would signify to a listener, the loss of the last beloved one. Then there were those who felt "lifted up" and chose to walk on the benches rather than on the floor, thinking nothing of walking from the pulpit to the door stepping from the back of one bench to another, and so on.

Another spiritual feast was yet in store for them. It was the feast of spiritual re-enforcement. Instead of having love-feast on Friday night of the next week the pastor, who arranged all things, considered it strengthening to his reinstatement, to have it associated as closely as possible with this meeting; so he announced it for the following evening.

It was at love-feast that all ill-feelings towards sister or brother were obliterated; hands were shaken as bits of bread were exchanged, and love reigned supreme. "Sis Hannah, w'at yer gwine ter do 'bout Sis Ang'line Skinner? Somehow I doan b'leve wid all her 'ligun, she'll brek bread wid yer."

"I'm goin to do my duty. I have no malice in my heart. Long ago the pastor showed his preference for Sis Lucy Ann Olmstead. You see all comes for the best any how. It ain't my nature to settle down to married life so early."

"Chile evy body ses you's get'n ole but yersef. You got jes nuf larnin to put on stylish airs." This exchange of words was between Miss Hannah Gibbs and Miss Maria Middleton, two maiden ladies, whose modesty and generosity were potent factors in constraining them to remain in a state of single blessedness. This was the evening for love-feast. The church was crowded. Bread had been passed and each was ready to "break with the other." The entire membership arose and began to break bread, while all joined in singing the following:

"Won't we have a happy time
There's a love-feast in' Heaven By'n Bye.
My Redeemer, My Redeemer,
There's a love-feast in Heaven By'n Bye."

"There's a love-feast in Heaven By'n Bye,
Eating of the honey and drinking of the wine,
There's a love-feast in Heaven By'n Bye.
    My Redeemer, My Redeemer,
There's a love-feast in Heaven By'n Bye."

By this time Sister Hannah Gibbs had made her way to
the altar, as that seemed the destination of all. They were
packed so closely now that as they rocked back and forth,
keeping time to the tune of the familiar song which was
interspersed with cries from the sisters who were happy, they
looked like one large body being drawn from right to left,
and between each vibration came a curtesy which too was
strictly in keeping with the melody of the song. Here she
was face to face with Sister Skinner, who for weeks had lifted
her skirts and held high her head to avoid contact, not even
a glance at the former. "May the good Lord bless you, Sister
Skinner," and with this she forced a crumb of bread into
Sister Skinner's hand; holding out her own to receive the
token of good feeling, and took advantage of the opportunity
to say, "Can't anybody see where the Reverend's affection is
centered? On nobody but Sister Lucy Ann Olmstead." They
shook hands, exchanged bits of bread and passed on to others.
During the evening the pastor was continually receiving
assurances of their appreciation for him.

As the crowd left the church they were full of the feast,
but among them was one whose heart was heavy. Sister
Skinner had hoped that her daughter would be the fortunate

one and had begun to feel confident that he would soon ask Miss Skinner to share his home.

"It's a monstrous undertakin', but today I goes over to Sis Olmstead's to larn de fac's," said Sister Skinner, after waiting several weeks for the minister's decided action in the matter.

"How yer do Sis Skinner I dunno how come I did'n fling dis water on yer, case no body never comes roun' that side o' the house.

"Ah, sorterso so. De sickness and trouble 'mongst folks seem mighty rapid. Did yer know Sis Mat Shepard mighty low? I felt lak you mought want ter go ter see her; so I jes stop ter tell you I'm goin' ter see her and git my clo'es on my way back home. It wouldn't do ter miss dryin' clo'es a day lak dis."

"Soon's I gits a moufful er coffee I'll be ready," said Mrs. Olmstead.

"W'at yer gwine do today? Wash I suppose," asked Mrs. Skinner.

"No, Luc' Ann'll wash, I'm'bliged ter do some sewin' to day. Fum all dat I kin see de Revend 'll tek her ter his home soon an' ef dere is anything I hates, it's ter see a nice gal go fum her home short o' clo'es an quilts."

"Yes, you's zackly right, Sis Olmstead," as if she knew the particulars. It was not her plan to ask questions, but to wait until the spirit moved Sister Olmstead and she would know all. This she did. After ministering to the sick according to their ability, they parted, Sister Skinner going for her clothes while Sister Olmstead went down to do a little "tradin." A few days later, brother Olmstead met the pastor as he was driving along the street:

"Revend, I want's ter talk wid yer."

"Whoa! how do you feel this morning, brother Olmstead?"

"No good feelin's t'wards yer. W'at yer mean by fool'n O'my gal? All de time I's been workin fur yer, eben to rushin in de enemy's camp, she seem powerful pleasin to yer choice 'mongst all de fine flowers, an' now w'en yer foundation quit rockin' an all pears peaceful, yer jis say ter her: ' 'Taint prudent fur me ter tek dat step.' Lemme tell yer man, yer done brek her heart, let lone how me an' her mammy done strain de las notch ter get artickles w'at's suitable fur dat persition. Luc' Ann's not de same.

"De po' chile nebber will kere fur nobody else: Her face done drap down lak dem Sisters on de hill. All she need is the veil, but I trust she nebber tek it." Brother Olmstead was not be toyed with, and the reverend saw it; so drove off rapidly, saying that he would see him again. A church meeting had been appointed for the next evening. This bit of news had spread through the village, and behind it followed brother Olmstead arousing the sympathy of all he met. When the subject was introduced at this meeting it was amazing how many had the same charge against the Reverend. Brother Olmstead told those assembled if they did not dismiss the pastor that he would put him out by force. It was decided by the majority that he be required to seek work elsewhere immediately.

Thus the Reverend E. Z. Cummings, D.D., passed from this active field of labor.

# BRO'R ABR'M
# JIMSON'S WEDDING
## *A Christmas Story*

*Pauline E. Hopkins*

It was a Sunday in early spring the first time that Caramel
Johnson dawned on the congregation of—Church in a pop-
ulous New England city.

The Afro-Americans of that city are well-to-do, being of a
frugal nature, and considering it a lasting disgrace for any
man among them, desirous of social standing in the community, not to make himself comfortable in this world's
goods against the coming time, when old age creeps on apace
and renders him unfit for active business.

Therefore the members of the said church had not waited
to be exhorted by reformers to own their unpretentious homes
and small farms outside the city limits, but they vied with
each other in efforts to accumulate a small competency urged
thereto by a realization of what pressing needs the future
might bring, or it might have been because of the constant
example of white neighbors, and a due respect for the dignity
which *their* foresight had brought to the superior race.

Of course, these small Vanderbilts and Astors of a darker
hue must have a place of worship in accord with their worldly
prosperity, and so it fell out that—church was the richest
plum in the ecclesiastical pudding, and greatly sought by
scholarly divines as a resting place for four years,—the extent
of the time-limit allowed by conference to the men who must
be provided with suitable charges according to the demands
of their energy and scholarship.

*Colored American Magazine* 4 (Dec. 1901): 103–12.

The attendance was unusually large for morning service, and a restless movement was noticeable all through the sermon. How strange a thing is nature; the change of the seasons announces itself in all humanity as well as in the trees and flowers, the grass, and in the atmosphere. Something within us responds instantly to the touch of kinship that dwells in all life.

The air, soft and balmy, laden with rich promise for the future, came through the massive, half-open windows, stealing in refreshing waves upon the congregation. The sunlight fell through the colored glass of the windows in prismatic hues, and dancing all over the lofty star-gemmed ceiling, painted the hue of the broad vault of heaven, creeping down in crinkling shadows to touch the deep garnet cushions of the sacred desk, and the rich wood of the altar with a hint of gold.

The offertory was ended. The silvery cadences of a rich soprano voice still lingered on the air, "O, Worship the Lord in the beauty of holiness." There was a suppressed feeling of expectation, but not the faintest rustle as the minister rose in the pulpit, and after a solemn pause, gave the usual invitation:

"If there is anyone in this congregation desiring to unite with this church, either by letter or on probation, please come forward to the altar."

The words had not died upon his lips when a woman started from her seat near the door and passed up the main aisle. There was a sudden commotion on all sides. Many heads were turned—it takes so little to interest a church audience. The girls in the choir-box leaned over the rail, nudged each other and giggled, while the men said to one another, "She's a stunner, and no mistake."

The candidate for membership, meanwhile, had reached the altar railing and stood before the man of God, to whom

she had handed her letter from a former Sabbath home, with
head decorously bowed as became the time and the holy place.
There was no denying the fact that she was a pretty girl;
brown of skin, small of feature, with an ever-lurking gleam
of laughter in eyes coal black. Her figure was slender and
beautifully moulded, with a seductive grace in the undulating
walk and erect carriage. But the chief charm of the sparkling
dark face lay in its intelligence, and the responsive play of
facial expression which was enhanced by two mischievous
dimples pressed into the rounded cheeks by the caressing
fingers of the god of Love.

The minister whispered to the candidate, coughed, blew
his nose on his snowy clerical handkerchief, and, finally,
turned to the expectant congregation:

"Sister Chocolate Caramel Johnson—"

He was interrupted by a snicker and a suppressed laugh,
again from the choir-box, and an audible whisper which
sounded distinctly throughout the quiet church,—

"I'd get the Legislature to change that if it was mine, 'deed
I would!" then silence profound caused by the reverend's
stern glance of reproval bent on the offenders in the choir-
box.

"Such levity will not be allowed among the members of
the choir. If it occurs again, I shall ask the choir master for
the names of the offenders and have their places taken by
those more worthy to be gospel singers."

Thereupon Mrs. Tilly Anderson whispered to Mrs. Nancy
Tobias that, "them choir gals is the mos' deceivines' hussies
in the church, an' for my part, I'm glad the pastor called 'em
down. That sister's too good lookin' fer 'em, an' they'll be
after her like er pack o' houn's, min' me, Sis' Tobias."

Sister Tobias ducked her head in her lap and shook her fat
sides in laughing appreciation of the sister's foresight.

Order being restored the minister proceeded:

"Sister Chocolate Caramel Johnson brings a letter to us from our sister church in Nashville, Tennessee. She has been a member in good standing for ten years, having been received into fellowship at ten years of age. She leaves them now, much to their regret, to pursue the study of music at one of the large conservatories in this city, and they recommend her to our love and care. You know the contents of the letter. All in favor of giving Sister Johnson the right hand of fellowship, please manifest the same by a rising vote." The whole congregation rose.

"Contrary minded? None. The ayes have it. Be seated, friends. Sister Johnson it gives me great pleasure to receive you into this church. I welcome you to its joys and sorrows. May God bless you, Brother Jimson?" (Brother Jimson stepped from his seat to the pastor's side.) "I assign this sister to your class. Sister Johnson, this is Brother Jimson, your future spiritual teacher."

Brother Jimson shook the hand of his new member, warmly, and she returned to her seat. The minister pronounced the benediction over the waiting congregation; the organ burst into richest melody. Slowly the crowd of worshippers dispersed.

Abraham Jimson had made his money as a janitor for the wealthy people of the city. He was a bachelor, and when reproved by some good Christian brother for still dwelling in single blessedness always offered as an excuse that he had been too busy to think of a wife, but that now he was "well fixed," pecuniarily, he would begin to "look over" his lady friends for a suitable companion.

He owned a house in the suburbs and a fine brick dwelling-house in the city proper. He was a trustee of prominence in the church; in fact, its "solid man," and his opinion was sought and his advice acted upon by his associates on the Board. It was felt that any lady in the congregation would be proud to know herself his choice.

When Caramel Johnson received the right hand of fellowship, her aunt, the widow Maria Nash, was ahead in the race for the wealthy class-leader. It had been neck-and-neck for a while between her and Sister Viney Peters, but, finally it had settled down to Sister Maria with a hundred to one, among the sporting members of the Board, that she carried off the prize, for Sister Maria owned a house adjoining Brother Jimson's in the suburbs, and property counts these days.

Sister Nash had "no idea" when she sent for her niece to come to B. that the latter would prove a rival; her son Andy was as good as engaged to Caramel. But it is always the unexpected that happens. Caramel came, and Brother Jimson had no eyes for the charms of other women after he had gazed into her coal black orbs, and watched her dimples come and go.

Caramel decided to accept a position as housemaid in order to help defray the expenses of her tuition at the conservatory, and Brother Jimson interested himself so warmly in her behalf that she soon had a situation in the home of his richest patron where it was handy for him to chat with her about the business of the church, and the welfare of her soul, in general. Things progressed very smoothly until the fall, when one day Sister Maria had occasion to call, unexpectedly, on her niece and found Brother Jimson basking in her smiles while he enjoyed a sumptuous dinner of roast chicken and fixings.

To say that Sister Maria was "set way back" would not accurately describe her feelings; but from that time Abraham Jimson knew that he had a secret foe in the Widow Nash.

Before many weeks had passed it was publicly known that Brother Jimson would lead Caramel Johnson to the altar

"come Christmas." There was much sly speculation as to the
"widder's gittin' left," and how she took it from those who
had cast hopeless glances toward the chief man of the church.
Great preparations were set on foot for the wedding festivities.
The bride's trousseau was a present from the groom and
included a white satin wedding gown and a costly gold watch.
The town house was refurnished, and a trip to New York
was in contemplation.

"Hump!" grunted Sister Nash when told the rumors,
"there's no fool like an ol' fool. Car'mel's a han'ful he'll fin',
ef he gits her."

"I reckon he'll git her all right, Sis' Nash," laughed the
neighbor, who had run in to talk over the news.

"I've said my word an' I ain't goin' change it, Sis'r. Min'
me. I says, *ef he gits her*, an, I mean it."

Andy Nash was also a member of Brother Jimson's class;
he possessed, too, a strong sweet baritone voice which made
him of great value to the choir. He was an immense success
in the social life of the city, and had created sad havoc with
the hearts of the colored girls; he could have his pick of the
best of them because of his graceful figure and fine easy
manners. Until Caramel had been dazzled by the wealth of
her elderly lover, she had considered herself fortunate as the
lady of his choice.

It was Sunday, three weeks before the wedding that Andy
resolved to have it out with Caramel.

"She's been hot an' she's been col', an' now she's luke
warm, an' today ends it before this gent-man sleeps," he told
himself as he stood before the glass and tied his pale blue silk
tie in a stunning knot, and settled his glossy tile at a becoming
angle.

Brother Jimson's class was a popular one and had a large
membership; the hour spent there was much enjoyed, even

by visitors. Andy went into the vestry early resolved to meet
Caramel if possible. She was there, at the back of the room
sitting alone on a settee. Andy immediately seated himself in
the vacant place by her side. There were whispers and much
head-shaking among the few early worshippers, all of whom
knew the story of the young fellow's romance and his disappointment.

As he dropped into the seat beside her, Caramel turned
her large eyes on him intently, speculatively, with a doubtful
sort of curiosity suggested in her expression, as to how he
took her flagrant desertion.

"Howdy, Car'mel?" was his greeting without a shade of
resentment.

"I'm well; no need to ask how you are," was the quick
response. There was a mixture of cordiality and coquetry in
her manner. Her eyes narrowed and glittered under lowered
lids, as she gave him a long side-glance. How could she help
showing her admiration for the supple young giant beside
her? "Surely," she told herself, "I'll have long time enough
to git sick of old rheumatics," her pet name for her elderly
lover.

"I ain't sick much," was Andy's surly reply.

He leaned his elbow on the back of the settee and gave his
recent sweetheart a flaming glance of mingled love and hate,
oblivious to the presence of the assembled class-members.

"You ain't over friendly these days, Car'mel, but I gits
news of your capers 'roun' 'bout some of the members."

"My—Yes?" she answered as she flashed her great eyes at
him in pretended surprise. He laughed a laugh not good to
hear.

"Yes," he drawled. Then he added with sudden energy,
"Are you goin' to tie up to old Rheumatism sure 'nuff, come
Chris'mas?"

"Come Chris'mas, Andy, I be. I hate to tell you but I have to do it."

He recoiled as from a blow. As for the girl, she found a keen relish in the situation; it flattered her vanity.

"How comes it you've changed your mind, Car'mel, 'bout you an' me? You've tol' me often that I was your first choice."

"We—ll," she drawled, glancing uneasily about her and avoiding her aunt's gaze, which she knew was bent upon her every movement, "I did reckon once I would. But a man with money suits me best, an' you ain't got a cent."

"No more have you. You ain't no better than other women to work an' help a man along, is you?"

The color flamed an instant in her face turning the dusky skin to a deep, dull red.

"Andy Nash, you always was a fool, an' as ignerunt as a wil' Injun. I mean to have a sure nuff brick house an' plenty of money. That makes people respec' you. Why don' you quit bein' so shifless and save your money. You ain't worth your salt."

"Your head's turned with pianorer-playin' an' livin' up North. Ef you'll turn *him* off an' come back home, I'll turn over a new leaf, Car'mel," his voice was soft and persuasive enough now.

She had risen to her feet; her eyes flashed, her face was full of pride.

"I won't. I've quit likin' you, Andy Nash."

"Are you in earnest?" he asked, also rising from his seat.

"Dead earnes'."

"Then there's no more to be said."

He spoke calmly, not raising his voice above a whisper. She stared at him in surprise. Then he added as he swung on his heel preparatory to leaving her:

"You ain't got him yet, my gal. But remember, I'm waitin' for you when you need me."

While this whispered conference was taking place in the back part of the vestry, Brother Jimson had entered, and many an anxious glance he cast in the direction of the couple. Andy made his way slowly to his mother's side as Brother Jimson rose in his place to open the meeting. There was a commotion on all sides as the members rustled down on their knees for prayer. Widow Nash whispered to her son as they knelt side by side:

"How did you make out, Andy?"

"Didn't make out at all, mammy; she's as obstinate as a mule."

"Well, then, there's only one thing mo' to do."

Andy was unpleasant company for the remainder of the day. He sought, but found nothing to palliate Caramel's treachery. He had only surly, bitter words for his companions who ventured to address him, as the outward expression of inward tumult. The more he brooded over his wrongs the worse he felt. When he went to work on Monday morning he was feeling vicious. He had made up his mind to do something desperate. The wedding should not come off. He would be avenged.

Andy went about his work at the hotel in gloomy silence unlike his usual gay hilarity. It happened that all the female help at the great hostelry was white, and on that particular Monday morning it was the duty of Bridget McCarthy's watch to clean the floors. Bridget was also not in the best of humors, for Pat McClosky, her special company, had gone to the priest's with her rival, Kate Connerton, on Sunday afternoon, and Bridget had not yet got over the effects of a strong rum punch taken to quiet her nerves after hearing the news.

Bridget had scrubbed a wide swath of the marble floor when Andy came through with a rush order carried in scientific style high above his head, balanced on one hand.

Intent upon satisfying the guest who was princely in his "tips," Andy's unwary feet became entangled in the maelstrom of brooms, scrubbing-brushes and pails. In an instant the "order" was sliding over the floor in a general mix-up.

To say Bridget was mad wouldn't do her state justice. She forgot herself and her surroundings and relieved her feelings in elegant Irish, ending a tirade of abuse by calling Andy a "wall-eyed, bandy-legged nagur."

Andy couldn't stand that from "common, po' white trash," so calling all his science into play he struck out straight from the shoulder with his right, and brought her a swinging blow on the mouth, which seated her neatly in the five-gallon bowl of freshly made lobster salad which happened to be standing on the floor behind her.

There was a wail from the kitchen force that reached to every department. It being the busiest hour of the day when they served dinner, the dish-washers and scrubbers went on a strike against the "nagur who struck Bridget McCarthy, the baste," mingled with cries of "lynch him!" Instantly the great basement floor was a battle ground. Every colored man seized whatever was handiest and ranged himself by Andy's side, and stood ready to receive the onslaught of the Irish brigade. For the sake of peace, and sorely against his inclinations, the proprietor surrendered Andy to the police on a charge of assault and battery.

On Wednesday morning of that eventful week, Brother Jimson wended his way to his house in the suburbs to collect the rent. Unseen by the eye of man, he was wrestling with a problem that had shadowed his life for many years. No one on earth suspected him unless it might be the widow. Brother Jimson boasted of his consistent Christian life—rolled his piety like a sweet morsel beneath his tongue, and had deluded himself into thinking that *he* could do no sin. There were scoffers in the church who doubted the genuineness of his pretensions, and he believed that there was a movement on foot against his power led by Widow Nash.

Brother Jimson groaned in bitterness of spirit. His only fear was that he might be parted from Caramel. If he lost her he felt that all happiness in life was over for him, and anxiety gave him a sickening feeling of unrest. He was tormented, too, by jealousy; and when he was called upon by Andy's anxious mother to rescue her son from the clutches of the law, he had promised her fair enough, but in reality resolved to do nothing but—tell the judge that Andy was a dangerous character whom it was best to quell by severity. The pastor and all the other influential members of the church were at court on Tuesday, but Brother Jimson was conspicuous by his absence.

Today Brother Jimson resolved to call on Sister Nash, and, as he had heard nothing of the outcome of the trial, make cautious inquiries concerning that, and also sound her on the subject nearest his heart.

He opened the gate and walked down the side path to the back door. From within came the rhythmic sound of a rubbing board. The brother knocked, and then cleared his throat with a preliminary cough.

"Come," called a voice within. As the door swung open it revealed the spare form of the widow, who with sleeves rolled above her elbows stood at the tub cutting her way through piles of foaming suds.

"Mornin', Sis' Nash! How's all?"

"That you, Bro'r Jimson? How's yourself? Take a cheer an' make yourself to home."

"Cert'nly, Sis' Nash; don' care ef I do," and the good brother scanned the sister with an eagle eye. "Yas'm, I'm purty tol'rable these days, thank God. Bleeg'd to you, Sister,

I jes' will stop an' res' myself befo' I repair myself back to the city." He seated himself in the most comfortable chair in the room, tilted it on the two back legs against the wall, lit his pipe and with a grunt of satisfaction settled back to watch the white rings of smoke curl about his head.

"These are mighty ticklish times, Sister. How's you continue on the journey? Is you strong in the faith?"

"I've got the faith, my brother, but I ain't on no mountain top this week. I'm way down in the valley; I'm jes' coaxin' the Lord to keep me sweet," and Sister Nash wiped the suds from her hands and prodded the clothes in the boiler with the clothes-stick, added fresh pieces and went on with her work.

"This is a worl' strewed with wrecks an' floatin' with tears. It's the valley of tribulation. May your faith continue. I hear Jim Jinkins has bought a farm up Taunton way."

"Wan' ter know!"

"Doctor tells me Bro'r Waters is comin' after Chris-mus. They do say as how he's stirrin' up things turrible; he's easin' his min' on this lynchin' business, an' it's high time—high time."

"Sho! Don' say so! What you reck'n he's goin' tell us now, Brother Jimson?"

"Suthin' 'stonishin', Sister; it'll stir the country from end to end. Yes'm, the Council is powerful strong as an organ-'zation."

"Sho! sho!" and the "thrub, thrub" of the board could be heard a mile away.

The conversation flagged. Evidently Widow Nash was not in a talkative mood that morning. The brother was disappointed.

"Well, it's mighty comfort'ble here, but I mus' be goin'."

"What's your hurry, Brother Jimson?"

"Business, Sister, business," and the brother brought his chair forward preparatory to rising. "Where's Andy? How'd he come out of that little difficulty?"

"Locked up."

"You don' mean to say he's in jail?"

"Yes; he's in jail 'tell I git's his bail."

"What might the sentence be, Sister?"

"Twenty dollars fine or six months at the Islan'." There was silence for a moment, broken only by the "thrub, thrub" of the washboard, while the smoke curled upward from Brother Jimson's pipe as he enjoyed a few last puffs.

"These are mighty ticklish times, Sister. Po' Andy, the way of the transgressor is hard."

Sister Nash took her hands out of the tub and stood with arms akimbo, a statue of Justice carved in ebony. Her voice was like the trump of doom.

"Yes; an' men like you is the cause of it. You leadin' men with money an' chances don' do your duty. I arst you, I arst you fair, to go down to the jedge an' bail that po' chile out. Did you go? No; you hard-faced old devil, you lef him be there, an' I had to git the money from my white folks. Yes, an' I'm breakin' my back now, over that pile of clo's to pay that twenty dollars. Um! all the trouble comes to us women."

"That's so, Sister; that's the livin' truth," murmured Brother Jimson furtively watching the rising storm and wondering where the lightning of her speech would strike next.

"I tell you what it is our receiptfulness to each other is the reason we don' prosper an' God's a-punishin' us with fire an' with sward 'cause we's so jealous an' snaky to each other."

"That's so, Sister; that's the livin' truth."

"Yes, sir; a nigger's boun' to be a nigger 'tell the trump

of doom. You kin skin him, but he's a nigger still. Broad-cloth, biled shirts an' money won' make him more or less, no, sir."

"That's so, Sister; that's jes' so."

"A nigger can't holp himself. White folks can run agin the law all the time an' they never gits caught, but a nigger! Every time he opens his mouth he puts his foot in it—got to hit that po' white trash gal in the mouth an' git jailed, an' leave his po'r ol' mother to work her fingers to the secon' jint to get him out. Um!"

"These are mighty ticklish times, Sister. Man's boun' to sin; it's his nat'ral state. I hope this will teach Andy humility of the sperit."

"A little humility'd be good for yourself, Abra'm Jimson." Sister Nash ceased her sobs and set her teeth hard.

"Lord, Sister Nash, what compar'son is there 'twixt me an' a worthless nigger like Andy? My business is with the salt of the earth, an' so I have dwelt ever since I was consecrated."

"Salt, of the earth! But ef the salt have los' its saver how you goin' salt it ergin'? No, sir, you cain't do it; it mus' be cas' out an' trodded under foot of men. That's who's goin' happen you Abe Jimson, hyar me? An' I'd like to trod on you with my foot, an' every ol' good fer nuthin' bag o' salt like you," shouted Sister Nash. "You're a snake in the grass; you done stole the boy's gal an' then try to git him sent to the Islan'. You cain't deny it, fer the jedge done tol' me all you said, you ol' rhinoceros-hided hypercrite. Salt of the earth! You!"

Brother Jimson regretted that Widow Nash had found him out. Slowly, he turned, settling his hat on the back of his head.

"Good mornin', Sister Nash. I ain't no hard feelin's agains' you. I'm too near to the kindom to let trifles jar me. My bowels of compassion yearns over you, Sister, a pilgrim an' a stranger in this unfriendly worl'."

No answer from Sister Nash. Brother Jimson lingered.

"Good mornin', Sister," still no answer.

"I hope to see you at the weddin', Sister."

"Keep on hopin'; I'll be there. That gal's my own sister's chile. What in time she wants of a rheumatic ol' sap-head like you for, beats me. I wouldn't marry you for no money, myself; no, sir; it's my belief that you've done goophered her."

"Yes, Sister; I've hearn tell of people refusin' befo' they was ask'd," he retorted, giving her a sly look.

For answer the widow grabbed the clothes-stick and flung it at him in speechless rage.

"My, what a temper it's got," remarked Brother Jimson soothingly as he dodged the shovel, the broom, the coalhod and the stove-covers. But he sighed with relief as he turned into the street and caught the faint sound of the washboard now resumed.

.     .     .     .     .

To a New Englander the season of snow and ice with its clear biting atmosphere, is the ideal time for the great festival. Christmas morning dawned in royal splendor; the sun kissed the snowy streets and turned the icicles into brilliant stalactites. The bells rang a joyous call from every steeple, and soon the churches were crowded with eager worshippers—eager to hear again the oft-repeated, the wonderful story on which the heart of the whole Christian world feeds its faith and hope. Words of tender faith, marvelous in their simplicity fell from the lips of a world-renowned preacher, and touched the hearts of the listening multitude:

"The winter sunshine is not more bright and clear than the atmosphere of living joy, which stretching back between our eyes and that picture of Bethlehem, shows us its beauty in unstained freshness. And as we open once again those chapters of the gospel in which the ever fresh and living picture stands, there seems from year to year always to come some newer, brighter meaning into the words that tell the tale.

"St. Matthew says that when Jesus was born in Bethlehem the wise men came from the East to Jerusalem. The East means man's search after God; Jerusalem means God's search after man. The East means the religion of the devout soul; Jerusalem means the religion of the merciful God. The East means Job's cry, 'Oh, that I knew where I might find him!' Jerusalem means 'Immanuel—God with us.' "

Then the deep-toned organ joined the grand chorus of human voices in a fervent hymn of praise and thanksgiving:

> "Lo! the Morning Star appeareth,
>    O'er the world His beams are cast;
> He the Alpha and Omega,
>    He, the Great, the First the Last!
> Hallelujah! hallelujah!
>    Let the heavenly portal ring!
> Christ is born, the Prince of glory!
>    Christ the Lord, Messiah, King!"

Everyone of prominence in church circles had been bidden to the Jimson wedding. The presents were many and costly. Early after service on Christmas morning the vestry room was taken in hand by leading sisters to prepare the tables for the supper, for on account of the host of friends bidden to the feast, the reception was to be held in the vestry.

The tables groaned beneath their loads of turkey, salads, pies, puddings, cakes and fancy ices.

Yards and yards of evergreen wreaths encircled the granite pillars; the altar was banked with potted plants and cut flowers. It was a beautiful sight. The main aisle was roped off for the invited guests, with white satin ribbons.

Brother Jimson's patrons were to be present in a body, and they had sent the bride a solid silver service so magnificent that the sisters could only sigh with envy.

The ceremony was to take place at seven sharp. Long before that hour the ushers in full evening dress were ready to receive the guests. Sister Maria Nash was among the first to arrive, and even the Queen of Sheba was not arrayed like unto her. At fifteen minutes before the hour, the organist began an elaborate instrumental performance. There was an expectant hush and much head-turning when the music changed to the familiar strains of the "Wedding March." The minister took his place inside the railing ready to receive the party. The groom waited at the altar.

First came the ushers, then the maids of honor, then the flower girl—daughter of a prominent member—carrying a basket of flowers which she scattered before the bride, who was on the arm of the best man. In the bustle and confusion incident to the entrance of the wedding party no one noticed a group of strangers accompanied by Andy Nash, enter and occupy seats near the door.

The service began. All was quiet. The pastor's words fell clearly upon the listening ears. He had reached the words:

"If any man can show just cause, etc.," when like a thunder-clap came a voice from the back part of the house—an angry excited voice, and a woman of ponderous avoirdupois advanced up the aisle.

"Hol' on thar, pastor, hol'on! A man cain't have but one wife 'cause it's agin' the law. I'm Abe Jimson's lawful wife, an' hyars his six children—all boys—to pint out their daddy." In an instant the assembly was in confusion.

"My soul," exclaimed Viney Peters, "the ol' sarpen'! An' to think how near I come to takin' up with him. I'm glad I ain't Car'mel."

Sis'r Maria said nothing, but a smile of triumph lit up her countenance.

"Brother Jimson, is this true?" demanded the minister, sternly. But Abraham Jimson was past answering. His face was ashen, his teeth chattering, his hair standing on end. His shaking limbs refused to uphold his weight; he sank upon his knees on the steps of the altar.

But now a hand was laid upon his shoulder and Mrs. Jimson hauled him up on his feet with a jerk.

"Abe Jimson, you know me. You run'd 'way from me up North fifteen years ago, an' you hid yourself like a groun' hog in a hole, but I've got you. There'll be no new wife in the Jimson family this week. I'm yer fus' wife an' I'll be yer las' one. Git up hyar now, you mis'able sinner an' tell the pastor who I be." Brother Jimson meekly obeyed the clarion voice. His sanctified air had vanished; his pride humbled into the dust.

"Pastor," came in trembling tones from his quivering lips. "These are mighty ticklish times." He paused. A deep silence followed his words. "I'm a weak-kneed, mis'able sinner. I have fallen under temptation. This is Ma' Jane, my wife, an' these hyar boys is my sons, God forgive me."

The bride, who had been forgotten now, broke in:

"Abraham Jimson, you ought to be hung. I'm goin' to sue you for breach of promise." It was a fatal remark. Mrs. Jimson turned upon her.

"You will, will you? Sue him, will you? I'll make a choc'late Car'mel of you befo' I'm done with you, you 'ceitful hussy, hoodooin' hones' men from thar wives."

She sprang upon the girl, tearing, biting, rendering. The satin gown and gossamar veil were reduced to rags. Caramel emitted a series of ear-splitting shrieks, but the biting and tearing went on. How it might have ended no one can tell if Andy had not sprang over the backs of the pews and grappled with the infuriated woman.

The excitement was intense. Men and women struggled to get out of the church. Some jumped from the windows and others crawled under the pews, where they were secure from violence. In the midst of the melee, Brother Jimson disappeared and was never seen again, and Mrs. Jimson came into possession of his property by due process of law.

In the church Abraham Jimson's wedding and his fall from grace is still spoken of in eloquent whispers.

.    .    .    .    .

In the home of Mrs. Andy Nash a motto adorns the parlor walls worked in scarlet wool and handsomely framed in gilt. The text reads: "Ye are the salt of the earth; there is nothing hidden that shall not be revealed."

# MIZERIAH JOHNSON: HER ARISINGS AND SHININGS

*Gertrude Mossell*

Andrew and Maria Johnson, a worthy colored couple living on the outskirts of a large town in Virginia, were the happy possessors of a baby girl. "What shall we name the baby?" had been the subject for discussion in this favored household for some weeks past.

Andrew Johnson came of a family that had "no mush of concession" in its make-up. He was possessed of that order of mind that once an idea had gained a footing in it, the more you argued against it, the more firmly fixed it became. Maria, his wife, was a novice in the art of matrimony and the full force of this fact had not yet dawned upon her, so argue she would and the more she argued a point the more stubborn Andrew became.

Maria had been for several days complaining of a "misery in her side." This complaint she had for two continuous weeks, sandwiched into all matrimonial conversations, along with the query, "What shall we name the baby?" At last Andrew said, jokingly, "I guess I'll name that baby 'Misery' for that pain in your side."

Maria was horror-stricken. At once the argument started and as usual Andrew got "set in the notion," which he bolstered up thus: "That white man that said, 'I wanted my first baby girl named they are always poorly, or so, or middlin', or have a misery in their side, they're never right

*Colored American Magazine* 4 (Jan.–Feb. 1902): 229–33.

well' was telling the truth, and Misery that baby shall be named."

Maria cried and protested in vain. She said, "I wanted my first baby girl named after myself, or rather "Riah" for short, and 'sides it would sound more stylish," but all to no purpose.

At last the day for the important ceremony arrived and the couple, the baby and the expectant friends, all sallied forth. At the font, Rev. Simon Colfax leaned forward (after taking the baby in his arms) and blandly asked the name. "Misery," said Andrew. "Riah," piped the little mother. The Rev. Simon was a little deaf, and catching a part of each name spoken, leaning forward, murmured questioningly, "Mizeriah?" Now whether the humor of the situation struck Andrew or whether in his heart he relented and determined to yield at last partially to the wishes of the little mother will never be known, but strong and firm came the reply, "Yes Mizeriah," and then came the words, "Mizeriah Johnson, I baptize thee," and the baby was named for good and all Mizeriah Johnson.

Mizeriah was a plump little nut-brown baby and she grew and thrived in spite of her name: all the misery in it never seemed to cause her one moment of trouble. Maria, the mother, used to sit and rock the little brown mite by the hour, singing her favorite hymn, beginning, "Arise and shine." Whether it was the baby's natural bent or whether the little mother sung it into the warp and woof of her spirit, no mortal man can tell, but by the time she could step the little Mizeriah exhibited a ceaseless desire to "rise and shine."

Fond of approbation to a fault she continually brought down wrath upon her small head by the display of these rising and shining qualities. With her head high up in the air, she would pass her parents and humble friends unnoticed.

The old folks complained that the little "Mizzy" went by them without even saying "howdy." Her little schoolmates formed rings and sung tauntingly, "Oh, Miss Johnsing turn me loose."

When she had grown a little older and was severely whipped by a larger girl in the schoolyard, "for doin' nuthin'," as she protested, the inquiry developed the fact that Mizzy was supposed to have been "puttin' on airs." "Yes she aired me and I slapped her," was the assailant's explanation of the whole matter.

Another method of making the high-minded little miss miserable, was to ring the changes upon her name in imitation of mother Maria's excited tones. "Mizzy, Mizz-ee, Mizeriah-Miz-er-riah, Riah, Ri-uh, you Mizeriah Johnson," until the little girl heartily detested her name.

All of these petty persecutions brought the tears continually to Mizzy's eyes, but did nothing toward curing her of the innate desire to rise and shine. Mizeriah often listened at night to her father arguing dogmatically on various subjects. The last time it had been on what was the most useful, a classical or an industrial education.

Andrew had been on the side of an industrial education. The first fruits of the little girl's listening came forth at the Literary Society where one of the older girls had taken Mizzy as a visitor. The argument started pro and con for industrial or classical education. In a lull of the discussion, Mizeriah took the side of industrial education and gave this illustration against the classical idea, as she had heard her father argue it:

"A woman was drownin' and she called out, sistence, sistence, instid of help, help, and so she got drowned cause the man on the bank didn't have no time to go git a dictionary to see what sistence meant." This unexpected speech from little Mizzy certainly electrified the audience, but it met with instant disapproval. The older and more conservative said Mizzy "was to forrid," and the younger and more radical, that she was "agin the using of big words." The President wishing to remain popular with all, waved his hand to Mizzy to be seated.

The second attempt of Mizzy to shine publicly fared very little better. She slipped off early and went to church during a revival service. The meeting grew enthusiastic and Mizzy determined not to hide her light under a bushel. One of her favorite hymns has a refrain, "Don't call the roll till I get there."

Now Mizzy understood fully the unpleasantness of missing this important ceremony at school. Another hymn recited "Hell is a dark and dismal place," and Mizzy also hated the dark.

Exhortation and song for the moving of sinners' hearts followed one after the other. Then came Mizzy's sweet soprano voice singing the refrain, "Don't call the roll till I get there." Line after line of the hymn was intoned; then came, "Hell is a dark and dismal place." And following it Mizzy again sung, "Don't call the roll till I get there."

A whole bench full of bad boys thereupon got to giggling and sister Martha Saunders marched them ignominiously down the centre aisle and out into the hallway. "Why you all have this way?" was the indignant query. "Mizzy Johnson singed, don't go to the bad place till she git there," was the unexpected reply. Up went sister Martha's hands in holy horror, and down to the parsonage the next morning sallied the good sister, and the pastor was kindly but firmly told, "he must stop Mizzy Johnson sittin' in the Amen corner and leaden hymns."

Our little girl grew somewhat discouraged after this, and some time had elapsed and the community had ceased to laugh at the little one's attempt to "rise and shine"; but the desire had remained in her heart and had grown with her growth and strengthened with her strength. But now Mizzy had at last finished the grammar school and two years of the High School lay behind under memory's lock and key.

The Woman's Missionary Society held a session during the Annual Conference. Volunteers were called upon to speak and once more Mizzy determined to rise and shine. Upon invitation she rose and spoke on "Answers to prayer." She quoted that story about the little girl who had been disobedient and was sent up stairs by her mother to pray over the matter, and who was not to return until she had received an answer to her prayers. When the mother returned and found the little miss in the parlor enjoying herself, she called her aside and asked, "Have you prayed and was your prayer answered?" "Yes," came the reply. "And what did the Lord say?" "Why he said, 'My Lord Molly, you ain't the wostest child in this whole world; get up and go right down stair.' "

Now this was Mrs. Sadie Jame's pet illustration and she looked daggers at poor Mizzy for usurping her rights.

Next came the invitation for solos. To this request Mizzy also responded by singing the "Last Rose of Summer," and as an encore, "Down on the Swanee River." These were another sister's especially favorite vocal offerings, so she was forced to decline to sing at all. And the spiteful murmur began to circulate, "Mizzy Johnson must be trying to rise and shine with a vengeance tonight."

It was promptly announced that no more invitations would be issued to volunteers at that session of the conference. But there was a worse fate still in store for these irate and jealous women. They had entirely overlooked the fact that the Sabbath School was to hold its exercises the last evening and that the tableaux might give Mizzy yet another opportunity to show her rising and shining qualities, both to her satisfaction and to their discomfiture. One after the other the tableaux appeared. Some home life, some romantic and others representative of historical groups.

Mizzy had longed for revenge on her jealous associates and she felt that the facts were propitious in the opportunity to appear in these tableaux. She had spent all her small earnings and pocket change for six months on her costume; she had secured, with no difficulty, the handsomest and most popular young man of the congregation to act as the groom, and they had kept their secret well as to the subject of the tableaux they would present that night.

So when the announcement was made the next tableau will be "Coming to the Parson," every neck was craned. Always a popular subject, who would give it tonight, was the query. The curtain rose and there stood Mizzy in her fleecy, fluffy bridal robes; her beautiful sparkling eyes, the wealth of lustrous, rippling waves of hair peeping from beneath the beautiful veil and bridal wreath, her tall, slender, but graceful figure set off to the best advantage by the clinging folds of her dress, and by her side the groom, manly in his bearing, looking pleased with the choice of a partner, if even only for one evening.

Friends and enemies looked with delight on the beautiful picture before them, then came round after round of deafening applause. The curtain rose a second and third time on the tableau, the success of the evening.

Now the young pastor had long secretly admired Mizzy, but had been kept from making his predilection public because of the church sisters' disapproval of Mizzy's rising and shining qualities. But tonight, with heart beating and throbbing so wildly as he looked upon the scene before him, he cast all doubt behind him. His heart so long wavering in allegiance toward these belligerent sisters, now gave the deciding vote against them and entirely in favor of Mizzy.

As the curtain rose a second time he glanced at the groom and as he viewed that gentleman's complacent smile, a great wave of jealousy swept through him. The curtain rose a third time; he could stand it no longer, and slipping inside the curtained enclosure where the performers would soon pass and where Mizzy with her arms laden with flowers soon came gliding swiftly by, he grasped her hands; all the love of his heart was in his eyes; in the tones of his voice. "O, Mizzy, Mizzy, I love you so my darling. Promise to be my wife."

Mizzy glanced up, not so greatly surprised; her woman's heart had discovered his secret long ago and resented his lack of faith in her. For an instant the shapely head tossed coquettishly and the desire to punish for past sins rose strong in her heart and shone forth from her beautiful eyes.

"Oh, Mizzy, promise me won't you? Promise, dear." For an answer, one little brown hand slipped softly into his own broad palm. He looked down again into the sweet eyes and read in their depths that he had won his heart's desire. Before another word could be spoken in drifted all the merry performers in the evening's entertainment, and the lover was forced to be content.

Just then an old classmate of the pastor entered the door. Mizzy's admirer gave her one parting glance and went to greet his friend. In his study he told him gleefully of his matrimonial prospects and dwelt, as all true lovers must, upon the charms of his intended bride. The visiting friend was invited to make a short closing address. While this part of the programme was being carried out the pastor was persuading Mizzy and her parents, Maria and Andrew, to let the tableau, "Coming to the Parson" be repeated as a reality. Mizzy left it all to her parents to decide.

Now Andrew and Maria had all along resented the disposition to flout their little daughter in the church work and fully realized that this ceremony would give complete triumph, so they willingly gave their blessings and consent. Smilingly they took their seats among the congregation. The visiting pastor requested silence and stated that there would now be a marriage ceremony performed. The organ pealed forth its glad notes of the wedding march; the curiosity of the congregation was aroused to its highest pitch; necks were again craned in vain attempts to solve this second mystery of the evening.

At last the door swung open and in came the bridal party; up to the altar they passed and there stood Mizzy Johnson, "coming to the parson" to be made the bride of a parson. All descriptions of silence fail to make clear the complete cessation of noise in that church; not a whisper or a cough; scarcely a breath was drawn while the service was performed.

Then and there Mizzy Johnson had her revenge. She had indeed "arisen and shone." All the years of taunts and persecutions, what were they to her at this moment. They lay behind her and her new found joy.

But the rising and shining of the new bride was of short duration on that charge, for sister Saunders circulated a petition asking for the removal of the young pastor at the close of the conference year.

The Bishop being a diplomat, advised the young brother to make the change, although he had many earnest supporters at his present mission.

When the good Bishop took Mizzy's small hand in his

upon her arrival at the new charge and said, "Sister Mizeriah, I hope you may rise and shine in good works, upon this, your new field of labor," a demure smile passed over the countenance of that little lady, but the good Bishop knew not the meaning thereof.

# THE OCTOROON'S REVENGE

*Ruth D. Todd*

He was a tall young fellow, with the figure of an athlete, extremely handsome, with short, black curls and dark eyes.

His companion was a beautiful girl, tall and slight, though exceedingly graceful, with masses of silken hair of a raven blackness, and with eyes large and dreamy, of a deep violet blue.

But while she was the daughter of one of Virginia's royal blue bloods, he was simply a young mulatto coachman in her father's employ.

The young girl was sitting on a mossy bank by the side of a shady brook while the young man lay at her feet. A carriage with a pair of fine horses stood just at the edge of the wood, across the roadway.

At last the young man spoke, looking up at the girl as he did so, and there was a world of anguish in his sad, dark eyes.

"Lillian, dearest, I am afraid that this must be our last day alone with each other."

"Oh, Harry dear, why so, what has happened? Does any one suspect us?" exclaimed the young girl as she moved swiftly from her seat and knelt by his side. He caught both her hands in his and covered them with kisses before he replied.

"No, dearest, nothing has happened as yet, but something may at any moment, Lillian darling." And the young man

*Colored American Magazine* 4 (March 1902): 291–95.

raised himself up and clasped the girl passionately to his heart. "It almost drives me mad to tell you, but I must go away."

"Oh, no! no! no! Harry, dear Harry, surely you do not mean what you are saying."

"Yes, darling, I must go! For your sake; for both of our sakes. Think dear one, it is quite possible that we may be found out some day, and then think of the shame and disgrace it will bring to you. Think what a blow it would give your father; what a blight it would cast upon an old and honored name. Shunned and despised by your most intimate friends, you would be a social outcast. They would lynch me, of course, but for myself I care not. It is of you that I must think, and of your father who has been so very kind to me. Dear heart, I would gladly lay down my life to save your pure and spotless name."

"Harry, dearest, although a few drops of Negro blood flows through your veins, your heart is as noble and your soul as pure as that of any one of my race. I would fain take you by the hand as my own, defying friends, father—defying the world, Harry, for I love you; and if you leave me I shall surely go mad! It would break my heart; it would kill me!" cried the girl, with frantic sobs.

"Oh, God! why was I ever born to wreck so pure and beautiful a heart as this? Why, oh, why is it such a crime for one of Negro lineage to dare to love the woman of his choice?"

"Darling, I wish that we had never met—that I had died before seeing your beautiful face—and then dear one you would be free to love and honor one of your own class; one who would be more worthy of you; at least, worthier than I, a Negro."

"To me, Harry, you are the noblest man on earth, and

Negro that you are, I would not have you changed. I only wish, dear, that I also was possessed of Negro lineage, so that you would not think me so far above you. As it is dear—perhaps it is but the teaching of Mammie Nell—but I feel something as though I belonged to your race, at any rate I shall very soon, for whither you go, there too I shall be."

"My darling—what strange words—what do you mean?" he asked anxiously.

"Simply this, that we can elope!"

"Oh, Lillian, dear one, you forget that you are the daughter of one of Virginia's oldest aristocrats!"

"Do not reproach me for that Harry. Have I not thought, and wept, and prayed over it until my eyes were dim and my heart ached? I tell you there is no other way. We could go to Europe. I have always longed to visit Italy and France. Oh, Harry! we could be so happy together!"

"Lillian! Lillian! oh, my dearest!" he cried as he drew her closer within his embrace and pressed passionate kisses on her upturned face. Then he as suddenly put her from him.

"No! No! I am but mortal; do not tempt me. It would be worse than cowardly to do this. I cannot! Oh God! I cannot!"

But the girl wound her beautiful arms around his neck and asked tenderly: "Not even for my sake, Harry? Not even if it was the only thing on earth that would make me happy?"

The soft arms clinging about his neck, the pleading eyes gazing into his, completely stole his senses. He could not draw her closer to him, but his voice shook with emotion as he answered:

"Lillian, I have said that I would die for you, if it would but make you happy. And the thought of taking you away— of making you my wife—drives me wild with joy. Will you trust yourself with me?"

"I am yours—take me to your heart," was her reply.

And he kissed her again passionately, almost madly; he called her sweetheart, wife, and many other endearing names.

\*    \*    \*    \*    \*

A week later the country for miles around was ringing with the news of Lillian Westland's elopement with her father's Negro coachman.

A posse of men and women scoured the country for miles around hoping to find the young people established in some dainty cottage. Cries of "lynch the Nigger, lynch the Nigger!" rang through the woods, and many were the comments, innuendoes and slighting words bestowed upon the young girl, who had been such a pet, but who had now outraged society so grossly.

It was a terrible shock to Lillian's white-haired aristocratic father. He had loved and worshipped his beautiful daughter and only child. But this madness, this ignominious conduct that his well beloved and petted darling had shown, crushed and dazed him, and placed him in a stupor from which it was impossible to arouse him. He shut himself up and refused to see even his most intimate friends.

The short, imploring, pitiful letter he received from Lillian, confessing all, and begging that in time her father would look upon her conduct a little less harshly, failed to animate him.

A month later, the news of the Hon. Jack Westland's death from suicide was announced by the entire press of that section. A deep mystery was connected with the suicide, of which vague hints were published in the daily papers. But nothing definite being known, the Westland mystery was soon forgotten by the world in general.

By only one person was the key of the mystery held, and

she was a servant, who had been in the Westland's employ for many years.

This servant was an octoroon woman of about thirty-five years of age. Her eyes were the most remarkable feature about her. They were large and dark: at times wild and flashing, and again gentle and appealing, which fact conveyed to one the idea of a most romantic history. Her straight nose, well cut mouth and graceful poise of her head and neck showed that she was once a very beautiful creature, as well as an ill-used one, to judge from her story which was as follows:

It was twenty years ago that I first took the position as chambermaid at Westland Towers; I was just sixteen years of age that day—June the 17th, 1875. My mother I never knew, but I was told by an aunt, an only relative of mine, that my mother had been a beautiful quadroon woman, and my father a member of one of Virginia's best families. My aunt having died while I was as yet but ten years old, the hardships and misery I experienced during my wretched existence between ten and sixteen, can better be imagined than described.

The filth and degradation of the low-class Negroes among whom, for lack of means, I was forced to live, disgusted me so that I grew to despise them. I held myself aloof from them and refused to take part in the vulgar frivolities which they indulged in, and occupied my spare moments in study, thereby evoking a torrent of anger and abuse upon my head, from the lowest Negroes. It was therefore with great relief that I accepted a position as chambermaid at Westland Towers, preferring to live as a servant with white people than to be the most honored guest of the Negroes among whom I had lived. I was young then, and the blood of my father who was a great artist, was stronger in me than that of my mother.

Naturally I hated all things dark, loathsome and disagreeable, and my soul thirsted and hungered for the bright sunshine, and the brilliancy and splendor of all things beautiful, which I found at the Westland Towers. It was one of the most magnificently beautiful places in Virginia.

The Westland family were of old and proud descent, and consisted of a father, son and a wizened old housekeeper. The son was a handsome man. In fact I will describe him as I saw him for the first time in my life. I was in the act of dusting his private sitting room, when I turned and saw this handsome young man standing in the doorway. The expression on his face was one of ardent admiration. His violet blue eyes, as they gazed into mine seeming to read my very soul, had a charm about them which drew me to him in spite of myself. His short curls, which lay about his high aristocratic forehead shone like bright gold, and a soft, light mustache hid a mouth which was better acquainted with a smile than a sneer. His figure was tall and stalwart, though as graceful as a woman's, and altogether, he impressed me as being by far the most handsome man I had ever seen.

He spoke to me pleasantly, kindly, and with a gentleness which seemed to thrill my very soul. I was young and foolish, unused to the ways of the world and of men, and when his blue eyes looked into mine, so appealingly, and his gentle, musical voice spoke to me so tenderly, telling me that I was the most beautiful girl in all the world, and that he loved me passionately, nay madly, adding that if I would only be his, he would place me in a beautiful house with servants, horses and carriages; telling me that I should have beautiful dresses and jewelry and that all within the household should worship me, I laid my head upon his breast and told him I would be his.

But when I asked him if we could not marry he replied

that it was impossible. That if he ever married one of colored blood, his father's anger would be so great as to cause his disinheritance, and that then he could not place his darling in a high position, adding that being born a gentleman, it would go hard with him to try to earn his own livelihood, all of which seemed to me a very fitting excuse. He also told me that it was not a marriage certificate or the words of a ceremony which made us man and wife. That marriages were made in Heaven, and if we loved each other and lived together, God would look down on us and bless our union, adding that he would always love me and never leave me. Oh, God! that was a bitter trial! I had no mother to advise me; no friend to go to for assistance, and the very thought of giving him up for the filth and degradation from which I came, tortured me for days, during which time my great love for him overcame all obstacles, and on the 4th of July, I found myself living in a luxury of love.

We lived together for eighteen months, during which time no sorrow came to me, save the death of a baby boy. Oh, they were happy days! I was assuredly the happiest girl in all Virginia. But there came evil times. His father died, and of course he had to leave me for a time to attend to important duties.

I was sorry for his father's death and I was also glad, thinking that now no obstacle being in the way, he would surely marry me. But in this I was doomed to bitter disappointment.

A young and beautiful lady, a distant cousin of his, stole his heart from me, and when I received a letter from him telling me that grave duties confronted him, and though it broke his heart to say it, he must part from me, offering me an annuity of five hundred dollars, a great lump rose in my throat which seemed to choke me. I felt my heart breaking.

The things before my eyes began to dance and gloat at me in my anguish. Then everything grew dark and I knew no more for several weeks. When I regained consciousness, my first impulse was to kill myself, but remembering that in a few months I would become a mother for the second time, I stayed my hand. I also accepted the annuity of five hundred dollars, thinking that if my little one lived, it would amount to a small fortune when of age. My love died, and in its stead lived hatred and thirst for vengence. I thought constantly of the words:

"Hell hath no fury like a woman scorned."

And likened them unto myself. I was young: I could be patient for years, but an opportunity presented itself sooner than I expected. Eight months before the birth of my child, which was a girl, Jack Westland married, and one year after his marriage, his beautiful young wife was called away by death, the cause of which was a tiny baby girl. The death of his young wife caused him such anguish that he shut himself up and would see no one. He would not even look upon the face of the poor motherless babe. He bade the housekeeper to procure a wet nurse for the infant, which was a delicate little thing, and as there were no other to be obtained, they sought me out and begged me to take the position as nurse.

I obstinately refused at first, but on learning that Jack would soon go abroad to try and divert his mind, I accepted; for an idea that would suit my purpose exactly, flashed through my brain. The two babies were almost exactly alike, both having violet blue eyes and dark hair. Indeed the only difference between them was that my baby was four months older. Supposing that the young heiress should die? Could I not deftly change the babies? I would try at all events.

Accordingly it was arranged that I should, as a competent

nurse go to some watering place on account of the young heiress' health.

All things went as I had hoped. The young heiress as I expected died, and I mourned her death as that of my own, and when I returned to Westland Towers, no one noticed any change, but that the sea air had improved the baby's health wonderfully.

When Jack returned home two years later, he saw a beautiful, blue eyed baby girl, with jet black curls about her little neck. He greeted me kindly, but there was no touch of passion in his voice. In fact he treated me as an exalted servant which made me hate him all the more.

"He was glad," he said "that I took such an interest in the welfare of little Lillian," and he asked me if there was any special thing that he could do to repay me. There was one thing I desired above all others, and that was the education of a mulatto lad of ten years of age, who worked about the stables. I asked him if he would send the lad to some industrial institution, which request he readily granted. There is but little more to tell. My little girl grew to be a beautiful young lady, the pet and leader among Virginia's most exclusive circle. But the teachings of her old mammie Nellie, she never forgot.

Her sympathy was always for the poor and lowly, and though there were scores of young men of aristocratic blood seeking her heart and hand, she preferred, as I intended she should, the colored youth, Harry Stanly.

"It was the result of this little episode of the change in the babies, which I related to Jack Westwood, after the elopement, that caused him to commit suicide, and as he leaves everything to his daughter Lillian, I hope we shall live happily hereafter," said Mammie Nellie, as she arose and rung for lights.

"My poor abused mother!" exclaimed both Harry and Lillian simultaneously, who had just joined her in New York City, as both threw a loving arm tenderly around her neck. "And now," said Lillian, "your revenge is complete. Let us close up the house, and go abroad. We can remain away several years, traveling and enjoying the beauties of the Old World. What do you say to this?"

"A capital idea," said Harry.

"As well as a practical one, for even here in New York race feeling sometimes runs very high!" exclaimed the octoroon avenger, with a curl of scorn about her mouth, and a triumphant light flashing from her beautiful dark eyes.

# AN EQUATION

*Gertrude H. Dorsey [Browne]*

Miss Sarah Gaudy sat at the desk in the college office examining the past month's records, and filling out the report blanks which were to be forwarded to the parents of each student.

Jessie Kirkland, the A Monitor, had told me confidentially that Miss Gaudy was especially constituted for "office work," and there was some legend abroad that she never stopped work at noon, but simply sucked the ink off the pen, and thereby derived sufficient nourishment to satisfy her hunger until dinner. This may, or may not, be true, but it is a fact, nevertheless, that she was poring over records when I entered the office to report for misbehavior.

"Well, Miss Grace, what can I do for you?" she said pleasantly.

"The assistant, Miss Maloney, sent me to report to you for misbehavior and for having this in my possession"; as I spoke I thrust forward a small piece of folded paper and stood defiantly awaiting results. She took it mechanically and opened it; then moved by a better impulse, she refolded and returned it to me. "Miss Grace, can you, a senior, justify yourself in sending or passing a note during class recitation when you know it is against the rules and must be recorded in this book? What does this note say?" I replied with some spirit: "I did not pass the note and I don't know anything about it, for it fell out of Viola's rhetoric and I picked it up,

*Colored American Magazine* 5 (Aug. 1902): 278–83.

just as Miss Maloney called the class, and she did not wait for an explanation, but sent me to you. I'm sorry to have troubled you about so small a matter, but I couldn't help it."

Poor little Miss Gaudy looked helplessly at the note and at me, and then we both smiled, and she said simply, "Read it." I was surprised and a little embarrassed to read in my own handwriting: "The product of the sum and difference of two quantities is equal to the difference of their squares," and this rather odd revelation was further endorsed by my name.

"My dear Miss Grace, what possible connection has the sum and difference of two quantities with your misconduct? You are studying trigonometry now, are you not?" she asked with a puzzled look. "Yes," I said. "I study trigonometry, but my room mate studies algebra and occasionally I help her in preparing her lessons, and in some unaccountable way that theorem has gotten into bad company. I like to go over those old principles and theorems." "Very well, you may return to the recitation room and tell Miss Maloney it was all a mistake," and Miss Gaudy resumed her interrupted task.

That day and that incident was the turning point in my school life, for, ever since, I have been prone to speak of events as happening before or since the day I was sent to the office to report.

After luncheon that same afternoon I received a note from Miss Gaudy asking if I could spend a few hours with her that afternoon and evening in correcting the algebra papers of the Sophomores. What girl of nineteen would not appreciate such a compliment, coming, as it did, from the gentlest and most winning of women? So as soon as I was excused from the music room, I went to the Office, where I spent a very busy hour, flattering myself all the while that if it had not been for me, those papers would never have been finished by the next day for the school inspector to examine.

And how very delightful it was, to be sure, to be allowed to talk whenever I pleased without the cruel formality of the recitation room staring me in the face like an evil genius.

Miss Gaudy, too, was so entertaining and talked freely of her anticipated visit from the inspector—Mr. Turner, whom she had never seen, but who she supposed was learned in all the wisdom of the Egyptians and was mighty in word and in deed.

Gradually even I entered into her enthusiasm, and more than once I found myself making computations on what Mr. Turner would be worth by the pound or cubic inch, but he always came out the Unknown Quantity.

After we had finished our task we went to the Principal's private sitting room and fared sumptuously on mustard sardines, Welsh rarebit, wafers, sweet pickles and chocolate.

Then it was, that I became skeptical on the subject of her lunching off the ink on her pen. Before I left she told me that the Board had promised her the aid of an assistant, after the next term, and she wondered if I would care for such a position. As I wished to continue my studies in music and German I was only too glad of the chance and thanked her for planning such an agreeable arrangement.

The next morning forty-three girls were in a flutter of excitement, and many and wild were the speculations on the Unknown Quantity, Mr. Turner. "He'll be sure to gaze on us very much as he would a spoiled copy book," declared Viola my chum. "Yes, and I know he's just full of ah's and big words, for they always are," came from another quarter.

"Of course, he'll wear nose glasses and will tell us how clever he was—'when he was a boy'—forty years ago, and did not begin to have the many advantages we enjoy, etc.," and thus they chatted until the A Monitor rang the bell and we went to chapel for worship.

If Mr. Turner had arrived, we saw nothing of him that morning, but as we were passing into the music-room, we heard laughing in the office, which certainly could not come from Miss Gaudy, "who had never been known to smile above a whisper," Viola said. At two o'clock the principal laid aside her "office" long enough to bring the visitor into the parlor to inspect us. We quite forgot our good manners when we beheld a young man, not a day over twenty-six (according to the A Monitor), "whose chin was but enriched with one appearing hair" and whose big brown eyes seemed to challenge laughing.

Well, he gave us a very jolly little talk about our work and he did not say "Ah" once, and moreover, he omitted the offending phrase, "when I was a boy." In fact, he addressed us very much on the "fellow-citizen" plan, and Jessie Kirkland proposed at the next class meeting to confer a degree upon him at once.

While we girls were discussing the inspector a half hour later and wondering if we could not find some excuse for reporting at the office, Miss Gaudy sent for me to come to her room. She met me at the door with "Oh, Miss Grace, it's so strange, Mr. Turner is an old, old pupil of my brother Thomas, and we are almost old friends, for I have often heard Thomas speak of Raymond Turner as one of the brightest boys in college, but I never dreamed of his being the inspector. However, this is his first year, and his first trip here. But what I want to tell you, is of an embarrassing mistake you have made in correcting those papers," and she handed me a paper whereon I had made the correction "$X = \frac{1}{4}$ the head of the Turner." "Oh, did he see it?" I asked. "Why certainly Miss Grace, he called my attention to it and laughed so heartily, I feared you all could hear him in the music room. After dinner you are to come to the office as he wishes to see you, and now I will not detain you longer," and she busied herself about the desk while I went to find Viola.

An hour later and (would you believe it?) I was sitting comfortably in the office talking to the inspector quite as much at my ease as I was when talking to Viola or a Freshman.

Commencement was near at hand and after that evening I had but little time to assist Miss Gaudy, although we met occasionally and she always had a smile or pleasant inquiry concerning my final, and for the ninety-ninth time she would offer me the use of her private library, or the benefit of her council.

After commencement, at which time, by the way, I received an appointment as regular assistant in the office, I spent a very delightful two weeks visit with Miss Gaudy and her brother at their home in Lexington. Mr. Turner was also a guest at the same time, and we each had the opportunity for becoming better acquainted.

Miss Gaudy never tired of telling the rest of the party about our calling Mr. Turner the Unknown Quantity, and even the quiet professor took delight in joking about it. One afternoon as we returned from an excursion to the woods for geological specimens I remarked that I was hungry, and was seconded by the others, so the professor started on a foraging expedition and returned soon, followed by a servant bearing a tray upon which were fresh rolls, milk and fruit. As he passed the fruit to the inspector and myself he solemnly repeated, "The same quantity may be added to both members of an equation without destroying the equality."

When my vacation was over I returned to the college and began my work, which although in time it became monotonous, was yet interesting and I enjoyed it. The suggestions and advice which Miss Gaudy, from a long experience, was able to give me, were so helpful and I began to appreciate the quiet, wise little principal, and to bless the mistakes which had been the means of drawing us together into such a warm and sympathetic friendship, as such friendships are really few.

The first term passed without incident, and we were nearing the close of the second, when one morning we were informed that the inspector would soon visit us and to have everything in readiness. Papers must be corrected, averages made out and report blanks filled, besides our other work must not be neglected, so we were very busy for a few days. However, the third term was almost at an end before he came.

Miss Gaudy received him with frank cordiality, and while he treated us with all respect, yet he was quite anxious to complete his task so that he might go, and addressed us all in the most perfunctory way. I was annoyed when I discovered how much I really cared whether he addressed me or not, so I assumed an indifference (which I did not feel) whenever his name was mentioned.

Vacation had come again and with my old enemy, Miss Maloney, and Miss Gaudy I attended the National Teachers' Association at Washington, D.C. We were sitting one morning in the large auditorium listening to a lecture by that wonderful man, Professor De Mott, when by a sly pinch on the arm and a little nod in the direction of the door, Miss Gaudy drew my attention to a group of ladies who had just entered. I had no trouble in recognizing the tall slender one as Viola Culver and the queenly beauty at her side as Jessie Kirkland.

The lecture did me no more good, and until I had managed by frantic and idiotic signs to attract the attention of three ushers and half the audience, I was as one deaf and dumb to all else. An usher made his way to me and I handed him my card with our hotel address, with the request that he would hand it to the persons who had just entered the hall. I then subsided into the depths of my program and remained an interested listener until the close of the session. As we passed out, we were accosted by Viola's friendly "Hello, Grace; what are you doing here? Oh, Miss Gaudy and Miss Maloney, how glad we are to see you, and just to think we have just been having no end of fun at your expense," and she passed her arm through mine and with Jessie and the rest bringing up the rear joined us in our walk to the car.

"Oh, Grace," she said, as soon as we were to ourselves, "I have made such a startling discovery, thanks to the stupid old policeman who misdirected us. You noticed we were late this morning. Well we just arrived last night and, of course, we had to be directed this morning which car to take for the hall, and the stupid fellow put us on the wrong car, which we did not know until we reached the government building, and as the crowd got off there, we did likewise, and I'm going again this afternoon and show you what I found. You little rogue, you keep your secrets as you do your seeds cakes, strictly to yourself. Why didn't you tell me about him and all the nice things he has said?" "About whom, Viola? What did you find? What secret have I kept from you?" I asked in bewilderment.

"O never mind, I have found out, and now you must give me your card so we can talk it out, in the good old way, in the privacy of a sitting room or chamber," she remarked, as the rest of the folks came to us. "I sent my card to you at the hall, by the usher, did you not get it?" I exclaimed. "Mercy, no, I'm sure I did not know you were here until I met you as we were coming out. Don't mind, Grace, I dare say you have more cards left, and one is quite as acceptable as another. Good bye, here comes our car; be ready by 2:30 and I'll come after you to show you one of the sights my investigating genius has discovered," and Viola and Jessie were soon seated in the car, and we walked a square further to the Pennsylvania Avenue line.

To Miss Gaudy I confided that part of Viola's conversation which mystified me and upon which I had placed grave fears of her sanity, but the little woman only smiled and remarked that Miss Viola had ranked first in our class, and was even then conducting a department in one of our best colleges.

We were discussing this subject in our room about two o'clock that afternoon when Miss Maloney entered, and gravely handed me a card with the words, "He's waiting in the parlor on the second floor." Why the card of Raymond Turner should be sent to me at that particular time I could not comprehend, so I hastily left the room and sought the second floor parlor.

He was alone, and as I entered he came forward with a pleased, expectant smile, which changed, as it encountered the look of annoyance and surprise on my face. "I was somewhat surprised to receive your card; the usher handed it to me as I entered the lecture hall this morning, and of course I am able to put but one construction on the case. You certainly meant that I should call, and you certainly know what such a summons means to me." He held out his hand as he spoke and in my astonishment, I forgot to take it, and simply stared at him, or perhaps glared would be the better word.

When I found my tongue, he was standing near the door, hat in hand, and was regarding me with an expression which might have been contempt and might have been pity. "There has been some mistake. I did not send my card to you and I know of no reason why your calling here would be of any special significance to either of us. Miss Gaudy would be glad to see you I do not doubt, but you really must excuse me as I have an engagement at 2:30 and it is nearly that now." With this rude speech, I returned to our room and soon afterwards Viola was admitted.

A half hour later and we were climbing the steps of a large building, and Viola with the confidence of a person "to the manor born" led the way to a gallery on the second floor, where in a glass case were exposed some thousands of written documents. Then she turned triumphantly to me and said, "This case of dead letters and rings and other valuables, was at the Exposition at—never mind where,—and has just been returned. You remember the day we girls went through the Government Building at the Chicago Exposition. Well, there was just such a case there and we read no end of queer letters to mothers, sons, sweethearts, Santa Claus, and every conceivable person or organization of persons. But this is much more interesting, as I'm sure you'll agree after reading the portion of this letter that is exposed," and she pointed to a sheet of legal cap, six inches of whose length was uncovered. I read: "and now Miss Moorman (I hope soon to enjoy the right of calling you Grace) I have attempted to convince you of the similarity that exists in our tastes, inclinations, etc, and to one in your position it is hardly necessary to quote, as authority, 'Only similar quantities can be united in one term.' I have told you all, and shall expect your reply not later than Thursday next. Until then, and always, I am,

Yours to command<br>Raymond Turner.

Sept. 18, 19——."

"There now, I knew you had been cheating me. If I am not very much mistaken, I met the self same gentleman, Raymond Turner, as I entered the vestibule going to your room. One of his many avowals has been misdirected or is free from guilt of ever having been directed, but what is one letter among a hundred, perhaps? Of course, you have been so absorbed in him that you could not give a thought to your poor old chum," she exclaimed mockingly, as I suddenly espied an envelope hanging just above the legal cap, upon which was written in the same handwriting "Grace Darling."

"Well, I'm afraid, Viola, if I stay here much longer, I'll find myself a central figure in one of your scatter-brain modern novels, so let's go at once. Who knows, there may be a round dozen of Grace Moormans and as many Raymond Turners as there are changes of the moon," and although this brave speech of mine was received with a contemptuous "Bah" by my companion, we each felt a delicacy about discussing the affair.

I turned the matter over in my mind and out of the confused mass of materials, I built the following theory: Mr. Turner had written me (there was no doubt in my mind of the identity of the person referred to in the letter at the Dead Letter Office) some time in September, and being absent-minded—poor fellow—had addressed Grace Darling instead of Grace Moorman, and there was nothing left to do but to send the letter to the Dead Letter Office, and as there was no possible chance for its identity to be learned, of course, it could be used along with thousands of others to help fill up space in Uncle Sam's cabinet of unclaimed or misdirected letters. I did not receive a second letter for the reason that Raymond is sensitive and did not care to presume upon an uncertainty. Certainly I shall call him Raymond. Who has a better right? As I was saying, he is sensitive, and hence his apparent indifference last May.

Who but Viola would have discovered that missing link? Viola has sharp, observant eyes, and I really believe I admired them more then than I ever did before. Wonder why? After a time, I suppose he thought I had reconsidered things, and sent my card to him in token of the same, and he had come, and alas,—he had gone. What could I do? Would I see him again? I was abruptly recalled to my surroundings by the information from Viola that she would now take the cable car, and would see me again after I had recovered from the shock she had been able to afford me.

I continued my walk alone to the hotel and with a guilty self-consciousness, I sought Miss Gaudy and told her all there was to tell. She listened very attentively to the entire story and then disappointed me at its close, by simply remarking: "While you were gone, I bought tickets for the concert for the three of us, and I hope you will be ready to go by seven." "She isn't a bit sympathetic, after all," I growled. "I would have found more consolation in telling my troubles to Miss Maloney."

I have never known just how it happened, but some few hours later as I sat in the concert hall, conversing in a low tone to—Raymond (it would have been rude to speak out loud, although several were doing it) it suddenly occurred to me that Miss Gaudy is sympathetic as well as diplomatic, for who else could have contrived to bring us together so soon after my discovery.

It must have sounded silly to those who sat near me to hear "him" say at the close of the program, "I insist, Grace, upon going to the Dead Letter Office now and you must accompany me." "The office has been closed since six o'clock, you 'Positive Quantity,' so you will have to wait awhile longer for an answer to the letter," and Miss Gaudy looked suspiciously at me, but I was waving my hand in the direction of some black plums, which I recognized as the property of Viola.

"But Grace, you must not take too many things for granted. How are you sure that his power of loving is not variable?" and Viola winked at Jessie who sat opposite me. "Why, don't you know, dear valedictorian, that 'All powers of a positive quantity are positive'?" I replied.

# FLORENCE GREY
## A Three-Part Story
## Part I

*Ruth D. Todd*

## CHAPTER I

It was nearly midnight as two gentlemen left a fashionable club in one of the most prominent avenues in Washington. One of the gentlemen, by name Percy Belmont, was considered good looking, but the other, Richard Vanbrugh, was very distinguished in appearance, and withal quite handsome. But there was about him an air that proclaimed him a man of rather fast habits, despite the fact that he would soon be thirty.

His eyes were as blue as the heavens above, with a certain amount of daring lurking in the corners. And his hair, which he always wore brushed carelessly back from his white, aristocratic brow, was of a chestnut brown. A rich, full mustache of the same color partly covered a beautifully cut mouth, which had about it a somewhat sarcastic expression. In stature he was above the average height, though proportionately built, and from the crown of his silk hat, to the tip of his patent leather boot, a gracefulness and an air of free and easy superiority moved with every turn of his fine figure.

"Shall we take a cab or walk, Percy?" asked Richard Vanbrugh, as both gentlemen stopped to strike a match with which to light their fragrant Havanas.

"The latter by all means," answered Percy Belmont. "A

cab is too confounded close on such an evening as this. By the by, Dick, it's quite a pleasant surprise to run across you at the Arlington when I thought you were abroad."

"Thanks, Percy, my boy, but I haven't been over a week yet, and I just arrived in Washington to-night. So thinking that I might run across some one I knew at the Arlington, I stopped in."

"And right glad I am that you did, for it gives me much pleasure to be the first to welcome you back to Washington again, albeit the season is far advanced. By the way Dick, while I have you I'd like to hear you say that you will come down to Belmont Grange and spend a few weeks with me next month."

"Thanks, nothing could give me more pleasure. Why, let's see! it's quite five years since I have been down to the Grange, isn't it, Percy?"

And both gentlemen as they walked leisurely along were so engrossed in each other's society that they failed to note which way they turned their footsteps, and suddenly found themselves in a less prominent avenue, but withal a very quiet and respectable thorough-fare.

In fact, one of the houses was brilliantly lighted, and before the entrance stood several carriages. Just as the gentlemen turned to retrace their footsteps, the door was opened and several negroes with soft laughter and pleasant adieus, descended the white marble steps and sought their different carriages.

Among the foremost was an elegant looking matron accompanied by a young girl who was tall, slight and exceedingly graceful, with the beauty of a goddess. The glare of an electric light fell full upon her face; and a painter would have likened it unto a queen of the night.

Her complexion was very fair, so fair that she had often

been mistaken for a white girl. She had a luxuriant growth of hair which was soft and brilliant, and as black as night; a pair of soft, lustrous dark eyes which looked forth innocently and frankly from 'neath long, silken lashes; a thin, straight nose, and a sweet mouth whose lips were as soft and as red as a blush rose. A black lace mantilla rested lightly upon her brilliant black hair and a lightweight evening wrap enveloped her slight form.

Her manner was gentle, sweet and very refined, and there was a grace and elegance about her that is only found in a gentlewoman.

Dick Vanbrugh gave an involuntary stare, thinking to himself that of all the beautiful and charming women he had ever seen this was by far the most beautiful as well as the most charming young girl in all the world.

Percy Belmont did not stare at the girl, but he did glance anxiously at Dick Vanbrugh, knowing the latter's weakness for pretty faces.

"By Jove, Percy, what a beautiful creature!"

"Yes, she is pretty," answered Percy, assuming a careless air.

Dick stared at him in infinite surprise.

"Pretty! Good Heavens, Belmont, you are quite as cold and impassive as ever! Why she is beautiful, fascinating, heavenly!" he exclaimed rapturously. Percy gave a careless laugh.

"Calm yourself, my dear Vanbrugh, or I'm afraid you'll lose your head."

Dick flushed slightly, but continued, though with less fervor.

"I'm afraid you'll think me an ass, Belmont, but I always was, you know, when a beautiful woman is the subject. But fancy calling such a lovely creature by the insignificant word pretty! By George, I have half a mind to call a cab and follow our fair friend's carriage."

"That would be quite useless; she would only treat any flirtations on your part with scorn and utmost contempt, for she is considered the pink of Negro aristocracy."

Vanbrugh gave a short laugh, which was his common mode of expressing incredulity.

"By Jove, [Belmont], that's a capital joke! As if any colored damsel, no matter how refined or elegant she may be, would treat the attentions of a gentleman with scorn; especially if the latter is by no means bad looking and—er—generous to a fault."

"My dear Dick, there are certain Negro families residing in Washington who are as proud as we are."

"Nonsense, I shall try this one at all events."

Percy's manner changed to one of earnestness; he laid his hand affectionately on Vanbrugh's shoulder.

"My dear fellow, you will oblige me by doing no such thing."

Vanbrugh bit his lip and waveringly asked: "No, and why not, pray?"

"Because the girl, whose name is Florence Grey, is a lady!"

"Oh, you know her, then?" he asked, with slight sarcasm.

"Yes, that is—I know of her. I know of her family, too. Their summer residence is about a half mile below Belmont Grange."

"How fortunate! And, of course you will be good enough to tell me more about this fair maiden."

"With pleasure, if you will spend the night with me."

"Certainly. I'll remain with you forever if you say so," laughed Dick, now in the best of humor, as both ascended the brown stone steps leading to the entrance of Percy's fashionable boarding place.

.   .   .   .   .

The fashionable widow Grey was a charming mulattress. Her husband had been a wealthy white man—a Yankee who had waived all caste aside and married the woman of his choice. For many years they had lived in Europe, their two children, James and Florence, being born there. But on account of his ill health, the doctor advised him to seek his native shores again. So he came to Washington and settled his family in a palatial residence on————Avenue, where, ten years previous to the opening of this story, he died.

His widow was heartbroken, and shut herself up in seclusion for two years; at the end of which time she bestirred herself to such an extent that she was very soon the leader of Negro society. Her son James, who was a tall, handsome young man of twenty-five, had just left college, and with the prefix of Dr. to his name, bade fair to be a very interesting as well as important personage in Negro business life.

Flossie, the beautiful young girl already described was twenty-two. She had finished her education, including a collegiate course, and was now doing her first full season in society.

Their country residence was quite an elegant affair, being an old two-story, white stone mansion, whose spacious halls and apartments had been modernized and fitted up with artistic taste, displaying luxury and elegance that would be admired by the most fastidious.

They moved in, or rather led, a class of the most reputable Negroes in Washington, and in summer their country residence was filled with the elite. This, Percy Belmont made his friend acquainted with, at the same time giving him to understand that they were a class of Negroes, who generally commanded respect, adding that for Vanbrugh to try and flirt with the beautiful Florence was the most abject folly.

Vanbrugh colored deeply, but there was an expression of daring in his handsome blue eyes, as well as a determination about his whole person as he replied:

"You mean well, my dear Belmont, and I daresay I ought to take your advice, but, you see, my dear boy, I have always been a shockingly bad fellow, and I fear some day that I'll go to the devil where I belong. So spare yourself any further advice and let's talk over old times."

And this conversation was never again referred to, Belmont, evidently, forgetting all about it, while on the contrary, it was impressed still more deeply on Vanbrugh's mind.

Richard Vanbrugh was born in Virginia of wealthy and aristocratic parents, who died when he was a mere lad, leaving him in the care of guardians who were too strict with him, and kept him in far more closely than was at all prudent with a lad of his temperament, so that when he became of age and felt himself his own master, he fell in with a set of fast young men and led a shockingly wild life.

There was no madness—no diabolical trick, that Dick Vanbrugh was not the originator of.

With women, he had always been a perfect pet; beginning from his old mammie nurse and only ending with the most fastidious society belle.

He was not exactly a prig, but from his earliest recollection women had petted and indulged him, so that it seemed only natural that those of his fancy should succumb to the charms of his handsome person, entrancing smiles and honeyed words.

And he had taken ardent fancy for this lovely colored girl, and did not mean that she should escape him.

In a month's time everyone in Washington would be seeking places of less intense heat. The Greys would, of course, leave for their country place, and as he had accepted Belmont's invitation to join him with a company of friends at the Grange, he was content to abide his time assuring himself that with a little patience he would certainly win her in the end. Never before had he beheld the girl whom he desired so ardently, and it would be no fault of his if he did not win her love in less than three months' time.

## CHAPTER II

It was a few days later, and everybody in Washington who moved in Afro-American society was discussing the greatest event of the season. A grand ball was to be given by the elegant widow Grey at her palatial residence on————Avenue.

It would be the best yet, and probably the closing event of a successful season.

Everybody who was anybody tried to secure invitations, for it was rumored that the ball would be given partly in honor of John Warrington, a young Northerner, a prominent young business man staying with the Greys. And as the young man was possessed of a snug fortune, handsome person and pleasing manners, he was considered a great "catch."

"My dear Jack," James Grey had playfully remarked, "I'm afraid you will have to enclose your heart in a steel case, or you may go back home minus it, for our girls down here in Washington are the fairest of the fair."

"Your words are very true, in one case at least, for I think that Miss Grey, your sister, is the most beautiful young lady I have ever met."

"Thanks, Jack, yes, Florence is very pretty, and the dearest sister on earth, but to-morrow night you will see some of the fairest girls the world has ever produced."

.　　.　　.　　.　　.

The night of the ball finally arrived and Mrs. Grey's rooms were very beautiful indeed. Trailing evergreens and floating ferns, through the interstices of which gleamed unveiled statues, and the distant murmur of wild, sweet music caused one to marvel and wonder if they were not in some enchanted palace.

James Grey had not been exaggerating when he assured Jack Warrington that the prettiest girls the world could produce would be at the ball, for the most beautiful faces, rich dresses and rare gems flashed brightness as they moved through the spacious ball-room.

But Florence, clad in a gown of chiffon and rich lace, with a bunch of scarlet roses in her hands and one nestling amid the coils of her brilliant black hair, was by far the most beautiful woman in the room.

"Prettiest girl in Washington."

"Who, Miss Grey?"

"Certainly, of whom else do you suppose I was speaking?"

Jack Warrington, standing back of a huge exotic plant heard this conversation go on between two foppish looking young men.

"Well, there's Sadie Payne, you know; you may have been speaking of her."

"Sadie, oh, she's the biggest flirt here."

"Probably, but there is no denying that she is pretty."

"Of course not; but of what advantage are her charms when a fellow can't get in edgeways."

"I don't know; Jim Grey seems to be making rapid progress with his wooing."

"Well, that isn't very singular. He and Sadie were children together; so the intimacy may be only friendship."

"But there is no denying that this chum of Jim's is sweet on Florence."

"By George, it's a shame! This Yankee shall not win our fairest flower without a hard struggle, for I, for one, shall be one of his antagonists. I shall go immediately to Miss Grey and beg the next dance." And both men disappeared amid the throng.

Warrington's first impulse was to seek his friend and put this bit of gossip to a test, but on second thought he remembered that he was engaged to dance the next with Florence, and he hastened to her instead.

Sadie Payne was a charming young girl. She was the only child of Mr. and Mrs. George Payne, a refined, though by no means wealthy couple, who resided about two blocks from the Greys. Mrs. Payne had been Mrs. Grey's dearest girl friend before either had married, and had always kept up the intimacy despite the fact that Mrs. Grey was exceedingly wealthy and Mrs. Payne not in the very best circumstances. And in summer either all three or else Sadie alone had been the guest of Mrs. Grey for two weeks or more. But for two years they had managed somehow to build a snug cottage not far from Mrs. Grey's summer residence, and the young folks were seldom, if ever, separated. It was almost a settled thing that James and Sadie would marry some day, but though it was gossiped with much fervor among their friends, no engagement had ever been announced. The young lady in question was very pretty, though by no means showy. She was possessed of a charming figure, not very tall, but by no means undersized, and a light brown complexion. Her hair was black and curly and worn in a fascinating style which she seldom, if ever, changed. But her chief charm lay in her eyes, which were large, bewitching, mirthful, tantalizing and as dark as night.

She was dressed in a simple gown of white organdie and surrounded by a group of young people who were ever at her beck and call, for being the most intimate girl friend of Miss Florence Grey, she was a very popular young girl.

So as the night grows old, the dances grow low down on the cards, the waiters in their white jackets, move less frequently through the well-bred crowd, and sundry elderly guests bid the hostess good night, feeling proud to be the departing guests of the best and most successful ball of the season.

# CHAPTER III

It was the first of July—quite two months later, and the Greys, as well as Percy Belmont, were established in their palatial summer residences.

The Greys were entertaining very few guests at present, for few of their friends were able to take in a full season's vacation.

Jack Warrington had promised to spend a few weeks with them, but his business would not allow him to indulge in this pleasure until August, and though the guests were few, the pleasures and amusements were many, and the young folks enjoyed themselves with utmost zeal.

Though Dick Vanbrugh had tried flirting with Florence several times, as he met her alone on the highway, his wooing was progressing very slowly—or rather—not progressing at all, for any advances on his part had been met with utmost scorn by that lovely young lady; indeed, she had shown him with an uplifting of her proud head and a flash of withering contempt from the beautiful dark eyes, that he was of utmost inconsequence to her.

This had angered—had piqued his vanity, but at the same time it had strengthened his desire to win her. She seemed more beautiful to him than ever, and while he was still trying to think of some plan with which to win her, it suddenly occurred to him that what Belmont had said was true. The girl was certainly a lady, and there was something a little special about her—a little touch of hauteur that repelled while at the same time it attracted, charmed, fascinated one. And he would have given her up, but somehow it seemed that the dark, liquid eyes haunted him; he could almost feel the touch of her soft, lustrous hair. She seemed to have thrown a spell about him, which, do as he might, he was unable to shake off.

Good Heavens! Was there no way of gaining this charming girl? And if there wasn't, would he never forget her? He had been petted and spoiled by some of the most fastidious society belles, and yet, not one of them had exerted such an influence over him. Could it be that he was in love with her? He, Richard Vanbrugh, the heir and last descendant of an old and aristocratic name, in love with a Negress?

"My God!" he cried, desperately, "Am I mad? Am I possessed of some strange delirium? Will I awake and find that I have been dreaming? No, oh no, it is only too true and I must tear her image from my heart and crush it!" he cried, beating his breast savagely in his great anguish. He lit a cigar and strolled out to the woods to try and quiet his nerves, and having found a quiet spot some little distance from the Grange he threw himself down disconsolately 'neath the refreshing shadow of a magnificent old oak. But a feeling of discomfort had taken possession of him, and he threw his cigar to the winds and groaned aloud in anguish. What should he do—what could he do! He could not make her his wife, and he dared not try another flirtation with her for fear of losing her forever. What he would say would come from his heart. And besides he could not bear to see the beautiful eyes flash with indignation, and the proud lips curl with infinite scorn. No, no, those eyes were made to glow with passion— those lips to give forth sweetest kisses. But would they be for him? A voice within him whispered: "No, they will not. They are for one of her own blood—a Negro."

His was a quick and passionate nature, and he was on his feet in a moment, and an expression of jealousy and fury flashed from his eyes as he clenched his fists and exclaimed aloud: "By heavens, I will not give her up! I will be d——— if I do!"

He had been so blinded by his passion that he had not seen the long, lank form of a Negro striding leisurely down the road towards him, and when the man addressed him, he started sharply and swore a terrible oath, asking furiously:

"Who are you, and what the devil do you want?"

The colored fellow, notwithstanding his lankness, was a rather good looking black man, and there was an expression in his keen eyes not unlike that in Vanbrugh's. In fact, this fellow, who was called "Long Tom" was a perfect dare devil—the terror of the Negro inhabitants down in the village. But, possessing a very pleasing manner, he smiled, showing two perfect rows of ivory teeth, bowed profusely, and answered:

"I beg de boss' pardin' if I 'sprised him, but I t'ought you was in trouble an' I mought be able to assist you. My name is Long Tom, sah," and he grinned significantly.

Vanbrugh scrutinized the fellow closely. "Long Tom," where had he heard that name before? Ah, yes, he was the devilish negro whom he had heard the fellows laughing about at the Grange. But why did the man think he could be of service to him? "You say that your name is Long Tom, and you thought I was in trouble?" asked Vanbrugh.

The man nodded.

"Then you are, so I have heard, a worthless young scoundrel! So tell me, pray, why in thunder did you imagine I needed your help?"

" 'Cos I'se de only one what could do it. But I am feared I made de boss mad, so good day, sah," and he turned to go.

"Stay!" commanded Vanbrugh, as a devilish idea flashed through his brain.

"Can I place confidence in you?"

"Oh, yes indeed, boss."

Vanbrugh looked him steadily in the eye for a moment, then said:

"Meet me here to-night at twelve o'clock sharp. I will be waiting for you. Leave me now, and remember: Silence is golden!" and shoving a crisp bank note into the man's hand, he pushed him gently towards the roadway.

## Part II

## CHAPTER IV

It was midnight. During the early part of the evening a heavy storm had been approaching, so that by now it was raging with all the fury of Hades. The wind blew with such cruel violence as to uproot trees and scatter destruction in its path. Great flashes of vivid lightning lit up the country for miles around and heavy thunder shook the earth with its deep and deafening roar. Accompanying this was a downpour of drenching rain, but despite this fact, Dick Vanbrugh, the elegant gentleman and Long Tom, the young Negro scoundrel, had both dared to brave its fury. Vanbrugh swearing as he drew his long ulster closer about him, that he would brave hell itself; and Long Tom being in very destitute circumstances, swore the same oath. So that by the time they reached their meeting place, both were possessed of decidedly bad tempers.

"Beastly night, this, my man," said Vanbrugh.

"Sartinly is, an' dangerous 'neath these trees, sah," answered Tom.

"I know, but where the devil can we go, fellow?" asked Vanbrugh, rather sharply.

"I was thinking dat de boss might not mind goin' round to my shanty, a little piece up de woods dar; I lives dar by myself."

"Anywhere out of this! Lead on!"

And both men struggled on until they reached the entrance of a lone cabin situated in the heart of the woods. Tom unlocked the door, and pushing it open so that Vanbrugh might enter first, apologetically said:

" 'Tain't much better in heah, but it's better'n bein' out in de rain, though."

Dick felt like telling the fellow to go to thunder, but instead he entered the place and cast a deprecating glance around at the few pieces of furniture (if two chairs, a table and an old ante bellum bedstead could be given that name) and asked Tom why the devil did he bring him to such a beastly hole!

To which Tom replied that " 'Tis de best place I knows on, and de gent could select a better if he has a mind to."

The elegant Richard Vanbrugh being exceedingly out of temper and growing more angry each moment, told Tom to

"Shut up!" that "He wanted none of his damned insolence," adding that it would be better if he appeared more respectful in the presence of a gentleman.

And Tom, being only a low-class Negro, followed this advice.

Meanwhile, Vanbrugh lit a cigar and paced the dusty floor back and forth; presently he drew off his ulster, threw it over the back of a chair and continued to pace the floor in moody silence.

By this time, the fire of pine bark and twigs which blazed on the old-fashioned hearth had sucked up the dampness of the apartment; and after a few more strides he went over to the fire and seated himself. He felt more comfortable now and in somewhat better humor.

"Well, Tom, it's about time to come to business now, unless we—that is, I—intend to remain here all night. Here is a cigar for you—and, about this business?" But here Vanbrugh hesitated. It was a nasty piece of business, but must be done.

"By thunder, I hate to confide in anyone, but then, this fellow is only a Negro, and will hold his tongue for fear of getting his neck broken, and besides I must have help from some one," he told himself. Then he said to Tom:

"Tom, you must have suspected something when you came upon me so suddenly this afternoon; so fire away and let me hear all about it."

Then Tom told him that he had followed him around for several days, and learned that he was trying to get in with the wench Florence—

But here Vanbrugh interrupted him sternly, almost fiercely, bidding him never to speak lightly of that young lady again or it would be the worse for him, adding:

"Yes, I have taken a fancy for her, but there is no way on

earth of winning her until she is in my power. But to accomplish that, I am afraid she will have to be abducted. And you, my man, are the only one who could do this."

Tom's keen eyes glistened like the bright orbs of some hideous reptile, but he said nothing, and Vanbrugh asked savagely:

"Well, and why the devil don't you answer me?"

Long Tom grinned diabolically, rubbed his hands together and replied:

"I'm thinkin' it's a mighty tough piece of business, an' if I gits ketched it'll go mighty hard wid me."

"You lie! What you want is money—and what I want is this girl Florence. You can kidnap her as easily as I can snap my fingers, and you will kidnap her if I pay you well. I will also add that money is of no consequence to me, and being very wealthy, I am always exceedingly liberal to those whom I employ. Am I plain enough, or do you wish to name your sum before you begin?"

"Oh, no, boss, no need of dat till after I gits her for you, and dat I kin do as soon as you likes."

"Very well then, here are my plans: Some time in August— I will see you later to set the date—some evening you are to kidnap this girl and—you know where the 'Haunted Towers' are? Well, you are to bring her there, where I will have a closed carriage in readiness, and once we get her in the carriage the rest will be quite easily managed. You are to drive us to a little country place of mine some ten or fifteen miles beyond the village—but enough of the plan, I will tell you everything when I am in a better temper. To-morrow I leave Belmont Grange; and I am to be seen by no one save you, in these parts again. And I will only see you once, which will be—let me see—on August the first, at midnight here in your cabin."

And the storm having, in the meantime, abated, Vanbrugh arose and drew on his long ulster. Then, taking out his wallet, he handed Tom five or six bank notes.

"This will do you until I see you again, so au revoir," and he was soon swallowed up in the darkness without.

# CHAPTER V

July had gone, and half of August. Mrs. Grey's summer residence was now filled with the most charming of guests.

It was a lovely day, being the month of August. It was hot, but not unpleasantly so, for a slight breeze, together with the refreshing shadows of the tall and wide-spreading old trees had helped to rob the day of its fervor. A party of young people had assembled together and gone to explore the ruins of the "Haunted Towers," which was about three-quarters of a mile from Grey's Villa.

There was a legend associated with the "Haunted Towers," from which it derived its name.

Many years ago, the "Haunted Towers," named then Wycliffe Towers, was the principal house of the county, and gallant men and beautiful women had danced, flirted and made merry through its spacious halls and apartments.

The last master was Philip Wycliffe, a handsome, though quick tempered young fellow, possessed of a jealous, passionate nature.

Philip married a beautiful girl, who was a born coquette.

One night they gave a grand ball, at which fete the beautiful, inconstant young wife flirted outrageously. When the ball was over and all the guests had departed, the young husband called his wife to task about her scandalous conduct.

Hot, bitter words ensued, whereupon Philip snatched his

father's sword from off the wall and plunged it through his wife's heart. With an agonized shriek she fell across the bed, her life's blood dyeing her white ball gown and the canopied bed as she fell.

When the young husband realized what he had done, he ran from the room screaming, "I have killed Pauline, my beautiful wife!" He still carried the sword in his hand, and just as he reached the entrance doors he stumbled and fell upon the sword, which, being still wet with the life blood of his wife, pierced his heart.

They buried the couple in the family vault and closed the old place up. No one has ever lived there since, and the superstitious and weak-minded declared that the place was haunted. Some had even gone so far as to declare that every night at about midnight one could hear the piercing shriek of a woman, then a little while after that, the agonized groan of a man's voice, a dull thud and then the hurrying of many feet and much lamenting, until after a while all sounds would die away and a ghostly silence reign.

This had caused no little terror among the Negroes and poor white people down in the village and at night it was absolutely impossible to induce the weak-minded ones to traverse the road which led past the Towers.

Richard Vanbrugh had heard this same legend, and it had strengthened his decision of having Florence brought there, for any noise they would cause would only make the Negroes take good care to avoid the place.

In the meantime, the pleasures and amusements at Grey's Villa continued to flow incessantly.

To-night one of the grandest lawn parties of the season would take place. Everything the Greys did was in proper style and of the first class.

Her lawn was decked beautifully to suit the occasion. Rows

of quaint Chinese lanterns were swung over head, and comfortable rustic seats and small tables were placed here and there throughout the spacious lawn.

At one end of the lawn a grand dancing pavilion was erected and decked with trailing evergreens and huge tropical plants. Here the lights were more brilliant than the dull red glare of the lanterns, for in some unique way an arch of brilliant lights was stationed just above the heads of the orchestra.

I have previously said that Florence was lovely, but tonight she seemed peerless in her strange young beauty. Her mass of brilliant black hair was coiled and pinned in a loose knot at the back of her queenly head, and her graceful figure was set off to advantage by a gown of rich black lace and flashing jet, from the low cut bodice of which rose her gleaming white shoulders and swan-like throat in charming loveliness.

The women envied her her beautiful face and queen-like carriage, while not a few of the men adored—worshipped the ground she trod upon.

Among the latter, Jack Warrington could be classed, for he was her constant shadow—her most ardent admirer, and Florence looked upon him with no little favor.

He was a tall, light fellow, with large grey eyes and curling black hair, and many were the admiring glances bestowed upon his graceful person as he moved through the crowd in search of the girl of his heart, with whom he was to dance the next dance.

"This is our next dance, Miss Grey," he whispered, when he had found her.

"Yes, I know, I had not forgotten," she answered, with one of her sweetest smiles. The next moment his arm was around her waist and they were slowly whirling away amid the crowd. For the moment he forgot all—everything, in the joy of being near, touching the girl he loved with all the intensity of his passionate soul. And when it was over, he led her out on the lawn in one of the most secluded spots so as to tell her of his love. It mastered, overpowered him so that he could contain himself no longer.

"Miss Grey—Florence," he began, his voice trembling with passion. "I have brought you here, away from all the crowd to tell you that I love you! Yes, I love you, Florence: I have loved you since the day I first met you. Won't you be my wife, dearest Florence?" For a moment he waited until the silence proved unbearable, and he felt that he must get her to raise her eyes to his at any cost. "Wait, darling. I have frightened you—I was too abrupt and you are angry with me, but oh Florence, the joy of having you all to myself overpowered me. Something within me—my heart whispered the words—I love you. And I cannot still its mad beating. Won't you come to my arms, dear Florence? Won't you rest your beautiful head upon my heart and whisper to me that you love me?" And with one hand he raised her beautiful face to his, while the other went gently around her waist.

"Ah, you do love me, Florence. I can see it in your eyes: speak to me, dear one."

For a moment her beautiful dark eyes gazed into his passionate orbs, then her head fell upon his breast, but not before he caught the faint whisper, "Ah, Jack, my Jack, how I do love you." And he drew her close to him in a passionate embrace and spent his kisses upon her upturned face, and called her his sweetheart, pet, and lastly his dear wife.

Florence was the first to awake from this beautiful dream, and with a little cry she whispered: "Oh, Jack, it is late—we must join the others now." "No, no, dearest, let me have you a little while longer; let's see, we are to dance the next together, and it is just beginning. We will sit it out. But you must be chilly; wait here a moment while I go and get you a shawl."

And after giving her another passionate embrace, he left her with the words: "I won't be gone long."

Florence lay back in her seat and closed her eyes so that her dream of love would appear more vivid. She wondered if there was another girl in all the world so happy as she, wondering if there was any other as loving and handsome as her Jack.

Suddenly she heard a slight noise, and slowly unclosing her eyes she turned her head to look; seeing nothing, she lay back again. In another moment she felt a hot breath close to her ear, and with a little cry, she started to her feet, at the same time she was caught in the strong embrace of a man who held a drugged kerchief to her nostrils. She tried to scream—to call Jack, but the words died on her lips; she gave a piteous moan—a suffocating gasp, and sank into unconsciousness.

# CHAPTER VI

Dick Vanbrugh was restlessly pacing the white sandy road which lay before the Haunted Towers. His covered carriage stood a little distance from the roadway, 'neath the dense shadows of the overhanging trees, through the interstices of which the moon gleamed like long slits of pale silver. There was an air of discontent about him as with both hands thrust into his trousers pockets and a frown on his handsome brow he would pause in the midst of his restless pacing and gaze expectantly into the distance.

He pulled out his watch and saw by the light of the pale,

round moon overhead that it was 12:30 o'clock. "I wonder what makes that confounded Negro so late?" he murmured to himself. "We will barely have time to reach Lesterville if he doesn't show up soon—ah, there he is now!" he exclaimed, as the form of Long Tom appeared in the middle of the road, with the girl Florence slung over his shoulder.

He withdrew behind the safe shadow of his carriage as Tom, struggling bravely on, drew nearer.

The rough jolting, together with the cool, refreshing night breeze had helped to revive the girl, who was now moaning piteously and struggling to free herself from the man's embrace. Her brain was clouded. She could remember nothing distinctly, but she did remember the party, the dance, and afterwards Jack's dear arms about her and his passionate love words in her ear. And then Jack left her—the strange noise, and, oh, God, that man! "Help, oh help!" she cried, fighting desperately to free herself. At the same time Vanbrugh rushed up, pretended to knock Long Tom down and received the girl, who had now fainted, in his arms. For a moment he held her passionately to his heart. "Ah, dear heaven, this one passionate embrace repays me for all that I have suffered! I would brave the world—all for her dear sake," he murmured fervently.

Long Tom had already clambered up to the coachman's seat, and had driven the horses around so that the carriage now stood in the road.

But just at this time the girl regained her senses, and with a faint cry, she staggered to her feet. "Jack! Jack! Oh, where am I!" she cried, gazing bewilderedly about her.

"Pardon me, miss, but an attempted insult has been played upon you, I fear; and I am indeed glad that I was near enough to render you my assistance," said Vanbrugh, in his most charming and gallant manner.

"Oh, thank you so much, sir, but you will not leave me. I—oh, my brain is so confused—but you will not let him touch me, sir?" she cried, piteously.

"Have no fear of that, miss. I will drive you home in my carriage if you will allow me that honor."

"Then you know who I am, sir?" she asked, trying to get a glimpse of his face. But that crafty gentleman kept his face averted.

"Pardon me, my dear young lady, but I think every one about the country here knows who Miss Florence Grey is," he answered, at the same time assisting her into the carriage. Then, springing in himself, he closed the door, and the rubber-tired vehicle rumbled noiselessly, though with great speed, down, instead of up the road. And Vanbrugh with a triumphant expression in his eyes, settled himself back in the dense shadow of the carriage.

Florence's brain was, by this time, growing clearer, and as she looked out the carriage window, she saw that the carriage was taking her from instead of to her home. With a faint cry, she turned to Vanbrugh, but a turn in the road had thrown the moonlight full upon his face, and she saw before her the man who had several times attempted a flirtation with her. Involuntarily, she started to her feet with an expression of indignation stamped upon her every feature.

"Sir! What does this mean!" she demanded.

"It means, dearest Florence, that I love you and want you to be my wife. I love you, Florence. I have loved you since the day I first saw you. Forgive me, my darling, but when I first beheld your beautiful face, I swore then that I would make you my beloved mistress, but when I attempted to flirt with you I saw that I could only win you by making you my wife. As I also saw that it was impossible to make you my wife until I had you in my power, I concluded to have you abducted so that I would have a chance to win your love. Be mine, dear Florence, and you shall have servants by the score. I will take you abroad, where the difference of color will not be questioned. You shall live in a palace amid a grove of orange trees, and with spacious balconies leading down to a bay as blue as the heavens above. Darling of my heart, if you will—"

During this passionate love avowal, the girl had remained standing with features as white and as immovable as a marble statue. And no pen could describe the expression of scorn and contempt that flashed from her beautiful eyes. And when he fell on his knees before her and attempted to catch her beautiful hands in his, she drew back with a scornful gesture and hissed:

"Wretch! Do not dare to touch me! Oh, I hate, I despise you! Let me out at once, or I shall scream for help!"

Dick Vanbrugh was confounded. That this colored girl had refused his offer of love and marriage, he, the Hon. Richard Vanbrugh, who could, with very little effort marry of the first society astounded, dazed him.

"Florence," he said, trying to gain one of her hands.

"Wretch! Dastard! Do not dare to touch me, I say! Stand aside, or else open this door and let me pass out of your hated presence!"

Vanbrugh had not dreamed that this beautiful creature was possessed of so much spirit. Her words stung, maddened him, while her beauty set his soul on fire; but with a great effort he calmed himself, and his voice was quite calm when next he addressed her.

"My dear Florence, calm yourself, for when you leave this carriage you will be either my promised wife or my prisoner. Why not be reasonable and leave it as my adored one?"

"Coward! Wretch! I would die first! I tell you I will never

marry you—no, never! For I hate you! Let me out or I shall scream for help!"

"That would be very foolish, as well as quite useless, for we are far beyond all hearing distance. Be seated, loved one, or I am afraid you will be quite exhausted by the time we reach our destination."

"Oh, God, what would you do! Surely, you would not take me away against my will! Ah, you would not—you could not be so heartless!"

"Heartless! Oh, my love, it is you who are heartless. I love you with the intensity of my soul! I love you better than my honor—better than my life," he exclaimed, with a passion that shook his whole person. Florence caught a glimpse of his passionate face, and, dastard that he was, a little pity stole into her heart for him; but remembering the cowardly trick he had played upon her, her hatred crushed it out.

"Why, oh why, can you not love or even pity me, Florence? I have suffered tortures since I first gazed upon your fatal beauty. But if you give me one good reason why you do not love me, I—oh, God, how it pains me to say it! But I will let you go."

"I cannot love you, sir," replied Florence as gently as she could, "because I love another, and even if I did not, I don't think that I could ever love you."

A jealous pang smote his heart, and with a smothered oath he hissed, his hot breath falling with fearful force on her neck:

"By heavens! No! I yield thee to no man! And by fair or foul means, I shall make you my wife!"

Thinking of the loving mother, devoted lover, and all of her dear friends and companions, the beautiful girl fell on her knees before him.

"Oh, sir, see, I kneel, I pray, I entreat you to let me go.

If there is one spark of manly feeling within your breast let me go to those I love and who love me. If I should give my consent to marry you, no good would result from such an unholy union."

How beautiful she looked. On her pale, upturned face he could not see the misery, he only saw her beauty which fascinated, stole his senses from him. He could scarcely control the impulse to clasp her to his heart, to kiss rapturously the soft, scarlet lips.

"My God, Florence, I would be mad to give you up. No I cannot, by heavens, I will not let you go! For I love you— you are dearer to me than heaven itself!"

"Oh, God," she cried, rising slowly to her feet, "Is there indeed no hope—no chance of escape from this villain whom I hate with all the intensity of my soul!" Then turning her white, set face to him, she said:

"Coward! I see there is no chance of escape, but my friends will some day come to my rescue, though if they should fail to find me, I shall never give up hope until my hair is gray and my back bent double, and death is staring me in the face. Now, do your worst, for I will never, never, change my decision."

"We shall see, my fair one," he answered, and the girl, not even glancing at him, seated herself in the corner of the vehicle, and gazed out of the window.

During this time the carriage had been speeding rapidly along the highway, and in two hours' time it stopped before the tall entrance gate of a beautiful, vine-clad villa.

Dick opened the door, alighted, and held out his hand to assist Florence, saying:

"Welcome to Lesterville, your future home, my darling: though this is but a playhouse to what I would give you if you would only say the word."

Florence answered him with not so much as a look, but sprung past his hand to the ground. It was chilly in the early morning atmosphere, and being clad in her low-cut evening gown, Florence shuddered slightly.

"What a brute I am," said Dick, and feeling in the carriage he drew forth a dark, though lightweight wrap and threw it about her shoulders as they proceeded towards the house. With a latch key he noiselessly opened the door: at the same time a fat, black, middle aged woman emerged from a doorway and approached them with loud and hearty exclamations:

"Lord, is dat you, Mr. Rich'd? None o' de oder sarvints is up yit. I hope yo' don't mind, sah, cos it's jest little af' five o'clock. Lord, is dis Miss Kate? Po' ting, she 'pears kind er tired."

"Yes, mammy, this is the much talked of Miss Kate. Show her to her room now: this long journey has fatigued both of us considerably."

"My po' boy, 'deed honey, jest you go to yer own room, an' af' I show Miss Kate hers, I'll make bof' on you a strong cup o' coffee."

This short dialogue did not surprise Florence; indeed, she was prepared for anything that might happen, for what dastard trick was this villain not capable of? But let come what may, she would put her faith and trust in the One who always looks down upon His little ones when they are in trouble.

## *Part III*

## CHAPTER VII

It took Jack Warrington quite a little while to find a wrap to put about his loved one's shoulders, and when he did find it he hastened to take it to her, but upon reaching the spot where he had left her, she was not there. "Perhaps," he told himself, "Some of the girls have carried her off; any way I shall ask Miss Payne."

Sadie was seated in the midst of a crowd of young men, flirting, as James always said, "to beat the band."

"I beg your pardon, Miss Payne, but have you seen Flor— Miss Grey?"

"Did I see Miss Grey? Dear me, when and how did you lose her?" she asked in mock surprise, and a mischievous twinkle in her bewitching eyes.

"My dear Jack, don't mind Sadie. She always pokes fun at everybody. Come and sit by me and join in this little discussion we are having, for I dare say Florrie will turn up pretty soon," put in James laughingly.

And not wishing to appear too disconcerted, Jack was forced to join in the merriment which was always sure to be found around the witty Sadie.

But as the time sped on and Florence failed to put in an appearance, James, as well as Jack grew anxious, and went in search of her. By this time two or three other girls, missing the sweet face, had also joined in the search. A servant was called and sent to the villa in search of her, but after a short while returned with the reply that Miss Florrie was not in the house.

"Nonsense," cried Mrs. Grey, trying to speak naturally, "Miss Florence must be in her room," and she hastily left the crowd, and went in search of Florence, herself.

But she returned quite hastily, and with much consternation, saying that she could not find the dear child anywhere, and wondering what possessed her to play so cruel a trick upon them. It was not like Florence to act so strangely.

By this time the dancing and gaieties had abruptly come to a halt, and even the musicians joined in the search for the missing girl.

Jack Warrington hastened to the little rustic seat in which he had left his darling, the crowd following closely. He was telling them why he left her there, when some one picked up a dainty bit of white lace and a few trampled roses.

"Good God, what does this mean?" exclaimed Jack, in an agonized voice as he stared at the articles just mentioned.

"What, oh, what is it?" asked Mrs. Grey, distractedly rushing up. "My heavens, they are the roses my darling carried in her hand, and that is her kerchief; Oh, God, what has happened to my dear one?"

Just then some one exclaimed, "Here is her fan!" and another, "Here are the roses and the much admired pearl-headed pin she wore in her hair!"

And for a while consternation and distraction reigned supreme.

But what followed can better be described by the insertion of a couple of extracts from the Washington newspapers:

"Negro Heiress Kidnapped"
Special to the Washington—(white)

Miss Florence Grey, the daughter of a respectable and well-bred Mulattress, has suddenly disappeared, and it is supposed that the young woman, who is a very beautiful

Octoroon, has been kidnapped. The Greys are very wealthy, and were staying at Grey's Villa, their summer residence, situated about twenty miles from Washington on the Virginia side. A garden or lawn festival was in progress at the time of the supposed abduction, which was brought to quite an abrupt and distracting termination, for the young woman was very highly esteemed by her own people and not a few of the whites.

From an Afro-American news edition:

> "The Abduction of Miss Florence
> Grey," our beautiful society belle."

Miss Florence Grey, our beautiful and accomplished society leader, has it is feared, been abducted from Grey's Villa, their magnificent country place.

Mrs. Estelle Grey, the young lady's widowed mother, and Dr. James Grey, her brother, are quite prostrated over this most unfortunate piece of ill luck, and have offered a reward of $500.00 for information of the whereabouts of the young lady.

A unique lawn party was going on at the time of this startling disappearance, which was brought abruptly and unceremoniously to an end, while all—even the musicians themselves, joined in the search for the missing girl, who is a great favorite with all who know her. Special detectives, William Wright and Henry K. Miller, have been despatched from this city, and are doing all in their power to find the missing one. Mr. John Warrington of the well-known firm of "Warrington and Carland" of Boston, was one of the young lady's most ardent admirers, and was in her company a short time before her disappearance. He is quite distracted, and is working like a hero to bring to light the mystery of this strange disappearance.

# CHAPTER VIII

"You, Susan! You Jinnie, you gals better git up an' come down stairs! 'Ere 'tis mos' five erclock—Miss Kate an' Mr. Rich'd done already come an' yo' all layin' in bed lek 'twas just night. 'Deed yo' better come down here at once!" screamed the voice of mammy, the black woman, after she had shown Florence to her room, and was bustling about the kitchen, preparing her "Mr. Richard and Miss Kate" a dainty luncheon. In a short time, two girls entered the kitchen, and with a quiet "Good mornin', Aunt Amy," proceeded to busy themselves with sundry duties.

One—the one called Susie—was a tall, dark girl about twenty years of age, and possessing a pleasing and quiet disposition, while the other was short, stout, and rather light complexioned with a jovial, fun loving disposition, and was always getting herself into mischief by, as her aunt always said—" 'tendin' to other folks' 'fairs."

"You said Mr. Vanbrugh and his cousin had arrived, Aunt Amy?" she asked, with much curiosity.

"Yas," replied her aunt.

"What an unusual hour for folks to arrive from an institution? Don't you think it seems strange?"

"Dat's Mr. Rich'd's business," replied her aunt, rather sharply. "I tells yo' 'bout niggers, dey never will have nothin' or be nothin' nowhow. Why? 'Cos every last one on um is too pizen meddlesome," and with her head well up in the air, and the tray of dainties in her hands, she indignantly left the kitchen.

She carried the tray to Dick's room first, and arranged daintily on a little table a plate of cold chicken, some home-made bread, fresh butter, a small pot of steaming, fragrant coffee and a pitcher of cream.

Vanbrugh thanked her, telling her that it seemed like old times to have her fixing things for him in such a motherly way, but that she had better take Miss Kate hers before the coffee got cold, cautioning her to answer no questions Miss Kate might see fit to ask, but to leave her to herself, until after she had rested, when by that time she would probably be all right. But on no account must she leave her mistress' door unlocked.

The woman, whom we shall hereafter call mammy, un-locked the door of Florence's sitting room, entered, arranged the contents of the tray on a small table and left the apartment, locking it after her.

The room was a large, well ventilated sitting-room, open-ing into a dainty bed-room beyond. The floor was of polished hard wood, in the centre of which was spread a rich Turkish rug, while some exceedingly comfortable chairs and a fine leather couch were arranged around with very good taste. A few good water colors decked the walls and cool, dainty curtains of the finest Swiss hung from the long bay windows.

When mammy entered, Florence had the windows hoisted and was searching about the room for some means of escape.

"Heah, honey, come 'long, eat yo' vittles 'fore your coffee gits cold." She said at the same time spreading the dainty repast on a small table.

Florence did not so much as glance in her direction, and the woman, murmuring, "Po' 'ting," left the room, not forgetting to lock the door after her.

After mammy was gone, Florence searched in vain for some means of escape, but her efforts were soon exhausted, and with a wild, heartrending cry, she threw herself down upon the leather couch. It was some moments afterwards that she heard the grating of a key in the door, and with a cry of alarm she started to her feet and found herself face to face with Vanbrugh.

"You—why are you here? Can you not leave me to myself for even a few moments?" she asked.

"So this is how you repay me for my love and gentle kindness, is it, Florence? Why, why do you compel me to speak harshly to you? Why not be reasonable and come to my arms as my adored one?"

"You forget," she said with icy coldness, "that I love and am beloved by one of my own race."

"It is you who must forget that, Florence," said Vanbrugh, impatiently. "You are mine—I yield you to no man! You shall never even see him again!"

"Oh, misery!" exclaimed she, burying her face in both hands.

Vanbrugh pushed a chair toward her, and she sunk into it, removing as with an effort, her hands from her face. Whatever struggle she had undergone was now passed, and her face was as calm, as white as a statue.

"Listen to me, Florence. You are in my power, and by lowering myself to the standard of a brute, I could force you to submit to anything that I might desire. It is in my power to ruin your character—to bring your proud spirit to the dust. I offered you my heart and hand, and with insolence you hurled them back into my face. And although, I love you still, that insult I shall never forget. I do not desire to marry you now, but I shall force you to live with me as my mistress, and when I am tired of you, when your character is spoiled and your beauty faded, you may go back to your lover and receive the insults you hurled at me." He stopped to see what effect his words carried, but her face wore an expression of mingled scorn and loathing that the meanest hound would have slunk from.

"I thought you a villain, but I had yet to learn what deeds of infamy you were capable of. I do not fear you, for if the worst comes I can but die. And I will die by my own hand before I submit to your brutish, degrading desires. But I will not die without a struggle. As heartless as your servants may be, I will appeal to them, for there may be one who still retains a spark of pity and would not stop to hesitate if one of their own race was in trouble."

"These servants as well as yourself are in my power. Listen, there is yet something else to learn. You are only fifteen miles from Grey's Villa, and yet no help will ever come to you. Your friends and associates, being only Negroes, would not dare to think of searching for you in the home of the Hon. Richard Vanbrugh, and even if they did, they would not know that I am staying at Lesterville until after my desires have been fulfilled.

"These servants here think that you are an insane cousin of mine, who went mad some years ago. They think that I have brought you here to try and recall your mind by bright, new scenes and my handsome person which you went mad over. Scream then, and they will pay no heed to your cries. Neither will any one else hear you, for few pass this way and there is not another villa within a mile of Lesterville. There-fore, you are in my power and must—will be forced to accede to my wishes."

"Villain—you have planned it well, but advance one step nearer me and I will bury this dagger in my heart, and you shall be held accountable for my murder." So saying, her small, white hand drew from the bosom of her black lace dress a jewelled dagger.

"Stay your hand, my beauty, I will give you three days to think the matter over, at the end of which time I shall come for my reward." And he left her as softly as he had approached her.

The moment the door closed upon him, Florence began to tremble with anguish and fear. "If I remain in this house, I am utterly in the power of this wretch. He has the key of my apartments in his possession. At the end of three days he said he would come again to, oh, God! he will force me to listen to his infamous proposals unless I—oh, God, it is terrible, terrible! Oh, Jack, Jack, could you only know what agony I am suffering! To die alone—oh, my heavens! Oh, merciful Father!" sobbed the girl in the anguish of her soul. So bitter was her grief that she had not heard the door open and a woman enter.

"Lord, honey, what's de matter? Pore Miss Kate, come to yo' ol' mammy nurse, honey," said mammy—for it was she who had entered, with genuine affection.

"My good woman, you will help me—you will have pity and help me to escape from this wretched place! See, I beg you to help me, on my bended knees. This man, Mr. Vanbrugh, has deceived you. I am not his cousin Kate as he made you believe—"

"Lord, chile, 'deed you is Miss Kate. You is her vary image; you has de same hair—de same eyes and dey are jest as wile as dey was when you was took away from here five years ago. So ef yo' ain't Miss Kate, dan who is yo'?"

"Oh, God, how can I make you understand! I am Florence Grey, a colored girl—"

" 'Deed yo' ain't no colud gal, chile, Lordy, lemme git out heah, 'cos I b'lieve yer done gone clean, spank crazy!" and mammy, with genuine fright, backed out of the apartment, slammed and locked the door, and with quick footsteps sought Vanbrugh, telling that gentleman that " 'Deed she was feared of Miss Kate, she was," and " 'twas her opinion dat Mr. Rich'd better take 'er back to the insti'shushion ware she come from," adding that "Ef he didn't take 'er back he'd have to send Susan to wait on 'er."

"Why, what is the matter? What has Miss Kate been doing?" asked Vanbrugh.

"Doin'? Good Lord, she is carryin' on very orful, indeed! Why, bless yo' soul, chile, she nearly tore all my close off—beggin' me to save her and glarin' erbout all 'cited like."

The situation was so ludicrous that Vanbrugh burst into a hearty laugh; and mammy, with a "Good Lord, what you see to laugh at?' indignantly flounced out of the room.

# CHAPTER IX

To hear that mammy was afraid of Florence was just exactly what Vanbrugh wanted. It would save him much trouble, while at the same time it would place that arrogant young person more firmly in his power. He rung the bell and asked Jennie, who answered it, to send Susie to him.

"Mammy tells me that she is afraid of Miss Kate; do you think that you could take mammy's place as waiting maid?" he asked, as Susie quietly entered the room.

"Yes, sir, I can," answered she, with quiet respect. "Knowing that Miss Kate is a harmless imbecile, I don't think you would be easily frightened by any of her strange actions, would you?"

"No, oh no, sir."

"You are a good, sensible girl," answered Vanbrugh, significantly, "and if you attend to your duties well, you shall be liberally rewarded. You may go now, but, one thing more, will you try to get that tiny dagger from her, and keep all dangerous weapons out of her reach? For I am afraid she might try to do herself bodily harm," and he handed the girl a silver coin, after which she thanked him, bowed respectfully, and withdrew.

Some moments afterwards she made Jennie, who, if she was a meddlesome Mattie and a chatterbox, could keep a secret, acquainted with the above conversation. "And another thing, Jennie, I don't believe this young lady is Mr. Vanbrugh's cousin at all."

"Why don't you think so, Susie?"

"I have my own reasons, as well as suspicions, and I will tell you exactly what I mean before the day is gone."

And do what she might, Jennie could get nothing more from the quiet Susie.

But to return to Florence—she had composed herself somewhat, and was seated in a rocker trying to interest herself in a book which she had picked up from the table. She had prayed to God and pleaded to humanity and both had turned a deaf ear. So, after all, she thought, though not without a degree of sadness, if the worst came, she could but die. How glad she was that she had her tiny, jewelled dagger in her possession. She had playfully placed it in her bosom last night while she was dressing for the lawn fete, and one of her girl friends had remarked that she looked like a Spanish princess; and another had picked up the tiny weapon and placed it in the folds of black lace, saying: "Now in truth you are a princess, for you have your jewels, dagger, and around you are gathered your pleading subjects and many gallant knights"; and during the fun and laughter that had ensued, she had forgotten to take it out.

Oh, how happy she was then—then! Why, it was only last night; but to the unhappy girl it seemed that days, weeks had

passed since Jack Warrington had clasped her in his strong
arms and whispering words of love and devotion, tenderly
asked her to be his wife, and she—but here the grating of
the key in the door harshly interrupted her. Good heavens,
had that wretch come back to torment her again? Could he
not leave her alone for even one hour? No, it was not
Vanbrugh, it was only the woman with the tray—her dinner
perhaps. But this was a new face, not that of the horrid old
woman, but the kind, sympathetic face of a young girl, and
Florence wondered if this girl possessed a heart as kind and
as sympathetic as was the dark though comely face.

Susie—for it was she—set the tray on a table and looked
up to encounter two beautiful, sad eyes gazing appealingly at
her. She started suddenly and with an expression of infinite
surprise, stared hard at Florence.

"She also thinks me mad, and is afraid of me," thought
Florence, while Susie was mentally exclaiming "I have seen
that face before! Ah, she is—I cannot be mistaken—Florence
Grey—she is certainly Florence Grey!"

"What is the matter? Do I frighten you also, girl?"

"No, oh no! no—no—you do not frighten me, but I have
seen your face before—you are Florence Grey, a girl of
color!" cried Susie excitedly.

With a glad cry, Florence fell upon her knees at the girl's
feet.

"Oh, God of mercy! You are right. I am Florence Grey,
and in the power of this wretch! But yours is a kind face—
you—you will not turn from me? You will help me to escape
from here?" she cried, frantically.

"With all my heart! But rise and calm yourself—we must
not be overheard,' said Susie, who had now regained her
usual quiet manner.

And Florence arose, and leading Susie into the dainty bed-room where they were not likely to be overheard, related to her her pitiful story, ending with:

"And you will help me? May God bless you, but you must have heard that I was very wealthy—and I will reward you liberally—richly if you will only help me to escape, for I fear I should indeed have gone mad if I remained here many more hours."

"Say no more, Miss Florence; my sister and I will do all in our power to help you. As for Aunt Amy, she is the kindest person I know, but being very ignorant, and Mr. Vanbrugh's nurse since the villain was an infant in long clothes, she would place his word above all—everything else."

And after telling Florence that she would come in again later in the afternoon to make some plan of escape, adding that it looked suspicious for her to remain with her too long, she left the apartment.

# CHAPTER X

Susie and Jennie Hill were orphans, whose parents had died within the same week of that dread disease, yellow fever. Both girls were attending the industrial institution at Hampton, Va., at the time, and as can be imagined, the death of both of their parents at the same time, was a sore trial to the young girls; for Susie was just sixteen and Jennie fourteen, and they were left penniless, as well as friendless, except for an aunt, who, as Susie has already said, was very kind to them.

The education of these two girls was brought to an abrupt— a cruel ending, and with as much heart as they had left they were forced to seek employment in Washington, the home of employment. Mammy procured situations for them in the

home of "fust class people and none o' yo' po' white trash,"
in which homes the girls had remained until Dick Vanbrugh
returned from abroad and made his plans known to mammy.

His plans were as follows:

Mammy was to procure two other servants, friends of hers,
if possible, and go down to Lesterville, one of his smallest
country villas, and make ready to receive him and his cousin
Kate, who had lost her reason five years ago, but whom he
was going to take to the country to try to restore her reason
by new scenery, fresh air, and his own presence. Susie had
often heard her aunt talking about this cousin, how, in
mammy's own words, "Mr. Rich'd wouldn't marry her and
the po' thing took it to heart so dat she run clean crazy, and
Mr. Rich'd took er to a private institshusion. But 'deed,
chile, Mr. Rich'd was mighty sorry for po' Miss Kate, so
shettin' de house up an' payin' fer my board 'twell he come
back he went to some place o' nother, I dunno whar. Dat
was five years ago, an' when he come home ergain an' tells
me to go down to Lesterville an' fix up tings for he an' Miss
Kate, I was most wile wid joy, bress his dear heart." But
mammy did not know that this same beautiful Miss Kate had
died two years after being placed in the institution.

Jennie's curiosity had been aroused to such a high pitch by
this piece of news that she had not formed any opinion
whatever as to the truth of Vanbrugh's plan, but Susie, on
the contrary, thought deeply, telling herself that as wild a
life as Mr. Vanbrugh had led it was not at all likely that he
would take an insane cousin, whom he had treated so cruelly,
out of an institution and sacrifice his pleasures for so vain an
attempt as that. "Good gracious, who can be silly enough to
believe such an absurd story?" she asked herself. But then,
Mr. Vanbrugh would reward them handsomely for their
services, and beside if there was very much villainy attached

to it who knew but what she and Jennie might not gain enough by their faithful services to help repair their interrupted education. She only needed two more years' study before she would graduate, and Jennie—poor, dear Jennie did so long to be a school teacher.

So they had come to Lesterville, and she, Susie, had found out that it was just as she had suspected. Richard Vanbrugh was still at his old tricks. And this time he had in his power the beautiful Florence Grey, a famous and well-loved girl who had shown so brightly in last season's world of fashion. Try to compel her—oh, the wretch! But even if Florence was only a pauper, she would run the chance of losing anything Vanbrugh might have given them by saving this sweet and beautiful young girl.

So she and Jennie quietly let themselves out of the house that evening about nine o'clock and with fleeting footsteps guided by human sympathy, and a brief instruction from Florence.

It was a beautiful night. The moon was just rising, and myriads of stars peeped forth from the cloudless blue heavens, some peeping through the branches of the tall, wide spreading trees which nearly met over the broad highway, down which the two girls who, with a prayer on their lips and fleeting footsteps, sped onward like two angels of mercy.

"Oh, I hope we won't be missed!" exclaimed Jennie.

"No danger of that until to-morrow morning, the thing to hope is that we may reach Grey's villa before morning. If we don't I fear for the worst," answered Susie, as she quickened her footsteps.

"We ought to reach there before morning; fifteen miles are not so many. Why, Sue, dear, we have often walked that distance in five hours."

"Yes, I know that Jennie; but as we do not know the exact

route, we may strike out on the wrong path and are liable to walk twice fifteen miles before we are through."

"Oh, God help us, I hope not!"

"So do I. But don't let's talk any more. It's too exhausting."

# CHAPTER XI

"My dear Jack, brace up; all hope is not yet lost. Mr. Miller tells me that he hopes to give us news of our lost one in a few hours," said a friend of Jack Warrington's early on the second morning after the abduction.

Jack was unable to sleep, and had come out early, and with this friend he was taking a stroll in the early morning air to try and quiet his nerves, which had been on the verge of mania ever since that fatal night. Presently they came upon Jim—Dr. Grey—who was standing against a tree, smoking a cigar and, it seemed, trying to compose his mind.

The others stopped, and all three engaged in an earnest conversation which they had carried on for about five minutes when somebody touched Jack's arm.

All three turned to look and saw two dust laden, excited young ladies.

"Pardon me, sirs, but would you kindly tell us if we are far from Grey's Villa?" asked Susie.

"Why, this is Grey's Villa," answered Jack, staring at them in wonderment.

"Then, oh, thank God, we have found her friends—You sir, must be Miss Florence Grey's brother!" exclaimed Susie, pointing at James.

And before anyone else could speak Jennie exclaimed excitedly:

"We have just left Miss Grey—she is in great trouble—is

in the power of an unscrupulous white man, and if you don't make haste you will be too late to save her."

"Oh, my God—do you hear, Jim! Oh, speak girl! tell us where she is that I can find my darling!" cried Jack, with the actions of an escaped lunatic.

Susie was quietly telling Dr. Grey the particulars, adding that he must procure the best horses he could find in order to reach Lesterville in time.

As will be imagined, the greatest excitement ensued for about ten minutes, at the end of which time a carriage with a smart lad in the coachman's seat, and Susie, Dr. Grey and John Warrington on the inside, tore madly down the road.

As it tore through the streets of the village, the well-shod feet of the thoroughbreds made such a noise that all who heard it ran to the doors, window, gates or whichever place was nearest, exclaiming, "A runaway horse!" "Good Lord, it's Grey's carriage!" "I wonder what's up now!" and many more exclamations.

Jennie had remained behind so as to break the news to Mrs. Grey, that lady receiving her in her arms as she would have received one of her most intimate friends: commanding the servants to bring the lady some refreshments, while with her own delicate hands she relieved Jennie of her dust laden garments, and on the whole, making her as comfortable as possible.

The news had spread rapidly. One of the servants from Grey's Villa had run down to the village and told one family of Negroes, and in a few moments, mind you, great crowds of men, women and children were gathered together in groups, in their houses, yards, pavements and even in the road, conversing, some loudly and vulgarly, others in excited whispers.

Some were saying that "Florence wasn't kidnapped no way,

but had run off wid a white man," others that "Dat I'd like
to 'cieve dat reward dem two gals would git," "Wonder what
time dey'll git back," "I'm jest dyin' to see Miss Florence
jest to see how she looks," "Spects she'll turn her nose up at
us now and hole her head high'n ever," and other remarks
too vulgar to repeat.

The reader perhaps would like to know what has become
of Long Tom. That gentleman, after driving Vanbrugh and
Florence to Lesterville, unharnessed and stabled the horses
and after receiving $500 in small bank notes to avoid suspi-
cion, walked to the nearest station, and boarding a train he
left for Washington. And, Negro like, after making a loud
display, left for a Northern city. It is well to add also that
he was killed—cut to death in a gambling affray some years
later.

# CHAPTER XII

"You Susan! You Jinnie! You all better come down stairs!
Here 'tis most seben erclock an' nare one un you up yit. I
bound if I comes up dere you'll come down quick 'nouf!"
exclaimed mammy, in her usual loud voice.

"Confound it! will she never stop yelling! How in thunder
is a fellow going to sleep!" He got up, threw on his dressing
robe and rung the bell angrily.

"Mammy, what the devil is the matter with you this
morning? I want you to shut up that noise yelling after those
accursed girls, and let me sleep!" he exclaimed angrily, as
mammy answered the ring.

"Lor' bless yo' soul, Mis' Rich'd, I can't get dem chil'en
up dis mornin' to save my life."

"Then go up and pitch them down; I don't care if you

break their d—— necks; Anyway, don't let me hear any more
of that infernal yelling!" and with this savage response he
shut the door, leaving that good old soul standing staring at
the panels of the latter object and wondering to herself "what
had come over Mr. Rich'd."

Meanwhile, all the sleep having left Vanbrugh's eyes by
this time, he began to slowly make his toilet, but was
startlingly interrupted in a very few moments by mammy,
who was knocking on his door and exclaiming that "Susan
and Jinnie can't be found nowhar!" and that "Miss Kate's
door was locked from de inside."

"The devil!" exclaimed Vanbrugh impatiently, "I'll be
there directly, mammy. Meanwhile, search the park and
neighboring woods."

"What in the—" but here he was interrupted by mammy's
voice saying that "de big gates was open and two white
gentlemen was drivin' in in a buggy."

Vanbrugh finished his toilet quick enough now, and was
on the verandah just in time to receive the two gentlemen
who had alighted from their phaeton and were ascending the
steps.

"Good morning, sir—Mr. Vanbrugh, I presume," said
one of the men. They were detectives Wright and Miller.
Vanbrugh bowed gallantly, saying in his cold, well bred
manner:

"Yes, I have the honor of bearing that title. What can I
do for you?"

"We, sir, are detectives Wm. Wright and Hr. Miller; we
are searching for a young lady by the name of Miss Florence
Grey. You, sir—"

Another interruption. This time it was the approach of a
carriage drawn by a pair of wild horses which came dashing
up the wide graveled drive and pulled up before them. Almost

before the carriage had stopped the door was thrown wide
and two young men alighted.

"By George, what does this mean!" exclaimed both detectives at the same time.

"Florence—my darling—have you found her?" cried both
men simultaneously.

"I beg your pardon, my friends, what does this abrupt
intrusion mean?" asked Vanbrugh in his cool and most scornful manner.

"Villain! wretch! I tell you, Mr. Miller, she is in this
house, suffering—perhaps dead!"

"This girl whom you seek—Florence Grey, is my mistress!" exclaimed Vanbrugh, insolently.

"You lie!" exclaimed James and Jack as with one breath.

"How dare you, you impudent Negro!" and Vanbrugh
drew a revolver and aimed it at Jack's head, but with a
lightning quickness, that young man knocked his hand back
with such force that the weapon went off, the discharge
passing through Vanbrugh's brain and he fell dead.

Meanwhile, Susie had alighted from the carriage by the
other door and unperceived by the men, had entered a side
door which led directly to Florence's apartments, and with
"It's I, Miss Florence; all's well, let me in," she had explained
briefly to Florence what was happening, had descended the
stairs and rushed out on the porch just in time to see the
revolver discharge.

Both girls gave a piercing shriek as Vanbrugh reeled and
fell heavily to the floor.

Jack caught Florence's fainting form in his arms, exclaim-
ing wildly, "Florence, darling, do not faint. It is I, Jack!
Good God, Jim, she doesn't know me! Water, girl, quick!
She is suffocating! Oh, Florence! oh, my love, my love!"

"Let me have her, Jack; she will be all right presently. She has only fainted, dear precious girl! How glad, how happy mother will be," said Dr. Grey.

The two detectives, unlike men of their profession, were as excited as the rest, while mammy, who had witnessed all, was on her knees crying, "Po' Mr. Rich'd! po' Mr. Rich'd!"

.   .   .   .   .

A few hours later Florence was gathered lovingly in a mother's arms, and many were the tears and rejoicings of that happy household.

Being only a girl of color no great stir was made over this awful tragedy, excepting through the newspapers. Those terrible mediums spread the news far and wide, one paper declaring that the beautiful Negress had run off with the Hon. Richard Vanbrugh of her own free will, and had caused him to commit suicide by deserting him and playing lady when caught up with.

But through it all Florence lived and shone as conspicuously as ever in her world of fashion, which received her with open arms.

And a year later she was the blushing bride of happy Jack Warrington, who took her to his Northern home, where very soon Mrs. Grey and James followed her, the latter bringing with him as his bride the winsome Sadie Payne.

Susie and Jennie were liberally rewarded, and with happy hearts and smiling faces they again took up their studies.

One more word. Mammy was mentioned in the Hon. Richard Vanbrugh's will as an old and faithful servant to whom was to be left $5,000, the rest of his large fortune to be divided up between different charitable institutions in case he had no wife.

Mammy was simply delighted, saying that "Mr. Rich'd allus was a good boy, and bless his dear heart, she'd soon jine him in heaven."

So with many good wishes and blessings we will leave our dear friends, hoping, as with the ending of a fairy tale, they may live very happily ever afterwards.

# THE TEST OF MANHOOD
## *A Christmas Story*

Sarah A. Allen
[Pauline E. Hopkins]

The shed door creaked softly, and Mark Myers stood for a moment peering into the semi-darkness of the twilight. He was a stalwart lad of about eighteen, with soft dark curls, big dark eyes, and the peach-like complexion of a girl, but he was only a Negro, what the colored people designate as "milk an' molasses, honey; neither one thing nor t'other," and he was leaving his home to try his fortune at the North.

One day Mark had carried a white gentleman's bag to the steamboat landing and as he loitered about the pier after pocketing a generous fee, the words of the patron in conversation with another white man sank in his heart:

"After all this wasted blood and treasure, the Negro question is still uppermost in the South. Why don't you settle it once and for all, Morgan?"

"We might were it not for the infernal interference of you Yankees, and amalgamation. The mulattoes are the curse of the South. We can't entirely ignore our brothers' cousins and closer kindred, so there you are."

"Your 'brothers and closer kindred' could settle the question themselves if they knew their power."

"How?" queried Morgan.

"Easily enough; when the white blood is pronounced enough, just disappear and turn up again as a white man. Half of your sectional difficulties would end under such a system."

"And would you—a white man—be willing to encounter

*Colored American Magazine* 5 (Dec. 1902): 114–19.

the risk that such a course would entail—the wholesale pollution of our race?" thundered the man called Morgan, in
disgust.

"Why not? You know the old saw,—Where ignorance is
bliss 'tis folly to be wise. Better that than a greater evil."

"You Northerners are a riddle—"

They passed out of sight and Mark heard no more, but
from that time he had thought incessantly of the stranger's
words, and at last he resolved to become a white man. And
one night when his mother lay peacefully sleeping, with no
foreshadowing of the sorrow in store for her, with a backward
look of regret and a tear stealing down his cheek, he had
stolen softly from the little cabin under the wide spreading
magnolia. At the top of the hill he paused for a last look and
then turned his face sorrowfully toward the great unknown
world, henceforth to be his only home. The day broke; the
sun rose; there was a stir of life all about him. How sweet
the air smelled; surely there could be no prettier mornings
up in the wonderful North to which he was journeying.

As he trudged along with his small bundle over his shoulder
he murmured to himself: "Mammy's up now, but she won't
miss me yet. I'm glad I chopped all that wood yesterday. It
ought ter last her a week an' better. The white folks all think
the world of her. They'll take keer on her tell I git settled;
then I'll write and tell her all about my plans."

He avoided the main roads and kept to the fields, thus
keeping clear of all chance acquaintances who might interfere
with his determination to identify himself with the white race.

The weary time passed on; days were merged into weeks,
when one morning, tired and fainting with hunger, Mark
found himself in the street of a great Northern metropolis,
homeless and nearly penniless. He walked through the thoroughfares with the puzzled uncertainty of a stranger doubtful

of his route, pausing at intervals to study the signs, feeling his heart sink as he watched the hurrying throng of unfamiliar faces. The scene was so different from his beautiful southern home that in his heart he cried aloud for the dear familiar scenes. Then he remembered and took up his weary tramp again and his search for a friendly face that he might venture to accost the owner for work. Night was approaching and he must have a place to sleep. As he neared the common, and its tranquil, inviting greenness burst upon his view, he determined that if nothing better presented itself, to pass the night there under the canopy of heaven.

As he neared Tremont street a gentleman passed him, evidently in a great hurry; scarcely had his resounding foot-steps ceased upon the concrete walk, when Mark noticed a pocket-book lying directly at his feet. He picked it up, opened it and saw that it was filled with bills of large denominations. "John E. Brown" was printed in gold letters upon one of the compartments.

Mark stood a second hesitating as to the right course to pursue; here was wealth—money for food, shelter, clothes— he sighed as he thought of what it would give him. But only for a moment, the next he was rushing along the wide mall at his utmost speed trying to overtake the gentleman whom he could just discern making his hurried way through the throng of pedestrians.

At the corner of Summer and Washington streets, Mark, breathless and hatless, caught up with the gentleman.

"Eh, what? My pocket-book?" ejaculated Mr. Brown, as he felt in all his pockets, and looked down curiously upon the forlorn figure that had tugged so resolutely at his arm to attract his attention.

"Now that was clever of you and very honest, my boy," said the great lawyer, gazing at him over his gold-rimmed spectacles. "Here's something for you," and he placed a bill in the lad's hand that fairly made the dark eyes bulge with surprise. "From the country, aren't you?"

"Yes, sir."

"I thought so. Honesty doesn't flourish in city air. Well, I haven't time to talk to you today. Come and see me to-morrow at my office; perhaps I can help you. Want a job don't you?"

"Yes, sir; I'm a stranger in Boston."

"Come and see me, come and see me. I'll talk with you. Good-day."

The lawyer went on his way. In one brief moment the world to Mark seemed spinning around. His breath came in quick struggling gasps, while wild possibilities surged through his brain, when he read the card in his hand which was that of a firm of lawyers whom he had often heard spoken of even in his far-off home.

The next morning Mark presented himself at the office and was kindly received by Mr. Brown. The lawyer glanced him over from head to foot. "A good face," he thought, "and pleasant way." Then he noted the neat, cheap suit, the well-brushed hair and clean-looking skin. Then he asked a few direct, rapid questions, which Mark answered briefly.

"What can you do?"

"Plow, make a garden an'—an' read and write," dropping his voice over the two last accomplishments.

The lawyer laughed heartily.

"What's your name?"

"Mark Myers, sir."

"Well, Mark, I like your face, and your manner, too, my lad, and although its contrary to my way of doing—taking a boy without a reference—because of your honesty you may set in as a porter and messenger here, if you've a mind to try the job; we want a boy just now, so you see you have struck it just right for yourself and me, too."

"If you are willing to take me, sir, just as you find me, I will do my best to please you," answered Mark, controlling his voice with an effort.

"Well, then, we'll consider it a bargain. I'll pay you what you are worth."

As Mark stepped across the threshold of the inner office and hung up his hat and coat he felt himself transformed. He was no longer a Negro! Henceforth he would be a white man in very truth. After all his plans, the metamorphosis had been accomplished by Fate. For the first time he seemed to live—to feel.

That night, he sat motionless beside the open window of the garret where he had found a lodging and planned his future.

"Oh, mammy," he cried at last, "if you knew you would forgive me. Some day you shall be rich—" He broke off suddenly and dropped his head in his hands. Did he mean this, he asked himself in stern self-searching. His mother could not be mistaken for a white woman—her skin was light, but her hair and features were those of a Negress. He shuddered at the gulf he saw yawning between them. Nothing could bridge it. From now on she should no more exist—*as his mother*—for he had buried his old self that morning, and packed the earth hard above the coffin.

As the months went by a curious change came to the lad. This new life—this masquerade, so to speak, had become second nature. He looked at life from a white man's standpoint, and had assumed all of the prejudices and principles of the dominant race. Out of the careless boy had come a wary, taciturn man. He availed himself of the exceptional school privileges offered by night study in Boston, and improved rapidly. One morning, Mr. Brown came to Mark with good news. He had promoted him from porter to clerk, with a corresponding increase in his salary.

That night, Mark dreamed he was at home with his mother. He felt the loving touch of her toil-worn dusky hands, and heard the caressing tones of her voice in its soft Southern dialect. Ah! there had been such infinite peace in the old, careless, happy life he had led there. Pictures came and went before his mental vision with startling distinctness. He saw the modest log-cabin, the sweet-scented magnolia-tree, the cotton fields, the sweeping long, gray moss hanging from the trees, the smell of the pines; he heard the cow-bells in the cane-brake, the hum of bees, and the sweet notes of the mocking-bird. He closed his eyes and could see the boys and girls dancing the old "Virginia reel":

"Dar's 'Jinny Put de Kittle On,' and' 'Shoo! Miss Pijie, Shoo!'
An' den 'King William Was King George's Son,'
'Blin' Man's Bluff,' an' 'Gimme Korner'; also 'Walk de Lo-
    nesum Road,'
'Whar de pint wuz gittin kisses—shorz yo' born,
De gals wuz dressed in hum'spun, long wid dar brogan shoes,
An' ef dar feet would tech yo',' you would feel,
'Do' de boys wore bed-tuck breeches, dese trifles wuz forgot,
While 'joyin' ub de ol' Virginny reel."

After that night he resolutely put by such thoughts; all his associates were white, and his life was irrevocably blended with the class far above the humble blacks. Months rounded into years. At the end of five years, Mark was on the road to wealth. He had studied law and passed the Bar. A fortunate speculation in Western land was the motive power that placed ten thousand dollars in his pocket.

"So unexpected a windfall might have ruined some men," Mr. Brown confided to his partner as they smoked an after dinner cigar at Parker's, "but no fear for Mark. His is an old head on young shoulders. He's bound to be a power in the country before he dies."

"How about a 'Co.,' Brown? ever thought of it in connection with the firm? We aren't growing any younger. What do you think of it?"

"Just the thing, Clark, Co. it is; and Myers is the man."

\*    \*    \*    \*    \*

The winter had set in early that year. Snow covered the ground from the first of December. The air was biting cold. The music of sleigh-bells, mingled with the voices of children playing in the streets. There was good skating on the frog pond and the Public Garden, where the merry skaters glided to and fro in graceful circles laughing and jesting merrily.

Down in the quarter where the colored people lived, Aunt Cloty sat most of the day looking drearily through the rusted iron railings of the area in a hopeless watch for a footstep that never came. Old, wrinkled, rheumatic, the patient face, and subdued air of the mulattress awakened sad feelings in the hearts of those who knew her story.

She had come North five years before searching for her son. At first she had been able to live in a humble way from her work as a laundress, but when sickness and old age laid their hands upon her, she had succumbed to the inevitable and subsisted upon the charity of the well-to-do among her neighbors, who had something to spare for a companion in poverty. After a time her case had come under the notice of the associated charities. At first it was determined to place the helpless creature in an institution where she could have constant attention, but her prayers and tears not to be "kyarted to de po'-house," had stirred the pity of the officials and at length the attention of Lawyer Brown's daughter Katherine had been directed to Aunt Cloty as a worthy object of charity. Miss Brown was delighted with the quaintness of the old Negress and her tender heart overflowed with pity for her woes, and so the helpless woman became a welcome charge upon the purse of the petted favorite of fortune. Since that time better days had dawned for Aunt Cloty.

The wealthy girl and the old mulattress grew to be great friends. Every week found Katherine visiting her protege, sitting in the tiny room, listening eagerly to her tales of the sunny South.

Aunt Cloty's turban always seemed the insignia of her rank and proud pretensions, for she declared there was "good blood" in her veins, and her majestic bearing testified to the truth of her words. When Cloty felt particularly humble, she laid the turban in flat folds on her head. In her character of a laundress, it was mounted a little higher. But when she received visitors, or called an enemy to account, the red flag of defiance towered aloft in wonderful proportion. So "Misse Katherine" could always read the signs of her protege's feelings in the build of the red turban.

Christmas week the turban lay in flat folds and Cloty mourned aloud.

"He mus' be daid. 'Deed, chile, he mus' be daid or he'd neber leave his ol' mammy to suffer," she cried as she rocked her frail body in the old wooden rocker. "Misse Katherine" sat patiently listening.

"You see, Misse, Sonny's da onlies' chile what I ebber had. De good Lawd sont him to me lak He done Isaac to Sary, in my ole age, an' sence de night he runned off I aint seed nuffin' but trouble. All dat fust ye'r I was spectin' him back again, an' when de win moan roun' my cabin endurin' o' de night, it seemed lak I hear him callin' fer me, an' I git up an open de do' ter listen, but it waz dark an' lonesome an' he wuzn't dar. So, at las' Marse Will, he sez ter me (Marse Will's one o' my white fokes, whar I dunn nurse for two ginerations, an' he call me mammy same as Sonny do,—so, Marse Will he sez to me, 'Mammy, Sonny's daid, or else he'd a written you whar he was. Sonny is allers been a good boy, an' he wouldn't act no sech way as this to you ef he was livin.' Yes, Misse, dat's what Marse Will, he tell me, an' it suttinly did seem reasonable, but somehow I cayn't b'lieve it." She paused, and opening an old carpet-sack always laid by her chair on the floor, drew from it a package. "Dis here is his leetle red waist an' de fus' par' o' britches he ebber wo'," she continued, displaying them to the young white girl with pride. "I fotch um Norf wif me kaze dey keeps me company up here all alone."

Misse Katherine's swimming eyes attested her sympathy.

"He wuz de pertes' youngster," continued the old woman, with an upward tilt of her turbaned head, "an' de day he put dese on he strut, Misse, same as er peafowil."

"Aunt Cloty, I've told my father of your son and he's going to institute a search for him. If he's alive he'll find him for you, rest assured of that."

"Gord bless you, honey; Gord bless you. A big gentleman like de judge, your pa 'll surely fin' him, fer I b'lieve Sonny's alive somedhere. Does I wanter see him?" and the woman's faded eyes held a joyous sparkle. "Does I wanter see him? why honey," coming close to the girl and unconsciously grasping her arm, "ef he was in prison, an' I couldn' git ter him no urrer way, I'd be willin' to crawl on my hands and knees ez fur agin ez I done come to git up Norf, jes' fur one look at him." For a moment she looked about her as though dazed, then some over-strained chord seemed to snap, and burying her face in her apron she sobbed aloud.

"Now, Aunty, don't," and the impulsive heiress threw her

soft arms about the forlorn figure and kissed the wrinkled
face. "Tomorrow is Christmas-eve, and I am coming for you
early in the day to take you home. You are to live with me
always after that, and if we don't find Sonny, you shall never
want while I live."

"I's hearn twell of fokes cryin' kase dey's happy, but I aint
neber done it twell now. Ef I kin jes fin' Sonny I'll be de
happies' old woman in de whole wurl."

And so it came about that Aunt Cloty was domiciled in the
home of Judge Brown.

\*     \*     \*     \*     \*

Christmas-eve in a great city is a wonderful sight. The
principal streets were in grand illumination. The shop windows were all ablaze, and through them came the vivid
coloring of holiday gifts, tinting the coldness with an idea of
warmth. It was a joyous pleasant scene; the pavements were
thronged, and eager traffic was going on. A band of colored
street musicians were passing from store to store stopping
here and there to sing their peculiar songs to the accompaniment of guitars, banjos and bones. One trolled out in a
powerful bass the notes of the old song:

> "The sun shines bright in my old Kentucky home,
> 'Tis summer the darkies are gay."

The familiar air fell upon the ears of a handsome dark-
eyed man as he took his way leisurely through the throng.
He paused a moment, dropped a coin in the hat extended for
contributions, laughed, and hastened on his way. Presently
he hummed the strain he had just heard in a rich undertone.
Then there floated through his mind the fragments of a poem
he had read somewhere:

"Hundreds of stars in the pretty sky;
   Hundreds of shells on the shore together;
Hundreds of birds that go singing by;
   Hundreds of bees in sunny weather.

"Hundreds of dewdrops to greet the dawn;
   Hundreds of lambs in the purple clover;
Hundreds of butterflies on the lawn;
   But only one mother the wide world over!"

"Pshaw!" exclaimed Mark Myers as he pulled himself together and brushed aside unpleasant memories.

Katherine Brown had been walking restlessly up and down the great reception room. The sound of the bell reached her. She stopped a moment, held her breath and listened. She heard Mark's voice in the hall and knew that her lover had come.

The servants were moving about in the back room, so she closed the folding-doors, and hid the Christmas tree, and sat down demurely waiting for him to come in, as if she had not indulged in a thought about the matter until then; though her heart was beating so tumultuously that a tuft of flowers among the lace on her bosom fluttered as if a breeze passed over it. The dainty room was redolent with the perfumes from a basket of tea-roses, Japan lilies and japanicas that had been sent to the lovely girl as her first Christmas gift in the morning. Their fragrance pervaded the whole room, and it seemed that the fair owner moved through the calm of a tropical climate when she came forward to receive her guest; for that portion of her dress that swept the floor was rich with lace and summer-like in its texture, as if the blast of a storm could never reach her.

"My darling, you scarcely expected me, I am sure," said Myers coming forward with hand extended and a world of lovelight in his dark eyes: "but nothing would keep me from you tonight, foolish fellow that I am."

"I should never have forgiven you if you had not come," replied the girl with arched tenderness. "Why, sir, I have waited a half-hour already."

"Wondering what I should bring you for a Christmas gift?"

"No, no—not that," she answered, turning her eyes on the basket of flowers and blushing like a rose. "That came this morning, and I would let them put nothing else in this room, for your roses turned it into a little heaven of my own."

"They will perish in a day or two at best. But I have really brought you something that will keep its own as long as we two shall love each other."

"So long! Then it will be perfect to all eternity."

Mark grew serious. Something in her words struck him with a thought of death; a chill passed over him.

"God forbid that it should not remain so while you and I live, Katherine; for see, it is the engagement-ring I have brought you."

A flood of crimson rose to her face. The little hand held out for the ring quivered like a leaf. She held the starlike solitaire in her hand a moment gazing on it with reverence, scarcely conscious of its beauty. It might have been a lot of glass rather than a limpid diamond for anything she thought of the matter, she only felt how solemn and sacred a thing that jewel was.

"No, you must put it on first," she said, resting one hand softly on his breast, and holding the ring toward him. "I shall always love it better if taken from your own fingers."

Myers gazing down into her face, read all the solemn and beautiful thoughts that prompted the action, and his own sympathetic nature was subdued by them into solemn harmony.

As he stood before her submitting one hand to her sweet will, he whispered: "And you are happy, my beloved?"

"Happy! Oh, Mark, if we could always be so, heaven would begin here with you. Nothing can part us now, we are irrevocably bound to each other forever. If only the whole world could be happy as we are tonight."

Her words jarred upon him an instant. His old mother's face rose before him as it had not done for years.

"Come," said Katherine, "let me show you the Christmas tree; they—papa and Aunt Cloty—are just finishing it."

As she spoke she threw wide the doors and in the midst of the glitter and dazzle he heard a voice scream out:

"Oh, my Gord! It's him! It's my boy! It's Sonny!"

Then panting excitedly, arms extended, the yellow face suffused with tenderness, Mark saw his mother standing before him.

After that scream came a deathly silence, Mark stood as if carved into stone, in an instant he saw his life in ruins, Katherine lost to him, chaos about the social fabric of his life. He could not do it. Then with a long breath he set his teeth and opened his lips to denounce her as crazy, but in that instant his eyes fell on her drawn face, and quivering lips. In another moment he saw his conduct of the past years in all its hideousness. Suddenly Judge Brown spoke.

"Mark, what is this? Have you nothing to say?"

He would not glance at Katherine. One look at her fair face would unman him. He turned slowly and faced Judge Brown and there was defiance in his look. All that was noble in his nature spoke at last.

Another instant his arms were about his fond old mother, while she sobbed her heart out on his breast.

# AFTER MANY DAYS
## *A Christmas Story*

### Fannie Barrier Williams

Christmas on the Edwards plantation, as it was still called, was a great event to old and young, master and slave comprising the Edwards household. Although freedom had long ago been declared, many of the older slaves could not be induced to leave the plantation, chiefly because the Edwards family had been able to maintain their appearance of opulence through the vicissitudes of war, and the subsequent disasters, which had impoverished so many of their neighbors. It is one of the peculiar characteristics of the American Negro, that he is never to be found in large numbers in any community where the white people are as poor as himself. It is, therefore, not surprising that the Edwards plantation had no difficulty in retaining nearly all of their former slaves as servants under the new regime.

The stately Edwards mansion, with its massive pillars, and spreading porticoes, gleaming white in its setting of noble pines and cedars, is still the pride of a certain section of old Virginia.

One balmy afternoon a few days before the great Christmas festival, Doris Edwards, the youngest granddaughter of this historic southern home, was hastening along a well-trodden path leading down to an old white-washed cabin, one of the picturesque survivals of plantation life before the war. The pathway was bordered on either side with old-fashioned flowers, some of them still lifting a belated blossom, caught in

*Colored American Magazine* 5 (Dec. 1902): 140–53.

the lingering balm of Autumn, while faded stalks of hollyhock and sunflower, like silent sentinels, guarded the door of this humble cabin.

Through the open vine-latticed window, Doris sniffed with keen delight the mingled odor of pies, cakes and various other dainties temptingly spread out on the snowy kitchen table waiting to be conveyed to the "big house" to contribute to the coming Christmas cheer.

Peering into the gloomy cabin, Doris discovered old Aunt Linda, with whom she had always been a great favorite, sitting in a low chair before the old brick oven, her apron thrown over her head, swaying back and forth to the doleful measure of a familiar plantation melody, to which the words, "Lambs of the Upper Fold," were being paraphrased in a most ludicrous way. As far back as Doris could remember, it had been an unwritten law on the plantation that when Aunt Linda's "blues chile" reached the "Lambs Of The Upper Fold" stage, she was in a mood not to be trifled with.

Aunt Linda had lived on the plantation so long she had become quite a privileged character. It had never been known just how she had learned to read and write, but this fact had made her a kind of a leader among the other servants, and had earned for herself greater respect even from the Edwards family. Having been a house servant for many years, her language was also better than the other servants, and her spirits were very low indeed, when she lapsed into the language of the "quarters." There was also a tradition in the family that Aunt Linda's coming to the plantation had from the first been shrouded in mystery. In appearance she was a tall yellow woman, straight as an Indian, with piercing black eyes, and bearing herself with a certain dignity of manner, unusual in a slave. Visitors to the Edwards place would at once single her out from among the other servants, sometimes asking some very uncomfortable questions concerning her. Doris, however, was the one member of the household who refused to take Aunt Linda's moods seriously, so taking in the situation at a glance, she determined to put an end to this "mood" at least. Stealing softly upon the old woman, she drew the apron from her head, exclaiming, "O, Aunt Linda, just leave your 'lambs' alone for to-day, won't you? why this is Christmas time, and I have left all kinds of nice things going on up at the house to bring you the latest news, and now, but what is the matter anyway?" The old woman slowly raised her head, saying, "I might of knowd it was you, you certainly is gettin' might saccy, chile, chile, how you did fright me sure. My min was way back in ole Carlina, jest befoh another Christmas, when de Lord done lay one hand on my pore heart, and wid the other press down de white lids over de blue eyes of my sweet Alice, O, my chile, can I evah ferget date day?" Doris, fearing another outburst, interrupted the moans of the old woman by playfully placing her hand over her mouth, saying: "Wait a minute, auntie, I want to tell you something. There are so many delightful people up to the house, but I want to tell you about two of them especially. Sister May has just come and has brought with her her friend, Pauline Sommers, who sings beautifully, and she is going to sing our Christmas carol for us on Christmas eve. With them is the loveliest girl I ever saw, her name is Gladys Winne. I wish I could describe her, but I can't. I can only remember her violet eyes; think of it, auntie, not blue, but violet, just like the pansies in your garden last summer." At the mention of the last name, Aunt Linda rose, leaning on the table for support. It seemed to her as if some cruel hand had reached out of a pitiless past and clutched her heart. Doris gazed in startled awe at the storm of anguish that seemed to sweep across the old woman's face, exclaiming,

"Why, auntie, are you sick?" In a hoarse voice, she answered: "Yes, chile, yes, I's sick." This poor old slave woman's life was rimmed by just two events, a birth and a death, and even these memories were hers and not hers, yet the mention of a single name has for a moment blotted out all the intervening years and in another lowly cabin, the name of 'Gladys' is whispered by dying lips to breaking hearts. Aunt Linda gave a swift glance at the startled Doris, while making a desperate effort to recall her wandering thoughts, lest unwittingly she betray her loved ones to this little chatterer. Forcing a ghastly smile, she said, as if to herself, "As if there was only one Gladys in all dis worl, yes and heaps of Winnes, too, I reckon. Go on chile, go on, ole Aunt Linda is sure getting ole and silly." Doris left the cabin bristling with curiosity, but fortunately for Aunt Linda, she would not allow it to worry her pretty head very long.

The lovely Gladys Winne, as she was generally called, was indeed the most winsome and charming of all the guests that composed the Christmas party in the Edwards mansion. Slightly above medium height, with a beautifully rounded form, delicately poised head crowned with rippling chestnut hair, curling in soft tendrils about neck and brow, a complexion of dazzling fairness with the tint of the rose in her cheeks, and the whole face lighted by deeply glowing violet eyes. Thus liberally endowed by nature, there was further added the charm of a fine education, the advantage of foreign travel, contact with brilliant minds, and a social prestige through her foster parents, that fitted her for the most exclusive social life.

She had recently been betrothed to Paul Westlake, a handsome, wealthy and gifted young lawyer of New York. He had been among the latest arrivals, and Gladys' happiness glowed in her expressive eyes, and fairly scintillated from every curve of her exquisite form. Beautifully gowned in delicate blue of soft and clinging texture draped with creamy lace, she was indeed as rare a picture of radiant youth and beauty as one could wish to see.

But, strange to say, Gladys' happiness was not without alloy. She had one real or fancied annoyance, which she could not shake off, though she tried not to think about it. But as she walked with Paul, through the rambling rooms of this historic mansion, she determined to call his attention to it. They had just passed an angle near a stairway, when Gladys nervously pressed his arm, saying, "Look, Paul, do you see that tall yellow woman; she follows me everywhere, and actually haunts me like a shadow. If I turn suddenly, I can just see her gliding out of sight. Sometimes she becomes bolder, and coming closer to me, she peers into my face as if she would look me through. Really there seems to be something uncanny about it all to me; it makes me shiver. Look, Paul, there she is now, even your presence does not daunt her." Paul, after satisfying himself that she was really serious and annoyed, ceased laughing, saying, "My darling, I cannot consistently blame any one for looking at you. It may be due to an inborn curiosity; she probably is attracted by other lovely things in the same way, only you may not have noticed it." "Nonsense," said Gladys, blushing, "that is a very sweet explanation, but it doesn't explain in this case. It annoys me so much that I think I must speak to Mrs. Edwards about it." Here Paul quickly interrupted. "No, my dear, I would not do that; she is evidently a privileged servant, judging from the rightaway she seems to have all over the house. Mrs. Edwards is very kind and gracious to us, yet she might resent any criticism of her servants. Try to dismiss it from your mind, my love. I have always heard that these old 'mammies' are very superstitious, and she may fancy that she has seen you in some vision or dream, but it ought not to cause you any concern at all. Just fix your mind on something pleasant; on me, for instance." Thus lovingly rebuked and comforted, Gladys did succeed in forgetting for a time her silent watcher. But the thing that annoyed her almost more than anything else was the fact that she had a sense of being irresistibly drawn towards this old servant, by a chord of sympathy and interest, for which she could not in any way account.

But the fatal curiosity of her sex, despite the advice of Paul, whom she so loved and trusted, finally wrought her own undoing. The next afternoon, at a time when she was sure she would not be missed, Gladys stole down to Aunt Linda's cabin determined to probe this mystery for herself. Finding the cabin door ajar, she slipped lightly into the room.

Aunt Linda was so absorbed by what she was doing that she heard no sound. Gladys paused upon the threshold of the cabin, fascinated by the old woman's strange occupation. She was bending over the contents of an old hair chest, tenderly shaking out one little garment after another of a baby's wardrobe, filling the room with the pungent odor of camphor and lavender.

The tears were falling and she would hold the little garments to her bosom, crooning some quaint cradle song, tenderly murmuring, "O, my lam, my poor lil' lam," and then, as if speaking to some one unseen, she would say: "No, my darlin, no, your ole mother will shorely nevah break her promise to young master, but O, if you could only see how lovely your little Gladys has growed to be! Sweet innocent Gladys, and her pore ole granma must not speak to or tech her, mus not tell her how her own ma loved her and dat dese ole hans was de fust to hold her, and mine de fust kiss she ever knew; but O, my darlin, I will nevah tray you, she shall nevah know." Then the old woman's sobs would break out afresh, as she frantically clasped the tiny garments, yellow with age, but dainty enough for a princess, to her aching heart.

For a moment Gladys, fresh and sweet as a flower, felt only the tender sympathy of a casual observer, for what possible connection could there be between her and this old colored woman in her sordid surroundings. Unconsciously she drew her skirts about her in scorn of the bare suggestion, but the next moment found her transfixed with horror, a sense of approaching doom enveloping her as in a mist. Clutching at her throat, and with dilated unseeing eyes, she groped her way toward the old woman, violently shaking her, while in a terror-stricken voice she cried, "O Aunt Linda, what is it?" With a cry like the last despairing groan of a wounded animal, Aunt Linda dropped upon her knees, scattering a shower of filmy lace and dainty flannels about her. Through every fibre of her being, Gladys felt the absurdity of her fears, yet in spite of herself, the words welled up from her heart to her lips, "O Aunt Linda, what is it, what have I to do with your dead?" with an hysterical laugh, she added, "do I look like someone you have loved and lost in other days?" Then the simple-hearted old woman, deceived by the kindly note in Gladys' voice, and not seeing the unspeakable horror growing in her eyes, stretched out imploring hands as to a little child, the tears streaming from her eyes, saying, "O, Gladys," not Miss Gladys now, as the stricken girl quickly notes, "you is my own sweet Alice's little chile, O, honey I's your own dear gran-ma. You's beautiful, Gladys, but not more so den you own sweet ma, who loved you so."

The old woman was so happy to be relieved of the secret burden she had borne for so many years, that she had almost forgotten Gladys' presence, until she saw her lost darling fainting before her very eyes. Quickly she caught her in her arms, tenderly pillowing her head upon her ample bosom, where as a little babe she had so often lain.

For several minutes the gloomy cabin was wrapped in solemn silence. Finally Gladys raised her head, and turning toward Aunt Linda her face, from which every trace of youth and happiness had fled, in a hoarse and almost breathless whisper, said: "If you are my own grandmother, who then was my father?" Before this searching question these two widely contrasted types of southern conditions, stood dumb and helpless. The shadow of the departed crime of slavery still remained to haunt the generations of freedom.

Though Aunt Linda had known for many years that she was free, the generous kindness of the Edwards family had made the Emancipation proclamation almost meaningless to her.

When she now realized that the fatal admission, which had brought such gladness to her heart, had only deepened the horror in Gladys' heart, a new light broke upon her darkened mind. Carefully placing Gladys in a chair, the old woman raised herself to her full height, her right hand uplifted like some bronze goddess of liberty. For the first time and for one brief moment she felt the inspiring thrill and meaning of the term freedom. Ignorant of almost everything as compared with the knowledge and experience of the stricken girl before her, yet a revelation of the sacred relationships of parenthood, childhood and home, the common heritage of all humanity swept aside all differences of complexion or position.

For one moment, despite her lowly surroundings and dusky skin, an equality of blood, nay superiority of blood, tingled in old Aunt Linda's veins, straightened her body, and flashed in her eye. But the crushing process of over two centuries could not sustain in her more than a moment of asserted womanhood. Slowly she lowered her arm, and, with bending body, she was again but an old slave woman with haunting memories and a bleeding heart. Then with tears and broken words, she poured out the whole pitiful story to the sobbing Gladys.

"It was this way, honey, it all happened jus before the wah, way down in ole Carolina. My lil Alice, my one chile had growed up to be so beautiful. Even when she was a tiny lil chile, I used to look at her and wonder how de good Lord evah 'lowed her to slip over my door sill, but nevah min dat chile, dat is not you alls concern. When she was near 'bout seventeen years ole, she was dat prutty that the white folks was always askin' of me if she was my own chile, the ide, as if her own ma, but den that was all right for dem, it was jest case she was so white, I knowd.

"Tho' I lived wid my lil Alice in de cabin, I was de housemaid in de 'big house,' but I'd nevah let Alice be up thar wid me when there was company, case, well I jest had to be keerful, nevah mind why. But one day, young Master Harry Winne was home from school, and they was a celebratin', an' I was in a hurry; so I set Alice to bringin' some roses fron de garden to trim de table, and there young master saw her, an' came after me to know who she was; he say he thought he knowed all his ma's company, den I guess I was too proud, an' I up an' tells him dat she was my Alice, my own lil' gel, an' I was right away scared dat I had tole him, but he had seen huh; dat was enough, O my pore lam!" Here the old woman paused, giving herself up for a moment to unrestrained weeping. Suddenly she dried her eyes and said: "Gladys, chile, does you know what love is?" Gladys' cheeks made eloquent response, and with one swift glance, the old woman continued, "den you knows how they loved each other. One day Master Harry went to ole Master and he say: 'Father, I know you'll be auful angered at me, but I will marry Alice or no woman'; den his father say—but nevah min' what it was, only it was enough to make young master say dat he'd nevah forgive his pa, for what he say about my lil' gurl.

"Some time after that my Alice began to droop an' pine away like; so one day I say to her: 'Alice, does you an' young master love each other?' Den she tole me as how young master had married her, and that she was afeard to tell even her ma, case they mite sen him away from her forever. When young master came again he tole me all about it; jest lak my gurl had tole me. He say he could not lib withou' her. After dat he would steal down to see her when he could, bringing huh all dese pritty laces and things, and she would sit all day and sew an' cry lak her heart would break.

"He would bribe ole Sam not to tell ole Master, saying date he was soon goin' to take huh away where no men or laws could tech them. Well, after you was bohn, she began to fade away from me, gettin' weaker every day. Den when you was only a few months ole, O, how she worshipped you! I saw dat my pore unhappy lil gurl was goin' on dat long journey away from her pore heart-broke ma, to dat home not made with hans, den I sent for young master, your pa. O, how he begged her not to go, saying dat he had a home all ready for her an you up Norf. Gently she laid you in his arms, shore de mos' beautiful chile dat evah were, wid your great big violet eyes looking up into his, tho' he could not see dem for the tears dat would fall on yo sweet face. Your ma tried to smile, reaching out her weak arms for you, she said: 'Gladys,' an' with choking sobs she made us bofe promise, she say, 'promise that she shall never know that her ma was a slave or dat she has a drop of my blood, make it

all yours, Harry, nevah let her know.' We bofe promised,
and that night young master tore you from my breaking
heart, case it was best. After I had laid away my poor unhappy
chile, I begged ole Master to sell me, so as to sen me way
off to Virginia, where I could nevah trace you nor look fer
you, an' I nevah have." Then the old woman threw herself
upon her knees, wringing her hands and saying: "O my God,
why did you let her fin me?" She had quite forgotten Gladys'
presence in the extremity of her distress at having broken her
vow to the dead and perhaps wrought sorrow for the living.

Throughout the entire recital, told between heart-breaking
sobs and moans, Gladys sat as if carved in marble, never
removing her eyes from the old woman's face. Slowly she
aroused herself, allowing her dull eyes to wander about the
room at the patch-work covered bed in the corner; then
through the open casement, from which she could catch a
glimpse of a group of young Negroes, noting their coarse
features and boisterous play; then back again to the crouching,
sobbing old woman. With a shiver running through her
entire form, she found her voice, which seemed to come from
a great distance, "And I am part of all this! O, my God,
how can I live; above all, how can I tell Paul, but I must
and will; I will not deceive him though it kill me."

At the sound of Gladys' voice Aunt Linda's faculties awoke,
and she began to realize the awful possibilities of her divulged
secrets. Aunt Linda had felt and known the horrors of slavery,
but could she have known that after twenty years of freedom,
nothing in the whole range of social disgraces could work
such terrible disinheritance to man or woman as the presence
of Negro blood, seen or unseen, she would have given almost
life itself rather than to have condemned this darling of her
love and prayers to so dire a fate.

The name of Paul, breathed by Gladys in accents of such

tenderness and despair, aroused Aunt Linda to action. She implored her not to tell Paul or any one else. "No one need ever know, no one ever can or shall know," she pleaded. "How could any fin' out, honey, if you did not tell them?" Then seizing one of Gladys' little hands, pink and white and delicate as a rose leaf, and placing it beside her own old and yellow one, she cried: "Look chile, look, could any one ever fin' the same blood in dese two hans by jest looking at em? No, honey, I has done kep dis secret all dese years, and now I pass it on to you an you mus' keep it for yourself for the res' of de time, deed you mus', no one need evah know."

To her dying day Aunt Linda never forgot the despairing voice of this stricken girl, as she said: "Ah, but I know, my God, what have I done to deserve this?"

With no word of pity for the suffering old woman, she again clutched her arm, saying in a stifled whisper: "Again I ask you, who was, or is my father, and where is he?" Aunt Linda cowered before this angry goddess, though she was of her own flesh and blood, and softly said: "He is dead; died when you were about five years old. He lef you heaps of money, and in the care of a childless couple, who reared you as they own; he made 'em let you keep his name, I can't see why." With the utmost contempt Gladys cried, "Gold, gold, what is gold to such a heritage as this? an ocean of gold cannot wash away this stain."

Poor Gladys never knew how she reached her room. She turned to lock the door, resolved to fight this battle out for herself; then she thought of kind Mrs. Edwards. She would never need a mother's love so much as now. Of her own mother, she dared not even think. Then, too, why had she not thought of it before, this horrible story might not be true. Aunt Linda was probably out of her mind, and Mrs. Edwards would surely know.

By a striking coincidence Mrs. Edwards had noticed Linda's manner toward her fair guest, and knowing the old woman's connection with the Winne family, she had just resolved to send for her and question her as to her suspicions, if she had any, and at least caution her as to her manner.

Hearing a light tap upon her door, she hastily opened it. She needed but one glance at Gladys' unhappy countenance to tell her that it was too late; the mischief had already been done. With a cry of pity and dismay, Mrs. Edwards opened her arms and Gladys swooned upon her breast. Tenderly she laid her down and when she had regained consciousness, she sprang up, crying, "O Mrs. Edwards, say that it is not true, that it is some horrible dream from which I shall soon awaken?" How gladly would this good woman have sacrificed almost anything to spare this lovely girl, the innocent victim of an outrageous and blighting system, but Gladys was now a woman and must be answered. "Gladys, my dear," said Mrs. Edwards, "I wish I might save you further distress, by telling you that what I fear you have heard, perhaps from Aunt Linda herself, is not true. I am afraid it is all too true. But fortunately in your case no one need know. It will be safe with us and I will see that Aunt Linda does not mention it again, she ought not to have admitted it to you."

Very gently Mrs. Edwards confirmed Aunt Linda's story, bitterly inveighing against a system which mocked at marriage vows, even allowing a man to sell his own flesh and blood for gain. She told this chaste and delicate girl how poor slave girls, many of them most beautiful in form and feature, were not allowed to be modest, not allowed to follow the instincts of moral rectitude, that they might be held at the mercy of their masters. Poor Gladys writhed as if under the lash. She little knew what painful reasons Mrs. Edwards had for hating the entire system of debasement to both master and slave.

Her kind heart, southern born and bred as she was yearned to give protection and home to two beautiful girls, who had been shut out from her own hearthstone, which by right of justice and honor was theirs to share also. "Tell me, Gladys," she exclaimed, "which race is the more to be despised? Forgive me, dear, for telling you these things, but my mind was stirred by very bitter memories. Though great injustice has been done, and is still being done, I say to you, my child, that from selfish interest and the peace of my household, I could not allow such a disgrace to attach to one of my most honored guests. Do you not then see, dear, the unwisdom of revealing your identity here and now? Unrevealed, we are all your friends——" the covert threat lurking in the unfinished sentence was not lost upon Gladys. She arose, making an effort to be calm, but nervously seizing Mrs. Edwards' hand, she asked: "Have I no living white relatives?" Mrs. Edwards hesitated a moment, then said: "Yes, a few, but they are very wealthy and influential, and now living in the north; so that I am very much afraid that they are not concerned as to whether you are living or not. They knew, of course, of your birth; but since the death of your father, whom they all loved very much, I have heard, though it may be only gossip, that they do not now allow your name to be mentioned."

Gladys searched Mrs. Edwards' face with a peculiarly perplexed look; then in a plainer tone of voice, said: "Mrs. Edwards, it must be that only Negroes possess natural affection. Only think of it, through all the years of my life, and though I have many near relatives, I have been cherished in memory and yearned for by only one of them, and that an old and despised colored woman. The almost infinitesimal drop of her blood in my veins is really the only drop that I can consistently be proud of." Then, springing up, an indescribable glow fairly transfiguring and illuminating her face, she said: "My kind hostess, and comforting friend, I feel that I must tell Paul, but for your sake we will say nothing to the others, and if he does not advise me, yes, command me, to own and cherish that lonely old woman's love, and make happy her declining years, then he is not the man to whom I can or will entrust my love and life."

With burning cheeks, and eyes hiding the stars in their violet depths, her whole countenance glowing with a sense of pride conquered and love exalted, beautiful to see, she turned to Mrs. Edwards and tenderly kissing her, passed softly from the room.

For several moments, Mrs. Edwards stood where Gladys had left her. "Poor deluded girl," she mused. "Paul Westlake is by far one of the truest and noblest young men I have ever known, but let him beware, for there is even now coming to meet him the strongest test of his manhood principles he has ever had to face; beside it, all other perplexing problems must sink into nothingness. Will he be equal to it? We shall soon see."

Gladys, in spite of the sublime courage that had so exalted her but a moment before, felt her resolution weaken with every step. It required almost a super-human will to resist the temptation to silence, so eloquently urged upon her by Mrs. Edwards. But her resolution was not to be thus lightly set aside; it pursued her to her room, translating itself into the persistent thought that if fate is ever to be met and conquered, the time is now; delays are dangerous.

As she was about to leave her room on her mission, impelled by an indefinable sense of farewell, she turned, with her hand upon the door, as if she would include in this backward glance all the dainty furnishings, the taste and elegance everywhere displayed, and of which she had felt so much a part. Finally her wandering gaze fell upon a fine picture of Paul Westlake upon the mantel. Instantly there flashed into her mind the first and only public address she had ever heard Paul make. She had quite forgotten the occasion, except that it had some relation to a so-called "Negro problem." Then out from the past came the rich tones of the beloved voice as with fervid eloquence he arraigned the American people for the wrongs and injustice that had been perpetrated upon a weak and defenseless people through centuries of their enslavement and their few years of freedom.

With much feeling he recounted the pathetic story of this unhappy people when freedom found them, trying to knit together the broken ties of family kinship and their struggles through all the odds and hates of opposition, trying to make a place for themselves in the great family of races. Gladys' awakened conscience quickens the memory of his terrible condemnation of a system and of the men who would willingly demoralize a whole race of women, even at the sacrifice of their own flesh and blood.

With Mrs. Edwards' words still ringing in her ears, the memory of the last few words stings her now as then, except that now she knows why she is so sensitive as to their real import.

This message brought to her from out a happy past by Paul's pictured face, has given to her a light of hope and comfort beyond words. Hastily closing the door of her room, almost eagerly, and with buoyant step, she goes to seek Paul and carry out her mission.

To Paul Westlake's loving heart, Gladys Winne never appeared so full of beauty, curves and graces, her eyes glowing with confidence and love, as when he sprang eagerly forward to greet her on that eventful afternoon. Through all the subsequent years of their lives the tenderness and beauty of that afternoon together never faded from their minds.

They seemed, though surrounded by the laughter of friends and festive preparations, quite alone—set apart by the intensity of their love and happiness.

When they were about to separate for the night, Gladys turned to Paul, with ominous seriousness, yet trying to assume a lightness she was far from feeling, saying: "Paul, dear, I am going to put your love to the test tomorrow, may I?" Paul's smiling indifference was surely test enough, if that were all, but she persisted, "I am quite in earnest, dear; I have a confession to make to you. I intended to tell you this afternoon, but I could not cloud this almost our last evening together for a long time perhaps, so I decided to ask you to meet me in the library tomorrow morning at ten o'clock, will you?"

"Will I," Paul replied; "my darling, you know I will do anything you ask; but why tomorrow, and why so serious about the matter; beside, if it be anything that is to affect our future in any way, why not tell it now?" As Gladys was still silent, he added: "Dear, if you will assure me that this confession will not change your love for me in any way, I will willingly wait until tomorrow or next year; any time can you give me this assurance?" Gladys softly answered: "Yes, Paul, my love is yours now and always; that is, if you will always wish it." There was an expression upon her face he did not like, because he could not understand it, but tenderly drawing her to him, he said: "Gladys, dear, can anything matter so long as we love each other? I truly believe it cannot. But tell me this, dear, after this confession do I then hold the key to the situation?" "Yes, Paul, I believe you do; in fact I know that you will." "Ah, that is one point gained, tomorrow; then it can have no terrors for me," he lightly replied.

Gladys passed an almost sleepless night. Confident, yet

fearful, she watched the dawn of the new day. Paul, on the contrary, slept peacefully and rose to greet the morn with confidence and cheer. "If I have Gladys' love," he mused, "there is nothing in heaven or earth for me to fear."

At last the dreaded hour of ten drew near; their "Ides of March" Paul quoted with some amusement over the situation.

The first greeting over, the silence became oppressive. Paul broke it at last, saying briskly: "Now, dear, out with this confession; I am not a success at conundrums; another hour of this suspense would have been my undoing," he laughingly said.

Gladys, pale and trembling, felt all of her courage slipping from her; she knew not how to begin. Although she had rehearsed every detail of this scene again and again, she could not recall a single word she had intended to say. Finally she began with the reminder she had intended to use as a last resort: "Paul, do you remember taking me last Spring to hear your first public address; do you remember how eloquently and earnestly you pleaded the cause of the Negro?" Seeing only a growing perplexity upon his face, she cried: "O, my love, can you not see what I am trying to say? O, can you not understand? but no, no, no one could ever guess a thing so awful"; then sinking her voice almost to a whisper and with averted face, she said: "Paul, it was because you were unconsciously pleading for your own Gladys, for I am one of them."

"What nonsense is this," exclaimed Paul, springing from his chair; "it is impossible, worse than improbable, it cannot be true. It is the work of some jealous rival; surely, Gladys, you do not expect me to believe such a wild, unthinkable story as this!" Then controlling himself, he said: "O, my darling, who could have been so cruel as to have tortured you like this? If any member of this household has done this

thing let us leave them in this hour. I confess I do not love
the South or a Southerner, with my whole heart, in spite of
this 'united country' nonsense; yes, I will say it, and in spite
of the apparently gracious hospitality of this household."

Gladys, awed by the violence of his indignation, placed a
trembling hand upon his arm, saying: "Listen, Paul, do you
not remember on the very evening of your arrival here, of
my calling your attention to a tall turbaned servant with the
piercing eyes? Don't you remember I told you how she
annoyed me by following me everywhere, and you laughed
away my fears, and lovingly quieted my alarm? Now, O
Paul, how can I say it, but I must, that woman, that Negress,
who was once a slave, is my own grandmother." Without
waiting for him to reply, she humbly but bravely poured
into his ears the whole pitiful story, sparing neither father
nor mother, but blaming her mother least of all. Ah, the pity
of it!

Without a word, Paul took hold of her trembling hands
and drawing her toward the window, with shaking hand, he
drew aside the heavy drapery; then turning her face so that
the full glory of that sunlit morning fell upon it, he looked
long and searchingly into the beautiful beloved face, as if
studying the minutest detail of some matchless piece of stat-
uary. At last he found words, saying: "You, my flower, is it
possible that there can be concealed in this flawless skin, these
dear violet eyes, these finely chiseled features, a trace of
lineage or blood, without a single characteristic to vindicate
its presence? I will not believe it; it cannot be true." Then
baffled by Gladys' silence, he added, "and if it be true, surely
the Father of us all intended to leave no hint of shame or
dishonor on this, the fairest of his creations."

Gladys felt rather than heard a deepened note of tenderness
in his voice and her hopes revived. Then suddenly his calm

face whitened and an expression terrible to see swept over it. Instinctively Gladys read his thought. She knew that the last unspoken thought was of the future, and because she, too, realized that the problem of heredity must be settled outside the realm of sentiment, her breaking heart made quick resolve.

For some moments they sat in unbroken silence; then Gladys spoke: "Good bye, Paul, I see that you must wrestle with this life problem alone as I have; there is no other way. But that you may be wholly untrammelled in your judgment, I want to assure you that you are free. I love you too well to be willing to degrade your name and prospects by uniting them with a taint of blood, of which I was as innocent as yourself, until two days ago.

"May I ask you to meet me once more, and for the last time, at twelve o'clock tonight? I will then abide by your judgment as to what is best for both of us. Let us try to be ourselves today, so that our own heart-aches may not cloud the happiness of others. I said twelve o'clock because I thought we would be less apt to be missed at that hour of general rejoicings than at any other time. Good bye, dear, 'till then." Absently Paul replied: "All right, Gladys, just as you say; I will be here."

At the approach of the midnight hour Paul and Gladys slipped away to the library, which had become to them a solemn and sacred trysting place.

Gladys looked luminously beautiful on this Christmas eve. She wore a black gauze dress flecked with silver, through which her skin gleamed with dazzling fairness. Her only ornaments were sprigs of holly, their brilliant berries adding the necessary touch of color to her unusual pallor. She greeted Paul with gentle sweetness and added dignity and courage shining in her eyes.

Eagerly she scanned his coutenance and sought his eyes, and then she shrank back in dismay at his set face and stern demeanor.

Suddenly the strength of her love for him and the glory and tragedy which his love had brought to her life surged through her, breaking down all reserve. "Look at me, Paul," she cried in a tense whisper, "have I changed since yesterday; am I not the same Gladys you have loved so long?" In a moment their positions had changed and she had become the forceful advocate at the bar of love and justice; the love of her heart overwhelmed her voice with a torrent of words, she implored him by the sweet and sacred memories that had enkindled from the first their mutual love; by the remembered kisses, their after-glow flooding her cheeks as she spoke, and "O, my love, the happy days together," she paused, as if the very sweetness of the memory oppressed her voice to silence, and helpless and imploring she held out her hands to him.

Paul was gazing at her as if entranced, a growing tenderness filling and thrilling his soul. Gradually he became conscious of a tightening of the heart at the thought of losing her out of his life. There could be no such thing as life without Gladys, and when would she need his love, his protection, his tenderest sympathy so much as now?

The light upon Paul's transfigured countenance is reflected on Gladys' own and as he moves toward her with outstretched arms, in the adjoining room the magnificent voice of the beautiful singer rises in the Christmas carol, mingling in singular harmony with the plaintive melody as sung by a group of dusky singers beneath the windows.

# THE FOLLY OF MILDRED
*A Race Story With a Moral*

Ruth D. Todd

"Mildred James is the most ill-bred girl in the neighborhood, and I think it would be very foolish as well as quite useless to include her name."

The speaker was Lillian Jones, a tall, pretty girl with light brown complexion. Her companion—the girl addressed—was Laura Claire, who, if not quite so pretty, was, nevertheless, graceful and tall, and her plain dark face was lighted by a pair of soft, lustrous, almost fascinating dark eyes.

"That is just where we differ, Lillie. We must not exclude Miss James—on the contrary, her name should head the list," answered Laura, as she regarded her with a steady, reproving look.

Both young girls were seated before a writing table which was strewn with paper, pens, ink, etc. Laura was writing and Lillian was glancing over and inspecting each little note which was intended for the different girls of their exclusive circle.

"My dear Laura," exclaimed Lillian, rather impatiently, "surely you can't be serious! Why, the mere name of this person would tend to spoil the reputation of the entire club. Do you forget all the slighting remarks that are made regarding her character?"

Laura laid down her pen and gazed steadily out of the window for quite a few moments before replying. Then turning her gentle eyes full upon Lillian, she said:

*Colored American Magazine* 6 (March 1903): 364–70.

"No, I have not forgotten the rumors afloat, and that is the very reason why she should belong to this club." Lillian gazed at her incredulously.

"Dear me, you are extremely exasperating sometimes! It would better become us to erase the name 'social' from our club and place 'reform' in its stead, it would certainly be more appropriate—from your point of view at all events. Besides, we could go around town and hunt up all the disreputable girls and reform them."

"Please spare me your sarcasm, Lillie, and listen to rea-son—." But Lillian interrupted her impatiently.

"I hate reasoning about Mildred James! You know your-self, Laura, that she is so conceited and overbearing that at times she scarcely notices either of us. I hate this "color line" nonsense within our own race. It's bad enough to have a dividing line between the Negro and the Caucasian, but when it comes to one Negro ignoring another simply because their Anglo-Saxon blood is not so prominent, I lose all patience as well as respect for them unless they are ignorant. And you know, Laura, that there is no excuse for Mildred James. She has an excellent education, and despite the whispered com-ments and slighting remarks upon her reputation, she moves in good circles!" exclaimed Lillian with ardor. Laura gazed at her with a significant smile, and when she had finished she quietly replied:

"You are right, I dare say. At all events, what you have just said has a ring of solid fact. But that doesn't show that we must exclude her name.

"She is well-educated, as you before stated, but she must join this club, as only through this medium can she be reduced to a sense of her shame. She must know that even though she is a graduate of the normal school, she is still extremely ignorant in many ways. She must be made to understand that her tastes and manners are forced and exaggerated, her mind decidedly uncultivated, and her morals in sad need of repair. It is not to be wondered at that the 'colored' American girl is regarded by the Anglo-Saxon as utterly devoid of all morality when such girls as Miss James (as well as many others I could name), display such shameful conduct and set such disgraceful examples. Must we, then, stand calmly by and receive upon our shoulders the burden of more unfortunate sisters' disgrace without one protest? Decidedly not! It is our duty to show the world that there are a countless number of virtuous dark-skinned women. And this we can only accomplish by co-operation. Together we must try to advise with and reform our straying sisters, at the same time leading the younger ones in the path of virtue and womanly modesty. Consequently, we must reach out our hands and grasp that of those who have not completely gone astray, through the medium of this club. For although it bears the title of "Social," yet morals, social reform, literature, elocution and later-day etiquette are to be studied deeply, and discussed thoroughly."

"I had not looked at it in that light, Laura. I don't suppose any of the other girls would have studied the subject so deeply either. Your arguments are extremely convincing. But there are many reform clubs for straying girls, besides, I don't think that any of the other girls will be so deeply impressed as to consent to receive Mildred James among us, for she is so conceited and overbearing that she is simply unendurable. Those that have gone astray we will let them be, for our duty is to try and keep others on the path of true and virtuous womanhood," argued Lillie.

"That's the way of the world, and the world is very hard and cold. Miss James belongs to the Christian Endeavor Society, and associates with the best of us in all church affairs.

She is not wholly lost. The good in her may yet predominate over the evil. Anyhow, our interest in her will show that we are at least Christians trying to do, and to teach others to do what is right and womanly, for to be a lady one must be a true and modest woman."

"You are positively incorrigible, and there is another drawback also. After all we have said, it is possible that she may not wish to join us. You know a great number of our girls are very dark, and Mildred may simply reply by a pert note, 'declined with thanks,' or something equally as impertinent," persisted Lillian.

"Oh well, that's quite a different aspect. I shall include her name, and if she declines to join us, then she must abide by the consequences, for mark me, Lillian, some day she will be sorry for her folly."

"And I for one will be downright glad to see the day that her proud spirit is humbled, for she is too overbearing for good luck!"

"We all have our faults, my dear Lillie, and yours, I'm sorry to say, is impetuosity. You must try to check that impulsive manner of yours and be not quite so hasty in your judgment of others. Whatever you think or may say of an erring girl, remember that a great deal depends upon what sort of home influence one has had," said Laura impulsively. But at that moment several girls came in and the conversation terminated abruptly.

*     *     *     *     *

Mildred James was truly a most beautiful girl. Her well developed figure was tall and graceful, and her complexion was exceedingly light. She possessed a wealth of luxuriant and rippling brown hair, and large, flashing brown eyes. She was also well educated and fashionable, though decidedly supercilious. Her mother, a stout, yellow woman, had done all in her power to (using one of the old woman's phrases), "make a lady o' Milly."

She had toiled early and late over the wash-tub and ironing board, and so far as education and dress was concerned, she had not labored in vain. But in her efforts she had over-looked—or rather was ignorant of the minor things which helped to form the character of a lady.

Aunt Dolly (as the old lady was generally called) had petted and spoiled Mildred all her life, so when Mildred had expressed her disgust of all manual toil, her mother had given in to her, inwardly assuring herself that some day "Milly'd be a great school teacher and take care of her ol' ma." And while Aunt Dolly bent over tubs of streaming, foamy suds in the kitchen, dainty Mildred played the piano in the parlor, or attended numerous church entertainments and parties.

Consequently while she was growing from girlhood into womanhood, all girlish confidences and minor things such as every mother should share with her daughter were withheld from Aunt Dolly and Mildred became a haughty, conceited, and overbearing creature, deeming even her mother far beneath her, as well as all others of darker hue. On account of her extreme whiteness of skin, she had obtained a position as typewriter in an Anglo-Saxon office, and many were the whispered comments bestowed upon her name. But whenever they were so unfortunate as to reach her ears, these whisper-ings only received a slight shrug of her dainty shoulders and her silent contempt.

Being so very beautiful it is not necessary to mention the fact that she possessed many admirers.

One of the most ardent was Robert Thompson, a rather handsome young man, though exceedingly dark, which last was, with Mildred, his only drawback. On the same evening that Lillian Jones and Laura Claire were discussing the events which transpired in the first part of the story, Mildred was making her toilette preparatory to attending a school reception, when her mother called to tell her that "Bob," Jinnie Thompson's boy, was "in the settin' room to see her."

She had taken great pains with her toilette, and when she entered the parlor with her hair caught back in a loose coil down on her neck, and clad in a perfectly fitting gown of the palest pink satin and rich black velvet ribbons, Robert thought that he had never before seen such a lovely woman.

And before he was aware of the fact he was at her side, telling her of his love for her and begging her to be his bride.

"My dear Robert, you must certainly be mad to carry on in this ridiculous fashion, why, you have hardly said good evening yet." She said this in her most careless manner, at the same time motioning to him to be seated.

"Oh Mildred darling, pray don't jest with me. I was never more serious before in my life. I love you, Mildred—"

"Stop right where you are, Bobby, for after I have talked this matter over with you and—er—shown you how ridiculous you can be at times, you may regret to have said so much. In the first place, you are poor as a church mouse, and you know that I must have money and plenty of it when I make up my mind to get married—" But Robert interrupted her, "I am not wealthy and that's a fact, but then I am on the road to make money, besides, I am going to be promoted to a higher office within a few weeks. My employer has just notified me, and the salary I'll receive will enable me to keep a wife in good circumstances. Oh Milly, think what you are saying! I love you well, and will try to make you a good husband."

"It's no use, Bobby, we were not made for each other. You

see I like you real well, but not well enough to trust my future with you. I—we should live miserably for I should never be satisfied to do housework, and you certainly could not afford to keep a servant. I—I am sorry, but I will be a sister to you," and although her countenance was quite serene, he could see that her eyes were mocking him.

"Great Scott, Mildred, this is no laughing matter with me, I am no boy to be jested with! I love you and asked you to be my wife and—you make a fellow feel like a—"

"If you are going to swear about this matter, I'll leave the room until you are through—"

"No—no—please don't go—I'm a brute, Mildred darling, say that you will be mine," he pleaded.

"Whether I will or not?" she asked, jeeringly.

"Good God, Mildred, I am not playing with you. Answer me! Will you be my wife?"

"No, I will not be your wife," she answered seriously enough now.

"Why won't you? I am sure you like me well enough; you have led me on shamefully."

"Do you want me to tell you the reason why?"

"Certainly."

"You are sure you won't be angry?"

"I'll try not to be."

"Very well then, you are too—dark, and you haven't got money enough," she replied, with her eyes on the carpet.

Robert did not start or make any outward show of his injured feelings, but the words stung him to the quick. He stood still regarding her scarlet, shamed countenance with an expression of incredulity. The scales fell from his eyes. Her beauty faded and he saw only a cold, heartless woman of the world. Instantly the rumors he had heard concerning her reputation returned to him. He had believed them false—

but she had just told him that money with her was a necessary article. She must then be her employer's—impossible! Mildred James, whom he had thought so sweet, so good and pure, this beautiful girl standing before him the—the mistress of some white man? Oh God it must be true! She had almost confessed it. And—he had asked her to be his wife. But she stole a frightened glance at his face.

"What's the matter, Bobby, are you angry? I—I love you—"

"Enough Miss James—do not make me despise you. I understand, it is well—good bye. Good bye—and may God forgive you—for I cannot!" he cried hoarsely as he reached for his hat and left the apartment. He found his way out alone, and as he was descending the front steps a man hurried past him up them and pulled the bell vigorously. It was Lemuel P. Flemings, one of—or rather—the favorite admirer of Mildred. He had come to escort her to the reception.

*   *   *   *   *

Lemuel Flemings was a good looking man. Tall, very light, with jet black curls and a handsome black moustache. He was from "up north," and was reputed to have lots of money. He had a smooth tongue and was a well spoken young man, and therefore with the girls "a great catch."

Aunt Dolly did not like him and cautioned Mildred against him.

"This here Lem Flemin's, he comes from God knows whar, fillin' you all young gals haid wid a lot ob nonsense en high perlutin' words twell you nigh 'bout gone crazy over 'im. 'Deed I like that ar boy o' Jinnie Thompson's a heap sight better an I'm positive he'll make you the best husband ef he is black. Black is honest, anyhow you knows mo' 'bout Bob en you do 'bout this Lem Flemin's."

But Mildred had flown into a passion, saying that Mr.

Flemings was not only a gentleman, but wealthy accordingly. That she supposed she was free to marry whom she chose. And that if she married Mr. Flemings she would live like a lady, whereby if she married Bobby, she would probably break her back over the wash tub and ironing board. But her mother had replied that "an old sheep knew the road and young lambs must learn the way," also "if she made her bed hard she must lay on it."

But nothing could move Mildred once she was bent on doing mischief, and she led him on as she had done many other young men with honest intentions.

But she had made up her mind to accept Lemuel and live in a whirl of gaiety and fashionable life as "That beautiful Mrs. Flemings," before whom all should bow.

So the engagement was announced on the same night that she had so coolly thrown Bobby over.

As Lillian Jones had predicted, Mildred had sent a dainty note to the club, "declining with thanks," on a plea of being too busy with sundry social duties to find time to attend the meetings.

"I knew she would do this!" exclaimed Lillie, as she and Laura were alone in the latter's sitting room.

"Poor girl, it's too bad; you see her mother has spoiled her to death, and she knows we have heard certain rumors, and how she threw poor Bobby over, so she thinks she will have no dealings with us whatever!" said Laura, sympathizingly.

"It's a mighty good thing she didn't, for I am sure she would have been snubbed shamefully. And the way she is leading Flemings around is perfectly disgraceful," exclaimed Lillie.

"Oh, not so shameful after all; you know she is engaged to him. You are so unjust, Lillie," pleaded Laura.

"Oh, I am not so kind hearted as you are, Laura. You were even kind enough to pick poor Bobby up after she had thrown him over."

"Oh Lillie!"

"Now please don't think I meant that as a slur. What I mean is that you are trying to comfort him with your at all times true sympathy, but," and she stole a sly glance of Laura's face, "you are losing your heart in an attempt to mend Bobby's."

"Am I? Well, I confess I always did like Bobby, and he says that he doesn't think he really loved Mildred. He was simply blinded, and after what she confessed to him, he was glad that she wouldn't accept him."

"Oh, what did she confess to him?" asked Lillian, consumed with curiosity.

"Why, he would not tell me. He said that whatever it was it caused him to lose all respect for her," answered Laura.

So Mildred was married and left town for a two months' wedding trip, and when she returned the latest news afloat was that Robert Thompson and Laura Claire were engaged to be married. It surprised her too, for she thought surely that Bobby would not get over his heart ache for at least a year, and it was hardly six months before he was actually engaged to be married. She loved Bobby better than she did her husband, but thought to get over it with her husband's great wealth.

But when six months of married life had gone by, and operations on the great Flemings mansion—which had been rumored was to be erected—had not begun, people began to talk and to say that "Lem Flemings wasn't what he was cracked up to be," and " 'Deed Lem didn't have nothin' nohow but education and high-perlutin' words." One old gossip went so far as to say that " 'Deed her old man often met Lem comin' out er Jayson's gambling rooms."

This was very true, for Lemuel was an inveterate gambler, and many were the nights that his beautiful young wife had waited his return in vain. This was a sore trial to Mildred, who had expected so much from this marriage, and when it became known that Robert Thompson had made a great deal of money of late and was building a beautiful house on —— — avenue, she soon began to look faded and old.

At the end of one year of married life Milly found herself the mother of a bouncing baby boy, the arrival of which brought Lemuel to a sense of shame, and for three months he devoted himself to his wife and babe. But the novelty of this wore off after a while and he took to the old life again. And people began to whisper that "Lem Flemings wouldn't rest twell he went to jail," and that "all of Milly's fine dresses and jewelry had been sold to pay Lem's gambling debts."

All of which was very true, and before Mildred had been married two years, she found herself a veritable slave, toiling like her mother before her, that her sweet young child might have bread to eat, while Robert Thompson and his dashing young bride lived in a whirl of fashionable society.

# BERNICE, THE OCTOROON

*Mrs. M.[arie] Louise Burgess-Ware*

## I

> "Learn to dissemble wrongs, to smile at injuries,
> And suffer crimes thou want'st the power to punish;
> Be easy, affable, familiar, friendly;
> Search and know all mankind's mysterious ways,
> But trust the secret of thy soul to none;
> This is the way,
> This only, to be safe in such a world as this is."
> —Rowe's Ulysses

"I'll not grieve longer over what may never be. Sometimes I think my lot hard, cruel, and unjust, then I remember that others suffer as keenly, if not more, than I."

These words were spoken by a beautiful girl, scarcely out of her teens. Her evenly developed head was covered with golden curls that reminded me of burnished gold, as the rays of sunlight fell upon them. Her blonde complexion, dainty mouth, and deep blue eyes completed one of the loveliest faces.

She lifted her tear-stained face, so like a Madonna's, filled

*Colored American Magazine* 6, pts. 1–4 (Sept. 1903): 607–26; 6, pts. 5–7 (Oct. 1903): 652–57.

with unutterable love. Rising, she exclaimed, "I must attend to my duties. I want no traces of tears on my face. Inquisitive little children may ask questions that perhaps will make my heart bleed." She bathed her swollen eyes, brushed back the curls from her forehead, and rang the bell which told the children recess was over. About forty little ones came marching into the school-room, all sizes and ages, and of every conceivable shade peculiar to the Negro race. Such bright faces, sparkling eyes and pretty teeth!

"Miss Bernice," as they called her, seemed to have good command of these little ones, although she appeared to be of a gentle, yielding temperament. Could you have looked into this country school-house, with its rude benches, ragged children and great inconveniences, you would have wondered what this college-bred lady was doing in the back woods of a Southern State, when a teacher less tenderly reared would have answered as well. Was it for money? Was it love of the race? The latter was the reason. This cultured octoroon, refined and fair as an Anglo-Saxon, was one of a despised race, and had only recently learned it.

Bernice Silva was a native of Ohio. Her father, a man of wealth and position, had married Pauline Blanchard twenty years before this story opens. She was the daughter of a wealthy Kentucky planter, and had been educated in a Western college, together with her sister, Mrs. Gadsden. The young couple were very happy, and when Bernice came with her wealth of golden curls, she was called "papa's sunbeam" by the delighted young father, whose life she crowned with joy.

All that wealth could bestow was lavished upon this child, and at a proper age, she, too, was sent to college. She became a great favorite with teachers and classmates, because of her winsome disposition and brilliant gifts as a student, her musical talent being of a very high order.

Mrs. Gadsden had a daughter Lenore who was also at college with Bernice. The two cousins were exact opposites in all things,—Lenore was as dark as Bernice was fair, as envious as Bernice was generous; she had a heart filled with jealousy and hatred for her beautiful cousin. Beautiful herself, her haughtiness repelled those who aspired to her friendship. This was more the result of over-indulgence, for after Mr. Gadsden's death, the child was given her own will in all things.

The winter after the girls were graduated was spent by both families in the picturesque town of St. Augustine, Florida. Society there was made up of many Northern and Southern aristocrats, who greeted with open arms two beautiful and accomplished young women, possessed of wealth and prestige. There was a flutter of expectancy throughout the little colony when cards were issued for a reception on Thanksgiving evening by Mrs. Silva, and the fortunate recipients counted themselves very lucky.

It was a night long remembered in St. Augustine. The spacious rooms were crowded by brave men and fair women. Flowers filled the air with fragrance, birds sang in gilded cages, fountains played, their perfumed waters falling in prismatic shades under constantly changing colored electrical lights; the dreamy, pulsating notes of the band were a welcome accompaniment to romantic conversation.

It was a memorable reception for all, but for Garrett Purnello life took a sudden change. The promising young barrister never again had eyes for a woman's fair face. He was much impressed by Bernice's beauty and modesty. He, with his passionate Spanish blood, loved her then and forever; she, with her pure heart returned his love unconsciously.

# II

Several days later, Bernice saw her father coming towards the house, accompanied by Mr. Purnello. They came immediately to the drawing-room where Mrs. Silva and her daughter were sitting. After the usual greetings, Mr. Silva said: "I brought Mr. Purnello home to lunch, and we have been having a lively discussion of the race question. This recent disfranchisement, and the attitude taken by the majority of our sound citizens towards the black men of this country, appears unjust to me. To be sure, the ignorant vote of any people is not fit to be counted, but still the Negro excites my pity. Ushered out of slavery into an unknown sphere of life, many have made themselves worthy to bear the name of citizen. And wholesale disfranchisement is to rob him almost of life itself. One wonders if mob law is not a stigma on our loved republic; this sweet land of liberty, the land of the noble free. It is as if the fatherhood of God and the brotherhood of man existed only in legends of Holy Writ. Peaceful black citizens are driven from their homes because a mob decides that they must leave a community. Is there no panacea for this evil, for evil it is?"

"To my mind, there is but one remedy," replied the younger man, "and that is being applied by Booker T. Washington and other advocates of Industrial Education. The masses of the blacks and the poor whites of our Southland must be educated, not only in books, but in trades and all those other things which crush out idleness and keep down vice. If we consider the matter seriously, we find that all this disturbance arises between the poor whites and the illiterate blacks. The intelligent Negro does not clamor for social equality; he is satisfied to be a leader of his people."

"What you say is true," replied Mr. Silva, "but it is an outrage to know that men are driven from their homes because they are Negroes. Debarred from all things which protect the white laborer, yet in spite of all this, they multiply and grow in mental and physical strength. Like the Jews they are favored of God, although despised by men. But this is dull conversation for the ladies; we will change the subject."

"But, papa," exclaimed Bernice, "I have read much concerning this matter; do not discontinue the conversation because mamma and I are here. I am sure that what involves the welfare of our country is interesting to us, and must be to all true women."

Garrett listened eagerly; it was rare to find so sweet a girl and one so young, finding attraction in words of wisdom and discretion. A pleasant hour was spent about the social board, and then the two gentlemen spent another enjoyable hour in the music room. Garrett was entranced by the wonderful gifts possessed by Bernice. Thus sped many pleasant days, merging into weeks, and it was soon plain to the onlooking world that the young people loved each other. It was the old, old story, ever fresh, ever new.

Lenore looked on with a heart swelling with envy and indignation. She was beautiful too; why was it that the only man she had ever felt she could love, found no attraction in her? That Bernice should take him from her filled her heart with most bitter thoughts. She clinched her hands in rage as she walked the floor of her room, and swore to part them.

Very soon the engagement of these popular young people was announced. Mr. Silva reluctantly consented to give his treasure to Garrett. All his affection was centered in this beautiful child, and he could not bear to think of trusting her happiness in a stranger's hands; but he smiled as he said to his wife—

" 'Thus it is our daughters leave us,
Those we love and those who love us.' "

# III

About six weeks after the betrothal, Mrs. Purnello and
Garrett took tea with Bernice. Mr. and Mrs. Silva had taken
a trip to Tuskegee Institute. They had given considerable
money for the education of the Freedmen, and so wished to
see this school of schools. Mrs. Gadsden was acting hostess,
and had planned a very pretty tea. Lenore had changed greatly
during the past few weeks, and everyone attributed it to
ill-health. In spite of this, she tried to assume her usual manner.

While they were enjoying the tea an old Negro servant
came into the room, with some tea cakes which had been
forgotten. Bernice smiled at her, and admired the pretty
bandana 'kerchief which she wore.

Mrs. Purnello, with a scornful smile, said quickly, "Bernice, don't admire these Negroes; they get beside themselves.
I despise them; if it were not for their labor, I would be glad
to have them swept out of existence."

Bernice was startled at such language from a lady's lips.
Garrett was mortified; he knew his mother hated Negroes,
and was oftentimes very eccentric about them. But such an
outburst startled him.

Bernice glanced at Mrs. Purnello and said, "You surely
could not have had a good old mammy for your nurse. Why
not let these people live and thrive? We are taught, and
pretend to believe that God created all alike; that Christ died
for all, and commands us as Christians to love our fellow
man. We are taught next to our duty to God, to love our

neighbor as ourselves. How can you entertain such a feeling in your bosom, and be a member of Christ's Church?"

"Law, Honey, you'se a Christian. Don' yer waste yer bref; she ain't got no 'ligion uv any kind. My sole dis minute am heap whiter'n her face," and the old woman shrugged her shoulders, and withdrew from the dining room.

Bernice looked pained. She was about to say something, when Mrs. Purnello said in her haughtiest manner, "Bernice, we will not discuss this subject further; you must relinquish some of your strange ideas about this matter. My son's future wife cannot hold such views. You have much to learn; I hope never to hear such expressions again in my presence."

"But, my dear madam, I have no desire to lay aside my good breeding nor my own convictions. I can never learn to be cruel to a race of people, who have never injured me. We have become rich through their toil," replied Bernice. "Their faults have not blinded me to their nobler qualities. They have hearts as tender as my own. All my life my heart has gone out to them, and when my parents have received appeals for help from their various homes and institutions of learning, I have longed to help them myself in some way."

Lenore had sat a silent spectator of the scene. Now she spoke.

"You can have your wish; nothing is easier, for you are one of them. Do you not know your mother is of Negro ancestry?"

For a moment dead silence followed her words. Bernice turned white to the lips. Garrett overcame his first anger and consternation with a laugh. He had seen through Lenore's jealousy for some time. But Mrs. Purnello held up both hands in horror. She moved away from Bernice, as if the air were contaminated.

Recovering herself by a great effort, Bernice smiled. She was not now the little girl whom every one thought so meek and gentle; her eyes sparkled, her air breathed defiance.

"How long have you known this, Lenore?"

"My parents have always known it," replied Lenore, now somewhat frightened at what she had done.

"Then, if one drop of that despised blood flows in my veins, loyal to that race I will be. I did not expect such a blow from you, Lenore."

The latter made no reply, but left the room, apparently satisfied with the mischief done.

"Garrett," said Mrs. Purnello, greatly agitated, "Bernice cannot expect you to fulfill your engagement under these unfortunate conditions. You cannot marry a Negro."

Garrett had been silent all through the storm aroused by Lenore's assertion. He faced his mother with unusual sternness on his handsome face.

"Mother, you have said enough; if you have no respect for us, have a little for yourself. Do not hide all that is womanly in you. Remember, Bernice is a woman, and has a woman's tender feelings, and it is not necessary to try to crush her. She is dearer to me than ever, because if she be really a Negro, she will need me more than ever. She may be good and pure, but she will be counted by many as no better than the most common type of her race. I will stand by her until death. I see in her all that is pure and lovely in woman. I love her with a love devoid of prejudice; it is too late for that to separate us."

"Then you are no longer my son."

"As you say, mother. A man's word is his bond. I am strong; she is weak. I will protect her. I am willing to give up even you, because you are wrong. Where is the warm feeling which should fill your bosom as a woman? I fear, mother, there is a touch of something unnatural and inhuman in your conduct."

"Bernice, let me appeal to you. Garrett is unreasonable and Quixotic. After the first few months of married life, he would become dissatisfied and unhappy. But if you will keep this matter secret, perhaps we can hide it from the world; but if you persist in allying your fortunes with Negroes, then our friendship must end. I love Garrett; I would like to see him happy, but I love my good name too well to wish him to marry into an alien race. As you value your future happiness, think well before you decide."

Bernice smiled. "My dear Mrs. Purnello, I see no difference between you and me; my tastes are as refined and cultured as yours. My skin is fairer than many of our acquaintances. My parents as cultured. Why should I be persecuted because mamma is of mixed origin? Did not God create all in His own image? Are we not taught that He is the father of all mankind? Because the despised blood of the Negro chances to flow through my veins, must I be trampled upon and persecuted? Let me ask you, how did it happen that your ancestors, whom you claim were so chivalrous and aristocratic, stooped to mix with an inferior race, and thus flood the country with the mulattoes, quadroons, and octoroons that are so bitterly despised by many of both races? Well may you blush when you think of such chivalry! My heart warms to the inferior race, and I will give all that I have in learning and culture, to follow in the footsteps of the great Teacher, who said, 'Inasmuch as ye have done it unto the least of these my brethren, ye have done it unto me.' "

Mrs. Purnello left the room without replying to Bernice.

Turning to Bernice, Garrett exclaimed passionately, "Think, Bernice, all that this means. Can you stand the snubs, insults, and temptations? My dear girl, you know not what you will have to encounter. Many will think you an Anglo-Saxon, and will treat you kindly, but if they find out what you really are, there is no ignorant Negro who will be treated more contemptuously. I cannot bear to think of it. Marry me, and forget all that has just happened."

"Garrett, I appreciate your kind thoughts for my welfare. I could not agree to anything but the right. Were I to accept your proposition I would feel like a woman wearing a mask. There is too much at stake. The sins of the fathers are surely visited upon the children. The Negro blood would show itself, if not in my children, in some of the coming generations. The so-called curse will follow us, and I would not blight your life. I know I have been beyond recognition all these years; others have been and others will be," replied Bernice sadly.

"I admire and love you more than ever; do not come to a hasty conclusion, even though you are right; you must not injure yourself. Talk with your parents, be guided by them; to-morrow we may be better able to decide what is best to be done under the circumstances. You are mine; I will never give you up this side of eternity."

He was sincere; this was no passing fancy. He loved her. He began to wonder why the white man should be the dominant race, and considered so far above his educated Negro brother. In his heart, he thought it unjust. He was deeply grieved and sorely perplexed in spirit. He thought of the passage of Scripture, "God is no respecter of persons." He wondered what it meant. His own sorrow was not to be compared with his sympathy for Bernice. When he thought of what she had been subjected to, the muscles of his face became rigid. The veins became prominent; his countenance showed the great anguish through which he was passing.

When Mr. Silva learned of the unwomanly conduct of Lenore, he was shocked; first of all, because of her treachery; secondly, because of the Negro blood in his wife's veins. It was true that Mrs. Silva and Mrs. Gadsden were only half-sisters. They were originally from Kentucky. Their father, Joseph Blanchard, had been a wealthy slave owner. He had educated them at the same college, and when, by accident, Beatrice had learned that Pauline's mother was her "mammy," she was too horrified to expose it. She loved her sister, and as the world was none the wiser, it was quietly covered up, and both daughters married well. Had Garrett Purnello loved Lenore, this story would never have been written.

Mr. and Mrs. Silva were grieved for Bernice. They cared nothing for themselves, but to have her life clouded in its springtime caused them much pain. They knew they could return to their Western home unmolested. But Bernice was determined not to sail under false colors, and had made up her mind to teach her people. She had a deep sense of right and wrong, and then, knowing the depth of the chasm existing between the two races, was not willing to remain in a false position. She knew nothing of her people, their manners and customs, nor the hardships which many had to endure. She did not dream of the discouragements awaiting her. She saw only their needs and her ability to help them. The ragged, ignorant, or unclean of either race, she had never come in contact with. She was ignorant of the vice that existed in the world; you can imagine her consternation at the sights she saw. After much persuasion, her parents consented to let her go to Maryland to teach a parish school. When our story opens she is in the schoolroom, trying to teach forty mischievous little children.

# IV

"Fairlily, sit down my dear," Bernice said, pointing to a little picanniny as black as midnight. Her head was covered with short, knotty hair, that looked as if a comb had never passed through it.

What a name for such a looking child. "Fairlily." She wondered where the mother got the name. Then there was a little boy named "Esther." He had an unusually large head and beautiful black eyes. His body was small and badly nourished, and the little creature seemed to have what is known as the "rickets." The next one that attracted her attention was as white as the others were black. Her face was freckled, her hair sandy and stringy. She looked very much out of place. Looking about her, Bernice noticed similar children scattered here and there. She thought this the most motley crowd she had ever seen; there were no two alike.

"And these are my people," she mused, "indeed it is a mixture. Where did they come from, and how did they become like this?" It never entered her pure mind that many of these knew no father; it did not dawn upon her that a race despising hers was at every opportunity flooding the country with children, born to be despised and persecuted. Some of these little ones were ragged and hungry, whose fathers lived in luxury, while their mothers were ignorant women who knew nothing of the development of their intellectual being, but allowed their animal natures to predominate, and brought forth children regardless of the laws of God or man. Immorality to these people had no meaning, and thus these poor little children's opportunities to become noble men and women, were very limited.

Bernice was the picture of a modern Priscilla in her simple black gown, white cuffs and apron. Her eyes were red from excessive weeping, her heart cried out in its loneliness, her task was very hard. Her boarding place was unlike her comfortable home. The log cabin had only three rooms, two of which were unfinished. Her room was the best in the house, and had a clean, bare floor, an old-fashioned bed covered with brilliantly colored quilts of various designs, a strip of home-made rag carpet answered for a mat, and two pine chairs and a table. The people around her were very sensitive, and she had to guard against hurting anyone's feelings, for they soon would brand her as an "eddicated and stuck-up yaller nigger." The food was coarse, the greens, which she ate very often, were a new article of food to her; the corn pones seemed heavy; the biscuits were a sore trial to her digestive organs, for she was used to home-made, light bread, and had never eaten very many biscuits. She had longed for a porterhouse steak, broiled and juicy, but that was unheard-of fare.

In spite of the many disadvantages, she labored on, teaching a Sabbath School in connection with her other work. It pleased her to see the children eagerly listening to the story she told them about the first Christmas. One little fellow with bright eyes, said, "Law, Miss Bernice, I never knew Christmas meant a thing more'n hanging up yer stockin's and gittin' presents. No one ever tole us anything else. Why, we gits up and runs across to Aunt Nancy and hollers, 'Christmas Gift!' She grins and says, 'You der same, honey,' and we all has a big time. Ma comes home from de white folks, and den we hear de chickens holler, and de eggs a beatin', and Miss Nicey, yer kin smell de egg nogg way down de road. I tastes de poun' cake right now."

Bernice smiled. She thought that there was no need of

going to Africa to do missionary work, there was plenty right here. Her sewing school was enjoyed not only by the little girls, but their mothers came also. One day each week she taught them how to cook and prepare food for the table in a scientific manner. Such poverty, ignorance and superstition as she saw among the lowest types! Christian education was sadly needed to save both soul and body. The public schools kept open only three or four months during the year, then to the pea-picking and other farming! Parents barely received money enough to provide for their large families, and the people were types of illiteracy. There were many strange customs which Bernice had never heard of, such as wakes. When the people died, in the dead hours of the night you would hear wild shrieks go up in the air, which would make you shudder, and then again you would hear a weird melody, followed by a loud prayer over the dead. Everyone at the wakes did not partake of the spirits of Frumenti, which almost always was there, but enough drank of it to give much life to the occasion.

The spiritual condition was bad; preachers were almost always called of God, but not very often educated and fitted for the work. The preacher was judged by the strength of his lungs, and oftentimes the number of big words which he used. A revival meant great excitement, exhortations, great shouting and much hilarity. Mourners went to the mourners' bench under the heat of a sermon which had vividly painted a picture of a burning lake, and his satanic majesty and his fiendish host standing ready with their cloven feet and pitch-forks to throw the victims into the lake before them. People who mourned often, wrestled for several days before Satan would leave their bodies, and when they felt him as he departed, they arose and made known their experiences to the remaining sinners.

Many might have thought this ludicrous, but Bernice thought it a sad sight in a Christian land. The Negroes whom she had seen during her life were not of this type; they were people whom education and Christianity had made intelligent men and women. She felt certain that religion scared into a person could not last after the excitement was over, and how she longed to instill into the little hearts under her control that God's Holy Word and His Spirit would make them better, if they would quietly ask him, and make up their little minds to do His will.

This town was twenty miles from any railroads, hence its backwardness.

Bernice had imported an organ. The little voices were so sweet and mellow, she often likened them to the mocking birds which warbled before her school door. Many of the people had never seen or heard an organ. How they did enjoy the music. It was not long before she learned to accompany their beautiful plantation melodies, although to a listener they are much sweeter without an instrument.

There was an interesting old lady who never missed a Sabbath. She led the melodies, and the children joined in with much fervor. Bernice could not help being touched by the weird tones and the soul-stirring words.

One Sabbath morning there was a funeral, and dear Aunt Martha led the music at the graveyard. They had all assembled around the grave; the air was filled with unearthly shrieks, the mourners were determined that everybody should know they were bereaved. Even in the midst of all the sorrow, there was something most amusing. One of the mourners had a red bandana handkerchief, wiping her eyes under a heavy crape veil. The minister committed the body to the ground, with a voice loud and trembling. Old Aunt Martha raised her tune.

Mother an' father, pray for me,
Mother an' father, pray for me,
Mother an' father, pray for me,
I've got a home in Galilee.

CHORUS
Can't yer live humble? praise King Jesus,
Can't yer live humble? dying Lamb.

The mourners wailed, the brothers shouted. Such a scene! Bernice had never witnessed the like before nor since. She looked towards her friend, Aunt Martha. Great drops of perspiration were rolling off her face, the tears were streaming down her cheeks, as she sang,

When you hear my coffin sound,
When you hear my coffin sound,
When you hear my coffin sound,
You may know I've gone around.

CHORUS
Can't yer live humble? praise King Jesus,
Can't yer live humble? dying Lamb.

There stood the old lady, under the shade of the trees, singing with all her might. Eighty-one years old, the mother of twenty-one children, unlettered, but trilling like a bird.


V


Bernice was an earnest Christian; she believed above all things in the preservation of the purity of womanhood. She wanted to make every woman the highest type of truth, beauty, and goodness. The scenes which she witnessed in her new surroundings were strange to her, and yet they were real. What

had she known of temptation—she who had been surrounded
by all that was pure and lovely, whose moral and religious
training had been of the highest order? She was unacquainted
with the ways of the outside world; her life had been lived
among those whose every thought had been for her and of
her. She knew nothing of the life of the lowly, of the sin
which surrounded them everywhere, of the temptations which
they resisted as well as yielded to. In her weak way she tried
to reach the hearts of the women to teach them by her example,
as well as by talks in her mothers' meetings, that if they
overcame temptation and repented of their sins then would
come real strength of character and true religion.

She had heard lectures by people engaged in work among
the black men. She had thought much of the degradation and
ignorance mentioned was exaggeration. She was entirely unprepared for the scenes which she encountered. Superstition
prevailed. There were signs for everything. The guinea hens
could not "holler" unless fallen weather was sure to follow.
An owl could not hoot in the tree before the house unless it
must be followed by a death in that family. The rooster could
not crow before the door unless hasty news followed, and if
he dared to strut away from the door and crow as he was
leaving what would be the result? Why, the news of a death
would soon reach the family. The dog must not howl, if so,
the neighborhood all wondered to whom this death warning
had been sent. These are only a very few of the many strange
signs Bernice listened to.

She visited the homes of the children, and when sickness
came it was she who knew just what to do for them, and how
to do it. She showed the old people many things that they
might do for the comfort of their suffering ones. She spent
many nights by the bedsides of the sick ones; she prayed for

them, comforted those who mourned, and in numerous ways brought sunshine into the homes.

There was one old mammy, "Aunt Lizzie," by name. She was one of those tall, well-built Negro women of pure blood, perfect in physique, and handsome in features. Her black skin was as smooth as satin, her teeth like pearl. She had a little daughter wasting away with consumption. Nor was it to be wondered at, for they lived in a two-room house, unfit for renting. There was a family of nine. Tina, the oldest, lay dying. The parents were what is known as "hardshell Baptists." They believed in foot-washing, and many other strange customs, known only to that set of Baptists. When Bernice came to care for her pupil, they looked on in wonder. Their house was very humble; it boasted of two beds in the front room and one in the kitchen. On one of the beds in the front room Tina lay, on the brink of eternity. The mother was washing, trying to obtain the means to provide extra comforts for Tina, the father working hard to earn the regular support of four dollars a week. Bernice made the room tidy, bathed the feverish child, and made her little delicacies. Tina grasped Bernice's hands as she lay dying, and exclaimed, "Oh, Miss Bernice, you've done tole me 'bout heaven, Jesus and the angels; tell Mammy too." And with Bernice's hands on her burning brow the child's spirit went into Paradise.

Bernice helped prepare her for burial, and if you can picture that family in its poverty and sorrow, the pine coffin, costing the paltry sum of seven dollars, the golden-rod and daisies which covered the coffin that contained the loving mother's child, you would feel that it is only too true that one-half the world knows not how the other half lives. The love in that ignorant yet tender heart would put to shame some of our more intelligent mothers. Then if you could

have looked into that church, and seen Bernice and her pupils
with their hands clasped, their heads bowed in prayer, and
the sweet voices chanting,

> "My God, my father, while I stray,
> Far from my home on life's rough way,
> O teach me from my heart to say,
> Thy will be done."

All these scenes reached Bernice's sensitive nature, and
drew her nearer to God and bound her more closely to her
poor, despised and ignorant people.

## VI

Three years rolled by, and Bernice longed for a change of
scene. She had not been away from Leeville since she came
there, and had it not been for the many periodicals which she
received weekly she would not have known what was happening in the outside world. Many of her classmates had corre-
sponded with her, and were much interested in what they
termed "her pious freak." She had been urged to spend
Christmas in Baltimore. After much consideration, she decided to go. She thought she would enjoy a farewell peep into
the world where once she had figured so prominently. Rita
Payne was delighted to see her; although she did not approve
of Bernice teaching in a Negro school, her love for her thus
far had remained unchanged. Any one who has lived in a gay
Southern city and seen its many beautiful women, and enjoyed
their hospitality, can realize what a delightful time Bernice
had.

She met the fashionable young men of the large Southern
metropolis, and received much attention from them. She

smiled as she thought of the stigma resting upon her. Such chivalry, such gallantry, but let it be even whispered that one drop of that blood coursed through her veins, she would be scorned and disgraced. This was only one of many instances which have happened in America.

She accepted the compliments and courtesy, smiling inwardly; her father's wealth was a great incentive to those who possessed good blood and small incomes.

During her stay, Rita gave a musicale. She wished her friends to hear Bernice sing. The young ladies in her circle wondered if she were really as talented as they had heard. They were obliged to admit that she was wondrously fair, but they did not wish to see anything above the ordinary in her music. But her voice was an exceedingly well-trained contralto, and when she stood before the cultured assemblage, even the most critical person had to admit the superior quality of her voice, and every one begged for an encore. Rita then placed "My Rosary" on the music stand, and Bernice began:

> "The hours I spend with thee, dear heart,
>     Are like a string of pearls to me,
> I count them over, every one apart,
>     My Rosary, my Rosary.
>
> Each hour a pearl, each pearl a prayer,
>     To still a heart in absence wrung,
> I tell each bead unto the end,
>     And there a cross is hung!
>
> O memories that bless and burn!
>     O barren gain and bitter loss!
> I kiss each bead, and strive at last to learn
>     To kiss the cross, Sweetheart! to kiss the cross!"

The pathos of her voice touched the hearts of nearly everyone who listened, and Bernice could barely finish. The memories within her soul did bless and burn, and she thought of how many times she had bowed her head and kissed the cross she bore. There passed before her mind's eye a picture of all that had transpired since she and Rita had practised together at college. She grew sick and faint at heart. Her visit was no longer pleasant to her; it was only a ghost of a happier past. Taking leave of Rita, after ten days' rest, she returned to Leeville, fully determined that Bernice Silva in that world could be no more, and she never intended to wear the mask again.

Returning to Leeville, she took up her old duties with renewed strength. The children were delighted to have her back again. There were times when she became discouraged and wished she might enter some convent and get away from everyone and everything; then she thought how cowardly it would be to shrink from life's duties.

The old people had planned to give her a party. It was equal to the one of which the talented Dunbar wrote in verse. Everybody came to the party, old and young, dressed in their best clothes. The cape bonnets were all done up freshly for the occasion, and the men's bosoms were ironed to a finish. Refreshments were served—fried chicken, Maryland biscuit, pound cake, potato custards, and 'possum, too, was there, fat and cooked to perfection. The people feasted, then they sang. How Bernice enjoyed the melodies! The tears rolled down her cheeks. They seemed so earnest; their rich voices, though untrained, were full of real music.

After they had sung to their hearts' content, speechmaking was next in order. The old men expressed themselves in the most elaborate manner, while the women when their turn came, made many informal gestures and courtesies. Bernice responded, and thanked them for the warm expression of their regard for her. She begged them to send their children to school regularly, and thus help her in her efforts to educate their children. She told them of the struggles of the race, the condition of the masses, and the necessity of improving their mental conditions in order to make them morally good. There was much headshaking and bowing, with an occasional "Amen." The old men thought her a godsend to their community.

# VII

The busy days grew into weeks. Summer passed and another winter. She attended strictly to her duties; nothing was left undone that would tend to the elevation of her people. Alas, like all human beings, she began to feel the great nervous strain. Instead of taking the rest she required, she often spent nights planning work for her girls and boys. One September evening she broke down with high fever and severe congestion of the brain. The doctor pronounced it typhoid fever. Each day the fever grew higher, until she became delirious and unmanageable. The cruel ravages of typhoid fever were visible in her beautiful countenance; her golden hair, which her father had loved to smooth, had to be shaved off, and now, in spite of all this, her life was despaired of.

Many an humble heart prayed for her recovery; more than one little barefoot child came to inquire for her. The people sent her fresh eggs, chickens, and anything that they thought tempting, but she tasted nothing. She was not even conscious of their existence. They sent for her parents; death seemed inevitable. Two colored trained nurses had come from Charleston, and she was being cared for by skilled hands.

No one knew anything of her past life. The doctor thought her one of God's missionaries, who had given her life to this work. The crisis was at hand; twenty-four hours would decide her condition. The doctor feared her parents would never see her alive; her beautiful, useful life seemed at an end, and he dreaded to impart the tidings to them.

Mr. and Mrs. Silva were at Newport, R. I., when they received the news. Garrett was with them; he had just arrived from his Southern home, and was anxious to learn Bernice's whereabouts. When the telegram was received, Mr. Silva was shocked. Mrs. Silva uttered no words, but collapsed completely. Garrett Purnello shook his head gravely as he said, "God is just, man is unjust. What a world of suffering man's injustice has caused right here."

When they arrived at Leeville the hack rolled up to the hotel and the strangers alighted. The whole village knew in an hour that the visitors had arrived. The hotel was only an apology, but they deposited their luggage, and repaired to Bernice's boarding place. The doctor, although a country physician, had graduated from Bellevue, and thoroughly understood his profession. He told them she had overdone, and had for several days before she had taken her bed, a kind of walking typhoid fever. The nurses were untiring in their efforts and all they could depend upon was Divine power.

Mr. Silva grew old in a few hours. He almost idolized his only child.

Garrett looked at Bernice; he was overcome. He knelt by the bedside, took the hot, feverish hand in his, pressed it to his lips.

"This is the result of Lenore's work. I wish she might see it," he murmured.

Mrs. Silva said nothing. She silently prayed for the preservation of her only child. "Thy will, not mine," she prayed, but her grief was intolerable.

Garrett bent over the sufferer, and as he watched the unconscious face, a spirit of rebellion swelled in his bosom.

It was soon replaced by a feeling of humble submission to Divine providence. He bathed her forehead with cool spring water, hoping to see her eyelids unclose. For hours he sat there, his heart filled with suspense. Finally his patience was rewarded. She opened her large blue eyes, tears rolled down her cheeks; she recognized him. It was the first intelligent expression that had been on her face for weeks. The doctor smiled. Garrett pressed her hand, and assured her that it were really he.

As yet Bernice had no knowledge of her parents' presence, and not until the next morning did they come to her. They feared the nervous shock would be too great. Sleep returned to the weary eyelids; she was on the road to recovery. Her joy at seeing her parents once more was boundless. They found no words to express their feelings. Her pale face showed how intensely she had suffered, but they were thankful that her life had been spared.

When she was able to be propped up on pillows, Garrett had a long story to tell her, and one evening as she was looking at the mountains in the distance, he drew his chair near her and began to tell her that which he had longed to tell her days before.

"Bernice," he began, "when we parted, I had a strange presentiment that my mother had not the character that stamped the caste of noble birth. I feared there was a mystery about her which ought to be fathomed. She was never able or willing to tell anything of her mother, only of her wealthy father. After her unwomanly conduct towards you, I decided to investigate the matter. She is my mother, but I could not overlook her unnecessary treatment of you. I have found that Negro blood flows in her veins; she is a mulatto, and has a living mother, whom she has cruelly ignored and disowned.

"I found my grandmother in Alabama, a smart old woman

who has brought into this world three beautiful daughters, whose father was her master. One was dead, the second is married to the principal of a large Negro school, and the third is my own mother. Her father sent her away to college, and during one of her vacations she met my father, a foreigner, who had not long been in America. She has never visited her mother since; her father gave her a large sum of money when she married. She was his favorite child, exactly like him in appearance and manners, and he was satisfied to see her well provided for. She inherited his arrogant ways, and very little, if any, of her mother's disposition."

"Did the old lady know she married well?" questioned Bernice.

"She knew it only too well, and many have been her heartaches, when she knew that her own child was no longer identified with her black kin-people. That child, Olivia, is my own mother. I asked my grandmother, for she is mine, if she would know Olivia if she saw her after all these years.

" 'Course I'd know my own child, honey. She is the image of her father, and 'though it's nearly thirty years since I've seen her, I'd neber fergit her.'

"I took the old lady to Florida," he continued, "and when my mother saw her she fainted. I needed no further proof of the truthfulness of the statements. I was ashamed of the cruel treatment which the dear old soul had received at her hands. I provided for her temporarily, and hastened to impart the tidings to you. You cannot imagine my sadness when I found you in this condition. But

> " 'There's never a day so sunny
> But a little cloud appears;
> There's never a life so happy
> But has had its time of tears;

Yet the sun shines out the brighter
When the stormy tempest clears.'

"God grant that the sun may smile graciously upon us after these years of sorrow."

Bernice had listened eagerly to his rehearsal, and in her heart pitied the woman who wished to lose her identity in this world, but would have to answer for living a lie, before Him who shall judge all folks righteously.

The doctor had told her that her teaching days were over; her health would permit it no longer. They decided to turn the work over to a mission board, and assist them to get someone to continue the work. The people wept when they learned that she would leave them,—the children flocked to see her. She was loath to leave them; her work had grown very dear to her. They succeeded in obtaining a graduate of an Industrial School, and after everything was satisfactorily arranged, Bernice, her parents and Garrett left the little village.

Bernice and Garrett were quietly married. He is a lawyer of much repute, and greatly beloved for the good he does for the race with which they are identified.

Lenore buried herself in a convent to atone for the wickedness she had done, if possible. She is known as Sister Jessie, she is no longer the haughty woman whom we knew, but a sweet Sister of Mercy. Bernice forgave her long ago. Mrs. Purnello never consented to be recognized as the old mammy's daughter; she continues to live in seclusion, while Garrett and Bernice have the old lady with them, who does all she can for "her dear chilluns," as she calls them.

# "AS THE LORD LIVES, HE IS ONE OF OUR MOTHER'S CHILDREN"

*Pauline E. Hopkins*

It was Saturday afternoon in a large Western town, and the Rev. Septimus Stevens sat in his study writing down the headings for his Sunday sermon. It was slow work; somehow the words would not flow with their usual ease, although his brain was teeming with ideas. He had written for his heading at the top of the sheet these words for a text: "As I live, he is one of our mother's children." It was to be a great effort on the Negro question, and the reverend gentleman, with his New England training, was in full sympathy with his subject. He had jotted down a few headings under it, when he came to a full stop; his mind simply refused to work. Finally, with a sigh, he opened the compartment in his desk where his sermons were packed and began turning over those old creations in search of something suitable for the morrow.

Suddenly the whistles in all directions began to blow wildly. The Rev. Septimus hurried to the window, threw it open and leaned out, anxious to learn the cause of the wild clamor. Could it be another of the terrible "cave-ins," that were the terror of every mining district? Men were pouring out of the mines as fast as they could come up. The crowds which surged through the streets night and day were rushing to meet them. Hundreds of policemen were about; each corner was guarded by a squad commanded by a sergeant. The police and the mob were evidently working together. Tramp, tramp, on they rushed; down the serpentine boulevard for nearly two miles they went swelling like an angry torrent. In front of

*Colored American Magazine* 6 (Nov. 1903): 795–801.

the open window where stood the white-faced clergyman they paused. A man mounted the empty barrel and harangued the crowd: "I am from Dover City, gentlemen, and I have come here to-day to assist you in teaching the blacks a lesson. I have killed a nigger before," he yelled, "and in revenge of the wrong wrought upon you and yours I am willing to kill again. The only way you can teach these niggers a lesson is to go to the jail and lynch these men as an object lesson. String them up! That is the only thing to do. Kill them, string them up, lynch them! I will lead you. On to the prison and lynch Jones and Wilson, the black fiends!" With a hoarse shout, in which were mingled cries like the screams of enraged hyenas and the snarls of tigers, they rushed on.

Nora, the cook, burst open the study door, pale as a sheet, and dropped at the minister's feet. "Mother of God!" she cried, "and is it the end of the wurruld?"

On the maddened men rushed from north, south, east and west, armed with everything from a brick to a horse-pistol. In the melee a man was shot down. Somebody planted a long knife in the body of a little black newsboy for no apparent reason. Every now and then a Negro would be overwhelmed somewhere on the outskirts of the crowd and left beaten to a pulp. Then they reached the jail and battered in the door.

The solitary watcher at the window tried to move, but could not; terror had stricken his very soul, and his white lips moved in articulate prayer. The crowd surged back. In the midst was only one man; for some reason, the other was missing. A rope was knotted about his neck—charged with murder, himself about to be murdered. The hands which drew the rope were too swift, and, half-strangled, the victim fell. The crowd halted, lifted him up, loosened the rope and let the wretch breathe.

He was a grand man—physically—black as ebony, tall, straight, deep-chested, every fibre full of that life so soon to be quenched. Lucifer, just about to be cast out of heaven, could not have thrown around a glance of more scornful pride. What might not such a man have been, if—but it was too late. "Run fair, boys," said the prisoner, calmly, "run fair! You keep up your end of the rope and I'll keep up mine."

The crowd moved a little more slowly, and the minister saw the tall form "keeping up" its end without a tremor of hesitation. As they neared the telegraph pole, with its out-stretched arm, the watcher summoned up his lost strength, grasped the curtain and pulled it down to shut out the dreadful sight. Then came a moment of ominous silence. The man of God sank upon his knees to pray for the passing soul. A thousand-voiced cry of brutal triumph arose in cheers for the work that had been done, and curses and imprecations, and they who had hunted a man out of life hurried off to hunt for gold.

To and fro on the white curtain swung the black silhouette of what had been a man.

For months the minister heard in the silence of the night phantom echoes of those frightful voices, and awoke, shuddering, from some dream whose vista was closed by that black figure swinging in the air.

About a month after this happening, the rector was returning from a miner's cabin in the mountains where a child lay dying. The child haunted him; he thought of his own motherless boy, and a fountain of pity overflowed in his heart. He had dismounted and was walking along the road to the ford at the creek which just here cut the path fairly in two.

The storm of the previous night had refreshed all nature and had brought out the rugged beauty of the landscape in all its grandeur. The sun had withdrawn his last dazzling rays from the eastern highlands upon which the lone traveler gazed, and now they were fast veiling themselves in purple night shadows that rendered them momentarily more grand and mysterious. The man of God stood a moment with uncovered head repeating aloud some lines from a great Russian poet:

> "O Thou eternal One! whose presence bright
> All space doth occupy, all motion guide;
> Unchanged through time's all devastating flight;
> Thou only God! There is no God beside
> Being above all beings, Mighty One!
> Whom none can comprehend and none explore."

Another moment passed in silent reverence of the All-Wonderful, before he turned to remount his horse and enter the waters of the creek. The creek was very much swollen and he found it hard to keep the ford. Just as he was midway the stream he saw something lying half in the water on the other bank. Approaching nearer he discovered it to be a man, apparently unconscious. Again dismounting, he tied his horse to a sapling, and went up to the inert figure, ready, like the Samaritan of old, to succor the wayside fallen. The man opened his deep-set eyes and looked at him keenly. He was gaunt, haggard and despairing, and soaking wet.

"Well, my man, what is the matter?" Rev. Mr. Stevens had a very direct way of going at things.

"Nothing," was the sullen response.

"Can't I help you? You seem ill. Why are you lying in the water?"

"I must have fainted and fallen in the creek," replied the man, answering the last question first. "I've tramped from Colorado hunting for work. I'm penniless, have no home, haven't had much to eat for a week, and now I've got a touch of your d——— mountain fever." He shivered as if with a chill, and smiled faintly.

The man, from his speech, was well educated, and in spite

of his pitiful situation, had an air of good breeding, barring his profanity.

"What's your name?" asked Stevens, glancing him over sharply as he knelt beside the man and deftly felt his pulse and laid a cool hand on the fevered brow.

"Stone—George Stone."

Stevens got up. "Well, Stone, try to get on my horse and I'll take you to the rectory. My housekeeper and I together will manage to make you more comfortable."

So it happened that George Stone became a guest at the parsonage, and later, sexton of the church. In that gold-mining region, where new people came and went constantly and new excitements were things of everyday occurrence, and new faces as plenty as old ones, nobody asked or cared where the new sexton came from. He did his work quietly and thoroughly, and quite won Nora's heart by his handy ways about the house. He had a room under the eaves, and seemed thankful and content. Little Flip, the rector's son, took a special liking to him, and he, on his side, worshipped the golden-haired child and was never tired of playing with him and inventing things for his amusement.

"The reverend sets a heap by the boy," he said to Nora one day in reply to her accusation that he spoiled the boy and there was no living with him since Stone's advent. "He won't let me thank him for what he's done for me, but he can't keep me from loving the child."

One day in September, while passing along the street, Rev. Stevens had his attention called to a flaming poster on the side of a fence by the remarks of a crowd of men near him. He turned and read it:

### $1,500 REWARD!

"The above reward will be paid for information leading to the arrest of 'Gentleman Jim,' charged with complicity in the murder of Jerry Mason. This nigger is six feet, three inches tall, weight one hundred and sixty pounds. He escaped from jail when his pal was lynched two months ago by a citizen's committee. It is thought that he is in the mountains, etc. He is well educated, and might be taken for a white man. Wore, when last seen, blue jumper and overalls and cowhide boots."

He read it the second time, and he was dimly conscious of seeing, like a vision in the brain, a man playing about the parsonage with little Flip.

"I knowed him. I worked a spell with him over in Lone Tree Gulch before he got down on his luck," spoke a man at his side who was reading the poster with him. "Jones and him was two of the smartest and peaceablest niggers I ever seed. But Jerry Mason kinder sot on 'em both; never could tell why, only some white men can't 'bide a nigger eny mo' than a dog can a cat; it's a natural antiperthy. I'm free to say the niggers seemed harmless, but you can't tell what a man'll do when his blood's up."

He turned to the speaker. "What will happen if they catch him?"

"Lynch him sure; there's been a lot of trouble over there lately. I wouldn't give a toss-up for him if they get their hands on him once more."

Rev. Stevens pushed his way through the crowd, and went slowly down the street to the church. He found Stone there sweeping and dusting. Saying that he wanted to speak with him, he led the way to the study. Facing around upon him suddenly, Stevens said, gravely: "I want you to tell me the truth. Is your real name 'Stone,' and are you a Negro?"

A shudder passed over Stone's strong frame, then he answered, while his eyes never left the troubled face before him, "I am a Negro, and my name is not Stone."

"You said that you had tramped from Colorado."

"I hadn't. I was hiding in the woods; I had been there a month ago. I lied to you."

"Is it all a lie?"

Stone hesitated, and then said: "I was meaning to tell you the first night, but somehow I couldn't. I was afraid you'd turn me out; and I was sick and miserable—"

"Tell me the truth now."

"I will; I'll tell you the God's truth."

He leaned his hand on the back of a chair to steady himself; he was trembling violently. "I came out West from Wilmington, North Carolina, Jones and I together. We were both college men and chums from childhood. All our savings were in the business we had at home when the leading men of the town conceived the idea of driving the Negroes out, and the Wilmington tragedy began. Jones was unmarried, but I lost wife and children that night—burned to death when the mob fired our home. When we got out here we took up claims in the mountains. They were a rough crowd after we struck pay dirt, but Jones and I kept to ourselves and got along all right until Mason joined the crowd. He was from Wilmington; knew us, and took delight in tormenting us. He was a fighting man, but we wouldn't let him push us into trouble."

"You didn't quarrel with him, then?"

The minister gazed at Stone keenly. He seemed a man to trust. "Yes, I did. We didn't want trouble, but we couldn't let Mason rob us. We three had hot words before a big crowd; that was all there was to it that night. In the morning, Mason lay dead upon our claim. He'd been shot by some one. My partner and I were arrested, brought to this city and lodged in the jail over there. Jones was lynched! God, can I ever forget that hooting, yelling crowd, and the terrible fight to get away! Somehow I did it—you know the rest."

"Stone, there's a reward for you, and a description of you as you were the night I found you."

Gentleman Jim's face was ashy. "I'll never be taken alive. They'll kill me for what I never did!"

"Not unless I speak. I am in sore doubt what course to take. If I give you up the Vigilantes will hang you."

"I'm a lost man," said the Negro, helplessly, "but I'll never be taken alive."

Stevens walked up and down the room once or twice. It was a human life in his hands. If left to the law to decide, even then in this particular case the Negro stood no chance. It was an awful question to decide. One more turn up and down the little room and suddenly stopping, he flung himself upon his knees in the middle of the room, and raising his clasped hands, cried aloud for heavenly guidance. Such a prayer as followed, the startled listener had never before heard anywhere. There was nothing of rhetorical phrases, nothing of careful thought in the construction of sentences, it was the outpouring of a pure soul asking for help from its Heavenly Father with all the trustfulness of a little child. It came in a torrent, a flood; it wrestled mightily for the blessing it sought. Rising to his feet when his prayer was finished, Rev. Stevens said, "Stone,—you are to remain Stone, you know—it is best to leave things as they are. Go back to work."

The man raised his bowed head.

"You mean you're not going to give me up?"

"Stay here till the danger is past; then leave for other parts."

Stone's face turned red, then pale, his voice trembled and tears were in the gray eyes. "I can't thank you, Mr. Stevens, but if ever I get the chance you'll find me grateful."

"All right, Stone, all right," and the minister went back to his writing.

.  .  .  .  .

That fall the Rev. Septimus Stevens went to visit his old New
England home—he and Flip. He was returning home the
day before Thanksgiving, with his widowed mother, who
had elected to leave old associations and take charge of her
son's home. It was a dim-colored day.

Engineers were laying out a new road near a place of
swamps and oozy ground and dead, wet grass, over-arched
by leafless, desolate boughs. They were eating their lunch
now, seated about on the trunks of fallen trees. The jokes
were few, scarcely a pun seasoned the meal. The day was a
dampener; that the morrow was a holiday did not kindle
merriment.

Stone sat a little apart from the rest. He had left Rev.
Stevens when he got this job in another state. They had voted
him moody and unsociable long ago—a man who broods
forever upon his wrongs is not a comfortable companion; he
never gave any one a key to his moods. He shut himself up
in his haunted room—haunted by memory—and no one
interfered with him.

The afternoon brought a change in the weather. There was
a strange hush, as if Nature were holding her breath. But it
was as a wild beast holds its breath before a spring. Suddenly
a little chattering wind ran along the ground. It was too weak
to lift the sodden leaves, yet it made itself heard in some way,
and grew stronger. It seemed dizzy, and ran about in a circle.
There was a pale light over all, a brassy, yellow light, that
gave all things a wild look. The chief of the party took an
observation and said: "We'd better get home."

Stone lingered. He was paler, older.

The wind had grown vigorous now and began to tear
angrily at the trees, twisting the saplings about with invisible
hands. There was a rush and a roar that seemed to spread
about in every direction. A tree was furiously uprooted and

fell directly in front of him; Stone noticed the storm for the first time.

He looked about him in a dazed way and muttered, "He's coming on this train, he and the kid!"

The brassy light deepened into darkness. Stone went upon the railroad track, and stumbled over something that lay directly over it. It was a huge tree that the wind had lifted in its great strength and whirled over there like thistledown. He raised himself slowly, a little confused by the fall. He took hold of the tree mechanically, but the huge bulk would not yield an inch.

He looked about in the gathering darkness; it was five miles to the station where he might get help. His companions were too far on their way to recall, and there lay a huge mass, directly in the way of the coming train. He had no watch, but he knew it must be nearly six. Soon—very soon—upon the iron pathway, a great train, freighted with life, would dash around the curve to wreck and ruin! Again he muttered, "Coming on this train, he and the kid!" He pictured the faces of his benefactor and the little child, so like his own lost one, cold in death; the life crushed out by the cruel wheels. What was it that seemed to strike across the storm and all its whirl of sound—a child's laugh? Nay, something fainter still—the memory of a child's laugh. It was like a breath of spring flowers in the desolate winter—a touch of heart music amid the revel of the storm. A vision of other fathers with children climbing upon their knees, a soft babble of baby voices assailed him.

"God help me to save them!" he cried.

Again and again he tugged at the tree. It would not move. Then he hastened and got an iron bar from among the tools. Again he strove—once—twice—thrice. With a groan the nearest end gave way. Eureka! If only his strength would hold out. He felt it ebbing slowly from him, something seemed to clutch at his heart; his head swam. Again and yet again he exerted all his strength. There came a prolonged shriek that awoke the echoes. The train was coming. The tree was moving! It was almost off the other rail. The leafless trees seemed to enfold him—to hold him with skeleton arms. "Oh, God save them!" he gasped. "Our times are in Thy hand!"

Something struck him a terrible blow. The agony was ended. Stone was dead.

      .    .    .    .    .

Rev. Stevens closed his eyes, with a deadly faintness creeping over him, when he saw how near the trainload of people had been to destruction. Only God had saved them at the eleventh hour through the heroism of Stone, who lay dead upon the track, the life crushed out of him by the engine. An inarticulate thanksgiving rose to his lips as soft and clear came the sound of distant church bells, calling to weekly prayer, like "horns of Elfland softly blowing."

      .    .    .    .    .

Sunday, a week later, Rev. Septimus Stevens preached the greatest sermon of his life. They had found the true murderer of Jerry Mason, and Jones and Gentleman Jim were publicly exonerated by a repentant community.

On this Sunday Rev. Stevens preached the funeral sermon of Gentleman Jim. The church was packed to suffocation by a motley assemblage of men in all stages of dress and undress, but there was sincerity in their hearts as they listened to the preacher's burning words: "As the Lord lives, he is one of our mother's children."

# MARJORIE'S SCHEME

*Kate D. Sweetser*

It was no great formal reception that Mrs. Groves was giving. It was just a cosy little "at home," to which were bidden a few kindred spirits, some literary women, a musician or two, who played and sang at intervals during the afternoon, a sprinkling of intimate friends, and half a dozen of the season's debutantes.

There was no attempt at wholesale decoration, but there were individual touches, characteristic harmonies, and contrasts here and there that betrayed the artist-spirit, which had planned the careless-seeming whole, and made of the little home a symphony of beauty.

Not the least attractive part of the scene was the group of girls gathered around the tea table, chatting and laughing as they sipped their tea.

"Who are those girls?" whispered an elderly lady to her hostess. "They do look so pretty in their spring gowns and big hats."

"In the corner? Oh, they are my 'rosebuds'; Meg Fleming, Elsie Browne, Jeanne Grey, and the Dunn girls, Madge and Rose."

"And the pretty girl pouring tea?"

"She is my favorite of them all—Marjorie Kane, Millionaire Kane's daughter. Doesn't she look sweet in that white gown? When you see one of those girls you usually find the other five, for they are perfectly inseparable. What they do

*Colored American Magazine* 6 (Dec. 1903): 879–81.

not do is not worth doing. They have tennis clubs, and
walking clubs, and gymnasium classes, and lunch clubs,
besides every other known and unknown sort of club. Talk
about society girls being base and indifferent!"

"That is Rob Kane with them—a queer fellow. He always
goes everywhere with them."

Patience has a limit, and that limit is not a very extended
one where a man and an afternoon tea are concerned, and
long before the girls were ready to leave, Jeanne noticed Rob
standing near them, in an attitude of martyr-like dejection,
watch in hand.

"Poor dear, he shall go home, so he shall," she said in a
mock sympathetic tone, and, turning to the others, said, as
she put her hand through Elsie's arm: "Come on, girls, every
one is going!"

"Then we are all to lunch with you on Thursday, Marj?"

"Indeed you are, and be sure to all come, for you know
its our last lunch for this season. Come early and stay late.
By the way, I have a scheme to propose to the club!"

A little more planning and talking, a suggestion from Rob
that he should not be dragged to "more than five hundred of
these things," and the group broke up.

As the girls left the room, more than one of the older
women turned away enthusiasm.

On the day of the luncheon Marjorie ran down for a last
look at the table before the girls came.

"Yes," she murmured, looking with admiration at the
fulfilment of her idea, "it is all right; now if they will only
be interested!"

Then the girls came in and interrupted her musing.

"Margie, you look sweet enough to eat," exclaimed Rose,
giving her a loving squeeze, as they walked in to the dining-
room arm in arm, and she said truly, for no picture could

have been prettier than fair Marjorie, with her golden hair fluffing all over her head, and the lilac of her gown heightening the pink and whiteness of her skin.

Certainly she was a beauty, and a very spoiled one, some said, but they were people who knew her slightly, or judged from their idea of what the only daughter of a millionaire must be.

An admiring "oh" burst from the girls, as they seated themselves around the table, the effect was so dainty and "Margie-esque," as Elsie put it.

Each one of this series of luncheons had been arranged as to table decorations in some one color, and Marjorie had chosen lilac—the King's Daughters' color—for hers.

The polished table was covered by lilac ribbons ending at each plate with an embroidered name on its fringed end. In the center of the table was a bank of fragrant violets, shading down into a circle of violets. On the candles were shades of maidenhair fern; all the little bonbon dishes were filled with candied violets, and at each plate lay a mass of those fragrant flowers.

"You extravagant wretch," exclaimed Meg. "I don't [know] which I love most, you or the violets!"

"It's just the sweetest of the whole set, Margie; how clever you were to think of it all," said Jeanne admiringly.

During luncheon the girls tried in vain to find out the new scheme, but the pretty hostess was so persistent in her refusals to say anything about it that the merry talk wandered off into other channels, touching on matters grave and gay, silly and sensible, sparkling with bright thought and ready wit.

All New Yorkers, born and bred, belonging to the same world of culture and society, their interests and friends were mainly the same, and they always had an unending amount of subject for discussion.

Lunch over, the girls settled themselves in Margie's sitting-room for an afternoon of cosy talk.

"Now, Marj, out with the scheme," said Elsie, curling herself up in an armchair, as Jeanne and Rose took possession of the divan, and the others settled themselves on the rugs that lay on the floor, their pet lounging place.

"Come, tell us what your little head has in it now," said Rose. "Are we all to go to China as missionaries, or—"

"Set up soup and coal kitchen in Union Square," interrupted Elsie.

"No, girls, I'll tell you what she wants—a subscription to buy Jack a catechism; he needs it badly enough!"

"Oh, yes, or a—"

"It's a new suit of clothes for her dear protegee, Mrs. Murphy."

"Rose," interrupted Marjorie, in a very earnest way, "did you ever meet a man whom you knew was often tempted to take too much wine?"

"Alas, my dear, I am afraid I have."

"Did you ever drink it with him?"

"Why, yes, I suppose so, at dinners and things."

"Jeanne, did you ever give up doing something you were very fond of because you knew it had a bad influence on the boys?"

"Why, of course not; I expect them to have strength of mind enough not to need my influence; but why this catechism, fair lady?"

Margie laughed; "I was just thinking, that's all. You see it began in this way—"

"The scheme! the scheme!" murmured Madge under her breath.

"One day long ago, just before I had the typhoid fever last winter, I was in my room, and I heard Rob and Jim

Crane talking in Rob's room. What brought up the subject I don't know, but I heard Rob say, 'Sisters! why, they're no good! They don't really care if a fellow goes to the devil or not, nor other fellows' sisters either, so far as I can see. They only want us to tote 'em around and amuse 'em!' "

"What a story!" exclaimed Rose indignantly.

"Then," continued Margie, "I heard Rob say, 'yes, sir, you bet we would be better men if they only helped us!"

"Pooh! I don't believe they would," said Jeanne contemptuously.

"Wait a minute, Jeanne. Then he went on: 'There's one girl in New York who could twist me around her little finger if she tried, and that's Jeanne Grey. It's a pity the girls don't know how much influence they have with us.' "

"There, Miss Jeanne, don't blush; I would not have told it if your ladyship had not been so scornful."

No answer came from Jeanne; all that could be seen of her face was the tip of a very red ear.

"I sat very still after this, trying not to lose a word Rob said, and he went on:—

" 'What man's going to refuse a glass of wine if a girl like Margie is sitting next to him smiling and drinking hers? I tell you they are responsible for the beginning of lots of the things they frown at when they get to be settled habits. If a girl will laugh at serious things, don't you suppose I will, too?'

"That was all I heard, but it set me thinking; then I was laid up with the typhoid for so long, and somehow I never had a chance to speak to you girls about it till now.

"I've thought about it in every possible way and manner, and I am firmly decided that no man would say such a thing if it were not true. They do have harder temptations to fight than we do, and I believe we have not helped them as we might. I propose," Margie's cheeks were bright red now, and her eyes sparkling with interest in her subject, "I propose that we try to show them that our ideal is high and that we will not come down to a lower level; they must come up to ours."

"But we will have to get up to the ideal ourselves first," sighed Meg.

"Of course, and it will not be easy, but I do honestly believe it will pay. I propose that we use all our power not to influence them to go one step in the wrong way, and to show them that we want friends that we can, first of all, respect. There are lots of little ways that we can help them if we stop and think about it, and I think it will do some good if they see that we are really willing to give up things for their sakes.

"We do a tremendous deal of frivoling about serious subjects that may not hurt us because we don't mean it, but it influences them.

"What do you say, girls, to being members of my Influence Ten? We are all Kings' Daughters; this will be our private branch."

"I am ready for anything, except to be eaten by a cannibal," said Madge.

"My dear," said Meg, with an effort at her usual light manner, "privately I have always thought good men very stupid, but if they are not all saints hereafter it shall not be my fault!"

"Alas, alack, I shall be obliged to have a complete house-cleaning, mental, moral and physical, before I try to scrub up other people's floors," said Rose laughingly, as they roused from their lounging positions when five o'clock chimed from the clock on the mantel, and they realized that the afternoon was over.

Margie went to a drawer and brought out six slender gold bracelets, padlocked each by a tiny cross of gold. "You see," she said, a smile flashing in her blue eyes, "I was so sure you would help me that I ordered these pledges to remind us as we wear them," adding in a lower voice: "Just think how much it will be worth if our influence ever brings one of the boys nearer—the King!"

Not a word more was said on the subject. The girls were thinking too seriously to speak of it lightly, and the good nights were very quietly said.

Then they went out to their various lives, went back into the whirl of people and things, whither we cannot follow them, but in each life there was from that day a new thought, that months and years wove into a controlling purpose. Theirs were, as the world goes, ordinary lives, but who dares say they were not changed, broadened by the resolution symbolized by the little gold crosses?

There's one thing sure. I know none of them ever suspected the reason for Margie's thinking so deeply on the subject, nor did they know why her engagement was not announced, or why Jack Dunning went West. But I—I knew, for I am Margie's brother Rob, and it's all right now, for Marj wears a ring on the proper finger, and Jack has a tiny cross on his watch chain.

I tell you what, my sister is a trump, and she has forgiven me long ago for listening on that day of her lunch party. Jeanne Grey is a pretty nice girl, too, after all!

# THE TAMING OF
# A MODERN SHREW

*Ruth D. Todd*

That Edward Reynolds was the most daring young fellow in
Liston was quite a settled fact. There was no mischief, no
diabolical trick that could frighten him off. As a boy he was
the terror of the town, for Liston was only a small town in
southern Arkansas, where the major number of the inhabitants
were Negroes.

Once, when he was quite a small lad, his companions had
dared him to jump from the high town bridge into the stream
below, and he had dared to do so with very fatal results.

That his neck hadn't been broken years before he arrived
at manhood was no fault of his; however, he had come out
of it all unscathed; a tall, perfectly built young man, as
handsome as a god. His complexion was a reddish brown,
his hair coarse, black, and as straight as an Indian's, and his
eyes, which were the most striking feature about him, were
large, fearless eyes, as black as night, and sparkling with
mischief, but a greater amount of daring.

Still, he was even-tempered, although his voice had a firm
and commanding ring. He was certainly the most popular
young fellow about town, and any one of the girls would
have been proud to call him her "young man." But this
youth, although not vain or egotistical, would have none of
them, that is, excepting a certain beautiful damsel named
Jennie Leigh, who, it seemed, would have none of him.

Jennie was the acknowledged belle of Liston. Her com-

*Colored American Magazine* 7 (March 1904): 191–95.

plexion was a trifle darker than Edward's, but she had soft, curly black hair, as fine and as glossy as silk, and large, bewitching, black eyes; in fact, many of the young men had been wont to declare that "Jennie Leigh's eyes always made a fellow feel deuced uncomfortable." She was fashionable, clever, witty, very charming, and possessed a temper that was, unlike Ed's, very uneven. In fact, when once aroused, she was a veritable shrew, though when things pleased her, there was not a young lady in Liston whose temper was so sweet or whose manner was gentler.

Edward was exceedingly fond of Jennie, in fact, had loved her when they were tots; and as a school girl, he had carried no other girl's books but Jennie's to and from the village school; and after both had graduated from the high school, the intimacy had never decreased. So it was quite evident that they would some day marry, despite the fact that they were forever "scrapping" with each other.

It was quite amusing to see them together, for Ed's temper was so even, and his vein of humor so tantalizing, that he always managed to arouse Jennie's ire. He had often asked her to marry him, a thing which any other young man would not dare to even think of, and Jennie had flatly refused Ed's every proposal.

But this fearless young man's courage never deserted him; his will was indomitable, and he inwardly avowed that Jennie Leigh should wed none save him. That he would win her or devote his whole life to the attempt, he was determined. One day when they were attending a certain afternoon garden party, Jennie had looked so lovely in a beautiful gown of some pale blue, soft material that Ed had blurted out in his abrupt fashion: "Oh, Jennie, won't you be mine?"

"Ed Reynolds, you are the silliest person I know. Every blessed time you see me, you ask me to 'marry you,' or 'be yours,' or something equally as stupid! You must think that I am going about looking for a husband, don't you?" she exclaimed impatiently.

"No, I did not think that, or I would have asked you nothing, because I'd have taken it for granted that I was your future spouse, and led you to the minister's years ago," answered Ed, gazing admiringly at her beautiful face and exquisite gown.

"Oh, you are just horrid, and sometimes I think I hate you," cried Jennie, angrily.

But Ed was so used to these angry outbursts of Jennie's that it would have seemed very unnatural if she had acted otherwise. They were seated on a little rustic seat quite out of "earshot," and Ed answered her, paying no attention whatever to her angry words:

"Gee, but that's a lovely dress you have on, Jennie. You look awfully sweet in it, Jen. I wish you belonged to me. Won't you tell me you will wed me, dear? Oh, please say yes, Jennie!" and he caught one of her soft little hands in his.

"Oh, Ed, don't be stupid; people are looking at us!" she cried, trying in vain to draw her hand away.

"Who cares?" answered he. "You know as well as they that I love you, Jen, have loved you all my life, and there isn't another girl that I'd even waste a thought on. I'm quite serious now, and if you send me away from you again, I'll do something desperate, I swear I will!"

"What will you do—commit suicide?" she asked, glancing mischievously up at him, for he had arisen now and with a slight frown upon his handsome face, and both hands thrust into his trousers pockets, he stood looking down upon her.

"Certainly not! Do you think I'm some darned idiot!" he exclaimed, indignantly.

"Men who are violently in love always commit suicide when the lady of their choice persistently refuses them."

"Let them, they're quite welcome, I'm sure. If they haven't got sense enough to bear up, they ought to die! What I'm going to do is to live and marry you."

"Oh, you are, are you? I'd like to see you without my consent."

"Oh, you'll consent all right."

"You are a conceited prig!" she cried, scornfully. "I'll show you whether I'll consent or not by accepting James Wilson the next time he asks me to marry him."

"What, that puppet! Has he asked you to marry him?"

"Why, of course he has. You are not the only person worthy of existence as yet," she exclaimed, indignantly.

"Why, confound him, if he even dares look at you again, I'll punch his head!" cried Ed, vehemently.

"Why, Ed Reynolds, you wouldn't dare. I'd hate you forever if you did such an ungentlemanly thing."

"I'd dare do anything for you. Oh, Jennie, dear Jennie, please say that you will be my own, my very own."

"You are absolutely incorrigible, Ed; do give me some rest."

"I will, when you promise to marry me, dear. Please say yes. Honest, I—I worship you. I don't know how on earth I can give you up. But I swear I'll leave town and never visit these parts again if you do not promise to marry me. I'm dead earnest this time. I know I've sworn to do all sorts of things time and again, but I'll—oh, Jennie, how can you be so cruel?"

"Cruel! Why I think I am extremely kind to you. There is not another person that I would allow to talk to me as you do, Ed Reynolds, but now I'll tell you what I will do."

"What will you do?"

"I'll marry you on one condition."

"Oh, name it! name it!" cried Ed, gladly.

"If you will write a novel or compose some poems worthy of notice, and have them published, I'll marry you—let's see—Easter."

"That's worse than cruel, Jennie. You know quite well that I'm not a literary chap, that I know nothing whatever of literature, and, er—you can't care anything for me if you ask me to do what you know is an impossibility."

"I never said I did care for you, did I?"

"But you do, don't you, Jen?"

"Do as I ask you to, and you will hear something that you have waited long to hear."

"Confound it, I'll try it, if I win or lose; I'd do anything to win you, dear Jennie."

And so it was announced that Jennie and Ed were to be married at Easter.

That was in September, and the last of March was drawing near before Ed was sure of winning his prize.

He knew that he would be very unsuccessful if he attempted such a serious thing as a novel, so he had tried his hand at poetry, but I'm afraid with very sad results. The following are specimens of his works:

> "It was a nice bright day in May,
> The birds were warbling out their lay,
> When everybody on that day
> Would stare at my girl named May."

This terminated quite abruptly, as though the writer was disgusted with such rubbish.

Then another:

Pathos

"My darling, I love you," the young man cried,
As he whispered these words to the maid at his side,
"If you will only say that you love me true,
I'll worship, adore you, my only dear Sue."

In fact this daring young man wasted a small fortune in
stationery, with the most disgusting results, when it suddenly
occurred to him to try his hand at nonsense poems, or stories
in modern slang. So he wrote this:

To Jennie

There was once a young chap called Bennie,
Who loved a sweet maiden named Jennie,
    Implored the lad, "Don't refuse me."
    Cried the maid, "You confuse me,
For I don't know my mind, if I've any."

Said she, "I can't quite discover,
Why you are such a persistent young lover,
    If you love me, dear Ben,
    Win fame with the pen,
And I'll wed you instead of another."

"No, no!" cried the lad with a shiver,
That shook him and stirred up his liver,
    "A pen I detest,
    Ask me anything else,
For I'd rather jump into the river."

Then the maid oped her eyes wide in surprise,
"For a lover," said she, "you're unwise,
    If you refuse my plan
    You're a nutty young man,
And for a dunce you'd take the first prize."

The lad thought the maiden was joking,
But instead with anger she was choking,

"To the river," she said,
"For you've such a thick head,
That I'm sure it needs a good soaking."

Then the lad left the maiden quite sadly,
Said he, "I want you so badly,
　　That I'll try at the pen,
　　If I'm successful, why then,
Will you have me?" cried the maiden, "Oh, gladly!"

This lad's brain was as thick as fog,
It was even as thick as a log,
　　For he thought that dear Jen,
　　When she mentioned the pen,
Could mean nothing excepting the hog.

So this bug-housed young man named Ben
Built him an enormous big pen,
　　And then he spent
　　Every blessed red cent
Invested in hogs, he told Jen.

Then Jennie thought sure he was broke,
And she thought this a freak of a joke.
　　"He's quite crazy," she said,
　　"He's off of his head,"
And she laughed till she thought she would choke.

But Ben made a big pile of money,
And Jen said, "It's just too funny,
　　But wed you I must,
　　Or with laughter I'll bust."
And she kissed him, and called him her honey.

Then Ed wrote a story in modern slang, as follows:

### To Jennie

Once upon a time there was a girl whose first name was
Jennie. She was the swellest girl among the whole bunch with

which she traveled. And there wasn't a chap in the whole neighborhood who wasn't dead gone on her. She wore such towering pompadours and such swell dresses she called gowns, and looked so much like a gorgeous queen that all the other girls turned green with envy, and the annoying disease called jealousy. And you can bet your life that this dusky damsel of the dreamy eyes was the only pebble on the beach. And as far as hot air was concerned, she could give more of that in ten minutes than any other girl could in fourteen hundred and ninety-eight hours. And she was quicker than lightning at spitting fire when a guy rubbed her the wrong way. She had no favorite guy that she doted on unless it was a swell-looking guy who lived near her, and who so persistently dogged this baby's cute little footsteps that she was forced to chew the taffy he gave her. This guy wore big-legged trousers and thought he looked wise and smart in rimless eye-glasses, which he donned after the maiden bade him do some intellectual stunts ere she would wed him.

It was a settled fact that this guy would win, so the other chaps all gave him a wide berth, but he failed to do these intellectual stunts, and was about to give the whole business up as a bad job, when it rushed through his noggin that all girls liked loads of presents and a plenty of dough, and when these were rushed in upon her she told him 'twas up to him to get the license, and she'd make the angel food with which to cholerize all of the guests, and the thing was completed in a swell church around the corner. Moral—Dough and a plenty of it is always the winning card.

He had no trouble to get Edson, the one and only colored editor in Liston, to promise to publish a nonsense poem or story in modern slang each week in his paper, and Ed hastened to the residence of his lady-love to tell her of his success.

"Oh, Ed, I think they are horrid!" cried Jennie, after she had read both poem and story.

"They are horrid, all right, but that's the only sort of literature now-a-days that makes a hit," answered Ed.

"I hope you are not going to have them published?" she asked anxiously.

"Of course I am. Do you suppose I'd give it up after seven long—almost intolerably long—months?"

"But surely you don't call this poetry or anything decent to read, even?"

"Sure—sure it is! It will make a hit all right."

"But why did you dedicate such horrid stuff to me? Oh, I think you are awful—just awful, and I hate you, Ed Reynolds!"

"You'll have to marry me, though," replied Ed, smiling triumphantly.

"I wouldn't marry you if there wasn't another man left," cried she, vehemently.

"You'll have to now. There's your promise that you'd wed me if I became successful, and I've leased a nonsense column in Edson's paper every week as long as I like to deal in literature," said Ed, quite complacently.

"Literature nothing. Why you know you wouldn't dare have such rubbish published, not if you cared anything for me."

"That's just why I'm going to have it published, because I think so much of you, I want the whole world to know. I shall sign my own name, Edward Benjamin Reynolds, in capital letters instead of a non-de-plume."

"Oh, you can't be serious, Ed."

"Never was more serious before in my life."

"Oh, Ed, please don't have it published, for my sake! The girls will all make the greatest joke of me. Oh, Ed, please don't!" she pleaded.

But Edward knew that he held the winning card in his

hand and he thought that now was the best time to get Jennie's consent to wed him in two weeks' time, so he firmly avowed that he'd have them published—that, in fact, Edson already had a type-written copy of them in his possession.

Then Jennie—the untamable, high-spirited Jennie Leigh— became quite meek and gentle, telling Ed that she would wed him on the morrow or whenever he wished if he would only promise her that he would not publish that awful stuff.

"But I won't marry you if you hate me, Jen," said Ed.

"You know that I love you, Ed, have always loved you, and could never live without you, dear, and if you loved me you would tear that paper up and throw it in the grate."

"Do you really love me, Jennie? Oh, Jennie, if I thought you cared enough to marry me Easter, I'd be the happiest man in Liston."

"And you wouldn't have them published?"

"Certainly not, darling."

"Then I am yours!" she cried, and Ed drew her to him, etc. etc.

On Easter morn, 'neath an arch of lilies, and surrounded by huge exotic plants in "St. James' Mission," Edward B. Reynolds and Jennie Leigh were happily wedded.

# THE AUTOBIOGRAPHY
# OF A DOLLAR BILL

*Lelia Plummer*

It was Christmas eve. The earth was covered with a white fluffy mantle. The snow gleamed brightly on the branches of the frozen trees, where a few brown little sparrows chirped cheerfully. The houses were covered with snow, and every few minutes might be heard the merry ringing of sleigh bells.

"Hullo," said ragged Jackie. "This is the kind of a Christmas for me, none o' yur mild dripping Christmases is this, but a good old-timer." The shivering little urchin addressed replied, that:

"As for them that has fires, a snowy Christmas was all right, but he was cold. Anyway," he concluded, "it ain't Christmas, it's only Christmas Eve, and I want to know what you're going to do when Christmas really comes?"

"Well," said Jackie, "just now I'm goin' to sell my papers and earn some stray cash; then I'm goin' to that little corner of the bridge and cuddle down, and to-morrer, I'll treat myself with my cash." So away he trudged, crying "Paper here, sir, *Daily News*, and special Christmas numbers!" But few seemed to hear the little one, so intent were all upon their Christmas shopping. But suddenly in crossing the street, Jackie lost his footing and nearly fell under the heels of a dashing pair of horses, which were drawing an elegant equipage up the street. The coachman sprang down and kindly raised the little arab in his arms. "Why youngster, you want

*Colored American Magazine* 7 (Dec. 1904): 726–28.

to be careful! Are you hurt?" Then the carriage door opened and a kind face looked out upon little Jackie, who was endeavoring to wrest himself from the coachman's arms.

"Are you hurt, little fellow?" a sweet voice asked. "No 'um," responded the blushing Jackie. Then seeing his rags, a kind hand drew forth some money from a bag and slipped it into the newsboy's hand. The coachman took his seat, and in a moment the carriage had passed on.

Jackie gazed upon the money in his dirty little hand, scarcely able to believe his own eyes. Yes, in that brown little palm lay a clear, crisp one dollar bill. Jackie hugged himself with delight, and clasping his dollar closely, danced off to resume his efforts to sell his papers. But people did not bother with Jackie any more that day, and when night came he had not sold one paper. Nevertheless his heart felt very light and he was happy. Many, many times during the day he had stolen a glance at the crisp little bill; and now when the bright and beautiful lights began to appear in the city street, he rushed off to his little niche in the bridge where he was pleased to curl himself up for the night. "This here's better'n them old homes where you'r all tucked and cuddled like a girl" he used to say to his young companions. There he cuddled down, still hugging closely his precious dollar bill and thinking of the pleasures it would bring him Christmas day. Suddenly, to his surprise, he heard a squeaking little voice call "Jackie, say Jackie!" Jackie rubbed his eyes and looked around. He saw no one. Suddenly it came again, and this time Jackie did not look for it, but said, "All right, here I am; what do you want anyway?"

"See here, Jackie," the voice continued, "I'm Mr. Dollar Bill and I want to tell you all about me. But hug me up nice and tight, for night is cold." Jackie tightened his clutch upon the precious bill. "Now, I first sprang into this world of

wonderful things in a place where I saw heaps of others just
like me. Oh my, there were so many of them that my eyes
just ached! And there were round little men who were very
bright looking but kept very humble before me, for they
seemed to know that they were not half so good or valuable
as I.

"Then there were some little silvery things, whom we
called, 'little dimes,' and I believe there were more of them
than any of us could ever imagine. Well, I stayed in this a
good while, until I got really tired; at last somebody far
larger and better clothed than you, Jackie, took me and put
me in a great big, hollow, cold place. If I had been alone I
would not have liked it at all, but there were lots of others
just like me, only none of the shining things were there. I
asked some of the more important men what it meant and
they said 'Little ones were to be seen and not heard' and that
I must live and learn. But I was not there long, for a great
broad hand came and hauled me out. I felt myself being
whirled through the air for a few moments, then I was
suddenly plunged into utter darkness. Ah Jackie! that was a
black moment for me. I could not tell where I was. For a
long while I felt as if I were moving. Then suddenly, I was
whisked out again and put into a little, wee box and felt
myself scudding along at a terrific rate. I wondered where I
was going. I was snatched from there just as suddenly, but
before I was again plunged into darkness, I caught a gleam
of bright and pretty things and a great moving mass of
people. Jackie, where was I?"

"Oh I guess somebody went to do some Christmas shopping
as they call it, with you and took you into one of those
beautiful stores."

"Very good" replied the bill complacently. "You're not a
bad little chap for your age, Jackie, not at all. Well, to

proceed with my tale, I met there an old friend, Jackie. Yes, my boy, an old friend, for I myself have had so many travels that I am beginning to feel old, though I look so bright and new. The last time I had seen him was when we lay in a great box together. He recognized me instantly and I began to talk to him. 'Hullo, old fellow!' I said, 'Here we are again. Now where have you been?' Then I noticed that beside him lay a very old and tattered gentleman, at whom I was inclined to turn up my nose, but bless me, Jackie, my friend seemed more inclined to notice the old one than he did me, the bright, the new and pretty. Just then came a ring and a click and my friend was gone. Then the old tattered fellow looked at me seriously and soberly for a few minutes, and began, 'An old fellow like myself, youngster, is really more valuable than a young one, like you. Oh! young ignorance, if you only knew the many and varied tales I could tell! Ha ha! youngster, you look as if you thought you knew something.' Then I blushed and looked down, for do you know, Jackie, I didn't just like the way the fellow was talking. But he kept on. 'Why, green one, I have travelled across rough waters, over green fields. I have been in the home of the rich, where there were many, many more like myself, and I have been in the homes of the poor, where there were none like myself. Little one, I have been where all was innocence and purity, and likewise where all was crime. Yes I have been snatched from wallets by crime-stained hands and been in the pockets of noted criminals. What phase of life have I not seen? I have been the poor man's joy, the miser's hoard, and until I fall in pieces, I shall continue to travel these rounds.' Ding, click! my acquaintance was gone.

"There were lots of other bills there, who, I do not doubt, were worthy of my notice, but really, Jackie, that last wonderful fellow had scarcely gone, when rude hands snatched me, sped me through space, and once more consigned me to gloom. But I did not mind the darkness so much this time, for I reflected upon the old one's story and hoped that I might live to be the ragged, worn old fellow he was. You see so much more of life, Jackie. While I studied and thought, I could hear sweet voices speaking and suddenly a kindlier and gentler hand gave me into your keeping. Some way or other I took a fancy to you directly. You seemed to treat a fellow as if he had some feeling and you had some consideration for it. I really like you, Jackie, and when Christmas morning comes and I am leaving you, for I suppose I must, do not grieve for I shall always be on the watch for you again."

"Oh no, You shall never go," cried Jackie with energy. He gave a start and sprang to his feet. It was early, early in the blessed Christmas morning and already the bells were chiming the birth of the Babe at Bethlehem. How they rang in Jackie's ears and heart.

"What! have I been dreaming all this? Not a bit of it! I heard that dollar just as plain as I hear these bells and I know that even if I part with my dear old bill, he'll be on the lookout for me and some day I'll have him again."

# THE BALANCE OF POWER

*Edith Estelle Bulkley*

"Winnie! Pretty Winnie!" screeched the poll parrot.

"Shut up, you infernal beast, till the right time, will you!" Carolton shouted.

The parrot tossed its head, looked wise, and closed with a hollow laugh.

"Oh, pretty Winnie!" it cried again saucily.

Carolton, thoroughly vexed, let the parrot have the nearest thing handy, and the parrot ceased its cries as a photograph rack, neatly folded, struck against its cage.

"Oh! Oh!" was all the parrot said.

Carolton prided himself that he was not cruel, so he amended by giving polly a cracker, although he took her out of the room and left her alone in the kitchen, closing the door between. He glanced at the clock as he returned to the room. Already ten—and Winnie due at half-past! Well, he was ready anyway—everything was in order, and he felt proud of his den.

"Everything," he said half aloud, "except this old rack." Carefully he picked up and unfolded the weapon which had defended him against polly's saucy tongue; a thrill passed over him such as he always felt when he handled it. He had, he acknowledged, many curios in his den, but not one that possessed a power like that. It wasn't new when he bought it of the gipsy woman, and many times since he would have given much to know its history; he recalled how she had

*Colored American Magazine* 8 (Jan. 1905): 8–12; 8 (Feb. 1905): 68–74.

forced him to buy it, so compelling were the flashes of her
black eyes. Who was it that had eyes that reminded him of
hers? Winnie, his fiancee, who, with her old nurse as chaperon, had promised to visit his den that morning. He arranged the room to the best order for his visitor, and displayed
all his curios.

Carolton took the rack and put it against the wall; the
knobbed corners, in the form of satyrs, made frightful
grimaces at him. He measured carefully the position of the
nail, so that the rack would hang correctly; he tried it here,
he tried it there. But alas! it was the same old trouble he had
always experienced when trying to hang it; it would not hang
evenly. Disgusted, he took it down.

"There is neither beauty of design nor accuracy of workmanship about it," he said grimly.

However, he again measured the distances on each side of
the nail; they were exactly even, and in a determined way,
he swung the rack for the last time upon it.

"Even if it doesn't balance in itself," he said, "perhaps I
can place the pictures so they will balance it." And this
reasoning, though faulty and wicked, seemed to satisfy him.

Diving down under his book case, he brought up a large
stack of photographs—his Bessies and Rosies and Kates and
Lauras, and down at the bottom, the largest one of all, that
of the widow. This last he took up almost caressingly, and
studied long. Handsome, but wicked, the face on the card
looked back at him, and he recalled the owner's words of the
previous morning when he had seen her off for Europe.

"I have not ruined you," she said. "Go back to your
Winnie. You will be happy with her, and I am never coming
back. To-night you will find it is Winnie you love." Carolton
knew by her eyes that she would never come again, and he
was glad. How glad too he was that Winnie would never

know about her; he knew she didn't, for surely she would have mentioned her, when that same night, true to the widow's words, he had sought Winnie, and obtained favor from her.

Half past ten! And Winnie had not come yet! Still he thought it kind of her to give him some grace, moments in which to put the finishing touches to his questionable arrangements. And he would quickly arrange the pictures on the rack, and settle down to await the coming of his gipsy queen, as he loved to call Winifred, with her (all black) eyes and blue-black hair. She was queenly made up, to be called a beauty prize.

Carolton took the small pictures and placed them in one corner of the rack—that fated rack! He tried to apply all his limited knowledge of the principles of balance, harmony, and rhythm. The one corner, where he had placed all the small pictures, swung to the side; Carolton quickly seized the large picture of the widow and placed it in the opposite diagonal corner. It seemed to produce a perfect balance—he watched eagerly—but no, it was heavy and overbalanced on the rack.

With a cry, Carolton snatched the pictures, then the rack, and tossed them together upon the sofa. Oh tell-tale rack! Here was his own life reproduced—himself the rack, crude and imperfect in itself, the widow, the one great influence in his life that overbalanced everything else, and whom he now hated. One gleam of hope remained. Could Winifred's picture produce the balance?

He hoped she would remember to bring it with her as she had promised. While he hoped and dreamed, footsteps were heard on the stairs. He knew it was Winnie coming—light, graceful Winnie, his gipsy queen.

The joy of her approach buoyed his spirits, and as she rapped, he called, "Come," and then in a playful mood hid quickly behind the portiere—he forgot it was translucent. He heard Winifred enter, followed by Alice—an excellent chaperon, Carolton thought, and not a bit curious. He waited with child-like impatience to hear what Winifred would say because of his absence, and he was quite surprised and disappointed at her silence. He soon tired and came forth.

"Sorry to keep you waiting so long," he said, at the same time greeting them.

"Then why didn't you come out from behind the portiere?" Winifred laughed. "You acted like you thought we were some of your creditors."

Carolton punished her by stealing a hair-pin and a kiss, but, being a man of honor, he lost no time in returning both.

"You are my creditor," he said finally, "for I am indebted to you for the pleasure of this visit."

"Oh, I assure you the 'pleasure is all mine,' " Winifred returned mockingly, throwing aside her fur, "isn't that what you men say?"

Carolton laughed, took her fur, and went to the kitchen to get polly whose hour of triumph had arrived.

"This is my mascot, companion, and love," he said, setting polly on a table.

"Ah then, so I have a rival!" Carolton winced all in a second, and he wasn't thinking of polly either.

"Yes, but an unambitious one, listen!"

"Polly! Pretty Polly!" screeched the bird.

"She is a knowing bird," Carolton remarked.

"Any polly can call itself pretty," Winifred answered, with feigned disgust.

"Yes, but listen," Carolton coaxed, uttering a swift prayer that polly might say the right thing. "Listen Winnie!" he repeated loudly, as if to encourage the bird.

"Winnie! Pretty Winnie!" Polly cried obediently and they

laughed, while Carolton heaped compliments upon the bird for its well-timed speech, lessons in which he had been giving it for days past.

In the joy of it all, Carolton forgot his sorrows of the previous hour; he was in a paradise now. Old Alice had found a shrine in the parrot while Carolton showed Winifred all over his den. He had meant to put the rack out of sight, before Winifred should come, but the idea had slipped his mind, so there it lay on the sofa with the pictures beside it, in full view. This was quite unfortunate too, for Winifred had eyes all around. Photographs, more especially a bachelor's photographs, are of great interest to girls, more so to the girl to whom he is engaged.

"What's this, Rae?" Winifred asked innocently enough.

"Oh that?" Carolton tried to laugh lightly, but failed miserably, sounding like the parrot, that at the very moment was laughing for Alice's amusement and edification. "Why that's a photograph rack and some pictures I was trying to put up."

"And you haven't an artist's eye for arrangement so you left it for me," Winifred finished.

"Yes," answered Carolton, glad of any escape from the truth.

He did not deem it necessary to explain how he had failed to make the rack balance. Winifred would find out all too soon that there was something radically wrong in the very construction of it. He watched the lines of her face as she took up the rack.

"Isn't it lovely, Rae," she said. "These satyrs seem to smile pleasantly at me. Somehow I feel as if I had seen the rack somewhere before."

"The woman I bought it of said there was none other like it in existence."

"Oh she only told you that to make a sale. Who was she?"

"A gipsy, and she had eyes and hair just like yours," Carolton answered promptly, and he noticed more closely than ever before the resemblance between his own Winifred and that gipsy woman.

"Thank you," Winifred returned with slight coldness.

"Oh, but your eyes and hair are beautiful!" Carolton hastened to explain.

"Oh, certainly," Winifred answered boldly.

Carolton thought her angry but she turned those black eyes in question upon him and laughed.

"I'm at fault, Rae," she said, "I had no business to be so personal. Now you be real good while I put the rack and pictures up."

"Did you bring the picture you promised me?" Rae asked eagerly.

"Well—maybe I did," Winifred replied with sufficient ignorance to assure him that she had. "Be patient."

Just as he had, earlier in the morning, Winifred unfolded the rack to its fullest length, admiringly. She turned it around with the back toward her, and saw how it fastened. She placed it on the same nail that Carolton had driven for it. She steadied it, then took her hand away. It hung there—a perfect balance.

"Doesn't it look lovely on the wall?" she said. "It is an adornment in itself—minus the pictures. And hasn't it a peculiar fastening at the back?"

"Yes," said Carolton, gazing at it, but for his life he would have sworn there was no such fastening when he had hung the rack. He took his chair again. Well, if he was the rack as he had called himself, at least he was not a hopeless case. Winnie had produced a balance in him. But how would it be with the pictures?

"Now," continued Winifred, laughing at her success, and

ready to achieve further victory, "I enjoin you, perfect silence while I place the pictures thereon. Do you promise? You see an artist must not be disturbed in his work."

"I promise."

Lucky it was for him and good it was of her, that she had enjoined him to silence, for how could he have kept his voice under normal control, as he saw her begin placing the pictures as he had—the small ones in the upper right hand corner. And when she had placed these to her liking, she too, like Carolton tried to produce a balance by placing the large picture of the widow at the bottom of the rack. It would not balance; she added one and another picture to the upper corner, and so on until all the small pictures were utilized, but ever the widow's picture overbalanced all.

All this time, Winifred had not even glanced at Carolton, being too intent on her work. At last in a vexed way, she spoke, though without turning.

"Isn't it funny you haven't enough smaller pictures to overbalance that large one?" Then, turning around, she shot the leading question:

"Who is she anyway?"

She caught the strange look on Carolton's face.

"Rae," she said, coming toward the Morris chair in which Carolton was sitting, "I don't like that picture." And there was something in her voice that went straight to Carolton's heart.

"Neither do I, Winnie—any more," he returned feebly.

"Is she the widow, Rae?" Winifred asked in a hushed tone. Alice was in the kitchen, where she had taken the parrot; Alice trusted her charge.

"Yes, Winnie," Carolton returned, "she is the widow," and he did not seek to learn who had told Winifred of her. "Throw her picture away, if you wish."

"No, Rae, I will not do that," Winifred replied quietly,

and she took, from a package she had brought, her own photograph. "Look Rae," she said to Carolton, who felt way down in the depths.

Carolton obeyed, and Winifred, going once again to the rack, placed, thereon, the photograph with those small ones in the upper corner. For the first time, the corner where the widow's picture had been placed, swayed the other way. Winifred Forrester had overbalanced the widow. Carolton looked radiant. He knew, now, that it wasn't only the picture of Winifred that overbalanced the widow's picture, but Winifred real flesh and blood, was more than conquering that evil influence.

The result was happy, and Carolton felt like a boy, as he laughed and joked with Winifred about the gipsy fortune-teller, of whom he had bought the rack. "He had not seen her since," he said.

"Nor," he added, "do I think she ought ever to come to me again with things to sell. You should have seen her coaxing me to buy it. Such eyes! 'You need it,' she said, 'it is your fortune, and is of use to no other person.' "

And, being in a good mood, Carolton jocosely told Winifred of his failure to hang the rack correctly. She laughed, but thought deeply upon the tale.

"Of course, Rae, if you got any other picture of the same weight as mine, it would have over-balanced the widow's. But isn't it funny, Rae" she added, and turned her black eyes full upon him, "isn't it funny that I should happen to be the one who held the balance of power?"


Two days later, Winifred stood, in the early morning, before her mirror. She wanted to see, she mused, if she looked any different from usual, on this, her twenty-first birthday.

"Not a bit," she said, looking at the face reflected in the mirror. "I have these same devilish black eyes," and she said it not coarsely, but with disappointment born of hopes unfulfilled. "Why haven't I eyes like other people? No wonder Rae said I have eyes like a gipsy; it was the truth of his words that hurt me."

Winifred turned away from the mirror, and looked in it no oftener than necessary. It was singular, she mused, how sensitive she had been of her eyes, since that morning in Rae's room. He had often called her a gipsy, but never before had he gone so far as to tell her she looked like a certain gipsy—and especially the one who had sold him the photograph rack.

That rack! She had seen Rae since that eventful morning, and from his light mention of the rack affair she could see that it meant nothing particular to him. Why, he just didn't know how to fasten the rack: and as to the balance of the pictures: why you can't strike a balance, if you haven't the proper weights. Well, such reasoning might be all right for Rae, but to her, her of the black eyes and blue black hair, this business was not an affair of a moment. How was it that she, Winifred Forrester, should be able to adjust things? And ever she answered her question with another. Is it, she thought, because I have eyes and hair like the gipsy who sold the rack?

Carolton had noticed with misgiving, Winifred's discomfort, and blamed himself, not for the mention of her eyes, but for his peculiar actions when the widow's picture had played such part in the affair. Winifred assured him over and over again that she never gave the widow a thought, and Carolton had finally to believe her, although he was not far from finding out the source of the trouble. Thus he had left her, the previous night, promising to come again the night of her birthday and scold her severely—he threatened playfully—if he did not find her in a happier mood.

And so it was, that Winifred, when she came down to

breakfast on her birthday morning, resolved to force herself to be bright, as a good preparation for the part she was to play in the evening; for certain it was, that a happy mood with her would be only a play, for Carolton's presence, since the rack affair, seemed only to increase the troubles of her heart.

"Where is papa?" she asked, when, on entering the dining room, she found the table set for one only.

"He has eaten and is in the library," the maid answered, "and he left word that you eat a hearty breakfast, and join him there immediately after."

Winifred obeyed, so far as eating her breakfast, though the heartiness of it may have been questionable, and then sought the library. That her father should send for her on this morning did not seem at all strange to her, for he was ever mindful of her birthday anniversaries, and celebrated them by not only external means, but food for thought.

Winifred rapped on the door lightly and entered without waiting for a reply. Mr. Forrester arose to greet his daughter and kissed her on both cheeks. Winifred settled herself in an arm chair near his desk.

"This, Winnie," Mr. Forrester began, "is the most important birthday yet. Can you tell me any reason why?"

"The only one I know of, papa," Winifred answered promptly, "is that I am a full-fledged woman, capable, at least so considered by law, of controlling my own money."

"Good!" Mr. Forrester answered smiling. "And now another!"

"Aren't you a little exacting?" Winifred asked frowning. "You are just like my old governess. Still if you persist," she added saucily, "another reason is, that this possibly is the last time you shall call Winnie Forrester to see you on her birthday anniversary."

Winifred laughed, as her father's countenance changed at the unexpected retort.

"Are things as serious as that?" he asked, "Well, I am beaten in my own game by my own daughter," he added good naturedly.

"You see," Winifred explained, "the minister warned us only last Sunday against tempting Providence too far. Never mind, papa," she consoled him, "remember it is your privilege to call henceforth Winnie Carolton to see you on her birthdays. Rae will come to see you to-night," she added meekly.

"Agreed?" Mr. Forrester replied satisfiedly, "And now to business!"

Winifred noticed the envelopes on the table, several of them addressed to her, and all containing business relative to her, which would be disclosed to her shortly. One envelope in particular she noticed; it read, "To be given Winifred on her 21st birthday," in a handwriting strikingly like her own. She was all curiosity and was thankful when her father picked this envelope up first.

"I think," he said, "we might as well attend to this one first," and his voice was strangely sad, "as on it depends all the rest of our business. Open it Winnie; it is your rightful property." And Mr. Forrester handed the envelope to Winifred.

With hands that trembled, Winifred broke the seal; she breathed easier when she found the envelope contained a mere picture—faded, yet sufficiently plain. It was the picture of a gipsy girl with eyes and hair like Winifred's mirror had reflected to her that morning; she was dark complexioned, but minus this difference, the exact likeness of Winifred herself.

"Who is it?" she asked softly.

"It is your mother," Mr. Forrester answered just as softly.

"But you told me you had no picture of her," Winifred protested incredibly.

"I haven't. That is yours. I have never seen it. All I knew was that it was her picture."

Winifred only remembered handing the picture to her father; after that, she was living over again the days of the week past. Why was it that all things conduced to lead up to that rack affair? Was she, an American girl apparently, to be confronted by gipsies and gipsy episodes all her life? So this gipsy was her mother!

"At least," she thought bitterly, "I have come honestly by my hair and eyes."

She started when her father called.

"If you care to hear it, Winnie," he was saying, "to-day is the day I recite to you your mother's history."

If she cared to hear it! Anything, she thought, to put an end to her miserable suspicions! For the answer she settled back more comfortably in her chair.

"You bear this, Winnie," Mr. Forrester said, more at ease, "more calmly than I thought you would. I dreaded to hand you that envelope."

"Papa," Winifred replied, "recent experience has prepared me for anything. Tell your story; then I'll tell mine. I have a strange presentiment that they will either coincide, or be complements." And she settled further back in her chair and closed her eyes, those all black eyes.

"Years ago," Mr. Forrester began, "I wandered in the west. I had a boy's love of adventure, and ample opportunity to seek it, added thereto. When I became of age, my father gave me my portion of his estate, and I determined to satisfy, in full, my desire for roaming. Boy as I was, I was man enough to take some of my money and invest it, and thankful to-day I am for it. The remainder of the money I kept for current needs. I roamed all over the west, which was much more a type of pioneer settlement then than it is to-day; I hunted, fished, in fact, lived a wild life, sleeping anywhere my wanderings happened to bring me, at the close of day."

Mr. Forrester was warming with the thrill that the memory of those days brought him. He paused, as if picturing the scenes in his mind.

"Go on," Winifred said, impatiently and almost commandingly. At her word, Mr. Forrester came somewhat to himself, though he would fain have forgotten for a while the living relic of his adventures, in the arm chair, and lived over in imagination all the old times.

"Go on," Winifred repeated louder, and opened her eyes, and flashed them at him compellingly. That was enough to restore him entirely to the present.

"But," he went on, and Winifred closed her eyes again, "I was the son of an English gentleman, and had only the desire for, and not the ability to withstand long, the hardships and privations necessary in such a life. What wonder, then, that I soon became ill, and one night, utterly exhausted, sank down before a gipsy camp."

The girl in the arm chair sighed wearily.

"What need," the man continued, "what need to recount all the days and nights in that gipsy camp? What need to tell you of the care I received, from one gipsy girl especially"——

"What need, indeed!" Winifred interrupted fiercely. "Haven't you told me enough already! Why have I not known this before? Twenty-one years I have lived in ignorance, without ever hearing my mother's name mentioned, or without ever seeing her picture. Where was the shame that she was my mother? And who," she added bitterly, "is so ignorant as not to know it, having once seen these eyes of mine?"

After this passionate outburst, Winifred again sighed—a sigh that came from her heart and passed all over her. It touched, too, the heart of Mr. Forrester, for he moved uneasily in his chair.

"Well, go on," Winifred said at last. "There is more yet. When did she die?"

"Five years ago."

"Five years ago!" Winifred interrupted again. "And I have believed her dead for at least nineteen! But go on, cruel one, nothing more you say can hurt me at all. Tell me all!" she commanded.

"Please do not reproach me for carrying out my wife's— your mother's wishes," Mr. Forrester only said, but there was a world of meaning in his voice.

Winifred felt the well-directed reproach.

"Excuse me, papa," she said penitently, "please go on."

"It was your mother's wish, Winnie, that you should know nothing of her until to-day."

"But where was she, papa, that I never saw her?"

"Let me go back some, that I may the better connect my story. You already guessed that I soon fell in love with my gipsy nurse, and on regaining my health, I succeeded in weaning her away from the camp, and married her. I immediately gave up roaming, and with my gipsy wife now fully civilized and Americanized, as I wrongly thought, set up housekeeping in a modern way. To be sure we lived somewhat reclusely, but I was happy, and, in my ignorance, thought that my wife was too. We had been married but a few months, when I noticed her failing physically. I called in perhaps a half-dozen different physicians, but not one apparently helped her. I have since been of the opinion that the doctors thought there had been something mysterious about her former life, although there was little about her dress or manner, that belied her being an American. But you see, she looked in feature, like a gipsy, and this fact naturally aroused some curiosity.

"When you were about two years old, her health became worse, and the real sadness of my life began. One evening she brought you over to me and left the room. She was, oh, so proud of you, for she said you were just like her, with enough of the American type about you to save you from the taunts of unkind people. As I said, on that evening, she brought you to me and left the room. Presently she returned, bringing with her a large box; it was the one thing she had brought with her when we were married. A peculiar key turned the lock of the box; once open, the inside disclosed numerous pieces of jewelry; in it also was that envelope, addressed by her, containing, she told me, that picture of herself, which you have to-day seen. She told me all of the contents of the box were for you when you were twenty-one. I will show you the box later. Let me finish my story now. I was blind, and did not realize for what reason she was telling me all this, but the realization came all too soon when, a week later, I came home to find her gone. Oh yes, she came back to tell me her reason; she could not, she said, stand the confinement of my mode of living; and I perceived the truth of her words, as I saw how much better she looked since she had gone back to her old life. Then too she told me, that for her to live with you, was to shame you; and she begged me to come east with you, to begin life over again. After a great mind struggle, I decided to yield to her wish. That night before our departure I shall never forget; she came for the last time to say good-bye to you."

"My poor mamma," Winifred murmured, as her father paused.

"Oh well," continued Mr. Forrester, "some there may be

who would call her heartless, wanton or what not; I say, however, it was for love of you that she left. She seemed to feel herself inferior to you, and wished not to stand in your light. When she turned to go out of the door, she took from her satchel, a photograph rack, and showed it to you. I remember it had knobs on it in the form of satyrs' heads, and you clutched two of them in your tiny hands. Then she turned to me and said, 'You see it? You'll hear of it again. It is her happiness pointing to you.' Then she left, taking the rack with her."

Mr. Forrester paused; Winifred did not move. Mr. Forrester raised a window; he did not attempt anything else in the way of restoring his stupefied daughter. The cool air fanned her cheeks.

"And the rest, papa," she asked faintly, motioning him to close the window.

"There is but little more, Winnie. She promised to keep me aware of her whereabouts; so we left the West, you and I. As we had lived somewhat reclusely gossipers got little for their amusement. She kept her word to me, and every once in a while, I got news of her. Once, only once, she came to this town, as a fortune-teller and peddler, and although I hunted high and low for her, I could not find her, but I have always been satisfied that she intended it so. Soon after, I received a letter from the West, written in an unfamiliar hand, telling of her death. I went on—you remember when I took my trip West—and the report was confirmed satisfactorily to me. That is all I know."

"But it isn't all I know," Winifred began, sitting straight up in her chair, and concluded her father's story by telling her own recent experience with the photograph rack. "Anyway," she ended, smiling, "it is all over now, and I am glad I know all. This afternoon, papa, we shall drive down town, and have arrangements made to have a likeness of my mother put in my locket by the side of yours. And the jewelry box, which you opened to get the picture out, I shall just peep into, and leave a thorough examination of it for another day."

After all, it had passed pleasantly enough—this recital of his wife's history, but Mr. Forrester decided there had been enough business transacted that day, and the rest should be left for another. Winifred tripped from the room with a lighter step than had been hers for a week past. It was all very simple now—this rack affair, and she was glad to be gipsy enough to settle her own and her lover's happiness. A sudden thought struck her, and she literally ran back to the library.

"Papa," she exclaimed, "Rae is coming to see you to-night, and you must tell him what you have to-day told me."

Mr. Forrester looked troubled; here was a new problem.

"You must!" Winifred cried, as he hesitated. "It is his business, and he shall know who and what he is marrying. If my misfortune is enough to change his affections, then let him go. His love shall be tested by a scale on which that of few others has been weighed."

She rose proudly; Mr. Forrester knew she was right.

"Right, as ever you are, my gipsy," he replied at last; and Winifred escaped quickly, fearing that he might detect a catch in her voice if she spoke further. What if Rae shouldn't love her any more—was the uppermost thought as she went down the corridor. It was alright to say "Then, let him go!" but—

The early evening of the same day found Winifred once more before her glass. She looked in it proudly now. What if her eyes were all black! Hadn't her mother had the same kind? Her mother's memory meant now so much to her.

"Marie," she called to her maid, "bring my red silk dress with the black girdle, my heavy gold chain and all my bracelets. Dress my hair low and put in the knot, this gold pin which was my mother's."

Marie made haste to obey.

"The first time," she said to herself, "I ever heard her speak of her mother!"

"Will you have all your bracelets on Miss?" Marie suggested, with emphasis on the "all."

"I will have all my bracelets on Marie," Winifred answered, with equal emphasis. "And quickly too, please. It is nearly eight now."

Marie had never experienced such impatient celerity on her mistress' part. Surely, she must be feeling the privileges of her twenty-one years! But Marie's ill-will, if she had any, passed quickly, as, when her mistress' toilet was complete, the mistress herself turned to her with a penitent:

"I'm sorry I was so cross Marie. And you're a dear good girl. Don't wait to undress me; you may go to bed any time."

"But miss," the maid protested, "that girdle does hook so peculiarly, I'm sure you'll need help to get it off."

"Never mind, Marie," Winifred laughed. "I'll tear it off rather than wake you up. You have been so patient with me while I have been so unreasonable." Then to herself, as she went down stairs, "This dress plays its part to-night only, and at the end of the evening, I shall either be so calm and content that I'll be willing to sleep, if necessary in my girdle and dress or I shall be so beside myself with sorrow that I shall be glad to tear my gipsy rig off."

A bell sounded as Winifred reached the last step; it marked the end of Carolton's interview with Mr. Forrester, and the beginning of his visit with Winifred. Tremblingly Winifred opened the drawing room door. "He either is or isn't, I either am or am not," she thought, with the meaning best known to herself. She entered the library where her father and Carolton were.

Carolton was the sole occupant of the room; he turned as Winifred entered. Winifred breathed hard but made no attempt at greeting. She stood up proudly to her full height and turned her eyes full upon him.

"You have heard," she said quietly, "who I am, and furthermore you see me as I am."

Carolton took in at a glance her whole dress, planned for the occasion.

All room for doubt of change in her lover's affections vanished as Carolton advanced and gathered Winifred in his arms.

"My true gipsy," he murmured, and it meant more to both of them than ever before.

"I just couldn't," Winifred confessed, as Carolton led her to the sofa, "I just couldn't bear to go into a new home, dragging behind me a skeleton to conceal in the closet."

# SCRAMBLED EGGS

*Gertrude Dorsey Brown[e]*

## [PART I]

It was Easter morning. Each room in the big house was in characteristic and suggestive attire. In the dining room and parlors large bouquets of Easter lilies and early violets were in evidence. The library had been temporarily converted into a kind of still life poultry show, for on the mantel and shelves sundry stuffed ducks and candy chickens shared common quarters with rabbits of doubtful origin and eggs of many sizes and all colors. In the dressing rooms, tidy house-maids were spreading out divers and costly arrays of feminine finery,—laces, bonnets and dresses. In the kitchen large baskets of fresh eggs hinted at the possibility of delicious omelets and muffins.

At seven o'clock the family and guests began to assemble in the sitting room, each in turn with bright happy faces and pleasant greetings, but the host, Mr. Grayson, was hungry. He wanted his breakfast; he was conscious that something was wrong, and his sensitive nature seemed to divine by intuition that the domestic economy of his establishment was in immediate danger of dissolution. Accordingly, he walked to the kitchen door and looked in. Everything was in scrupulous order, but no where to be seen was cook or serving

*Colored American Magazine* 8, pt. 1 (Jan. 1905): 31–38; 8, pt. 2 (Feb. 1905): 79–86.

maid. The fire was not yet lighted in the range, and alas! no signs of breakfast did he see.

"What can this mean,—where the deuce is Mandy and Bess?" soliloquized the bewildered Mr. Grayson. He rang the servants' bell several times but without response, save from his wife who now came rushing into the entry to inquire into the cause of such delay. Her husband explained, and then added, "It just seems that if we want any breakfast to-day we must prepare it ourselves or wait for the Lord to work a miracle, for there isn't a servant in sight."

"Well I do declare!" and Mrs. Grayson seated herself on the meal bin and for the twentieth time in as many hours, she made a diligent search through her store of resources for some solution to this new problem. Finally she arose and bidding her husband return to their guests she gathered up the train of her elegant gown and hurried from the house. In fifteen minutes she returned, accompanied by an old colored lady and a young girl.

"Now Aunt Caddy, I want you and Lulu to—"

"Look here Mrs. Grayson! Before the war when I belonged to you'uns I was 'Aunt Caddy,' but now I'm 'Mrs. Caroline Somebody' and please, you jes' call me that hereafter." The quiet dignity with which the old lady gave this gentle rebuke awakened both pity and respect.

"Well you must excuse me—I—I didn't know your name in full—At any rate please get us up some breakfast as soon as possible. Thank goodness there are plenty of fresh rolls and butter and cream. Just fry some ham and some potatoes, and cook some eggs, yes, boil some, and fry some, and poach a few and scramble some for the children, and make an omelet or two, and some coffee and—"

—"Run along honey' I know how to get an Easter Breakfast and that mighty quick, so don't you worry."

An hour later at 8:30 the family were summoned to the dining room, where true to her promise and profession, Mrs. Caroline Somebody had not only provided the prescribed articles, but a tempting tray of hot muffins and fried chicken.

Mr. Grayson exchanged satisfied glances with the lady who presided so gracefully at his board and mentally congratulated himself upon such a valuable possession.

"My wife," he was prone to say, "is equal to any emergency in the domestic government of the house. She is so graceful and competent in discharging her social duties, and on the whole as handsome a woman as there is in Georgia."

It was seven o'clock that evening before husband and wife were free to discuss together the proceeding of a most unusual day. Fortunately the guests and Miss Dora were "invited out" for the evening—Aunt Effie and Malcolm had gone to church and the twins were safely stored away for the night, each with a stomach full of hard boiled eggs and a mind filled with wonderful recollections of the Easter tide.

"Now Elizabeth, do sit in this easy chair with me for an hour or so. Poor little wife, you look so tired,—and Oh, that ugly frown that sits so comfortably on your pretty brow. Tell me dear of what you are thinking?" and Mr. Grayson took a seat beside his adored Elizabeth, and gently smoothed out the frown on her face.

"Really Merrit, it is hard to explain, but the sum of matter is—I'm worried and perplexed about Aunt Caddy. She actually frightens me sometimes and some how she makes me feel so uncomfortable. When the cook and Bessie left us so unceremoniously, my only resource was a call upon the services of Aunt Caddy.—Now do you know she refuses to be called Aunt Caddy any more? To-day she told me to call her Mrs. Caroline Somebody."

"Mrs. Caroline Fiddlesticks! nonsense! And you have al-

lowed that foolishness to worry you all day?—You see Lizzie
it is but another phase of the subject that is agitating not only
the individual, the family and the community, but it is
stirring up the whole state. What must be done for these ex-
slaves who are too poor to live independently of us and who
must yet dictate terms of moral and social propriety that
would raise the hair of an imperialist?—I say, 'crush them.'
I have no patience with such mistaken ideas of citizenship, as
are advanced in the legislature by such fellows as Slaughter
and Owens. I shall never consent for my daughter Dora, to
make an alliance with young Slaughter while he advocates the
principles of a doctrine so foreign to the education and so
distasteful to the nature of all Southern gentlemen. Do you
not see in this foolish revolt of Aunt Caddy a spirit of—'I—
am—as—good—as—you, Sir?' Lewis struck the keynote when
he presented his bill providing for separate traveling apartments and for certain restrictions in the suffrage of these
people. Now I shall go a step further and shall bring before
the municipal council a petition to grant the whites either
separate street cars or the reservation of a distinct section of
a car, and absolute control of the theatres, concert halls and
public parks. Social equality will never do. One drop of the
African blood is, in my estimation, sufficient cause for ostra-
cism. Education and all the adornment of music, art, literature and travel can never fully eradicate from our minds the
thought that but one drop of blood can make a Negro, and
'Once a Negro, always a Negro.' There! my dear, I have
finished," and Mr. Grayson looked expectantly at his wife as
if he had rather anticipated a round of applause or at least
some favorable comment.

"Well Merrit, your ideas and mine usually coincide, but
in this instance I am bound to disagree, at least I am not in
harmony with your proposed method of dealing with these

true but simple minded creatures. Aunt Caddy is a type of one class of Negroes who certainly has proved its legitimate title to our respect and confidence. She has been well raised and for honesty and faithful service was rewarded with treachery. My greatest regret is that my own father wronged her as he did."

"Lizzie you are supersensitive."

"Why do you say so?"

"For the reason that you imagine your father did wrong when he disposed of his own property as he thought best. Aunt Caddy's daughter, although a quadroon and a very beautiful child, deserved no exemption from the lot or condition of the blackest African slave, and in selling her he simply exercised the right of every slave holding gentleman in the South. It but brings us back to the original hypothesis—'Once a Negro, always a Negro.'—But let us not discuss the subject any further, and do not let the whims of a half-witted old woman worry or in any way annoy my dear little wife. Not for every Negro in the world would I willingly spare one of your sweet smiles, or see a frown upon this handsomest of all faces," and bending over, the fond husband kissed his wife and bade her good-night.

One month later, the entire state was talking over the wonderful victory of the youngest member of the legislature. How did Slaughter manage it? What right had he, what right had any one, to rule the vote, to induce men to defeat the very bill that they were bound by their constituents to support? But Slaughter did it, and the "keynote" struck by Lewis, received such an astounding shock that after wandering disconsolately over the heads of quandom admirers it suddenly suffered a complete loss of identity.

Flushed with a triumph of a hard earned victory, yet modest in claiming the reward that he felt awaited him, the young giant, Slaughter, presented himself at the Grayson mansion and inquired for Miss Dora. Merrit Grayson, dignified and stern-faced, met the young man who had dared much that he might gain more, and in unqualified terms forbade him the premises and any future communication with his daughter, and by way of further admonition, he added, "Young man, be careful hereafter how you use for your own glory and selfish ambition, the talent you have derived from an honorable Southern ancestry. Your father whom we respected and loved, and your mother who gave all of her vast fortune to the cause that we loved but lost, are thrice blessed in that they do not live to see their son a bigot in a false position."

"Respect for myself, and for those who like yourself differ with me politically—forbids that I say to what extent this same heresy of which I am accused, exists in your own family. Some day, God only knows when, I firmly believe that you will reap the benefits that will result to us, as a people, from the defeat of Mr. Lewis' bill. As for your daughter, I love her—yes quite as much as you loved her mother when you were my age, but I refuse to sacrifice principle and every true conviction, for the boon of a sweet help mate who must ever afterward regard me as a coward and one unworthy of her confidence. You need fear no future intrusion on my part, for as a gentleman I expect you to acquaint your family of our interview. Good afternoon," and Mr. Slaughter, late of Atlanta, returned on the evening train to his city office.

Next afternoon two little girls were jumping rope on the lawn in front of a neat little cottage, and as a carriage rolled by, both children stopped their play and stared in opened-mouth wonder.

"Why that were Miss Dora, or I done seen a spirit," said one.

"It were Miss Dora, or this chile has done swallowed a gopher sure"—replied the other.

"How you reckon it feels to be took like she is? Sam say las' night that she were all broken up and they have to get a 'pasition' to come and take the spell off'en her."

"Sam don't know; he only hear say—I knows, cause my Aunt Caddy were over there when it happened. She aint got no spell and she ain't got the janders, nor the measles nor nothing like us cullud folks gets. It's somethin' 'fectin' on the heart and the stomach, Aunt Caddy say," responded the proud possessor of the correct diagnosis of the case.

The other little girl eyed her companion knowingly and then said simply—"How do it ail her?"

"Why she jes cry all the time and won't go no where, and can't eat nothing," said Miss Importance.

"Lordy! is it ketchin?"

"Not with cullud folks."

"I'm mighty glad, fer I'd hate like all get out, to have to cry all the time and not eat any grub, and stay in bed all day—that's worse'n our baby, for if it do cry a heap and can't walk, it got a bottle milk to chew on every time it wants it. T'aint so bad after all to be cullud, least it aint so resky, but there! our baby's crying and course I got to go in and sing it back to sleep." Soon the rich voice of a little girl was heard singing:

> "Bringing in the sheeps,
> Bringing in the sheeps,
> We shall come rejoicing,
> Bringing in the sheeps."

At an open window in an office in the ware-house opposite, sat Merrit Grayson, holding in his hand a petition conceived, composed and circulated by himself. It was to be presented

to the city council at its next meeting and was signed by
hundreds of influential citizens. The sudden illness of Dora
Grayson had made it impossible for him to present it the
night before as he had intended. The conversation of the little
girls had been distinctly heard by himself and his three clerks,
and it awakened in the father a train of new thoughts. Had
he been cruel in his attempt to be just? Was Dora's illness
really serious? Did his wife fully sympathize with his method
of righting a fancied wrong? Was his a position ethical, or
ethical? For some time he sat very still and mused over the
situation while he tapped the petition monotonously against
his forehead. He was aroused by the unceremonious banging
of the door and the sudden appearance of Sam—the man of
all work.

"Mister Grayson your wife sent me to say that you are
wanted at home, and to stop by the drug store and get some
oil of olives grease, and to come straight home and don't stop
no where."

"What's the trouble Sam?"

"Your two twin children, sir."

"My God Sam, can't you tell me what is wrong, what has
happened to the twins?"

"They was botherin' around where 'Liza was boilin' the
soft soap and natchelly they took on fire"—but the excited
father had rushed from the building and Sam, unexpectedly
deprived of the privilege of inflicting further torture, sauntered out of the office.

A scene of confusion presented itself at the home of the
Graysons. Aunt Effie with her best Holland apron tied hind
part before, across her generous proportions, met her brother
at the door with a look of "I-alone-have-escaped-to-tell-you."

Malcolm was hitching the doctor's horse to a prop that
helped to support a clothes line. Dora was making linen

bandages from a whole bolt of unbleached muslin, and no where did the unhappy man see the light of sanity but in the eyes of his faithful wife who very quietly, very calmly, drew him into the cool sitting room and explained the case. The twins had been burned, and with what serious results they would know after the doctor had completed his examination. Thanks to God and Mrs. Caroline Somebody that the little dears were not then disfigured and unrecognizable corpses. Aunt Caddy had saved their lives at the risk of her own, and was now lying unconscious in the room over head, attended by Lulu, her granddaughter, and Aunt Effie's maid. The doctor had done all in his power to relieve the pain and to make the dying woman as comfortable as possible; and then the parents, hand in hand, went softly into the darkened nursery where two little sufferers were groaning in the restless sleep that an opiate produces. The medical man with the brief statement—"painful but not serious"—passed out of the room and sought the bed of the old colored lady. Tears of gratitude mingled with tears of sorrow flowed, as Mr. and Mrs. Grayson sat beside those little iron beds and thought of the noble sacrifice that had been made to keep from their hearts the bitter experience of a fireside containing two vacant chairs.

Supper time came and went and gradually the house became quiet and its inmates composed. The summon which all were expecting, did not come until almost midnight, and then the maid softly opened the door of the sitting room, and motioning to Mr. and Mrs. Grayson—"Come," and silently they followed her into the presence of death. The seal of the "Great Beyond" was stamped upon the wrinkled yellow face, but intelligence and perfect composure shone in the keen grey eyes, and when she began to speak, the truth of all she said was impressed upon her hearers. The maid was dismissed and the doctor left the room, while in a solemn voice, Mrs. Caroline Somebody began her remarkable testimony.

"I have so much to say to you, and though my time is short, I know the good Lord is goin' to let me tell you all of it. Never mind honey, about my pillow—the burn don't hurt now, I've gone clear past all aches and pains and have stepped into the healing, cooling stream of the River of Life. Forty years ago when I lived on the large plantation with Master and Missus I laid aside the robes of the righteous and not until this very day have I called upon the name of the Lord. Now I see all of my wickedness, and now I know I done scrambled more eggs than I ever intended.

"You see it was like this. Missus was took sick one Easter morning and it was at the town house and nobody was handy to wait on her but me. When Miss 'Lisbeth was born old Doctor Slaughter hand her to me and say—'Caddy you take keer of the baby and keep it in your room for awhile until your mistress is better. She's too nervous to have it around her just yet.' Well I was nervous too, but I took the little thing and I done for it all that I could do. That very night my own child was born—a pretty plump little girl, as much like missus' babe as could be 'ceptin' mine had darker hair and much more of it. Old Hannah waited on me and both the children, as much as she could until master bring three or four of the slaves in from the plantation. He come in to see me directly he come back, and he was in powerful bad humor. He say: 'Look here, Caddy, I done left you to take care of my wife while I gone for more servants and what you mean by gettin' sick now and leavin' my wife all alone? I tell you I won't stand no sech airs. Soon as you git up I reckon you'll want to have your brat take all your 'tention and that'll be a excuse for not looking after your young mistress. But

my chile comes first, and I reckon the first trader comes along
can have yours and take the keer of it offen your shoulders.'
At first I was too surprised to say anything, then my Spanish
come to the top. I reckon you don't know that my father was
Spanish—well he was. Then I up and says to master:

" 'Kernel Claybourn, you wouldn't dar'st to sell my child,
for you know that both these children are your own flesh and
blood and you know you wouldn't sell the one any sooner
than you would the other.' He looked at me kind a hard like
and then he come up to the little crib where both babies lay
and say, kind a' soft like: 'Caddy, which of these children
belong to your mistress?'

"Now, Hannah had just had time to dress one of them
before she was obliged to go get breakfast, and that one was
mine, because it happened to be awake. I wanted to see how
it would look in the fine clothes that belonged to 'Lisbeth,
and Hannah had dressed it up so cunning, while poor little
'Lisbeth was still asleep in a plain little muslin slip. Well, I
could see there was mischief in master's eye and I reckon I
got some of the same stuff in mine, for I reached over, past
my own baby and picked up little 'Lisbeth and I said to him:
'Now, jest look here, Mast' Claybourn, if my poor little girl
had on a fine dress like your'n and was all fixed up, wouldn't
she be jest as white, jest as pretty as that chile? Aint my baby
as good as missus' baby?' Then he grab up the other baby
and say: 'No, not by a damn sight, is your young 'un as good
as this,' and he walked out of the room with it and gave it to
Molly, who had just come, and tole her to take good care of
it and as soon as the doctor come to carry it to its mother.
Hannah was kept in the kitchen after that and little black
Betty looked after me, so no body but me knew of the
exchange. A few days after this master sent for me to come
to the liberry. I was pretty weak but I went, and when I got

there he said: 'Caddy, you been sick long enough now, so I want you to get breakfast, for Hannah has to go away to help out over at Jedge Whites' during Miss Jessie's wedding. You seem to think because we always been good to you that you are a great somebody, but it's a mistake. You ain't nobody more'n the rest of your kind. I might as well tell you first as last that I done sold your baby up-river to a speculator in Memphis. Don't do any bad actin' over this affair for it won't count, and jist you turn around in the kitchen and make yourself as useful as you ken; and mind you scramble my eggs for my breakfast. I like them scrambled best.'

"When I left that room I seem to see everything I saw when I had the swamp fever. I knew I was almost as sinful as master, but I was so glad that I had done jest the sort of sinning that I had."

"Good God," broke from the lips of Mr. Grayson, who in the midst of this confession looked longingly and hungrily at his wife, who in turn had drawn her chair nearer to the bed and in a moment had clasped the almost lifeless hand, and whispered "Mother—my own poor mother."

"It does not matter," continued the dying woman, "how long I was getting that breakfast, nor how often I kept saying over and over, 'I certainly done scrambled your eggs.' I cried over dear little 'Lisbeth, when they took her away next day, and then I took mighty sick in my head and Hannah said I didn't know beans from a cock-roach for five weeks. From the day that I began to get better until now, I don't seem to see anything or hear anything but scrambled eggs. Everything around me is mixed with yellow and white. When the war broke out and word came to us that master was sick with yellow fever, up in Tennessee, I jest said to myself, 'Serves him right, he always would have scrambled eggs, and now let the yellow fever mix itself all through and through that

white-livered coward,—yellow and white still makes yellow.
Just a little bit of yellow and a lot of white, and bless you it
ain't white no more.' When mistress began to droop and pine
away, I reckon I saw that same yellow mixin' up with the
white in her eyes, and though the doctor said it was janders,
I knew it was scrambled eggs.

"My time is almost up, but I want to ask you, Mr.
Grayson, what you going to do for my daughter? Is she still
your wife; is her children your children? I ain't claimin' no
relation to yours, but your family is bound to be relations of
mine. Now when I'm gone will you leave my daughter and
her family to go to the dogs? Will you have your wife ride
in a dirty car with the very lowest of 'cullud' people while
you sit back in a first class coach and smoke a cigar? Will
you take her to an opera, or one of them song concerts and
let her sit in the peanut ring, while you are in a fine box?
When you enter a hotel or one of them fine eating rooms,
will you call the manager aside and say: 'Take this Negro
woman back behind the screen to a side table, while I sit with
my friends at the first table by the door?'

"When your sons, the twins, become men, will you follow
them to the voting place and say: 'You shall vote for this
man,' or 'you shan't vote for that man, because you have no
right to choose for yourself. You must vote as I think best?'

"When an honest white man comes and asks you for your
daughter, Dora, are you going to say: 'She is a Negro and
any one can have her,' or will you say, 'She is my only
daughter and no man is quite worthy of her?'

"If your son, Malcolm, is accused of some awful crime,
will you join in the cry of 'Lynch him, string him up, he is
only a Negro and he don't need a trial?' Tell me, Merrit
Grayson, how do you intend to use your share of scrambled
eggs?"

With suffering and intense pain written upon every feature, and with a trembling voice, the miserable man answered:

"Before God, I will do all for my family that man can do. I shall continue to love and protect my dear wife and my children, and I shall try to be more just to my fellow men. 'Tis a hard lesson you have taught me but I believe I have learned it well. My wife and my family are, regardless of Negro blood, as good, as pure, and as capable as any family on God's green earth."

He stopped, giving his wife a nod, pointed toward the east window. It was dawn,—and yellow streaks from the rising sun were mingling with the first white lights. A soul was passing away, and the feeble voice, before it was forever silent, softly said: "Yellow and white—scrambled eggs."

# PART II

"'Tis thy wedding morning
Shining in the skies
    Bridal bells are ringing
    Bridal songs arise
Opening the portals
Of thy Paradise
    Arise, sweet maid, arise."

The windows of the bed chambers on the second floor were soon filled with eager faces and each delighted listener inquired of the other from whence came this bridal chorus so early in the morning.

Dora Grayson stood on the balcony over-looking the garden, and from that vine-covered nook she discovered that several white robed creatures had taken possession of the little arbor that faced the balcony and stood directly under the window of her own bed chamber. But to her, the chorus meant nothing and with an abstracted half sigh, she turned to re-enter the large French window of her dressing room, but that space was occupied by the ample figure of her aunt Effie.

"Why Dora Grayson, what are you doing up and dressed so early: and in this solemn looking black gown? Why child, this is your wedding morning and even now the bridesmaids and flower girls are singing your bridal. Come quick, throw this opera cape over your shoulders and while I bring the rose bowl you must make your courtesy and for mercy sake look happy. 'Mr. Choppang' couldn't help writing another funeral march if he could see you now. It's enough to make an American weep, much less a heathen Chinaman," and with a gentle but resolute push, Aunt Effie parted the vines and drew Dora forward.

"The bride! the bride! how lovely," and laughing and dancing gayly below the jolly serenaders threw kisses at Dora while she, with a graceful movement, from the handsome rose jar showered bridal roses upon them. Whether from the effort required to do this, or for some other reason, the beautiful white opera cape became disengaged from its fastenings and slipped to the floor, leaving a pale faced girl in a simple blace [word illegible in original text]—alone on the balcony,—superstitious people might have said it was an evil omen, but of course no superstitious people were there. Carl Slaughter entering the yard at that moment saw his betrothed and breathing a fervent "God bless her" started for the house, but was met by Merrit Grayson and the two stopped to exchange greetings. The latter did not look like the same man who had one year before forbade him the premises and denied him all future association or communication with his daughter. That Merrit Grayson had long ceased to exist. It had been a trying year and by no means was it an easy task to make the change and reformation in thought, word and action that he had done.

Any coward can avoid unpleasant issues by professing to adopt popular ideas; by saying green is pink because public sentiment says so. But it requires a real hero to yield stubborn prejudices and preference to a conviction inspired by the unsubstantiated testimony of one whom he considers in every way his inferior.

True to his promise to Mrs. Caroline Somebody, Mr. Grayson had tried to undo the wrong he had started, for he realized that to pursue the course he had undertaken he must give up all that was nearest and dearest—a sacrifice upon the very altar he had erected whereon he had designed that other men's liberties should perish. After talking it over with his wife, he decided to go to Atlanta, call upon Mr. Slaughter and apologize for his actions. The young lawyer received him politely if not cordially and after listening in wonder to the retraction of statements most emphatically advocated such a short time before, he thanked Merrit Grayson for his offer of renewed friendship and boldly asked permission to see Miss Dora.

A great wave of crimson suffused the face of the strong man, and his emotions overcoming him he burst into tears, "O Slaughter for God's sake, as you live, as you prize your manhood, do not betray this sacred confidence, and were it not that my daughter loves you—No, by the eternal God—no—I would not tell you this secret," exclaimed the excited father.

"Your confidence is safe with me, although I do not know

for what reason you should distress yourself thus—" replied the lawyer.

Merrit Grayson briefly told the story he had heard from the lips of the dying woman, and with a look half of sorrow half of defiance, faced the man who wished above all else to become his son-in-law. "Now Slaughter you professed to love Dora, before this, what do you think of it since you know her to be a—I can't say the word? Excuse me but I never made a practice of saying colored people, and Negress hardly seems appropriate, it is so much like tigress. But since you know, that things are not what they have seemed, tell me truly if your love is as unchanged and as sincere, as is the character of my oldest-born? I am her father, and I wish above all else to protect her and the rest of my family, who are, mind you, as good as any and better than most people under the heavens above."

For a few minutes the room was as silent as a tomb, then Carl Slaughter with a peculiar expression on his face arose— and taking a key from his pocket unlocked the door to a private drawer in his desk and took therefrom a small book which he proceeded to open and finally placed before the other, with the remark—"This was my father's diary and among other things concerning his professional career I found the statements I place before you. I have known of this for some time, and in that fact alone you may be better convinced of my love for Dora. Read for yourself."

It was an old style memoranda with a substantial morocco case and although the writing was yellow, yet it was perfectly legible and easily read.

Under date of Easter Sunday, April 18—was written.— "Attendance upon Mrs. Clayborne, etc—Strange experience with a servant called Hannah. She stopped me in the hall one evening as I was leaving the Clayborne house and told me she wanted to tell me something no one else must hear. I stepped into the library and closed the door for I saw by the excited features that the poor creature was in great distress.

" 'Mars Slaughter, Missus done sent for me to come and show the gal Molly how to dress de baby, and shore as I'm alive that ain't missus' baby a' tall. Hit's Caddie's baby for I done dressed it my self yestidy in dem very close and more-soever, I knows them babies apart. This'in is sure cullored and ain't missus' baby, but she done seen it now and say hit got eyes like hits pap', and mouf like hits granny and she done put a little ring on its finger and say hit must stay there till the finger out grow it, for she say she put it on with a wish.'

"I tried to persuade Hannah that she must be mistaken but she would not have it so, and as nothing else would satisfy her I promised to speak to the Col. about it the next day. That night I was called to Montgomery and it was some days later before I again visited the Claybornes. The horror I saw in the eyes of Hannah and the manner in which she watched my movements convinced me that she had something to say. I made an excuse for sending her for my case, and as she returned I met her in the dressing room.

" 'Oh Mars Slaughter! Mars Clayborne done gone and sold his own baby and left this here'n for missus. He and Caddie must a got things mixed for he sure done sold the wrong child and its gone up river to the Lord-don't-know-where.'

"The earnestness of the poor creature, and a thorough knowledge of the caprices of a mother about to be robbed of her child, led me to make an investigation, first cautioning Hannah to say nothing to any one of her discovery. I sought out Col. Clayborne and stated the case to him. He flatly refused to credit it and declared he believed this so-called discovery, but a put-up-job to cause him trouble. Hot words followed and then and there I severed my connections with Clayborne. He made no effort so far as I know to follow up, or locate the child he had sold, and as a physician my position was little better than that of father confessor, for I dared not push matters without better testimony than that of a slave,— a slave's mere suspicion. Heaven will reveal all things, but God knows I believe that somewhere in this Southland—a slave—a pure white child is in bondage, and that child is the daughter of Col. Ellwood Clayborne."

Merrit Grayson, his face white, and his features strained, yet with a certain dignity, closed the little book and returned it to Carl Slaughter. "Well my boy, if my daughter's happiness depends upon you, then make her happy, and if ever you feel that you cannot do so, I"—but he did not finish for the men had been so engrossed in their mutual sorrow that they had not heard the opening of the door of the outer office some fifteen minutes before, and now when it closed with a bang, both gentlemen sprang to their feet and hurried to the hall. A discharged office clerk was just stepping into the elevator. Slaughter turned a trifle pale, and then said—"If agreeable to your daughter I will call to-morrow evening."

This interview and others that followed were soon productive of definite arrangements for an early marriage, and a consequent trip to Europe. The time was fixed for June 1st, and now that day had arrived. After the celebration of the old custom of awakening the bride with the singing of the bridal, the different members of the family prepared in their own way for the festivities of the day.

The twins—Raymond and Marcellus—were bringing gladness to the hearts and sweet-meats to the stomachs of a crowd of urchins who had solicited "errand work" at the kitchen door. Small corners of cake, and pans of icing with

stray pieces of ham and chicken wings, were rapidly disappearing, while Ray and Marc entertained the children with
accounts of the inner workings of the great event. "I reckon
you'uns won't allow we'uns to git a look at the bright grooms,"
and one little fellow looked wistfully at Ray as he munched
the cookie in his dirty little hand, but Ray unheeding the
warning look from Marc, stoutly declared "O yes we will.
Its to be at the big church and every one who comes and
brings one of our tickets is sure to get in, cause my aunt Effie
told me so." Then a bright idea occurring to him, he called
his brother aside and unfolded his plan, which meeting the
instant approval of the practical Marc, away ran the twins
while the urchins, their number augmented by the arrival of
a strange, hungry looking young man, wondered how and by
what means the tickets spoken of could be obtained. They
had not long to wait, for the boys soon returned with a box
containing twenty engraved cards which bore this simple
statement:

"Please present this card at the church."

In some manner the idea was soon understood and the
tickets began to sell like hot cakes, for from three to ten
cents, according to the reputed wealth of the purchaser.

Little Edna Clayborne, who with the year-and-a-half-old-
baby, had joined the crowd, was anxiously watching the sale,
and trying to decide upon some plan whereby she too, might
witness Miss Dora's marriage. Then remembering her own
valued possession—an Angora kitten—she bounded away
leaving Isaac Orlando to the tender mercies of his fellow
scamps.

When Edna returned she marched boldly up to the twins
and demanded: "A kitten's worth of tickets." This demand
was met with a shout of derision from the spectators, while
the youthful merchants, cast into doubt by the problem of a

satisfactory adjustment of such a purchase, examined the cat, and as it was a beautiful creature and promised new diversion they decided it was worth three tickets. The tickets thus disposed of, the children separated, and little Edna was wearily "luggin" the baby home to the favorite strains of "Bringing in the sheeps" when she was accosted by the stranger who had watched the sale a few minutes before.

"I say sissy, I'll give you a quarter for one of them tickets you just got" and the piece of silver was temptingly held out to the ex-owner of the Angora. Edna eyed him suspiciously and then said loftily, "Who is you, and is you 'spectable?"

"Never mind about me—I'm his royal Nibs of Nibbsville. Just you hand over one of them cards before I cut yer ears off"—replied the man.

Thus appealed to and seeing no way of escape, the card was given in exchange for the quarter and the baby was gently admonished to hurry along, cause the beans would sure burn, if he didn't.

It was five o'clock in the afternoon, and the large crowd gathered at the church bore evidence of the popularity of the couple about to be married.

To be sure, some surprise was evinced when the ushers seated two rows of little black girls and boys and when Edna and the baby, duly arrayed in their Sunday best, were seated beside the fashionable Mrs. Norman Rossin, that worthy dame, in the name of her departed ancestry—requested the usher to please find other accommodations for the "persons" who sat beside her.

The bridal party finally arrived and with the usual pomp and ceremony of such occasions, each participant took his place and the minister began the sacred service.

In the midst of that silence which follows the words "Speak now," a young man arose from no one knew where, and distinctly said, "I forbid the bans. It is an illegal act in this state for any minister of any religious denomination to marry a colored or Negro woman to a white man. Dora Grayson has Negro blood in her veins and you dare not perform this ceremony."

The effect was all that could have been desired from such a malicious source. Merrit Grayson had arisen and faced the accuser, and then white and shaking in every limb, he had sunk back into the seat. Slaughter and his best man, had involuntarily reached for the hip pocket, and then helplessly dropped their arms. The minister, with blazing eyes, and threatening attitude in stern words, commanded the young man to come forward and produce proof of his assertion. But proof came from another source.

Dora Grayson, dignified, sweet, composed, turned to the minister and in clear tones said—"It is true, let us not listen to the story of the past, now. If this ceremony cannot proceed under the conditions we may at least withdraw in peace."

Slaughter, the lion of the senate, the pet of the club, the wit of the banquet, led from the church, past the pews of the proudest and wealthiest the girl whom he loved but whom the laws of his state forbade him to marry. Crushed yet resolute, defeated yet defiant, the groom-elect handed the girl into the waiting carriage and was driven back to the Grayson home. The family soon followed, and in which face was the most misery, the most suffering, would be hard to decide. The guests went to their own homes and no one save the minister and the strange young man remained. The latter explained very glibly that at one time he was a clerk in the office of Carl Slaughter, and after being dismissed he had returned one day for a talk with his former employer and hearing him in conversation with another gentleman in his private office, he had seated himself and thus heard the story of that skeleton which occupied the spare closet at the Grayson home.

He had taken a run up from Atlanta the day before, hoping to see Slaughter and exact quieting money from him, but finding an easier way of humiliating Mr. Slaughter and the rest of them big-bugs he had abandoned the former plan and procured an entrance card to the church and now he guessed their cake was all dough. In disgust the minister turned abruptly from the informer and was about to leave the church when one of the trustees approached and desired an interview.

"If all this stuff is true, we might as well get through with the unpleasant part at once. This church does not fellowship Negroes, and as senior trustee I shall call a meeting and have this settled before we lose our best members."

"My God! my God! and has the church no place in it for such as we have just seen denied the privileges of the most sacred of its ordinances? God forbid that I wear the holy garments only to deny the faith that I am trying to instil in others. I see the whole thing now. We are the servants of the world, we are the most abject slaves of mammon, we are crucifying our Lord daily, and I for one, shall begin now to ask God's mercy upon me, chief of sinners, that I know myself to be." The minister knelt at the deserted railing of the altar and poured out his soul before the God of Sabaoth. The trustee, bored and uncomfortable, took his hat and went out.

For three weeks after the sensational revelation at the fashionable church very little was seen of any of the members of the Grayson family. It was known that Slaughter had returned to Atlanta, but for how long and for what purpose, none could say. In fact society canvassed and gossiped the affair in a guarded way, for openly it avoided any direct investigation. It felt that its own foundations were of such a nature that it must handle with care any stones which came within its way.

Mrs. Norman Rossin, upon her return from the church walked straight to the library, took from its shelf the large family Bible and carried it to her room and never again was it seen by any member of her household.

Mrs. Grayson and Dora seemed strangely self possessed. Malcolm spent most of his time with his favorite pony, the twins tried to adapt themselves to the new order of affairs by acquiring a knowledge of the life of little colored boys. When no one was near they took turns in calling each other "nigger" just to see how it felt. To Aunt Effie the blow was mortal. She had been kept in ignorance of everything until disclosure was made at the church and then she had done what she usually did at a crisis—fainted. Afterward when her brother told her the facts she became hysterical and blamed Aunt Caddy for all their misery, and now at the end of three weeks she was reduced to a mere nonentity.

The family was seated at the table and the fish was being served when a servant entered and handed a letter to Mr. Grayson. He glanced over it and laid it by his plate, then picking it up and reading it a second time the full significance of it burst upon him and in a frenzy he tore the sheet into bits.

"The Rev. Mr. Voorhees regrets his inability to accommodate my sons at his private school, for the next term," and he abruptly left the room. His wife did not tell him that upon her dresser lay three envelopes, each containing some such insult. The first was from Capt. and Mrs. Benjamin, recalling their invitation to dinner, but assigning no reason. Another was from Madame Carée, announcing her regrets that she could no longer accommodate the ladies at her dressmaking establishment; the last, and worst of all, was from the man-of-all-work, Sam.

He wished her to know that they had treated him well, but it was a matter of "principle" with him, and he would not work for "cullord folks. As long as you was white it was all right, and if you'en is ever white again, just send for me and I'm your man, but I won't work for no niggers if I knows it," and thus Sam's resignation was filed.

The minister called and although the call was not a pleasant one, yet his unspoken sympathy and love went far towards the soothing of the ruffled sea.

Judge White's son, Ben, came often and stayed late with Malcolm, and several ladies made it known in various ways that they were friends of the family in spite of reverses.

One morning Dora came into the sitting room with such a radiant face that every one asked what good news she bore.

"It is a message I received from Carl, in the first place. He says, he has arranged everything and we may all start for Europe next week if we can get ready in time. He has put papa's business in the hands of a capable agent and there is nothing left to do, but to get ready for our vacation.

"My second cause for joy is this: I think we all have been very silly to spend so much time weeping and mourning over the fact that we are of Negro extraction. Are we not as good as we were before we found this out? If not it is our own fault. Have we changed in our love for each other? Have our feet become larger or our lips thicker or have horns begun to grow on our heads? If we have endured insults and calumny, it has been only for three or four weeks. Think what it has been to those around us, who have endured these things not three weeks only, but all their lives. We have ourselves heaped upon them some of the very burdens which now threaten to overcome us. If I am a Negro, from this day forward I mean to be just as persevering, just as ambitious, just as successful, as the white Dora Grayson of a year ago. After our marriage, Carl and I shall return to this same place and live before these people the lives of two honest God-fearing citizens, and the right people will recognize and encourage us too."

Ten days later when the family left for New York, a little colored girl stood on the deserted porch holding to her breast an Angora kitten. She watched the carriage as it drove out of sight and taking a corner of her gingham apron she wiped the tears from her eyes and then turned to Isaac Orlando with the philosophic remark:

"If poor Miss Dora and them boys is not white, then they is the most respectable colored folks in the world, and if they finds they can't pass for white where they is going, maybe they kin fix it so as Mr. Grayson an' Mr. Carl can pass for colored."

# THE BETTER LOOKING

*Gertrude Dorsey Brown[e]*

"There is a certain social clique in many small towns that merits the ambiguous epithet of 'up-to-date.' There are certain gentlemen who are occupying positions several degrees below that of senator, who are yet prone to consider themselves lords of creation, but for unprecedented presumption this case of Clarice Jones beats the record," and Miss Mildred handed the morning paper to Miss Elizabeth and advised her to examine the personals.

Miss Elizabeth glanced hurriedly over the first page and then became deeply interested in the fourth, while her sister sewed vigorously on the pajama and waited for some recognition of the wisdom of her comment.

"That sounds good," murmured Miss Elizabeth.

"What sounds good?" snapped Mildred.

"Why this new kind of cream fudge served with candied cherries and pistache; I can just imagine how delicious it must be," said Elizabeth smacking her lips.

"I must say Elizabeth Lucas, you are the most exasperating creature I ever saw. Here I gave you the paper to read a personal, and you have been wasting this time reading the recipes, finding some expensive way to get the stains out of the old table cloth and I dare say hunting up the market quotations for butter and cheese, ascertaining the exact time for the trains to go and come, and informing yourself gen-

*Colored American Magazine* 8 (March 1905): 146–50.

erally on such topics as will be of no earthly or heavenly value to you," and with an indignant bounce the younger sister left the room.

Her words had the desired effect, however, for Elizabeth began dutifully to hunt the personal column and having found it, read the advertisement of Clarice Jones:

> "Wanted—Correspondent with view to matrimony, by refined and educated lady—good looking—sweet voiced and owning extensive property, etc., etc."

This description was even too much for her to pass by without some word of protest.

"Refined and educated lady—indeed,—any person who says, 'pizen' for poison, and 'taters' for potatoes—pshaw! Good-looking—humph!

"Owning extensive property—ha! ha! She must refer to her feet and her pompadour for they are extensive enough land knows," and Miss Elizabeth continued to read the personals.

Suddenly jumping up and clasping her hands she rushed to the door, and almost fell into the arms of Mildred who was just returning to the room.

"O Mildred, we're in it too," she screamed.

"In what?"

"In the paper among the personals."

"In the paper among the fiddle-sticks. What ails you? Do you want the smelling salts? Is it your nose or your instep that hurts!" and Mildred, the younger, looked half sorrowfully at the excited Elizabeth who still protested that the paper contained a personal that concerned them.

"Here is the piece, and you read it for yourself if you can't believe me," and sure enough with many little catches of the breath Miss Mildred read the following:

'Will the two attractive ladies who made purchases at
Roberts' music store yesterday morning call on or address
Mrs. B. S., Hotel White, Room 28, third floor? That there
be no mistake the taller of the ladies wore a dark tailor-made
suit and walking hat, her companion who was the better
looking of the two, wore white shirt waist and brown walking
skirt. It is important that this receive attention.'

"So I am the taller of the two attractive ladies and quite
naturally you are the better looking and we constitute the
Alpha and Omega of this important advertisement. Really
Bess, this is all your fault, for in my very bones I felt that
your buying that copy of 'The Angels' Serenade,' when you
can neither sing nor play it, was a piece of extravagance, but
you never will listen to my superior advice, although I am
your younger sister."

Miss Elizabeth received the sisterly caress that always
followed invectives of the petulant Milly, and then walked to
a small escritoire and took from it a roll of music which had
not been opened since its purchase the previous day.

However instead of "The Angels' Serenade," the roll
contained the written copy of the celebrated "Intermezzo
from Cavalleria Rusticana," as prepared for the violin and
clarionet.

"O I see it all—I made a mistake and picked up the wrong
roll. Evidently Mrs. B. S. has my music and I have hers,
and it will be no harm for you to run down to the Hotel and
exchange it for me," and Elizabeth smiled most bewitchingly
upon Mildred, who although in no wise deceived or flattered
was yet strongly in favor of gratifying her curiosity to see the
person who dared to say that she was not as good looking as
her sister.

It was four o'clock, and Tom, the porter, was just leaving
the hotel to meet the 4:20 train, when a tall, neatly dressed

lady presented herself at the office desk and asked to see the register. The obliging clerk dipped the stub pen into the ink and extended it to her, which courtesy she refused by adroitly remarking, "I am looking for a friend."

Yes it was there: Mrs. Brownlee Stuffæ. Room 28—3rd floor.

As she entered the elevator a sudden sense of the awfulness of her position rushed upon her, but it was now too late to retreat, and when she knocked at No. 28, she felt in all respects equal to the occasion.

She opened the door in response to the summons to enter, and beheld a sweet faced woman seated by the window before a music rack; and on the floor beside it, lay a violin, and a music roll,—the exact duplicate of the one she carried. The lady arose and advanced, and with an encouraging bow said, "You are the lady, doubtless, with whom my son made an exchange of music rolls at Roberts' store yesterday. Do be seated and let me tell you how thankful we are that you saw and answered our 'ad' in the paper." While Miss Mildred surrendered the roll Mrs. Stuffæ continued:

"You see my son is first violin in the Metropolitan orchestra and as his copy of the intermezzo had been misplaced, we had not time to send for another which contained both parts, so Mr. Roberts kindly consented to make the necessary copy, and by mistake it was given to you I suppose.—Ah here he comes now," and the door opened and a young man entered. Mildred recognized the person who had held the door for her and Elizabeth to pass out the music store, but her manner was perfectly formal and stiff as Mrs. Stuffæ undertook the honors—"My son, Mr. Brownlee—Miss—"

"Lucas," supplied Mildred.

While Mr. Brownlee was delivering himself of the usual formulæ, Miss Lucas was secretly annoyed to think that so handsome a young man would dare advertise her in the paper as less beautiful than Elizabeth.

They were on the whole very friendly people but Mildred refused to overlook their one great error, and even when Mrs. Stuffæ thrust upon her two reserved seat tickets for the evening concert, she mentally vowed that the person who occupied seat No. 74 at the Grand Opera that night would in every particular be as lovely as the holder of coupon 75.

The result of this determination was so emphatically impressed upon the mind of the first violin and his mother, who occupied seat 73, that after being introduced to Miss Elizabeth at the close of the program, they went back to the hotel and for half an hour discussed the Misses Lucas, especially the tall, proud Miss Mildred.

Exchange of courtesies soon followed, and during the week of the grand concerts, a friendship was formed between the families of Mrs. Brownlee Stuffæ and Mr. Daniel Lucas, which certainly was more substantial than those usually formed upon the basis of a newspaper advertisement.

During the months which followed the departure of the Stuffæs, an occasional square envelope contained the message which kept Miss Mildred informed of the movements of the first violin, and wherever "Intermezzo from Cavallaria Rusticana;" or "Angel Serenade" appeared on the program, they were underscored in a most pronounced way.

One evening in May while Elizabeth was reading the paper she espied a second pathetic appeal from Miss Clarice Jones to the general masculine public.

It seems that her wants had not yet been gratified notwithstanding the good looks, sweet voice and extensive property.

"Really Mildred, I am sorry for the poor soul, and hope she will find what she wants in the way of a correspondent."

"I don't pose for a philanthropist myself but I mean to

help that woman in some way," and Miss Mildred answered the door bell while Elizabeth pushed forward the best chair and shook out the cushion with a deft hand.

"Well who would have thought of seeing Mr. Stuffæ to-day? but here he is," was the introductory speech of Milly, as she advanced with her guest into the room.

Instead of explaining his unexpected visit at the beginning, the first violin was ready to go before he ventured the information—

"I am hunting some one who can take the place of our soprano. She was called to Boston to-day and we give a concert to-morrow evening at the Normandy, in Columbus, and we must find a substitute."

A wicked gleam was in the eye of Mildred as she gave Elizabeth a warning glance, and then smoothing down the ruffles of her pretty dimity she very modestly offered her services to the young man.

"O Miss Mildred, can you help me out," he exclaimed.

"I do not sing myself, but I read in one of the late papers the advertisement of an accomplished lady with a sweet voice and as I happen to know her, I'm sure I could make arrangements for you to meet her and you might be able to procure her"—and again the eyes of one sister said to the other, "Say one word if you dare."

"I will give you her address and a note of introduction," and while Mildred left the room to write the address of Miss Clarice Jones, Miss Elizabeth was left to entertain the visitor.

Her determination that the plans of her sister should not succeed, urged her to remark, as soon as they were alone:

"Mr. Stuffæ, I beg that you do not put any dependence upon the services of the sweet-voiced lady of whom Milly speaks. Actually her voice is—well not at all what you expect, and this is only a little joke of Milly's."

"We will settle matters in my way," he laughed as Milly re-entered the room, and handed him the note of introduction.

"I have decided to ask Miss Elizabeth to accompany me and hear the lady sing, as she has such excellent taste I am sure her assistance will be of value to me, so please get your hat and we will go."

Again the eyes of the younger sought the eyes of the elder, but for once Elizabeth wore the serene look of the just, "who knoweth his duty and doeth it," and as she passed into the hall she said sweetly, "I'll not be gone very long, dear, you may depend upon that."

Miss Clarice Jones was not at home to all appearances but as her callers were about to leave, the lady with the sweet voice entered the yard from the rear, and catching sight of the gentleman, she hastily cast aside her apron, gave the extensive pompadour an affectionate pat and with a voice like the echo from a frenzied Zobo shrieked at him:—

"I reckon you're the chap from Rileyville who wants to marry me, and as you're not bad looking, jest come in a spell and may be I'll have you."

Without a word, but with a dangerous look in the eyes which said "This is the most unkindest cut of all," Mr. Stuffæ wheeled around and led Miss Elizabeth from the yard.

Even Job in his misery was allowed comforters, and why need the first violin go comfortless?

How thoroughly he was comforted we can only surmise from the short conversation that Miss Milly overheard as she lowered the window.

"But Jack I did not think you cared for me, I am not nearly so clever or so attractive as Milly, and, and—"

"And what, darling?"

"Just think, we became acquainted through the newspaper,"

Mildred closed the shutters with a bang and in mimic disgust muttered—

"I never did believe in newspaper personals but she ought to, for he still clings to his first impression, 'her companion is the better looking,' and in spite of all I can do or say, she is the better looking."

# THE GIFT OF THE STORM

*Frances Nordstrom*

The night was dark and a great storm raged upon the sea. The wind blew loud and shrill, and the waves tossed and beat against the shore in angry fury.

The people of the island were shut tightly in their little huts soundly sleeping, as such a storm as this was no stranger to the hardened, sea-bred fishermen and their families.

The only light to be seen burned brightly in the tower of the light-house some little way from the island down the coast, where Captain Grey, the keeper of the tower, stood with his field glasses at a small window anxiously scanning the angry waters.

Grey was a man of some sixty-nine or seventy years, and in his prime had been the commander of a larger merchantman, but advancing age and health compelled him to retire from active service, to forsake the deeps he loved for comparative shallows, but where with the "lip, lipping of the waters" still about him the regnant passion of his life for their companionship reigned grimly on.

The room in which he stood was small and bare, graceless of the little comforts and touches which women give, significant in its mute way of the two lives within it, for on a cot asleep lay the figure of a man. It were easy for the trained physiognomist to trace the relationship existent between these two, to recognize them as father and son, but no scientific

*Colored American Magazine* 8 (Apr. 1905): 190–93.

probe can sound the depths of human affection, and between them was an affinity of interest and a singleness of mind and heart bred of simple living and past trials borne together.

The old man stood for some moments silently gazing out into the darkness, then with a sigh and a mutter of "it's being a bad night," took his seat beside a little pine table and dropped his white head upon his withered hands.

Suddenly he roused, and, after a keen glance at the sleeper, pulled open a small drawer and took out a picture at which he looked long and sadly. Then gradually his eyes filled with tears and his hands trembled so that the bit of cardboard rustled in their grasp.

The bright and winsome face of a young girl looked up into his own, a girl of about seventeen years, with large mutinous eyes and a wealth of wavy dark hair. It was a promise, in the way that all faces are promises or histories, the promise of a quick, ardent, imperious and highly sensitive creature. What possibilities lurked in the red, resolute lips, what dreams lay hidden in the white brow. The quaint, home-cut gown fitted the dainty figure to perfection, grace and youth sat smiling on the throne of life, and the heart of the man who gazed was as ashes in his breast.

Eighteen years ago that night the old salt had seen this winsome "wee thing" become the wife of his only son, Addison, with grave misgiving, for though he owned her charm and lingered almost with as much tenderness as her lover upon her beauty, his graver judgment, ripened by a wider experience of the world than had come to his boy, told him that no happiness could ensue from the match, for Bess West was a flirt and a romp, already spoiled by the adulation of men and the jealousy of maidenkind. However, with the insistence which only the very young and the very old possess,

Addison had swept aside tender opposition, and with the
magnificent egotism of manhood entered upon that estate
which makes or mars most of his kind—marriage.

He was a fine, steady-going fellow, and his girl wife held
all that was best of him in the white hollow of her dimpled
hand, but not many months had elapsed, nor the glamor of
the honeymoon quite faded, before he began to recognize the
grave mistake they had both made. Her demands for excitement, what she was pleased to call "life," appalled the serious-
minded, determined benedict, for considering his straitened
circumstances and narrow opportunities, it was borne in upon
him that he could not meet her expectations nor satisfy her
temperament. The island life was dull, the fisher folk were
so also, and mingling with his pain and regret at her rest-
lessness and carping, was the recluse's fear of the mighty,
pulsating world which lay far beyond his ken.

A year passed, a year of disagreements and some recrimi-
nation, and then there entered into the home that which
should have healed all differences and smoothed for both the
way back to marital felicity. But matters grew from bad to
worse, and one night, after a bitter quarrel over a mere trifle,
Bess Addison disappeared from her home, taking her baby
with her.

Wounded to the quick and smarting with a new sense of
public shame, Addison refrained for a week from following
her. Content in the thought that she had returned to her
parents in a miff, he awaited some word or message, light as
thistle-down, he told himself, but all sufficient to bring him
to her, glad to take, if need be, whatever blame her haughty
nature demanded. But the days sped without the white message
of peace, and with a new fear working in his fevered brain
he sought her, to find that she had left him indeed, and, in
the companionship of some visiting tourists, completely dis-

appeared. Vainly he followed, vainly he endeavored to trace her. Money, the great silencer of human tongue, had locked such lips as might have aided him, and with rage and despair consuming him he had returned to the drudgery of the light-house and the companionship of his father. Many times, unable to stand the sickening silence and the fears which only the loving heart can know for others cast upon unknown waters, he had started blindly out to follow her, but always a sense of duty to his fast fading father and a species of grim contempt for his own unsurmountable weakness, had con-spired with him to drag him back to the island—and the winds and the waves told him nothing.

The man who had been sleeping suddenly awoke and started to his feet, but the captain, engrossed with his thoughts, sat on until a hand was laid upon his shoulder and a voice exclaimed,

"What are you doing, father?"

And then Addison Grey's eyes caught his wife's picture, a thing he had not seen for years.

The lines about his mouth tightened, over the prematurely grave face a pallor stole.

"Where did you get this, father?" he demanded, taking it up and devouring it with eager eyes.

"I have had it for a long time, Addison," explained his father. "I kept it from you as I felt sure it would only pain you, lad."

The younger man attempted to laugh. It ended in a groan. What use to masquerade with one who knew the secrets of his soul? He sat down weakly, shaken to the foundations of his very being. To think that an echo should rouse the ghost of his past—a picture, an insensate bit of paper! In the silence which followed, feeling was more eloquent than words. At last he spoke in a queer, concentrated voice.

"I was wrong in marrying her. What had I to offer a beautiful woman? And even when she made me see it, I was too stupid to make some other opening for us—to take her away—so she left me. I wronged her, but I loved her; I love her yet. And the child—the child! The long, empty years, father!"

The dull roar of a cannon boomed out to sea. The two men looked into each other's faces and passed in an instant out of the unrecoverable past into the strenuous present. The signal of distress came nearer and deepened into a steady repetition.

"A ship on the rock!" exclaimed Addison, hurriedly thrusting the photograph away. "The life-saving crew will be out soon. Good bye, I'm off with the boys."

He was right. Lights began to glimmer along the shore. Shouting men ran hither and thither, and the voices at times encouraging and advising one another rose over the roar of the storm. After many vain attempts Addison managed to launch a boat and, after a desperate struggle with the waters, reach the main shore, where he was quickly accepted as part of the first crew to the rescue. It was a battle for life, and every strained muscle responded to the uttermost before the ship was reached, but not before she had dashed repeatedly upon the rocks and was sinking fastly. Only a few remained upon the fated vessel. Many boats had been lowered, but the black waters swallowed them and those in them went down to death.

Clinging to a broken spar was the figure of a woman. She was rapidly losing strength, and suddenly she dropped. The water splashed and covered her, but brawny arms were outstretched and quick hands drew her into the boat. A lad and two sailors were also caught as they rose to the surface, and, after some further futile search, the life-boat pulled for the shore. It was even a more difficult struggle. The fiends who wait on human destruction were with the elements, and inch by inch the hardy fishermen fought their way to safety with the human cargo, until willing helpers on the shore rushing to their help cheated the cruel sea of its prey.

Addison carried the woman he had been most instrumental in saving to a nearby house, leaving her in the charge of a good fish-wife, and then, with affectionate impulse, stirred perhaps by the earlier scene of the night, started out in the face of protest and danger for the light-house and his father.

The morning dawned bright and clear. The sea was calm—the placid, rippling calmness which seems to succeed its fury and mark its attempt once more to soothe the minds of those who live upon it into a species of infatuated confidence.

The house to which Addison had borne his burden was quiet, and a species of enforced anxiety encompassed its members. Several times Mother Allen looked into a room where a woman lay exhaustedly sleeping, but no sigh or sound issued forth, and at last she stole into the room and bent anxiously over the sleeper. The old woman started and drew back.

"Where have I seen that face before?" she muttered. "It ain't no stranger to me."

A decidedly beautiful girl lay before her. The raven hair, curling in wet ringlets about her, threw into sharp contrast a white face and dark, silky lashes. The lips were parted, the short upper one with its overripe fullness suggesting a haunting memory. Mother Allen stood gazing fixedly at her charge, the look of fright deepening on her kindly features. Hurriedly she left the room to return in about half an hour with Addison Grey. He tramped in timidly. A look of embarrassment softened the chill face, and the evident shrinking of the strong, self-reliant character from praise or notice was visible in each motion. It had occurred to him that this waif of the waters would offer him reward, or submerge him in a torrent of grateful words, and both were equally distasteful.

"What do you want with me here?" he exclaimed when it dawned upon him that the woman still slept. "I will see her again. This is no place—no time—"

But the fish-wife caught him by the arm.

"Wait," she cried in trembling accents. "Wait, man. May be my sight's failing me, and it may be I'm plum crazy, but—look at her, look at her."

And with that the old woman ran out of the room.

He looked and staggered back, every drop of blood in his body rushed to his heart.

"Great God!"

A haze fell over his eyes. Surely death was such as this— and then he found he had slipped to his knees beside the bed and the girl had moved. As she did so Addison caught a tiny gold chain worn around the white throat with a small locket attached. Mechanically he opened it and looked—looked straight into his own eyes.

The locket fluttered unheeded to the floor, and Addison Grey gathered his sleeping child to his breast and sobbed aloud.

# BLOOD MONEYS
# OF LA PETEI'

*Gertrude Hayes [Dorsey] Brown[e]*

La Petei', whether French or Italian or both does not matter,
La Petei' was a foreigner—a stranger in a strange land.

The shaggy over hanging eyebrows were of themselves
forbidding, but the sullen mouth, the hair-lip was positively
menacing. He sat in the miserable court on the door curbing,
and without seeming to notice his surroundings, watched the
one gate through which passed the promiscuous and motley
crowd of those who inhabited the tenements of the foreign
section. Now an Italian wheeling a banana cart, now the
Jewish miser who drove the junk wagon, two Polish women
with bright red scarfs and immense bundles balanced on their
heads; and again, a Syrian lad feeding pistachio nuts to a
large green parrot,—and children, O so many children—La
Petei' saw them all as they passed in and out.

His wicked little eyes, alert and bright took in the scene
and yet no one would have thought that he was conscious of
his surroundings. Once only did he show signs of life. From
the balcony overhead a woman descended to the court below.

Madame Fanchaux—in the remnants of a once handsome
gown made in dear old Paris—paused in the middle of the
dirty walk, and, looking up at the window above, threw a
kiss and waved her hand, before joining the crowd of bread
winners who jostled and pushed in the busy street.

La Petei' watched the trim figure of the little French
seamstress as it dodged in and out, disappeared, reappeared—

*Colored American Magazine* 9 (Oct. 1905): 567–70.

and finally was lost; then rising awkwardly he strode into the room he called home.

A child scarcely six years old sat upon the floor idly playing with a crucifix and clay pipe. It certainly was La Petei's own son, in spite of the yellow hair and attractive face.

"More dinner," the child said.

La Petei' dived into the pocket of his greasy velveteen jacket and threw a banana to the boy.

"Hungry, no more nanna, tired nanna, want sweet wound thing like Louie," and he pointed significantly across the court to that part of the building where lived Madame Fanchaux and her crippled son.

The father, moved by the appeal for food from the one being on earth whom he loved, took the child into his arms and in that one fierce embrace made a vow to himself that he would bring home sweets to his Alon' such as Louie had never tasted. As he sat the child down he noticed the crucifix and hastily crossing himself fled from the building.

Why did the Wicked One keep urging him on? Ah "sweet wound thing like Louie," that was what made him do it. Yes, yes Alon' must have food.

He had stolen bananas and black bread from Aldragio' time and again, and he had brought home his piece of bologna from the free lunch, but now Alon' should have sweets.

Swiftly the man walked; looked neither to right nor left, but straight to the narrow street where the foreign shops were clustered.

La Petei' hurried along the row and finally stopped at a small apothecary shop. He boldly opened the door, and to the little wizened woman who accosted him from behind the counter he demanded:

"Where ze La Terrore?

"Ze La Terrore' not in town. He no live here anyhow," replied the woman eyeing him suspiciously.

"La Terrore', here I say," and approaching nearer he mumbled something to which there was an instant reply from behind the screen at the back of the shop.

"Gott" was all the woman said but La Petei' passed behind the screen and through the small door into the large room where sat the La Terrore'.

For the next fifteen minutes the two men talked rapidly, fiercely, in an unknown tongue. The argument was at its height when another person entered the shop and the noise behind the screen stopped instantly.

At last La Petei' came out into the front of the store and offered to the old woman a slip of paper.

She looked at it and without a word opened the money safe and counting out a roll of bills handed them to him.

Now Alon' could have sweets for a month, ah yes and a pretty green jacket with a scarlet tie and he should have three large candles to burn before the Virgin at early mass. Had he, La Petei', not earned the money and was it not then in his pocket with his hand on it?

Ah surely—but the ugly Louie with the hump on his back—his mother would not have to work so hard now to buy him nice things for La Petei' had sold the little cripple to the doctor from his own country who could mount his twisted bones and sell them again to the big college.

"Ah—ze pore devile, he haf to die one day, why not now! Ze La Terrore' not give moneys very big but it buy sweets for Alon'," and La Petei' quite satisfied with his deal, which he did not regard as a crime, sauntered over to the bridge, and stood gazing into the water.

"Man fool—big fool to fall in water to die, ugh!" and he shuddered and walked off.

Poor little Alon', quite lonely and eager for a companion, wandered around the deserted court for an hour and then thought of Louie the French boy who sat by the window all

day and did nothing but look at beautiful pictures and eat
sweet confecto from a little pink box. He wished he was a
cripple with a hump on his back and a pink box with sweet
things.

Then he ran into the house and taking his little pillow,
stuffed it into his blouse, and mimicking as best he could the
antics of a little cripple, hobbled into the court.

Around and around he gamboled, using a broom stick for
a crutch and allowing one leg to hang limp, as Louie did.

Finally two swarthy men took a position in the gate and
watched Alon' as he hopped about.

"Have ye got the dope ready?" one man asked of the other.

"Yes,—thet ez the kid now," replied the other.

"Well, don ye mek no bunkle of it. Git him pat, and 'en
come on afor the mater comes back. I'll be jest around the
corner and when this job is done me and you goes to clover
right quick," so saying the first man disappeared and the
second boldly approached Alon'.

His method, whatever it was, of attracting the child and
gaining its confidence, succeeded and he picked him up and
hurried from the court.

Half an hour later La Petei' entered the same gate, his
pockets full of bundles and in his hands a large basket of
fruits and sweets for his Alon', his darling Alon'.

He paused at his door and looked guiltily across the court
at the window on the second floor. "Deo—est Louie?"

Yes, that looked like the French cripple.—Why yes, he
was waving his hand to La Petei' and beckoning him to come
up.

La Petei' entered his room and called Alon' at first tenderly
and then loudly, but no response.

Where could the child be?

Ah! the rogue, he must be at the Italian's, watching them
sort the fruit. He would go to see.

In and out of the rooms, in the fruit cellars and in the sheds the father hunted, yet no one had seen Alon'. At last after a two hours search Madame Fanchaux rushed into the little room and earnestly begged La Petei' to listen to the story her boy Louie had to tell of two dark men who took Alon' away with them. Louie had seen the men talking at the gate and he saw one of them approach Alon' who was trying to be a cripple with an ugly hump like he—Louie.

The man had given him a pretty flower which he smelled and then Alon' went all pale and closed his eyes and the man carried him away.

La Petei', the truth at last filtering through his dull head, screamed and swore and raved and shook his fist at Louie, and opening his blouse, flung a roll of money at poor frightened madame.

"Tis ze blood moneys—my son, my poor Alon' he come not again, he smell ze poison of La Terrore' and now he with ze Virgin—Curse ze crooked devile who sits by ze windy. I go and fall in ze water—I sell to La Terrore' no more—I die—I eat waters and die—O my son, my Alon'."

In vain did they try to reason with him and try to understand his ravings. Some one sent for a policeman but before he came, La Petei' had gone, no one knew where.

Next morning very early a child was laid on the cot in the room where La Petei' had lived.

The child had yellow hair, and the white cold face was attractive if not pretty. Death had been kind to the little fellow and left no cruel marks upon his features. No one saw who brought him home, but later, many saw the black wagon draw up to the door and take away little Alon' to the morgue where side by side lay father and son.

One drowned, the other murdered.

A small pillow fell from the blouse of the child as he was carried into the morgue.

The little tragedy created some excitement for the time, but the same crowds pass daily in and out of the gate—the Italians, Poles, Jews, Norwegians and Syrians. The little French seamstress still goes back and forth to work but she does not wave and throw kisses to the boy who sat by the window.

For that same boy has a new pair of patent crutches and every Sunday he burns three candles before the Virgin.

# A CASE OF MEASURE
# FOR MEASURE

*Gertrude Dorsey Brown[e]*


## CHAPTER I
## WANTED—LEOPARD SPOTS

"Please, Ora, do try to discover or invent something that
will make me look like the real thing. I can't just explain to
you, but I am sure it is only for the novelty of the thing,
and not for any burlesque on your race. I don't think you
ought to feel offended or act ugly about such a harmless thing
as our 'little colored ball.' "

Agnes Hein regarded her maid, Ora Marshall, with evident awe and with plain apprehension, but the colored girl,
recognizing her advantage, continued to brush the luxuriant
hair and deigned no word of reply.

"Ora?"

"Well, Miss Agnes."

"Will you do it? *Please?*"

"I suppose I *could* if I tried."

"Well please try."

"Let me see; if I understand you, the case is simply this:
Your Navajo Club has been invited to Savannah by a social
club there, who are giving a colored ball, and wish you each
to represent a colored person, and—"

*Colored American Magazine* 10, chs. 1–2 (Apr. 1906): 253–58; 10, chs. 3–
4 (May 1906): 301–4; 11, ch. 5 (July 1906): 25–28; 11, chs. 6–7 (Aug.
1906): 97–100; 11, ch. 8 (Sept. 1906): 167–72; 11, chs. 9–10 (Oct. 1906):
281–84.

"That's it, that's it exactly."

"Now tell me what *class* of colored people are supposed to be represented?" inquired the maid.

"Why, just anybody, no particular class, in fact I didn't know there was a social scale among your people. Of course we don't mean that extremely bad set like Chick Clark, or Cad Riley. Just a gang of ordinary cotton pickers, laundresses, cooks, hotel waiters and Pullman porters,—oh, most anything that is decent and comical," and again Miss Agnes looked half timidly at her servant.

"I am a maid, and is my position decent and comical? Is that what you mean?" asked Ora.

"Oh, the position would do all right, but the person in it makes all the difference in the world. You are certainly decent—the most decent girl I can imagine, but comical—never. You are not just like other maids I have had, for while you are not altogether solemn, you are so perfectly correct or so correctly perfect that I can't quite get used to you. You are a genuine treasure, for you do your work so well and seem to fall in with my ways so intelligently and so readily, and yet I cannot command you. I am sure to request instead of command. Now Katie was kind hearted enough, but a hundred times a day she would look silly and say, 'Why Law, I forget that,' or 'Deed and double I sure didn't hear ye.' You don't know how annoying it is to have such a girl around one.

"Lettie was good enough at times, but I couldn't trust her; for while she wasn't dishonest she was officious, and she used to dress in my, not *second* best, but very *best* clothes and go places in them, and all that, and I couldn't stand it. What I've endured and suffered with my maids, if written out, would make the old martyrs pale with jealousy.

"You see, Ora, I don't want my face smeared up with

burned cork or anything black and greasy. I want to be a pretty light brown-skin like—well, like you, and can't you think of something that will do?"

"I'll see what I can find, Miss Agnes, and will let you know. There is, at present, no great market demand for stuff to turn people darker, most people being as dark as they care to be," replied Ora, dryly.

Miss Hein's toilet being completed, the maid and mistress separated for the rest of the morning, but by neither was the "colored ball" forgotten.

# CHAPTER II
# WINNING HER WAY

Ora Marshall was not any ordinary maid, for ordinary maids are not collegiate graduates; neither do they prepare themselves systematically to be real companions of those whom they serve.

A blind and ready acquiescence to every opinion, and a servile agreement with whatever is proposed, whether senseless or profound, these were not the qualities that won for Ora the respect and regard of those by whom she was employed. Never seeming herself to forget that she was a servant, never presuming upon the good will of the family, she yet inspired its members with a wholesome regard for her opinions and a disregard for the position she occupied as maid.

Mrs. Van Leiter, the housekeeper, like the rest of her kind, believed that the proper care of the home and the servants was the one and only divine calling. Others, as ministers of the gospel, evangelists, etc., were well enough in their places, but how on earth could they reach an age of usefulness, unless some one kept house while they studied and prepared for work?

But it came to pass that Mrs. Van, the divinely called, was favorably impressed with the "new colored girl," and before the first month had passed had asked her opinion on various subjects and in several instances had ordered her conduct accordingly.

The household servants, more or less clannish, at first resented this superior ladies' maid, but as each in his turn found his dislike rebound to his own confusion or discomfiture in one way or another, she was quietly accepted as an unnecessary evil, and in time proved herself a very necessary blessing. When the horses ran away and James the coachman was violently thrown to the ground, it was not the hand that rocked the cradle in his pretentious cottage that ministered to the wounded members. The cold compresses which reduced the swelling and eased the patient until the arrival of a physician, were prepared and applied by the same hand that bandaged the broken leg of Rastus, the fierce thoroughbred.

A knowledge of hydrotherapy and its practical uses were the means of breaking down the last barrier that existed between Ora and Jerusha the cook, for Jerusha's outraged sense of social precedence was not easily appeased, nor was her heart reached by any common avenue. It happened this way. Jerusha became the victim of an earache, a very severe, a most painful earache, one that refused to be comforted by the different remedies that were tried, and when her long suffering husband presented the case and asked permission to call in the minister to pray for the offending member, he explained: "Ye see, dis here ain't no common yereache, fer I done squeezed de drap of blood from a black betty bug in her yere and, fore de Lawd that didn't do no good noways."

"Well what do you suppose is the matter with it?" the housekeeper inquired.

"De debbil, de ungodly debbil," briefly announced William.

"Why William, what makes you think the devil is in it?"

"Well, ye see, Rusha has allys had him in her tongue, and sense she has begun to grow so fat, natcherly de debbil spread wid de rest of her, and now it done retched her yere, fore de Lawd, and nothin' short o' 'mazin' grace goin' ter cure her. Dat's why I done suaded her to get de parson.

"Rusha sure do fuss a lot an' natcherly makes me feel mos' as bad as"—

But William proceeded no further, for with a shriek of pain poor Jerusha ran into the room and throwing herself into a chair poured forth entreaties, invectives and unspeakable groans in such profusion that Mrs. Van, realizing her utter lack of succor, rang for Ora, and with a feeling of entire security, demanded that she do something immediately for "that poor creature."

After the incoherent recital of her woes, Jerusha submitted to the simple but effective treatments which followed, and when the pain became quieted she remarked half in scorn, half in admiration, "Who'd a thought biled water and a timpertoor would a made my yere feel so good, and me a biling water every day ob de year. I declar I sure do feel like a baby takin' his fust nap," and in a few minutes the gentle snoring of the recent sufferer attested the perfection of the old lady's simile.

"Now, William, you may get some laudanum. Mrs. Van Leiter, can you spare a small piece of that medicated cotton, for while she sleeps we will forestall a second attack by stopping up that ear?" said Ora.

William returned shortly with a bottle containing a brown fluid, and on the label was the unmistakable skull and cross bones and the name in large letters, "LAUDANUM."

Quiet and peace at last restored, the patient happily disposed of, and the housekeeper more than ever proud of her profession, the maid returned to the sewing room and spent the remainder of the evening darning the refractory hosiery of her mistress. No wonder Miss Hein considered her a treasure, for who would ever recognize this dainty silken hose as the rag she had discarded because the buckle of her slipper had torn a small right angle into the instep. Here was art as well as knowledge, for the rent had been drawn neatly together and the unsightly right angle served as a part of the letter H that was heavily and skillfully embroidered over the tear.

"Really, Ora, the hose belong to you; but since you have put my initial instead of your own on them, and it is done so beautifully, I must appear selfish and keep them, while you really must take this dollar for your trouble," and the silver coin was laid in the maid's hand, who entered it on her day book as extra change.

Small wonder, at the monthly reckoning, the regular salary of $20 was augmented to $28.85.

While in the midst of settling her accounts Ora was interrupted by the shuffling of feet and the customary "fore de Lawd" of William, who stood just inside the door bowing awkwardly and looking fearfully from right to left.

"Fore de Lawd, Miss lady, I sure done done it now. Dat stuff I fetched ye for Rusha's yere ain't no more launam den sugar cane is hoss redish. Dat stuff Rusha done made herself, an' put hit in de ole launam bottle, and its for to put on hay."

"To put on hay? What did she mean by making something to put on hay? I don't understand," and Ora looked at William as at something bereft of reason.

"I doan mean hay, I means hai, or what it is dat de Lawd let grow on our haids. Dat stuff sure make gray hai turn and be black again, and now fore de Lawd, Rusha say some o' hits got on her face and she's afeered she's goin' to be some darka den she ca'h to be. Kaint you do somefin to hep her out?" And the appeal in the old man's eyes spoke eloquently of the travail of his soul.

"I can't imagine how a stain, however dark, can possibly effect Jerusha's complexion. Hers is a black that defies comparison and er or est can mean nothing when attached to it." This was the mental comment of Ora as she followed the sorrowing husband to the little room over the kitchen.

"Heah ye come," screamed Jerusha from the banister, as she beheld the two ascending the stairs. "Maybe ye think biled water'll take de black offen my face, same as it took de debbil out of my yere."

"Quite an idea, Jerusha, I have been wondering just what to do, and now you mention it I believe some very hot water with two or three lemons squeezed into it will make you look quite like yourself again," and suiting the action to the words a generous application of the solution removed every vestige of stain and reduced Jerusha to a state of admiration bordering on insanity.

"How quare you is, anyways. Jest put hot lemonade on my face, and I 'clar I'm a light brown skin once mo. I isn't stuck up none ober my hai and my culla, but I is powerful proud that the good Lawd didn't make me as black as some is," with a significant look at William, who protested feebly against the implied affront to his color by scratching his head and saying, "Fore de Lawd, Rusha, I kaint be so berry many colors darka den you is, I sure kaint."

"All right, Willium," loftily, "yit you kin see you isn't as fair as I is," and Ora turned away in disgust from a conver-

sation that certainly occurs oftener than is necessary among
all classes of colored people.

The question of color and hair is as freely discussed among
the educated men and women of color as it is among those
who have had small chance to know better. How often does
the Negro prove himself an enemy to himself and yet stoutly
declares against a white person who snubs him? Race prejudice
will never, can never die out as long as the Negro forces the
black man back and puts the light or mulatto man forward,
for the sole reason of a shade or degree of color.

Can we hope to see the great problem solved, so long as
our working men and women refuse to hire themselves to
those of the race who need and are willing to pay for their
services? Dare we to expect the infant of to-day to become
the man of to-morrow, when we tolerate, nay, perpetuate the
hated words "nigger," "coon," and "darkey," in the bosoms
of our families? We sing them, we play them, we hang them
on our walls, and yet we call ourselves "the repairers of the
breech, the restorers of paths to dwell in." As Ora thought
bitterly of these things, consistency appeared more than ever
before the pearl of great price.

But here, at a most unexpected place and time, was to be
found the means of granting Miss Hein's latest request. This
hair dye of Jerusha's must answer the purpose and pave the
way for this young white lady to appear as she desired at the
"colored ball" in Savannah. Since the week before the maid
had been importuned every morning for this same aid that
now presented itself, and should she not avail herself of this
opportunity?

Quick to decide and as quick to act, Ora retraced her steps
and after a diplomatic parley with the owner, secured the
bottle and returned to her rooms.

Three days later, having tested upon her own arm the

merits of the dye, the maid delivered the preparation into the hands of her mistress, who was leaving that day for Savannah.

Miss Agnes Hein had for several nights slept with her hair plaited into many small braids, each braid having been previously immersed in quince seed curline, and now when Ora carefully unplaited the braids, the crisp, kinky locks certainly looked uncomfortably like those given by the Creator to the despised race, and as she worked a feeling of indignation took possession of her and mentally she consigned the white colored ball to the same depths of contempt that she reserved for such unhealthy compositions as "Red Rock" and "The Clansman." But if such thoughts were entertained by maid, they were plainly no part of the happy meditation of mistress, who as she contemplated her partial transformation, and noted with satisfaction the bushy mass, skillfully twisted and turned under, in the very style she had seen worn by Katie, the ex-maid, became more and more anxious to assume the entire outfit. Without objection or hesitation the dye was massaged into the soft white skin, and when all was finished the result was astonishing even to Ora, and so gratifying was it to Miss Hein that she forthwith gave permission for the maid to spend the rest of the time as suited her best, and included a five dollar bill as a testimonial of her appreciation.

When the carriage drove up to the front entrance and James announced that it lacked but forty minutes of train time, Miss Agnes ran to her room and rang for Ora.

"I want to be un-Negroed," she laughingly explained to Nellie Griffin, who was to accompany her to the city, but the laugh died in a violent death when search was made over the house, but Ora Marshall could not be found.

"Oh, heavens! what shall I do?" wailed the girl, as soap and water failed to erase the stain.

"Oh, merciful heavens!"

# CHAPTER III
# CHARLEY GALE

The billiard room of the club was fast filling up with its usual patrons, the balls were rolling merrily, and through the haze of smoke from the dozen pipes, the white shirt fronts and the sparkle of costly gems, bespoke the presence of wealth and even extravagance.

At small tables in another room, men were seated playing cards and sipping wines from tiny glasses, while white aproned waiters moved softly about refilling glasses or removing empty ones to side tables.

"Queer thing, about that avenue affair," remarked an elderly man to a group of smokers sitting apart by one of the large windows.

"Yes, very queer. First time any nigger escaped the hemp who ventured on the avenue," replied a mannish looking youth.

"Where do the police think he has gone?" inquired a third.

"Haven't heard, but I am strongly inclined to a belief that the police know as little about that fellow as that fellow does about the crime," continued the elderly gentleman. "Fact is, gentlemen, that fellow Gale came here from Boston two years ago with my wife's sister and I saw much of him. He made himself useful around my law office and I observed him carefully, and in my opinion he is not the sort of Negro to commit such a crime."

"The sort, did you say?" questioned the youth.

"Yes, sir, I repeat, Charles Gale is not that sort of Negro, or I am no judge of men," replied the first speaker.

"This is a question of niggers and not of men," blurted

out the other, as he elevated his feet to a position on the window sill several degrees higher than the yellow fuzz on his upper lip which he fondly hoped might some day be dignified by the name of mustache. "Take him at his best and, as my friend, Mr. Dixon, says, he is *one* sort, and that is a very *bad* sort, a *damned* bad sort. How any man can speak of niggers as *men*,—well, it puzzles me."

"When you become a man, my boy, you will put away childish things and possibly learn several things which now in your immature state appear as mysteries;" and while the chuckle was still going around Judge King summoned a clerk and ordered for himself and a half dozen gentlemen suppers in a private dining room.

Percival Smith stared stupidly after the retiring party and savagely brushed his upper lip as he realized that his opinions had been so lightly regarded—in fact had been ridiculed.

Once inside the cozy little apartment the conversation was again resumed, nor was it a one-sided argument, for several of the men held views very similar to those of Smith, although they respected the judge and regarded him as a man who knew whereof he spoke.

"I'll admit, gentlemen," said their host, "I am one of those tender creatures who infest every decent community, with a certain amount of God-given conscience, and I am not ashamed to again repeat my conviction that that boy Gale had no hand in the avenue crime, and his disappearance is a matter which your own common sense tells you was deuced timely. He knows how men accused as he is are dealt with, and doubtless had some objections to Manila hemp as a neck ornament. But we won't discuss this any further, especially as these are colored men who are waiting on us; here comes one now."

"Why that's only Dummy," laughed one of the men. "Haven't you heard, Judge, of our latest acquisition? Then

hear of the annexation of Dummy to the working force of
Ocean View Club. Like Jonah's gourd, he sprung up in the
night and was fully equipped with references which installed
him chief tabber of the juices before morning."

"When did it happen?" asked the Judge.

"Oh, 'bout a week ago. We fellows were sitting around a
jinny in the card room when Thomas came in and told us we
were missing something by not being in the office to witness
the moving pictures up-to-date. Young Howard naturally
connected moving pictures with women and butterfly dances,
and before Thomas could explain, half the boys were on their
way to the office. Then Thomas tells how a young darky
mute is trying to get himself engaged as a waiter at the bar,
and by the time he has finished his antics, in comes the gang
bringing Dummy along, and Dummy is here to stay. Knows
every juice and its combinations, knows how to keep his eyes
open and his mouth shut, and now a fellow can have as
private a talk as he wishes and get properly served at the
same time, without danger of hearing his remarks parroted
about among the fellows who shine his shoes and pour his
coffee," and the speaker sized up the "acquisition" with an
approving eye.

Judge King, from his position at the table, commanded a
side view of the young colored man as he stood at the side
board deftly arranging glasses and sorting liquors, and although the man was of ordinary build and stature, he yet had
the unmistakable mien of one who dignified any office he
might choose to hold.

An hour spent at the table, another at bridge, and the
frown on the Judge's face relaxed and a new light dawned on
his face. "Here, Joseph, get me a mint julep, and tell Dummy
to fix it up. No, keep the change, only let Dummy fix it for
me," and when the julep arrived and had been duly quaffed

by the best authority on juleps, as well as criminal law, in the state, W. J. King, a peculiar smile on his face, took his hat and stick from the attendant and bade the company good night.

As he neared his beautiful residence, in the up-town fashionable district, he saw a cab driving away and three women were disappearing into the hall. "More company, I'll be bound," and the laughter that greeted him as he entered his drawing room, at least satisfied him that here were women enough to furnish ten houses of that size with noise and gaiety galore.

"O, papa, isn't it just too funny? Agnes and Nelly have just come, and please look at Agnes. Isn't she great? Just listen: You know she has a maid that is the envy of us all, and she got her all fixed up for our ball for to-morrow night, and she looked so comical that she kept the stuff on and came over with Nell as Nell's maid. They've had all kinds of larks and I'm sure Agnes will make the hit of the ball."

Miss Julia King enjoyed the joke and was so excited over it that she mixed her pronouns indiscriminately and the Judge was at a loss to know whether Agnes or the maid or both were involved in the disguise and the consequent lark. It was not until the clock struck twelve that Julia was reminded that her guests must be tired, and showed them to their rooms.

"Now, Ora, for goodness sake stay close while I am disguised in this fashion. If you hadn't hit upon that plan of passing me off for a maid we never could have made that 7:50 train, but now that we are here, I don't mind you taking hold at once and getting this stain off my face, for I must look decent when I go down to breakfast."

The lemons, hot water and liquid of potassa with which the skin was gently massaged finally worked the desired results and Miss Hein fell asleep at two o'clock, while Ora Marshall sat by the dressing table reading from several papers the account of the dastardly crime, and the unsuccessful search for the "brutal Negro, Charley Gale," who committed the crime.

"Charley Gale is innocent; of this I am sure, but poor boy, I fear he has made a mistake by showing these white people that he has working machinery in full operation in his head as well as his hands." Was it while visiting in Alabama Hall, or was it while domiciled at proud old Burton Chapter, that she had heard some one singing these words to the tune of the Marseillaise:

> "It is the march of education
>     That leads in triumph o'er the land,
> That makes the glories of a nation
>     By training heart and head and hand."

Very likely she had heard it both places, but the campus opposite Burton Chapter was the one spot where, in their Senior robes, she and Charley Gale had exchanged the vows of heart, head and hand with another meaning and with other thoughts than those now occupying her mind. She turned the electric button with a click and sought the comfort and rest she so much needed.

# CHAPTER IV
## IN THE SNUGGERY

Breakfast over, the Judge took his newspaper and retired to a certain corner of the back veranda, which from long association had become known as the Snuggery, and here he smoked and read and dozed.

From time to time a servant passed the retreat or a guest

wandered by in an aimless way that guests have of roaming about the house and grounds. Once only did Mr. King fear intrusion, and that was when Julia and Tom, on their way to the tennis court, brought a crowd of girls directly to the spot where he was pretending to sleep, and in mock gravity his daughter's voice warned the giggling girls, on pain of banishment, to make no noise, for "behold this is the sanctum sanctorum of my beloved father."

"It used to be the spanktum spanktorum of your beloved brother," Tom replied irrelevantly, at which the Judge stirred uneasily and the girls laughed outright. When the laughing had died away to what the Judge supposed a safe distance, he very cautiously opened his eyes and reached for his pipe.

"Excuse the intrusion, Mr. King, but here is a message for you which is of the utmost importance, and which I promised to deliver at once."

William King looked at the colored girl who stood before him and then laughingly remarked, "By Jove, if you are a Navajo I don't recognize you, and if you ain't a Navajo I don't know you, so, in any event you have the better of yours obediently."

"I am Miss Hein's maid, Ora Marshall, and my errand certainly concerns you quite as much as my presence bewilders you," and this time the note was taken from her hand and hastily read:

> "Can you arrange to meet me at once—*privately*—on very important business?—M. J."

And at the bottom of the sheet a postscript was attached: "Should you have any difficulty in determining my identity, bearer of this note is instructed to enlighten you."

"Surely a day of mystery, for M. J. might mean a score of things, in fact anything from Mary Jane to Meandering

Jack, but to neither of them do I owe allegiance, and I'll have to ask for that enlightenment which you are instructed to give." Very shrewdly the old gentleman regarded the girl and no expression of her face escaped him.

"You said, Mr. King, that M. J. might mean a score of things," and leaning over the taborette so that no word could be overheard by a chance listener, she whispered, "Might it not mean 'Mint Julep?' "

# CHAPTER V
## ACQUIRED—LEOPARD SPOTS

When Judge King emerged from his den and joined the young people who were having luncheon, his manner, always polite and hospitable, was nevertheless not quite up to the standard. Tom's easy wit was allowed to pass unchallenged, and the salad course received small attention from one who regarded it the essential of luncheon, but perhaps the greatest digression from the beaten track was noticed when the judge arose without excuse or apology and hailed a colored maid who was crossing the lawn.

"Hi there, Miss—Miss Marshall."

The maid stopped and the judge lost no time in joining her and walking to the gate, where he remained in earnest conversation for fifteen or twenty minutes.

As evening drew near, the gay party dispersed, the young men going in a body to the club, where their various "make-ups" were effected, and the girls placing themselves under treatment from maids and skilled hairdressers. Jerusha's invention was very much in demand, as it was found that so little was required to give the desired effect. When finally the giggling, ludicrous crowd of "colored belles" assembled in the front hall the judge drew a silent comparison between the extremes of all that was gaudy and ridiculous—the mantles that covered his daughter and those with her, who represented the culture, refinement and wealth of the South, and the tidy but modestly attired maids, "original Negroes," who represented the illiterate, uncouth, the poor, the despised. One class was an exaggerated type, a burlesque, metamorphosed into that which must forever remain unclassified and nondescript.

The other class was neither more nor less than a legitimate example of those people who engage to make an honest living, whether in the livery of maid or housekeeper.

> "The time is out of joint, O cursed spite
> That ever I was born to set it right,"

quoth the judge as he re-entered his den and locked the door.

The carriages have arrived, the Dinahs, Chloes, Hannahs and Mirandys were handed in by their respective Sambos, Calebs, Remuses and Jaspers, and the house was left in comparative silence.

"Now is my time to look around and see that everything is in order for the company I am expecting. I believe I'll step outside and put that longest ladder up to the back hall window and forget about it and leave it there. Then I think I'll loosen the wire screen at the window, and perhaps it would be just as well to accidentally leave a dim light in the front hall, and Miss Marion's door might be left carelessly open and a few of these diamonds put here and there, in order to facilitate matters. Just why women—good looking white women—should wish to dress like Julia and Marion have rigged out, is too much for me, but for scamps like Tom and his crowd, well there might be some method in such madness, after all." Coolly locking the door Mr. King strolled out into the yard and lighting a cigar, took a leisurely course up the avenue, although a half hour later he entered the side gate and slipped quietly into a small Summer house which commanded a view of both front and side entrances. The Summer house was already occupied by two persons, and when a third and fourth arrived the whispered words "mint julep" instantly secured for them a seat in this mysterious council chamber.

In striking contrast with the dark Summer house was the brightly lighted banquet hall, where the "Seasiders" were lavishly entertaining the "Navajos" and "Jolly Friars" from the neighboring cities. As Ora gazed over the assembly from the balcony, where some half dozen maids were watching their mistresses do their parts in this comedy of errors, she wondered if in any part of the civilized world there were colored people who dressed and acted as did the dancers below. Such startling combinations. One group presented sufficient material in that line to have sent whole generations of artists into a state of hopeless insanity, and yet that same group was composed of men and women who were considered connoisseurs of art. She was not surprised to hear one maid say to a companion, "Betty, if I thought I ever looked like these people do, and Bob looked like these men, I'd sure kill myself."

But now a signal from the gentlemen's cloak room on the opposite side of the house, and Miss Marshall no longer saw the rainbow of color, nor heard the shouts of laughter. She vanished into the dressing room, secured a shawl and slipped quietly down the stairs, pausing an instant to listen at the street door and then passing out. A gentleman assisted her into a cab and springing in beside her, closed the door with a bang.

"Did you see him?" she whispered.

"Yes indeed. Working like a charm," came the answer.

"Tell me how you managed."

"H.N.O.$_3$."

"H.N.O.$_3$ what?"

"Put it in that mess of pottage you gave me."

"Well, what then? I don't seem to comprehend," and Ora waited anxiously for the information which was forthcoming.

"Well, it was like this. From the time I overheard him and young Smith plan to make this robbery, I felt convinced that I was on the right track of the fellow in the other case, in my case. So I fixed up what the boys call a loaded cocktail, and by the time that had been disposed of my man talked very glibly from both ends of his tongue. In the meantime in comes Mr. Tom grinning from ear to ear, and tells Smith and Henderson about Miss Agnes coming here all stained up like a nice looking colored girl, and immediately I saw that Henderson was becoming intensely interested, but still had sense enough left to keep his own counsel. Then I sent the message to you to meet me when I came off duty at the address on the bluff, for I was sure that if Miss Hein was in the city, you were also. The Judge knew me by the julep I fixed up, for he taught me how to compound it, and after I had overheard a part of his conversation, in which he expressed a belief in my innocence, I felt that I could trust him. You know the rest. He acted the man to the letter, and it is surprising how soon the report spread among the men that some of the famous stuff would be in the ladies' dressing room to-night. The Judge arranged for me to come over and make the punch, and Mr. Tom put in a word on the quiet to certain parties that for a small bit of change he could get some of that stain from Miss Hein's maid, to help out in case any one feared his color would fade before the evening was over. This is the place where Dummy got his master-stroke. A maid smuggled a bottle to him when she came to the hall for ice. Dummy takes the bottle, puts in some diluted H.N.O.$_3$ and sets it on the dresser in the men's smoking room, and then hunts a label and puts on it, and waits patiently for the fish to bite.

"Masterson is the first one to take the bait and then a couple of strangers from your own town, and just when I was beginning to despair in glides the heavenly twins, Smith and Henderson, and they both use the precious fluid on their faces and arms and necks, while Dummy stands by looking as blank and unconcerned as a brand new set of scratch tablets. Shortly after this the darky bootblack, Mr. Tom, comes in, and receiving the countersign from me promptly captures the bottle and returns it, almost empty, to you, while I am left to watch the movements of those two devils.

"At last Henderson goes for his stick and says as he passes Smith in the doorway, 'Come on, Pete, lets you and me go and get somethin' to wet our chops,' and after some foolish attempts to mimic colored men Pete accepts and out they go. Then I signal for you, and here we are at the side gate of Judge King's home."

They quickly alighted and were soon lost in the dense foliage that surrounded the Summer house. The sound of the departing cab could still be heard when other signs were heard and the figures of the two men darted into the yard from the front carriage drive and fled to the rear, always keeping in the shadow of the house.

After a few minutes the watchers in the arbor heard a husky whisper.

"I say, Perce, it's dead easy."

"Which way?"

"Why some old dunce of a nigger has left a good stout ladder up against the back porch. Come on, lets try it," and up the ladder went the speaker, while the one addressed as Perce stood at the foot and waited for developments.

Two or three minutes passed before the words were received from overhead: "This is the easiest thing I ever tackled. Not a nigger in sight. Old screen came out like a rotten barrel head, and nothing to do but 'walk into my lady's bower' and here I go. Come on, if you want to get that money you need and escape the wrath of the old governor." But the latter part was lost upon Perce, for he was already half way up the ladder.

Two very rough looking colored youths in rough clothes and slouch hats moved cautiously up the hall of the mansion and slipped into a room whose door stood ajar.

"Now wouldn't this fill your granny's pipe?" whispered one, as he seized a diamond ring and slipped it into his vest pocket.

"That may fill your granny's pipe, but this here little jeweled ticker's going to fill my bank book," replied his companion.

"Listen. What was that?"

"Nothing, gentlemen, only a little light on the subject to help you find some other filling for your worthless carcasses— well, by jingo, if they aint niggers. Young Smith didn't miss it by far when he said last night that niggers aint men," and Judge King, revolver in hand, surveyed the captured pair and motioned for the three or four men who stood in the room to advance and secure them.

Taken so unawares, no resistance was offered till one of the men opened the hall door and called, "Bring the rope, boys, we've caught the niggers dead to rights and here's where we have a tree party."

"O I say, fellows, this is a step too far," remonstrated the larger of the two criminals. "This is only a joke which we can explain, and you'd better go a little slow on this rope business."

"Gentlemen" (it was the polite, even voice of Judge W. J. King), "before you take charge of your prisoners, leave them with my son, and come into the dining room and have a good mint julep. A particular friend of mine, whom we call Dummy, is preparing the same, and it will surely put life into you and serve you for the work you have on hand."

# CHAPTER VI
# TO THE RESCUE

"Hello! Give me police headquarters."

"This you, Captain McDowell?"

"Well, this is King, and I want to know if you have your men detailed for the rescue? Yes, they're caught all right."

"What?"

"Well, send them along pretty lively now, captain, for they are about to leave my house. Yes, over by the bridge."

The receiver was hung up as the leader of the lynching party ordered a "forward march," and two miserable wretches were hurried out a rear entrance half fainting and scarcely able to plead for that mercy which is so seldom granted to colored men who are charged with crime, and never to those who are caught with the goods.

What, though the men said they could explain, that they were guilty of nothing worthy of death, the Charley Gale case was freely quoted and offered a precedent which could not well be denied. He was accused of entering the bed chamber of a white woman, a guest at an avenue hotel, and although the woman's screams had frightened him away almost as soon as his presence became known, yet it was argued he could have gone there but for one purpose, and no one thought of it as an attempted robbery, for a Negro can have but one intent, one motive for entering the secret chamber of a white woman.

"I say," began Smith in a feeble treble, "can't you fellows listen to a man for a minute? For God's sake do."

"This is a case of niggers, not of men," was the laconic reply.

"Pretty brisk now boys, before any one comes along to complex things. There's the bridge. Get that rope ready, and remember the middle beam." The leader held grimly to the smaller captive and issued his commands in a voice that a novice could scarcely assume.

"Who the devil are those men on horses coming up this way? Police? Ah come on. Swing these niggers. What?

"Who demands them? Look out now, we caught these fellows and we're going to see the thing through.

"What say? Judge King? The devil he did. Did you hear that, boys? King's turned softie and telephoned the police, and here they are three to our one to rescue two worthless villains. Let 'em have 'em, we'll come around and serenade them when we can pick up a decent number of men to sing the right song. Lord! how I wish we had a few like young Percival Smith with us to help this through from principle." The crowd dispersed after some further parley, and the younger of the two prisoners was lifted into a patrol wagon in a dead faint, while the other wiped his brow with a white linen handkerchief and whispered, "Gee, I call that great in King. He's the only brick I've seen south of the M. & D. line."

At headquarters the prisoners were searched and such things

as were found were carefully registered and laid in a drawer in the sergeant's desk to remain until the hearing in the morning.

"Put this fellow Henderson in No. 18. No, never mind that window in the corridor. He's safe enough in 18."

"But they threaten to come after them to-night. Hadn't we better—ah, put 'em in the new part?"

"Who's running this office? I reckon I said No. 18, and No. 18 it'll be. That new part wasn't made for everybody."

"What'll we do with this," pointing to the inert object at his feet.

"Take him to the tank and spray him with the ice cold. That'll fetch him. Then put him in with Pete—the darky in 32, and he'll keep him company until morning."

This dialogue passed between the sergeant and the turnkey, and the prisoners were disposed of accordingly.

When poor Finnegan beheld the white body of the "dirty nager" he crossed himself and made a solemn vow to touch not another drop of "spirits" this side of his own wake.

What his victim thought, upon gaining consciousness and finding himself in a close cell with a large, coarse Negro occupying the only cot, and snoring in a way that defies description—well, let us content ourselves by supplying the void with our own imaginings.

# CHAPTER VII
## MORE WORMWOOD

Ora Marshall shall once again behold the gay panorama at the "Negro ball" and almost doubted her senses when she thought of all that she had witnessed during the hour and a half that she had been absent. She scarcely recognized Miss

Hein when that lady presented herself at the dressing room and in some excitement asked to be prepared at once for her return journey.

"Miss Agnes have you not used more of that dye since I last saw you?" inquired the maid.

"Yes, I did, and so did the other girls, as far as the stuff would go. O we've had such slathers of fun. Why Ora you look so funny, what is the matter?"

"O, Miss Agnes, I fear you have used too much."

"Too much? Why, won't it come off?"

"I'm afraid not, right away."

"It simply must come off, and right this minute, too," and the usually sweet tempered girl began to warm up with the old patrician blood of her German ancestors.

"Now get this stuff off quick," authoritatively. "Camile Smith had a party made up to return home in her father's private car; Percy and that chum of his were going along, but they are not here and she has 'phoned to the club and the depot and can't locate them, so she has asked Nell and me to go in their stead. The car leaves at 3:10 and it is 2:00 now, so you see you must have me ready in time. Tom has gone up to King's to make our excuses and get our traps, and he'll meet us at the station with them. O, Julia, we've had such a royal time, and if it wasn't for the rest of the crowd I'd stay until to-morrow, but it'll be such fun to go back with the rest. My goodness, Ora, get another lemon and some more of that liquid of potash, or whatever it is, and do make haste. I'm sure I look,—why Nell, what's wrong?" as a dusky maid began to weep hysterically.

"That pesky dye won't come off. Rose has tried her best and just see my face. Camile is having the same trouble and unless something is found mighty sudden we're Daughters of Dahomey for keeps.

"O, Agnes, why did you make us do it? You knew I didn't want to be very black in the very first, and here I am black and nappy and no way to become Christianized again," wailed the pet of the Griffin family.

"For heaven sake, Ora, why don't it come off? Why I look blacker than Jerusha this very minute, and poor dainty Nell is worse yet than I am. Oh, my! Oh, heavens! Oh, mercy!" and Miss Hein was in unmistakable tears, while Camile Smith looked on in a stoney, uncomprehending way at the frantic efforts of maids to restore fallen mistresses.

"O come on, girls, Tom says you have only a half hour for that train, and what's the difference if you go in Mr. Smith's private car? When you get home you can easily get that stain off and who'll be the wiser or the worser," the voice of Julia King sounded soothingly through the confusion that reigned supreme, and before long the weeping, wailing, contending occupants of the dressing room were being hurried to the station. The gates were still open and they crowded through.

"There stands a couple of porters. I believe I'll ask them to direct us to our car," and Miss Smith stepped briskly forward, but what was her surprise when she discovered in the porters none other than Robert Brister and George McClelland, companions in misery, as it soon developed by their story.

"Like a couple of fools we put some infer—I mean some indelible stuff, that was in the dressing room, on our faces and it won't come off. I've got to report at 8:30 at the bank and this 3:10 is the only train that will get me in in time and here's McClelland, attorney for the prosecution in that Stidell case, due at the court house at 9:30 A.M.," dramatically explained Robert.

"Well, why don't you go and get on the train, if you must

go. Isn't that the train on the third track," inquired Agnes, innocently.

McClelland wondered at the entire lack of penetration which some females possess on occasions that require so little reasoning, and very slowly, very impressively he replied:

"Miss Hein, they won't accept us on the through train. We'll have to wait until 3:45 and travel in the Jim Crow."

"The Jim Crow? O heavens," chorused the girls, while hysterical giggles began again to threaten supremacy.

"I say, boys, you might go over with us in papa's car, if you can find it, for it's almost time. It ought to be coupled to the 3:10 now; why there it is, the 'Camila,' third coach from the baggage. Come one, come all, and when we are fairly started we'll sing the song of Moses and the lamb."

What use to argue and coax and beg with the colored porter who stood guard at the steps.

"Ladies and gentlemen, don't think I'd turn my own color down, but this is strictly a white man's outfit and you can't work no dodge on me. Why this car b'longs to Major Smith, and only his daughter and her crowd of friends is invited to participate."

In vain did Camile plead and threaten and get very angry and abusive. The regular conductor, attracted to the scene by the high pitched and angry voices, inquired sharply of the porter what it meant, and what he heard satisfied him that it was an extraordinary case.

"Why, you surely can tell by our voices and—well, our diction, that we are not Negroes," returned Nell.

"Let me tell you, young lady, that game won't work. A little bit of college and a whole lot of ambition has made colored girls the equal of white girls in voice and diction. Look at the Sampsons and Clarkes right here in Savannah. If you didn't know so much diction you wouldn't be trying now to get on this private car. Time now for us to start and not one of you gets on my car."

"O, Sam, can't you see I'm Miss Smith and this is Miss Hein and"—

"She sure do look like a hen," grinned Sam as he placed his step on the platform and proceeded to lock the vestibule doors.

The train glided out of the depot and the Navajos were left standing on the platform in various stages of insanity and chagrin.


# CHAPTER VIII
# THE JIM CROW

The guard at the gate refused to allow the crowd of Navajos to stand out on the track nor would he unlock the gates and let them reenter the depot, and so it happened when the 3:45 arrived at the station 50 minutes late, a motley wrangling set of supposed Negroes were huddled in the rear platform.

"Let's do the thing up in the right way and have some fun out of it," advised one.

"No, let's go in for our rights, and if the best accommodations are taken, we'll make such a glorious row that we'll soon possess the land," replied another.

The Jim Crow, in its usual position next to the baggage car, looked very much like the two day coaches at the rear, and without further protestation they mounted the steps and entered upon the genuine experiences of thousands of colored men and women who daily patronize the Southern railroad.

"Why this isn't so bad I'm sure," ventured one of the girls.

"When the conductor comes in and gives us a little more

light and some air it—O heavens—you brute—find a seat; don't you see this one is occupied," as a foul-smelling burley colored man lunged forward and dropped heavily beside dainty little Nell.

"Yah! yah! you is de limit," laughed the man good naturedly, and yet making no attempt to move.

Had the hateful stain not hid it, a very pale faced little woman would have been seen to gather up her belongings and pass the man who had seated himself beside her, but once in the aisle, alas for poor Nell.

The train, with one great jolt began its Northern journey and she was thrown, dignity and all, against another colored man who was coming up the aisle. The stranger politely lifted his hat and assisting her to a vacant seat, placed her scattered possessions on the seat beside her, and gravely asked if there was any further service he could offer her.

"Yes, I want that ruffian put off this car," she almost cried as she pointed to the usurper, who now having full possession appeared to have forgotten "de limit" and with one foot on the window sill and the other on the back of the forward seat was preparing to smoke a cob pipe, which gave every evidence of being as disagreeable as its owner.

The gentleman, for it was a gentleman who was thus appealed to, looked from the man in the seat ahead, to the indignant, odd looking woman.

"Ah! You are no doubt a stranger to our customs; have you never encountered the rough element before? Did that fellow dare to insult you? What is wrong, may I ask, and if it is anything I can rectify I shall be happy to do so."

"Why that brute forced himself into my seat. Of course he insulted me."

"Indeed lady, that is an ordinary offense, and one that we are powerless to suppress."

"Why don't you colored people keep such things from getting on the trains. Why I wouldn't ride with them at all if I were a Negro," and Nellie's eyes blazed defiantly, regardless of the peculiar manner in which the stranger regarded her.

"Do you mean to say you are not a Negro?" he inquired, looking at her respectfully but nevertheless incredulously.

"O I forgot—of course I am not a Negro—certainly not, but you don't understand the situation. I fear you will laugh and I shall too, before I am half through, but here goes the story"—and Miss Griffin plunged into the recital of the strange adventures of the Navajos.

In the mean time Miss Smith and Miss Hein were encountering situations both novel and interesting, yet nothing new to the patrons of Jim Crow cars.

Camile and another young lady bent upon having their own rights seated themselves in a section vacant of human occupant, but containing an innocent looking carpet bag— one of the kind so often seen carried by poor whites and colored people from the rural districts in the South.

"Let's push that old sack under the seat," said Camile, and suiting the action to the word she gave a vicious kick with the toe of her smart Oxford, and with the kick came the unmistakable squeal of a small pig, and with the squeal of the pig came the emphatic scream of two young Navajos.

"O heavens? It's a pig or something else. O what an awful place"—and out in the aisle the ladies hurried.

At the back of the car McClelland sat moodily gazing out of the window, but as Miss Smith and her companion came stumbling up to where he sat, with what grace he could master under the circumstances he ushered them into his seat and sitting on the dusty steam-coil coolly quoted:

"If you'll have a coon for a beau
I'll have a Navajo."

Agnes Hein began to feel that she was fortunate even if
she was compelled to ask a share of the seat beside a colored
lady.

The wealthy girl, not realizing that it was impolite, nor
discourteous, was silently "sizing up" her seat mate, in fact
had reached the conclusion that her teeth were very even and
white, that her hands were manicured in the correct style,
that she was reading a nicely bound copy of the Rubaiyat and
that her feet were small and well shod, when the "masher"
appeared.

The professional masher for want of a better name and
occupation, has become well known and understood by the
majority of travelers and is everywhere recognized by a kind
of trade mark which he carries in his face as well as in his
manner of dressing.

It was one of the genuine brotherhood who with a smile,
intended for encouragement, but really filling all the requirements of an emetic—presented himself before the unsuspect-
ing Agnes.

"Let me see, I believe I met you once, but your name—
what might your name be?" gazing boldly into her face.

Taken by surprise, she returned the gaze and answered
weakly—"No sir, I'm Miss Hein; I don't think you did."

"Of course I ought to know you, I've been down about
Floridy nigh all summer and lowed I'd go up this a way for
a spell and maybe I'd marry if I can git the sort of woman I
want. Lem me see I bleeve yor a travelin the lonesome road
yorself," seating himself on the arm of the chair in that
offensive way which only the masher has mastered.

The young colored lady quietly closed her book and turning

around beckoned to a young man sitting several seats to the rear.

"Mr. Paine will you kindly see that this man does not annoy us any longer?" The request was made so calmly and the answer was so promptly given that even now Miss Hein cannot recall just what did happen. The man who a moment before was perched on the arm of the chair was escorted to the seat by the door in such an energetic manner that he forgot to make any further arrangements for his companion— along the lonesome road, and the remaining chapters in that autobiography, at least Agnes was saved the torture of hearing.

She turned to thank the stranger beside her and was met by a frank smile and a careless "O that's all right" which encouraged her to inquire:

"Did you ever hear of such impudence before?"

"O, many times," her companion replied.

"Why I didn't know that people are so rude on these kind of cars."

"Didn't you? Well some are worse than others, but he is bad enough."

"I suppose you know all about them."

"Any one who travels as we are forced to, can not help but know something of the rough element."

Miss Hein became thoughtful, and finally suggested:

"Why don't you colored people who act like ladies and gentlemen protest against riding with such roughs?"

"Why don't we colored people who are ladies and gentlemen get that justice from white people that will recognize a decent from an indecent element? Why are we all classed together? What plan would you suggest whereby railroad officials might be able to tell at a glance who is and who is not entitled to ride in a first-class Jim Crow car? Why are we riding in one now?"

"Why I'm here because they won't allow us on the other coach."

"Exactly. You are here because you are colored," responded the other.

"But I'm not a Negro, really,"—began Miss Hein, and immediately she saw her mistake, for the Rubaiyat was opened promiscuously and she received no more attention from the person beside her.

Half an hour later and Mr. Paine interrupted her reverie by saying:

"A friend of yours, a Miss Griffin, is occupying an entire seat near the rear, and asks if you will not come and share it with her," and as Agnes rose he added, "I hope the change will be a mutual benefit."

"A mutual benefit? What could he mean?"

She had not long to wonder, for when Nellie became talkative she went at it with the same thoroughness that characterized her plans for entertaining, and in a short time Agnes had heard all about the ruffian who smoked that strong pipe, and about the knight gallant who had given up his seat, and who, by the way, had studied psychology and every other ology, and was now teaching electrical engineering in a colored university at or near Atlanta, and his friend, Miss Pollard,—the very girl with whom she had been seated—an associate teacher in the industrial department of the same school.

"They are not Northern Negroes either, Agie, they and those two young girls with the black plumes, all are educated Southern men and women. I'll tell you, after all it's no mistake, this educating of our Negroes. Why, that Mr. Paine is quite a gentleman and I've felt quite at home talking to him. I've told him all about our being white, and when I mentioned Ora's name as being your maid he seemed then to stop doubting my veracity and sanity, and said he thought you would feel more comfortable among your own people, and right now—by the way they are laughing—I believe he is telling that Pollard girl about us."

Nellie chattered so incessantly that not until now did she pause to hear the account Agnes had to give of the masher and his subsequent mashing.

Each agreed that the Jim Crow might do for a certain class of colored people, but was hardly the place for all.

"I have often wondered why Negroes make such a fuss about the separate cars, for those who are educated disclaim any and all ambition of the race to force itself upon us socially, and I have always felt that separate coaches and churches gave them the chance to be alone and to enjoy their politics and religion in their own peculiar way. Now I see where the reason lies. They say they do not blame the white men who own and operate the Rail Roads for protecting their families and friends from the offensive and insulting things which we have had to endure, but they contend for that which their tickets represent—first class accommodations—whether separate or not.

"It's a perplexing question, but it seems to me if they were prepared financially to become stockholders, or enter into an independent organization of their own, the matter could be satisfactorily adjusted—at least it seems so to me," and while this Griffinian philosophy was slowly becoming comprehensive to Miss Hein—Nell had begun to formulate a scheme whereby her father might help in some way to correct the Jim Crow evil.

Robert Brister had been in earnest conversation with the conductor ever since that worthy had collected the tickets.

"'Twas a hard job," he explained afterward "but after I had told him some things about myself and a few more concerning himself he finally agreed that I knew him and that I am who I am. But to help us out of the scrape, he was powerless to move, so long as we remained Negroes, moreover he laughed over the affair and seemed to consider it a joke worthy of repetition in the Sunday Journal, I didn't care for myself, but it seems a shame that the girls must be written up and cartooned in every old paper that comes from the press."

It is needless to recount all of the incidents of that trip. How the calls for breakfast on the dining car were not repeated in the car occupied by colored people. How at certain stations bandanned women in soiled kitchen aprons crowded on the car and in loud voices demanded seats which when obtained were filled with an odor that might be named attar of pig stye. How gray-haired men of ante-bellum days offered their seats to ladies with a grace that, if borrowed from the folks at the "big house," was none the less the attribute of the true gentleman. How Negro men or women quietly talked upon subjects supposed to interest only the favored few.

Courtesies were extended as freely and received as gratefully as among the elect. Conditions such as the many must needs bear, for the few, were cheerfully complied with and endured.

The lesson was not without its moral, and when at 8:10 the members of the Navajos party left the train, they felt that there was small need of crossing the ocean to study in Italy and Russia the social conditions of the peasantry, nor do we need a Tolstoy or a Gorky to awaken us to the sense of duties that the rich owe to the poor. A compulsory ride of seventy-five miles on the average Jim Crow is all the Tolstoy, Gorky or Disraeli that the uninformed citizen need have.

Thanks to the thoughtful maid Ora, three closed carriages were in waiting at the station for the young ladies, who were by this time tired, hungry and disheartened. Having gone ahead with the baggage and Mr. Tom King, Miss Marshall had experienced no difficulty in gaining admission to the Smith private car, and after disposing of the various boxes and bundles busied herself preparing for the comfort of Miss Hein.

Thus it happened that the train was several miles from Savannah before she knew of the misfortune that had befallen the extempore Negroes, for she supposed they were lunching in the dining car.

Sam told the story of the defeated plans of a bunch of duskies who had tried to "do" him, and of the way he had wisely refused to be "done," and then the full significance of the situation burst upon Ora.

The matter was reported to Mr. Smith when he emerged from his berth at 6 A.M., and being of a nervous temperament he succeeded in working himself up to such a degree of excitement that he would listen to no reason and admit of no justifiable excuse. Why had his daughter ever attempted such a disgraceful disguise? Was she not satisfied to know that she was born of as good blood as that which flowed in any of the royal houses of Europe?

Why did not Sam know his business well enough to have admitted Miss Camile, even though she had come dressed as Cleopatra and was attended by monkeys instead of servants? He would have recognized her, he knew. Why didn't Sam call him and allow him to decide the case? What was the South coming to? Would young people continue to be fools and idiots in spite of the improved educational system? and thus ad infinitum.

The directions for meeting the Jim Crow were given by Ora, for she alone understood what the trip was and how it must be accomplished by her mistress and her companions.

Mrs. Hein, an invalid, was spared the disquieting details of her daughter's ignominious return, and pleading a headache Miss Agnes kept her room until after dusk, and during that period called "candle light" she visited her mother, although it must be confessed that before the lights were brought she escaped quietly to her room.

"A letter for you, Miss Agnes," and while that lady sat disconsolately before her dressing table Ora removed the breakfast tray and placed the mail and morning papers before her.

"Here, Ora, my head aches so furiously, won't you read this letter for me? My eyes burn, and I feel so weak and everything looks double." That the girl was truly ill no one could doubt. The stubborn refusal of the stain to yield to the many treatments that had been employed was fast working mischief on the sensitive, delicate nerves of its victims. The maid broke the seal and read the following letter:

# CHAPTER IX
## "THE DENOUEMENT A LA JULIA"

Savannah, Ga.

Dear Agnes:

I can't wait for you to read in the papers the many happenings of the past few hours. Do you know there was a burglary committed at our house the night of the ball? Well Ora can tell you about the main points of the affair, as she happened to be there, but the sequel—O—goodness—This morning the burglars had their hearing and what do you think?—Well they turned out to be white men—not Negroes as every one supposed—and now Agnes have you any idea who they were? Of course you haven't, but its all so romantic

or so funny or so awful I don't know which. I confess I am
fuddled. I hardly know how to express myself. Anyhow the
boys who attempted to rob our house, both come from
excellent families and belong to our set, in fact, but for mercy
sake don't mention it, one of them is a first cousin of Camille
Smith, and the other has been paying attentions to Marion
ever since he met her. Papa thinks however, that it was
Marion's jewels that attracted him, in the first place, for you
know she inherited the old family jewels of the Latrosse's of
New Orleans, besides her mother's wedding jewels. ·

But Marion is so careless and unless papa insisted upon it
she would never take the trouble to keep her valuables in the
safe. I am digressing, but try dear to be patient with me. As
I started to say, the boys had their hearing this morning at
least one of them did, for when the turnkey went into
Percival's cell with his breakfast he found him very ill indeed.
He jabbers a lot of French nursery rhymes which his grandmother taught him years ago, and the doctor says he is not
only delirious but he fears he has lost his reason entirely. The
black is still on his face and arms but he is positively identified
as Percy Smith. His father refuses to go to see him or to
allow him to be brought home, but his poor dear mother
stays with him constantly and won't believe that he is actually
guilty of breaking into our house. You know Agnes, I don't
know very much about legal terms and can't exactly understand the details of the trial, but at the hearing to day there
were many startling developments. Papa and Tom were both
there of course and they told us that a colored fellow who
used to work for us, Charley Gale, was the principal witness
against them. I wondered how a Negro could qualify as chief
accuser in a case against two white men, and right there came
in surprise No. 1. Gale is a graduated lawyer and has been
admitted to the bar. Just think of it. He came here first with

aunt Joe about two years ago and stayed several months, then he returned to his home in the north and began his practice. Shortly afterward he obtained his first really important case. It involved the legality of certain claims to a large estate in the South. Certain documents had the appearance of forgery and fraud and although the fact seemed very apparent, yet it could not be proved without an actual finding of the originals. Gale being ambitious to succeed and win a name for himself, secured a postponement of the trial, and himself undertook to find the original deeds or certificates or whatever they were.

He was convinced that his suspicions were well founded when he discovered on reaching Nashville that he was followed by the principal claimant Henderson, but he continued his journey. It was at Augusta where he met his first defeat. The officials wouldn't allow him to examine the records without a certain amount of red tape, and when at last he did get them, the main ones had been taken away and were said to be filed in the vaults of the county auditor, which official was then taking a much needed vacation. To be sure a white man's money and influence had arranged this matter. Then Gale came here and consulted with papa and together they laid plans for getting those papers. Papa advised Charley to seek employment at a certain hotel on the Avenue, and thus cover his movements as much as possible. Fate or providence or some mere chance sent Henderson to Savannah and to the identical hotel. He recognized Gale shortly after his arrival and not knowing to what extent he had succeeded in his quest, resolved to put him out of his way. In the meantime papa had gone to Augusta and without arousing any suspicion had examined the court records which strangely enough were not locked in the vaults of the auditor's office, and secured an exact copy of the originals, duly stamped and sealed. He brought them home and sent for Charles and I supposed they both felt very much elated over the affair, at any rate papa insisted upon the making of julep and punch and even Marion and myself were invited down,—to add grace to the occasion, I suppose. Charley didn't leave here until ten o'clock, but at eight the next morning we heard of the crime that had been committed at the hotel and of how he had been accused of it by one of the guests. The guest who so positively identified him was no other than Will Henderson and the woman's description tallied exactly with Gale's appearance. Our ball being planned for the near future, and with company and other things I didn't concern myself very much with the matter. To be sure he was only a Negro and I couldn't be expected to look at it in the way I do this case of Percy who is a true blue vein.

Papa says this morning it was proved beyond a doubt that Will Henderson impersonated Gale and even stole some of his clothes to wear, in order to carry out the disguise, and as seen in the dim light by the guest, he looked very much like the accommodating waiter who brought her coffee and toast. Henderson has wilted completely—and now for surprise No. 2. Marion, our dear sweet Marion, it seems has actually become engaged to this Henderson but because of my own affair had agreed to say nothing of her engagement until after Robert and I are married. When papa told us at luncheon of the trial, Marion—because of her French blood or in spite of it—without fainting or screaming (as I am sure I should have done) went to her room and returned shortly with a small jewel case which she opened and O Agnes!—the most exquisite diamond ring with two of those oriental rubies set on either side—a priceless treasure.

She almost flung it at Tom and said,

"Take it, and let it be a witness against the wretch, I shall waste no sentiment upon him.

This must be the very ring that was mysteriously stolen from the hotel a few days ago."

Papa asked her where she got it and she said Henderson gave it to her to seal their betrothal. Well papa and Tom went down immediately and made the proper inquiries and it is just as Marion thought. The ring belongs to a guest at the hotel, but for Marion's sake it is to be hushed up.

Henderson has been bound over with three or four indictments against him. It may be months before he has his trial in the regular court. When he does, suppose you and Nell come over,—your maid has to come as a witness—but for the sake of all that is holy, don't come as Negroes. I'm so sick of that miserable ball, and I don't want ever again to act the foolish part that I did once.

Marion and I have always been more or less proud of the healthy tan and sunburn which we acquire every summer, but from this time and on, Julia King wears a sun bonnet in summer and carries a parasol.

I am tired of writing now, but my mind is relieved. Would you mind calling up Robert—that is Mr. Brister, and telling him I will drop him a line later on and please tell him about this stupid fuss that is going on—there's a dear girl.

Love to your dear mamma and any of the girls you see— and remember, Agie dear, you are the recipient of the longest letter ever written by yours devotedly—    JULIA SNEAD KING

P.S.—Of course I have written longer letters to Robert but that doesn't count.

P.S.—You would be surprised to know how much law I

have learned in a very short time—"Falsely charging or imputing to one the commission of some crime is libelous"— hence Will Henderson is guilty of libel—malicious libel, so Tom says. If I had time I could tell you all about felony, larceny, embezzlement and burglary and you could easily see that Henderson is an arch sinner and has committed nearly everything that papa and Tom can find in Blackwell.

Papa says Mrs. Smith is entirely to blame, for she has always pampered Perce and allowed him too much rope. He has already wasted the greater part of her personal wealth and had been making heavy inroads upon Mr. Smith's account. Recently Mr. Smith stopped Percy's allowance at the National, and it was for funds to continue his gambling deals with Henderson that led the poor boy to commit burglary.

P.S.—O say Agie that face dye of yours was doctored, that is, it was fixed up, by Charles Gale in order to catch Smith and Henderson in the act of impersonating Negroes. It was papa's idea. Gale put nitric acid in diluted form in it and it caused the chemical change.

Take some good strong coffee and any good alkali and rub the effected parts and the stuff will come off—I don't understand it, but any how papa does.

P.S.—I am now really and truly going to close.

# CHAPTER X
# NEGRO CITIZENSHIP ACCORDING TO CHARLEY GALE

"I don't see how I shall get along without you Ora," the pale convalescent sat in a chair piled high with pillows and looked

very forlorn as she watched the movements of the nurse—
Ora had been her constant attendant during eight weeks of
brain fever, and now when the patient was pronounced out
of danger, she felt no longer compelled to remain.

Charley Gale—the young colored lawyer, who had just
won his first case, who had cleared himself of an awful
charge, and had succeeded in bringing to justice a most
dangerous criminal, had written her only a few days before
and had used the very same phrase, now so piteously uttered
by Miss Hein. The two years spent in the South had served
a double purpose. It had corrected several erroneous impressions on both sides—The employer had found a really competent servant in one who was properly educated, and had
found her neither conceited nor officious. The employee had
found a singular willingness on the part of her employer, to
recognize worth and to treat with respect one who gave them
honest labor for honest hire.

Traditions and sectional differences which make the South,
Southern and the North, Northern are not removed in a day
nor by an individual effort, and Ora Marshall felt two days
later as she bade good-bye to the Hein household that her
personal share of the race problem so far as it affected these
people, had been solved to the satisfaction of both.

The fee recieved from the Henderson case was a sufficient
guarantee of what must follow and the lovers were quietly
married in Savannah after the conclusion of the trial.

Henderson received fifteen years—the maximum sentence—through the influence of Judge King to whom half
way measures were less than useless.

Mr. and Mrs. Charles Gale were importuned to remain
in Savannah until after the marriage of Miss King, but no
persuading could induce the young man to mix another mint
julep.

Mint juleps had served their purpose and henceforth he declared that nothing, not even a julep should tempt him from what was strictly in accord with his and his wife's ideas of Negro citizenship.

When the Negro shall have completed for himself a civilization equal to any nation or race of men, when he shall have attained the highest and noblest of purposes, when his going in, and coming out is no longer [word illegible in original text] with an eye of suspicion or envy, then, and not until then will he have the time to sip mint juleps and indulge in the things which after a ripe civilization, denote the first steps of decline.

"You see Judge," Charles explained on the eve of his departure, "the colored man in order to gain recognition must not only be the equal but the superior of his white competitor. If he learns a trade he must know it so thoroughly that he can explain the theory and demonstrate the practice better than the white man who runs in opposition to him, or ten to one the other fellow will get the paying patronage.

"But this kind of talk no doubt is like giving the second gift kindergarten beads to a new born babe. He doesn't see them, he can't apply them and he doesn't even notice when they slip from his fingers. My wife's uncle, Charley Marshall in Virginia has expressed the thing a little more plainly. He says the colored man is unfitted financially to spring very many or elaborate surprises upon the nation, and with much labor and no rest must patiently nourish his plan until it becomes a plant—a tangible, living being, and then his white benefactors may water it, weed it and help it to grow."

"I may be letting second gift beads slip from my fingers, but if this check for $500 will help along the plant you are

cultivating—then take it, and may God bless you"—replied
the Judge.

He walked away but turned sharply at the gate and called
back to the young man on the steps—"Hi there Charley—Be
sure the plant you are watching contains at least a few olive
branches."

# THE LUCK OF LAZARUS

*Grace Ellsworth Tompkins*

"Yas, honey, dem shawks sho' must a be'n pison mean fish; yas, indeedy. Whuffo' yo' say dey chuck poak into de watah?"

"For the sharks to eat, Aunt Jane."

"But, chile, whuffo' dey want to feed sech mean trash?"

"O, they poison the pork first, Aunty, and the sharks die."

"Dat's somefin' like; dat's somefin' like. Umph! Wal, goodbye, honey; sorry yo' gwine; come en' read to me ag'in 'bout de shawks."

The child ran across the yard to the great house, leaving the black woman to get her supper. She poured hot water on some coffee grounds which had already done service once, drew from the ashes a hot ash cake and poured over it some bacon gravy. Then she began her meal, elbow propped on the table, cup in hand. To an outsider the darkness of the cabin blended with the blackness of the hand and arm, leaving the cup apparently suspended in the air.

As Jane ate, she mused.

"Pison de poak en' den feed it to 'em. Dat is sho' de way to do wif sech trash. En' ain't dat dawg ez mean ez any fish dat evah swum? Ah is clean frazzled outen my wits wif him. He eat de aigs en' he kills de chickens, en' yes' d'y he scratch up all my flowah baids. Ah gwine do it."

So the next morning Aunt Jane went up to the great house and asked the mistress for some poison.

"A want de stronges' kine yo' got, Miss Helen."

*Colored American Magazine* 12 (Apr. 1907): 283–84.

"What can you want with poison, Aunt Jane?"

"Ah doan' want to tell yo' ef yo' doan' mine, Missus. Ah ain't gwine to do much hahm wif it."

So Miss Helen went to the kitchen closet, and presently emerged with a tablespoon of powder in a paper. Aunt Jane took it, with thanks, and departed.

That night she took from a shelf a piece of pork, into which she cut gashes, which she filled with the powder. This pork she took out into the yard and laid on the ground, having carefully seen that the fowls were in their yard. She then went indoors, muttering: "He ain't gwine chase my cat to-night."

She slept later than usual the next morning, and was awakened by sounds of weeping outside her door. She arose, looked out of the window, and saw a small Negro boy of about seven years sitting beside an exceedingly sick dog.

Aunt Jane, who had a very soft place in her heart for children, hastily dressed and went into the yard.

"Whuffo' yo' cryin', chile?" she asked.

"Becuz mah dawg is dyin'; mah po' Towse, what ah loves. Mah po,' po' Towse!" and the child wept again.

"Doan' cry, chile; we'll do somefin' fo' Towse, ef we even has to go fo' de doctah. Wait till ah gits Missus."

Missus appeared and looked at the dog.

"He'll get well," she announced; "I gave you some mustard and baking soda, Aunty, instead of poison." And she went away, leaving Aunt Jane to comfort the child. She took him in her arms and carried him into the cabin, where she gave him some breakfast. When Towser was seen to rise and walk with unsteady steps, she said: "Now, ah gwine tek yo' home. Whah yo' live? Ah doan' seem to know yo'."

"Ah doan' want to go home," said the child.

"Why doan' yo'? Woan' yo' mammy worry?"

"Ah ain' got no mammy; on'y a 'ooman what mah paw ma'ied when mah maw died. She beats me en' sthaves me en' Towse. Lemme stay heah."

"Why, chile," said Aunt Jane, "de Lawd knows ah'd like to keep yo', but mebbe dey say no."

"No dey won't; she'll be glad to git rid o' me, en' paw'll be glad to git me away whah ah woan' git beat. Yo' ask 'em."

So, with a small boy clinging to her hand and a wobbly dog following at her heels, Aunt Jane proceeded in the direction of the child's home. At the door they were greeted by a voice, saying: "Why yo' bring strange niggahs heah, yo' Laz'rus yo'? Git from befo' me, bofe of yo'."

But Aunt Jane held her ground.

"Ah wants dis boy to bring up fo' mah own," she said, peaceably.

"Wal yo' kin have him. Ah doan' want him."

"Whah his paw? Ah'm gwine ask him, too."

"No need o' dat; ah say yo' kin; but he's in de woodshed."

So to the woodshed went Aunt Jane and Lazarus, where they found "paw" chopping wood. When Aunt Jane stated her desires concerning Lazarus, the man took the child in his arms and was silent for a moment. Then he said:

"Yo' want to go, sonny?"

"Yas, paw," said Lazarus.

"Wal, it gwine be mighty hahd for me to let yo' go, but ah kain' beah to have yo' beat all de time, en' ah kain' always be 'round to pertect yo'. Yo' kin have him, ma'am, en' ah know by yo' face yo'll be kind to him. Lazzy, yo' paw'll come to see yo' sometimes; be a good boy." Then, kissing him, he sat the child down and turned sadly to his work.

A happy woman is Aunt Jane and a blissful child is Lazarus; while in the sunshine before the cabin door sleeps a reformed dog, with all unseemly desires weeded out, and the cat and chickens are safe.

# THE VOICE OF
# THE RICH PUDDING

*Gertrude D.[orsey] Browne*

The door bell rang furiously, and Mr. Willis, who was in the act of blowing out the light, hastily retraced his steps down the hall, and stopped at the front door.

"Who's there?"

"Father's dead," came the answer, in an excited, childish voice.

Mr. Willis lost no time in drawing the bolts and unlocking the door, but the messenger had vanished and further questioning was impossible.

"Who the deuce was that kid, and why did he come to tell me about it at eleven o'clock?" and as he walked slowly back to his bed chamber he reviewed his limited list of acquaintances and wondered who could possibly consider his friendship and sympathy of sufficient moment that he should be notified at this hour of their loss.

"Now, let's see, there's Tyler, I've known him longer than any one else here, but since when did he become a father? and O—pshaw! I might as well dress and get myself collected. Jones has a family and is tolerably fond of me, but it's a long walk for one of his kids at this time of night. Guess I'll call up and find out the particulars. Yes, I'm afraid it is Jones. Poor old fellow, of course they'd send for me to look after things until his folks can be communicated with. I'll go right down and call up. These telephones are a great thing. Thank God! he didn't say Estella is dead."

*Colored American Magazine* 13 (Oct. 1907): 305–9.

Mr. and Mrs. Sarter were roaming about in the sweet land of Nod when they were recalled to things present and terrestrial by loud knocking at their door.

"Go down Jim, for mercy's sake, and find out what's the matter," Mrs. Sarter advised.

The sleepy man very ungraciously stumbled down the stairs, through the sitting room into the parlor and peered through the window at a small white figure on the porch.

"Hey, sonny, what's the row?" he yelled through the window.

"Mother's dead!"

"Whose mother? Mine or Annie's?" screamed Mr. Sarter as he dashed to the door and threw it open.

No one answered him for the porch was empty. In the sitting room, as he returned, he found his wife seated on the floor rocking to and fro moaning and groaning in a most distressing manner.

"Did you hear him Annie? It's so sudden and we're so unprepared for it."

"Oh, Jim, is it my mother?"

"I don't know, but its somebody's mother."

"There now, don't be foolish. If it ain't my mother why would any one come and wake us up in the middle of the night?" responded Mrs. Jim.

"There's just a possibility that should my own mother die, the folks would remember to notify her only son," sarcastically from Jim.

"We won't quarrel Jim, dear, don't be a bear, but if it should be poor, dear, devoted Mama, O——" and the crying began afresh.

"Now, see here, Annie, you might as well calm yourself, for we don't know whether it's proper to laugh or cry."

"We don't, hey? Well maybe you don't. If it's your mother

you'll know it's proper to cry, and if it's mine, you'll laugh——
——O, you beast," wailed Mrs. Sarter.

"I'm going out to Hunters' to see if there's anything wrong, and on the way back I'll stop at your mother's," with which announcement Mr. Sarter slammed the front door.

"He needn't been so grumpy, I guess I stumped my toe against that old rocker hard enough to make a stone image cry," and Mrs. Sarter limped painfully to the switch and turned on the light.

At eleven P.M. Miss Stella Warner had left her sister Alice and brother-in-law Horace and retired to her room, not to sleep, but to "think it all out."

"I don't see why we can't. I'm no infant, and I don't care a snap whether he's high church or low church or any church at all, he suits me, so there! Calls us sinners, just as if he is accusing angel of the judgment." Thus ran the tearful meditations of Stella.

"Horace, I think it is perfectly ridiculous to stand in their way just on account of the slight difference in their church service. For the love of goodness let them alone, and let us get back home. I know little Marie wants to see us. I shouldn't wonder if, because of the stand you take in this matter, something should happen to Marie in our absence, which will always cause us to associate the two affairs."

Pretty Alice Thordeau was half angry with her resolute husband, but far from allowing her indignation to get the better of her prudence, she diplomatically brought into the subject the name and possible welfare of their three-year-old daughter Marie.

"Alice, I am resolved to do my duty by my ward. If Mr. Willis cannot consent to conform with the requirements of the high church, I can not consider his proposal for the hand of Estella. If they are so unwise as to do this thing without my consent, Estella loses a fortune and need expect nothing from me." Mr. Thordeau spoke with the earnest decision of a conscientious man.

"Of course, Horace, you have the say so, but just suppose Marie should ever be left to the care of a guardian and that guardian was a—was a—a Mormon or a—a—"

"Impossible!" impatiently replied Horace. "Utterly impossible, why do you suppose I would ever commit Marie into the hands of any person of whose character I was not certain? Really, Alice, you flatter my judgment by conceiving of such impossible conditions."

"Well, at any rate, father didn't make our church and mode of worship a handicap for Estella, and I'm sure he would hardly appreciate the wisdom of keeping them apart on that issue. If I thought that Marie would be compelled to eat fish on Friday or burn incense to an ebony god, why I should cry my eyes out, I know."

"Very likely," was the dry return. Then with kindness, "Alice, don't confuse our personal affairs with the question we are considering, Marie is not an orphan and God knows—What was that?"

Some one tapping on the window. A faint, but persistent tap. As Mr. Thordeau opened the hall door a voice in the darkness greeted him with the words:

"Baby is dead."

"What is it, Horace?" asked Alice, coming into the hall.

"Baby is dead," he answered in a hoarse whisper. "Come—let us go—If we hurry we can catch the midnight express. Why, in the name of all that is holy, are we here, anyhow?"

But Alice, the emotional, the hysterical, was running out after the messenger.

"Here, stop! whose baby is dead? My Marie isn't dead,

stop," she cried as she ran and stumbled over the shrubbery, down the avenue and out upon the street.

"Absurd—simply impossible. Oh, it must have been one of Myrtle's children—the baby—why of course—little Elizabeth. What a pity, but then the Lord knows best." She stopped at the end of the street and considered whether it was best to go on or to return to Mr. Thordeau, who by this time was thoroughly excited. Finally deciding upon the latter course, she hurried back to the house.

"Listen, Horace, have some reason. That was a child who spoke to you, and it couldn't be our Marie, she is with mother in Dayton, and telegrams don't yell at a man in the dark. They are always written or typewritten on paper. Why, it must be one of your cousin's children, the baby—little Elizabeth, no doubt. We might go over there and see what we can do, for Myrtle is utterly prostrated, I know." All the time she was talking, Alice had been making hurried preparations to visit the stricken home, and, as they entered the hall, they were joined by Stella, who insisted upon accompanying them.

"I don't know why that call should upset me as it did, I might have known it wasn't Marie, but all the same I— well—I want to get back home. I'm convinced that converting sinners from the errors of their ways isn't my forte, but mind, Miss Estella, I'm exempt from all reproach if it doesn't result harmoniously," remarked Mr. Thordeau.

Alice and Estella were both unprepared for such a concession from such a stubborn source, and the remainder of the walk was made in complete silence.

When they reached the Smith residence they found it enveloped in darkness. In response to a light rap Otis Smith's head appeared at an upstairs window and his sleepy voice inquired:

"Who's there?"

"Why, it's us," inelegantly replied Horace. "We thought we'd come over and see—and I mean ask—that, is—Say how's your baby? She ain't dead or nothing, is she?"

"For God's sake! hold on a minute and I'll be down."

The head was withdrawn and a few minutes later Otis walked out on the veranda.

"Say, what's the fun? I don't seem to understand this death notice racket. About ten minutes ago Myrt went over to her mother's to see if Helen is dead. Some one came here and made noise enough to wake up the kids, and that's going some—and when Myrt asked what was the trouble, he said her sister or my sister or some sister was dead, and Myrt just threw her rain coat over her shoulders and ran, and left me to look after Elizabeth."

The quartet sank on the steps, overcome by the mystery, and compared notes as they were able.

"Listen, there comes some one now, maybe its the bird of evil omen," cautioned Stella. But when the solitary figure of a man was about to pass them by she called after it, "O, Mr. Willis is that you?"

"It certainly is I, but why this select gathering at the witching hour of night?" he asked as he greeted the other occupants of the veranda steps.

"Who's dead?" abruptly asked Horace. "Have you heard of any deaths to-night, Mr. Willis?"

"Quite a number, I should say, but I can't tell you who."

"For instance," persisted the imaginative Horace.

"Well, for instance, I am informed that father is dead, and I just met Jim Sarter and he is trying to locate a dead mother, having satisfactorily accounted for his own and his wife's mother," was the good natured reply of Willis.

While he was talking, the telephone in the hall began to ring, and Otis answered it.

"That you, Myrt? Come on home, get one of the boys to come with you. Yes—yes—I know. Whose sister? O, is that so? No! Who! Me? You bet I ain't dead. O, rot. It's a shame—why it's the rumest game I ever heard or saw played. Yes. Good-bye."

When he rejoined the company on the steps Otis mopped his perspiring brow.

"O, Lord, my mother is on her way over here to put pennies on my waxen eyelids, and I'm afraid I don't make a very successful corpse just now. At least I can't be one of the silent kind."

"Say, let's all go home and go to bed," advised Alice, to whom each new development was a separate and distinct shock.

"Kind a reminds a fellow of the passover or the ten virgins or the Johnstown flood or something—don't it?" asked Otis as he bade his guests good night and soothed the fretful crying of little Elizabeth.

\*     \*     \*     \*     \*

The supper bell had rung the second time and the tea was in danger of cooling, before the Rev. Harvey Reynolds and wife entered the dining room. Their son Max—a lad of thirteen—was impatiently awaiting them, and amusing himself in the meantime by deftly balancing a dessert spoon on the edge of a cut glass candlestick.

Rev. Reynolds led his wife to the head of the table, placed her chair, and rang the bell, requesting the maid to serve.

"That was a singular experience I must say—very singular,

but quite a pretty little ceremony, Willa, did you not think
so?"

"Very pretty, indeed, dear, and O, wasn't she happy?"

"The gentleman, Mr. Thordeau, rather impressed me as
being a somewhat zealous person. He didn't seem to hesitate
about giving her away, like they sometimes do," remarked
the minister.

"After all, the dream of life is happiness and if the reality
is more than the dream how very happy they ought to be,"
Mrs. Reynolds responded.

"Dream? What dream, Mama?" Max inquired.

"Why, dear, the dream that we are speaking of is the
dream of two happy hearts made one," laughed his mother.

"O, shucks, I wouldn't give my dream for a dozen old
hearts as happy as a bunch of tops."

"Well son, if you've had such a pleasant dream relate it to
us. I'm sure we always find pleasure in your dreams.

"I think they supply the lack of printed fiction to which I
am not a generous subscriber," added his father.

"Well, sir, last night I dremp—"

"Dreamed, you mean, dear," corrected Rev. Reynolds.

"Well, then, I dreamed that Mr. Morehead took me into
the Western Union, where I've always wanted to be, and he
made a messenger boy out of me.

"O, shucks, if you could of seen me hustling.

"The telegrams, it seems, were written out on a blackboard
and I had to learn ten or more at a time. They was all about
people dying. Mr. Morehead would let me study 'em for a
while and then he'd say, 'Run to So and So's and tell 'em
their father's dead or sister's dead, and stop at What's his
Name on your way back and tell 'em the baby's dead.' O,
shucks, I almost ran myself to death. When I got up this
morning I was so sore and tired I could hardly dress."

"Please excuse me," weakly interposed Mrs. Reynolds.

She left the room, but was gone only a few minutes—with horror she gasped:

"Look, Harvey! see this boy's gown, it's muddy and grass stained and the sheets of his bed—there, there, father, don't give him another bit of that rich pudding."

# GUESTS UNEXPECTED
## A *Thanksgiving Story*

*Miss Maude K. Griffin*

Ina Scott-Craven settled among the rich cushions of her luxurious divan with a distinct sense of well-being. She was a widow with a generous income, left by a man whom she married solely because he was rich. Mr. Scott-Craven had been a very convenient husband, generous and indulgent; so she bore him no grudge when he died a few years after their marriage, leaving her free and contented with life.

In society Mrs. Scott-Craven was neither popular nor unpopular; the paragraphs for which she furnished comment in the smart weeklies devoted more space to her bridge and motor achievements than to her dinners and receptions. She was extremely selfish, but not ill-natured. Her conversation never expanded beyond the recognized topics of the day in her set, racing, chiffons, bridge and motoring, with stray remarks on new books, plays and spicy gossip on the marriages, deaths, debts and divorces of her dearest friends and acquaintances.

Among the new books lately received by Mrs. Scott-Craven was one devoted to the slums, sent by a new acquaintance. The author was soon to lecture in a fashionable drawing-room, and in order to converse intelligently with her during the subsequent reception Mrs. Scott-Craven deemed it the correct thing to skim through the pages of her gift.

The book was written in the most lurid vein, the heroes and heroines being represented as hopelessly wicked, the men

*Colored American Magazine* 14 (Nov. 1908): 614–16.

drunken and brutal; the women miserable in appearance and light in conduct.

A perusal of the chapters did not increase Mrs. Scott-Craven's charity nor was she inspired with a desire to help humanity. The pleadings of the author were overdone and she turned with loathing from the description of a state of things which can only be described as bestial, remarking, "How dreadful!"

A servant entered to interrupt her thoughts, and noticing a frown upon the none too handsome countenance of her mistress, hastened to announce that the decorators had finished their work of preparing the dining and reception rooms for the Thanksgiving dinner dance to take place on the following day.

"Very well, Juliette," said Mrs. Scott-Craven. "Tell the decorators to go, and if there are later changes I will telephone for them to return. And, by the way, Juliette," continued the mistress, "you need not come again for two hours. I do not feel well, and hope to go to sleep before dressing for Mrs. Barlow's dinner this evening."

Juliette, a demure damsel, with a coquettish expression in her small, dark eyes, retired, closing the door softly.

Mrs. Scott-Craven, conscious of the luxury of oncoming sleep, reclined deeper among the cushions and straightened out the folds of the beautiful Persian silk dressing gown, which had been a gift from her late husband. The richness of the gown made her think of the donor in a desultory way, but soon she ceased to think connectedly; a great whiteness seemed to spread around her and sleep coursed warmly through her veins.

In her subconsciousness Mrs. Scott-Craven saw gradually moving toward her divan a tall, white-clad form, like that of a conventional male angel with great white feather wings. He was the conventional angel of pictorial art, and yet he reminded her, whimsically enough, of a handsome young man whom she had noticed with the author of the book on slum life a few days ago.

"You must come with me," said the angel, with an air of authority, and she rose upward, followed him without further protest. It was not until they arrived in a strange section of the city that it occurred to her she was attired in dressing gown and slippers. But she was under the influence of the angel and powerless to help herself or offer the least resistance. The streets were narrow and dirty, and the rookeries parading under the names of tenements ill-smelling and stuffy. Following her guide, without a question, she ascended four or five flights of break-neck steps, finally reaching a squalid apartment of two rooms which they entered without the formality of a knock at the door.

On a couch lay a woman, not older than forty-two or three years, though wasted by disease until she appeared sixty. Three small children, the picture of poverty, were gazing pitifully into her face, one of them crying for a piece of bread. An old stove in a corner of the room contained an ordinary bit of candle, which sent out the only heat the occupants of the room felt, while furnishing light at the same time.

Mrs. Scott-Craven, obeying a motion command of the angel, surveyed the dismal picture and her heart sank within her.

Hearing a slight sigh from another corner of the room, she turned to see from whom it escaped, astonished to recognize—as well as she could by the miserable candle light—the figure of a beautiful young girl snuggling to her breast, in an effort to keep it warm, a young baby. Her hair was fluffed out on either side of her head, covering the top halves of her ears, and caught up at the back in an unpretentious knot. Her features were thin, but beautiful, her eyes a mystery, her mouth a flower and her hands, despite the signs of hard work, well shaped and well kept. The expression she wore was one of indescribable sadness; one could easily guess that the responsibility of the entire household devolved upon her and the task was too much for her strength as well as the little money she received for the two or three days' work she was fortunate enough to secure every week.

Mrs. Scott-Craven finally perceived that the little group noticed neither her, her strange attire nor her stranger companion. She evidently was in the spirit world. What would happen next?

The angel left the dingy little tenement, walking a little in front of her, but moving along with swift even strides. Gaining the street, she was led through first one alley and another, interrupting their walks with visits to homes each worse than the preceding one.

Thoroughly frightened and sick at heart, she summoned courage and said:

"I wish you would tell me the meaning of all this? Am I mad or are these people merely visionaries?"

For answer the angel took her by the hand, spread his great bird-like wings and for one giddy moment they hung in space.

"Br-rr, it is freezing here," cried the terrified Mrs. Scott-Craven; "my dressing gown has shrunk to my ankles and the pattern has all washed out. An air journey is worse than traveling through the frightful streets below."

"It is not an air journey," replied the angel. "It is your mental atmosphere. If your inner life had been large and full and beautiful, your outer covering would have been luxuriant. As you may be said to have had no inner life at all, your

mental poverty is shown in your scanty drapery. In all of
your lifetime you have never made an effort to make those
around you happy. The hungry you have turned from your
door; the poor you have oppressed."

Then suddenly as they had ascended, the angel released her
hand and she felt herself speeding through space, helpless
and alone.

"Save me! Save me!" she cried, almost paralyzed with fear.

"What is it, Madame?" asked the surprised voice of Juliette.

It was some time before Mrs. Scott-Craven realized that
she had been asleep and dreaming.

A few minutes later Mrs. Scott-Craven received a call
from her "Lady of the Slums," as she called the writer of the
settlements. And still unstrung by the memory of her vision,
she begged to be excused to keep her dinner engagement.

"I have a surprise for you, however," said she to her guest
in parting. "I am recalling the invitations to my Thanksgiving
dinner dance to-morrow, and my plans, without any rear-
rangement whatever, are subject to your disposal for your
unfortunate charges. My invitations number fifty, but you
can increase the number to suit your needs and in future
draw upon me for any assistance needed."

The astonishment of Mrs. Scott-Craven's new friend was
too great for words, but it did not compare with the sensation
created by the announcement in the newspapers the next
morning that one of the wealthiest women in the city, who
had always attracted society's attention by her independence
of action, had decided to abandon the pleasures of a fashionable life to devote her time entirely to work among the poor.

# EMMY

*Jessie Fauset*

## I

"There are five races," said Emmy confidently. "The white
or Caucasian, the yellow or Mongolian, the red or Indian,
the brown or Malay, and the black or Negro."

"Correct," nodded Miss Wenzel mechanically. "Now to
which of the five do you belong?" And then immediately
Miss Wenzel reddened.

Emmy hesitated. Not because hers was the only dark face
in the crowded schoolroom, but because she was visualizing
the pictures with which the geography had illustrated its
information. She was not white, she knew that—nor had she
almond eyes like the Chinese, nor the feathers which the
Indian wore in his hair and which, of course, were to Emmy
a racial characteristic. She regarded the color of her slim
browns hands with interest—she had never thought of it
before. The Malay was a horrid, ugly-looking thing with a
ring in his nose. But he was brown, so she was, she supposed,
really a Malay.

And yet the Hottentot, chosen with careful nicety to represent the entire Negro race, had on the whole a better
appearance.

"I belong," she began tentatively, "to the black or Negro
race."

*Crisis* 5, pts. 1–4 (Dec. 1912): 79–87; 5, pts. 5–9 (Jan. 1913):
134–42.

"Yes," said Miss Wenzel with a sigh of relief, for if Emmy had chosen to ally herself with any other race except, of course, the white, how could she, teacher though she was, set her straight without embarrassment? The recess bell rang and she dismissed them with a brief but thankful "You may pass."

Emmy uttered a sigh of relief, too, as she entered the schoolyard. She had been terribly near failing.

"I was so scared," she breathed to little towheaded Mary Holborn. "Did you see what a long time I was answering? Guess Eunice Lecks thought for sure I'd fail and she'd get my place."

"Yes, I guess she did," agreed Mary. "I'm so glad you didn't fail—but, oh, Emmy, didn't you mind?"

Emmy looked up in astonishment from the orange she was peeling.

"Mind what? Here, you can have the biggest half. I don't like oranges anyway—sort of remind me of niter. Mind what, Mary?"

"Why, saying you were black and"—she hesitated, her little freckled face getting pinker and pinker—"a Negro, and all that before the class." And then mistaking the look on Emmy's face, she hastened on. "Everybody in Plainville says all the time that you're too nice and smart to be a—er—I mean, to be colored. And your dresses are so pretty, and your hair isn't all funny either." She seized one of Emmy's hands— an exquisite member, all bronze outside, and within a soft pinky white.

"Oh, Emmy, don't you think if you scrubbed real hard you could get some of the brown off?"

"But I don't want to," protested Emmy. "I guess my hands are as nice as yours, Mary Holborn. We're just the same, only you're white and I'm brown. But I don't see any difference. Eunice Lecks' eyes are green and yours are blue, but you can both see."

"Oh, well," said Mary Holborn, "if you don't mind—"

If she didn't mind—but why should she mind?

"Why should I mind, Archie," she asked that faithful squire as they walked home in the afternoon through the pleasant "main" street. Archie had brought her home from school ever since she could remember. He was two years older than she; tall, strong and beautiful, and her final arbiter.

Archie stopped to watch a spider.

"See how he does it, Emmy! See him bring that thread over! Gee, if I could swing a bridge across the pond as easy as that! What d'you say? Why should you mind? Oh, I don't guess there's anything for us to mind about. It's white people, they're always minding—I don't know why. If any of the boys in your class say anything to you, you let me know. I licked Bill Jennings the other day for calling me a 'guiney.' Wish I were a good, sure-enough brown like you, and then everybody'd know just what I am."

Archie's clear olive skin and aquiline features made his Negro ancestry difficult of belief.

"But," persisted Emmy, "what difference does it make?"

"Oh, I'll tell you some other time," he returned vaguely. "Can't you ask questions though? Look, it's going to rain. That means uncle won't need me in the field this afternoon. See here, Emmy, bet I can let you run ahead while I count fifteen, and then beat you to your house. Want to try?"

They reached the house none too soon, for the soft spring drizzle soon turned into gusty torrents. Archie was happy— he loved Emmy's house with the long, high rooms and the books and the queer foreign pictures. And Emmy had so many sensible playthings. Of course, a great big fellow of 13 doesn't care for locomotives and blocks in the ordinary

way, but when one is trying to work out how a bridge must
be built over a lop-sided ravine, such things are by no means
to be despised. When Mrs. Carrel, Emmy's mother, sent
Céleste to tell the children to come to dinner, they raised
such a protest that the kindly French woman finally set them
a table in the sitting room, and left them to their own devices.

"Don't you love little fresh green peas?" said Emmy
ecstatically. "Oh, Archie, won't you tell me now what difference it makes whether you are white or colored?" She peered
into the vegetable dish. "Do you suppose Céleste would give
us some more peas? There's only about a spoonful left."

"I don't believe she would," returned the boy, evading the
important part of her question. "There were lots of them to
start with, you know. Look, if you take up each pea separately
on your fork—like that—they'll last longer. It's hard to do,
too. Bet I can do it better than you."

And in the exciting contest that followed both children
forgot all about the "problem."


# II


Miss Wenzel sent for Emmy the next day. Gently but
insistently, and altogether from a mistaken sense of duty, she
tried to make the child see wherein her lot differed from that
of her white school-mates. She felt herself that she hadn't
succeeded very well. Emmy, immaculate in a white frock,
her bronze elfin face framed in its thick curling black hair,
alert with interest, had listened very attentively. She had
made no comments till toward the end.

"Then because I'm brown," she had said, "I'm not as good
as you." Emmy was at all times severely logical.

"Well, I wouldn't—quite say that," stammered Miss Wenzel miserably. "You're really very nice, you know, especially nice for a colored girl, but—well, you're different."

Emmy listened patiently. "I wish you'd tell me how, Miss Wenzel," she began. "Archie Ferrers is different, too, isn't he? And yet he's lots nicer than almost any of the boys in Plainville. And he's smart, you know. I guess he's pretty poor—I shouldn't like to be that—but my mother isn't poor, and she's handsome. I heard Céleste say so, and she has beautiful clothes. I think, Miss Wenzel, it must be rather nice to be different."

It was at this point that Miss Wenzel had desisted and, tucking a little tissue-wrapped oblong into Emmy's hands, had sent her home.

"I don't think I did any good," she told her sister wonderingly. "I couldn't make her see what being colored meant."

"I don't see why you didn't leave her alone," said Hannah Wenzel testily. "I don't guess she'll meet with much prejudice if she stays here in central Pennsylvania. And if she goes away she'll meet plenty of people who'll make it their business to see that she understands what being colored means. Those things adjust themselves."

"Not always," retorted Miss Wenzel, "and anyway, that child ought to know. She's got to have some of the wind taken out of her sails, some day, anyhow. Look how her mother dresses her. I suppose she does make pretty good money—I've heard that translating pays well. Seems so funny for a colored woman to be able to speak and write a foreign language." She returned to her former complaint.

"Of course it doesn't cost much to live here, but Emmy's clothes! White frocks all last winter, and a long red coat—broadcloth it was, Hannah. And big bows on her hair—she has got pretty hair, I must say."

"Oh, well," said Miss Hannah, "I suppose Céleste makes

her clothes. I guess colored people want to look nice just as much as anybody else. I heard Mr. Holborn say Mrs. Carrel used to live in France; I suppose that's where she got all her stylish ways."

"Yes, just think of that," resumed Miss Wenzel vigorously, "a colored woman with a French maid. Though if it weren't for her skin you'd never tell by her actions what she was. It's the same way with that Archie Ferrers, too, looking for all the world like some foreigner. I must say I like colored people to look and act like what they are."

She spoke the more bitterly because of her keen sense of failure. What she had meant to do was to show Emmy kindly—oh, very kindly—her proper place, and then, using the object in the little tissue-wrapped parcel as a sort of text, to preach a sermon on humility without aspiration.

The tissue-wrapped oblong proved to Emmy's interested eyes to contain a motto of Robert Louis Stevenson, entitled: "A Task"—the phrases picked out in red and blue and gold, under glass and framed in passepartout. Everybody nowadays has one or more of such mottoes in his house, but the idea was new then to Plainville. The child read it through carefully as she passed by the lilac-scented "front yards." She read well for her age, albeit a trifle uncomprehendingly.

"To be honest, to be kind, to earn a little and to spend a little less;"—"there," thought Emmy, "is a semi-colon—let's see—the semi-colon shows that the thought"—and she went on through the definition Miss Wenzel had given her, and returned happily to her motto:

"To make upon the whole a family happier for his presence"—thus far the lettering was in blue. "To renounce when that shall be necessary and not be embittered"—this phrase was in gold. Then the rest went on in red: "To keep a few friends, but these without capitulation; above all, on the same given condition to keep friends with himself—here is a task for all that a man has of fortitude and delicacy."

"It's all about some man," she thought with a child's literalness. "Wonder why Miss Wenzel gave it to me? That big word, cap-it-u-la-tion"—she divided it off into syllables doubtfully—"must mean to spell with capitals I guess. I'll say it to Archie some time."

But she thought it very kind of Miss Wenzel. And after she had shown it to her mother, she hung it up in the bay window of her little white room, where the sun struck it every morning.

## III

Afterward Emmy always connected the motto with the beginning of her own realization of what color might mean. It took her quite a while to find it out, but by the time she was ready to graduate from the high school she had come to recognize that the occasional impasse which she met now and then might generally be traced to color. This knowledge, however, far from embittering her, simply gave to her life keener zest. Of course she never met with any of the grosser forms of prejudice, and her personality was the kind to win her at least the respect and sometimes the wondering admiration of her schoolmates. For unconsciously she made them see that she was perfectly satisfied with being colored. She could never understand why anyone should think she would want to be white.

One day a girl—Elise Carter—asked her to let her copy her French verbs in the test they were to have later in the day. Emmy, who was both by nature and by necessity independent, refused bluntly.

"Oh, don't be so mean, Emmy," Elise had wailed. She hesitated. "If you'll let me copy them—I'll—I tell you what I'll do, I'll see that you get invited to our club spread Friday afternoon."

"Well, I guess you won't," Emmy had retorted. "I'll probably be asked anyway. 'Most everybody else has been invited already."

Elise jeered. "And did you think as a matter of course that we'd ask you? Well, you have got something to learn."

There was no mistaking the "you."

Emmy took the blow pretty calmly for all its unexpectedness. "You mean," she said slowly, the blood showing darkly under the thin brown of her skin, "because I'm colored?"

Elise hedged—she was a little frightened at such directness.

"Oh, well, Emmy, you know colored folks can't expect to have everything we have, or if they do they must pay extra for it."

"I—I see," said Emmy, stammering a little, as she always did when she was angry. "I begin to see for the first time why you think it's so awful to be colored. It's because you think we are willing to be mean and sneaky and"—with a sudden drop to schoolgirl vernacular—"soup-y. Why, Elise Carter, I wouldn't be in your old club with girls like you for worlds." There was no mistaking her sincerity.

"That was the day," she confided to Archie a long time afterward, "that I learned the meaning of making friends 'without capitulation.' Do you remember Miss Wenzel's motto, Archie?"

He assured her he did. "And of course you know, Emmy, you were an awful brick to answer that Carter girl like that. Didn't you really want to go to the spread?"

"Not one bit," she told him vigorously, "after I found out why I hadn't been asked. And look, Archie, isn't it funny, just as soon as she wanted something she didn't care whether I was colored or not?"

Archie nodded. "They're all that way," he told her briefly.

"And if I'd gone she'd have believed that all colored people were sort of—well, you know, 'meachin'—just like me. It's so odd the ignorant way in which they draw their conclusions. Why, I remember reading the most interesting article in a magazine—the *Atlantic Monthly* I think it was. A woman had written it and at this point she was condemning universal suffrage. And all of a sudden, without any warning, she spoke of that 'fierce, silly, amiable creature, the uneducated Negro,' and—think of it, Archie—of 'his baser and sillier female.' It made me so angry. I've never forgotten it."

Archie whistled. "That was pretty tough," he acknowledged. "I suppose the truth is," he went on smiling at her earnestness, "she has a colored cook who drinks."

"That's just it," she returned emphatically. "She probably has. But, Archie, just think of all the colored people we've both seen here and over in Newtown, too; some of them just as poor and ignorant as they can be. But not one of them is fierce or base or silly enough for that to be considered his chief characteristic. I'll wager that woman never spoke to fifty colored people in her life. No, thank you, if that's what it means to belong to the 'superior race,' I'll come back, just as I am, to the fiftieth reincarnation."

Archie sighed. "Oh, well, life is very simple for you. You see, you've never been up against it like I've been. After all, you've had all you wanted practically—those girls even came around finally in the high school and asked you into their clubs and things. While I—" he colored sensitively.

"You see, this plagued—er—complexion of mine doesn't tell anybody what I am. At first—and all along, too, if I let them—fellows take me for a foreigner of some kind—Spanish or something, and they take me up hail-fellow-well-met. And then, if I let them know—I hate to feel I'm taking them in, you know, and besides that I can't help being curious to know what's going to happen—"

"What does happen?" interrupted Emmy, all interest.

"Well, all sorts of things. You take that first summer just before I entered preparatory school. You remember I was working at that camp in Cottage City. All the waiters were fellows just like me, working to go to some college or other. At first I was just one of them—swam with them, played cards—oh, you know, regularly chummed with them. Well, the cook was a colored man—sure enough, colored you know—and one day one of the boys called him a—of course I couldn't tell you, Emmy, but he swore at him and called him a Nigger. And when I took up for him the fellow said—he was angry, Emmy, and he said it as the worst insult he could think of—'Anybody would think you had black blood in your veins, too.'

" 'Anybody would think right,' I told him."

"Well?" asked Emmy.

He shrugged his shoulders. "That was all there was to it. The fellows dropped me completely—left me to the company of the cook, who was all right enough as cooks go, I suppose, but he didn't want me any more than I wanted him. And finally the manager came and told me he was sorry, but he guessed I'd have to go." He smiled grimly as at some unpleasant reminiscence.

"What's the joke?" his listener wondered.

"He also told me that I was the blankest kind of a blank too—oh, you couldn't dream how he swore, Emmy. He said why didn't I leave well enough alone.

"And don't you know that's the thought I've had ever since—why not leave well enough alone?—and not tell people what I am. I guess you're different from me," he broke off wistfully, noting her look of disapproval; "you're so complete and satisfied in yourself. Just being Emilie Carrel seems to be enough for you. But you just wait until color keeps you from the thing you want the most, and you'll see."

"You needn't be so tragic," she commented succinctly. "Outside of that one time at Cottage City, it doesn't seem to have kept you back."

For Archie's progress had been miraculous. In the seven years in which he had been from home, one marvel after another had come his way. He had found lucrative work each summer, he had got through his preparatory school in three years, he had been graduated number six from one of the best technical schools in the country—and now he had a position. He was to work for one of the biggest engineering concerns in Philadelphia.

This last bit of good fortune had dropped out of a clear sky. A guest at one of the hotels one summer had taken an interest in the handsome, willing bellboy and inquired into his history. Archie had hesitated at first, but finally, his eye alert for the first sign of dislike or superiority, he told the man of his Negro blood.

"If he turns me down," he said to himself boyishly, "I'll never risk it again."

But Mr. Robert Fallon—young, wealthy and quixotic—had become more interested than ever.

"So it's all a gamble with you, isn't it? By George! How exciting your life must be—now white and now black—standing between ambition and honor, what? Not that I don't think you're doing the right thing—it's nobody's confounded business anyway. Look here, when you get through look me up. I may be able to put you wise to something. Here's my card. And say, mum's the word, and when you've made your pile you can wake some fine morning and find yourself famous simply by telling what you are. All rot, this beastly prejudice, I say."

And when Archie had graduated, his new friend, true to his word, had gotten for him from his father a letter of introduction to Mr. Nicholas Fields in Philadelphia, and Archie was placed. Young Robert Fallon had gone laughing on his aimless, merry way.

"Be sure you keep your mouth shut, Ferrers," was his only enjoinment.

Archie, who at first had experienced some qualms, had finally completely acquiesced. For the few moments' talk with Mr. Fields had intoxicated him. The vision of work, plenty of it, his own chosen kind—and the opportunity to do it as a man—not an exception, but as a plain ordinary man among other men—was too much for him.

"It was my big chance, Emmy," he told her one day. He was spending his brief vacation in Plainville, and the two, having talked themselves out on other things, had returned to their old absorbing topic. He went on a little pleadingly, for she had protested. "I couldn't resist it. You don't know what it means to me. I don't care about being white in itself any more than you do—but I do care about a white man's chances. Don't let's talk about it any more though; here it's the first week in September and I have to go the 15th. I may not be back till Christmas. I should hate to think that you— you were changed toward me, Emmy."

"I'm not changed, Archie," she assured him gravely, "only somehow it makes me feel that you're different. I can't quite look up to you as I used. I don't like the idea of considering the end justified by the means."

She was silent, watching the falling leaves flutter like golden butterflies against her white dress. As she stood there in the old-fashioned garden, she seemed to the boy's adoring eyes like some beautiful but inflexible bronze goddess.

"I couldn't expect you to look up to me, Emmy, as though I were on a pedestal," he began miserably, "but I do want you to respect me, because—oh, Emmy, don't you see? I love you very much and I hope you will—I want you to—oh, Emmy, couldn't you like me a little? I—I've never thought ever of anyone but you. I didn't mean to tell you all about this now—I meant to wait until I really was successful, and then come and lay it all at your beautiful feet. You're so lovely, Emmy. But if you despise me—" he was very humble.

For once in her calm young life Emmy was completely surprised. But she had to get to the root of things. "You mean," she faltered, "you mean you want"—she couldn't say it.

"I mean I want you to marry me," he said, gaining courage from her confusion. "Oh, have I frightened you, Emmy, dearest—of course you couldn't like me well enough for that all in a heap—it's different with me. I've always loved you, Emmy. But if you'd only think about it."

"Oh," she breathed, "there's Céleste. Oh, Archie, I don't know, it's all so funny. And we're so young. I couldn't really tell anything about my feelings anyway—you know, I've never seen anybody but you." Then as his face clouded— "Oh, well, I guess even if I had I wouldn't like him any better. Yes, Céleste, we're coming in. Archie, mother says you're to have dinner with us every night you're here, if you can."

There was no more said about the secret that Archie was keeping from Mr. Fields. There were too many other things to talk about—reasons why he had always loved Emmy; reasons why she couldn't be sure just yet; reasons why, if she were sure, she couldn't say yes.

Archie hung between high hope and despair, while Emmy, it must be confessed, enjoyed herself, albeit innocently enough, and grew distractingly pretty. On the last day as they sat in the sitting room, gaily recounting childish episodes, Archie suddenly asked her again. He was so grave and serious that she really became frightened.

"Oh, Archie, I couldn't—I don't really want to. It's so lovely just being a girl. I think I do like you—of course I like you lots. But couldn't we just be friends and keep going on—so?"

"No," he told her harshly, his face set and miserable; "no, we can't. And, Emmy—I'm not coming back any more—I couldn't stand it." His voice broke, he was fighting to keep back the hot boyish tears. After all he was only 21. "I'm sorry I troubled you," he said proudly.

She looked at him pitifully. "I don't want you to go away forever, Archie," she said tremulously. She made no effort to keep back the tears. "I've been so lonely this last year since I've been out of school—you can't think."

He was down on his knees, his arms around her. "Emmy, Emmy, look up—are you crying for me, dear? Do you want me to come back—you do—you mean it? Emmy, you must love me, you do—a little." He kissed her slim fingers.

"Are you going to marry me? Look at me, Emmy— you are! Oh, Emmy, do you know I'm—I'm going to kiss you."

The stage came lumbering up not long afterward, and bore him away to the train—triumphant and absolutely happy.

"My heart," sang Emmy rapturously as she ran up the broad, old-fashioned stairs to her room—"my heart is like a singing bird."

# IV

The year that followed seemed to her perfection. Archie's letters alone would have made it that. Emmy was quite sure that there had never been any other letters like them. She used to read them aloud to her mother.

Not all of them, though, for some were too precious for any eye but her own. She used to pore over them alone in her room at night, planning to answer them with an abandon equal to his own, but always finally evolving the same shy, almost timid epistle, which never failed to awaken in her lover's breast a sense equally of amusement and reverence. Her shyness seemed to him the most exquisite thing in the world—so exquisite, indeed, that he almost wished it would never vanish, were it not that its very disappearance would be the measure of her trust in him. His own letters showed plainly his adoration.

Only once had a letter of his caused a fleeting pang of misapprehension. He had been speaking of the persistent good fortune which had been his in Philadelphia.

"You can't think how lucky I am anyway," the letter ran on. "The other day I was standing on the corner of Fourth and Chestnut Streets at noon—you ought to see Chestnut Street at 12 o'clock, Emmy—and someone came up, looked at me and said: 'Well, if it isn't Archie Ferrers!' And guess who it was, Emmy? Do you remember the Higginses who used to live over in Newtown? I don't suppose you ever knew them, only they were so queer looking that you must recall them. They were all sorts of colors from black with 'good' hair to yellow with the red, kinky kind. And then there was Maude, clearly a Higgins, and yet not looking like any of them, you know; perfectly white, with blue eyes and fair hair. Well, this was Maude, and, say, maybe she didn't look good. I couldn't tell you what she had on, but it was all right, and I was glad to take her over to the Reading Terminal and put her on a train to New York.

"I guess you're wondering where my luck is in all this tale, but you wait. Just as we started up the stairs of the depot, whom should we run into but young Peter Fields, my boss's son and heir, you know. Really, I thought I'd faint, and then I remembered that Maude was whiter than he in looks, and that there was nothing to give me away. He wanted to talk to us, but I hurried her off to her train. You know, it's a queer thing, Emmy; some girls are just naturally born stylish. Now there are both you and Maude Higgins, brought up from little things in a tiny inland town, and both of you able to give any of these city girls all sorts of odds in the matter of dressing."

Emmy put the letter down, wondering what had made her grow so cold.

"I wonder," she mused. She turned and looked in the glass to be confronted by a charming vision, slender,—and dusky.

"I am black," she thought, "but comely." She laughed to herself happily. "Archie loves you, girl," she said to the face in the glass, and put the little fear behind her. It met her insistently now and then, however, until the next week brought a letter begging her to get her mother to bring her to Philadelphia for a week or so.

"I can't get off till Thanksgiving, dearest, and I'm so lonely and disappointed. You know, I had looked forward so to spending the 15th of September with you—do you remember that date, sweetheart? I wouldn't have you come now in all this heat—you can't imagine how hot Philadelphia is, Emmy—but it's beautiful here in October. You'll love it, Emmy. It's such a big city—miles and miles of long, narrow

streets, rather ugly, too, but all so interesting. You'll like
Chestnut and Market Streets, where the big shops are, and
South Street, teeming with Jews and colored people, though
there are more of these last on Lombard Street. You never
dreamed of so many colored people, Emmy Carrel—or such
kinds.

"And then there are the parks and the theatres, and music
and restaurants. And Broad Street late at night, all silent with
gold, electric lights beckoning you on for miles and miles.
Do you think your mother will let me take you out by
yourself, Emmy? You'd be willing, wouldn't you?"

If Emmy needed more reassurance than that she received
it when Archie, a month later, met her and her mother at
Broad Street station in Philadelphia. The boy was radiant.
Mrs. Carrel, too, put aside her usual reticence, and the three
were in fine spirits by the time they reached the rooms which
Archie had procured for them on Christian Street. Once
ensconced, the older woman announced her intention of taking
advantage of the stores.

"I shall be shopping practically all day," she informed
them. "I'll be so tired in the afternoons and evenings, Archie,
that I'll have to get you to take my daughter off my hands."

Her daughter was delighted, but not more transparently
so than her appointed cavalier. He was overjoyed at the
thought of playing host and of showing Emmy the delights
of city life.

"By the time I've finished showing you one-fifth of what
I've planned you'll give up the idea of waiting 'way till next
October and marry me Christmas. Say, do it anyway, Emmy,
won't you?" He waited tensely, but she only shook her head.

"Oh, I couldn't, Archie, and anyway you must show me
first your wonderful city."

They did manage to cover a great deal of ground, though

their mutual absorption made its impression on them very doubtful. Some things though Emmy never forgot. There was a drive one wonderful, golden October afternoon along the Wissahickon. Emmy, in her perfectly correct gray suit and smart little gray hat, held the reins—in itself a sort of measure of Archie's devotion to her, for he was wild about horses. He sat beside her ecstatic, ringing all the changes from a boy's nonsense to the most mature kind of seriousness. And always he looked at her with his passionate though reverent eyes. They were very happy.

There was some wonderful music, too, at the Academy. That was by accident though. For they had started for the theatre—had reached there in fact. The usher was taking the tickets.

"This way, Emmy," said Archie. The usher looked up aimlessly, then, as his eyes traveled from the seeming young foreigner to the colored girl beside him, he flushed a little.

"Is the young lady with you?" he whispered politely enough. But Emmy, engrossed in a dazzling vision in a pink décolleté gown, would not in any event have heard him.

"She is," responded Archie alertly. "What's the trouble, isn't to-night the 17th?"

The usher passed over this question with another—who had bought the tickets? Archie of course had, and told him so, frankly puzzled.

"I see. Well, I'm sorry," the man said evenly, "but these seats are already occupied, and the rest of the floor is sold out besides. There's a mistake somewhere. Now if you'll take these tickets back to the office I can promise you they'll give you the best seats left in the balcony."

"What's the matter?" asked Emmy, tearing her glance from the pink vision at last. "Oh, Archie, you're hurting my arm; don't hold it that tight. Why—why are we going away from the theatre? Oh, Archie, are you sick? You're just as white!"

"There was some mistake about the tickets," he got out, trying to keep his voice steady. "And a fellow in the crowd gave me an awful dig just then; guess that's why I'm pale. I'm so sorry, Emmy—I was so stupid, it's all my fault."

"What was the matter with the tickets?" she asked, incuriously. "That's the Bellevue-Stratford over there, isn't it? Then the Academy of Music must be near here. See how fast I'm learning? Let's go there; I've never heard a symphony concert. And, Archie, I've always heard that the best way to hear big music like that is at a distance, so get gallery tickets."

He obeyed her, fearful that if there were any trouble this time she might hear it. Emmy enjoyed it thoroughly, wondering a little, however, at his silence. "I guess he's tired," she thought. She would have been amazed to know his thoughts as he sat there staring moodily at the orchestra. "This damnation color business," he kept saying over and over.

That night as they stood in the vestibule of the Christian Street house Emmy, for the first time, volunteered him a kiss. "Such a nice, tired boy," she said gently. Afterward he stood for a long time bareheaded on the steps looking at the closed door. Nothing he felt could crush him as much as that kiss had lifted him up.

## V

Not even for lovers can a week last forever. Archie had kept till the last day what he considered his choicest bit of exploring. This was to take Emmy down into old Philadelphia and show her how the city had grown up from the waterfront—

and by means of what tortuous self-governing streets. It was a sight at once dear and yet painful to his methodical, mathematical mind. They had explored Dock and Beach Streets, and had got over into Shackamaxon, where he showed her Penn Treaty Park, and they had sat in the little pavilion overlooking the Delaware.

Not many colored people came through this vicinity, and the striking pair caught many a wondering, as well as admiring, glance. They caught, too, the aimless, wandering eye of Mr. Nicholas Fields as he lounged, comfortably smoking, on the rear of a "Gunner's Run" car, on his way to Shackamaxon Ferry. Something in the young fellow's walk seemed vaguely familiar to him, and he leaned way out toward the sidewalk to see who that he knew could be over in this cheerless, forsaken locality.

"Gad!" he said to himself in surprise, "if it isn't young Ferrers, with a lady, too! Hello, why it's a colored woman! Ain't he a rip? Always thought he seemed too proper. Got her dressed to death, too; so that's how his money goes!" He dismissed the matter with a smile and a shrug of his shoulders.

Perhaps he would never have thought of it again had not Archie, rushing into the office a trifle late the next morning, caromed directly into him.

"Oh, it's you," he said, receiving his clerk's smiling apology. "What d'you mean by knocking into anybody like that?" Mr. Fields was facetious with his favorite employees. "Evidently your Shackamaxon trip upset you a little. Where'd you get your black Venus, my boy? I'll bet you don't have one cent to rub against another at the end of a month. Oh, you needn't get red; boys will be boys, and everyone to his taste. Clarkson," he broke off, crossing to his secretary, "if Mr. Hunter calls me up, hold the 'phone and send over to the bank for me."

He had gone, and Archie, white now and shaken, entered his own little room. He sat down at the desk and sank his head in his hands. It had taken a moment for the insult to Emmy to sink in, but even when it did the thought of his own false position had held him back. The shame of it bit into him.

"I'm a coward," he said to himself, staring miserably at the familiar wall. "I'm a wretched cad to let him think that of Emmy—Emmy! and she the whitest angel that ever lived, purity incarnate." His cowardice made him sick. "I'll go and tell him," he said, and started for the door.

"If you do," whispered common sense, "you'll lose your job and then what would become of you? After all Emmy need never know."

"But I'll always know I didn't defend her," he answered back silently.

"He's gone out to the bank anyhow," went on the inward opposition. "What's the use of rushing in there and telling him before the whole board of directors?"

"Well, then, when he comes back," he capitulated, but he felt himself weaken.

But Mr. Fields didn't come back. When Mr. Hunter called him up, Clarkson connected him with the bank, with the result that Mr. Fields left for Reading in the course of an hour. He didn't come back for a week.

Meanwhile Archie tasted the depths of self-abasement. "But what am I to do?" he groaned to himself at nights. "If I tell him I'm colored he'll kick me out, and if I go anywhere else I'd run the same risk. If I'd only knocked him down! After all she'll never know and I'll make it up to her. I'll be so good to her—dear little Emmy! But how could I know that he would take that view of it—beastly low mind he must have!" He colored up like a girl at the thought of it.

He passed the week thus, alternately reviling and defending himself. He knew now though that he would never have the courage to tell. The economy of the thing he decided was at least as important as the principle. And always he wrote to Emmy letters of such passionate adoration that the girl for all her natural steadiness was carried off her feet.

"How he loves me," she thought happily. "If mother is willing I believe—yes, I will—I'll marry him Christmas. But I won't tell him till he comes Thanksgiving."

When Mr. Fields came back he sent immediately for his son Peter. The two held some rather stormy consultations, which were renewed for several days. Peter roomed in town, while his father lived out at Chestnut Hill. Eventually Archie was sent for.

"You're not looking very fit, my boy," Mr. Fields greeted him kindly; "working too hard I suppose over those specifications. Well, here's a tonic for you. This last week has shown me that I need someone younger than myself to take a hand in the business. I'm getting too old or too tired or something. Anyhow I'm played out.

"I've tried to make this young man here,"—with an angry glance at his son—"see that the mantle ought to fall on him, but he won't hear of it. Says the business can stop for all he cares; he's got enough money anyway. Gad, in my day young men liked to work, instead of dabbling around in this filthy social settlement business—with a lot of old maids."

Peter smiled contentedly. "Sally in our alley, what?" he put in diabolically. The older man glared at him, exasperated.

"Now look here, Ferrers," he went on abruptly. "I've had my eye on you ever since you first came. I don't know a thing about you outside of Mr. Fallon's recommendation, but I can see you've got good stuff in you—and what's more, you're a born engineer. If you had some money, I'd take you into

partnership at once, but I believe you told me that all you
had was your salary." Archie nodded.

"Well, now, I tell you what I'm going to do. I'm going
to take you in as a sort of silent partner, teach you the business
end of the concern, and in the course of a few years, place
the greater part of the management in your hands. You can
see you won't lose by it. Of course I'll still be head, and after
I step out Peter will take my place, though only nominally I
suppose."

He sighed; his son's business defection was a bitter point
with him. But that imperturbable young man only nodded.

"The boss guessed right the very first time," he paraphrased
cheerfully. "You bet I'll be head in name only. Young
Ferrers, there's just the man for the job. What d'you say,
Archie?"

The latter tried to collect himself. "Of course I accept it,
Mr. Fields, and I—I don't think you'll ever regret it." He
actually stammered. Was there ever such wonderful luck?

"Oh, that's all right," Mr. Fields went on, "you wouldn't
be getting this chance if you didn't deserve it. See here, what
about your boarding out at Chestnut Hill for a year or two?
Then I can lay my hands on you any time, and you can get
hold of things that much sooner. You live on Green Street,
don't you? Well, give your landlady a month's notice and
quit the 1st of December. A young man coming on like you
ought to be thinking of a home anyway. Can't find some nice
girl to marry you, what?

Archie, flushing a little, acknowledged his engagement.

"Good, that's fine!" Then with sudden recollection—"Oh,
so you're reformed. Well, I thought you'd get over that.
Can't settle down too soon. A lot of nice little cottages out
there at Chestnut Hill. Peter, your mother says she wishes
you'd come out to dinner to-night. The youngest Wilton girl

is to be there, I believe. Guess that's all for this afternoon, Ferrers."

## VI

Archie walked up Chestnut Street on air. "It's better to be born lucky than rich," he reflected. "But I'll be rich, too— and what a lot I can do for Emmy. Glad I didn't tell Mr. Fields now. Wonder what those 'little cottages' out to Chestnut Hill sell for. Emmy—" He stopped short, struck by a sudden realization.

"Why, I must be stark, staring crazy," he said to himself, standing still right in the middle of Chestnut Street. A stout gentleman whom his sudden stopping had seriously incommoded gave him, as he passed by, a vicious prod with his elbow. It started him on again.

"If I hadn't clean forgotten all about it. Oh, Lord, what am I to do? Of course Emmy can't go out to Chestnut Hill to live—well, that would be a give-away. And he advised me to live out there for a year or two—and he knows I'm engaged, and—now—making more than enough to marry on."

He turned aimlessly down 19th Street, and spying Rittenhouse Square sat down in it. The cutting November wind swirled brown, crackling leaves right into his face, but he never saw one of them.

When he arose again, long after his dinner hour, he had made his decision. After all Emmy was a sensible girl; she knew he had only his salary to depend on. And, of course, he wouldn't have to stay out in Chestnut Hill forever. They could buy, or perhaps—he smiled proudly—even build now, far out in West Philadelphia, as far as possible away from Mr. Fields. He'd just ask her to postpone their marriage—

perhaps for two years. He sighed a little, for he was very much in love.

"It seems funny that prosperity should make a fellow put off his happiness," he thought ruefully, swinging himself aboard a North 19th Street car.

He decided to go to Plainville and tell her about it—he could go up Saturday afternoon. "Let's see, I can get an express to Harrisburg, and a sleeper to Plainville, and come back Sunday afternoon. Emmy'll like a surprise like that." He thought of their improvised trip to the Academy and how she had made him buy gallery seats. "Lucky she has that little saving streak in her. She'll see through the whole thing like a brick." His simile made him smile. As soon as he reached home he scribbled her a note:

"I'm coming Sunday," he said briefly, "and I have something awfully important to ask you. I'll be there only from 3 to 7. 'When Time let's slip one little perfect hour,' that's that Omar thing you're always quoting, isn't it? Well, there'll be four perfect hours this trip."

All the way on the slow poky local from Harrisburg he pictured her surprise. "I guess she won't mind the postponement one bit," he thought with a brief pang. "She never was keen on marrying. Girls certainly are funny. Here she admits she's in love and willing to marry, and yet she's always hung fire about the date." He dozed fitfully.

As a matter of fact Emmy had fixed the date. "Of course," she said to herself happily, "the 'something important' is that he wants me to marry him right away. Well, I'll tell him that I will, Christmas. Dear old Archie coming all this distance to ask me that. I'll let him beg me two or three times first, and then I'll tell him. Won't he be pleased? I shouldn't be a bit surprised if he went down on his knees again." She flushed a little, thinking of that first wonderful time.

"Being in love is just—dandy," she decided. "I guess I'll wear my red dress."

Afterward the sight of that red dress always caused Emmy a pang of actual physical anguish. She never saw it without seeing, too, every detail of that disastrous Sunday afternoon. Archie had come—she had gone to the door to meet him— they had lingered happily in the hall a few moments, and then she had brought him in to her mother and Céleste.

The old French woman had kissed him on both cheeks. "See, then it's thou, my cherished one!" she cried ecstatically. "How long a time it is since thou art here."

Mrs. Carrel's greeting, though not so demonstrative, was no less sincere, and when the two were left to themselves "the cherished one" was radiant.

"My, but your mother can make a fellow feel welcome, Emmy. She doesn't say much but what she does, goes."

Emmy smiled a little absently. The gray mist outside in the sombre garden, the fire crackling on the hearth and casting ruddy shadows on Archie's hair, the very red of her dress, Archie himself—all this was making for her a picture, which she saw repeated on endless future Sunday afternoons in Philadelphia. She sighed contentedly.

"I've got something to tell you, sweetheart," said Archie.

"It's coming," she thought. "Oh, isn't it lovely! Of all the people in the world—he loves me, loves me!" She almost missed the beginning of his story. For he was telling her of Mr. Fields and his wonderful offer.

When she finally caught the drift of what he was saying she was vaguely disappointed. He was talking business, in which she was really very little interested. The "saving streak" which Archie had attributed to her was merely sporadic, and was due to a nice girl's delicacy at having money spent on her by a man. But, of course, she listened.

"So you see the future is practically settled—there's only

one immediate drawback," he said earnestly. She shut her eyes—it was coming after all.

He went on a little puzzled by her silence; "only one drawback, and that is that, of course, we can't be married for at least two years yet."

Her eyes flew open. "Not marry for two years! Why— why ever not?"

Even then he might have saved the situation by telling her first of his own cruel disappointment, for her loveliness, as she sat there, all glowing red and bronze in the firelit dusk, smote him very strongly.

But he only floundered on.

"Why, Emmy, of course, you can see—you're so much darker than I—anybody can tell at a glance what you—er— are." He was crude, he knew it, but he couldn't see how to help himself. "And we'd have to live at Chestnut Hill, at first, right there near the Fields', and there'd be no way with you there to keep people from knowing that I—that—oh, confound it all—Emmy, you must understand! You don't mind, do you? You know you never were keen on marrying anyway. If we were both the same color—why, Emmy, what is it?"

For she had risen and was looking at him as though he were someone entirely strange. Then she turned and gazed unseeingly out the window. So that was it—the "something important"—he was ashamed of her, of her color; he was always talking about a white man's chances. Why, of course, how foolish she'd been all along—how could he be white with her at his side? And she had thought he had come to urge her to marry him at once—the sting of it sent her head up higher. She turned and faced him, her beautiful silhouette distinctly outlined against the gray blur of the window. She wanted to hurt him—she was quite cool now.

"I have something to tell you, too, Archie," she said evenly.

"I've been meaning to tell you for some time. It seems I've been making a mistake all along. I don't really love you"— she was surprised dully that the words didn't choke her— "so, of course, I can't marry you. I was wondering how I could get out of it—you can't think how tiresome it's all been." She had to stop.

He was standing, frozen, motionless like something carved.

"This seems as good an opportunity as any—oh, here's your ring," she finished, holding it out to him coldly. It was a beautiful diamond, small but flawless—the only thing he'd ever gone into debt for.

The statue came to life. "Emmy, you're crazy," he cried passionately, seizing her by the wrist. "You've got the wrong idea. You think I don't want you to marry me. What a cad you must take me for. I only asked you to postpone it a little while, so we'd be happier afterward. I'm doing it all for you, girl. I never dreamed—it's preposterous, Emmy! And you can't say you don't love me—that's all nonsense!"

But she clung to her lie desperately.

"No, really, Archie, I don't love you one bit; of course I like you awfully—let go my wrist, you can think how strong you are. I should have told you long ago, but I hadn't the heart—and it really was interesting." No grand lady on the stage could have been more detached. He should know, too, how it felt not to be wanted.

He was at her feet now, clutching desperately, as she retreated, at her dress—the red dress she had donned so bravely. He couldn't believe in her heartlessness. "You must love me, Emmy, and even if you don't you must marry me anyway. Why, you promised—you don't know what it means to me, Emmy—it's my very life—I've never even dreamed of another woman but you! Take it back, Emmy, you can't mean it."

But she convinced him that she could. "I wish you'd stop, Archie," she said wearily; "this is awfully tiresome. And, anyway, I think you'd better go now if you want to catch your train."

He stumbled to his feet, the life all out of him. In the hall he turned around: "You'll say good-by to your mother for me," he said mechanically. She nodded. He opened the front door. It seemed to close of its own accord behind him.

She came back into the sitting room, wondering why the place had suddenly grown so intolerably hot. She opened a window. From somewhere out of the gray mists came the strains of "Alice, Where Art Thou?" executed with exceeding mournfulness on an organ. The girl listened with a curious detached intentness.

"That must be Willie Holborn," she thought; "no one else could play as wretchedly as that." She crossed heavily to the armchair and flung herself in it. Her mind seemed to go on acting as though it were clockwork and she were watching it.

Once she said: "Now this, I suppose, is what they call a tragedy." And again: "He did get down on his knees."

# VII

There was nothing detached or impersonal in Archie's consideration of his plight. All through the trip home, through the long days that followed and the still longer nights, he was in torment. Again and again he went over the scene.

"She was making a plaything out of me," he chafed bitterly. "All these months she's been only fooling. And yet I wonder if she really meant it, if she didn't just do it to make it easier for me to be white. If that's the case what an insufferable cad she must take me for. No, she couldn't have cared for me, because if she had she'd have seen through it all right away."

By the end of ten days he had worked himself almost into a fever. His burning face and shaking hands made him resolve, as he dressed that morning, to 'phone the office that he was too ill to come to work.

"And I'll stay home and write her a letter that she'll have to answer." For although he had sent her one and sometimes two letters every day ever since his return, there had been no reply.

"She must answer that," he said to himself at length, when the late afternoon shadows were creeping in. He had torn up letter after letter—he had been proud and beseeching by turns. But in this last he had laid his very heart bare.

"And if she doesn't answer it"—it seemed to him he couldn't face the possibility. He was at the writing desk where her picture stood in its little silver frame. It had been there all that day. As a rule he kept it locked up, afraid of what it might reveal to his landlady's vigilant eye. He sat there, his head bowed over the picture, wondering dully how he should endure his misery.

Someone touched him on the shoulder.

"Gad, boy," said Mr. Nicholas Fields, "here I thought you were sick in bed, and come here to find you mooning over a picture. What's the matter? Won't the lady have you? Let's see who it is that's been breaking you up so." Archie watched him in fascinated horror, while he picked up the photograph and walked over to the window. As he scanned it his expression changed.

"Oh," he said, with a little puzzled frown and yet laughing, too, "it's your colored lady friend again. Won't she let you go? That's the way with these black women, once they get hold of a white man—bleed 'em to death. I don't see how you can stand them anyway; it's the Spanish in you, I suppose. Better get rid of her before you get married. Hello—" he broke off.

For Archie was standing menacingly over him. "If you say another word about that girl I'll break every rotten bone in your body."

"Oh, come," said Mr. Fields, still pleasant, "isn't that going it a little too strong? Why, what can a woman like that mean to you?"

"She can mean," said the other slowly, "everything that the woman who has promised to be my wife ought to mean." The broken engagement meant nothing in a time like this.

Mr. Fields forgot his composure. "To be your wife! Why, you idiot, you—you'd ruin yourself—marry a Negro—have you lost your senses? Oh, I suppose it's some of your crazy foreign notions. In this country white gentlemen don't marry colored women."

Archie had not expected this loophole. He hesitated, then with a shrug he burnt all his bridges behind him. One by one he saw his ambitions flare up and vanish.

"No, you're right," he rejoined. "White gentlemen don't, but colored men do." Then he waited calmly for the avalanche.

It came. "You mean," said Mr. Nicholas Fields, at first with only wonder and then with growing suspicion in his voice, "you mean that you're colored?" Archie nodded and watched him turn into a maniac.

"Why, you low-lived young blackguard, you—" he swore horribly. "And you've let me think all this time—" He broke off again, hunting for something insulting enough to say. "You Nigger!" he hurled at him. He really felt there was nothing worse, so he repeated it again and again with fresh imprecations.

"I think," said Archie, "that that will do. I shouldn't like to forget myself, and I'm in a pretty reckless mood to-day. You must remember, Mr. Fields, you didn't ask me who I was, and I had no occasion to tell you. Of course I won't come back to the office."

"If you do," said Mr. Fields, white to the lips, "I'll have you locked up if I have to perjure my soul to find a charge against you. I'll show you what a white man can do—you—"

But Archie had taken him by the shoulder and pushed him outside the door.

"And that's all right," he said to himself with a sudden heady sense of liberty. He surveyed himself curiously in the mirror. "Wouldn't anybody think I had changed into some horrible ravening beast. Lord, how that one little word changed him." He ruminated over the injustice—the petty, foolish injustice of the whole thing.

"I don't believe," he said slowly, "it's worth while having a white man's chances if one has to be like that. I see what Emmy used to be driving at now." The thought of her sobered him.

"If it should be on account of my chances that you're letting me go," he assured the picture gravely, "it's all quite unnecessary, for I'll never have another opportunity like that."

In which he was quite right. It even looked as though he couldn't get any work at all along his own line. There was no demand for colored engineers.

"If you keep your mouth shut," one man said, "and not let the other clerks know what you are I might try you for awhile." There was nothing for him to do but accept. At the end of two weeks—the day before Thanksgiving—he found out that the men beside him, doing exactly the same kind of work as his own, were receiving for it five dollars more a week. The old injustice based on color had begun to hedge him in. It seemed to him that his unhappiness and humiliation were more than he could stand.

# VIII

But at least his life was occupied. Emmy, on the other hand, saw her own life stretching out through endless vistas of empty, useless days. She grew thin and listless, all the brightness and vividness of living toned down for her into one gray, flat monotony. By Thanksgiving Day the strain showed its effects on her very plainly.

Her mother, who had listened in her usual silence when her daughter told her the cause of the broken engagement, tried to help her.

"Emmy," she said, "you're probably doing Archie an injustice. I don't believe he ever dreamed of being ashamed of you. I think it is your own wilful pride that is at fault. You'd better consider carefully—if you are making a mistake you'll regret it to the day of your death. The sorrow of it will never leave you."

Emmy was petulant. "Oh, mother, what can you know about it? Céleste says you married when you were young, even younger than I—married to the man you loved, and you were with him, I suppose, till he died. You couldn't know how I feel." She fell to staring absently out the window. It was a long time before her mother spoke again.

"No, Emmy," she finally began again very gravely, "I wasn't with your father till he died. That is why I'm speaking to you as I am. I had sent him away—we had quarreled— oh, I was passionate enough when I was your age, Emmy. He was jealous—he was a West Indian—I suppose Céleste has told you—and one day he came past the sitting room—it was just like this one, overlooking the garden. Well, as he glanced in the window he saw a man, a white man, put his arms around me and kiss me. When he came in through the side door the man had gone. I was just about to explain— no, tell him—for I didn't know he had seen me when he began." She paused a little, but presently went on in her even, dispassionate voice:

"He was furious, Emmy; oh, he was so angry, and he accused me—oh, my dear! He was almost insane. But it was really because he loved me. And then I became angry and I wouldn't tell him anything. And finally, Emmy, he struck me—you mustn't blame him, child; remember, it was the same spirit showing in both of us, in different ways. I was doing all I could to provoke him by keeping silence and he merely retaliated in his way. The blow wouldn't have harmed a little bird. But—well, Emmy, I think I must have gone crazy. I ordered him from the house—it had been my mother's—and I told him never, never to let me see him again." She smiled drearily.

"I never did see him again. After he left Céleste and I packed up our things and came here to America. You were the littlest thing, Emmy. You can't remember living in France at all, can you? Well, when your father found out where I was he wrote and asked me to forgive him and to let him come back. 'I am on my knees,' the letter said. I wrote and told him yes—I loved him, Emmy; oh, child, you with your talk of color; you don't know what love is. If you really loved Archie you'd let him marry you and lock you off, away from all the world, just so long as you were with him.

"I was so happy," she resumed. "I hadn't seen him for two years. Well, he started—he was in Hayti then; he got to New York safely and started here. There was a wreck—just a little one—only five people killed, but he was one of them.

He was so badly mangled, they wouldn't even let me see him."

"Oh!" breathed Emmy. "Oh, mother!" After a long time she ventured a question. "Who was the other man, mother?"

"The other man? Oh! that was my father; my mother's guardian, protector, everything, but not her husband. She was a slave, you know, in New Orleans, and he helped her to get away. He took her to Hayti first, and then, afterward, sent her over to France, where I was born. He never ceased in his kindness. After my mother's death I didn't see him for ten years, not till after I was married. That was the time Emile—you were named for your father, you know—saw him kiss me. Mr. Pechegru, my father, was genuinely attached to my mother, I think, and had come after all these years to make some reparation. It was through him I first began translating for the publishers. You know yourself how my work has grown."

She was quite ordinary and matter of fact again. Suddenly her manner changed.

"I lost him when I was 22. Emmy—think of it—and my life has been nothing ever since. That's why I want you to think—to consider—" She was weeping passionately now.

Her mother in tears! To Emmy it was as though the world lay in ruins about her feet.


# IX

As it happened Mrs. Carrel's story only plunged her daughter into deeper gloom.

"It couldn't have happened at all if we hadn't been colored," she told herself moodily. "If grandmother hadn't been colored she wouldn't have been a slave, and if she hadn't been a slave—That's what it is, color—color—it's wrecked mother's life and now it's wrecking mine."

She couldn't get away from the thought of it. Archie's words, said so long ago, came back to her: "Just wait till color keeps you from the thing you want the most," he had told her.

"It must be wonderful to be white," she said to herself, staring absently at the Stevenson motto on the wall of her little room. She went up close and surveyed it unseeingly. "If only I weren't colored," she thought. She checked herself angrily, enveloped by a sudden sense of shame. "It doesn't seem as though I could be the same girl."

A thin ray of cold December sunlight picked out from the motto a little gilded phrase: "To renounce when that shall be necessary and not be embittered." She read it over and over and smiled whimsically.

"I've renounced—there's no question about that," she thought, "but no one could expect me not to be bitter."

If she could just get up strength enough, she reflected, as the days passed by, she would try to be cheerful in her mother's presence. But it was so easy to be melancholy.

About a week before Christmas her mother went to New York. She would see her publishers and do some shopping and would be back Christmas Eve. Emmy was really glad to see her go.

"I'll spend that time in getting myself together," she told herself, "and when mother comes back I'll be all right." Nevertheless, for the first few days she was, if anything, more listless than ever. But Christmas Eve and the prospect of her mother's return gave her a sudden brace.

"Without bitterness," she kept saying to herself, "to renounce without bitterness." Well, she would—she would. When her mother came back she should be astonished. She would even wear the red dress. But the sight of it made her weak; she couldn't put it on. But she did dress herself very carefully in white, remembering how gay she had been last Christmas Eve. She had put mistletoe in her hair and Archie had taken it out.

"I don't have to have mistletoe," he had whispered to her proudly.

In the late afternoon she ran out to Holborn's. As she came back 'round the corner she saw the stage drive away. Her mother, of course, had come. She ran into the sitting room wondering why the door was closed.

"I will be all right," she said to herself, her hand on the knob, and stepped into the room——to walk straight into Archie's arms.

She clung to him as though she could never let him go.

"Oh, Archie, you've come back, you really wanted me."

He strained her closer. "I've never stopped wanting you," he told her, his lips on her hair.

Presently, when they were sitting by the fire, she in the armchair and he at her feet, he began to explain. She would not listen at first, it was all her fault, she said.

"No, indeed," he protested generously, "it was mine. I was so crude; it's a wonder you can care at all about anyone as stupid as I am. And I think I was too ambitious——though in a way it was all for you, Emmy; you must always believe that. But I'm at the bottom rung now, sweetheart; you see, I told Mr. Fields everything and——he put me out."

"Oh, Archie," she praised him, "that was really noble, since you weren't obliged to tell him."

"Well, but in one sense I was obliged to——to keep my self-respect, you know. So there wasn't anything very noble about it after all." He couldn't tell her what had really happened. "I'm genuinely poor now, dearest, but your mother sent for me to come over to New York. She knows some pretty all-right people there—she's a wonderful woman, Emmy—and I'm to go out to the Philippines. Could you—do you think you could come out there, Emmy?"

She could, she assured him, go anywhere. "Only don't let it be too long, Archie—I—"

He was ecstatic. "Emmy—you—you don't mean you would be willing to start out there with me, do you? Why, that's only three months off. When—" He stopped, peering out the window. "Who is that coming up the path?"

"It's Willie Holborn," said Emmy. "I suppose Mary sent him around with my present. Wait, I'll let him in."

But it wasn't Willie Holborn, unless he had been suddenly converted into a small and very grubby special-delivery boy.

"Mr. A. Ferrers," he said laconically, thrusting a book out at her. "Sign here."

She took the letter back into the pleasant room, and A. Ferrers, scanning the postmark, tore it open. "It's from my landlady; she's the only person in Philadelphia who knows where I am. Wonder what's up?" he said incuriously. "I know I didn't forget to pay her my bill. Hello, what's this?" For within was a yellow envelope—a telegram.

Together they tore it open.

> "Don't be a blooming idiot," it read; "the governor says come back and receive apologies and accept job. Merry Christmas.
>
>                                   "Peter Fields."

"Oh," said Emmy, "isn't it lovely! Why does he say 'receive apologies,' Archie?"

"Oh, I don't know," he quibbled, reflecting that if Peter hadn't said just that his return would have been as impossible as ever. "It's just his queer way of talking. He's the funniest chap! Looks as though I wouldn't have to go to the Philippines after all. But that doesn't alter the main question. How soon do you think you can marry me, Emmy?"

His voice was light, but his eyes—

"Well," said Emmy bravely, "what do you think of Christmas?"

# MY HOUSE AND A GLIMPSE
# OF MY LIFE THEREIN

*Jessie Fauset*

Far away on the top of a gently sloping hill stands my house.
On one side the hill slopes down into a valley, the site of a
large country town; on the other it descends into a forest,
thick with lofty trees and green, growing things. Here in
stately solitude amid such surroundings towers my dwelling;
its dull-red brick is barely visible through the thick ivy, but
the gleaming tops of its irregular roof and sloping gables
catch the day's sunlight and crown it with a crown of gold.

An irregular, rambling building is this house of mine,
built on no particular plan, following no order save that of
desire and fancy. Peculiarly jutting rooms appear, and un-
suspected towers and bay-windows,—the house seems almost
to have built itself and to have followed its own will in so
doing. If there be any one distinct feature at all, it is that
halls long and very broad traverse the various parts of the
house, separating a special set of rooms here, making another
division there. Splendid halls are these, with fire places and
cosy arm-chairs, and delightful, dark corners, and mysterious
closets, and broad, shallow stairs. Just the place in winter for
a host of young people to gather before the fire-place, and
with popcorn and chestnuts, stories and apples, laugh away
the speeding hours, while the wind howls without.

The hall on the ground floor has smaller corridors that
branch off and lead at their extremity into the garden. Surely,
no parterre of the East, perfumed with all the odors of Araby,

*Crisis* 8 (July 1914): 143–45.

and peopled with houris, was ever so fair as my garden! Surely, nowhere does the snow lie so pure and smooth and deep, nowhere are the evergreen trees so very tall and stately as in my garden in winter! Most glorious is it in late spring and early June. Out on the green, green sward I sit under the blossoming trees; in sheer delightful idleness I spend my hours, listening to the blending of wind-song with the "sweet jargoning" of little birds. If a shower threatens I flee across my garden's vast expanse, past the gorgeous rosebushes and purple lilacs, and safe within my little summer-house, watch the "straight-falling rain," and think of other days, and sighing wish that Kathleen and I had not parted in anger that far-off morning.

When the shower ceases, I hasten down the broad path, under the shelter of lofty trees, until I reach one of my house's many doors. Once within, but still in idle mood, I perch myself on a window-seat and look toward the town. Tall spires and godly church steeples rise before me; high above all climbs the town clock; farther over in the west, smoke is curling from the foundries. How busy is the life beyond my house! Through the length of the long hall to the window at the opposite side I go, and watch the friendly nodding of tall trees and the tender intercourse of all this beautiful green life. Suddenly the place becomes transformed—this is an enchanted forest, the Forest Morgraunt—in and out among the trees pass valiant knights and distressed ladies. Prosper le Gai rides to the rescue of Isoult la Desirous. Surely, the forest life beyond my house is full of purpose and animation, too.

From the window I roam past the sweet, familiar chambers, to the attic staircase, with its half-hidden angles and crazy old baluster. Up to the top of the house I go, to a dark little store-room under the eaves. I open the trap-door in the middle of the ceiling, haul down a small ladder, mount its deliciously wobbly length, and behold, I am in my chosen domain—a queen come into her very own! If I choose I can convert it into a dread and inaccessible fortress, by drawing up my ladder and showering nut-shells and acorns down on the heads of would-be intruders. Safe from all possible invasion, I browse through the store of old, old magazines and quaint books and journals, or wander half-timidly through my infinite unexplored land of mystery, picking my way past heaps of delightful rubbish and strong, secret chests, fancying goblins in the shadowy corners, or watching from the little windows the sunbeams play on the garden, and the grey-blue mist hanging far-off over the hollow valley.

From such sights and fancies I descend to my library, there to supplement my flitting ideas with the fixed conception of others. Although I love every brick and little bit of mortar in my dwelling, my library is of all portions the very dearest to me. In this part of the house more than any place else, have those irregular rooms been added, to receive my ever-increasing store of books. In the large room,—the library proper,—is a broad, old-fashioned fire-place, and on the rug in front I lie and read, and read again, all the dear simple tales of earlier days, "Mother Goose," "Alice in Wonderland," "The Arabian Nights"; here, too, I revel in modern stories of impossible adventure. But when a storm rises at night, say, and the rain beats and dashes, and all without is raging, I draw a huge, red arm-chair before the fire and curl into its hospitable depths.

> "And there I sit
>   Reading old things,
> Of knights and lorn damsels,
>   While the wind sings—
>   Oh, drearily sings!"

Off in one of the little side-rooms stands my desk, covered with books that have caught my special fancy and awakened my thoughts. This is my *living*-room, where I spend my moods of bitterness and misunderstanding, and questioning, and joy, too, I think. Often in the midst of a heap of books, the Rubaiyat and a Bible, Walter Pater's Essays, and "Robert Elsmere" and "Aurora Leigh," and books of belief, of insinuation, of open unbelief, I bow my head on my desk in a passion of doubt and ignorance and longing, and ponder, ponder. Here on this desk is a book in which I jot down all the little, beautiful word-wonders, whose meanings are so often unknown to me, but whose very mystery I love. I write, "In Vishnu Land what Avatar?" and "After the red pottage comes the exceedingly bitter cry," and all the other sweet, incomprehensible fragments that haunt my memory so.

High up on many of the shelves in the many rooms are books as yet unread by me, Schopenhauer and Gorky, Petrarch and Sappho, Goethe and Kant and Schelling; much of Ibsen, Plato and Ennius and Firdausi, and Lafcadis Hearn,— a few of these in the original. With such reading in store for me, is not my future rich?

Can such a house as this one of mine be without immediate and vivid impression on its possessor? First and most of all it imbues me with a strong sense of home; banishment from my house would surely be life's most bitter sorrow. It is so eminently and fixedly mine, my very own, that the mere possession of it,—a house not yours or another's, but mine, to live in as I will,—is very sweet to me. It is absolutely the *chey soi* of my soul's desire. With this sense of ownership, a sense which is deeper than I can express, a sense which is almost a longing for some unknown, unexplainable, entire possession—passionate, spiritual absorption of my dwelling—

comes a feeling that is almost terror. Is it right to feel thus, to have this vivid, permeating and yet wholly intellectual enjoyment of the material loveliness and attractiveness of my house? May this not be perhaps a sensuality of the mind, whose influence may be more insidious, more pernicious, more powerful to unfit me for the real duties of life than are other lower and yet more open forms of enjoyment? Oh, I pray not! My house is inexpressibly dear to me, but the light of the ideal beyond, "the light that never was on sea or land," is dearer still.

This, then, is my house, and this, in measure, is my life in my house. Here, amid my favorite books, and pictures, and fancies, and longings, and sweet mysteries, shall old age come upon me, in fashion most inglorious, but in equal degree most peaceful and happy. *Perhaps*—that is! For after all my house is constructed of dream-fabric, and the place of its building is—*Spain!*

# HIS MOTTO

*Lottie Burrell Dixon*

"But I can't leave my business affairs and go off on a fishing trip now."

The friend and specialist who had tricked John Durmont into a confession of physical bankruptcy, and made him submit to an examination in spite of himself, now sat back with an "I wash my hands of you" gesture.

"Very well, you can either go to Maine, now, at once, or you'll go to—well, as I'm only your medical, and not your spiritual advisor, my prognostications as to your ultimate destination would probably have very little weight with you."

"Oh well, if you are so sure, I suppose I can cut loose now, if it comes to a choice like that."

The doctor smiled his satisfaction. "So you prefer to bear the ills of New York than to fly to others you know not of, eh?"

"Oh, have a little mercy on Shakespeare, at least. I'll go."

And thus it was that a week later found Durmont as deep in the Maine woods as he could get and still be within reach of a telegraph wire. And much to his surprise he found he liked it.

As he lay stretched at full length on the soft turf, the breath of the pines filled his lungs, the lure of the lake made him eager to get to his fishing tackle, and he admitted to himself that a man needed just such a holiday as this in order to keep his mental and physical balance.

*Crisis* 8 (Aug. 1914): 188–90.

Returning to the gaily painted frame building, called by courtesy the "Hotel," which nestled among the pines, he met the youthful operator from the near-by station looking for him with a message from his broker. A complicated situation had arisen in Amalgamated Copper, and an immediate answer was needed. Durmont had heavy investments in copper, though his business was the manufacture of electrical instruments.

He walked back to the office with the operator while pondering the answer, then having written it, handed it to the operator saying, "Tell them to rush answer."

The tall, lank youth, whose every movement was a protest against being hurried, dragged himself over to the telegraph key.

"'S open."

"What's open?"

"Wire."

"Well, is that the only wire you have?"

"Yep."

"What in the dickens am I going to do about this message?"

"Dunno, maybe it'll close bime-by." And the young lightning slinger pulled towards him a lurid tale of the Wild West, and proceeded to enjoy himself.

"And meanwhile, what do you suppose is going to happen to me?" thundered Durmont. "Haven't you ambition enough to look around your wire and see if you can find the trouble?"

"Lineman's paid to look up trouble, I ain't," was the surly answer.

Durmont was furious, but what he was about to say was cut off by a quiet voice at his elbow.

"I noticed linemen repairing wires upon the main road, that's where this wire is open. If you have any message you are in a hurry to send, perhaps I can help you out."

Durmont turned to see a colored boy of fifteen whose entrance he had not noticed.

"What can you do about it," he asked contemptuously, "take it into town in an ox team?"

"I can send it by wireless, if that is sufficiently quick."

Durmont turned to the operator at the table.

"Is there a wireless near here?"

"He owns one, you'll have to do business with him on that," said the youth with a grin at Durmont's unconcealed prejudice.

It would be hard to estimate the exact amount of respect, mingled with surprise, with which the city man now looked at the boy whose information he had evidently doubted till confirmed by the white boy.

"Suppose you've got some kind of tom-fool contraption that will take half a day to get a message into the next village. Here I stand to lose several thousands because this blame company runs only one wire down to this camp. Where is this apparatus of yours? Might as well look at it while I'm waiting for this one-wire office to get into commission again."

"It's right up on top of the hill," answered the colored boy. "Here, George, I brought down this wireless book if you want to look it over, it's better worth reading than that stuff you have there," and tossing a book on the table he went out followed by Durmont.

A couple of minutes' walk brought them in sight of the sixty-foot aerial erected on the top of a small shack.

"Not much to look at, but I made it all myself."

"How did you happen to—construct this?" And Durmont really tried to keep the emphasis off the "you."

"Well, I'm interested in all kinds of electrical experiments, and have kept up reading and studying ever since I left school, then when I came out here on my uncle's farm, he let me rig up this wireless, and I can talk to a chum of mine down in the city. And when I saw the wire at the station was gone up, I thought I might possibly get your message to New York through him."

They had entered the one room shack which contained a long table holding a wireless outfit, a couple of chairs and a shelf of books. On the walls were tacked pictures of aviators and drawings of aeroplanes. A three-foot model of a biplane hung in one corner.

"Now if he is only in," said the boy, going over to the table and giving the call.

"He's there," he said eagerly, holding out his hand for the message.

Durmont handed it to him. His face still held the look of doubt and unbelief as he looked at the crude, home-made instruments.

"Suppose I might as well have hired a horse and taken it into town." But the sputtering wire drowned his voice.

"And get on your wheel and go like blazes. Tell 'em to rush answer. This guy here thinks a colored boy is only an animated shoe-blacking outfit; it's up to us to remedy that defect in his education, see!" Thus sang the wires as Durmont paced the floor.

"I said," began the nervous man as the wires became quiet. "I—" again the wire sputtered, and he couldn't hear himself talk. When it was quiet, he tried again, but as soon as he began to grumble, the wire began to sputter. He glanced suspiciously at the boy, but the latter was earnestly watching his instruments.

"Say," shouted Durmont, "does that thing have to keep up that confounded racket all the time?"

"I had to give him some instructions, you know, and also keep in adjustment."

"Well, I'll get out of adjustment myself, if that keeps up."

Durmont resigned himself to silence, and strangely enough, so did the wire. Walking around the room he noticed over the shelf of books a large white card on which was printed in gilt letters:

> "I WILL STUDY AND MAKE READY,
> AND MAY BE MY CHANCE WILL
> COME."    ABRAHAM LINCOLN.

Durmont read this, and then looked at the boy as if seeing him for the first time. Again he looked at the words, and far beyond them he saw his own struggling boyhood, climbing daily Life's slippery path, trying to find some hold by which to pull himself up. And as he watched the brown skinned boy bending over the instruments, instinct told him here was one who would find it still harder to fight his way up, because of caste.

"Ah!"

The exclamation startled him. The boy with fones adjusted was busily writing.

"Well, has that partner of yours got that message down at his end yet?"

"Yes, sir, and here is your answer from New York."

"Why, it's only been half an hour since I wrote it," said Durmont.

"Yes, that horse wouldn't have got into town yet," grinned the boy.

Durmont snatched the paper, read it, threw his cap in the air, exclaiming: "The day is saved. Boy, you're a winner. How much?" putting his hand in his pocket suggestively.

"How much you owe to my help, I don't know," answered the lad sagely. "I offered to help because you needed it, and I was glad of the chance to prove what I believed I could do. I'm satisfied because I succeeded."

Durmont sat down heavily on the other chair; his nerves

couldn't stand much more in one afternoon. To find himself threatened with a large financial loss; to have this averted by the help of the scientific knowledge of a colored boy, and that boy rating the fact of his success higher than any pecuniary compensation—he had to pull himself together a bit.

His eyes fell on the motto on the wall. He read it thoughtfully, considered how hard the boy had worked because of that, his hopes of the future based on that; saw the *human* element in him as it had not appealed to him before, and then turning something over in his mind, muttered to himself, "It's nobody's business if I do."

He got up, and walking over to the boy, said: "What's your name?"

"Robert Hilton."

"Well, Robert, that motto you've got up there is a pretty good one to tie to. You certainly have studied; you have made yourself ready as far as your resources will permit, and I'll be hanged if I don't stand for the 'chance.' In the manufacturing of electrical instruments you could have great opportunity for inventive talent, and in my concern you shall have your chance, and go as far as your efficiency will carry you. What do you say, would you care for it?"

"I'd care for it more than for any other thing on earth, and am very grateful for the chance."

"The chance wouldn't be standing here now if you had not had the inclination and the determination to live up to those words on the wall."

# HOPE DEFERRED

*Mrs. Paul Lawrence Dunbar*
*[Alice Dunbar-Nelson]*

The direct rays of the August sun smote on the pavements of
the city and made the soda-water signs in front of the drug
stores alluringly suggestive of relief. Women in scant garments, displaying a maximum of form and a minimum of
taste, crept along the pavements, their mussy light frocks
suggesting a futile disposition on the part of the wearers to
keep cool. Traditional looking fat men mopped their faces,
and dived frantically into screened doors to emerge redder
and more perspiring. The presence of small boys, scantily
clad and of dusky hue and languid steps marked the city, if
not distinctively southern, at least one on the borderland
between the North and the South.

   Edwards joined the perspiring mob on the hot streets and
mopped his face with the rest. His shoes were dusty, his
collar wilted. As he caught a glimpse of himself in a mirror
of a shop window, he smiled grimly. "Hardly a man to
present himself before one of the Lords of Creation to ask a
favor," he muttered to himself.

   Edwards was young; so young that he had not outgrown
his ideals. Rather than allow that to happen, he had chosen
one to share them with him, and the man who can find a
woman willing to face poverty for her husband's ideals has a
treasure far above rubies, and more precious than one with
a thorough understanding of domestic science. But ideals do
not always supply the immediate wants of the body, and it

*Crisis* 8 (Sept. 1914): 238–42.

was the need of the wholly material that drove Edwards wilted, warm and discouraged into the August sunshine.

The man in the office to which the elevator boy directed him looked up impatiently from his desk. The windows of the room were open on a court-yard where green tree tops waved in a humid breeze; an electric fan whirred, and sent forth flashes of coolness; cool looking leather chairs invited the dusty traveler to sink into their depths.

Edwards was not invited to rest, however. Cold gray eyes in an impassive pallid face fixed him with a sneering stare, and a thin icy voice cut in on his half spoken words with a curt dismissal in its tone.

"Sorry, Mr.—Er—, but I shan't be able to grant your request."

His "Good Morning" in response to Edwards' reply as he turned out of the room was of the curtest, and left the impression of decided relief at an unpleasant duty discharged.

"Now where?" He had exhausted every avenue, and this last closed the door of hope with a finality that left no doubt in his mind. He dragged himself down the little side street, which led home, instinctively, as a child draws near to its mother in its trouble.

Margaret met him at the door, and their faces lighted up with the glow that always irradiated them in each other's presence. She drew him into the green shade of the little room, and her eyes asked, though her lips did not frame the question.

"No hope," he made reply to her unspoken words.

She sat down suddenly as one grown weak.

"If I could only just stick it out, little girl," he said, "but we need food, clothes, and only money buys them, you know."

"Perhaps it would have been better if we hadn't married—"

she suggested timidly. That thought had been uppermost in her mind for some days lately.

"Because you are tired of poverty?" he queried, the smile on his lips belying his words.

She rose and put her arms about his neck. "You know better than that; but because if you did not have me, you could live on less, and thus have a better chance to hold out until they see your worth."

"I'm afraid they never will." He tried to keep his tones even, but in spite of himself a tremor shook his words. "The man I saw to-day is my last hope; he is the chief clerk, and what he says controls the opinions of others. If I could have gotten past his decision, I might have influenced the senior member of the firm, but he is a man who leaves details to his subordinates, and Mr. Hanan was suspicious of me from the first. He isn't sure," he continued with a little laugh, which he tried to make sound spontaneous, "whether I am a stupendous fraud, or an escaped lunatic."

"We can wait; your chance will come," she soothed him with a rare smile.

"But in the meanwhile—" he finished for her and paused himself.

A sheaf of unpaid bills in the afternoon mail, with the curt and wholly unnecessary "Please Remit" in boldly impertinent characters across the bottom of every one drove Edwards out into the wilting sun. He knew the main street from end to end; he could tell how many trolley poles were on its corners; he felt that he almost knew the stones in the buildings, and that the pavements were worn with the constant passing of his feet, so often in the past four months had he walked, at first buoyantly, then hopefully, at last wearily up and down its length.

The usual idle crowd jostled around the baseball bulletins. Edwards joined them mechanically. "I can be a side-walk fan, even if I am impecunious." He smiled to himself as he said the words, and then listened idly to a voice at his side, "We are getting metropolitan, see that!"

The "That" was an item above the baseball score. Edwards looked and the letters burned themselves like white fire into his consciousness.

> STRIKE SPREADS TO OUR CITY.
> WAITERS AT ADAMS' WALK OUT
> AFTER BREAKFAST THIS MORNING.

"Good!" he said aloud. The man at his side smiled appreciatively at him; the home team had scored another run, but unheeding that Edwards walked down the street with a lighter step than he had known for days.

The proprietor of Adams' restaurant belied both his name and his vocation. He should have been rubicund, corpulent, American; instead he was wiry, lank, foreign in appearance. His teeth projected over a full lower lip, his eyes set far back in his head and were concealed by wrinkles that seemed to have been acquired by years of squinting into men's motives.

"Of course I want waiters," he replied to Edward's question, "any fool knows that." He paused, drew in his lower lip within the safe confines of his long teeth, squinted his eye intently on Edwards. "But do I want colored waiters? Now, do I?"

"It seems to me there's no choice for you in the matter," said Edwards good-humoredly.

The reply seemed to amuse the restaurant keeper immensely; he slapped the younger man on the back with a familiarity that made him wince both physically and spiritually.

"I guess I'll take you for head waiter." He was inclined to be jocular, even in the face of the disaster which the morning's strike had brought him. "Peel off and go to work. Say, stop!" as Edwards looked around to take his bearings, "What's your name?"

"Louis Edwards."

"Uh huh, had any experience?"

"Yes, some years ago, when I was in school."

"Uh huh, then waiting ain't your general work."

"No."

"Uh huh, what do you do for a living?"

"I'm a civil engineer."

One eye-brow of the saturnine Adams shot up, and he withdrew his lower lip entirely under his teeth.

"Well, say man, if you're an engineer, what you want to be strike-breaking here in a waiter's coat for, eh?"

Edwards' face darkened, and he shrugged his shoulders. "They don't need me, I guess," he replied briefly. It was an effort, and the restaurant keeper saw it, but his wonder overcame his sympathy.

"Don't need you with all that going on at the Monarch works? Why, man, I'd a thought every engineer this side o' hell would be needed out there."

"So did I; that's why I came here, but—"

"Say, kid, I'm sorry for you, I surely am; you go on to work."

"And so," narrated Edwards to Margaret, after midnight, when he had gotten in from his first day's work, "I became at once head waiter, first assistant, all of the other waiters, chief boss, steward, and high-muck-a-muck, with all the emoluments and perquisites thereof."

Margaret was silent; with her ready sympathy she knew that no words of hers were needed then, they would only add to the burdens he had to bear. Nothing could be more bitter than this apparent blasting of his lifelong hopes, this seeming lowering of his standard. She said nothing, but the pressure of her slim brown hand in his meant more than words to them both.

"It's hard to keep the vision true," he groaned.

If it was hard that night, it grew doubly so within the next few weeks. Not lightly were the deposed waiters to take their own self-dismissal and supplanting. Daily they menaced the restaurant with their surly attentions, ugly and ominous. Adams shot out his lower lip from the confines of his long teeth and swore in a various language that he'd run his own place if he had to get every nigger in Africa to help him. The three or four men whom he was able to induce to stay with him in the face of missiles of every nature, threatened every day to give up the battle. Edwards was the force that held them together. He used every argument from the purely material one of holding on to the job now that they had it, through the negative one of loyalty to the man in his hour of need, to the altruistic one of keeping the place open for colored men for all time. There were none of them of such value as his own personality, and the fact that he stuck through all the turmoil. He wiped the mud from his face, picked up the putrid vegetables that often strewed the floor, barricaded the doors at night, replaced orders that were destroyed by well-aimed stones, and stood by Adams' side when the fight threatened to grow serious.

Adams was appreciative. "Say, kid, I don't know what I'd a done without you, now that's honest. Take it from me, when you need a friend anywhere on earth, and you can send me a wireless, I'm right there with the goods in answer to your S. O. S."

This was on the afternoon when the patrol, lined up in

front of the restaurant, gathered in a few of the most disturbing ones, none of whom, by the way, had ever been employed in the place. "Sympathy" had pervaded the town.

The humid August days melted into the sultry ones of September. The self-dismissed waiters had quieted down, and save for an occasional missile, annoyed Adams and his corps of dark-skinned helpers no longer. Edwards had resigned himself to his temporary discomforts. He felt, with the optimism of the idealist, that it was only for a little while; the fact that he had sought work at his profession for nearly a year had not yet discouraged him. He would explain carefully to Margaret when the day's work was over, that it was only for a little while; he would earn enough at this to enable them to get away, and then in some other place he would be able to stand up with the proud consciousness that all his training had not been in vain.

He was revolving all these plans in his mind one Saturday night. It was at the hour when business was dull, and he leaned against the window and sought entertainment from the crowd on the street. Saturday night, with all the blare and glare and garishness dear to the heart of the middle-class provincial of the smaller cities, was holding court on the city streets. The hot September sun had left humidity and closeness in its wake, and the evening mists had scarce had time to cast coolness over the town. Shop windows glared wares through colored lights, and phonographs shrilled popular tunes from open store doors to attract unwary passersby. Half-grown boys and girls, happy in the license of Saturday night on the crowded streets, jostled one another and pushed in long lines, shouted familiar epithets at other pedestrians with all the abandon of the ill-breeding common to the class. One crowd, in particular, attracted Edwards' attention. The girls were brave in semi-decolleté waists, scant short skirts and exaggerated heads, built up in fanciful designs; the boys with flamboyant red neckties, striking hat-bands, and white trousers. They made a snake line, boys and girls, hands on each others' shoulders, and rushed shouting through the press of shoppers, scattering the inattentive right and left. Edwards' lip curled, "Now, if those were colored boys and girls—"

His reflections were never finished, for a patron moved towards his table, and the critic of human life became once more the deferential waiter.

He did not move a muscle of his face as he placed the glass of water on the table, handed the menu card, and stood at attention waiting for the order, although he had recognized at first glance the half-sneering face of his old hope—Hanan, of the great concern which had no need of him. To Hanan, the man who brought his order was but one of the horde of menials who satisfied his daily wants and soothed his vanity when the cares of the day had ceased pressing on his shoulders. He had not even looked at the man's face, and for this Edwards was grateful.

A new note had crept into the noise on the streets; there was in it now, not so much mirth and ribaldry as menace and anger. Edwards looked outside in slight alarm; he had grown used to that note in the clamor of the streets, particularly on Saturday nights; it meant that the whole restaurant must be prepared to quell a disturbance. The snake line had changed; there were only flamboyant hat-bands in it now, the decolleté shirt waists and scant skirts had taken refuge on another corner. Something in the shouting attracted Hanan's attention, and he looked up wonderingly.

"What are they saying?" he inquired. Edwards did not answer; he was so familiar with the old cry that he thought it unnecessary.

"Yah! Yah! Old Adams hires niggers! Hires niggers!"

"Why, that is so," Hanan looked up at Edwards' dark face for the first time. "This is quite an innovation for Adams' place. How did it happen?"

"We are strike-breakers," replied the waiter quietly, then he grew hot, for a gleam of recognition came into Hanan's eyes.

"Oh, yes, I see. Aren't you the young man who asked me for employment as an engineer at the Monarch works?"

Edwards bowed, he could not answer; hurt pride surged up within him and made his eyes hot and his hands clammy.

"Well, er—I'm glad you've found a place to work; very sensible of you, I'm sure. I should think, too, that it is work for which you would be more fitted than engineering."

Edwards started to reply, but the hot words were checked on his lips. The shouting had reached a shrillness which boded immediate results, and with the precision of a missile from a warship's gun, a stone hurtled through the glass of the long window. It struck Edwards' hand, glanced through the dishes on the tray which he was in the act of setting on the table, and tipped half its contents over Hanan's knee. He sprang to his feet angrily, striving to brush the dèbris of his dinner from his immaculate clothing, and turned angrily upon Edwards.

"That is criminally careless of you!" he flared, his eyes blazing in his pallid face. "You could have prevented that; you're not even a good waiter, much less an engineer."

And then something snapped in the darker man's head. The long strain of the fruitless summer; the struggle of keeping together the men who worked under him in the restaurant; the heat, and the task of enduring what was to him the humiliation of serving, and this last injustice, all culminated in a blinding flash in his brain. Reason, intelligence, all was obscured, save a man hatred, and a desire to wreak his wrongs on the man, who, for the time being, represented the author of them. He sprang at the white man's throat and bore him to the floor. They wrestled and fought together, struggling, biting, snarling, like brutes in the dèbris of food and the clutter of overturned chairs and tables.

The telephone rang insistently. Adams wiped his hands on a towel, and carefully moved a paint brush out of the way, as he picked up the receiver.

"Hello!" he called. "Yes, this is Adams, the restaurant keeper. Who? Uh huh. Wants to know if I'll go his bail? Say, that nigger's got softening of the brain. Course not, let him serve his time, making all that row in my place; never had no row here before. No, I don't never want to see him again."

He hung up the receiver with a bang, and went back to his painting. He had almost finished his sign, and he smiled as he ended it with a flourish:

> WAITERS WANTED. NONE BUT
> WHITE MEN NEED APPLY

Out in the county work-house, Edwards sat on his cot, his head buried in his hands. He wondered what Margaret was doing all this long hot Sunday, if the tears were blinding her sight as they did his; then he started to his feet, as the warden called his name. Margaret stood before him, her arms outstretched, her mouth quivering with tenderness and sympathy, her whole form yearning towards him with a passion of maternal love.

"Margaret! You here, in this place?"

"Aren't you here?" she smiled bravely, and drew his head towards the refuge of her bosom. "Did you think I wouldn't come to see you?"

"To think I should have brought you to this," he moaned.

She stilled his reproaches and heard the story from his lips. Then she murmured with bloodless mouth, "How long will it be?"

"A long time, dearest—and you?"

"I can go home, and work," she answered briefly, "and wait for you, be it ten months or ten years—and then—?"

"And then—" they stared into each other's eyes like frightened children. Suddenly his form straightened up, and the vision of his ideal irradiated his face with hope and happiness.

"And then, Beloved," he cried, "then we will start all over again. Somewhere, I am needed; somewhere in this world there are wanted dark-skinned men like me to dig and blast and build bridges and make straight the roads of the world, and I am going to find that place—with you."

She smiled back trustfully at him. "Only keep true to your ideal, dearest," she whispered, "and you will find the place. Your window faces the south, Louis. Look up and out of it all the while you are here, for it is there, in our own southland, that you will find the realization of your dream."

# THE FAIRY GOODWILLA

*Minnibelle Jones,*
WRITTEN WHEN SHE WAS TEN YEARS OF AGE

In the good old days when the kind spirits knew that people trusted them, they allowed themselves to be seen, but now there are just a few human beings left who ever remember or believe that a fairy ever existed, or rather does exist. For, dear children, no matter how much the older folks tell you that there are no fairies, do not believe them. I am going to tell you now of a dear, good fairy, Goodwilla, who has been under the power of a wicked enchanter called Grafter, for many years.

Goodwilla was once a very happy and contented little fairy. She was a very beautiful fairy; she had a soft brown face and deep brown eyes and slim brown hands and the dearest brown hair that wouldn't stay "put," that you ever saw. She lived in a beautiful wood consisting of fir trees. Her house was made of the finest and whitest drifted snow and was furnished with kind thoughts of children, good words of older people and everything which is beautiful and pleasant. She was always dressed in a white robe with a crown of holly leaves on her head. In her hand she carried a long magic icicle, and whatever she touched with this became very lovely to look upon. Snowdrops always sprang up wherever she stepped, and her dress sparkled with many small stars.

The children loved Goodwilla, and she always welcomed them to her beautiful home where she told them of Knights and Ladies, Kings and Queens, Witches and Ogres and

*Crisis* 8 (Oct. 1914): 294–96.

498

Enchanters. She never told them anything to frighten them and the children were always glad to listen. You must not think that Goodwilla always remained at home and told the children stories, for she was a very busy little fairy. She visited sick rooms where little boys or girls were suffering and laid her cool brown hands on their heads, whispering beautiful words to them. She touched the different articles in the room with her magic icicle and caused them to become lovely. Wherever she stepped her beautiful snowdrops were scattered. At other times she went to homes where the father and mother were unhappy and cross. She was invisible to them, but she touched them without their knowing it and they instantly became kind and cheerful. Other days she spent at home separating the good deeds which she had piled before her, from the bad deeds. So you see with all of these things to do Goodwilla was very busy.

Now, there was an old enchanter who lived in a neighboring wood. He was very wealthy, but people feared him, although they visited him a great deal. His house was set in the midst of many trees, all of which bore golden and silver apples. The house was made of precious metal and the inside was seemingly handsome. But looking closely one could see that the beautiful chairs were very tender and if not handled rightly they would easily break. Music was always being played softly by unseen musicians, but one who truly loved music could hear discords which spoiled the beauty of all. In fact, everything in his palace, although seemingly beautiful, if examined closely, was very wrong. Grafter, which was the enchanter's name, spent all of his time in instructing men how to be prosperous and receive all that they could for nothing. He did not pay much attention to the children, although once in a while a few listened to his evil words. He was always very busy, but somehow he did not at all times

get the results he expected. He scratched his head and thought
and thought. Finally, one day he cried, "Ah, I have it, there
is an insignificant little fairy called Goodwilla who is meddling
in my affairs, I'll wager. Let me see how best I can overcome
her." The old fellow who could change his appearance at
will, now became a handsome young enchanter and looked so
fine that it would be almost impossible for the fairy herself
to resist him. He made his way to her abode and asked for
admittance to her house. She gladly bade him enter, for,
although she knew him, she thought she could persuade him
to forego his evil ways and win men by fair means.

Now something strange happened. Every chair that Grafter
attempted to take became invisible when he started to seat
himself and he found nothing but empty air. After this had
happened for a long while, he became so angry that he forgot
the part he was trying to play and acted very badly indeed.
He stormed at poor Goodwilla as if she had been the cause
of good deeds and kind words to vanish at his touch. "You,
Madam," said he, "are the cause of this, and I know now
why I cannot be successful in my work. You fill the children's
heads full of nonsense and when I have almost persuaded the
fathers to do something which will benefit them as well as
their children, these brats come with their prattle and undo
all that I have done. Now I have stood it long enough. I
shall give you three trials, and if you do not conquer, you
shall be under my power for seven hundred years."

The Good Fairy listened and felt very grieved, but she
knew that Grafter was stronger than she, as minds of men
turned more to his commanding way than they did to hers.
Nevertheless she determined to do her best and said, "Very
well, Grafter, I shall do as you wish and if I do not succeed
I am in your hands, but later everything will be all right and
I shall rule over you." Grafter, who had not expected this,

now became alarmed and thought by soft words he could perhaps coax her to do his way, but Goodwilla was strong and would not listen to his cajoling and flattering. "Then, Madam," he said, "I shall force you to perform these tasks or be my slave:

"First, you must cause all of the people in the world to help and give to others for the sake of giving and not for what they shall receive in return.

"Secondly, you must cause all of the rich to help the poor instead of taking from them to swell their already fat pocketbooks, and thirdly, you must cause men and women to really love for love's sake and not because of worldly reasons."

The poor little fairy sighed deeply, for she knew that she could not perform these tasks in the three days that Grafter had allowed her. She talked to the children, but they were being dazzled by Grafter since he had become so handsome. Goodwilla continued to work though, and had just commenced to open men's eyes to Grafter as he really was, when the three days expired.

She was immediately whisked off by the wicked old fellow, who chuckled with glee. He did not know that there were many people in whose hearts a seed had been planted (which would grow) by this good little fairy and that she herself had a plan for helping all when she was released. Grafter, after having locked her up, departed on his way rejoicing. He has been prosperous for a long, long time, but the seven hundred years are almost up now, and soon Goodwilla will come forth stronger and more beautiful than ever with the children as her soldiers.

# BREAKING THE COLOR-LINE

*Annie McCary*

"Coach Hardy has selected for the two-mile relay team to go against Gale, Carter, Pratt, Staunton and Thacker, to run in the order named. Payne, you will 'sub'."

"Captain Pratt, I certainly object to that nigger's presence on the team. Whom do I mean? Thacker, of course, he's a nigger, and no southern gentleman would compete against or run with a nigger and I—"

"Now, Staunton, none of your southern idiosyncrasies go here," cut in Pratt. "You know we want to win that relay, and Gale is priming her best half-milers for the race and since Thacker can do the half in less than two minutes, take it from me, so long as I'm captain, he runs."

"Then I quit," and red as a beet, Staunton sat down.

"Quit, then, if you want to!" thundered Pratt.

"Hold on, Pratt, we're all white fellows together and there's no need of our having a row over a colored chap. You know, I'm from Texas anyway, and I want to say that here in Starvard we've never had any colored fellows on the track team in the three years I've been here, and I'm hanged if I see why we've got to start now. These niggers are always trying to get out of their place," said Payne, the junior who had been crowded off the team by Thacker.

"Well by Jove, he seems to have pushed you out of *your* place on the team. He's beaten you more than once in the time trials and—"

"Just a minute," a calm voice put in, and Thacker came

*Crisis* 9 (Feb. 1915): 193–95.

into the meeting. "I did not hear the beginning of this discussion, but I did hear some remarks and I judge that I am considered objectionable as a member of the relay because of—surely not the color of my skin [for he was as fair as any of the other fellows there] but because I have Negro blood in my veins." Every man was breathless. "Let me say this one thing, that *nigger* or not, I have won the place on the team but rather than cause any discord which might end in Starvard's losing the meet to Gale, I'll quit!" he swung on his heel and strode from the gym.

As the door slammed the storm broke.

"I didn't know he was colored," said one.

"Well, he is," answered Staunton.

"Well, he's whiter than you both in skin and in heart, Phil Staunton," yelled Pratt.

"You are insulting me, you Yank," and Staunton sprang at Pratt. The other men jumped in and held the two apart. Finally, quiet was restored and Payne was replaced on the team.

The meet was to come off a week from the coming Saturday. This was on Wednesday. Saturday, Gale had a dual meet with East Point, and Pratt and the coach, Hardy, went down to look over Gale's two-mile relay team and get a general line on the rest of the men. Silently they watched Gale win 69 to 20. On the return to Wainbridge, Hardy said: "Pratt, you fellows are all sorts of fools to let that man Thacker get off the team. Why, he's the fastest half-miler I've seen. I bet you he walks away with the half—if his heart isn't taken out by this dirty work," he added in an undertone.

"Hardy, you know I did all I could but he stuck out. He's as proud as the deuce, and as for those Southerners, they stuck out, too. They're always trying to make it hard for these colored boys. Oh, they make me sick!"

"Well, he's going to win that half in a walk, although

Price ran a pretty race against those soldiers. Well, here's my jumping off place, Pratt," and the coach swung off the trolley.

"Curse the luck! Hardy doesn't want to own it, but we can't beat that Gale team."

The day of the meet came. Gale was down, brimming over with confidence, for the news that the crack half-miler on the relay was not going to run had spread like wild fire. Gale had no opinion, Starvard was divided.

At 1:30 the pistol cracked for the start of the hundred yard dash. Gale took first, but Starvard got second and third. Engle, of Gale, won the 120 hurdles, Wilson and Desmond, of Starvard, second and third. In the broad jump Bates and Hines of Starvard took first and third, but again Gale took first in the hammer throw.

The quarter-mile was next. In a close and exciting race Chalmers of Starvard "brought home the bacon" in 50 flat. Starvard began to hope. She grew frantic as she landed first in the high jump, although Gale took second and third.

Then came the half mile. The pride of Gale, Price's equal, Simpson, followed by his teammates, Parsons and Terry, sprang out to toe the mark. James and Keele threw off their crimson sweaters and a third Starvard man stepped up. It was Thacker. He was an ideal half-miler, five feet eleven inches, lean of face, broad shouldered, slender waisted, and with great long tapering legs. Simpson was short and stocky with a choppy stride with which he hoped to break Thacker.

All six got off to a good start. Thacker set the pace for the first lap. Then he seemed to slow up and Simpson and Terry drew up. Terry was now two feet ahead of Thacker, and Simpson stride and stride, with Parsons pushing him hard. Keele was out of it. As they turned in the last stretch, pandemonium broke loose in the Gale stands. Starvard cheered

on her men. Thacker had seen Staunton leer at him and his
heart gave a great jump and his feet responded to the call.
His big lead was gone and it would be no easy matter to get
in first in the short distance remaining. Teeth set, head back,
he began a great sprint. With forty yards to go Terry and
Simpson were leading, Terry a good two feet in front of
Simpson and Thacker a yard behind. Three great strides and
the red and blue jerseys were neck and neck. The stands were
hushed. Nothing was heard but the pat-pat-pat of the spikes
on the cinders. All three runners were straining every muscle,
calling on their reserve strength, holding on by sheer nerve.
Five great jumps and Thacker toppled over a winner in 1:58
flat, Simpson dropped a hand's breadth behind, and Terry
was all in as he fell across.

Starvard cheered and cheered Thacker. Rooters jumped
from the stands to pat Thacker on the back. Hardy drove
them off and arm in arm he and Thacker went to see to a
rub down.

"All out for the 220 high hurdles!" Payne and Gardner
showed Starvard's crimson, while Kittredge and Fields wore
the Gale blue. Payne was showing an easy first with Gardner
and Fields neck and neck, with Kittredge a good third. As
Payne took the last hurdle, Starvard's cheers turned to groans,
for Payne stumbled and fell. In a flash he was up, just to
limp across the finish behind Gardner, who was trailing the
Gale man. Gloom pervaded the Starvard stands when the
news spread that Payne, the anchor man of the two-mile relay
was out with a sprained ankle. Second and third in the 120
high hurdles gave Starvard four points to Gale's five. Gale
took first and third in the mile and first in the pole vault.

There was but one event left on the program—the two-
mile relay. In the stands it was figured that Gale was three
points to the good: Starvard 48, Gale 51.

"Who's going to take Payne's place?" was the question in the Starvard stands. Then calls for "Thacker! Thacker!" came from the crimson supporters. For if Starvard took the relay, the meet was hers by a scant two points. If Gale won, the meet was *hers*, together with the Eastern championship.

"Hardy, do you suppose Thacker *could* run *another* half against Price, who is perfectly fresh?"

"Pratt, I'd think you fellows would be so ashamed of the dirt you've done Thacker that you'd go hide yourselves. I won't ask him, I'll tell you, but—" here the coach looked straight into Pratt's eyes, "I bet you he'll run, and mark my words, he'll beat Price, if it kills him. Now, go ask him."

Pratt came back looking relieved. "All right, Hardy!"

Carter toed the mark against Steen, the first Gale runner. Crack! went the pistol, off they sped.

"Staunton, Thacker takes the baton from you," called Pratt. Staunton looked sullen. Down the home stretch came Carter and Steen, Carter giving Pratt a good five-yard lead which he held and increased by five, and then Staunton took up the running. Archer brought joy to Gale as he cut down Staunton's lead yard by yard. Then he tore down to give Price an eight-yard start. Thacker snatched the baton from Staunton and sped away on a seemingly impossible task.

"Can he catch him? Will he hold out?"

Thacker seemed to be oblivious to the fact that the heat was terrific, of everything indeed, but the eight-yard lead he had to cut down. What difference did it make that his throat was parched, his head was splitting, that Price was the fastest man in the East and this was *his* first year in collegiate circles? He had to win. He had to make good, even under handicaps. Starvard thundered encouragement as he tore after the flying Price. After the first hundred yards, he began a terrific pace. His feet seemed to barely touch the ground. All thoughts of his blood gone, Starvard cheered him on: "Keep it up! Thack, old boy, go it! Come on, old man!"

He heard nothing. He thought he had cut down the lead by two yards. He prayed for strength: "Oh, Lord, just let me catch him and I can pass him!" On and on they flew. No cheering now, for the stands had settled down to watch a match between two strong men. The great stadium was silent save for the crunching of the cinders. Thacker was crawling up, foot by foot. Yard after yard was covered at this murderous pace. Around the last turn they sped, Price running easily, Thacker glassy-eyed, hollow-cheeked but still flying. One hundred yards to go—Thacker's breath was coming hot and fast, his knees felt as if they must give way, yet he spurred his failing strength for one last great sprint. He again increased his speed, to the amazement of the stands. Half-way down he seemed almost gone. Forty yards—two more yards to make up on Price, who, although tiring was beginning a spurt. Twenty-five yards—he was just behind Price but his chin had dropped on his chest, his mouth hung open, and his eyes were blinded with tears as he felt unable to pass Price, laboring at his side. Eight yards—he was growing weaker stride by stride, but Price had slipped an inch or so behind. Thacker no longer heard the heavy breathing of Price and raised his eyes to see whether he was in front. Nothing in front but that bit of worsted which marked the finish. He threw up his arms and Hardy caught him as he fell unconscious, breasting the tape, and breaking the color line.

# POLLY'S HACK RIDE

*Mrs. Emma E. Butler*

Polly Gray had lived six and one-half years without ever having enjoyed the luxury of a hack ride.

The little shanty, merely an apology for a house, in which she lived with her parents, sat in a hollow on the main road in the village, at least fifteen feet below the road; and when Polly sat or stood at the front window up stairs, she watched with envy the finely dressed ladies and gentlemen riding by on their way to the big red brick building on the hill.

On several occasions her secret longing got the best of her, and she mustered all the self control of which her nature boasted to keep from stealing a ride on behind, as she had seen her brothers do on the ice wagon, but the memory of the warm reception usually awaiting the little male Grays, accompanied by predictions of broken necks, arms, legs, etc., caused her little frame to shiver.

Who then could say that Polly was wanting in sisterly love when she exulted in the fact that she was going to a funeral? What did it matter if Ma Gray was heart-broken, and Pa Gray couldn't eat but six biscuits for his supper when he came home and found the long white fringed sash floating from the cracked door knob?

Polly reviewed the events leading up to her present stage of ecstasy: Ma Gray had sent in hot haste for Aunt Betty Williams, who came with question marks stamped on her face, and when she found Ella, the two-year-old pet of the

*Crisis* 12 (June 1916): 84–85.

family in the throes of death she was by far too discreet to say so but advised Ma Gray to put her down. Polly had then become afraid and had run down stairs. She felt it—yes, sir—she felt it 'way down in her "stummik!" Something was going to happen, so when Ma Gray appeared at the head of the stairs with eyes swollen, and still a-swellin', and told her in a shaky voice to go to school for the children, she knew it had happened.

She started off at break-neck speed but, undecided just as to the proper gait for one bearing a message of such grave importance, she walked mournfully along for a while, then as the vision of a hack and two white horses arose, she skipped and finally ran again until she reached the school-house.

The afternoon session had just begun, as she timidly knocked on the door of the class-room where the two elder Grays were "gettin' their schoolin' "; and when the teacher opened the door, she beheld a very dirty little girl blubbering, "Ella's dead; Mamma's cryin'. Kin Bobby and Sally cum home?"

Master Bobby and Miss Sally were dismissed with the reverence due the dignity of their bereavement, and on their way home they proceeded to extract such bits of information as they deemed suitable for the occasion: "Were her eyes open or shut? Had she turned black yet? Did Aunt Betty cry too? Did Mamma fall across the bed as the breath was leaving her body?" Whereupon Miss Polly, being a young lady of a rather keen imagination upon which she drew, and drew heavily in times of need, gave them quite a sensational version of the affair, and by the time they reached home they were fully prepared to grieve with a capital "G." Sally ran to Ma Gray and with a shriek, threw both arms around her neck, while Bobby fell on his knees by the deceased Ella, imploring her to come back and be his baby sister once more.

Aunt Betty told her next door neighbor afterwards that she had her hands full and her heart full too, trying to quiet them. And if the smell of fried liver and onions had not reminded Bobby that it was near dinner time, she really couldn't tell how she should have managed them.

As plateful after plateful of liver, onions and mashed potatoes disappeared, the raging storm of grief subsided in the hearts of the young Grays, and by the time dinner was over Bobby was kept busy unpuckering his lips to suppress a whistle, and Sally had tried several bows of black ribbon on her hair to see which one looked best.

After the dishes were cleared away, and Ma Gray was scouring the floor in a solution of concentrated lye, water and tears, Uncle Bangaway, a retired deacon in the Baptist church, stepped in to pay his respects.

Uncle Bangaway was considered a fine singer in his younger days and was quite proud of the accusation, so he proceeded to express his sympathy for Ma Gray in the words of his favorite hymn, kept in reserve for such occasions:

> "Wasn't my Lord mighty good and kind?
>   O Yeah!
> "Wasn't my Lord mighty good and kind?
>   O Yeah!
> "Wasn't my Lord mighty good and kind
> "To take away the child and leave the mother behind?
>   "O Yeah! O Yeah! O Yeah!"

When he finished singing Ma Gray stopped crying to smile on him. It seemed that the hymn brought to her mind certain facts that were well worth considering.

On the morning of the day appointed for the funeral, a dark cloud hung over the village when Polly awoke, and her heart sank within her. Oh! If it should rain! Every hack she had ever seen on a rainy day had the curtains down, and there was no use riding in a hack if you had to have the curtains down. Anyhow, she began to dress, and before she was half through the sun began to peep through the clouds, and finally it shone brightly; and so did Miss Polly's face.

Who, then, could not pardon the cheerful face she brought down stairs where the funeral party was gathered? Dressed in a new black dress, new shoes, new hair ribbon, even new gloves, and a hack ride scheduled for the next two hours, was enough to make her very soul shine.

She hardly heard the minister as he dwelt at length on the innocence of childhood; nor his reference to Him who suffered the little ones to come unto Him; but the closing strains of "Nearer My God To Thee" seemed to awaken her from pleasant dreams.

When the funeral procession started out Polly felt very sad, but the tears wouldn't come and, of course, "you can't make 'em come, if you ain't got no raw onions."

Now, it fell to her lot to sit in the hack with her great uncle, "Uncle Billings" Ma Gray called him, but Polly often wondered why Pa Gray spoke of him as "Uncle Rummy."

One of the many reasons for Polly's aversion to Uncle Billings was because of his prompt appearance before dinner every Sunday, when he would call her mother's attention every time she, Polly, took another doughnut or cookie. So you may be sure her spirits fell when she realized the state of affairs.

On the way to the cemetery neither found much to say to the other, but when they started home Uncle Billings began to lecture Polly concerning her apparent indifference to the family bereavement; during which discourse Polly sat without hearing one word, as her mind was otherwise engaged. She was trying to think of some manner in which to attract the attention of the Higdon girls as she passed the pump; she knew they would be there.

Before her plans were matured, however, the red bonnet of Cecie Higdon loomed up at the corner, and standing right behind her were Bessie and Georgia Higdon and Lucy Matthews.

Now was her chance! Now or never! So she sprang from her seat, leaned far out of the window, and gave one loud "Whee!" to the girls, waving her black-bordered handkerchief meanwhile.

Uncle Billings had just dropped off in a doze, and Polly's whoop brought him out of it so suddenly that he could find nothing more appropriate to say than, "Hush your noise, gal!" when with a sudden jerk the hack stopped and they were home.

As Polly alighted from the hack, she began to realize how, as a mourner, she had lowered her dignity by yelling from the window like a joy-rider, and she was not a little uneasy as to how Ma Gray would consider the matter should old Rummy inform her. So during supper she cautiously avoided meeting his eye, and as soon as she had finished eating she ran upstairs to change her clothes.

Here her mother found her later, with her head resting on the open Bible, and when she tried to awaken her she said, "Yes'm, just tell him not to drive quite so fast."

# "BITS"
## A Christmas Story

### Helen G. Ricks

The feathery snowflakes came hurrying down simply because it was the day before Christmas and not because there was any intention on their part to remain. It was late afternoon and the holiday bustle had only partially subsided.

Pushing through the crowds at the railway station a young girl emerged, muffled up to the ears in furs, with a girlish face wreathed up to the eyes in smiles. It was very evident with her that Christmas was coming. At the gate entrance she inquired about her train. The *train was gone!* To stand there stupidly gazing at the official who certainly was not responsible helped matters not at all. Of course, it meant a "wire" and a wait until next morning. To a girl who was bent on meeting a bunch of college friends at a house party Christmas morning, the laconic information concerning the means of her transportation came not joyously. The tears which filled her brown eyes were definitely feminine. And then a little smile slipped out from somewhere and she proceeded to the Western Union office.

She was pushing through the door leading out to the busy street when a little brown hand caught at her skirt.

"Evenin' Herald, Lady?"

The girl looked down.

"Why, little fellow, you're crying. I can't let you take my pet indulgence away from me like that. Tell me about things, dear." And she brushed a perfectly good little tear out of the

*Crisis* 13 (Dec. 1916): 64–66.

corner of her eye—the one that had refused to be chased when the smile came.

"It's—it's that I've just *got* to sell out tonight. It's—it's oranges for Bits."

By this time the ragged little coat-sleeve was serving wonderfully as a handkerchief.

"Come, come, little lad, stand over here out of the crowd. Somehow I don't understand. Who is Bits?"

"Why, he's all I'm got—that's all."

"Oh, I see! Can't you tell me more about him and your own little self? Maybe I can *buy you out?*"

The childish face stared up into the girl's with an incredulity that was not at all concealed.

"Mean it, or jes' kiddin'?"

"Yes, dear, I *do* mean it. Tell me."

"It ain't so awful much to tell you 'bout where we live, 'cause we ain't roomin' in any manshun. Bits an' Spatch an' me all sleeps on a cot in Mis' Barney's basement, an' we gets our feed from Greeley's grocery when we *gets* it. Spatch is jes' beany 'bout weenies—swellest little *poor* dog you ever seen. We ain't got no folks but jes' ourselves, an' Spatch. Somehow, though, Bits hits it off with the papers—he's onto *his* job all right. I'm littler than him an' folks lots of time passes me up. We ain't never had *heaps*, but we has allus been happy, 'cause Bits says it's the only way to top off things. He's sick, though, now—he jes' all to oncet took down an' they bustled him off to the hospital. He looked right spruce an' cleaned up in that white bed when I went to see him, but say, he was *some* sick. They told me I could come back tonight, an' I wanted *awful* hard to take him oranges 'cause tomorrer's Christmas. But you see, I'm down to six cents, less'n I sell out. Guess I wasn't a game thoroughbred, like

when you saw me cryin'—bet you Bits wouldn't a done it!
My name's Rodney, but folks as knows me calls me Pep,
'cause some days I hits it off right spunky—specially when
they're hot on—on Spatch's trail—he's one-eyed."

With the ingeniousness of the small boy he related the
history of himself, Bits and Spatch. And the girl understood.

"Rodney, I'm going to buy you out and we'll dispose of
these Heralds someway. You lead the way because we must
get these oranges to Bits. May I go with you, please, to see
your brother?"

"Well, I should jes' bet you *can!* It ain't so far, but I spect'
as how you'll better take the car. I'm only got six cents, but
I'll boost you up an' pop the conductor a half-dime an' beat
it faster than the car an be *waitin'* for you."

"Thank you, dear, for wishing for me to ride, but oh, I'd
love to walk with you if I may."

"Say, you are *some* great—know it?" And the look of
gallant appreciation over-spread the boy's face.

"Maybe if you're this good for walkin'—maybe you wouldn't
mind cuttin' over two blocks with me. I promised Spatch
that *he* could go tonight."

"Certainly! Are you cold, dear?"

*"Should say not*—too excited!"

They were reaching the quarter of the city very unfamiliar
to the girl. Faithfully she followed the little figure striding
along manfully with a bundle of "Evenin' Heralds" tucked
under one arm.

" 'Lo, kids!"

They had passed a bunch of little street children.

"That's *my* bunch. They was some starin'—huh? Wonderin'
'bout *you*, I guess."

Finally they had reached a tenement house.

"Can't ast you in, but I'll be right down soon as I untie him. An'—an' shall I leave these papers? She could use them for kindlin'."

"Oh, yes, by all means! I'll wait for you."

In an incredibly short space of time a boy with a dog was retracing his steps down the street in company with the girl.

"Ain't he a dog fer you? Spatch is the cut'off for 'Dispatch'—one of the old papers. We're *pardners!*"

His new friend smiled understandingly.

At the fruit stand they purchased the oranges.

"Say! but you're *some* lady. I'll bet Bits will like you heaps. What made you good to me today?"

"Why, my dear! I just love all the little boys and girls of my race. I just wanted to help you if I could, just a little bit."

They had now reached the hospital. The girl, the small boy and the dog entered the building. It so happened that the lady visitor was not a stranger to the hospital force, consequently Spatch was graciously accorded a permit.

"How is the little lad, nurse?"

"The crisis came four nights ago—he will recover. He's been waiting for his little brother—go right in."

The white hospital cot was near the window and a shaft of light fell across the face which instantly became illumined with a smile when Spatch and Pep uttered their effusive greetings.

"Well, if here ain't the little kid and Pardner! How's business? Sleep cold last night, Pep?"

"*Should say not!* So warm, almost had to hist the window!"

The tail of Spatch wagged perilously near the sack of oranges purposely concealed at the foot of the bed.

Bits smiled, and then his eyes fell on the girl standing a

little away from the bed. He turned towards Pep, and in a voice a trifle weak and very much puzzled, exclaimed: "Pep, who's the swell skirt? She with you?"

"She's *some* lady!" A smile followed his words, absolutely appreciative. "She bought me out an' then come clear here jes' to see you. Can't you shake? She's a—a friend of *mine.*"

In the course of a few minutes *she* was irrevocably taken into the partnership with Bits, Pep and Spatch. After the neighborhood news had been imparted and all preliminaries completed, the oranges were presented. The smile from Bits more than paid their real value.

All too soon the nurse came to announce the close of visiting hours.

"Pep, old feller, cover up good tonight. Give Pardner a weenie and please take three of these oranges for yourself— tomorrer's Christmas. Stick it out! I'll be back to the old job soon. They're bully to me here."

The girl bent over the little sick-a-bed laddie.

"Bits, is there a single Christmas wish of yours that I could fulfill, dear? Please let me try."

"Mighty nice of you. I think you've done a heap now. But there is—is something. It's the little kid there. I've heard about juvenile officers an' their doin's. Mebbe *somebody* could get a home for him. He's a smart little chap, Miss, an' deserves a chance. When I get well I'd work to help for his keep. Could you get him in?"

"Yes, dear, I've been thinking of Rodney all the way over here. Fortunately I know the very people to secure him a home. And I have a friend who has charge of a settlement house, and I am going to take him there tonight so he won't be lonesome. It's warm there, and they'll be good to him— they really would be happy to have him come. Plenty of boys there, and games, and a Christmas tree. I'll be there myself for a while. Now, have a good sleep and don't worry about him. Spatch is going, too. Good-bye."

As they turned to look back once more at the door, a smile from Bits was following them. Outside Pep hesitated.

"Look here, I've *lied*—yes, I've told a ripper! I was freezin' cold last night—I give the blanket to my Pardner here."

"I understand, laddie. Tomorrow is Christmas. We're going down town on this car and I'm going to fit you out in some real warm clothing for your Christmas present, Rodney. And then tonight you, and Spatch, and I, are going to the settlement house. There, other little colored children are having a Christmas tree, and games, and fun! And there isn't going to be any more paper selling for you, or Bits, but you're going to have a real home and a chance to go to school. I have friends who will help me. Are you willing, dear?"

Two little cold hands ecstatically clasped themselves over one of the girl's, and two little tears of joy made two little tracks on his childish brown face.

"I guess you're the 'Christmas Angel' I heard 'bout oncet. Gee! but you're touchin'!"

The happiness that reigned in his little heart that Christmas eve is not to be described in words. Pep appreciated.

On Christmas morning a car stopped outside the settlement house and the girl bounded out to return leading a small boy, refreshed and happy and followed by a one-eyed canine disciple.

All arrangements had been made and both boys were to be located in a private home with a fair chance. A young doctor, the very dearest friend of the girl's, had consented to look after her charges in her holiday absence. It was he who opened the door of the car as they approached.

"Good morning, little chap! Merry Christmas!"

"Ditto"—this last from Pep, and an exhilarating bark from Spatch.

"Rodney, this is Dr. Weston—*our friend.*"

When they reached the ward, one bound and Pep was at the side of the bed.

"Know me, Bits? *Some looker,* ain't I? Had one spludge las' night—too big almost to talk about. She done it all. *She's an angel!* Now, hold your breath while I tell you the biggest ever! She's found a home for you, an' me, an' Spatch, an' we're goin' to *school,* an'—an' *she means it!*"

The "Christmas Angel" and the doctor came nearer the bed. Professionally he reached for the pulse and all the friendliness possible was in his greeting.

"Well, little friend, I'm in the partnership, too, and we're going to get you well in ten days!"

Bits smiled first at one and then at the other appreciatively.

"You two don't know how I thank you for myself an' the kid! I can't tell you. Just give us the chance—we'll prove up the claim!" Determination and gratitude were in his face.

"I'm glad if you're pleased, Bits. You are both going to be my little brothers, and Spatch here (at this opportune moment there was an appreciative tail-wag) is going to be our mascot. I must hurry now to catch the train, for I'm going away for three days. Dr. Weston is going to give Rodney a 'big day,' and I think he has a surprise for Bits. Good-bye, dear!"

There was a kiss left on the warm forehead. A little hand shot out from the covering.

"*You're* the best Christmas I ever had! I—I just wish I could whisper to you, some thin'—"

The girl bent down. Two arms went around her neck, two words from a little heart filled with gratitude slipped out—

"Merry Christmas!"

# MAMMY
## *A Story*

*Adeline F. Ries*

Mammy's heart felt heavy indeed when (the time was now two years past) marriage had borne Shiela, her "white baby," away from the Governor's plantation to the coast. But as the months passed, the old colored nurse became accustomed to the change, until the great joy brought by the news that Shiela had a son, made her reconciliation complete. Besides, had there not always been Lucy, Mammy's own "black baby," to comfort her?

Yes, up to that day there had always been Lucy; but on that very day the young Negress had been sold—sold like common household ware!—and (the irony of it chilled poor Mammy's leaden heart)—she had been sold to Shiela as nurse to the baby whose birth, but four days earlier had caused Mammy so much rejoicing. The poor slave could not believe that it was true, and as she buried her head deeper into the pillows, she prayed that she might wake to find it all a dream.

But a reality it proved and a reality which she dared not attempt to change. For despite the Governor's customary kindness, she knew from experience, that any interference on her part would but result in serious floggings. One morning each week she would go to his study and he would tell her the news from the coast and then with a kindly smile dismiss her.

So for about a year, Mammy feasted her hungering soul with these meagre scraps of news, until one morning, contrary

*Crisis* 13 (Jan. 1917): 117–18.

to his wont, the Governor rose as she entered the room, and he bade her sit in a chair close to his own. Placing one of his white hands over her knotted brown ones, he read aloud the letter he held in his other hand:

"Dear Father:—

"I can hardly write the sad news and can, therefore, fully appreciate how difficult it will be for you to deliver it verbally. Lucy was found lying on the nursery floor yesterday, dead. The physician whom I immediately summoned pronounced her death a case of heart-failure. Break it gently to my dear old mammy, father, and tell her too, that the coach, should she wish to come here before the burial, is at her disposal.

"Your daughter,
"SHIELA."

While he read, the Governor unconsciously nerved himself to a violent outburst of grief, but none came. Instead, as he finished, Mammy rose, curtsied, and made as if to withdraw. At the door she turned back and requested the coach, "if it weren't asking too much," and then left the room. She did not return to her cabin; simply stood at the edge of the road until the coach with its horses and driver drew up and then she entered. From that time and until nightfall she did not once change the upright position she had assumed, nor did her eyelids once droop over her staring eyes. "They took her from me an' she died"—"They took her from me an' she died"—over and over she repeated the same sentence.

When early the next morning Mammy reached Shiela's home, Shiela herself came down the road to meet her, ready with words of comfort and love. But as in years gone by, it was Mammy who took the golden head on her breast, and patted it, and bade the girl to dry her tears. As of old, too, it was Mammy who first spoke of other things; she asked to be shown the baby, and Shiela only too willingly led the way to the nursery where in his crib the child lay cooing to itself. Mammy took up the little body and again and again tossed it up into the air with the old cry, "Up she goes, Shiela," till he laughed aloud.

Suddenly she stopped, and clasping the child close she took a hurried step towards the open window. At a short distance from the house rolled the sea and Mammy gazed upon it as if fascinated. And as she stared, over and over the words formed themselves: "They took her from me an' she died,"— "They took her from me an' she died."

From below came the sound of voices, "They're waiting for you, Mammy,"—it was Shiela's soft voice that spoke— "to take Lucy—you understand, dear."

Mammy's eyes remained fixed upon the waves,—"I can't go—go foh me, chile, won't you?" And Shiela thought that she understood the poor woman's feelings and without even pausing to kiss her child she left the room and joined the waiting slaves.

Mammy heard the scraping as of a heavy box upon the gravel below; heard the tramp of departing footsteps as they grew fainter and fainter until they died away. Then and only then, did she turn her eyes from the wild waters and looking down at the child in her arms, she laughed a low, peculiar laugh. She smoothed back the golden ringlets from his forehead, straightened out the little white dress, and then, choosing a light covering for his head, she descended the stairs and passed quietly out of the house.

A short walk brought Mammy and her burden to the lonely beach; at the water's edge she stood still. Then she shifted the child's position until she supported his weight in her hands and with a shrill cry of "Up she goes, Shiela," she lifted him above her head. Suddenly she flung her arms forward, at the same time releasing her hold of his little body. A large breaker caught him in its foam, swept him a few feet towards the shore and retreating, carried him out into the sea—

A few hours later, two slaves in frantic search for the missing child found Mammy on the beach tossing handfuls of sand into the air and uttering loud, incoherent cries. And as they came close, she pointed towards the sea and with the laugh of a mad-woman shouted: "They took her from me an' she died!"

# "THERE WAS ONE TIME!"
## A Story of Spring

### Jessie Fauset

## [I]

"There was one time" began the freckled-faced boy. Miss
Fetter interrupted him with emphasis—"but that is not idi-
omatic, our expression for *il y avait une fois* is 'once upon a
time.' The value of a translation lies in its adequacy." And
for the fiftieth time that term she launched into an explanation
of the translation of idioms. The class listened with genial
composure—the more she talked, the less they could read.
She reached her peroration. "Do you understand, Master
Reynolds?"

The freckled-faced boy, who had been surreptitiously con-
sulting his vocabulary, turned deftly back to the passage.
"Yes'm," he nodded. "There was one time"—he began again
unabashed.

Miss Fetter sighed and passed on to another pupil. Between
them all there was evolved in hopelessly unsympathetic English the story of a dainty French shepherdess who growing
tired of her placid sheep left them to shift for themselves one
gorgeous spring-day, donned her sky-blue dress, traversed
the sombre forest and came to another country. There she
met the prince who, struck with her charm and naiveté, asked
her to play with him. So she did until sunset when he escorted
her to the edge of the forest where she pursued her way home

*Crisis* 13, pts. 1–3 (April 1917): 272–77; 14, pts. 4–5 (May 1917): 11–
15.

to her little thatched cottage, with a mind much refreshed and "garlanded with pleasant memories."

The pupils read, as pupils will, with stolid indifference. The fairy-tale was merely so many pages of French to them, as indeed it was to Miss Fetter. That she must teach foreign languages—always her special detestation—seemed to her the final irony of an ironic existence.

"It's all so inadequate," she fumed to herself, pinning on her hat before the tiny mirror in the little stuffy teachers' room. She was old enough to have learned very thoroughly all the aphorisms of her day. She believed that all service performed honestly and thoroughly was helpful, but she was still too young to know that such was literally true and her helplessness irked her. See her, then, as she walked home through the ugly streets of Marytown, neither white nor black, of medium height, slim, nose neither good nor bad, mouth beautiful, teeth slightly irregular, but perfect. Altogether, when she graduated at eighteen from the Business High School in Philadelphia she was as much as any one else the typical American girl done over in brown, no fears for the future, no regrets for the past, rather glad to put her school-books down for good and decidedly glad that she was no longer to be a burden on her parents.

Getting a position after all was not so easy. Perhaps for the first time she began to realize the handicap of color. Her grade on graduation had been "meritorious." She had not shone, but neither had she been stupid. She had rarely volunteered to answer questions, being mostly occupied in dreaming, but she could answer when called on. If she had no self-assurance, neither had she a tendency to self-belittlement. Her English, if not remarkable, was at least correct; her typewriting was really irreproachable; her spelling exact; and she had the quota of useless French—or German—

vocabulary which the average pupil brings out of the average
High School. Perhaps it was because she had lived all her
life in a small up-town street in a white neighborhood and
played with most of the boys and girls there, perhaps it was
because at eighteen one is still idealistic that she answered
advertisement after advertisement without apprehension. The
result, of course, was always the same; always the faint shock
of surprise in the would-be employer's voice, the faint stare,
the faint emphasis—"You! Oh no, the position is not open
to—er—you." At first she did not understand, but even when
she did she kept futilely on—she *could* not, she *would* not
teach—and why does one graduate from a Business High
School, if one is not to be employed by a business firm?

That summer her father, a silent, black man, died and her
decisions against teaching fled. She was not a normal school
graduate, so she could not teach in Philadelphia. The young
German drummer next door told her of positions to be had
in colored schools in the South—perhaps she could teach her
favorite stenography or drawing in which she really excelled.
Fate at that point took on her most menacing aspect. Nothing
that was not menial came her way, excepting work along lines
of which she knew nothing. Her mother and she gave up the
little house and the two of them went to service. Those two
awful years gave Anna her first real taste of the merciless
indifference of life. Her mother, a woman of nerveless and,
to Anna, enviable stolidity found, as always, a refuge in inapt
quotations of Scripture. But Anna lived in a fever of revolt.
She spent her days as a waitress and her evenings in night
school trying feverishly to learn some of those subjects which
she might have taught, had she been properly prepared. At
the end of two years the change came carelessly, serenely, just
as though it might always have happened. The son-in-law of

Mrs. Walton, for whom she worked, passed through town late one night. The family had gone out and for want of something better he had, as he ate his solitary dinner, asked the rather taciturn waitress about her history. She had told him briefly and he had promised her, with equal brevity, a position as drawing teacher in a colored seminary of which he was a trustee. Anna, stunned, went with her mother to Marytown. Just as suddenly as it started, the struggle for existence was over, though, of course, they were still poor. Mrs. Fetter found plenty of plain sewing to do and Anna was appointed. But Fate, with a last malevolence, saw to it that she was appointed to teach History and French, which were just being introduced into the seminary. She thought of this as she opened her mother's gate,—the irony of the thing made her sick. "Since my luck was going to change, why couldn't I have been allowed to teach mechanical drawing," she wondered, "or given a chance at social work? But teaching French! I suppose the reason that little shepherdess neglected her sheep that day was because *they* were French."

## II

Still one cannot persist in gloom when it is April and one is twenty-six and looks, as only American girls, whether white or brown, can look, five years younger. Anna hastening down the street in her best blue serge dress, her pretty slim feet in faultless tan shoes, felt her moodiness, which had almost become habitual, vanish.

The wearing of the blue dress was accidental. She had come down to breakfast in her usual well-worn gray skirt and immaculate shirt-waist in time to hear her small cousin,

Theophilus, proclaim his latest enterprise. A boy was going to give him five white mice for his pen-knife and he was going to bring them home right after school and put them in a little cage. Pretty soon there'd be more of them——"they have lots of children, Aunt Emmeline, and I'm going to sell them and buy Sidney Williams' ukulele, and"——

"Indeed you are going to do no such thing," exclaimed Anna, her high good humor vanishing. "Mother, you won't let him bring those nasty things here, I know. As for keeping them in a cage, they'd be all over the house in no time."

But Mrs. Fetter, who loved Theophilus because he was still a little boy and she could baby him, opined that foxes and birds had their nests. "Let's see the cage, Philly dear, maybe they can't get out."

The rest had followed as the night the day. Theophilus, rushing from the table, had knocked Anna's cup of cocoa out of her hand and the brown liquid had run down the front of the immaculate blouse and settled in a comfortable pool in her lap.

"Oh well," her mother had said, unmoved as usual, "run along, Anna, and put on your blue serge dress. It won't do you any harm to wear it this once and if you hurry you'll get to school in time just the same. You didn't go to do it, did you, Philly?"

Theophilus, aghast, had fled to the shelter of his banjo from which he was extracting plaintive strains. He played banjo, guitar and piano with equal and indeed amazing facility, but as his musical tastes were surprisingly eclectic, the results were at times distressing. Anna, hastening out, a real vision now in her pretty frock, an unwonted color in her smooth bronze cheeks, heard him telling his aunt again about the ukulele which Sidney Williams owned but couldn't play.

"It's broke. Some folks where his father works gave it to him. Betcher I'll fix it and play it, too, when I get hold of it," his high voice was proclaiming confidently.

"I suppose he will,"—thought his cousin, "I hope that North street car won't be hung up this morning. He ought to make a fine musician, but, of course, he won't get a chance at it when he grows up." The memory of her own ironic calling stung her. "He'll probably have to be a farmer just because he'll hate it. I do wish I could walk, it's so lovely. I wish I were that little shepherdess off on a holiday. She was wearing a blue dress, I remember."

Well, her mind leaped up to the thought. Why shouldn't she take a day off? In all these six years she had never been out once, except the time Theophilus had had the measles. The street car came up at this point, waited an infinitesimal second and clanged angrily off, as if provoked at its own politeness. She looked after it with mingled dismay and amusement. "I'd be late anyway," she told herself, "now that I've lost that car. I'll get a magazine and explore the Park; no one will know."

Two hours of leisurely strolling brought her to Hertheimer Park, a small green enclosure at the end of the ugly little town. Anna picked her way past groups of nurse-maids and idlers looking in newspapers for occupation which they hoped they would never find. She came at last to the little grove in the far side of the Park where the sun was not quite so high and, seating herself near the fountain, began to feed the squirrels with some of the crackers which she had bought in one of the corner groceries.

Being alive was pretty decent after all, she reflected. Life was the main thing—teaching school, being colored, even being poor were only aspects, her mind went on. If one were just well and comfortable—not even rich or pampered—one could get along; the thing to do was to look at life in the large and not to gaze too closely at the specific interest or activity in hand. Her growing philosophy tickled her sense of humor. "You didn't feel like that when you were at Mrs. Walton's," she told herself bluntly and smiled at her own discomfiture.

"That's right, smile at me," said an oily voice, and she looked up to see one of the idlers leaning over the back of her bench. "You're a right good-lookin' gal. How'd you like to take a walk with me?"

She stared into his evil face, fascinated. Where, where, where were all the people? The nurse-maids had vanished, the readers of newspapers had gone—to buy afternoon editions, perhaps. She felt herself growing icy, paralyzed. "You needn't think I mind your being a nigger," went on the hateful voice, "I ruther like 'em. I hain't what you might call prejudiced."

This was what could happen to you if you were a colored girl who felt like playing at being a French shepherdess. She looked around for help and exactly as though at a cue in a play, as though he had been waiting for that look a young colored man stepped forward, one hand courteously lifting his hat, the other resting carelessly in his hip-pocket.

"Good afternoon, Miss Walker," he said, and his whole bearing exhaled courtesy. "I couldn't be sure it was you until you turned around. I'm sorry I'm late, I hope I haven't kept you waiting. I hope you weren't annoying my friend," he addressed the tramp pleasantly.

But the latter, with one fascinated glance at that hand still immobile in that suggestive hip-pocket, was turning away.

"I was jus askin' a direction," he muttered. "I'll be going now."

# III

The two young colored people stared at each other in silence. Anna spoke first—

"Of course, my name isn't Walker," she murmured inadequately.

They both laughed at that, she nervously and he weakly. The uncertain quality of his laughter made her eye him sharply. "Why, you're trembling—all over," she exclaimed, and then with the faintest curl of her lip, "you'd better sit down if you're as much afraid as all that," her mind ended.

He did sit down, still with that noticeable deference, and, removing his hat, mopped his forehead. His hair was black and curly above a very pleasant brown face, she noted subconsciously, but her conscious self was saying "He was afraid, because he's colored."

He seemed to read her thoughts. "I guess you think I'm a fine rescuer," he smiled at her ruefully. "You see, I'm just beginning to recover from an attack of malarial fever. That is why I pretended to have a gun. I'm afraid I couldn't have tackled him successfully, this plagued fever always leaves me so weak, but I'd have held him off till you had got away. I didn't want him to touch you, you seemed so nice and dainty. I'd been watching you for sometime under the trees, thinking how very American you were and all that sort of thing, and when you smiled it seemed to me such a bit of all right that you should be feeling so fit and self-confident. When I saw the expression on your face change I almost wept to think I hadn't the strength to bash his head in. That was why I waited to catch your eye, because I didn't want to startle you and I didn't have strength for anything but diplomacy."

She nodded, ashamed of her unkindness and interested

already in something else. "Aren't you foreign?" she ventured, "You seem different somehow, something in the way you talk made me feel perhaps you weren't American."

"Well I am," he informed her heartily. "I was born, of all places, in Camden, New Jersey, and if that doesn't make me American I don't know what does. But I've been away a long time, I must admit, that's why my accent sounds a little odd, I suppose. My father went to British Guiana when I was ten; but I got the idea that I wanted to see some more foreign countries, so when I was fifteen I ran away to England. You couldn't imagine, a girl like you, all the things I've seen and done, and the kinds of people I've known. I had such an insatiable thirst for adventure, a sort of compelling curiosity."

He paused, plainly reminiscent.

"I've picked up all sorts of trades in England and France— I love France and it was my stay there that made me long so much to get back to America. I kept the idea before me for years. It seemed to me that to live under a republican form of government, with lots of my own people around me, would be the finest existence in the world. I remember I used to tell a crowd of American chaps I was working with in France about it, and they used to be so amused and seemed to have some sort of secret joke."

Anna thought it highly probable.

He looked at her meditating. "Yes, I suppose they had— from their point of view but not from mine. You see," he told her with an oddly boyish air of bestowing a confidence, "life as life is intensely interesting to me. I wake up every morning—except when I have malarial fever"—he interrupted himself whimsically—"wondering what I'll have to overcome during the day. And it's different things in different environments. In this country it's color, for instance, in another it might be ignorance of the native tongue.

"When I came back to New York I was a little non-plussed, I must confess, at the extraordinary complexes of prejudice. I went to a nice-looking hotel and they didn't want me a bit at first. Well, I pick up the idiom of a language very quickly and I suppose at this point my English accent and expression out-Englished most Englishmen's. After a bit the clerk asked where I hailed from and when I told him Manchester, and displayed my baggage—only I called it luggage—all covered with labels, he said 'oh, that was different,' and gave me a room just as right as you please. Well it struck me so peculiarly idiotic to refuse your own country-man because he is brown, but to take him in, though he hasn't changed a particle, because he hails from another country. But it gave me a clue."

"Yes?" she wondered.

"You see, it made me angry that I had allowed myself to take refuge under my foreign appearance, when what I really wanted to do was to wave my hat and shout, 'I'm an American and I've come home. Aren't you glad to see me? If you only knew how proud I am to be here.' The disappointment and the sting of it kept me awake all night. And next day I went out and met up with some colored fellows—nice chaps all right—and they got me some rooms up in Harlem. Ever see Harlem?" he asked her,—"most interesting place, America done over in color. Well it was just what I wanted after Europe.

"But it struck me there was a lack of self-esteem, a lack of self-appreciation, and a tendency to measure ourselves by false ideals." He was clearly on his hobby now, his deep-set eyes glowed, his wide, pleasant mouth grew firmer.

"Your average British or French man of color and every Eastern man of color thinks no finer creature than himself ever existed. I wanted to tell our folks that there is nothing more supremely American than the colored American, nothing more made-in-America, so to speak. There is no supreme court which rules absolutely that white is the handsomest color, that straight hair is the most alluring. If we could just realize the warmth and background which we supply to America, the mellowness, the rhythm, the music. Heavens," he broke off, "where *does* one ever hear such music as some of the most ordinary colored people can bring out of a piano?"

Anna, thinking of Theophilus, smiled.

"And there's something else too," he resumed. "The cold-bloodedness which enables a civilized people to maim and kill in the Congo and on the Putumayo, or to lynch in Georgia, isn't in it with the simple kindliness which we find in almost any civilized colored man. No people has a keener, more rollicking humor, and the music—

"Excuse my ranting," he begged, all apology, "but I get so excited about it all. Did you ever read any Pater?" he asked her abruptly.

"No," she told him shamefacedly—Pater was not included in her High School English and she had read almost no literature since.

He nodded indifferently. "Well, in 'The Child in the House,' the chap says if he had his way he wouldn't give very poor people 'the things men desire most, but the power to realize and taste at will a certain desirable, clear light in the new morning.' That's me," he concluded, too earnest to care about grammar. "I'd give us the power to realize how wonderful and beautiful and enduring we are in the world's scheme of things. I can't help but feel that finally a man is taken at his own estimate."

They were silent a moment, watching a flock of pale, yellow butterflies waver like an aura over a bed of deep golden crocuses.

"Have you told your views to many people?" Anna asked him a trifle shyly. His mood, his experiences, his whole personality seemed so remote from anything she had ever encountered.

"No," he told her dryly. "I haven't done anything. I came from New York down to this town to visit my aunt, my mother's youngest sister—she's as young as I am, by the way, isn't that funny? And I've had the malarial fever ever since. I get it every spring, darn it!" He ended in total disgust.

"You might tell me something of yourself. We'll probably never see each other again," he suggested lingeringly, with just the faintest question-mark in his voice.

But Anna didn't catch it, she was too absorbed in the prospect of having some one with whom to discuss her perplexities. She launched out without a thought for the amazing unconventionality of the whole situation. "And so," she finished, "here I am painfully teaching French. I don't make enough to allow me to go to summer school and I don't seem to make much progress by myself." He seemed so terribly competent that she hated to let him know how stupid she was. Still, it was a relief to admit it.

"I know," he comforted her. "You needn't feel so very bad, there are some things that just don't come to one. I'm a mechanical engineer and I can read any kind of plans but it worries me to death to have to draw them."

"Why, I can draw," she told him—"anything."

Their first constraint fell upon them.

He tried to break it. "If you teach," he asked her, "What are you doing here? Wednesday isn't a holiday, is it?"

She broke out laughing. "No, it's too funny! You wouldn't

believe how it all happened"—and she told him the story of
the little shepherdess. "And this morning my little cousin
spilt cocoa all over my school clothes and I had to put on my
blue dress. It made me think of the little shepherdess and
here I am."

He was watching her intently. How charming she was
with all that color in her face. Comely, that was the word for
her and—wholesome. He was sure of it.

"How did the story end?" he wondered.

She didn't know, she told him, shamefaced anew at her
stupidity. "You know it is to hard for me, every year we
read a new book and I never get a chance to get used to the
vocabulary. And so the night before I just get the lessons out
for the next day. I teach six preparations, you see, three in
history and three in French. And it takes me such a long
time I never read ahead. I simply cannot get the stuff," she
explained, much downcast.

"I've tried awfully hard; but you know some people have
absolutely no feeling for a foreign language. I'm one of them!
As for composition work"—she shook her head miserably,
"I have to dig for it so. The only thing is that I *can* feel
whether a translation is adequate or not, so I don't mind that
part of the work. But when we got that far in this story the
head language teacher—crazy thing, she's always changing
about—said to lay that aside and finish up all the grammar
and then go back and do all the translating. I've never looked
at the story since. All I know," she ended thoughtlessly, "is
that the shepherdess played and talked with the prince all day
and he took her to the edge of the forest at sunset—what's
the matter?" she broke off.

"You didn't tell me," he said a trifle breathless, "that she
met a prince."

"Didn't I? Well she did—and it's four o'clock and I must

go. My mother will be wondering where I am." She held
out her ungloved hand, shapely and sizeable and very comely.
It took him some time to shake hands, but perhaps that was
one of his foreign ways.

She had gone and he stood staring after her. Then he
settled back on the bench again, hat over his eyes, hands in
his pockets, long legs stretched out in front of him.

"Of course," he was thinking, "you can't say to a girl like
that, 'well, if you're playing shepherdess let me play your
prince?' Wasn't she nice, though, so fine and wholesome—
and colored. What's that thing Tommy was playing last night
with that little Theophilus somebody? Oh yes,"—he hummed
it melodiously:

" *'I'm for you, brown-skin.'* "

# IV

Not until June did Anna encounter the little shepherdess
again.

She settled down the night before the lesson was due to
read it with a great deal of interest. Her meeting with "the
prince," as she always called the strange young man, had left
on her a definite impress. She wondered if ever she would
meet him again, and wished ardently that she might. Her
naiveté and utter lack of self-importance kept her from feeling
piqued at his failure to hunt her up. She wondered often if
life still seemed interesting to him, found herself borrowing
a little of his high ardor. On the whole, her attitude toward
"the adventure," as she loved to call it, was that of the little
shepherdess and she brought back from that day only a mind
"garlanded with pleasant memories."

Perhaps, she thought fancifully that Thursday evening, the

shepherdess meets the prince again and he gives her a position as court artist. And she opened the little text to find out. But that lesson was never prepared, for Theophilus came in at that point with a bleeding gap in his head, caused by falling off a belated ice wagon. The sight of blood always made Mrs. Fetter sick, so Anna had the wound to clean and bind and Theophilus to soothe and get to bed.

So as it happened all she could do was to underline the new words and get their meaning from the vocabulary and trust to the gods that there would be no blind alleys in construction.

Anyone but Anna would have foreseen the end of that fairy-tale. For the prince, with the utter disregard for rank and wealth and training which so much fails to distinguish real princes, sought out the little shepherdess, who had been living most happily and unsuspectingly with her little sheep and her "so pleasant souvenirs" (so said Miss Selena Morton in translation), and besought her to marry him and live forever in his kingdom by the sea.

" 'Oh, sky!' " (thus ran Miss Morton's rendition for the French of "Oh, heavens!"). " 'Oh, sky!' exclaimed the shepherdess, and she told him she would accompany him all willingly, and when the prince had kissed her on both jaws they went on their way. And if you can find a happier ending of this history it is necessary that you go and tell it to the Pope at Rome." Thus, and not otherwise, did Miss Selena Morton mutilate that exquisite story!

But Miss Fetter was too amazed to care. Moreover, Tommy Reynolds and some of the other pupils had translated very well. Perhaps the work in grammar had been the best thing, after all—and perhaps she, too, was becoming a better teacher, she hoped to herself wistfully.

"I'm very much pleased with the work you've done to-day," she told the class. "It seems to me you've improved greatly—particularly Master Reynolds."

And Master Reynolds, who was cleaning the black-boards, smiled inscrutably.

All the way home Anna pondered on something new and sweet in her heart.

"But just think—the first part of the story had come true, why shouldn't the second? Oh, I wish, I wish—" She rushed into the "front-room," where Theophilus sat, his small broken head bandaged up, picking indefatigably at his banjo, and hugged him tumultuously.

He took her caress unmoved, having long ago decided that all women outside of aunts and mothers were crazy. "Look out, you'll break my new strings," he warned her. And she actually begged his pardon and proffered him fifteen cents towards the still visionary ukulele.

One can't go far on the similarity between one incident in one's life and the promise of a French fairy-tale. "Still things do happen," she told herself, surprised at her own tenacity. "Think of how Mr. Allen came into Mrs. Walton's that night and changed my whole life." She went to bed in a maze of rapture and anticipation.

Her mother was interested in a bazaar and dinner for the bazaar workers in the Methodist Church, but she had quarrelled with one of the sisters and she meant to go and arrange her booth and come back, so she shouldn't have to eat at the same table with that benighted Mrs. Vessels.

"I'd rather eat stalled oxen by myself all my days," she told her daughter Saturday morning, "than share the finest victuals at the same table as Pauline Vessels."

"Oh, mother," Anna had wailed, "how *can* you say such things? 'Stalled oxen' *is* the choice thing, the thing you are supposed to want to eat. You've got it upside down."

"Well, what difference does it make?" her mother had retorted, vexed for once. "I'm sure I shouldn't like the stuff, anyway. They'd probably be tough. Don't you let Philly stir out of this house till I come back, Anna. I don't want him to hurt hisself again. Do you think you can manage everything? I swept all the rooms yesterday but the kitchen. There's only that to scrub and the dusting to do."

Anna nodded. She was glad to be alone, glad to have work to do. She sent Theophilus out to clean up the side yard. She could hear him aimlessly pattering about.

"Ann," he called. She had finished scrubbing and all the dusting, too, except in the "front-room," which her mother *would* keep full of useless odds and ends—sheaves of wheat, silly bric-a-brac on what-nots. Ordinarily she hated it, but to-day—"to be alive"—her mind, not usually given to poetical flights, halted—"to be alive," no, "to be *young*," that was it, "to be young was very heaven." And he *had* said in the queerest way, "you didn't say she met a prince." If she could just find out something about him, who he was, where he lived, who *was* his mother's youngest sister. Why, what had she been thinking about to let two months go by without making any inquiry? True, she didn't know many colored people in Marytown, she had never bothered—she had been so concerned with her own affairs—but her mother knew everybody, positively, and a question here or there! Oh, if he only knew how the story ended! She became poetical again—"Would but some winged angel ere too late." She had to smile at that herself. Yet the winged angel was on the way in the person of Theophilus. He couldn't have adopted a more effective disguise.

"Ann," he called again. "C'n I go fishin' now with Tommy Reynolds? I've found all these nice worms in the garden, they'll make grand bait. Aunt (he pronounced it like the name of the humble insect) won't mind. She'd let me go 'n the air'll be good for my head," he wheedled.

Anna, dusting the big Bible, hardly turned around. "No," she told him vigorously, "you can't go, Philly. You must stay till mother comes—she'll be here pretty soon, and you wash your hands and study your lessons a bit. Your last report was dreadful. Tommy Reynolds is only one year older than you and there he is in the second year of the seminary and you still in the graded schools. He plays, but he gets his lessons, too."

And then Theo began to rustle his wings, but neither he nor his cousin heard them.

"Oh, pshaw!" he retorted in disgust. "Tommy don't get no lessons. Someone around his house's always helpin' him— he don't do nothin'. Why, his mother always does his drawin' for him."

"I don't know about his drawing," retorted his cousin, "but I know he does his French. He had a beautiful lesson yesterday. Don't laugh like that, Theophilus, it gets on my nerves."

For Theophilus was laughing shrilly, which perhaps drowned the still louder rustling of the wings.

"There you go," he jibbed, "there you go. He doesn't do his French at all, his uncle does it for him; he did it Thursday night when I was there. I heard him and I ain't tellin' any tales about it, neither," he put in, mistaking the look on her face, "for he said you'd be interested to have him do it for Tommy. He said he'd tell you about it the next time he saw you."

"Theophilus Jackson, you're crazy. I never saw Tommy Reynolds' uncle in my life. I don't even know where they live."

"Well, he's saw you," the child persisted and hesitated and

looked puzzled—"though he did ask an awful lot of questions about you as if he didn't know you. Well, I don't know what he meant, but he did Tommy's French for him, I know that!" he ended in defiance.

Some faint prescience must have come to her mind, for she spoke with unwonted alertness. "He asked about me?" she insisted. "Sit down here, Theo, and tell me all about it. Who is his uncle?"

"Oh, I don't know, you needn't hold me so tight. I ain't goin' to go. Uncle Dick, Tommy calls him, Uncle Dick somethin'—oh—Winter—Mr. Richard Winter I heard Mrs. Reynolds call him. 'Now see here, Mr. Richard Winter,' she said to him—and she's his aunt, Anna, ain't that funny?—and he's bigger'n she and older, I guess, 'cause she looks awful young. I thought aunts were all old like Aunt Em."

She was sure now, and this miserable little boy had known all along. She alternately longed to shake him and hug him. She restrained both desires, knowing that the indulgence of either would dam the fount interminably.

"Go on, Philly," she begged him. "Maybe I can get Sid Williams to let you have the ukulele right away and you can pay him on the installment plan."

"Well, ain't I tellin' you? Tommy and me, we wanted to go to the movies and his mother said, 'No,' he'd got to get all his lessons first, and Tom winked at me and said he had 'em all, and his mother said, 'Not your French,' and Tommy said, 'Well, Uncle Dick's well again now, c'n I ask him to-night?' And just then his uncle walked in and said, 'Hullo, what's it all about?'—he talks so funny, Anna, and Tommy said, 'Please do my translation!' His mother said, 'Not till he's reviewed the first part; then, he hasn't seen the part for two months, because he's been studying something else.' And his uncle said, 'All right, hurry up, kid, because I must

pack, I've got to go away again to-morrow.' And that was
when Tommy's mother said, 'Well, Mr. Richard Winter,
do you own the railway? Why don't you stay in one place?
You've been here and gone again four times in the last two
months!' And he said, 'Oh, Nora, I'm looking for something
and I can't find it.' And she said, 'Did you lose it here?'—
and he answered, awful sad, 'I think I did.' Why doesn't he
buy another one, whatever it is, Cousin Anna?"

"I don't know, dear. Go on—did he say anything else?"

"Uh, huh—my but your face is red! And he said, 'Hit it
up, Thomas-kid,' and Tommy opened the book and began to
read all the silliest stuff about a lady in a park tending goats
in a blue dress, and he said, his uncle did, 'What's that?
What's that?' and he snatched the book away and looked at
it, and he said in the funniest voice, 'I thought you said you
were studyin' German all along. I never realized till this
minute. Who's your teacher, Thomas?' And Tommy said *you*
was. And he said, 'What does she look like?' Tommy said,
'She's awful cute, I must give her that, but she is too darn
strict about her old crazy French,' and I said you was my
cousin, and I told him not to get gay when he talked about
you and if you was strict he needed it. And Mr. Winter said,
'Right-oh!' and asked me a lot of questions, and I said, no,
you weren't pretty, but you were awful nice looking and had
pretty skin and little feet, and he asked me did I ever spill a
cup of cocoa in your lap."

She was on the floor now, her arms around him. "And
what else, Philly. Oh, Philly, what else?"

"Lemme go, Ann, ain't I tellin' you?" He wriggled himself
free. "Oh, yes, and then he said, 'Where does she live?' I
said, 'With me, of course,' and he said, 'Here, in Marytown?'
and I said, 'Yes, 37 Fortner street, near North,' and he
said—oh, he swore, Ann—he said, 'My God, to think she's

been here all this time. Here, boy, gimme that book,' and he sat down and started to read the old silly stuff to Tommy, and I ran out and jumped on the ice wagon and got my head busted. And will you get me the ukulele, Anna?"

She would, she assured him, get him anything, and he could go fishing and she would explain to Aunt Emmeline. "And here, take my apron upstairs with you. Why didn't you tell me before, Philly?"

"Well, what was there to tell, Anna?" he asked her, bewildered.

## V

As soon as her mother should come in she'd bathe and dress and go out—but where? After all she was a girl, she must stand still, she didn't even know Mrs. Reynolds. But she could go by the house—yes, but he was to go away Friday, Theo said—why he *had* gone. Well, he would come back.

The gate clicked. At least, she could tell her mother. But she was crazy—she had only seen him once—well, so had the shepherdess seen the prince only once. Her mother would *have* to understand. What an age she was talking to one of those old Dorcas society sisters! She ran to the door and, of course, it was he on the steps, his hand just raised to knock.

Together they entered the room, silent, a little breathless. Even *he* was frightened. As for Anna—

"You knew I was coming," he told her. "I didn't find out until Thursday. Somehow I thought you lived in another town. You know you said the shepherdess had come such a long, long way, and I thought that meant you had too, and I was afraid to ask you. Oh, I've hunted and hunted, and Tommy, the rascal, told me he was crazy about German because he wanted some illustrated German books he saw in my trunk, and I thought he was studying it," he rushed on breathlessly. "And Thursday night I had to go right away to New York to be sure about something, before I dared to talk to you. And I'm to be a social settlement worker, and I can talk and talk and tell people about all those things," he ended lamely.

Anna stood silent.

"Anna, I thought, I hoped, I wondered"—he stammered. "Oh, do you think you could go with me—I want you so. And don't say you don't know me, we've always known each other, you lovely, brown child." His eyes entreated her.

But she still hung back. "*You* could talk to people about those wonderful things, but I, what could I do?"

"After the war," he explained to her, "we could go back to Europe and I could build bridges and you could draw the plans, and after we had made enough money we could come back and I could preach my gospel—for nothing."

"But, till then?"

"Till then," he whispered, "you could help me live that wonderful fairy-tale. Dear, I love you so"—and he kissed her tenderly, first on one cheek and then on the other.

"On both jaws," she whispered, a bit hysterically.

So then he kissed her on her perfect mouth.

Just then her mother, bidding Sister Pauline Vessels an amicable good-bye at the gate, came up the walk. So, hand in hand, they went to tell her about the happy ending.

# AUNT CALLINE'S SHEAVES

*Leila Amos Pendleton*

No, indeed, chile, I never did believe in taking things frum dead people. You know Aunt Calline Juniper was my mother-in-law and a grander one never hopped, so when she died, me and May Jane Juniper, which married her other son, was awful sorry. We certainly was. As for Uncle John, her husband, he just took on turrible. Everybody loved Aunt Calline and they sent lots of flowers to the funeral and three sheaves of wheat.

Now I never could bear the sight of sheaves of wheat, less they was at the mill, and when all them sheaves come rollin' in to Aunt Calline, I begun to look at 'em cross-eyed. I was in hopes, though, that everybody would forget 'em and they'd be left in the simitary. But no sooner was Aunt Calline covered up than here comes the undertaker with a long face and all three of them sheaves.

Uncle John took 'em very solemn-like, handed one to me and one to May Jane and says, "Chillun, always keep these to 'member Calline. I'll keep one and when I die, Sally, you must take it, as you're the oldest." Ever notice how people are always making you presents of things you hate? "Laws," thinks I to myself, "this is worse than Chrismus." I groaned down in my toes, but didn't say anything outward, and here goes May Jane and me home loaded down with wheat. They was the biggest sheaves I ever seen,—they was small-sized shocks, in fact.

*Crisis* 14 (June 1917): 62–63.

Well, after I got that wheat home, I didn't have a place to put it and every time I cleaned up, I had it to move. "No, indeed," thinks I to myself, "I'll never have a chance to forget Aunt Calline." Finally, the thought struck me to have the sheaf framed, because though I never could like it any better, it would at least be out of the way.

And what do you think that man charged to frame it? Ten dollars! Ten whole dollars! It certainly do seem funny to me how folks are always laying to rob bereaved mourners. Seems like they've made up their minds to git all they can out of you while you're kinder unconscious-like. But I wasn't that much of a mourner, so I carries my wheat home without a frame, and then me and that sheaf has it. Every time I went into the settin' room I was either knocking it down or pickin' it up until I was sick and tired of the sight of it.

One day, about six months after Aunt Calline died, just as I was haulin' that sheaf around, May Jane came in. "May Jane," says I, "how do you like your sheaf?" "Don't like it a tall, Sally." "Well," says I, "I've got a plan, and if you'll stand by me and say nothin', I think we kin fix Aunt Calline's sheaves." So the day when Uncle John and Georgie, which is my husband, and Samyell, which is May Jane's, went over to Rushtown to the hog-killin', I sent for May Jane. "M. J.," says I when she got there; "the men are gone for the day and now's our time. Wrap up your sheaf with a plenty of paper and bring it over here."

When May Jane came back, I had my sheaf all bound up so you couldn't tell what it was, and my hat and coat on. "Sally," says May Jane, very solemn, "What on earth are you going to do?" Says I, "May Jane, foller me." So out we goes with them great bundles and all the neighbors peepin' through their blinds and wonderin' what we had and where we was goin'.

I led May Jane to the horse-cars and as the line ended at our street we set there a while before the car started, both of us feelin' very funeral-like and neither sayin' a word, though May Jane kept a eyein' me as if she wanted to ask some questions. But I kep' lookin' straight ahead with a long face, so she didn't say nothin'.

All of a sudden the conductor broke out singin' "Bringin' in the Sheaves," and the driver joined in the chorus. I never have known how they happened to strike on that hem, but it was too much for us. We looked at each other and then we burst out, and we laughed untel we couldn't see. The driver started up his horses and the conductor looked at us as if he thought we was daft, but that did not hender us from laughin'.

As soon as she could speak, May Jane says, "Sally Ann Juniper, you have just got to tell me what you're goin' to do." "May Jane," says I, "we air goin' to carry these sheaves right straight to Aunt Calline. That's what. When people gives things to dead people, they wants 'em to have 'em. That's why they gives 'em sheaves and pillers and pams and such instid of pincushions and calendars and postcards, and I believe in lettin' dead people have everything that belongs to 'em." May Jane got pop-eyed but she never said a word.

So we carried that wheat out and laid it on Aunt Calline's grave and I hope she feels satisfied. We do if she don't. But one quare thing about it is that neither Georgie nor Samyell has ever inquired after them tributes. I believe in my soul that they was just as tired of 'em as we was. As for Uncle John, he went to desperate courtin' of that little sixteen-year-old Simmins gal just six weeks after Aunt Calline had been put away. He tried to git Cannie Simmins to accept him as a husband, and his sheaf as a bokay, but she wouldn't have neither, so that wheat offering is still willed to me. But if I should be the longest liver, I mean to see to it that sheaf number three is left in the simitary on top of Uncle John.

# LENORA'S CONVERSION

*Edna May Harrold*

It all started on the day Gaynell, Lenora, and I decided to pay our first visit to Mrs. Holman, whose husband had just been assigned to the pastorate of our church. I had dressed and was waiting when Lenora came with the news that Gaynell was at home with an aching tooth, but that she would join us in an hour's time if she felt better. So Lenora and I prepared to relieve the tedium of waiting with a game of cards, mother being absent. We were just beginning the second game of "Seven Up" when foot-steps sounded on the walk. Discovery was imminent; quickly stuffing the deck of cards into my blouse pocket I seized the morning paper and was reading reports of the cotton and zinc markets to Lenora when mother came in.

An hour had passed and Gaynell had not come. Lenora and I started out to pay our call without her. The Reverend Mr. Holman, himself, answered our ring and ushered us very courteously into the parlor where Mrs. Holman sat knitting. After we had talked awhile, she asked us if we were Christians and seemed pained when we said, "No." Then she asked us if we would not care to give our souls to God. Lenora sighed and murmured something about wishing to do better, but I said nothing because for some reason I was beginning to feel uneasy. Then Mr. Holman spoke: "There is no reason why these dear children should not become

*Crisis* 15 (Feb. 1918): 171–73.

soldiers for Christ," he said. "God wants the lambs in His fold. Now is the time to give Him your hearts; now, while they are tender and comparatively free from sin."

"There is no time like the present," said Mrs. Holman, rising. "Reverend, pray that these darling girls' hearts may be touched, and that they may accept the Master now."

So we all knelt down and as the pastor opened his mouth to pray I shifted my position just a little and—luck of the luckless—those cards fell out of my pocket!

Well, as real authors say: "Let us draw a curtain over the painful scene that followed." Somehow I managed to get away from that house, but not before I had been shown several reasons why I, if no one else in town, needed religion badly.

The following Sunday Mr. Holman started a revival. The services lasted a week and on the last night Lenora joined the church. When Mr. Holman asked her to testify, she said she felt so happy and wished her sinful companions would follow her step. Her heart, she said, was too full for words; then she began to sing: "Though Your Sins Be As Scarlet," looking straight at me! Gaynell chuckled right out, but I sat there hating everybody and *especially* that unknown person who invented the first card game.

Lenora's conversion caused much happiness among the older members of the church, but most of her young friends took a different view of the situation. Lenora had always been a jolly girl, popular with nearly everyone, but now her conduct showed a marked change. She shunned all of the girls except Gaynell and myself, and into our unhappy ears she was continually pouring tales of the Joys of Salvation and imploring us to give up the pleasures of this wicked world before it was too late.

"Lenora," I said, one day after she had spent half an hour or more pitying our unsaved state, "you talk like Gaynell and

I are simply steeped in sin. I'm not saying a word against you having religion, but I really don't see what we have done that is so very, very sinful."

"You really don't, Belle?" Lenora asked, and her eyes narrowed. "Well, maybe you have forgotten that miserable card episode, but I haven't and never shall."

Of course, that made me furious, and I said: "No, Miss Angel, I haven't forgotten that 'card episode,' as you call it, and I know you haven't. Nor have Mr. Holman and Mrs. Holman forgotten. It didn't make any difference to any of you that I cried myself sick and apologized a dozen times. It seems to me that if you all had so much religion you'd forget it and forgive me, too, instead of always throwing it in my face!"

Gaynell said, "Belle, be careful"; but Lenora replied very gently: "I'm only telling you for your own good, and I'll forgive all you have said to me because 'Blessed are ye when men shall revile you,' you know," and she walked off, leaving me too angry for words.

"Gaynell," I said, "I know it's wrong, but I do wish something would happen to bring Lenora down from her pedestal. If Mr. and Mrs. Holman could only see that their idol's feet are made of clay, my cup of joy would overflow."

"I know how you feel," said Gaynell, "but nothing will ever happen to Lenora. She doesn't go any place, but to church." And so we were plunged into despair, forgetting that the darkest hour is just before the dawn.

Then about ten days before school opened Mrs. Greenway issued invitations to a dance in honor of her son, Henry, who was going away to begin his first term in college. It rained during the whole of the day set for the dance, but when night came the weather cleared and the stars twinkled in the sky and I was glad just to be alive.

552 *Edna May Harrold*

Gaynell and I went to the dance together. We didn't say much, but deep in my heart I was thinking of Lenora and I know Gaynell was, too. I remembered how she loved dancing and I couldn't help feeling glad I wasn't converted when I thought of all Lenora was going to miss that evening.

The first ten minutes or so after we arrived at Mrs. Greenway's, we were very busy getting our dance cards filled.

Then the music started and everyone was searching through the crowd for their partner for that dance, when Gaynell clutched my arm.

"For mercy sakes," she whispered, "look, it's Lenora!"

It *was* Lenora.

And even as I looked, amazed, I saw Henry Greenway approach her eagerly and whirl her away in the dance.

Lenora's backsliding created as much comment as her conversion. The Reverend Mr. Holman and his wife prayed over their fallen idol and bade her think of the fate of those who set their faces toward the Light and then turned back. Some of the old people said it was a wonder that Lenora had held out as long as she did, considering Gaynell and myself. Others said Lenora didn't have much religion in the first place, or she would not have lost it so easily. I inclined to the last opinion myself, but I said nothing, for I was glad Lenora had ceased trying to be an angel and had become human once more.

# AT THE TURN
# OF THE ROAD
## *A Story*

*Helen G. Ricks*

At the turn of the road,
  There'll be luck to share;
At the turn of the road,
  Silver and gold and a dream to spare,
And a host of sunny sweet days and fair,
  And all that you wish for most out there,
At the turn of the road.

It wasn't Christmas Day, but it was *Christmas* in the heart of
Mr. Jimps. There seemed never a time when there wasn't
some sort of a smile on his wholesome brown face. Sometimes
it was one of those right-up-from-the-heart smiles; sometimes
just one of those sudden-willing smiles,—but always a smile.

Many a spring with violets and robins, many a summer
with June and summer loveliness; many an autumn with
symphonies in gold and brown; many a winter in snowy
whiteness had all come and gone; but each had found Mr.
Jimps contented in the little hut at the turn of the road.

Pedestrians of every type through many years had stopped
to talk to this village character as they had passed and always
had left him filled with a newer zeal and a keener happiness.
Mr. Jimps possessed the great gift of human understanding
and in his heart there lived nothing but a love for his

*Crisis* 17 (Dec. 1918): 64–66.

fellowmen. There was in his kindly face an expression of his own ideals. The encouragement which he had so generously given to individuals all along the way was never to be measured.

On this particular afternoon it was snowing, seemingly with the one thought of preparedness for the Christmas Day, which was only two days distant. The old man sat nodding by an eastern window, pipe between his teeth, glasses tilted perilously on his nose, and an open book on his knee. Finally he aroused himself.

"Well, a-noddin' still and a-snowin' still. Fire all low and supper-time. Mr. Jimps, it looks like you had better oust yourself together smartly-soon."

Busied with the reflections of the duties before him, he had not seen the stranger approaching the hut (struggling up the snow-covered road), and was a little startled when the rap came.

"Howdy, friend. Come in and warm yourself. I'll have a blaze sputtering in a slim few minutes. Are you in a hurry?"

"There is no hurry, my friend," was the laconic reply.

Commonplaces were exchanged during the simple meal, and the stranger rose to go.

"I thank you, Mr. Jimps, for your generous hospitality to me, a stranger. Before leaving you, may I ask you a question?"

"As many as you wish, my friend."

"Why do you *always* smile?"

"Because it is the easiest way, I find."

"Perhaps it is better, but how find it easier? I find nothing in all the world worth smiling for."

"What? With Christmas coming!—aye, even with Christmas gone!"

"Mr. Jimps, I have come to the place where the morning of another day is never welcome."

"Sit down, friend. Let me tell you a story."

Outside the flakes of snow descended noiselessly. Inside the hut there was a stillness. Tenderly Mr. Jimps laid down his pipe.

"There came a day into my life when I not only felt the meaning of your words but lived them. It seems to me that when an unhappiness comes, it comes only after some great happiness has just passed. A month before *she* had given me her promise of fidelity and love. I had been saving all along with just a hope,—saving for the little home our dreams had built. Young we were and happy. She was a woman wonderful,—the greatest gift God ever gave to man. I remember the night of her promise. There were cornflowers,—cornflowers of an unforgettable spring. We do not know what love is,—we know it just *is*. But the story!

"I had just finished high school two years before and had been doing all kinds of jobs in the little town, earning the dollars required to pay for the little farm where we were both to be just happy. One particular job was that of janitor in the largest bank. My mother and I lived alone. Returning one night from work I entered my home where officers of the law stood waiting to arrest me. Seven hundred dollars had been stolen from the bank. I was accused. Our home had been searched. My saving budget contained just two hundred dollars. The sentence was fifteen years. During that time my mother died, and the girl—her heart broke first and then she passed away. That was fifty years ago, my friend.

"For years I wandered only with a bitterness burning in my heart,—a bitterness toward man and his injustice. With all the heart-break, there never came a bitterness toward God. Still when birds sang, their songs seemed a mockery to me. The most beautiful of melodies seemed just like little lost tunes too tired to die. Even the sunshine hurt. I hated everything. My life seemed useless,—as useless as a Jimpson weed; so I called myself plain Mr. Jimps.

"Then twenty years after my Shadow, sick and heart-sore, I came to a stranger's cabin,—just as you have come to mine. It was two days before Christmas, and, yes,—it was snowing. While we were sitting there a gust of wind blew open the door and blew in the tiniest sprite of a lad, all snow covered, all smiles. 'Hey, Grandpa. It's a booster out there for sure, but I got your tobacco and the other stuff.' And then he noticed me and removed his cap. 'Evenin', sir.' I nodded and spoke to the child in my usual tone. 'Pardon me, mister, but didn't you forget to smile?' "

Mr. Jimps wiped a tear from the corner of his eye, rememberingly.

"Friend, from that hour on I have been *always* smiling. Why not? There were more heart breaks than my own. After all, it was a love-world; and there could come a peace from simply mending hearts. The friendly comfort of that old man and the radiant cheer from that child-heart, untouched, warmed the littleness of my own worn heart.

"After leaving the shelter of that home I wandered through the snow until I came to this poor hut on Christmas Day. From that day until this have I lived here, my friend—here at the turn of the road. My little garden furnishes my living and my friends of the wayside, who come, furnish me my pleasures. People have wondered how life could slip by me, leaving of its joys and sorrows scarcely a trace. It has been because I have been happy in trying to be happy in smiling at the shadows and the sunshine both. And so each day I sit here waiting patiently for the Joy I feel shall come someday to me—at the turn of the road."

The guest of the roadside hut rose falteringly. "Mr. Jimps, your words have been both a salvation and a happiness. Someday I shall return." The stranger *smiled* his farewell from the door as he trudged on his way.

Christmas morning came in a flurry of snowflakes. Mr. Jimps after clearing away the breakfast dishes spread out the numerous parcels, ribbon-wrapped and otherwise, that had come the day before. Few of his wayside acquaintances and friends from the village had forgotten his roadside cordiality. His old heart was indeed cheered as he viewed these tokens of appreciation.

The last package unopened lay at the end of the table. It was a copy of Henry Van Dyke's story of "The Other Wise Man." On the flyleaf was this inscription: "To him, who in his kindly way opened forever the heart of a stranger of yesterday."

Mr. Jimps smiled understandingly as he turned the pages. A few hours later he looked up from his new book and through the eastern window. A figure was plodding faithfully through the snow. The old man opened the door and looked out.

"Hey! over there," called a fresh young voice. "The turn of this old road has got me fussed *some more!* Know any old guy around here by the name of Jimps?"

"This is the offender. How best can I serve you, this Merry Christmas?"

"Merry Christmas, yourself—here's a 'special.' I've been tracking around here an hour or two. Oh, no, thanks—must be moving on."

The envelope slid to the floor as Mr. Jimps held shakingly the letter from the old attorney's son.

Chelsea, Virginia,
December 17, 1916.

James Avery—

Dear Friend:—

For ten years we have sought vainly to locate you. The thief of fifty years ago confessed, exonerating you entirely. In the Citizens Savings Bank ten thousand dollars is accredited to your name,—a gift from the stockholders and the towns-people. This is not an effort to make amends—no amends can be made.

We beg you to return to your home and honor its citizens.

Very truly yours,

HOWARD KILTHROP, JR.

Mr. Jimps sat down before the fire. Two tears fell, one on the wrinkled brown hand, and one on the crumpled white linen sheet. Tenderly he smoothed out the letter and smiled.

"Fifty years! but it came—at the turn of the road."

# MARY ELIZABETH
## *A Story*

*Jessie Fauset*

Mary Elizabeth was late that morning. As a direct result, Roger left for work without telling me good-bye, and I spent most of the day fighting the headache which always comes if I cry.

For I cannot get a breakfast. I can manage a dinner,—one just puts the roast in the oven and takes it out again. And I really excel in getting lunch. There is a good delicatessen near us, and with dainty service and flowers, I get along very nicely. But breakfast! In the first place, it's a meal I neither like nor need. And I never, if I live a thousand years, shall learn to like coffee. I suppose that is why I cannot make it.

"Roger," I faltered, when the awful truth burst upon me and I began to realize that Mary Elizabeth wasn't coming, "Roger, couldn't you get breakfast downtown this morning? You know last time you weren't so satisfied with my coffee."

Roger was hostile. I think he had just cut himself, shaving. Anyway, he was horrid.

"No, I can't get my breakfast downtown!" He actually snapped at me. "Really, Sally, I don't believe there's another woman in the world who would send her husband out on a morning like this on an empty stomach. I don't see how you can be so unfeeling."

Well, it wasn't "a morning like this," for it was just the beginning of November. And I had only proposed his doing what I knew he would have to do eventually.

*Crisis* 19 (Dec. 1919): 51–56.

I didn't say anything more, but started on that breakfast. I don't know why I thought I had to have hot cakes! The breakfast really was awful! The cakes were tough and gummy and got cold one second, exactly, after I took them off the stove. And the coffee boiled, or stewed, or scorched, or did whatever the particular thing is that coffee shouldn't do. Roger sawed at one cake, took one mouthful of the dreadful brew, and pushed away his cup.

"It seems to me you might learn to make a decent cup of coffee," he said icily. Then he picked up his hat and flung out of the house.

I think it is stupid of me, too, not to learn how to make coffee. But, really, I'm no worse than Roger is about lots of things. Take "Five Hundred." Roger knows I love cards, and with the Cheltons right around the corner from us and as fond of it as I am, we could spend many a pleasant evening. But Roger will not learn. Only the night before, after I had gone through a whole hand with him, with hearts as trumps, I dealt the cards around again to imaginary opponents and we started playing. Clubs were trumps, and spades led. Roger, having no spades, played triumphantly a Jack of Hearts and proceeded to take the trick.

"But, Roger," I protested, "you threw off."

"Well," he said, deeply injured, "didn't you say hearts were trumps when you were playing before?"

And when I tried to explain, he threw down the cards and wanted to know what difference it made; he'd rather play casino, anyway! I didn't go out and slam the door.

But I couldn't help from crying this particular morning. I not only value Roger's good opinion, but I hate to be considered stupid.

Mary Elizabeth came in about eleven o'clock. She is a

small, weazened woman, very dark, somewhat wrinkled, and a model of self-possession. I wish I could make you see her, or that I could reproduce her accent, not that it is especially colored,—Roger's and mine are much more so—but her pronunciation, her way of drawing out her vowels, is so distinctively Mary Elizabethan!

I was ashamed of my red eyes and tried to cover up my embarrassment with sternness.

"Mary Elizabeth," said I, "you are late!" Just as though she didn't know it.

"Yas'm, Mis' Pierson," she said, composedly, taking off her coat. She didn't remove her hat,—she never does until she has been in the house some two or three hours. I can't imagine why. It is a small, black, dusty affair, trimmed with black ribbon, some dingy white roses and a sheaf of wheat. I give Mary Elizabeth a dress and hat now and then, but, although I recognize the dress from time to time, I never see any change in the hat. I don't know what she does with my ex-millinery.

"Yas'm," she said again, and looked comprehensively at the untouched breakfast dishes and the awful viands, which were still where Roger had left them.

"Looks as though you'd had to git breakfast yoreself," she observed brightly. And went out in the kitchen and ate all those cakes and drank that unspeakable coffee! Really she did, and she didn't warm them up either.

I watched her miserably, unable to decide whether Roger was too finicky or Mary Elizabeth a natural-born diplomat.

"Mr. Gales led me an awful chase last night," she explained. "When I got home yistiddy evenin', my cousin whut keeps house fer me (!) tole me Mr. Gales went out in the mornin' en hadn't come back."

"Mr. Gales," let me explain, is Mary Elizabeth's second husband, an octogenarian, and the most original person, I am convinced, in existence.

"Yas'm," she went on, eating a final cold hot-cake, "en I went to look fer 'im, en had the whole perlice station out all night huntin' 'im. Look like they wusn't never goin' to find 'im. But I ses, 'Jes' let me look fer enough en long enough en I'll find 'im,' I ses, en I did. Way out Georgy Avenue, with the hat on ole Mis' give 'im. Sent it to 'im all the way fum Chicaga. He's had it fifteen years,—high silk beaver. I knowed he wusn't goin' too fer with that hat on.

"I went up to 'im, settin' by a fence all muddy, holdin' his hat on with both hands. En I ses, 'Look here, man, you come erlong home with me, en let me put you to bed.' En he come jest as meek! No-o-me, I knowed he wusn't goin' fer with ole Mis' hat on."

"Who was old 'Mis,' Mary Elizabeth?" I asked her.

"Lady I used to work fer in Noo York," she informed me. "Me en Rosy, the cook, lived with her fer years. Old Mis' was turrible fond of me, though her en Rosy used to querrel all the time. Jes' seemed like they couldn't git erlong. 'Member once Rosy run after her one Sunday with a knife, en I kep 'em apart. Reckon Rosy musta bin right put out with ole Mis' that day. By en by her en Rosy move to Chicaga, en when I married Mr. Gales, she sent 'im that hat. That old white woman shore did like me. It's so late, reckon I'd better put off sweepin' tel termorrer, ma'am."

I acquiesced, following her about from room to room. This was partly to get away from my own doleful thoughts—Roger really had hurt my feelings—but just as much to hear her talk. At first I used not to believe all she said, but after

I investigated once and found her truthful in one amazing statement, I capitulated.

She had been telling me some remarkable tale of her first husband and I was listening with the stupefied attention, to which she always reduces me. Remember she was speaking of her first husband.

"En I ses to 'im, I ses, 'Mr. Gale,—' "

"Wait a moment, Mary Elizabeth," I interrupted, meanly delighted to have caught her for once. "You mean your first husband, don't you?"

"Yas'm," she replied. "En I ses to 'im, 'Mr. Gale! I ses—' "

"But, Mary Elizabeth," I persisted, "that's your second husband, isn't it,—Mr. Gale?"

She gave me her long-drawn "No-o-me! My first husband was Mr. Gale and my second is Mr. *Gales*. He spells his name with a Z, I reckon. I ain't never see it writ. Ez I wus sayin', I ses to Mr. Gale—"

*And it was true!* Since then I have never doubted Mary Elizabeth.

She was loquacious that afternoon. She told me about her sister, "where's got a home in the country and where's got eight children." I used to read Lucy Pratt's stories about little Ephraim or Ezekiel, I forget his name, who always said "where's" instead of "who's," but I never believed it really till I heard Mary Elizabeth use it. For some reason or other she never mentions her sister without mentioning the home, too. "My sister where's got a home in the country" is her unvarying phrase.

"Mary Elizabeth," I asked her once, "does your sister live in the country, or does she simply own a house there?"

"Yas'm," she told me.

She is fond of her sister. "If Mr. Gales wus to die," she told me complacently, "I'd go to live with her."

"If he should die," I asked her idly, "would you marry again?"

"Oh, no-o-me!" She was emphatic. "Though I don't know why I shouldn't, I'd come by it hones'. My father wus married four times."

That shocked me out of my headache. "Four times, Mary Elizabeth, and you had all those stepmothers!" My mind refused to take it in.

"Oh, no-o-me! I always lived with mamma. She was his first wife."

I hadn't thought of people in the state in which I had instinctively placed Mary Elizabeth's father and mother as indulging in divorce, but as Roger says slangily, "I wouldn't know."

Mary Elizabeth took off the dingy hat. "You see, papa and mamma—" the ineffable pathos of hearing this woman of sixty-four, with a husband of eighty, use the old childish terms!

"Papa and mamma wus slaves, you know, Mis' Pierson, and so of course they wusn't exackly married. White folks wouldn't let 'em. But they wus awf'ly in love with each other. Heard mamma tell erbout it lots of times, and how papa wus the han'somest man! Reckon she wus long erbout sixteen or seventeen then. So they jumped over a broomstick, en they wus jes as happy! But not long after I come erlong, they sold papa down South, and mamma never see him no mo' fer years and years. Thought he was dead. So she married again."

"And he came back to her, Mary Elizabeth?" I was overwhelmed with the woefulness of it.

"Yas'm. After twenty-six years. Me and my sister where's got a home in the country—she's really my half-sister, see

Mis' Pierson,—her en mamma en my step-father en me wus
all down in Bumpus, Virginia, workin' fer some white folks,
and we used to live in a little cabin, had a front stoop to it.
En one day an ole cullud man come by, had a lot o' whiskers.
I'd saw him lots of times there in Bumpus, lookin' and peerin'
into every cullud woman's face. En jes' then my sister she
call out, 'Come here, you Ma'y Elizabeth,' en that old man
stopped, en he looked at me en he looked at me, en he ses to
me, 'Chile, is yo' name Ma'y Elizabeth?'

"You know, Mis' Pierson, I thought he wus jes' bein'
fresh, en I ain't paid no 'tention to 'im. I ain't sed nuthin'
ontel he spoke to me three or four times, en then I ses to
'im, 'Go 'way fum here, man, you ain't got no call to be
fresh with me. I'm a decent woman. You'd oughta be ashamed
of yoreself, an ole man like you.' "

Mary Elizabeth stopped and looked hard at the back of
her poor wrinkled hands.

"En he says to me, 'Daughter,' he ses, jes' like that,
'daughter,' he ses, 'hones' I ain't bein' fresh. Is yo' name
shore enough Ma'y Elizabeth?'

"En I tole him, 'Yas'r.'

" 'Chile,' he ses, 'whar is yo' daddy?'

" 'Ain't got no daddy,' I tole him peart-like. 'They done
tuk 'im away fum me twenty-six years ago, I wusn't but a
mite of a baby. Sol' 'im down the river. My mother often
talks about it.' And, oh, Mis' Pierson, you shoulda see the
glory come into his face!

" 'Yore mother!' he ses, kinda out of breath, 'yore mother!
Ma'y Elizabeth, whar is your mother?'

" 'Back thar on the stoop,' I tole 'im. 'Why, did you know
my daddy?'

"But he didn't pay no 'tention to me, jes' turned and walked
up the stoop whar mamma wus settin'! She was feelin' sorta

porely that day. En you oughta see me steppin' erlong after
'im.

"He walked right up to her and giv' her one look. 'Oh,
Maggie,' he shout out, 'oh, Maggie! Ain't you know me?
Maggie, ain't you know me?'

"Mamma look at 'im and riz up outa her cheer. 'Who're
you?' she ses kinda trimbly, 'callin' me Maggie thata way?
Who're you?'

"He went up real close to her, then, 'Maggie,' he ses jes'
like that, kinda sad 'n tender, 'Maggie!' And hel' out his
arms.

"She walked right into them. 'Oh,' she ses, 'it's Cassius!
It's Cassius! It's my husban' come back to me! It's Cassius!'
They wus like two mad people.

"My sister Minnie and me, we jes' stood and gawped at
'em. There they wus, holding on to each other like two pitiful
childrun, en he tuk her hands and kissed 'em.

" 'Maggie,' he ses, 'you'll come away with me, won't you?
You gona take me back, Maggie? We'll go away, you en
Ma'y Elizabeth en me. Won't we, Maggie?'

"Reckon my mother clean fergot my stepfather. 'Yes,
Cassius,' she ses, 'we'll go away.' And then she sees Minnie,
en it all comes back to her. 'Oh, Cassius,' she ses, 'I cain't
go with you, I'm married again, en this time fer real. This
here gal's mine and three boys, too, and another chile comin'
in November!' "

"But she went with him, Mary Elizabeth," I pleaded.
"Surely she went with him after all those years. He really
was her husband."

I don't know whether Mary Elizabeth meant to be sarcastic
or not. "Oh, no-o-me, mamma couldn't a done that. She wus
a good woman. Her ole master, whut done sol' my father
down river, brung her up too religious fer that, en anyways,

papa was married again, too. Had his fourth wife there in Bumpus with 'im."

The unspeakable tragedy of it!

I left her and went up to my room, and hunted out my dark-blue serge dress which I had meant to wear again that winter. But I had to give Mary Elizabeth something, so I took the dress down to her.

She was delighted with it. I could tell she was, because she used her rare and untranslatable expletive.

"Haytian!" she said. "My sister where's got a home in the country, got a dress looks somethin' like this, but it ain't as good. No-o-me. She got hers to wear at a friend's weddin',— gal she was riz up with. Thet gal married well, too, lemme tell you; her husband's a Sunday School sup'rintender."

I told her she needn't wait for Mr. Pierson, I would put dinner on the table. So off she went in the gathering dusk, trudging bravely back to her Mr. Gales and his high silk hat.

I watched her from the window till she was out of sight. It had been such a long time since I had thought of slavery. I was born in Pennsylvania, and neither my parents nor grandparents had been slaves; otherwise I might have had the same tale to tell as Mary Elizabeth, or worse yet, Roger and I might have lived in those black days and loved and lost each other and futilely, damnably, met again like Cassius and Maggie.

Whereas it was now, and I had Roger and Roger had me.

How I loved him as I sat there in the hazy dusk. I thought of his dear, bronze perfection, his habit of swearing softly in excitement, his blessed stupidity. Just the same I didn't meet him at the door as usual, but pretended to be busy. He came rushing to me with the *Saturday Evening Post*, which is more to me than rubies. I thanked him warmly, but aloofly, if you can get that combination.

We ate dinner almost in silence for my part. But he praised everything,—the cooking, the table, my appearance.

After dinner we went up to the little sitting-room. He hoped I wasn't tired,—couldn't he fix the pillows for me? So!

I opened the magazine and the first thing I saw was a picture of a woman gazing in stony despair at the figure of a man disappearing around the bend of the road. It was too much. Suppose that were Roger and I! I'm afraid I sniffled. He was at my side in a moment.

"Dear loveliest! Don't cry. It was all my fault. You aren't any worse about coffee than I am about cards! And anyway, I needn't have slammed the door! Forgive me, Sally. I always told you I was hard to get along with. I've had a horrible day,—don't stay cross with me, dearest."

I held him to me and sobbed outright on his shoulder. "It isn't you, Roger," I told him, "I'm crying about Mary Elizabeth."

I regret to say he let me go then, so great was his dismay. Roger will never be half the diplomat that Mary Elizabeth is.

"Holy smokes!" he groaned. "She isn't going to leave us for good, is she?"

So then I told him about Maggie and Cassius. "And oh, Roger," I ended futilely, "to think that they had to separate after all those years, when he had come back, old and with whiskers!" I didn't mean to be so banal, but I was crying too hard to be coherent.

Roger had got up and was walking the floor, but he stopped then aghast.

"Whiskers!" he moaned. "My hat! Isn't that just like a

woman?" He had to clear his throat once or twice before he could go on, and I think he wiped his eyes.

"Wasn't it the—" I really can't say what Roger said here,— "wasn't it the darndest hard luck that when he did find her again, she should be married? She might have waited."

I stared at him astounded. "But, Roger," I reminded him, "he had married three other times, he didn't wait."

"Oh—!" said Roger, unquotably, "married three fiddle-sticks! He only did that to try to forget her."

Then he came over and knelt beside me again. "Darling, I do think it is a sensible thing for a poor woman to learn how to cook, but I don't care as long as you love me and we are together. Dear loveliest, if I had been Cassius,"—he caught my hands so tight that he hurt them,"—and I had married fifty times and had come back and found you married to someone else, I'd have killed you, killed you."

Well, he wasn't logical, but he was certainly convincing.

So thus, and not otherwise, Mary Elizabeth healed the breach.

# EL TISICO *

*Anita Scott Coleman*

"What is patriotism?" shouted O'Brady, the Irish engineer, as peppery as he was good-natured. He was showing signs of his rising choler faster and faster as the heated argument grew in intensity.

He argued that it was a thing men put before their wives, and Tim held that it couldn't be compared with love-making and women.

"Cut it, boys, and listen to this," broke in Sam Dicks, a grizzled old trainman, who had more yarns in his cranium, than a yellow cur has fleas on a zig-zag trail between his left ear and his hind right leg.

"Fire up," roared the crowd of us.

The debate on patriotism had started between O'Brady and Tim Brixtner in the Santa Fé restroom. It was a typical scene,—the long paper-strewn table occupying the center space, and sturdy sons of America—hard-muscled, blue chinned, steady-nerved, rail-road men—lounging around it. Over in the alcove, upon a raised platform, three colored men, who styled themselves, "The Black Trio," were resting after their creditable performance. They had given us some of the best string music from banjo, mandolin, and guitar, I have ever heard.

One of them, a big, strapping, ebony fellow, minus an arm, had a baritone voice worth a million, headed under

* The Consumptive.

*Crisis* 19 (March 1920): 252–53.

different color. He sang "Casey Jones"—not a classic—but take it from me, a great one among our kind. He sure sang it. . . .

A colored youngster, whom they carried about with them, had just finished passing the hat. It had been all both hands could do to carry it back to "The Black Trio." I, myself, had flung in five bucks, the price I'd pay, maybe, to go to a swell opera.

The guy who played the banjo was a glowing-eyed, flat-chested fellow with a cough, which he used some frequent.

I lit my pipe, and O'Brady and Brixtner and the rest lit theirs. Sam Dicks was about to begin when the "Trio" showed signs of departing. He left us with, "Wait a bit boys," and went to them. He gave the glad hand to the glowing-eyed, coughing one, with a genuine friendship grip. He came back ready for us.

"In the early nineties I was working with Billy Bartell, the greatest daredevil and the squarest that ever guided a throttle. We made our runs through that portion of the country which is sure God's handiwork, if anything is. It always strikes me as being miraculous to see the tropic weather of old Mex and the temperate weather of our U.S., trying to mix as it does along the border. It gives us a climate you can't beat—but the landscape, sun-baked sand, prairie-dog holes, and cactus with mountains dumped indiscriminately everywhere, all covered by a sky that's a dazzle of blue beauty, is what I call God's handiwork, because it can't be called anything else.

"At one of our stops in one of Mexico's little mud cities, a colored family,—father, mother, and baby—boarded the train. The woman was like one of those little, pearly-grey doves we shoot in New Mexico, from August to November— a little, fluttery thing, all heart and eyes.

"When they got on, their baby was a mere bundle, so no

one noticed its illness. But it was soon all aboard that a sick kid was on. He *was* a sick kid, too: so sick that every mother's son on that train felt sorry and wanted to do something.

"The mother's eyes grew brighter and brighter, and the father kept watching his kid and pulling out his big, gold watch. The baby grew worse.

"In some way, as the intimate secrets of our heart sometimes do, it crept out that the family was trying to get over to the U.S. side before the baby died. We still had an eight hour run, and the baby was growing worse, faster than an engine eats up coal.

"The mother's eyes scanned the country for familiar signs. Every time I passed through that coach and saw her, I was minded of the way wounded birds beat their wings on the hard earth in an effort to fly. To all our attempted condolence, she replied with the same words:

" 'If he lives until we get home—if he lives till we get home.'

"Billy Bartell always knew who his passengers were. He used to say he didn't believe in hauling whole lots of unknown baggage. So he knew that we carried the sick kid. We passed word to him that the kid was worse, and what his parents were aiming for.

"Well, boys, after that, our train went faster than a whirligig in a Texas cyclone. The landscape—cactus, prairie-dog holes, and mountains, rolled into something compact and smooth as a khaki-colored canvas, and flashed past us like sheets of lightning. We steamed into Nogales. The depot was on the Mexican side, but the coach with the sick kid landed fair and square upon American sod.

"The little colored woman with her baby in her arms, alighted on good old American turf. She turned in acknowledgement to the kindness she had received, to wave her hand at the engine and its engineer, at the coaches and all the passengers, at everything, because she was so glad.

"If the kid died, it would be in America—at home."

Old Dicks paused a moment before querying, "Boys, did you get it?"

"You bet," spoke up Brixtner. "That's patriotism. Now, Pat O'Brady! 'Twasn't no man and woman affair either," he cried, eager to resume their interrupted debate.

"Wait a minute, fellows," pleaded Dicks, "wait."

"I want to know, did the kid live?" somebody asked.

"That's what I want to tell," said Dicks.

"Eh, you Tim! Cut it, cut it. . . ."

"That little banjo picker was the kid whose parents did not want him to die out of sight of the Stars and Stripes."

A long-drawn "phew" fairly split the air,—we were so surprised.

"Yes," said he, "and he has never been well, always sick. He's what the Mexicans call, 'el Tisico.' "

"Scat. . . . He isn't much of a prize!"

"What's he done to back up his parents' sentiments?"

"He sure can't fight." These were the words exploded from one to the other.

"Do you know what 'The Black Trio' do with their money?" asked Dicks, pride modulating his voice.

"Well—I—guess—not," drawled someone from among the bunch.

"Every red cent of it is turned into the American Red Cross—do you get me?" And old Dicks unfolded the evening paper and began to read.

"Be Gad, that's patriotism, too," shouted O'Brady. "Can any son-of-a-gun define it?"

# THE SLEEPER WAKES
## *A Novelette in Three Instalments*

*Jessie Fauset*

## [I]

Amy recognized the incident as the beginning of one of her phases. Always from a child she had been able to tell when "something was going to happen." She had been standing in Marshall's store, her young, eager gaze intent on the lovely little sample dress which was not from Paris, but quite as dainty as anything that Paris could produce. It was not the lines or even the texture that fascinated Amy so much, it was the grouping of colors—of shades. She knew the combination was just right for her.

"Let me slip it on, Miss," said the saleswoman suddenly. She had nothing to do just then, and the girl was so evidently charmed and so pretty—it was a pleasure to wait on her.

"Oh no," Amy had stammered. "I haven't time." She had already wasted two hours at the movies, and she knew at home they were waiting for her.

The saleswoman slipped the dress over the girl's pink blouse, and tucked the linen collar under so as to bring the edge of the dress next to her pretty neck. The dress was apricot-color shading into a shell pink and the shell pink shaded off again into the pearl and pink whiteness of Amy's skin. The saleswoman beamed as Amy, entranced, surveyed herself naively in the tall looking-glass.

*Crisis* 20, pts. 1–2 (Aug. 1920): 168–73; 20, pt. 3 (Sept. 1920): 226–29; 20, pts. 4–5 (Oct. 1920): 267–74.

Then it was that the incident befell. Two men walking idly through the dress-salon stopped and looked—she made an unbelievably pretty picture. One of them with a short, soft brown beard,—"fuzzy" Amy thought to herself as she caught his glance in the mirror—spoke to his companion.

"Jove, how I'd like to paint her!" But it was the look on the other man's face that caught her and thrilled her. "My God! Can't a girl be beautiful!" he said half to himself. The pair passed on.

Amy stepped out of the dress and thanked the saleswoman half absently. She wanted to get home and think, think to herself about that look. She had seen it before in men's eyes, it had been in the eyes of the men in the moving-picture which she had seen that afternoon. But she had not thought *she* could cause it. Shut up in her little room she pondered over it. Her beauty,—she was really good-looking then—she could stir people—men! A girl of seventeen has no psychology, she does not go beneath the surface, she accepts. But she knew she was entering on one of her phases.

She was always living in some sort of story. She had started it when as a child of five she had driven with the tall, proud, white woman to Mrs. Boldin's home. Mrs. Boldin was a bride of one year's standing then. She was slender and very, very comely, with her rich brown skin and her hair that crinkled thick and soft above a low forehead. The house was still redolent of new furniture; Mr. Boldin was spick and span—he, unlike the furniture, remained so for that matter. The white woman had told Amy that this henceforth was to be her home.

Amy was curious, fond of adventure; she did not cry. She did not, of course, realize that she was to stay here indefinitely, but if she had, even at that age she would hardly have shed tears, she was always too eager, too curious to know, to taste

what was going to happen next. Still since she had had almost
no dealings with colored people and knew absolutely none of
the class to which Mrs. Boldin belonged, she did venture
one question.

"Am I going to be colored now?"

The tall white woman had flushed and paled. "You——" she
began, but the words choked her. "Yes, you are going to be
colored now," she ended finally. She was a proud woman, in
a moment she had recovered her usual poise. Amy carried
with her for many years the memory of that proud head. She
never saw her again.

When she was sixteen she asked Mrs. Boldin the question
which in the light of that memory had puzzled her always.
"Mrs. Boldin, tell me—am I white or colored?"

And Mrs. Boldin had told her and told her truly that she
did not know.

"A—a—mee!" Mrs. Boldin's voice mounted on the last
syllable in a shrill crescendo. Amy rose and went downstairs.

Down in the comfortable, but rather shabby dining-room
which the Boldins used after meals to sit in, Mr. Boldin, a
tall black man, with aristocratic features, sat reading; little
Cornelius Boldin sat practicing on a cornet, and Mrs. Boldin
sat rocking. In all of their eyes was the manifestation of the
light that Amy loved, but how truly she loved it, she was not
to guess till years later.

"Amy," Mrs. Boldin paused in her rocking, "did you get
the braid?" Of course she had not, though that was the thing
she had gone to Marshall's for. Amy always forgot essentials.
If she went on an errand, and she always went willingly, it
was for the pure joy of going. Who knew what angels might
meet one unawares? Not that Amy thought in biblical or in
literary phrases. She was in the High School, it is true, but

she was simply passing through, "getting by" she would have said carelessly. The only reading that had ever made any impression on her had been fairy tales read to her in those long remote days when she had lived with the tall, proud woman; and descriptions in novels or histories of beautiful, stately palaces tenanted by beautiful, stately women. She could pore over such pages for hours, her face flushed, her eyes eager.

At present she cast about for an excuse. She had so meant to get the braid. "There was a dress—" she began lamely, she was never deliberately dishonest.

Mr. Boldin cleared his throat and nervously fingered his paper. Cornelius ceased his awful playing and blinked at her short-sightedly through his thick glasses. Both of these, the man and the little boy, loved the beautiful, inconsequent creature with her airy, irresponsible ways. But Mrs. Boldin loved her too, and because she loved her she could not scold.

"Of course you forgot," she began chidingly. Then she smiled. "There was a dress that you looked at *perhaps*. But confess, didn't you go to the movies first?"

Yes, Amy confessed she had done just that. "And oh, Mrs. Boldin, it was the most wonderful picture—a girl—such a pretty one—and she was poor, awfully. And somehow she met the most wonderful people and they were so kind to her. And she married a man who was just tremendously rich and he gave her everything. I did so want Cornelius to see it."

"Huh!" said Cornelius who had been listening not because he was interested, but because he wanted to call Amy's attention to his playing as soon as possible. "Huh! I don't want to look at no pretty girl. Did they have anybody looping the loop in an airship?"

"You'd better stop seeing pretty girl pictures, Amy," said

Mr. Boldin kindly. "They're not always true to life. Besides, I know where you can see all the pretty girls you want without bothering to pay twenty-five cents for it."

Amy smiled at the implied compliment and went on happily studying her lessons. They were all happy in their own way. Amy because she was sure of their love and admiration, Mr. and Mrs. Boldin because of her beauty and innocence and Cornelius because he knew he had in his foster-sister a listener whom his terrible practicing could never bore. He played brokenly a piece he had found in an old music-book. *"There's an aching void in every heart, brother."*

"Where *do* you pick up those old things, Neely?" said his mother fretfully. But Amy could not have her favorite's feelings injured.

"I think it's lovely," she announced defensively. "Cornelius, I'll ask Sadie Murray to lend me her brother's book. He's learning the cornet, too, and you can get some new pieces. Oh, isn't it awful to have to go to bed? Good-night, everybody." She smiled her charming, ever ready smile, the mere reflex of youth and beauty and content.

"You do spoil her, Mattie," said Mr. Boldin after she had left the room. "She's only seventeen—here, Cornelius, you go to bed—but it seems to me she ought to be more dependable about errands. Though she is splendid about some things," he defended her. "Look how willingly she goes off to bed. She'll be asleep before she knows it when most girls of her age would want to be in the street."

But upstairs Amy was far from sleep. She lit one gas-jet and pulled down the shades. Then she stuffed tissue paper in the keyhole and under the doors, and lit the remaining gas-jets. The light thus thrown on the mirror of the ugly oak dresser was perfect. She slipped off the pink blouse and found two scarfs, a soft yellow and a soft pink,—she had had them in a scarf-dance for a school entertainment. She wound them and draped them about her pretty shoulders and loosened her hair. In the mirror she apostrophized the beautiful, glowing vision of herself.

"There," she said, "I'm like the girl in the picture. She had nothing but her beautiful face—and she did so want to be happy." She sat down on the side of the rather lumpy bed and stretched out her arms. "I want to be happy, too." She intoned it earnestly, almost like an incantation. "I want wonderful clothes, and people around me, men adoring me, and the world before me. I want—everything! It will come, it will all come because I want it so." She sat frowning intently as she was apt to do when very much engrossed. "And we'd all be so happy. I'd give Mr. and Mrs. Boldin money! And Cornelius—he'd go to college and learn all about his old airships. Oh, if I only knew how to begin!"

Smiling, she turned off the lights and crept to bed.

## II

Quite suddenly she knew she was going to run away. That was in October. By December she had accomplished her purpose. Not that she was the least bit unhappy but because she must get out in the world,—she felt caged, imprisoned. "Trenton is stifling me," she would have told you, in her unconsciously adopted "movie" diction. New York she knew was the place for her. She had her plans all made. She had sewed steadily after school for two months—as she frequently did when she wanted to buy her season's wardrobe, so besides her carfare she had $25. She went immediately to a white Y.W.C.A., stayed there two nights, found and answered an advertisement for clerk and waitress in a small confectionery and bakery-shop, was accepted and there she was launched.

Perhaps it was because of her early experience when as a tiny child she was taken from that so different home and left at Mrs. Boldin's, perhaps it was some fault in her own disposition, concentrated and egotistic as she was, but certainly she felt no pangs of separation, no fear of her future. She was cold too,—unfired though so to speak rather than icy,—and fastidious. This last quality kept her safe where morality or religion, of neither of which had she any conscious endowment, would have availed her nothing. Unbelievably then she lived two years in New York, unspoiled, untouched, going to her work on the edge of Greenwich Village early and coming back late, knowing almost no one and yet altogether happy in the expectation of something wonderful, which she knew some day must happen.

It was at the end of the second year that she met Zora Harrisson. Zora used to come into lunch with a group of habitués of the place—all of them artists and writers Amy gathered. Mrs. Harrisson (for she was married as Amy later learned) appealed to the girl because she knew so well how to afford the contrast to her blond, golden beauty. Purple, dark and regal, developed in velvets and heavy silks, and strange marine blues she wore, and thus made Amy absolutely happy. Singularly enough, the girl, intent as she was on her own life and experiences, had felt up to this time no yearning to know these strange, happy beings who surrounded her. She did miss Cornelius but otherwise she was never lonely, or if she was she hardly knew it, for she had always lived an inner life to herself. But Mrs. Harrisson magnetized her— she could not keep her eyes from her face, from her wonderful clothes. She made conjectures about her.

The wonderful lady came in late one afternoon—an unusual

thing for her. She smiled at Amy invitingly, asked some
banal questions and their first conversation began. The acquaintance once struck up progressed rapidly—after a few
weeks Mrs. Harrisson invited the girl to come to see her.
Amy accepted quietly, unaware that anything extraordinary
was happening. Zora noticed this and liked it. She had an
apartment in 12th Street in a house inhabited only by artists—
she was no mean one herself. Amy was fascinated by the new
world into which she found herself ushered; Zora's surroundings were very beautiful and Zora herself was a study. She
opened to the girl's amazed vision fields of thought and
conjecture, phases of whose existence Amy, who was a builder
of phases, had never dreamed. Zora had been a poor girl of
good family. She had wanted to study art, she had deliberately
married a rich man and as deliberately obtained in the course
of four years a divorce, and she was now living in New York
studying by means of her alimony and enjoying to its fullest
the life she loved. She took Amy on a footing with herself—
the girl's refinement, her beauty, her interest in colors (though
this in Amy at that time was purely sporadic, never consciously encouraged), all this gave Zora a figure about which
to plan and build a romance. Amy had told her the truth,
but not all about her coming to New York. She had grown
tired of Trenton—her people were all dead—the folks with
whom she lived were kind and good but not "inspiring" (she
had borrowed the term from Zora and it was true, the Boldins,
when one came to think of it, were not "inspiring"), so she
had run away.

Zora had gone into raptures. "What an adventure! My
dear, the world is yours. Why, with your looks and your
birth, for I suppose you really belong to the Kildares who
used to live in Philadelphia, I think there was a son who ran
off and married an actress or someone—they disowned him

I remember,—you can reach any height. You must marry a
wealthy man—perhaps someone who is interested in art and
who will let you pursue your studies." She insisted always
that Amy had run away in order to study art. "But luck like
that comes to few," she sighed, remembering her own plight,
for Mr. Harrisson had been decidedly unwilling to let her
pursue her studies, at least to the extent she wished. "Anyway
you must marry wealth,—one can always get a divorce," she
added sagely.

Amy—she came to Zora's every night now—used to listen
dazedly at first. She had accepted willingly enough Zora's
conjecture about her birth, came to believe it in fact—but
she drew back somewhat at such wholesale exploitation of ·
people to suit one's own convenience, still she did not probe
too far into this thought—nor did she grasp at all the infamy
of exploitation of self. She ventured one or two objections,
however, but Zora brushed everything aside.

"Everybody is looking out for himself," she said airily. "I
am interested in you, for instance, not for philanthropy's
sake, but because I am lonely, and you are charming and
pretty and don't get tired of hearing me talk. You'd better
come and live with me awhile, my dear, six months or a
year. It doesn't cost any more for two than for one, and you
can always leave when we get tired of each other. A girl like
you can always get a job. If you are worried about being
dependent you can pose for me and design my frocks and
oversee Julienne"—her maid-of-all-work—"I'm sure she's a
stupendous robber."

Amy came, not at all overwhelmed by the good luck of
it—good luck was around the corner more or less for everyone, she supposed. Moreover, she was beginning to absorb
some of Zora's doctrine—she, too, must look out for herself.
Zora *was* lonely, she *did* need companionship; Julienne *was*
careless about change and odd blouses and left-over dainties.

Amy had her own sense of honor. She carried out faithfully her share of the bargain, cut down waste, renovated Zora's clothes, posed for her, listened to her endlessly and bore with her fitfulness. Zora was truly grateful for this last. She was temperamental but Amy had good nerves and her strong natural inclination to let people do as they wanted stood her in good stead. She was a little stolid, a little unfeeling under her lovely exterior. Her looks at this time belied her—her perfect ivory-pink face, her deep luminous eyes,—very brown they were with purple depths that made one think of pansies— her charming, rather wide mouth, her whole face set in a frame of very soft, very live, brown hair which grew in wisps and tendrils and curls and waves back from her smooth, young forehead. All this made one look for softness and ingenuousness. The ingenuousness was there, but not the softness—except of her fresh, vibrant loveliness.

On the whole then she progressed famously with Zora. Sometimes the latter's callousness shocked her, as when they would go strolling through the streets south of Washington Square. The children, the people all foreign, all dirty, often very artistic, always immensely human, disgusted Zora except for "local color"—she really could reproduce them wonderfully. But she almost hated them for being what they were.

"Br-r-r, dirty little brats!" she would say to Amy. "Don't let them touch me." She was frequently amazed at her protégée's utter indifference to their appearance, for Amy herself was the pink of daintiness. They were turning from MacDougall into Bleecker Street one day and Amy had patted a child—dirty, but lovely—on the head.

"They are all people just like anybody else, just like you and me, Zora," she said in answer to her friend's protest.

"You *are* the true democrat," Zora returned with a shrug. But Amy did not understand her.

Not the least of Amy's services was to come between Zora

and the too pressing attention of the men who thronged about her.

"Oh, go and talk to Amy," Zora would say, standing slim and gorgeous in some wonderful evening gown. She was an extraordinarily attractive creature, very white and pink, with great ropes of dazzling gold hair, and that look of no-age which only American women possess. As a matter of fact she was thirty-nine, immensely sophisticated and selfish, even, Amy thought, a little cruel. Her present mode of living just suited her; she could not stand any condition that bound her, anything at all *exigent*. It was useless for anyone to try to influence her. If she did not want to talk, she would not.

The men used to obey her orders and seek Amy sulkily at first, but afterwards with considerably more interest. She was so lovely to look at. But they really, as Zora knew, preferred to talk to the older woman, for while with Zora indifference was a rôle, second nature by now but still a rôle—with Amy it was natural and she was also a trifle shallow. She had the admiration she craved, she was comfortable, she asked no more. Moreover she thought the men, with the exception of Stuart James Wynne, rather uninteresting—they were faddists for the most part, crazy not about art or music, but merely about some phase such as cubism or syncopation.

Wynne, who was much older than the other half-dozen men who weekly paid Zora homage—impressed her by his suggestion of power. He was a retired broker, immensely wealthy (Zora, who had known him since childhood, informed her), very set and purposeful and very polished. He was perhaps fifty-five, widely traveled, of medium height, very white skin and clear, frosty, blue eyes, with sharp, proud features. He liked Amy from the beginning, her childishness touched him. In particular he admired her pliability—not knowing it was really indifference. He had been married twice; one wife had divorced him, the other had died. Both marriages were unsuccessful owing to his dominant, rather unsympathetic nature. But he had softened considerably with years, though he still had decided views, was glad to see that Amy, in spite of Zora's influence, neither smoked nor drank. He liked her shallowness—she fascinated him.

Zora had told him much—just the kind of romantic story to appeal to the rich, powerful man. Here was beauty forlorn, penniless, of splendid birth,—for Zora once having connected Amy with the Philadelphia Kildares never swerved from that belief. Amy seemed to Wynne everything a girl should be— she was so unspoiled, so untouched. He asked her to marry him. If she had tried she could not have acted more perfectly. She looked at him with her wonderful eyes.

"But I am poor, ignorant—a nobody," she stammered. "I'm afraid I don't love you either," she went on in her pretty troubled voice, "though I do like you very, very much."

He liked her honesty and her self-depreciation, even her coldness. The fact that she was not flattered seemed to him an extra proof of her native superiority. He, himself, was a representative of one of the South's oldest families, though he had lived abroad lately.

"I have money and influence," he told her gravely, "but I count them nothing without you." And as for love—he would teach her that, he ended, his voice shaking a little. Underneath all his chilly, polished exterior he really cared.

"It seems an unworthy thing to say," he told her wistfully, for she seemed very young beside his experienced fifty-five years, "but anything you wanted in this world could be yours. I could give it to you,—clothes, houses and jewels."

"Don't be an idiot," Zora had said when Amy told her. "Of course, marry him. He'll give you a beautiful home and position. He's probably no harder to get along with than anybody else, and if he is, there is always the divorce court."

It seemed to Amy somehow that she was driving a bargain—how infamous a one she could not suspect. But Zora's teachings had sunk deep. Wynne loved her, and he could secure for her what she wanted. "And after all," she said to herself once, "it really is my dream coming true."

She resolved to marry him. There were two weeks of delirious, blissful shopping. Zora was very generous. It seemed to Amy that the whole world was contributing largesse to her happiness. She was to have just what she wanted and as her taste was perfect she afforded almost as much pleasure to the people from whom she bought as to herself. In particular she brought rapture to an exclusive modiste in Forty-second Street who exclaimed at her "so perfect taste."

"Mademoiselle is of a marvelous, of an absolute correctness," she said.

Everything whirled by. After the shopping there was the small, impressive wedding. Amy stumbled somehow through the service, struck by its awful solemnity. Then later there was the journey and the big house waiting them in the small town, fifty miles south of Richmond. Wynne was originally from Georgia, but business and social interests had made it necessary for him to be nearer Washington and New York.

Amy was absolute mistress of himself and his home, he said, his voice losing its coldness. "Ah, my dear, you'll never realize what you mean to me—I don't envy any other man in the world. You are so beautiful, so sweet, so different!"

## III

From the very beginning *he* was different from what she had supposed. To start with he was far, far wealthier, and he had, too, a tradition, a family-pride which to Amy was inexplicable. Still more inexplicably he had a race-pride. To his wife this was not only strange but foolish. She was as Zora had once suggested, the true democrat. Not that she preferred the company of her maids, though the reason for this did not lie *per se* in the fact that they were maids. There was simply no common ground. But she was uniformly kind, a trait which had she been older would have irritated her husband. As it was, he saw in it only an additional indication of her freshness, her lack of worldliness which seemed to him the attributes of an inherent refinement and goodness untouched by experience.

He, himself, was intolerant of all people of inferior birth or standing and looked with contempt on foreigners, except the French and English. All the rest were variously "guineys," "niggers," and "wops," and all of them he genuinely despised and hated, and talked of them with the huge intolerant carelessness characteristic of occidental civilization. Amy was never able to understand it. People were always first and last, just people to her. Growing up as the average colored American girl does grow up, surrounded by types of every hue, color and facial configuration she had had no absolute ideal. She was not even aware that there was one. Wynne, who in his grim way had a keen sense of humor, used to be vastly amused at the artlessness with which she let him know that she did not consider him good-looking. She never wanted him to wear anything but dark blue, or sombre mixtures always.

"They take away from that awful whiteness of your skin," she used to tell him, "and deepen the blue of your eyes."

In the main she made no attempt to understand him, as indeed she made no attempt to understand anything. The result, of course, was that such ideas as seeped into her mind stayed there, took growth and later bore fruit. But just at this

period she was like a well-cared for, sleek, house-pet, delicately nurtured, velvety, content to let her days pass by. She
thought almost nothing of her art just now, except as her
sensibilities were jarred by an occasional disharmony. Likewise, even to herself, she never criticized Wynne, except
when some act or attitude of his stung. She could never
understand why he, so fastidious, so versed in elegance of
word and speech, so careful in his surroundings, even down
to the last detail of glass and napery, should take such evident
pleasure in literature of a certain prurient type. He fairly
revelled in the realistic novels which to her depicted sheer
badness. He would get her to read to him, partly because he
liked to be read to, mostly because he enjoyed the realism
and in a slighter degree because he enjoyed seeing her shocked.
Her point of view amused him.

"What funny people," she would say naively, "to do such
things." She could not understand the liaisons and intrigues
of women in society novels, such infamy was stupid and silly.
If one starved, it was conceivable that one might steal; if one
were intentionally injured, one might hit back, even murder;
but deliberate nastiness she could not envisage. The stories,
after she had read them to him, passed out of her mind as
completely as though they had never existed.

Picture the two of them spending three years together with
practically no friction. To his dominance and intolerance she
opposed a soft and unobtrusive indifference. What she wanted
she had, ease, wealth, adoration, love, too, passionate and
imperious, but she had never known any other kind. She was
growing cleverer also, her knowledge of French was increas-
ing, she was acquiring a knowledge of politics, of commerce
and of the big social questions, for Wynne's interests were
exhaustive and she did most of his reading for him. Another
woman might have yearned for a more youthful companion,
but her native coldness kept her content. She did not love

him, she had never really loved anybody, but little Cornelius Boldin—he had been such an enchanting, such a darling baby, she remembered,—her heart contracted painfully when she thought as she did very often of his warm softness.

"He must be a big boy now," she would think almost maternally, wondering—once she had been so sure!—if she would ever see him again. But she was very fond of Wynne, and he was crazy over her just as Zora had predicted. He loaded her with gifts, dresses, flowers, jewels—she amused him because none but colored stones appealed to her.

"Diamonds are so hard, so cold, and pearls are dead," she told him.

Nothing ever came between them, but his ugliness, his hatefulness to dependents. It hurt her so, for she was naturally kind in her careless, uncomprehending way. True, she had left Mrs. Boldin without a word, but she did not guess how completely Mrs. Boldin loved her. She would have been aghast had she realized how stricken her flight had left them. At twenty-two, Amy was still as good, as unspoiled, as pure as a child. Of course with all this she was too unquestioning, too selfish, too vain, but they were all faults of her lovely, lovely flesh. Wynne's intolerance finally got on her nerves. She used to blush for his unkindness. All the servants were colored, but she had long since ceased to think that perhaps she, too, was colored, except when he, by insult toward an employee, overt always at least implied, made her realize his contemptuous dislike and disregard for a dark skin or Negro blood.

"Stuart, how can you say such things?" she would expostulate. "You can't expect a man to stand such language as that." And Wynne would sneer, "A man—you don't consider a nigger a man, do you? Oh, Amy, don't be such a fool. You've got to keep them in their places."

Some innate sense of the fitness of things kept her from

condoling outspokenly with the servants, but they knew she was ashamed of her husband's ways. Of course, they left—it seemed to Amy that Peter, the butler, was always getting new "help,"—but most of the upper servants stayed, for Wynne paid handsomely and although his orders were meticulous and insistent, the retinue of employees was so large that the individual's work was light.

Most of the servants who did stay on in spite of Wynne's occasional insults had a purpose in view. Callie, the cook, Amy found out, had two children at Howard University— of course she never came in contact with Wynne—the chauffeur had a crippled sister. Rosa, Amy's maid and purveyor of much outside information, was the chief support of her family. About Peter, Amy knew nothing; he was a striking, taciturn man, very competent, who had left the Wynnes' service years before and had returned in Amy's third year. Wynne treated him with comparative respect. But Stephen, the new valet, met with entirely different treatment. Amy's heart yearned toward him, he was like Cornelius, with short-sighted, patient eyes, always willing, a little over-eager. Amy recognized him for what he was; a boy of respectable, ambitious parentage, striving for the means for an education; naturally far above his present calling, yet willing to pass through all this as a means to an end. She questioned Rosa about him.

"Oh, Stephen," Rosa told her, "yes'm, he's workin' for fair. He's got a brother at the Howard's and a sister at Smith's. Yes'm, it do seem a little hard on him, but Stephen, he say, they're both goin' to turn roun' and help him when they get through. That blue silk has a rip in it, Miss Amy, if you was thinkin' of wearin' that. Yes'm, somehow I don't think Steve's very strong, kinda worries like. I guess he's sorta nervous."

Amy told Wynne. "He's such a nice boy, Stuart," she pleaded, "it hurts me to have you so cross with him. Anyway don't call him names." She was both surprised and frightened at the feeling in her that prompted her to interfere. She had held so aloof from other people's interest all these years.

"I *am* colored," she told herself that night. "I feel it inside of me. I must be or I couldn't care so about Stephen. Poor boy, I suppose Cornelius is just like him. I wish Stuart would let him alone. I wonder if all white people are like that. Zora was hard, too, on unfortunate people." She pondered over it a bit. "I wonder what Stuart would say if he knew I was colored?" She lay perfectly still, her smooth brow knitted, thinking hard. "But he loves me," she said to herself still silently. "He'll always love my looks," and she fell to thinking that all the wonderful happenings in her sheltered, pampered life had come to her through her beauty. She reached out an exquisite arm, switched on a light, and picking up a hand-mirror from a dressing-table, fell to studying her face. She was right. It was her chiefest asset. She forgot Stephen and fell asleep.

But in the morning her husband's voice issuing from his dressing-room across the hall, awakened her. She listened drowsily. Stephen, leaving the house the day before, had been met by a boy with a telegram. He had taken it, slipped it into his pocket, (he was just going to the mail-box) and had forgotten to deliver it until now, nearly twenty-four hours later. She could hear Stuart's storm of abuse—it was terrible, made up as it was of oaths and insults to the boy's ancestry. There was a moment's lull. Then she heard him again.

"If your brains are a fair sample of that black wench of a sister of yours—"

She sprang up then thrusting her arms as she ran into her pink dressing-gown. She got there just in time. Stephen, his face quivering, was standing looking straight into Wynne's smoldering eyes. In spite of herself, Amy was glad to see the boy's bearing. But he did not notice her.

"You devil!" he was saying. "You white-faced devil! I'll make you pay for that!" He raised his arm. Wynne did not blanch.

With a scream she was between them. "Go, Stephen, go,— get out of the house. Where do you think you are? Don't you know you'll be hanged, lynched, tortured?" Her voice shrilled at him.

Wynne tried to thrust aside her arms that clung and twisted. But she held fast till the door slammed behind the fleeing boy.

"God, let me by, Amy!" As suddenly as she had clasped him she let him go, ran to the door, fastened it and threw the key out the window.

He took her by the arm and shook her. "Are you mad? Didn't you hear him threaten me, me,—a nigger threaten me?" His voice broke with anger, "And you're letting him get away! Why, I'll get him. I'll set blood-hounds on him, I'll have every white man in this town after him! He'll be hanging so high by midnight—" he made for the other door, cursing, half-insane.

How, *how* could she keep him back! She hated her weak arms with their futile beauty! She sprang toward him. "Stuart, wait," she was breathless and sobbing. She said the first thing that came into her head. "Wait, Stuart, you cannot do this thing." She thought of Cornelius—suppose it had been he— "Stephen,—that boy,—he is my brother."

He turned on her. "What!" he said fiercely, then laughed a short laugh of disdain. "You are crazy," he said roughly, "My God, Amy! How can you even in jest associate yourself

with these people? Don't you suppose I know a white girl
when I see one? There's no use in telling a lie like that."

Well, there was no help for it. There was only one way.
He had turned back for a moment, but she must keep him
many moments—an hour. Stephen must get out of town.

She caught his arm again. "Yes," she told him, "I did lie.
Stephen is not my brother, I never saw him before." The
light of relief that crept into his eyes did not escape her, it
only nerved her. "But I am colored," she ended.

Before he could stop her she had told him all about the
tall white woman. "She took me to Mrs. Boldin's and gave
me to her to keep. She would never have taken me to her if
I had been white. If you lynch this boy, I'll let the world,
your world, know that your wife is a colored woman."

He sat down like a man suddenly stricken old, his face
ashen. "Tell me about it again," he commanded. And she
obeyed, going mercilessly into every damning detail.

## IV

Amazingly her beauty availed her nothing. If she had been
an older woman, if she had had Zora's age and experience,
she would have been able to gauge exactly her influence over
Wynne. Though even then in similar circumstances she would
have taken the risk and acted in just the same manner. But
she was a little bewildered at her utter miscalculation. She
had thought he might not want his friends—his world by
which he set such store—to know that she was colored, but
she had not dreamed it could make any real difference to
him. He had chosen her, poor and ignorant, out of a host of
women, and had told her countless times of his love. To

herself Amy Wynne was in comparison with Zora for instance, stupid and uninteresting. But his constant, unsolicited
iterations had made her accept his idea.

She was just the same woman she told herself, she had not
changed, she was still beautiful, still charming, still "different." Perhaps that very difference had its being in the fact of
her mixed blood. She had been his wife—there were memories—she could not see how he could give her up. The
suddenness of the divorce carried her off her feet. Dazedly
she left him—though almost without a pang for she had only
liked him. She had been perfectly honest about this, and he,
although consumed by the fierceness of his emotion toward
her, had gradually forced himself to be content, for at least
she had never made him jealous.

She was to live in a small house of his in New York, up
town in the 80's. Peter was in charge and there were a new
maid and a cook. The servants, of course, knew of the
separation, but nobody guessed why. She was living on a
much smaller basis than the one to which she had become so
accustomed in the last three years. But she was very comfortable. She felt, at any rate she manifested, no qualms at
receiving alimony from Wynne. That was the way things
happened, she supposed when she thought of it at all. Moreover, it seemed to her perfectly in keeping with Wynne's
former attitude toward her; she did not see how he could do
less. She expected people to be consistent. That was why she
was so amazed that he in spite of his oft iterated love, could
let her go. If she had felt half the love for him which he had
professed for her, she would not have sent him away if he
had been a leper.

"Why I'd stay with him," she told herself, "if he were
one, even as I feel now."

She was lonely in New York. Perhaps it was the first time

in her life that she had felt so. Zora had gone to Paris the
first year of her marriage and had not come back.

The days dragged on emptily. One thing helped her. She
had gone one day to the modiste from whom she had bought
her trousseau. The woman remembered her perfectly—"The
lady with the exquisite taste for colors—ah, madame, but you
have the rare gift." Amy was grateful to be taken out of her
thoughts. She bought one or two daring but altogether lovely
creations and let fall a few suggestions:

"That brown frock, Madame,—you say it has been on
your hands a long time? Yes? But no wonder. See, instead of
that dead white you should have a shade of ivory, that white
cheapens it." Deftly she caught up a bit of ivory satin and
worked out her idea. Madame was ravished.

"But yes, Madame Ween is correct,—as always. Oh, what
a pity that the Madame is so wealthy. If she were only a poor
girl—Mlle. Antoine with the best eye for color in the place
has just left, gone back to France to nurse her brother—this
World War is of such a horror! If someone like Madame,
now, could be found, to take the little Antoine's place!"

Some obscure impulse drove Amy to accept the half proposal: "Oh! I don't know, I have nothing to do just now.
My husband is abroad." Wynne had left her with that
impression. "I could contribute the money to the Red Cross
or to charity."

The work was the best thing in the world for her. It kept
her from becoming too introspective, though even then she
did more serious, connected thinking than she had done in
all the years of her varied life.

She missed Wynne definitely, chiefly as a guiding influence
for she had rarely planned even her own amusements. Her
dependence on him had been absolute. She used to picture
him to herself as he was before the trouble—and his changing

expressions as he looked at her, of amusement, interest, pride, a certain little teasing quality that used to come into his eyes, which always made her adopt her "spoiled child air," as he used to call it. It was the way he liked her best. Then last, there was that look he had given her the morning she had told him she was colored—it had depicted so many emotions, various and yet distinct. There were dismay, disbelief, coldness, a final aloofness.

There was another expression, too, that she thought of sometimes—the look on the face of Mr. Packard, Wynne's lawyer. She, herself, had attempted no defense.

"For God's sake why did you tell him, Mrs. Wynne?" Packard asked her. His curiosity got the better of him. "You couldn't have been in love with that yellow rascal," he blurted out. "She's too cold really, to love anybody," he told himself. "If you didn't care about the boy why should you have told?"

She defended herself feebly. "He looked so like little Cornelius Boldin," she replied vaguely, "and he couldn't help being colored." A clerk came in then and Packard said no more. But into his eyes had crept a certain reluctant respect. She remembered the look, but could not define it.

She was so sorry about the trouble now, she wished it had never happened. Still if she had it to repeat she would act in the same way again. "There was nothing else for me to do," she used to tell herself.

But she missed Wynne unbelievably.

If it had not been for Peter, her life would have been almost that of a nun. But Peter, who read the papers and kept abreast of the times, constantly called her attention, with all due respect, to the meetings, the plays, the sights which she ought to attend or see. She was truly grateful to him. She was very kind to all three of the servants. They had the easiest "places" in New York, the maids used to tell their friends.

As she never entertained, and frequently dined out, they had a great deal of time off.

She had been separated from Wynne for ten months before she began to make any definite plans for her future. Of course, she could not go on like this always. It came to her suddenly that probably she would go to Paris and live there— why or how she did not know. Only Zora was there and lately she had begun to think that her life was to be like Zora's. They had been amazingly parallel up to this time. Of course she would have to wait until after the war.

She sat musing about it one day in the big sitting-room which she had had fitted over into a luxurious studio. There was a sewing-room off to the side from which Peter used to wheel into the room waxen figures of all colorings and contours so that she could drape the various fabrics about them to be sure of the best results. But today she was working out a scheme for one of Madame's customers, who was of her own color and size and she was her own lay-figure. She sat in front of the huge pier glass, a wonderful soft yellow silk draped about her radiant loveliness.

"I could do some serious work in Paris," she said half aloud to herself. "I suppose if I really wanted to, I could be very successful along this line."

Somewhere downstairs an electric bell buzzed, at first softly, then after a slight pause, louder, and more insistently.

If Madame sends me that lace today," she was thinking, idly, "I could finish this and start on the pink. I wonder why Peter doesn't answer the bell."

She remembered then that Peter had gone to New Rochelle on business and she had sent Ellen to Altman's to find a certain rare velvet and had allowed Mary to go with her. She would dine out, she told them, so they need not hurry. Evidently she was alone in the house.

Well she could answer the bell. She had done it often enough in the old days at Mrs. Boldin's. Of course it was the lace. She smiled a bit as she went down stairs thinking how surprised the delivery-boy would be to see her arrayed thus early in the afternoon. She hoped he wouldn't go. She could see him through the long, thick panels of glass in the vestibule and front door. He was just turning about as she opened the door.

This was no delivery-boy, this man whose gaze fell on her hungry and avid. This was Wynne. She stood for a second leaning against the door-jamb, a strange figure surely in the sharp November weather. Some leaves—brown, skeleton shapes—rose and swirled unnoticed about her head. A passing letter-carrier looked at them curiously.

"What are you doing answering the door?" Wynne asked her roughly. "Where is Peter? Go in, you'll catch cold."

She was glad to see him. She took him into the drawing room—a wonderful study in browns—and looked at him and looked at him.

"Well," he asked her, his voice eager in spite of the commonplace words, "are you glad to see me? Tell me what do you do with yourself."

She could not talk fast enough, her eyes clinging to his face. Once it struck her that he had changed in some indefinable way. Was it a slight coarsening of that refined aristocratic aspect? Even in her subconsciousness she denied it.

He had come back to her.

"So I design for Madame when I feel like it, and send the money to the Red Cross and wonder when you are coming back to me." For the first time in their acquaintanceship she was conscious deliberately of trying to attract, to hold him. She put on her spoiled child air which had once been so successful.

"It took you long enough to get here," she pouted. She was certain of him now. His mere presence assured her.

They sat silent a moment, the late November sun bathing her head in an austere glow of chilly gold. As she sat there in the big brown chair she was, in her yellow dress, like some mysterious emanation, some wraith-like aura developed from the tone of her surroundings.

He rose and came toward her, still silent. She grew nervous, and talked incessantly with sudden unusual gestures. "Oh, Stuart, let me give you tea. It's right there in the pantry off the dining-room. I can wheel the table in." She rose, a lovely creature in her yellow robe. He watched her intently.

"Wait," he bade her.

She paused almost on tiptoe, a dainty golden butterfly.

"You are coming back to live with me?" he asked her hoarsely.

For the first time in her life she loved him.

"Of course I am coming back," she told him softly. "Aren't you glad? Haven't you missed me? I didn't see how you *could* stay away. Oh! Stuart, what a wonderful ring!"

For he had slipped on her finger a heavy dull gold band, with an immense sapphire in an oval setting—a beautiful thing of Italian workmanship.

"It is so like you to remember," she told him gratefully. "I love colored stones." She admired it, turning it around and around on her slender finger.

How silent he was, standing there watching her with his sombre yet eager gaze. It made her troubled, uneasy. She cast about for something to say.

"You can't think how I've improved since I saw you, Stuart. I've read all sorts of books—Oh! I'm learned," she smiled at him. "And Stuart," she went a little closer to him, twisting the button on his perfect coat, "I'm so sorry about it all,—about Stephen, that boy you know. I just couldn't help interfering. But when we're married again, if you'll just remember how it hurts me to have you so cross—"

He interrupted her. "I wasn't aware that I spoke of our marrying again," he told her, his voice steady, his blue eyes cold.

She thought he was teasing. "Why you just asked me to. You said 'aren't you coming back to live with me—' "

"Yes," he acquiesced, "I said just that—'to live with me.' "

Still she didn't comprehend. "But what do you mean?" she asked bewildered.

"What do you suppose a man means," he returned deliberately, "when he asks a woman to live with him, but not to marry him?"

She sat down heavily in the brown chair, all glowing ivory and yellow against its sombre depths.

"Like the women in those awful novels?" she whispered. "Not like those women!—Oh Stuart! you don't mean it!" Her very heart was numb.

"But you must care a little—" she was amazed at her own depth of feeling. "Why I care—there are all those memories back of us—you must want me really—"

"I do want you," he told her tensely. "I want you damnably. But—well—I might as well out with it—A white man like me simply doesn't marry a colored woman. After all what difference need it make to you? We'll live abroad—you'll travel, have all the things you love. Many a white woman would envy you." He stretched out an eager hand.

She evaded it, holding herself aloof as though his touch were contaminating. Her movement angered him.

Like a rending veil suddenly the veneer of his high polish cracked and the man stood revealed.

"Oh, hell!" he snarled at her roughly. "Why don't you

stop posing? What do you think you are anyway? Do you suppose I'd take you for my wife—what do you think can happen to you? What man of your own race could give you what you want? You don't suppose I am going to support you this way forever, do you? The court imposed no alimony. You've got to come to it sooner or later—you're bound to fall to some white man. What's the matter—I'm not rich enough?"

Her face flamed at that—"As though it were *that* that mattered!"

He gave her a deadly look. "Well, isn't it? Ah, my girl, you forget you told me you didn't love me when you married me. You sold yourself to me then. Haven't I reason to suppose you are waiting for a higher bidder?"

At these words something in her died forever, her youth, her illusions, her happy, happy blindness. She saw life leering mercilessly in her face. It seemed to her that she would give all her future to stamp out, to kill the contempt in his frosty insolent eyes. In a sudden rush of savagery she struck him, struck him across his hateful sneering mouth with the hand which wore his ring.

As *she* fell, reeling under the fearful impact of his brutal but involuntary blow, her mind caught at, registered two things. A little thin stream of blood was trickling across his chin. She had cut him with the ring, she realized with a certain savage satisfaction. And there was something else which she must remember, which she *would* remember if only she could fight her way out of this dreadful clinging blackness, which was bearing down upon her—closing her in.

When she came to she sat up holding her bruised, aching head in her palms, trying to recall what it was that had impressed her so.

Oh, yes, her very mind ached with the realization. She lay back again on the floor, prone, anything to relieve that intolerable pain. But her memory, her thoughts went on.

"Nigger," he had called her as she fell, "nigger, nigger," and again, "nigger."

"He despised me absolutely," she said to herself wonderingly, "because I was colored. And yet he wanted me."


# V


Somehow she reached her room. Long after the servants had come in, she lay face downward across her bed, thinking. How she hated Wynne, how she hated herself! And for ten months she had been living off his money although in no way had she a claim on him. Her whole body burned with the shame of it.

In the morning she rang for Peter. She faced him, white and haggard, but if the man noticed her condition, he made no sign. He was, if possible, more imperturbable than ever.

"Peter," she told him, her eyes and voice very steady, "I am leaving this house today and shall never come back."

"Yes, Miss."

"I shall want you to see to the packing and storing of the goods and to send the keys and the receipts for the jewelry and valuables to Mr. Packard in Baltimore."

"Yes, Miss."

"And, Peter, I am very poor now and shall have no money besides what I can make for myself."

"Yes, Miss."

Would nothing surprise him, she wondered dully. She went on "I don't know whether you knew it or not, Peter, but I am colored, and hereafter I mean to live among my own people. Do you think you could find me a little house or a little cottage not too far from New York?"

He had a little place in New Rochelle, he told her, his manner altering not one whit, or better yet his sister had a four-room house in Orange, with a garden, if he remembered correctly. Yes, he was sure there was a garden. It would be just the thing for Mrs. Wynne.

She had four hundred dollars of her own which she had earned by designing for Madame. She paid the maids a month in advance—they were to stay as long as Peter needed them. She, herself, went to a small hotel in Twenty-eighth Street, and here Peter came for her at the end of ten days, with the acknowledgement of the keys and receipts from Mr. Packard. Then he accompanied her to Orange and installed her in her new home.

"I wish I could afford to keep you, Peter," she said a little wistfully, "but I am very poor. I am heavily in debt and I must get that off my shoulders at once."

Mrs. Wynne was very kind, he was sure; he could think of no one with whom he would prefer to work. Furthermore, he often ran down from New Rochelle to see his sister; he would come in from time to time, and in the spring would plant the garden if she wished.

She hated to see him go, but she did not dwell long on that. Her only thought was to work and work and work and save until she could pay Wynne back. She had not lived very extravagantly during those ten months and Peter was a perfect manager—in spite of her remonstrances he had given her every month an account of his expenses. She had made arrangements with Madame to be her regular designer. The French woman guessing that more than whim was behind this move drove a very shrewd bargain, but even then the pay was excellent. With care, she told herself, she could be free within two years, three at most.

She lived a dull enough existence now, going to work steadily every morning and getting home late at night. Almost it was like those early days when she had first left Mrs. Boldin, except that now she had no high sense of adventure, no expectation of great things to come, which might buoy her up. She no longer thought of phases and the proper setting for her beauty. Once indeed catching sight of her face late one night in the mirror in her tiny work-room in Orange, she stopped and scanned herself, loathing what she saw there.

"You *thing!*" she said to the image in the glass, "if you hadn't been so vain, so shallow!" And she had struck herself violently again and again across the face until her head ached.

But such fits of passion were rare. She had a curious sense of freedom in these days, a feeling that at last her brain, her senses were liberated from some hateful clinging thralldom. Her thoughts were always busy. She used to go over that last scene with Wynne again and again trying to probe the inscrutable mystery which she felt was at the bottom of the affair. She groped her way toward a solution, but always something stopped her. Her impulse to strike, she realized, and his brutal rejoinder had been actuated by something more than mere sex antagonism, there was *race* antagonism there—two elements clashing. That much she could fathom. But that he despising her, hating her for not being white should yet desire her! It seemed to her that his attitude toward her—hate and yet desire, was the attitude in microcosm of the whole white world toward her own, toward that world to which those few possible strains of black blood so tenuously and yet so tenaciously linked her.

Once she got hold of a big thought. Perhaps there *was*

some root, some racial distinction woven in with the stuff of which she was formed which made her persistently kind and unexacting. And perhaps in the same way this difference, helplessly, inevitably operated in making Wynne and his kind, cruel or at best indifferent. Her reading for Wynne reacted to her thought—she remembered the grating insolence of white exploiters in foreign lands, the wrecking of African villages, the destruction of homes in Tasmania. She couldn't imagine where Tasmania was, but wherever it was, it had been the realest thing in the world to its crude inhabitants.

Gradually she reached a decision. There were two divisions of people in the world—on the one hand insatiable desire for power; keenness, mentality; a vast and cruel pride. On the other there was ambition, it is true, but modified, a certain humble sweetness, too much inclination to trust, an unthinking, unswerving loyalty. All the advantages in the world accrued to the first division. But without bitterness she chose the second. She wanted to be colored, she hoped she was colored. She wished even that she did not have to take advantage of her appearance to earn her living. But that was to meet an end. After all she had contracted her debt with a white man, she would pay him with a white man's money.

The years slipped by—four of them. One day a letter came from Mr. Packard. Mrs. Wynne had sent him the last penny of the sum received from Mr. Wynne from February to November, 1914. Mr. Wynne had refused to touch the money, it was and would be indefinitely at Mrs. Wynne's disposal.

She never even answered the letter. Instead she dismissed the whole incident,—Wynne and all,—from her mind and began to plan for her future. She was free, free! She had paid back her sorry debt with labor, money and anguish. From now on she could do as she pleased. Almost she caught herself saying "something is going to happen." But she checked herself, she hated her old attitude.

But something *was* happening. Insensibly from the moment she knew of her deliverance, her thoughts turned back to a stifled hidden longing, which had lain, it seemed to her, an eternity in her heart. Those days with Mrs. Boldin! At night,—on her way to New York,—in the work-rooms,— her mind was busy with little intimate pictures of that happy, wholesome, unpretentious life. She could see Mrs. Boldin, clean and portly, in a lilac chambray dress, upbraiding her for some trifling, yet exasperating fault. And Mr. Boldin, immaculate and slender, with his noticeably polished air— how kind he had always been, she remembered. And lastly, Cornelius; Cornelius in a thousand attitudes and engaged in a thousand occupations, brown and near-sighted and sweet— devoted to his pretty sister, as he used to call her; Cornelius, who used to come to her as a baby as willingly as to his mother; Cornelius spelling out colored letters on his blocks, pointing to them stickily with a brown, perfect finger; Cornelius singing like an angel in his breathy, sexless voice and later murdering everything possible on his terrible cornet. How had she ever been able to leave them all and the dear shabbiness of that home! Nothing, she realized, in all these years had touched her inmost being, had penetrated to the core of her cold heart like the memories of those early, misty scenes.

One day she wrote a letter to Mrs. Boldin. She, the writer, Madame A. Wynne, had come across a young woman, Amy Kildare, who said that as a girl she had run away from home and now she would like to come back. But she was ashamed to write. Madame Wynne had questioned the girl closely and she was quite sure that this Miss Kildare had in no way incurred shame or disgrace. It had been some time since

Madame Wynne had seen the girl but if Mrs. Boldin wished, she would try to find her again—perhaps Mrs. Boldin would like to get in touch with her. The letter ended on a tentative note.

The answer came at once.

My dear Madame Wynne:

My mother told me to write you this letter. She says even if Amy Kildare had done something terrible, she would want her to come home again. My father says so too. My mother says, please find her as soon as you can and tell her to come back. She still misses her. We all miss her. I was a little boy when she left, but though I am in the High School now and play in the school orchestra, I would rather see her than do anything I know. If you see her, be sure to tell her to come right away. My mother says thank you.

Yours respectfully,
CORNELIUS BOLDIN

The letter came to the modiste's establishment in New York. Amy read it and went with it to Madame. "I have had wonderful news," she told her, "I must go away immediately, I can't come back—you may have these last two weeks for nothing." Madame, who had surmised long since the separation, looked curiously at the girl's flushed cheeks, and decided that "Monsieur Ween" had returned. She gave her fatalistic shrug. All Americans were crazy.

"But, yes, Madame,—if you must go—absolument."

When she reached the ferry, Amy looked about her searchingly. "I hope I'm seeing you for the last time—I'm going home, home!" Oh, the unbelievable kindness! She had left them without a word and they still wanted her back!

Eventually she got to Orange and to the little house. She sent a message to Peter's sister and set about her packing.

But first she sat down in the little house and looked about her. She would go home, home—how she loved the word, she would stay there a while, but always there was life, still beckoning. It would beckon forever she realized to her adventurousness. Afterwards she would set up an establishment of her own,—she reviewed possibilities—in a rich suburb, where white women would pay and pay for her expertness, caring nothing for realities, only for externals.

"As I myself used to care," she sighed. Her thoughts flashed on. "Then some day I'll work and help with colored people—the only ones who have really cared for and wanted me." Her eyes blurred.

She would never make any attempt to find out who or what she was. If she were white, there would always be people urging her to keep up the silliness of racial prestige. How she hated it all!

"Citizen of the world, that's what I'll be. And now I'll go home."

Peter's sister's little girl came over to be with the pretty lady whom she adored.

"You sit here, Angel, and watch me pack," Amy said, placing her in a little arm-chair. And the baby sat there in silent observation, one tiny leg crossed over the other, surely the quaintest, gravest bit of bronze, Amy thought, that ever lived.

"Miss Amy cried," the child told her mother afterwards.

Perhaps Amy did cry, but if so she was unaware. Certainly she laughed more happily, more spontaneously than she had done for years. Once she got down on her knees in front of the little arm-chair and buried her face in the baby's tiny bosom.

"Oh Angel, Angel," she whispered, "do you suppose Cornelius still plays on that cornet?"

# MARY

Helen Pepper

*All booklets are published
thanks to the generosity of the supporters
of the Catholic Truth Society*

CATHOLIC TRUTH SOCIETY

PUBLISHERS TO THE HOLY SEE

# Contents

ISBN 978 1 78469 553 8

# Introduction

This book will accompany Mary, the Mother of Jesus, as she follows in her son's footsteps on the Via Dolorosa. The purpose is not simply to define the Stations of the Cross from her perspective, but to experience them with her.

We join Mary as she traces Jesus' journey on his way to Calvary to be crucified. We see through her eyes the suffering Jesus endured and take a moment to reflect upon Jesus' great sacrifice. We join her in the realisation of the purpose of Jesus' ministry: the crucifixion as a necessity to redeem humanity from the bondages of sin, and as a prelude to the glory of the Resurrection.

Mary's own journey begins much earlier, at the Annunciation. Here the Angel Gabriel intimates the unique importance of her role in our salvation, as the miracle of the incarnation takes place in her womb (*Lk* 1:26-38). Mary is a simple girl from a humble background who demonstrates true faith in God and his plan. She is the ultimate disciple, as although she does not fully understand what she is being asked to do, she is the Lord's willing servant. Her fate is declared by Simeon during Jesus' presentation: "And a sword will pierce your own soul too" (*Lk* 2:25). But the depth of suffering involved for Mary, and the literal truth of this metaphor, only becomes fully clear on her road to Calvary.

On this journey, Mary must have contemplated the life she shared with her son. Her role is exalted, but unspeakably hard. Mary's mission embodies both joy and suffering, from the birth of her child, to seeing him die in the most barbaric way. We focus on Mary's emotions on witnessing Jesus' immediate anguish but also narrate back to different stages in her life with Jesus, those joys and sufferings they shared together.

It is a venerable tradition within the Catholic faith to seek Mary's perspective on her son. It is through Mary's eyes that we can best see the humanity and the divinity of Christ. Her agony in his death is balanced by her willingness to put her faith in the Lord and his plan. She is a model of dignity, discipleship and duty.

Pope Francis said, "Where there is a mother, there is tenderness. By her motherhood, Mary shows us that humility and tenderness are not virtues of the weak but of the strong." Mary's perspective is so powerful in viewing Christ because she sees him as a mother looking at her beloved child. She allows us to experience his death in human terms: Mary grieves with the raw pain that any parent would suffer at the loss of a child. Mary has endured as much as any person can, but she remains steadfast. From this we gain spiritual strength as we feel humility and tenderness at Christ's sacrifice for us. We embody this love and anguish like a parent losing a child. We become pilgrims with a greater love for Christ and humanity. Mary's own motherly love and faithful devotion act as a way we can mirror our own love for Christ and the Church.

Mary's relationship with Jesus is unique. It is because of this that we trust in Mary and she is able to intercede on our behalf. It is because of this that we trust in Mary; she is the Mother of the Church, and through her maternal and protective embrace we ask her for help as we strive to change our own lives and become better disciples. Furthermore, Mary's clarity in understanding what the Lord had planned for her can be emulated by us in our own lives if we imitate her faith and courage. In times of difficulty we should trust in the Lord's plan for us, knowing that hope will triumph from hopelessness.

As we join Mary on the way to Calvary, may we bear witness to all the events that took place. May we open our hearts and strive to mirror Mary's motherly love and devotion. May we take a moment to reflect on Christ's great sacrifice for us, but also to embrace his great love for humanity, appreciating all he has done and continues to do for us.

# First Station
## Jesus is condemned to death

**Leader:** We adore you, O Christ, and we praise you.
**All:** Because by your Holy Cross you have redeemed the world.

My cherished son, as you stand on trial before Pilate, alone and afraid, fear not for my heart is with you. When you face the crowd that rejects you, fear not for my hand is holding on to yours. When you hear that you are sentenced to the most barbaric death, fear not for nothing can separate my love from you. For I was alone and afraid, a young virgin with no understanding of how or why I was chosen. I was judged for how you came into being. I cried when I was rejected. But I clung to the words uttered by the Angel Gabriel, "Fear not Mary, for you have found favour with the Lord. And you will conceive and bear a son." I trusted in the Lord and his path for me. So, too, should you trust in the path he has prepared for you.

### Reflection

**Leader:** May we all "fear not" in times of alienation, rejection and judgement, and instead find strength and courage by trusting in the Lord. For nothing can separate his love from us.

---

**All:** Our Father… Hail Mary… Glory be to the Father…
**Leader:** Jesus Christ Crucified,
**All:** Have mercy on us.

## Second Station
# Jesus takes up the cross

**Leader:** We adore you, O Christ, and we praise you.
**All:** Because by your Holy Cross you have redeemed the world.

I am watching you lift up the cross. The cross you will soon be nailed to. Your face looks calm and in control. You fully accept the Father's will. I, too, remember completely accepting his will. "Behold, I am the servant of the Lord; let it be to me, according to your word." I didn't understand how it could be, how could I? But I carried you willingly in my womb. I trusted in God's plan for me, just as I continue to trust him now. You begin to walk. I follow you through the crowds, carrying my heavy heart.

## Reflection

**Leader:** May we all be the servant of the Lord and accept willingly the role God has laid out for us, trusting in the Lord with all our hearts.

**All:** Our Father… Hail Mary… Glory be to the Father…
**Leader:** Jesus Christ Crucified,
**All:** Have mercy on us.

# Third Station
# Jesus falls the first time

**Leader:** We adore you, O Christ, and we praise you.
**All:** Because by your Holy Cross you have redeemed the world.

I cry out as I watch you fall. I can see the pain in your face, but you get up. The cross seems so heavy across your shoulders. You never falter from what you have to do. Even as your body fails, you have a strength that radiates.

You have always had this ability to bring hope. Even when you were wrapped in swaddling clothes, lying in a manger, strangers travelled great distances to be close to you. The Shepherds said, "A saviour has been born; he is the Messiah, the Lord." The Magi came bearing gifts and worshipped at your feet. In such hopelessness, as this, you continue to fill me with hope.

## Reflection

**Leader:** May we all strive for hope in times of hopelessness and know we can do all things through him who strengthens us.

**All:** Our Father… Hail Mary… Glory be to the Father…
**Leader:** Jesus Christ Crucified,
**All:** Have mercy on us.

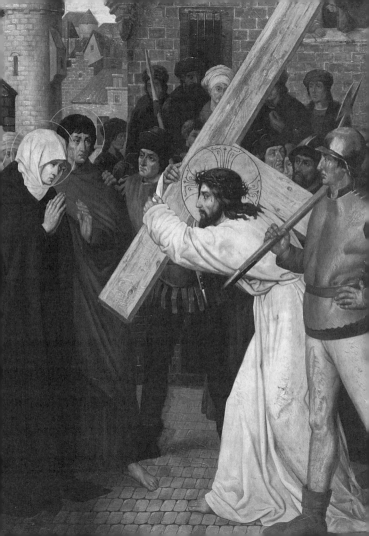

# Fourth Station
## Jesus meets his mother

**Leader:** We adore you, O Christ, and we praise you.
**All:** Because by your Holy Cross you have redeemed the world.

We embrace. You address me, "Mother", and I hear a slight sadness in your voice as you speak. I realise that this could be our last moment together. It reminds me of all those times I held you as a child: we were strangers in a foreign land, and I had to protect you. But I know that now I must remain silent. I cannot help you now.

You know that you must complete your Father's will. The Almighty has done great things and I see in your eyes that you truly trust in the Lord's plan. As the guards wrench you from me, I am joined by some of the women who loved you and they try to comfort me.

### Reflection

**Leader:** May we all remember our mothers who protected and loved us. But remember that the Lord ensures we are never alone in our time of need. We will be comforted.

---

**All:** Our Father… Hail Mary… Glory be to the Father…
**Leader:** Jesus Christ Crucified,
**All:** Have mercy on us.

# Fifth Station
## Simon of Cyrene helps Jesus carry the cross

**Leader:** We adore you, O Christ, and we praise you.
**All:** Because by your Holy Cross you have redeemed the world.

I watch you grow weary. The guards shout at you to hurry. They are getting frustrated with the pace at which you walk. They are so cruel. One of the guards pulls a man away from his sons and tells him to help you.

He is from a different country; I don't know him, but he looks like a disciple of yours. You take comfort in him as he lifts some of the weight from you.

Do not feel ashamed that you have needed the help of another, but take refuge in his kindness. For I have been helped in my journey with you. In my husband, Joseph, I have gained acceptance and protection. Through my cousin Elizabeth I have found joy, for she told me, "Blessed are you among women and blessed is the fruit of your womb."

### Reflection

**Leader:** May we all take refuge in the kindness of others as we journey with Christ in our lives; and like Simon, Joseph and Elizabeth, may we be prepared to help others as they take up the burden of their own crosses.

**All:** Our Father... Hail Mary... Glory be to the Father...
**Leader:** Jesus Christ Crucified,
**All:** Have mercy on us.

## Sixth Station
## Veronica wipes the face of Jesus

**Leader:** We adore you, O Christ, and we praise you.
**All:** Because by your Holy Cross you have redeemed the world.

I see a woman come towards you. She is crying. The guards let her take her cloth and wipe your face. You find a moment's relief in this caring act. The burning sun beats down on your raw body. I want nothing more than to make this pain end. This woman shows you such tenderness and devotion.

I have been amazed by the level of devotion you have instilled in those around you. I have accepted it, but never fully understood. For others have said such wondrous things about you. That you will be great. And that you are the salvation of the world. These things I have treasured and have pondered in my heart daily. Your face now and forever shall be embossed in my heart.

### Reflection

**Leader:** May we follow the example of St Veronica and show constant devotion to the Lord. May we follow Mary and treasure and ponder the mystery of Jesus in our own hearts.

**All:** Our Father... Hail Mary... Glory be to the Father...
**Leader:** Jesus Christ Crucified,
**All:** Have mercy on us.

# Jesus falls the second time

**Leader:** We adore you, O Christ, and we praise you.
**All:** Because by your Holy Cross you have redeemed the world.

You fall for a second time. Your body is weak from thirst and exhaustion. My heart is completely torn. I want this journey to end. But how can a mother want to see an end such as this? I am filled with sorrow at the very thought of what is to come.

You falling has taken me back to a happier time, when we presented you at the Temple. Joseph brought two turtle-doves as a sacrifice. I was so pleased with you, as you had grown in wisdom and stature, and found favour in God. An old man named Simeon rushed towards us; he knew how special you were, his eyes had seen your salvation. But he warned us of your fate. "This one is destined for the fall and rising of many in Israel and a sword will pierce your own heart." I am watching in agony as you fall. But with trepidation and hope as you rise up.

## Reflection

**Leader:** May we all remember those who fall in life and encourage them to have faith in the Lord in helping them rise up in times of strife.

---

**All:** Our Father... Hail Mary... Glory be to the Father...
**Leader:** Jesus Christ Crucified,
**All:** Have mercy on us.

# Eighth Station
## Jesus meets the women of Jerusalem

**Leader:** We adore you, O Christ, and we praise you.
**All:** Because by your Holy Cross you have redeemed the world.

I am not alone in my torment. Others in the crowd are weeping. You stop and speak to a group of women who are lamenting your fate. Even in your own suffering, you show them such love and compassion. I have learnt that you see all those who do the will of God as your family.

Once when you were teaching you were hustled away from me. I was with your brothers and sisters. At the time, it hurt that you could not meet with us, but I see now that others needed you. You said then, "Whoever does the will of my Father in heaven is brother, and sister and mother."

My idea of family has changed. I am not alone in my grief. These women mourn for you as I mourn for my child, and they grieve as bitterly for you as I grieve for my firstborn son. You are hustled on and continue to walk forward.

## Reflection

**Leader:** May we all rejoice in our Church family and love those who are our mothers, brothers and sisters in Christ.

**All:** Our Father... Hail Mary... Glory be to the Father...
**Leader:** Jesus Christ Crucified,
**All:** Have mercy on us.

# Ninth Station
## Jesus falls the third time

**Leader:** We adore you, O Christ, and we praise you.
**All:** Because by your Holy Cross you have redeemed the world.

I feel a rush of panic as you fall yet again. I've felt like this before, when you were a child. It was at the Passover Festival. We were on our way home from Jerusalem and had travelled a whole day when we realised you were not with us. We returned and searched for you. Eventually we found you. You were sitting in the Temple surrounded by teachers, and they were listening to you! My relief turned to bewilderment. You were calm and unfazed by our worry. You said you were in your Father's house. You had such authority, and I felt such calm that you were safe.

I watch as a guard bends down and pushes you roughly. I wish that I could feel such calm now and keep you safe. But once more you look calm and unfazed, as though you are heading back to your Father's house.

### Reflection

**Leader:** May we all listen to the teachings of Christ, and trust in him to help us up more times than we fall.

**All:** Our Father… Hail Mary… Glory be to the Father…
**Leader:** Jesus Christ Crucified,
**All:** Have mercy on us.

# Tenth Station
## Jesus is stripped of his garments

**Leader:** We adore you, O Christ, and we praise you.
**All:** Because by your Holy Cross you have redeemed the world.

How simple dice can cause such humiliation! You are stripped, and the guards take pleasure in gambling for your clothes. You are shamed by your nakedness, but without your garments your body is still cloaked in purple and red wounds. I long to shield and protect you from this mockery.

Some people in the crowd goad you into performing a miracle to save yourself. You once turned water into wine, yet you stand helpless before them. You look so vulnerable. I feel a burst of anger inside of me for they did not see the signs of who you are. Yet this truly awful and humiliating death will be their salvation.

### Reflection

**Leader:** We pray for those who are sick, wounded and vulnerable, trusting that the Lord will give them strength and healing.

---

**All:** Our Father… Hail Mary… Glory be to the Father…
**Leader:** Jesus Christ Crucified,
**All:** Have mercy on us.

# Jesus is nailed to the cross

**Leader:** We adore you, O Christ, and we praise you.

**All:** Because by your Holy Cross you have redeemed the world.

The guards encircle you. They hammer nails into your hands and feet. I watch as they lift up your cross. You are like a lamb who has been led to the slaughter. You refuse as they offer you wine vinegar. I want you to take it to your lips but you won't let your pain be dulled. Others are crucified next to you, one on your right and one on your left. Even they hurl insults at you.

You see me standing in front of you. You call out to me: "Woman, here is your son." You are not talking about yourself, but about a different man – the disciple you call the beloved. To him you say "Son, behold your mother." I am overcome with sadness: you are irreplaceable, you are my only son. But your disciple reaches out to me with kindness, and I take his hand. For although you will shortly leave me, I am not to lose what it means to be a mother. I will provide love to all those who believe in you.

## Reflection

**Leader:** May we all share in the suffering of Christ like a mother watching her child, so we can understand the sacrifice needed to deliver us from sin. May we love one another in the knowledge that we are all some mother's child, but also loved by Mary, who extends her maternal embrace to us all.

**All:** Our Father… Hail Mary… Glory be to the Father…

**Leader:** Jesus Christ Crucified,

**All:** Have mercy on us.

# Twelfth Station
## Jesus dies on the cross

**Leader:** We adore you, O Christ, and we praise you.
**All:** Because by your Holy Cross you have redeemed the world.

Even in your final moments of life you forgive those who crucify you and mock you. How much kindness and love is in your heart! Darkness suddenly covers the land. You cry out. "Father into your hands, I commend my spirit." I realise now that this was always part of the Lord's plan. Generations will call me blessed. My soul extols the Lord.

You look up and your spirit leaves your body. Your eyes are lifeless and you hang limply on the cross. The ground shakes. I feel afraid. The Centurion next to us glorifies the Lord; he has seen who you truly are. The soldiers who killed you place a sword into your side to check you are dead and it pierces my own soul sevenfold.

### Reflection

**Leader:** May we remember the sacrifice that Jesus made for us and join our prayers with his cries from the cross.

**All:** Our Father… Hail Mary… Glory be to the Father…
**Leader:** Jesus Christ Crucified,
**All:** Have mercy on us.

## Thirteenth Station
# Jesus is taken down from the cross

**Leader:** We adore you, O Christ, and we praise you.
**All:** Because by your Holy Cross you have redeemed the world.

You are gently lifted down from the cross by those that believe in you. They place you tenderly into my lap. I hold your body and see your blood. Our journey together is ending and now I will be carrying on without you. I look down at your beautiful body, not a bone is broken. So fragile. I hold you close against me.

I am bursting with sorrowful love. I hear your voice from inside of me, words you have said before: "Very truly I tell you, you will weep and mourn while the world rejoices. You will grieve, but your grief will turn to joy." In this moment of sorrow, I feel I will never rejoice or be glad again. But I am hopeful in the Lord and his promises to me.

## Reflection

**Leader:** May we join Mary as she mourns in the death of her son. May we remember those who have mourned for a child and rejoice in the day when they will meet again.

**All:** Our Father… Hail Mary… Glory be to the Father…
**Leader:** Jesus Christ Crucified,
**All:** Have mercy on us.

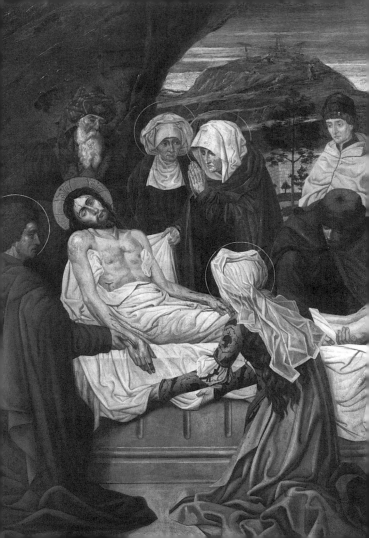

## Fourteenth Station
# Jesus is laid in the tomb

**Leader:** We adore you, O Christ, and we praise you.
**All:** Because by your Holy Cross you have redeemed the world.

Your body is lifted from me. Even in death, others show you such love and devotion. Joseph of Arimathea, a respected member of the council, has prepared for your burial. He has asked Pilate if he can take your body. Your body is bound in the linen cloths that are infused with myrrh and spices. I've smelt these spices before, at your birth. They were a gift then and are a gift now.

I realise that there is a time for everything. A time to give birth and a time to die. A time to tear down, and a time to build up. A time to weep, and a time to laugh. They place you in a rock-hewn tomb. I watch as a stone is rolled against the door of the tomb.

As the day of the Sabbath begins, I am suddenly not afraid. I am filled with awe-inspiring hope and joy as I wait for the time when you will rise up and I will meet you again.

## Reflection

**Leader:** May we all emulate the faithfulness of Mary as we wait in hope for the risen Christ, rejoicing in the day when he will meet us all again.

**All:** Our Father… Hail Mary… Glory be to the Father…
**Leader:** Jesus Christ Crucified,
**All:** Have mercy on us.

# Marian Prayers
## Hail Mary

The first two lines are the Salutation of the Archangel Gabriel to the Blessed Virgin Mary the future mother of Jesus. The next four lines are the words of Elizabeth, her cousin; the addition of the word 'Jesus' is attributed to Pope Urban IV (1261–64), while the concluding petition reached its present form in 1514.

Hail, Mary, full of grace,
the Lord is with thee.
Blessed art thou
   among women,
and blessed is the fruit
   of thy womb, Jesus.
Holy Mary, Mother of God,
pray for us sinners,
now and at the hour
   of our death.

Amen.

Ave María, gratia plena,
   Dóminus tecum.
Benedícta tu in muliéribus,
et benedíctus fructus
   ventris tui, Iesus.
Sancta Maria, Mater Dei,
ora pro nobis peccatóribus,
   nunc et in hora mortis
   nostræ.

Amen.

# Hail, Holy Queen

Attributed to several sources, the probable author is Herman the Lame (1013–1054), a monk of Reichenau Abbey in Germany.

Hail, Holy Queen,
  Mother of Mercy,
hail, our life, our sweetness
  and our hope!
To thee do we cry, poor
  banished children of Eve.
To thee do we send up
  our sighs, mourning
  and weeping in this vale
  of tears!
Turn then, most gracious
  Advocate,
thine eyes of mercy
  toward us,
and after this, our exile,
show unto us the blessed
fruit of thy womb, Jesus.
O clement, O loving,
O sweet Virgin Mary!

V. Pray for us,
O holy Mother of God.

R. That we may be made
worthy of the promises
  of Christ.
Amen.

Salve, Regína,
Mater misericórdiæ,
vita, dulcédo et spes nostra,
  salve.
Ad te clamámus,
  éxsules fílii Evæ.
Ad te suspirámus
  geméntes et flentes
in hac lacrimárum valle.
Eia ergo, advocáta nostra,
illos tuos misericórdes óculos
  ad nos convérte.
Et Iesum benedíctum
  fructum ventris tui,
nobis, post hoc exsílium,
  osténde.
O clemens, O pia,
  O dulcis Virgo María!
V. Ora pro nobis,
  Sancta Dei Genitrix.
R. Ut digni efficiamur
  promissionibus Christi.

Amen.

# 1st January
# Solemnity of Mary, the Holy Mother of God

This feast of the Blessed Virgin Mary, the Theotokos, or Mother of God, is held on the first day of the New Year, the Octave day of Christmas. It celebrates Mary's motherhood of Jesus, and the term Theotokos or God-bearer was adopted by the First Council of Ephesus (431), in order to safeguard the Divinity and humanity of Christ.

## *Collect from the Missal*

O God, who through the fruitful virginity
  of Blessed Mary
bestowed on the human race
  the grace of eternal salvation,
grant, we pray,
that we may experience the intercession of her,
through whom we were found worthy
to receive the author of life,
our Lord Jesus Christ, your Son.
Who lives and reigns with you
  in the unity of the Holy Spirit,
one God, for ever and ever.

Amen.

# 31st May
## The Visitation of the Blessed Virgin Mary

The Visitation commemorates the meeting between Mary and her cousin St Elizabeth at Ein Kerem, just outside Jerusalem. Feeling the presence of his Divine Saviour, St John the Baptist leapt in his mother's womb on the Blessed Virgin's arrival. Following St Elizabeth's words of greeting, Our Lady proclaimed the Magnificat, a hymn praising the Lord for all that he had done for his handmaid and expressing her attitude of faith and humility.

### *Collect from the Missal*

Almighty ever-living God,
who, while the Blessed Virgin Mary
  was carrying your Son in her womb,
inspired her to visit Elizabeth,
grant us, we pray,
that, faithful to the promptings of the Spirit,
we may magnify your greatness
with the Virgin Mary at all times.
Through our Lord Jesus Christ, your Son,
who lives and reigns with you
  in the unity of the Holy Spirit,
one God, for ever and ever.

Amen.

### *Concluding Prayer from the Liturgy of the Hours*

Almighty, ever-living God,
you inspired the Blessed Virgin Mary,
when she was carrying your Son,
to visit Elizabeth.
Grant that, always docile to the voice of the Spirit,
we may, together with our Lady, glorify your Name.
Through our Lord Jesus Christ, your Son,
who lives and reigns with you and the Holy Spirit,
one God, for ever and ever.

Amen.

# 15th September
## Our Lady of Sorrows

This feast originated as a memorial of the Seven Sorrows of Mary, most of which were linked to the events of Good Friday, when she stood at the foot of the cross. We remember that the Blessed Virgin had to live through the personal tragedy of seeing her Son die. She had a unique share in our redemption, offering her Son's life to the Lord, trusting that it was part of his plan.

### *Collect from the Missal*

O God, who willed that,
when your Son was lifted high on the Cross,
his Mother should stand close by and share
  his suffering,
grant that your Church,
participating with the Virgin Mary in the Passion
  of Christ,
may merit a share in his Resurrection.
Who lives and reigns with you in the
  unity of the Holy Spirit,
one God, for ever and ever.

Amen.

# 25th December
# The Nativity of the Lord

Christmas Day is the culmination of the Advent Season, and the glorious commemoration of the Birth of Our Lord Jesus Christ of the Blessed Virgin Mary. His birth was foretold by the prophets, and long awaited. Our Lady and St Joseph travelled to Bethlehem for a census, and it was here that Jesus was born. But it happened in silence, poverty and humility, and the first people to see the Infant Christ were poor shepherds.

## Mass during the Day
### *Collect from the Missal*

O God, who wonderfully created the dignity,
  of human nature
and still more wonderfully restored it,
grant, we pray,
that we may share in the divinity of Christ,
who humbled himself to share in our humanity.
Who lives and reigns with you
  in the unity of the Holy Spirit,
one God, for ever and ever.

Amen.

### *Concluding Prayer from the Liturgy of the Hours*

God our Father,
our human nature is the wonderful work
  of your hands,
made still more wonderful by your work
  of redemption.
Your Son took to himself our manhood,
grant us a share in the godhead of Jesus Christ,
who lives and reigns with you and the Holy Spirit,
God for ever and ever.

Amen.

# Has this book helped you?

Spread the word!

@CTSpublishers

/CTSpublishers

ctscatholiccompass.org

Let us know!
marketing@ctsbooks.org
+44 (0)207 640 0042

Learn, love, live your faith.
**www.CTSbooks.org**